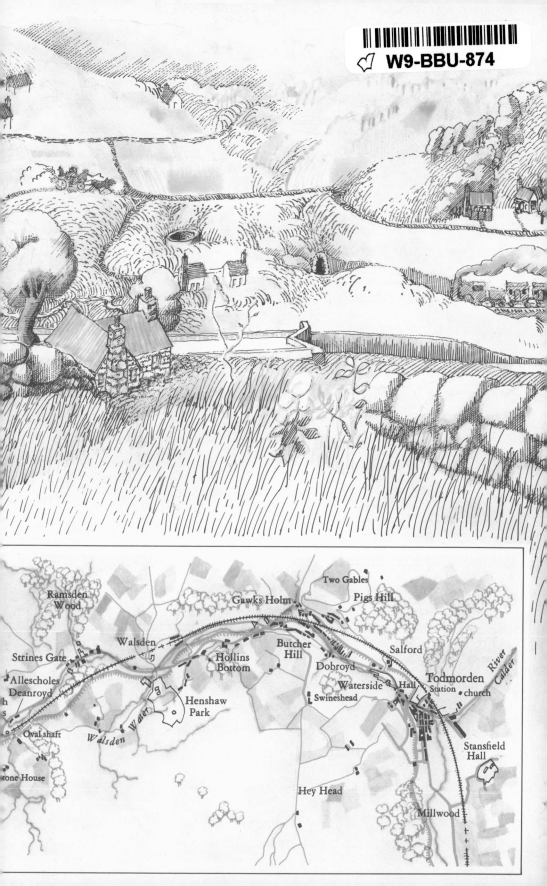

# *The* WORLD FROM ROUGH STONES

# *The* WORLD FROM

## *Malcolm Macdonald*

# ROUGH STONES

*Alfred A. Knopf* 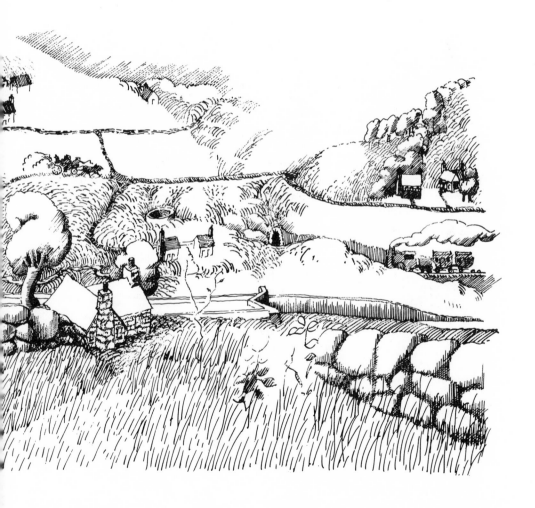 *New York 1975*

*This is a Borzoi Book*
*published by Alfred A. Knopf, Inc.*

Copyright © 1974, 1975 by Malcolm Macdonald
Endpaper and title page illustrations
Copyright © 1975 by Alfred A. Knopf, Inc.
All rights reserved under International and Pan-American Copyright Conventions. Published in the United States by Alfred A. Knopf, Inc., New York. Distributed by Random House, Inc., New York. Originally published in Great Britain by Hodder and Stoughton Limited, London.

Library of Congress Cataloging in Publication Data
Macdonald, Malcolm, (date)
The world from rough stones.
I. Title.
PZ4.M13484Wo3 [PR6063.A1692] 823'.9'14 74–21296
ISBN 0–394–49434–2

Manufactured in the United States of America

First American Edition

# PART ONE

Manchester

# Chapter 1

Nora lived a nightmare as she stood among the dripping carcasses of the butcher's mart and waited to see if her tactics had worked; all she could do now was hide, as still and as silent as the hanging sides of beef and pork. If she had been right, nothing would happen; but if she had been wrong. . . . She was surprised at how exciting it was to know that her life really stood in the balance.

The blue man. The man with the blue bandanna. Pat Connally. He was the one who would kill her. They said he kept a golden guinea sewn into the lining of that blue bandanna and he used the weight of it to swing it around your neck and strangle you.

What a fool she had been to try to blackmail Charley Eade! "Charley, you're keepin' ten quid a week for your own pocket out of this business. From now on I want two and a half for me!"

*Fool!* she raged at herself, standing silent and hardly breathing among the gently swaying carcasses. *Idiot! Stupid halfwit! Numskull!*

Thank God young Tony, Charley's assistant, had told her in time—even though he hadn't really meant to. Tony thought the idea of killing her was just a big joke. "See them two men talking to Charley Eade? He's paying them to kill thee! That one with the blue bandanna, Pat Connally, he's a killer! He does half the paid-up killings in Manchester, that Pat Connally." And then with great glee he told her how—the trick with the guinea weight.

As soon as she was convinced that Tony was not just pulling her leg, she turned, picked up her shawl, and walked away. She had to get away from the market; and then she'd have to get away from Manchester. But first the market.

It cost every mite of her courage not to run. She had to walk briskly enough to attract some slight attention. She forced herself to nod, smile, exchange a fleeting word with the porters, clerks, and salesmen who had befriended her these last three weeks—a pretty young girl of eighteen, with a strong body, no family, and a good head for figures, can soon make a long tally of friends, even in so short a time, among market men. She had to lay an easily identifiable trail to the street. And there she had to vanish from Manchester as completely as if a giant hand had plucked her from the earth.

It all depended on how soon Charley Eade woke up to her absence. The nearer she got to the exit, the harder she fought her impulse to run.

But the hardest part was still to come. She reached the outside without being followed. A blear pink dawn suffused the sky away to the east, far off above Rochdale and Oldham. But here, above the city, still stretched the deep purple of the dying night. Away in the distance the cathedral clock struck five. The dark invited her to escape. Surely she could dash now to her lodging, retrieve the money she'd already blackmailed out of Charley Eade—or at least the six pounds that were left after last Saturday's booze-up—and run! It was so tempting that she almost obeyed the urge.

Dozens of people in her situation would have done so. Six pounds! A year's wages for a scullery maid. She knew dozens who would have gone back to get it before running. But people like that were the already defeated. Their destiny lay at the bottom of this rat fight. And what put them there and kept them there was the tendency to make such choices. An instinct sharpened by years of struggle upward through that throng warned her off.

If Eade had gone so far as to hire these two to attend to her, he'd not rest if he thought she was near. They'd watch her lodging even after it was relet. They'd make their way there at once, as soon as they were sure she'd left the market building. There would certainly be no time for her, hampered by her skirts, to return there, make her way upstairs, take out the panel by the door, and scrabble among the earth filling for the thread that led to the little bag with six sovereigns in it—not to do all that *and* make her escape.

So what they intended as a bait for her she would turn into a lure for them. But first she had to be sure that they had left.

As silent as her shadow, she slipped along the outside wall of the market building, threading her way carefully among the broken crates and chests, the discarded bales, the rotting vegetables, drunks, dead cats, rats, and ordure that gathers around civilized mankind. Then came the dangerous part. Having laid the trail to the outside, she had to get back in—unseen. Once they were convinced she had left, they'd never look inside for her. But it had to be in a part of the market where she was not known: the butchers' mart. In less than ten seconds she could get from the back exit to a secure place among the carcasses. But if in that time one of them came searching that way, or someone who knew her saw her, it would all be up. That was the risk in her plan.

The nearer she drew to the back exit, the louder the screams grew. They were killing the last of the pigs on the cobbles of the apron around the door. One jerked its death spasms over a great vat of steaming blood. Its predecessor silently endured a dowsing of boiling water. Another, even longer dead, appeared to sigh as its innards tumbled out into a tall barrel. Another, already shaved, hung gleaming and silent, turning this way and that, seeming to shiver in the flaring gaslight, waiting to be carried in. Beside it, deep in the shadows, Nora watched.

The squealing stopped. The last of the pigs was yielding the last of its blood. The raucous voice of the bloodpudding maker's wife carried on into the silence as she and the pigkiller haggled on—just as they haggled here every morning of the working week. Oblivious to it all, a drunken girl in a faded blue dress wove an erratic course among the vats and the dead and dying pigs. She paid attention to no one; and none—save Nora—attended her. She had passed well out of the circle of light when she fell heavily among some broken tea chests. She did not rise. Nora noted the position; the girl was about her own size and build. Her clothing could be useful.

A porter came and took up the glistening carcass; it hung over his shoulder looking oddly human. Using him as cover, Nora entered the building from which she had so recently escaped.

She grasped the layout with one quick sweep of her eyes. The newly killed pigs were to the right, nearest the door. The porter would head that way. Beyond hung those killed earlier, together with some sides of beef that had already hung a week. At the farther end of this section selling had just begun; a small knot of butchers and cooks surrounded the auctioneer.

The worst moment came when the porter turned aside with his carcass. The sanctuary she sought was only yards away, but there, turning from the crowd near the auctioneer, was one of the killers. She saw his blue bandanna! Or was it? In the bright light she could not be sure. And now it was too late for her to move.

She stood looking at the nearest carcasses as a butcher's daughter might look, she hoped, and waited for the man to pass. As he drew level she turned casually to face him. A vast relief welled up within her: he was not the man! He had a blue bandanna but he was not the man. More important though, she noticed how he screwed up his eyes and peered toward the doors as if he could only just make them out. Of course! There were three big flares around the auctioneer. Anyone coming from that end would think it pretty dark down here. She, coming in from the outside, had been led into the contrary error. Whoever he might be, the man with the bandanna had not even noticed her.

Fearless now, she slipped among the carcasses and waited for the real pursuer to come by. She was certain he would. They were of the mob and they knew their trade. They'd make a rapid search of the market. Go straight to her lodging. Then, finding her not yet returned, one would stay there while the other came back here for a further search and new instructions. The twenty or so minutes they were away would be the safe time, the only safe time, for her to make good her escape.

Curiously enough, it was only when she stood securely hidden that she felt the usual signs of fear—the racing heart and sinking stomach. Until then she had acted and thought in the coolest of spirits; if she had felt any emotion, it had been a kind of mad joy. To be hunted and to outwit your pursuers was to turn the tables and to become, in a way, a kind of hunter yourself. A hunter-from-in-front. You had the power. You dictated the play. You escaped. They lost you. The true hunter was always the one that did *not* lose.

Escape! But where? Sam, her younger brother, had gone back to Leeds last year and was now in service there somewhere. He'd always see her settled. But could she find him? In any case, there must be some of her father's family left in Leeds. That's where she'd have to go. Certainly there was no point in trying to go back to the mills in Stockport. Eade and his two would trace her back there with no difficulty. In fact, she hoped they would; it would let her get away to Leeds that much more easily.

She came back to her present surroundings with a jolt—and froze. The man with the blue bandanna—the real one this time—was standing not three yards from her. Standing. Not moving. Freakishly his eyes stared straight into hers. *He cannot see me,* she thought as she fought down the panic that had thrust her heart and lights up into her gullet. It's much too dark. It's not possible.

The man bit his lip and turned away to the exit. Nora counted thirty, forcing herself to count slowly, imagining herself walking through treacle and counting one for each footfall. She was so relieved to reach thirty that she almost relaxed her guard and walked out; but that same survivor's instinct held her back. She edged her face slowly out for a quick peep. It was the saving of her, for the man still stood in the doorway, letting his eyes grow dark-accustomed, looking right and left, giving no sign of leaving.

Soon it became clear that he was waiting; probably the other man was working his way around the outside—the way Nora had crept. And indeed, before long, the other came breathlessly up from the shadows, heading for his companion in the doorway. He shook his head as he walked. At this the bandanna man set off for the main roadway, leaving his companion to follow close on his heels. Neither gave so much as a backward glance at the market building.

A crowd of drovers came out of one of the offices, up beyond the auctioneer; warm with hospitality they made for the door. As soon as they were past, Nora slipped out from among the carcasses and walked as if she were a straggler from their band, just in case one of the pursuers looked back. A drover turned and, seeing her, fell behind a pace or two and grabbed her around the waist. She smiled encouragement and joined the group, to shouts of bawdy approval.

But when they were well out of the light she slipped away and ran off into the darkness. The drover took three or four loud, laughing steps after her but made no genuine effort to follow. When their laughter had faded around the corner, she doubled back and sought for the crates where the girl in the blue dress had fallen. Blue was going to be her lucky colour this morning, after all!

She imagined it would be a matter of moments to get the unconscious girl's dress off and change it for her own. In fact it took ten gruelling minutes, for nothing is less co-operative than a full-grown adult dead to the world. And all the while the sky was getting paler and the risk of discovery grew.

But she managed in the end. It was a wrench to part with her lovely red worsted dress and the dark brown shawl. And she despised the faded blue cotton thing and single petticoat she was to take in exchange. It hung so slack and straight that her boots peeped out beneath the hem. What was worse, her toes, in their turn, peeped out of the boots. On the brighter side, the borrowed clothes were much freer of vermin than Nora had feared. As a final touch she let down and disarranged the black coils of her well-kept hair.

At last, rising drunkenly from the spot where she had changed, she staggered off into the sooty dawn. When she risked a backward glance, she saw a dog sniff at the bare toes of the unconscious girl. Then it lifted its leg and staled them. The girl's utter stillness made Nora think of death.

Thoughts of death had not been far away all spring and summer—what with the death of her father and then the terrible, terrible deaths of the two young children. She must shut that out. She could talk about it in company, and even sound quite matter-of-fact; but she must not think about it. Thinking could never bring them back.

Of course, she could not help it.

"Dad!" she whispered at the eastern sky.

And the eastern sky shivered asunder in a sea of hot salt. And she remembered his strong body and his gentle voice. And she remembered how home was always where he was, even when it held no food and he was desperate with the worry. And she remembered the ruin that followed his death and how there was never any more home. And she thought of the mess she had made of everything because he was not there to stop her. And more than anything she wanted someone to whom she could turn and just whisper, "Sorry." Someone big like him. She wanted to start again.

But when she was out on the Oldham road, bound off for Leeds, and the sun was up, and the birds sang, and the day promised to be hot, she said to herself that this *was* a way of starting again. She remembered that her father was in a pauper's grave in the abandoned cemetery beyond Littleborough.

"I'll give it a last tending afore I tramp back to Leeds," she said. And the thought came like a great comfort.

# *Chapter 2*

**Walter** had almost gained the shade of the tree plantation before he saw Nora. A sweat flushed his back. Drops of it slithered down his spine. He had to rest. She sat on the low stone wall as if carved from it, looking enviably cool in the dappling sun whose contrasts of light and shade had hidden her. She was a labouring girl, big-boned, young, but with a good skin.

"That's the best employment today," he said when he was sure of her class.

"I'd like to be the lass ye were thinking of. Ye looked right through me."

She smiled. Good teeth, too. Quite pretty. She'd be about eighteen.

"Yes," he said. "My thoughts were . . . miles away."

His engineer's instinct had almost led him to put it into furlongs and chains. He touched the stone wall.

"These stones *are* hot."

She stood up. Her long blue dress fell straight from her waist; she must be wearing only a single petticoat.

"Sit here," she said. "Stones have cooled under me skirt."

She walked a few steps with no obvious purpose. Her limbs swung easily, as countrywomen's limbs do—especially those who carry bundles on their heads. She looked steadily at him.

He sat where she had been.

"Oh—cold under your skirts, is it?" he asked.

He carefully hid his lust until a price was set. He turned away from her level grey gaze. Inside he shivered. His heart began to race.

"I didn't mean that," she said wearily.

"Need a little warming?" he persisted. Some good clothes and a few months away from the sun and weather would transform her; she'd be a damned handsome girl.

"I've a belly needs meat," she said.

"Ah."

This was it.

"It'd cost thee. I can't frig with the likes of thee for naught."

"Three bob," he said, looking away at the horizon. "Three and six if ye really please."

"Five," she said, "I'm no regular gay girl. I'm not lightly given."

Prudence and lust fought for him. He ducked to let a bumblebee pass; briefly his eye held a frozen image of it, laden with orange pollen.

He turned to her and thought he saw a kindred longing in her face. It ought to have made him insist on his offer but it had the contrary effect.

"Four and six," he said. "Five's all I've got and I'll not be left without coin."

Now that their bargain was certain, she looked at him more closely, seeking some attraction to make his intimacy less distasteful. Only once before in her life had she been reduced to such desperate measures; and then it had taken six pennyworth of gin to ease the contract.

He was on the tall side. Slender, but wiry, too. There was muscle there if he wanted to use it. He had a long, angular face with a firm chin, chiselled lips, and bright, roving eyes. They were stripping her where she stood. The thought excited her, and she began actually to want him.

Her manner changed at once. She grinned and stretched. He could sense every plane of her flesh beneath that thin blue dress and petticoat. He walked past her and took her wrist, meaning to lead her to the cornfield near by. But she shook free and stood her ground. He turned back. Until this moment her face had stood out, light against the shade of the tree plantation. Now, seen from within that shade, she became a dusky silhouette against the sunstruck hills and trees beyond. Her grey-brown eyes glinted dully a message he could not read; had she been weeping? Then, as she smiled again, her teeth shone like dim gemstones. Now it was she who held forth her hand. He took it.

"We can go in here," she said.

"Is it not private property?"

She laughed.

"Private enough," she said. "We'll get no complaint from its owners. I'll warrant thee that."

Even in the heart of the plantation there was no relief from the torrid afternoon.

"Here's a level place," he said.

She snorted—was it a laugh?

A stone outcrop, three-quarters covered with turf and weed, promised an adequate bed. Her hobnail boots grated as she turned to loosen her clothes. He rolled his jacket for the small of her back and spread his waistcoat for her head. He turned to face her. Their eyes met. Again he shivered for lust. She, too, was possessed. He was suddenly so absorbed by her that he forgot precisely what to do. For an unreal age they bent down, down, down toward that bed. In that same daze he threw her skirts above her waist.

The sudden hot reek of that unwashed body threw him into a frenzy. He tried to thrust his hands up under her dress, beyond her waist, but the twine was still too tight.

"Wait!" she said, laughing as she fiddled urgently with the knot.

He could not wait. He ripped open his buttons and threw himself over her. She was hot and very smooth. He spent himself at once, almost without joy.

She stopped laughing. She stopped breathing. Her lips went thin with anger.

She looked up at him in venomous disappointment and struck repeatedly at his shoulder. "No," she kept saying. "No! No . . ."

He jigged again, clasping her to stop that punching.

"That was only starters, sweet," he said. "I'll not stop." Inwardly he wondered why he bothered.

Her joy was as sudden as her rage, and as natural. Unable to get at her breasts either via her waist or down her tight sleeves, he caressed them through the thin material of her dress, astonished at the voluptuousness of it.

She moaned, beginning her ecstasy. He drove slower, deeper, spinning her out. It was a long, long crescendo that almost brought him to spend again.

Then, the animal gone, he envied her delirium and cursed the body that had spent itself so quickly. It was all so meaningless. Why had he stopped here at all? Now he would be exhausted—and with four more hot miles to walk.

She stirred in terminal exhaustion. He looked at her, eyes shut, smiling to herself, almost pretty. He lay upon the huge bolster of her body, suddenly conscious of the odour and sweat that bathed them both. He rolled off and, with the stench strongly in his nostrils, fell at once into a mindless slumber.

It cannot have lasted long, perhaps not above five minutes. He awoke to disperse the cloud of flies that had settled on him. The girl was still beside him, now sitting up, looking at him with a strangely level gaze. He did up his buttons and sat half facing her. "Why look at me like that?" he asked.

For answer she opened her hand. A sovereign glinted in her palm. "I found yon there." She pointed where her head, and his waistcoat, had hung back over the stone.

"I'm vexed what's to be done with it. It can't be yourn for ye said ye hadn't but a crown about ye. So . . . ?"

"It must have fallen from my waistcoat pocket," he said.

"Oh aye."

"They say wagered money's soon forgot. And it's true, for that's how I won it. I forgot I had it, for it cost me nothing to get."

The coin gleamed between them still. He looked at her boots; one thin sole had parted from its uppers. The hobs were worn to little metal flecks.

"You keep it," he said.

Nora let it lie there, as if he had offended her. "I must've pleased," she said.

Was she joking?

"Don't joke, girl . . . what's your name?"

"Me what?"

"Name. Your name?"

"Oh! Molly. They call us Molly," she lied.

"Well, listen, Molly, you turned a very common, brutish act into . . ." How could he put it to her? " . . . a glimpse of paradise."

"Oh aye," she giggled.

"So don't spoil it."

"Right, master. To be sure, master." She reacted facetiously to his tone of command.

"Didn't it take you that way at all?" he asked.

"I never knew it any other way," she said simply.

"By the by," he said, "I'm Walter." He always liked them to think of him as himself.

She nodded, her thoughts elsewhere.

Still the coin shone between them.

"For God's sake, pick it up," he said. "It lies there like an accusation."

She stared at it sullenly. "The way ye gives it us makes us feel cheaper than what we settled on first."

"You have sensibilities above your station," he sneered. "Look at your boots. Ye could get a new pair *and* a good meal for that."

At last she picked it up, but without urgency, as if it had been a dead leaf. "Aye. Well," she said. "I'm bound for Leeds, so I can't say nay."

Then there was an extraordinary optical illusion: where the coin had lain was a crisply carved, old-fashioned letter E. He had to twist his head to be sure the carving was real.

"Someone's cut his name here," he said.

It was her turn to look puzzled. "Well, that's not strange," she said.

"A letter 'E.' L—Y—E . . . lyes . . . in—ter. . . . Ye gods! 'Here lyes interred' . . . It's someone's grave. Nicholas Everett's grave."

"I thought ye knew. It's the old churchyard."

"No. Ye gods! I thought it was a grove. A plantation. We've desecrated a grave. Hundreds of graves. How could I not have seen!"

He knew well enough why he had failed to notice.

"Eeee," she said. "One minute thou art glimpsing paradise. Next minute it's desecration!"

She lay down again, totally relaxed. Sunlight dappled a pattern of blunted lace across her.

"Thank the gods I didn't know. What were you doing out here?"

"Tending our dad's grave. He were the last to be interred here. I thought as I'd give it a last tending afore I tramped back." She did not open her eyes.

"Is he long dead?"

"Four month." She wondered why she lied; he had died before last Christmas.

"A great loss. A grievous loss."

She looked old suddenly. The hand in her pocket turned the sovereign over and over. She opened her eyes and stared unseeing at the pale green canopy that shimmered above. When she spoke it was in a glum, low register, with a voice no longer feminine.

"Aye. He were more than a father to us. Me mam died of birth fever when I were fourteen. He frigged with us then, while he lived. Mebbe that's why me mind were on it when ye stopped by."

Walter hardly breathed. He knew then that she had spoken the truth when she had said she was not "lightly given." She was a rank novice. Everyone knew that the poor had their own disgusting ways. The things he'd seen among the navvies—even beasts would die of shame. But when their girls wanted to earn a shilling or two by catering for people of taste and quality, they soon learned what to hide and what to show. This Molly creature hadn't even taken her first lesson. He cursed himself for giving her a pound; that fatal detumescent generosity of his. He felt defiled.

"I'm saying why thou had me that easy," she added.

She thought again of her father. Poor, lonely man, failing slowly at everything he tried—except at loving them, all five of them, crammed in that wretched one room. What could this fine gentleman, who could afford to wager whole sovereigns, and who had only to show the glint of gold to get anything he wanted . . . what could he possibly . . . ?

She had to stop thinking like that. Always thinking of her father. It did no good.

"But . . . your own father!" he said.

"Aye. And a good father. Nay, lad—ye knows nothing, your sort. He worked hisself into yon grave. Fendin' for us. Me and the family."

"How many were you?" Walter steered her from the subject.

"Five."

"And now? Where are you all now?"

"The bairns is dead. One died of rats. With rat bites, ye know. Me brother went into service in Leeds last October. And me other brother's transported."

"What for?"

"Forming a trade union, a 'combination.' Administering an illegal oath. Damn fool!"

"What did the other one die of? The other . . . bairn?"

Her lips tightened.

"Well," he said, "no business of mine, I suppose." He began to arrange his clothing.

"I couldn't help it," she said, now looking at him. "I had to go out. To earn. I had to get to market. Weren't no fault of mine there weren't no door to the hovel. Coroner said that. The hovel weren't no more nor a pig-pen itself."

"I see," he said. "He strayed."

"She. Aye, she strayed. Right into the jaws of Tom o' Jones's boar as weren't penned. There were naught left but one arm to bury."

"Dear God!" he said. "Ye gods."

Still the thought of this girl and her father seethed within him. "But . . . you and your father! Weren't you afraid of conceiving? Didn't you get with child?"

She took his tone as a challenge. Her lip curled in scorn. "Child! There was none come to term. They was nothing but little kittens. Meagre wrecklings born dead and soon cold. And sooner forgotten. I tell thee— thou hasn't lived, thy sort."

He could not tell if she was sad or past all anger. He said nothing, though his eyes were fixed upon her face. What terrible revelations! What a terrible existence they hinted at! He wondered at the force that drove such people to survive. The thought struck him: Perhaps even now a new life, half his, was kindling in her—to be born, to survive plague and disease, to worm its way up through the gauntlet of human cruelty and indifference, to eat its meagre fill, to get drunk, to frig, beget, and die. The futility of human existence was encompassed within the few cubic yards of air, earth, and flesh immediately around him—even the vanity of the half-deciphered legend in the stone. What a farce!

He stood up. "I have work to finish," he said. "Keep the sovereign. Get some better boots."

She smiled but did not rise. Only half her mind was on him. She swished her skirts above her ankle and grinned wryly at her boots. Renewed lust faintly stirred him.

"If you're making for Leeds," he said, "you'll want the canal. That's the easiest way over to Todmorden."

She smiled indulgently, unfurling his waistcoat and dusting it before she passed it to him. He liked seeing her hands moving over the cloth. The next female hands to do that, he realized, would be Arabella's. He tried to feel ashamed of this conjunction of thoughts.

"Aye. Mebbe they'd say nothing to thee. But they put dogs on us at Oldham Cut. Towpath's private property, ye see. I'll take the packhorse trail. That's the best road."

"Oh, they'd chase me off, too, Molly. Canal folk have no love of railroad men. You'd best hurry. There's thieves up on top there."

"Thieves!" Now her scorn was frank. "What've I got that—" And then she remembered her sovereign. "Oh aye!" It was a very young girl who bit her lip with such exaggeration and grinned up at him.

"I said, didn't I—soon forgot!"

"Eeeee!" She stood up, dusting herself off with those same firm hands.

"If you want to stop this side till morning, there's a navvy gang you'd find shelter with . . ."

"Navvies! I'd as soon sup with the devil."

"Ah," he told her, "this one's different. They sleep under a roof. No rowdies. Between one randy and the next, they're churchwardens. Ask for Lord John. That's what they call him. Say Gaffer Thornton sent you."

# Chapter 3

The afternoon was almost done by the time Nora reached the cutting for Summit Tunnel. This part of the line, east of Littleborough, was not yet open, though it ran as far as the drift for the tunnel; only supplies and company men used the track. And Nora.

As she strode in her shoddy boots along the new roadbed, she sang aloud, "I walked by the brook, I walked by the mill . . ." From time to time her mind's eye roved back over the sullied land behind her—the flats that ran far into Cheshire, beyond where she had ever been. Dimly she remembered when she, a girl of ten, had come this way from Leeds with her father. Eight years ago. The number of factory chimneys must have doubled since then, or trebled. Ahead the hills and dales were an even dimmer memory. But somewhere among them was Leeds. Home. Her memory of that was an unfinished patchwork, parts blank, parts filled in minutest detail. The cottage, the clacking loom, the smell of wet wool, their own green field in Hunslet with its ragged edge on dirty little Dow Beck, just before the river Aire swallowed it. There were railways there now, people said. She wouldn't know the place. But she would; of that she was sure.

"Can ye tell us where Lord John's at work?" she asked a labourer at the foot of the cutting.

"Aye, luv. Who sent thee?"

"Gaffer called Thornton."

"Him what's engineer up at Summit?"

"Mebbe."

"Oh ah. He told thee to ask for Big Lord John, then? Gaffer Thornton?"

He seemed to have no purpose in persisting so. She wearied of him.

"Aye. He told us."

The man began to move away. "He's just round the cutting there," he said as he walked. Then he stopped. "He's working the first drift of Summit Tunnel. But ye must wait till he comes out. They'll stand no wench in a drift. No wench underground, ye see."

"Aye. I can wait for him."

Before the tunnel's mouth she climbed a ladder up the side of the cutting, ten feet or so, to reach the sun. There she sat astraddle a rock and waited.

From deep in the tunnel came the clang of iron on iron, well muted by distance. Heralded by a long swelling rumble, a horse emerged at the trot, pulling a line of tubs laden with millstone muck from the driftway. The noise almost masked a deeper and more distant roar, like a far-off thunderclash.

Even before the navvy with the horse stopped, Nora knew that something about the second noise was wrong. It had been too loud and too long. On the far side of the cutting two others, sorting some shuttering for the masons, also stopped. All three listened to the silence. Then they ran to the tunnel entrance. The two sorters sprinted straight into the dark. The horseman put fingers in his mouth and blew an urgent, piercing whistle. A blacksmith and his attendants, down near the mouth of the cutting, stopped and took up the whistle until a gang setting out a stone wall to the south of the track, even farther away, dropped their work and came running. At the same time another gang sprinted down from the first shaft up on the moor. The urgency of it thrilled Nora and she stood up to gain a better view of the tunnel mouth.

The navvy who had deserted the horse now reappeared, this time with a boy beside him. Both ran to the tubs and tipped them straight out onto the track. For the first time the horse looked around, surprised at this break in routine.

Hard behind them came a giant of a man, the ganger. It could only be Lord John. He was naked to the waist and plastered with rock dust, so that he moved and stood like a stone carving brought to life. His skin showed bare only around his eyes and on his brow and along the forearms that had wiped them. He halted, blinking at the lowering sun before he turned east, toward the moor.

"You! Slen!" he called to a navvy running down from the top.

"Aye?" The other halted.

"Where's Gaffer?"

"Over Rough Stones, or Todmorden. He'll not be back until morning."

"Then go get him. Tell him there's a fall of five hundred ton or more at the west driftway."

"Right. Any dead?"

"Pengilly trapped."

The man called Slen turned and ran, a long, loping stride he could sustain for hours. The horseman and the lad rehitched the horse to the up-line end of the tubs and started for the dark of the tunnel. Lord John searched both banks of the cutting with eyes just grown used to the light. He saw Nora.

"Wench," he called.

"Aye?"

"Can ye run? Are ye crippled?"

"I can run."

"Then up to the top of the cutting ye go. There's a farm there, a furlong distant." Nora was already scrambling toward the top. He lifted his voice to follow her. "Beg as many wet sacks as ye can run with. Don't load thyself down."

"I'll not be gone long." Already she was at the top.

"Farmer's a sour crab. Tell'm there's men dead and men a-dying and we need sacks to cover the gunpowder."

She kicked off her boots and pounded barefoot along the cattle track to the farm. It led among great banks of spoil, twisting, turning, denying her any distant view. What she at first took to be a farm proved to be an almost completed chapel—a small, eight-windowed building with *Wesleyan Providence 1839* carved in plain script over the door head. Of masons or other workmen there was no sign. She turned to the field opposite and at once saw the farmer. He stood with his back to her but glanced about at the sound of her approach. He scanned her quickly up and down, from bare feet to dirty bonnet, before he turned back to his oats.

"Are you the master?" she asked, gasping for breath.

"And if I am?" He did not turn but reached a scrawny brown arm for more ears of ripening oat.

"Pray ye, sir, there's trouble in the tunnel. They're afraid the gunpowder's going off and can they have some wet sacks?"

He pulled the oat ears and tumbled their seed into his left palm. "They can blow themselves to Kingdom Come and to Hell, see if I care! And *thee's* trespassing," was all he said.

"But sir! There's men a-dying."

Ponderously he lifted the seed to his nose and sniffed. *"All* of 'em, I hope. Men! They're bloody vermin. I hate 'em."

"But they want aid!" Nora was shocked at his callousness.

"They shoulda thought of that on their last drunken randy—when they tore down my hedges and fired the poultry run."

"Ah, well," said Nora, searching for a different argument. "It isn't just the men, see. If that powder was to blow, it'd take half the hillside with it. This land of thine and all."

The man threw back his head and laughed, scattering the oats to the wind. "Oh ah! What they got buried then? Liverpool Arsenal? Enough powder to blow the hillside! Thou art talking to a Waterloo gunner, lass."

"Ye'll not help then?" Still she could not believe it.

He turned to her and spoke in a different tone. "I'll help thee. Pretty young wench likes of thee shouldn't lack for help."

That was when she saw the crucifix around his neck. Without thought she spoke. "I'll tell the priest on thee." And she made to leave.

"Yer what?" His voice told her she'd struck home.

"I said I'll tell the priest ye left men dyin' when I asked ye for help."

He paused long enough to see that she meant it. "Ye'd best take three or four. Up in the yard. Ask for Tom. Tell'm what ye want."

She was running before he had finished. *Mawrode Farm* said a notice on the gate, decorated at each end with a crucifix. Tom, old and spiritless, took her to a rat-infested shed built against a big cow barn. She snatched the top three sacks off the pile and turned—only to face the farmer, blocking the door. He grabbed them from her and held them for inspection, one by one. Two, almost whole, he threw back on the pile. The third, well rat-tattered, he gave back to her.

"Two more like this, Tom," he instructed.

Exasperated at his slowness, she joined the old man in his search. Dust of hemp, dried mud, and rat dung danced in the air. The papist farmer's hands circled her waist.

"Piss off," she said, hammering down on his left wrist. He laughed.

She and the old man found two more tattered sacks simultaneously. She snatched them and ran, rolling them about the one she already had. At the gate she paused only to soak them at a stone trough half filled with hot green water. Living things in it nudged her fingers.

Tom, without a glance at her, returned to scraping the yard with his wooden shovel. The farmer watched her all the way out of sight.

Soaked from bosom to ankle with sticky water squeezed from the rotting sacks, she slithered and slipped down the bank to the rock of the cutting wall, where the makeshift ladder led down to the track bed. As she reached the permanent way the horseman and tubbing came clattering out, laden again.

"He sent us for wet sacks," she said, hoping the man would take them.

"Take 'em in." He nodded at the tunnel. "Fire's out but they might still want it."

"Me! In there!"

He began to tip the first tub. "I can't," he said. "Don't linger. 'Tis bad luck, a wench in a drift. Stop where the rail stops."

Unwilling, she set off into the gloom. In a curious way it grew light ahead of her as she walked, so that pitch black had turned paler by the time she reached it. A dusty, mineral smell grew stronger as she followed the long left-hand curve. Soon the wide brick vault of the mouth gave way to the cramped tunnel of the drift itself. Here she caught the first sounds of iron shovels scraping on the rock. It was feverish, with none of that measured rhythm of navvies on a twelve-hour stint.

The warm sacking grew dank and chill in the gloom. The best place to walk was on the continuous course of stone beneath the rails. She was surprised that light still filtered this deep into the tunnel, for the entrance was long out of sight around the curve. The frenzied shovelling was now close at hand, so close that she wondered whether or not they were at work in the dark. The dust caught at her throat and made her cough. There was also a reek of wet, charred wood.

She was almost at the fall before she saw the candles. The swirl of the dust brought them into and out of visibility. She could not see the men she heard so clearly; but from time to time a black shape darted between the lights and her.

"Eyoop!"

Lord John stepped toward her from the dark. He held a shaded oil lamp where its light fell upon her.

"I've gotten them sacks," she shouted over the din.

"Grand," he called. "Feel before thee with thy foot."

She slid her boot along the rail. It came up hard against a low wall of stone.

"End of the line," he said. "Stop there."

She edged to one side, to find the debris-littered rock of the tunnel floor. Now her eyes began to make out faint detail. Her tongue had grown claggy with dust, and the grit crunched between her teeth. She could see that most of the men were working at one part of the fall, for they were in a kind of cavern, much larger than the driftway she had come in by.

Suddenly amid the broken shuttering and the tumbled rock she saw an arm, then part of a naked body. Both were the same greyish ochre as the rock. It moved. She gave a little cry. Two of the men stopped their digging and stared in her direction.

By chance the injured man rolled over. Blood was running from his nose. He moaned. One of the men staring at her returned to the task of digging him out. The other began to walk toward her.

Lord John tugged at the sacks. "Over here," he said.

"Who let a bloody wench in this drift?" the approaching navvy asked.

Lord John, ignoring him, held forth a guiding hand. "Can ye see, lass?" he asked.

"Fookin' wench. No right in a drift."

"You—Visick!" Lord John spoke without looking at him. "There's Pengilly there trapped. So less of thy bloody gassing."

" 'Tis ill luck." He hunched his shoulders and lurched forward.

Still Lord John ignored him. "We've had today's ill luck, see thee. Get Pengilly out afore he croaks." He turned as he led Nora to the opposite end of the cavern and added as a slight placation: "She stopped afore the line."

Visick argued no further.

"There's only three," Nora said, wondering now if it was any use at all. "He were tight as a packhorse girth, yon farmer."

"Three'll do. Lay 'em over them barrels. That's gunpowder in them barrels."

"Eee," she said. The thought of that vast power so close by was daunting. Her eyes were now well adapted to the dark and she could make out fine detail—not where she was looking but all around. She could see a pile of burned shuttering, now a sodden mass of wet charcoal, perilously near the explosive. Lord John arranged the sacks.

"So," he said. "Safe! Aye—ye'd best steam back out sharp like. There'd be trouble if ye stayed. Wait for us by . . ."

"Trouble now," Nora interrupted.

Visick had come up to them again. "If she stops, we're out. Down fookin' tools and out."

"She's already going, ye ignorant friggin' fugitive. Lass!"

She turned. "Aye?"

"See thee by the tunnel mouth. Not be long until we're done here."

"Mebbe."

Unseen by her he smiled at the suggestion that she might not wait.

# *Chapter 4*

The sun was well down by the time they emerged. As daylight and fresh air hit them, they hacked and coughed and spat the grit from their throats. Lord John was among the last to come out, leading the stretcher party. Dust shrouded the unconscious man, unstained by fresh bleeding.

Now that John stood close by her in daylight, he seemed unreal. She knew she was tall for a girl, but he towered at least a foot above her. And his body was like a tree trunk. Such men, she thought, had vanished with her infancy. She wondered what he really looked like under all that dust. "Eee, sorry lass!" he said. "It took a blue month." He cleared his throat and spat a shimmering gobbet high into the evening sunlight. "Eh! Yer chest gets fair closed up with dust. What's yer name?" His eyes appraised her; she could tell he fancied what he saw.

"What do ye mean?"

"What do they call thee?"

"Oh. Nora. Nora Telling. Thou art Lord John, I know. Why'd they call thee Lord?"

He heard the tremble in her voice. "Thou art diddering with cold! Soaked to the buff. I should've known. Should've thought. Breeze can be grim if thou art wet."

They walked again when the stretcher party had gone by.

"Aye," she said. "It's what they call a Robin Hood breeze. It were warm before the sun went behind yon bank."

"Cutting!" he corrected her. "Not bank. We did that. None of nature's work. Well—thou come along of us and dry. I daresay a good helping of beef'll warm thee, eh?"

"Beef!" For her it was a distant memory.

"Aye. When'd thou last eat?"

"I had a shive of bread and a latherick of bacon yesterday noon."

"Well—thou art with navvyin' folk now. Thou'll get a bite to eat, and warmth. And beer. And company. And a shakedown."

He walked tall, with a patrician confidence. No man's my master, was his air. Just to be beside him was a kind of warmth; and though she had eaten so little, she felt a new vigour as she matched him stride for stride.

It was exciting, too, to walk among these men. They were like an army of prizefighters, well fed, well boozed, and fearless. With their sinews of iron they had punched that great hole in the mountain behind. Then she remembered the one who had complained at her being in the drift.

"Won't they mind?" she asked.

As he wondered what she meant his eyes roved without stealth over the wet clothes that clung to her. "Mind?"

The apathy in his voice and the frankness of his inspection warmed her. She liked the thought that this man wanted her. That hasty scrabble back in the graveyard with what-they-call-him had, she now realized, done nothing for her. She shivered with pleasure at the notion of passing the night with this Lord John.

"Him yonder." She nodded at Visick.

"Oh—him what threatened blue murder in the drift! Nay! There's fifteen men here mebbe owe thee their lives this night. They'll not mind. Where's yer boots?"

"I kicked 'em off up on the brow. Got shut on 'em. They was done."

"Mebbe *his*'ll fit thee." He nodded toward the stretcher. "Them Cornishmen is all little."

"Is he dead?" she asked.

"Nay. Lost a leg. Dead drunk, that's all. That's what kept us that long. Couldn't find his leg. There's two men still looking. Mebbe his boots'll fit thee. If they find it. It'll be a week or two until he needs boots, I fancy."

"Poor bugger," she said. "All that blood."

"They got more blood than what we have. Cornishmen. All that fish. Ever see a fisherman from Hull bleed?"

She hadn't.

"They got a lot of blood and all. Same thing. I sent for a surgeon. If he'll come."

They were almost clear of the cutting now. The gangs were thinning out as men in ones and twos stopped off at makeshift homes beside the line. Some were rough shelters of heaped boughs and tarpaulin; some were stouter huts of dry stone and turf. A few navvies had made pitched roofs of rotproofed ties burrowed from the pile at the mouth of the cutting. In the now-breezeless evening greenstick smoke rose from a dozen fires. Women stood alone by their hovels, or in subdued groups, watching the stretcher party go by. Even the children were momentarily hushed. Only the babies cried on, heedless. She smelled meat—beef, mutton, boiling bones. Her flesh suddenly craved and she weakened at the knees.

John spoke again. "How did thou badger yon sacks from him up there? Yon farmer? Tight as a nun's arse, he is."

"Aye!" she agreed. Already it seemed an age ago. "He weren't going to give us aught. I told him the land would blow up under him, but he just laughed."

John laughed too. "Aye, thou were fetchin' it far there."

"Then I saw as he had a cross round his neck, so I thought as he might be a papist. Cross on a chain, it were. So I told him I'd go and tell his priest about him leaving men to die as was in peril of their lives and asking help. So then he give us the sacks. Even then he sought through forty to pick out the worst—them as was all rotten and torn."

John stopped and stared at her, as if he searched for something caught in her eyes. "Thou said that to him!"

"What?"

"About goin' to a priest?"

"Aye. Why? I'd have gone and all."

"Well—thou art a girl of real calibre, Nora."

The way he said it made her proud. Her father had always said of his loom that it was "of real calibre." But, because it might appear that she was putting on airs to admit to such understanding, she said: "Oh aye. We used to have one of them but me sister went and broke it."

He ignored this deviation: "I take off my hat. There's not many now with such spirit. Talking to a gaffer like that."

"Gaffer?" She had never thought of the farmer as a gaffer. "He were nothing but an ill-thriven farmer. Ignorant as thee and me. I've spoken to *thy* gaffer, though."

"Mine?"

"Aye—Mr. Walter Thornton. He put me on to this working of thine."

John laughed. "Thornton! He's no gaffer of mine. Railway engineer. Company servant. I'll tell thee, Nora . . ." He paused.

"What?"

Whatever he had been going to add he thought better of it. "It will keep," was all he said. "Wait till we've supped."

The horse, eager for oats, passed them. Each foot unerringly found a tie. The navvy sat slouched on its shoulders; together they formed a single deep-blue shape against the orange of the setting sun. For a while after it passed, she and John had to swish away a swarm of midges.

"See yon shanty?" He nodded toward a stoutly boarded timber hut with four glazed windows and an iron chimney. "Mine. Big Lord John's Palace. As they call it."

"Nay!" she said. "I thought navvies lay rough."

A breathless youth, barefoot, ran up behind them.

John turned and stopped. "Aye, lad?"

"I . . ." he gasped.

"Get thy breath. Thou's been to the surgeon?"

"Aye . . . and he'll not come . . . he asked if it were . . . navvies . . . and he'll not come."

"Thou said it were Lord John's gang?"

"Aye. He said he'd not come, not if it was Lord Melbourne's gang."

John looked coldly at the distant hills, as if seeking a safe path through them. "I shoulda sent thee, Nora."

"I'll go *now* if thou wish it." His confidence filled her with assurance. For a moment she felt she could, indeed, talk the surgeon round.

He laughed as he turned to her. Not in mockery. More in admiration. It made her want to help him even more, and she understood the effortless command he had over all these other huge and dangerous men.

"Nay," he said, implying thanks. He was serious again. "I'll do what I can. As well as any bloody surgeon." Then he added enigmatically: "This is what must change, lass. One day. It's wrong."

A distant shout behind them made them turn. Two navvies were running out of the cutting, one of them bearing something aloft. Folk streamed from huts and hovels to cheer them from the edge of the permanent way. There was a good deal of laughter, too.

"Pengilly's leg," said the lad.

When the two runners drew level, the one bearing the leg—part of a calf and a booted foot—threw it at the gang around the stretcher. There it was neatly caught and passed from hand to hand until one of them laid it, almost tenderly, beside the still unconscious Pengilly.

Their callousness disgusted Nora—but not absolutely; something in her was eager to share their high-spirited contempt for danger, mutilation, and death.

"That'll cheer him when he wakes," John said. "They'll have a mock funeral tonight. Any excuse for a booze-up." He began to walk again. "See what I can do. Nora—in yon palace there ye'll find an old woman name of Meg. Tell her Lord John sent thee. Lad'll go with thee. Tell her she's to give him me cautering irons and spirit stove. The lad knows. And tell her thou art to have me best overcoat while thy rags are off to dry."

She and the lad made for the hut.

"One thing," he called after her. "Thou's got thy pair of boots now!"

# *Chapter 5*

She gorged herself that suppertime, putting down almost as much beef and ale as Lord John. A corner of the shanty was partitioned off, by rough wooden lockers on the one side and heavy curtains on the other. Outside, the furniture was all crates and packing cases; it lasted as long as someone's casual drunkenness permitted. The men and their women slept in hammocks or on straw mattresses. But inside Lord John's area was real furniture: a bed, all of four feet wide, with a hair mattress and blankets; a scrubbed table; two stout chairs; two pewter candlesticks not yet lighted; and an oak chest, smaller than the nautical kind but, like it, bound in brass and with a lock. She felt privileged to be sitting and eating in there with him.

Washed and changed he looked almost a gentleman. He certainly behaved like one—helping her into her seat, making the old woman serve her first, and things like that. And he took such an interest in her, too. Whatever she said he found some way of turning into another question— about her, her family, her life. And though she knew it was all just a way of passing the time until he took her over to the bed, it was kind and good of him to make her feel so interesting. Yet, funnily enough, he said almost nothing about himself; there weren't many men like that.

He held up the ale jug. "Shall I pour more ale?"

"Nay!" She put a hand over her mug. "I've supped plenty. And I've eaten till I'm nigh burst. Eee—I've not had beef since . . ." She could not remember.

"When?" he prompted.

"Since circuit preacher come to sup," she said, not certain it was true. "One Sunday, backend of last year."

"When thy father were still alive."

"Aye. Just afore he died."

"And ye had beef in plenty afore that?" He suddenly noticed that his hand still held aloft the jug; he poured himself a bare pint, what they call a woolsorter.

"Nay," she said. "Me dad were a handloom weaver. If we'd not had five acres we'd have starved long since. Even then it were cat-collop and chimpins mainly."

"Have ye—" he interrupted.

But she was already speaking on: "If we ate flesh at all . . . have I what?"

"Nay. Go on." He downed most of the ale.

"I said if we ate flesh at all, it were pig."

She brushed some hair from her forehead; he thought she was mopping her brow. "It's hot in here," he said. "What say we go out for a stroll on them banks?"

She wondered why, with a good bed and a thick curtain, he'd want to go out and frig among the grass and rabbit dung. "Aye," she said, standing up and easing the twine that girthed her waist. "It were right grand last night, with the moon out and all. It were that big and red."

"Oh aye," he said, smiling a pretended innocence. "Ye like it big and red, do ye?"

She giggled and dug him with her elbow. Then she realized they had not said grace. "Hold fast."

She did not bow her head but turned it up to an imaginary sky. "Thank thee, Lord, for what we've gotten. If more we'd had, more we'd eaten. Amen."

"Amen," he said and parted the curtain for her.

Ironic cheers greeted them. The navvy who had been playing a jig on his concertina broke at once into "The Yorkshire Ram." They were still roaring out its chorus as John and Nora stepped outside.

"They're not like navvies," she said.

"That they are not. They're Stevenson's lads—*my* lads." He spoke with unaffected pride as he led the way across the line to the banks beyond. "Have ye still got the land?"

"Nay," she said. "Sold it. To pay the lawyer for defending me brother when he got took for swearing a combination. Bugger got his hands on the title deeds and pled me brother guilty. There weren't naught as I could do." She spoke as poor folk speak of floods and famines and other acts of God.

"What've ye done since?"

"Looked after the bairns until they died. Worked in the mills down Stockport, then in the markets in Manchester. I've just done gathering . . ."

"Markets! What did ye do there?" His interest was more than merely polite.

"Figurework," she said proudly. "I like figurework. And I've gotten the head for it. Up to Cocker, as they say."

"Oh? What made thee leave?"

"Gaffer there. He were on the swindle. He thought I'd be too soft to see it." She snorted. "Ill-thriven fool! I saw it first day! He were keeping ten quid a week off takings of hundred 'n fifty. I don't see why he's not caught. Unless they're all at it down there."

"Seven percent!" he marvelled.

"Six and two-thirds," she corrected automatically.

He laughed. "And then he found out thou knowed?"

Now she was scornful: "Found out! I bloody told him. I said I'd want two ten and he could keep seven ten."

"Ye what!" He was taken aback.

"I did. I thought it were generous."

"Ye don't lack for stomach, Nora, but, eee, ye want teaching!"

"Mebbe," she conceded. "He paid us three weeks. Then one of the lads tipped us that gaffer were arrangin' for us to get killed. He's that mean, see thou, copper and gold give him cramp in the hand."

John laughed. "I don't blame him! So—here ye be."

They had reached the highest of the banks. A bright silver moon picked out the land as clear as day, though it was still dark enough to show the gleam of factory windows in Littleborough and Rochdale and even in distant Manchester. Nora thought briefly of the days she had ached and sweated among the looms, inhaling the cotton lint until each breath was a struggle. Of the thousands of women and children now so placed she thought not at all.

"There's no night left," John said. "Not from Manchester to Leeds. Even on the darkest ye can always see them things glimmerin'." He nodded at the factories.

"Aye," she said. "I thought as I'd tramp back to Leeds afore winter falls."

He sniffed. "What did'st do with the seven guineas thou got in the market?"

"Thou art asking a lot." She wished she could see his face more clearly.

"Not in idleness, Nora. I have a purpose."

"Why do they call thee Lord John?"

Laughing he threw himself upon a bank and patted the grass beside him.

"It were Lord Muck once. I worked a twelve-set on me own. For a bet, see."

"What's a twelve-set?"

"I filled twelve tubs of muck. Twenty-seven yards. Cubic yards. Say thirty-four tons of muck." He sought for terms she could grasp. "Pair of good men in a twelve-hour'll do fourteen tubs. I done twelve on me own. So they called us Lord Muck. Every navvy's gotten his name. There's none goes by his given name."

"Why not?"

He spoke for effect: "We're breakin' ground that none has opened since the world and time began. There's spirits there undisturbed. They'd have us if they knew our given names."

"Oh aye." She did not think him serious.

"That's what the lads say, anyway. For meself I'd say there's bodies above ground and all, some way more solid than spirits, as would grab us if *they* knew our given names!"

"Ah," she said with more conviction.

"I can talk like a lord, if I'm minded to," he said.

"Go on then."

He crossed arms behind his head, closed his eyes, and recited: "It is with most agonized heart and mind I presume to address these few lines to your lordship's notice, whom I have had the honour of knowing by sight these many years . . ."

Her giggles rose to a crescendo, drowning his plea. "Know what thou sounds like?"

"A begging letter," he said. "I once made a good screw"—he dropped back into his affected speech—"a tolerable living, a tolerable living, harkee, writing begging letters."

"Eee! Give over! Begging letters! I know what thou sounds like."

"What then?"

"Church of England! Church of England sounds just like thee."

The thought delighted him. "Very good! I'll wager thou could talk just the same if thou wanted."

"Me? Nay. That I could not."

"Go on!"

"Nay, I shan't."

"Say 'five.' "

"Ffff—" she began. "Nay!"

"Go on."

"Thou say it again."

"F i v e," he said deliberately.

"F i v e," she mimicked perfectly.

"Bloody marvellous!" he said, genuinely astonished.

She giggled. She knew she could talk like Manchester or Stockport well enough to gull the folk there; but she had never tried to talk like a nob.

"Say it again," he urged.

"Five," she said, not quite so perfectly when she lacked his model to copy.

"Say 'thousand,' " he continued.

"Thousand." Again it was perfect. She giggled, again in surprise at herself.

"Thou'll do." He was completely serious. "Thou art gifted, lass. Thou has gifts thou never dreamed on."

"Nay, don't mock," she said, misjudging his tone in the dark. "Anyway, what're thou so quick to know about us for then?" And when he did not answer at once, she prompted, "Thou said thou had reasons."

"I know," he said, still pondering. "All right. I'll tell thee. The fall in the drift, in the tunnel today . . ."

"Aye?"

"That little accident is going to domino our contractor, Mr. Skelm. It's the beggar's staff for him now, see thee."

"Nay." She was horrified.

"Failed brickie. Failed builder. And now failed navigation contractor. Or railroad contractor. He'll be sold up—dish, pan, and doubler."

She could not understand his relish. "But won't ye all be out of work? If the contractor's dished up?" He chuckled but did not at once speak. "What'll ye do?" she prompted.

"Skelm's in debt to these gangs two hundred 'n fifty pound, give or take. I'll tell thee what I'll do. I'm going to pay his debt for him. That's what."

"Hoooo! Lord John Muck! Why—it's only two hundred 'n fifty!"

He did not respond to her banter. "Oh—I've gotten it."

"Where," she said, deliberately overeager. She began to search through the pockets of his coat, which she was still wearing.

"Ye'll not find it there. Give over! Anyway—aren't thy own rags dry yet? Nay—give over." His voice was edged with anger but she did not notice.

Her search produced a small silver box. It gleamed in the moonlight as she held it for him to snatch. He did not take the bait. "That's mine and all. Give over, I say!"

She sniffed it. "Snuff. And silver, too." She ran a fingernail across the lid. "What's that? All them squiggles?"

"Put it back, please," he said, still not joining her game.

"Duke of Bridgewater's agent had one of them."

"Back, please!"

She yielded, no longer seeking to taunt him. "He were our landlord down Stockport," she said as she put the snuffbox back in his pocket.

"I'll buy out Skelm's debt on condition he assigns me the contract to finish Summit Tunnel."

At last she realized he was perfectly serious. "What's that worth?" she asked, eager to make up for her disbelief.

"To him? Bloody millstone round his neck. To me and my lads? Five more months for the drift, a year after that for the tunnel. To me meself? Profit on . . . hundred thousand pound? Belike more." She drew in her breath sharply. "Aye! Food for thought, lass. Food for thought."

"He'll never do it. Will he?"

"He's going to have to. See thee, he's not been entirely honest—and I'm not entirely ignorant of that fact. Nor am I unwilling to use it. Anyway— the reason I was asking thee all that was . . . I mean, when ye said ye could do figurework . . . "

"I can," she said. "I know ye'd not think it, to look at us. But me dad taught us. Them five acres—I sold all the produce off of them in the market. When I were so high."

"Everything?"

"Money. And bargaining—I'd badger anyone down, or up, as I wanted. That's why Charley Eade took us on in Manchester. He said he'd never seen a body figure as quick as I could."

"What's seven percent of sixteen and four?" he asked. It was a sum for which most people would have needed a minute or two with pencil and paper.

She thought only briefly before replying, "Nigh on one and two." Thinking aloud she added, "And ye'd be . . . fourpence . . . fourpence ha'penny in the pound too rich if ye multiplied up from that. If you was the taker."

"Eh! Thou'll do, lass!" He was delighted—something more than delighted. "No doubt about it."

"I love figures," she said. "It's like pattern and colours." She wished she could explain it properly.

He grasped her arm briefly, to stress his words. "See thee—if I can hook this contract, I'm going to need someone who can do figurework. It's not that I can't do it meself. But I can't do it *all*. Not on me own."

"Straight?" she said, beginning to feel excited. "Not just gas?"

"Thou'll see. I was saying—I'll need someone who can . . . see thee, there'll be quantities to survey, materials, provisions, things to buy. I need a factotum."

"Oh ah? That's another of them things me sister broke."

Impatience crept into his voice; he was eager to make his point. "A clerk. A help. Another right hand. I tell thee, Nora, this is an age for fortunes. There's brass to be made on the railroads. Brass for common folk that would turn kings and queens of past ages green with envy." She smiled at the thought of it. "Aye," he went on, "ye may pull all the faces ye will, ye may doubt it—but I tell thee: we can be rich!"

"We?"

"Me. Thee. This gang if they can stand the race. All this navigation work that's going on now—all this cuttin' and bankin' and driftin' and sinkin'—it's nothing. Nothing. Not compared to what's going to be. And this business of contracting out to little men, five furlongs here, half a tunnel there, ten fathoms of ventilation somewhere else, all to some little half-bankrupts like Skelm and the other petty barons on this line—it's no way. No way at all."

There was no urgency in his voice now. In fact he spoke almost without expression, forcing her to hold her breath and concentrate. "What should they do then?" she asked.

"They? Do?" He chuckled softly. "Nay—it'll happen anyway. Ye can see it ten mile off if ye've gotten the vision. Big men are going to rise—men as can organize not *one* gang, not *ten* gangs, but whole armies of navvies. Take this line, Manchester & Leeds. Can ye think of anything more daft than cutting it in little parcels and giving it out to two—three dozen little men? Nay—it should be one big man. One organizer. One central purchaser who can strangle suppliers if they try it on with prices—see thee—brick, stone, rail, timber and all. Screw 'em down to the rock bed."

"Buy at pit bottom. Sell at pit head."

"Aye."

"Me dad always said that." Then, to break the silence and change his solemn mood, she added, "So—thou art Duke of Wellington!"

But he was not to be so diverted. "Mock on. One day mebbe thou'll remember I said it. One day there'll be armies of navvies, ten for every one as fought at Waterloo, on both sides. It's not just *this* country, Nora. It's the whole world. Look what's going on in Manchester. Ye can't turn your back but they've knocked up five more mills."

"And Leeds," she said.

"Aye. And Sheffield and Birmingham and London. It's the same down south, ye know. Mills, foundries, works—the whole country's one cauldron of molten iron. But I'll tell thee this, too: It's a bloody one-horse Derby. There's none else at it. We're the only ones. There's English navvies in France now. And Germany. Laying railroad. It'll not be long afore it's the rest of the world. They'll come to us. There's none else they can ask. That's where our fortune's coming from—not gold buried in a bloody tropic island, but gold buried in the future. Waiting while we grow toward it. Do ye see?''

By now he had entirely won her over. The thought that the navvy ganger beside her was perhaps some future civilian Wellington provoked no hint of mockery. "I'm thinking thou'll do it," she said.

"No thinking. I know I will. No doubt on it. I'll do it!"

Suddenly the most important aim in her life was to claim whatever he had offered her a while ago. "I'll be thy fac—toe—whatnot."

"Factotum." He said it as if she was already recruited. "Thou never said what thou did with yon seven guineas from the market."

"I boozed it." She wanted to lie about the part she had spent but found herself not daring to. "I been right down in the doldrums since I were left on me own. It isn't like me, boozing. Eh, but there's times when ye're that low, ye just . . . give way. Whatever's in ye makes ye . . . just give way." Then she remembered the pound Walter had given her; surely she could lie about that? How else could she explain it? "I've still got one pound saved. Look away."

He obeyed. She had tied the sovereign into her shimmy, over her stomach. To get it she had to open his topcoat and turn her shimmy up from the lower hem. While she fiddled with the string that closed the makeshift pouch she looked up to meet his level gaze. "Do ye see somethin' ye fancy?" she asked. But she was coy enough to keep her thighs together.

He smiled but did not answer. Nor did he look away. He knew he wanted her, yet he wished it were not all so inevitable, so taken for granted.

She enjoyed his scrutiny and made no haste to finish undoing the knot. Eventually it gave and she caught the coin as it fell. "There!" She passed it to him, proud of her carelessness.

"A warm golden sovereign!" He fondled it with his lips. "I've never known warmer. What'll ye do with that?"

"Thou keep it," she said impulsively, surprising even herself.

"What?"

"Aye!" She spoke firmly to smother his disbelief—and her own. "Put it in thy fund. Then I'll be thy partner—not just thy . . . what thou said. Fac—toe—thing."

He paused, aware that she was offering something much less explicit than a mere pound. He gazed long at her but she did not flinch. "Very well," he said. "Aye. For sure. Tell us, Nora, what would thou do with a fortune?"

"Eh! I'd have a big house and a park. Me own park, trees and all. And servants in powdered wigs . . ." Then, remembering this was no mere daydream but a distinct possibility, she added, ". . . And I'd have a pump right in the kitchen! Bugger goin' out into the yard!" His laughter hurt her. "All right, Mister Buckstick—what would thou do?"

He took her question seriously, to atone for his unfeeling mirth. "There's naught but one end for money, Nora. For me. Power. Power to change things. To sweep away the old order and make something new. Make a better world for folk. And for meself. They try doin' it through parliament and through unions but there's no success that way. Power first. Then ye can be free to act. Wealth's naught but a dungheap; spread it and thou's made fertilizer." To her surprise he stood and stretched. His joints cracked. "Nay, but I'm getting desperate old. By! The moon does make black shadows!" He scanned about them as if he had personally arranged the landscape. "Ye could put an army in them shadows—and lose 'em. Footpad's friends."

"Aye," she said with unambiguous invitation. "There's a lot could happen in them shadows as folk wouldn't challenge!"

He laughed, kindly this time, and, stooping, lifted her as if she had no weight. Before she found her balance his arms were about her. She did not even try to stand. Her lips poised, darted, and shivered over the stubble of his face like a sucking bee on clover. He responded when they settled on his lips, but she was away again, nipping his ears and pushing his head down from behind so that she could kiss his eyelids. His breathing told her the effect she made. She had not known such happiness since . . . when? She had *never* known such happiness.

"Eee—thou art a canty wench, Nora!" he said. "A right fizzer." He imprisoned her head between his hands and made to kiss her firmly.

"Stop thy gas!" she said and reached a hand down to his front.

But before she could release the tension there he drew away. "Nay," he said, unaccountably lost for words. "I mean . . . not . . ."

"Whassup?" she said. "I never wanted lovin' more. And I'm nake-i-bed under me shimmy. Look!"

Coat wide apart, shimmy held high, she discovered herself to him. Then, on a sudden impulse, she turned herself to face the moon. The feeling was so blissful that, for a moment, she fell under the enchantment of her own senses, ignoring him. She closed her eyes and began a slight barefoot dance upon the soft turf, humming notes that never quite resolved themselves into a tune—or, rather, notes through which many tunes threaded a memory. Her act set lust at a distance and kindled in her a desire far less easy to requite.

He held out his hand. "Come on," he said.

Still swaying and humming, she dropped the shimmy, buttoned up her coat, and took his hand. The mood had died leaving barely an echo. They might have been strangers, but for their clasped hands.

"I should've told thee," he said. "When I was tidying Pengilly's leg, Thornton sent word. I'm to meet him in the drift at ten thirty. Thy Mister Thornton."

That jerked her back to reality!

"Harken thee." She squeezed his hand to give her words emphasis. "He's none of *mine*. Thou's no cause to say that. I chanced to meet him this side Littleborough. We chanced to walk along the railroad at same time. He chanced to say that if I was fearful to tramp over Summit in the dark, to ask for Big Lord John as had a gang of right churchwardens. But that were XYZ-and-parcel. There were naught more. Naught."

He marvelled at the fluency of her lying—for she was not to know that the sovereign she had given him and that now lay in his trouser pocket had lain there not twenty hours before. Thornton had won it from him in a wager that very morning. There was no mistaking the two nicks, one deep, one shallow, in its edge; they were just as his thumbnail remembered them.

"Say no more," he said and gave her hand a squeeze. "I'll be back in a crack. Thou may stop in yon bed of mine this night. If thou still has a mind to it!"

# Chapter 6

He needed no light to guide him to the ventilation cavern in the drift—he who had supervised every foot of the digging. The steady gleam of a bullseye lantern, being played slowly over the rock face, told him the engineer had already arrived. The lantern turned several times toward the driftway; but the rays were too feeble for Thornton to identify John Stevenson.

"Lord John?" he asked when the other was almost in the cavern.

"Aye, sir. I'm a touch late."

"One of your men hurt, I hear. I see some blood over there."

"Pengilly. Lost a leg. Below the knee, so it could be worse." He sucked in his breath sharply and scanned the disordered rubble. "Nay, but it's a sorry business, this, sir."

Thornton spoke with little heat. "As if this tunnel weren't plagued enough. We've had an invert failure at the top end, too."

Secretly Stevenson was pleased. The more trouble for Skelm, the better for him. All he said was, "Aw—I'd not heard."

"This afternoon. It's that blue shale. I knew it was trouble."

"Much, is it?"

Thornton nodded dourly. "Almost an inch!"

Stevenson drew a sharp breath with what he hoped was proper sympathy.

"It'll mean two more courses of brick," Thornton went on. "I don't know! Where's it going to end? And now this! It cannot rain but it pours. This'll put Skelm back."

Stevenson took his chance. "Beggin pardon, sir. Skelm's out. This'll domino Skelm or I'm a Spaniard."

"Hah! Since when?" Threat of disaster often made the engineer almost jocular, John observed.

"The minute this lot fell. He's been at the far end these weeks past. A nudge like this were all he could take. All and more."

Thornton looked round with sudden interest. "You seem to know his business well."

"I've a right to. I lent him a hundred quid not a month back to meet wages for my gang."

"The devil you did!" Thornton, smiling, shook his head in amazement. "But if what you say is true, this is serious. Most decidedly serious. The tender's accepted now. The company's capitalized. We have to find someone to take it on at . . . well, the tendered price. If not . . . it'll be all merry hades!"

He realized now that it would mean an emergency Board meeting; and with Gooch, the senior engineer away, it would be his lot to lay the news before them. His heart slowed at the prospect. He hardly heard what Stevenson was saying; all he caught was the final sentence: " . . . And I'm minded to take on the contract meself."

"You!" Thornton blurted the word too quickly to suppress the mockery in it. But Stevenson merely smiled.

"Aye—I've more to show than ever Skelm had."

His confidence unnerved Thornton, who did not know whether to patronize the ganger or treat him seriously. "I can't see the Board agreeing to that."

It was an unexpected setback for Stevenson: "Ye mean Skelm couldn't just assign the contract to me?"

"No, of course not. Not if he really *is* bankrupt. You are quite sure?"

"No doubt. Not a shade. So . . . it'd be for the Board to determine. Not Skelm?"

"I don't relish telling them."

"Might be better, like, if you was to go with a remedy in hand. If you was to . . ."

But again Thornton was not listening. He spoke, thinking aloud: "Be a meeting *tomorrow,* of course. Emergency meeting. Of all they can muster."

"If you was to put a word in first and then let me speak for meself."

"Me? What could I say?"

"D'ye not think I could measure to it then?"

Thornton decided to let the fellow down lightly. "Yes. Or yes and no. Yes—I think you could . . . I *know* you could . . . get the gangs working. You could organize. Better than Skelm. You'd follow your trades through better. You know the job better. And for my part, speaking as an engineer for Mr. Gooch on this section, I can think of nothing would make me sleep easier nights than to have you on this driftway. But fellow—it takes more than that! Takes capital. Working capital. And that's where I must regretfully say no. I do not think . . ."

"I've got some saved," Stevenson said, relishing the surprise he was about to spring.

The note of contemptuous patronage crept back into Thornton's voice. "Yes. I'm sure. But hardly . . ."

"How much did Skelm have?"

"He lodged a note of hand, a banker's note of hand, good for ten thousand." Thornton hoped this intelligence would show Stevenson the sort of impossible desires he was chasing.

"Ten thousand!" Stevenson shouted. "He never had ten hundred—and one of them was mine!"

Thornton let the echoes die before he spoke—gently he hoped, but firmly. "It's not a matter of hundreds, you see. It's going to . . ."

"How much do they want?"

"How much?"

"Aye. The Board. What'll they want to see?"

Thornton turned his torch back to the broken face of rock, to indicate they must end this idle talk and start their proper business. "Well," he said absently, "if Skelm failed with ten—whether he had it or no—they'll want something the colour of twelve, I should think."

"I've got ten." Stevenson joined in the aimless search of the rock face.

Thornton repeated with martyred patience. "I'm talking about thousands. Twelve *thousand.*"

"Aye." Stevenson sucked a tooth. "I've got ten thousand." He slipped his fingers behind a thin flange of loose rock. "I'll lodge a note of hand from my London bankers, Bolitho & Chambers of Dowgate in the City. Good for ten thousand." He pulled the rock loose, creating a toy avalanche of grit. A less practised deceiver would have made it twelve thousand, but Stevenson knew that if ever doubt seized Thornton, it would be stilled by the fact that the claim was for a mere ten and it was made within moments of hearing that ten would be insufficient. Also, to be sure, he enjoyed sailing close to the wind.

"Jesting apart?" Thornton was wary now.

"Never jest on brass."

"You're worth many times more than I!" The idea made Thornton uncomfortable.

"What's more to the matter is that me plus ten thousand is worth Skelm plus forty."

"You're probably right. But it's unlikely the Board will see it in that light."

"Even if you speak for me?"

Thornton did not at once reply. "I'll do my best," he said at length. Then he turned full face to Stevenson. "Who are you?" he asked. "They call you Lord John. But who are you really?"

Now it was Stevenson whose smile was patronizing. "Ye'll pardon me, but that's my affair. No offence meant and none taken I hope. I could, however, show the chairman, Sir . . . Sir . . ." He pretended to fish for the name.

"Sir Sidney Rowbottom."

"Aye. Him or the reverend gentleman, Doctor Prendergast—under oath of secrecy—I could show either a letter of patronage from . . . one in a high place, a peer of the realm and close to the queen. Our present queen." He made a sudden expansive gesture to bring Thornton some way into the secret circle he had set up. "I trust ye'll be able to be discreet on this yourself, sir."

"Why . . ." The change took Thornton aback. "Yes . . . to be sure . . ."

"I think it'd satisfy 'em. The meeting's to be in Manchester, I take it?"

"Yes . . . yes . . . at the Miles Platting offices."

"It's nothing so very grand, sir. So if you'll speak out for me and how I can organize the lads and see the working through, I'll fire the other broadside—the credentials and particulars."

"Ye know what you're taking up?" Thornton reasserted himself. "I still expect this driftway finished by Christmas. Two thousand eight hundred and eighty-five yards. You know that."

Stevenson pretended to be thinking aloud: "Well—this'll make number one shaft blind. And with number thirteen blind already, there'll be only twelve shafts to work from." Thornton nodded agreement. "So we'll only have twenty-six faces to work."

"At most. Fourteen shaft is almost through to the end drift now."

Stevenson reached the tip of his thumb into his moustache, ruffled it, then smoothed it with a knuckle. Thornton watched anxiously.

"You and me shall walk every yard of it on Boxing Day," he promised at last.

"*This* year." Thornton persisted.

"This year of grace, eighteen hundred and thirty-nine."

Thornton grinned broadly. "You can survey this sorry heap of rubble" —he played the torch once more over the rock, bringing it to rest on the bloodstained area—"the ruin of one contractor, and say that!"

"I can, sir." Stevenson's tone was strangely perfunctory. He seemed more concerned to cover the marks of the blood. He kicked unstained muck over it and even bent to raise larger rocks with his hands to lay upon that patch of brown. Curious, Thornton now shone his lamp on the other's profile. Stevenson was totally absorbed. Only when the last trace of blood was covered did he return to their conversation.

Thornton said, "Then, by George, you have my vote!"

"Thank you, Mr. Thornton, sir. I'm counting on it," Stevenson replied. But he spoke as though *that* had been a foregone conclusion.

Then, omitting only the mention of Nora and her part in it, he gave the engineer his account of the events leading up to and following the explosion.

Ten minutes later they were out in the blinding moonlight.

"My! It's brighter than day after that stygian dark in there," Thornton said. He greatly wanted to reopen the topic of Stevenson's bid for main contractor and wondered how the other had managed to close it so completely.

"Look! Yon bank's alive with rabbits," Stevenson said. "Ye'd think they knew they was safe from poaching. Night like this."

"They'll not be safe long."

"Oh?"

"No. I'm told they're to break up the warren tomorrow."

The two men began to walk out along the cutting. "It's happening everywhere now. We broke up two down in Hertfordshire last summer. Big ones, too. Just in our one valley. Taken over the country as a whole, they must be ploughing up hundreds. About time too. The rabbits are a menace."

"What'll poor folk be doing for meat?" Stevenson threw a lump of ballast at the bank, narrowly missing a large buck.

"Hard luck! They'll not thieve it anymore, that's certain. There's talk now of fitting whole ships out with ice-making engines and chambers insulated from the heat in which to bring frozen meat from Australia. I suppose it will happen one day. I can't say I'd relish frozen meat, but no doubt it will be a boon to the poor."

"Mebbe," Stevenson said, already planning the night's work ahead.

"Incidentally," Thornton chattered on, "talking of the poor—met a young girl this afternoon, tramping up this way, coming up from Little-borough. Handsome girl, too. Name of Molly. Tramping over to Leeds with her toes sticking out of her boots. I . . . uh . . . told her she might get a bite and some shelter with you." He looked for a response.

Some time passed before Stevenson said flatly, "Aye. She's there now." Then turning suddenly, he added, with every sign of innocent curiosity: "Did ye tumble with her, sir?"

"I *beg* your pardon!" Thornton's hesitation and then his overreactive bluster turned a near certainty into one that was absolute.

"She had a sovereign hid about her—the which, if she got it off of you, were seventeen shilling too much."

That, too, found an easy target. "You presume too far, fellow," the engineer said thinly. Then, in even less certain tones he added: "Did . . . er . . . *she* tell you so?"

"Nay." Stevenson let him infer that the very idea was unthinkable.

"Well . . ." Thornton, smiling again, was all breezy assurance. "There was nothing of that sort. The very idea! And a pound, too! Hah! There's better in St. George's Street at half as much."

An outsider would have thought their laughter had a common cause.


# *Chapter* 7


That same bright moon lay across the bed and Nora's sleeping form. Only her hand and arm extended into the light, but a softer reflection bathed the rest of her. It dimmed the redness of her hands and the weather stains upon her face. It lent her hair a lustre that daylight would dull, and effaced the lines of care that these last years had etched. It was a more innocent girl, a Nora-who-might-have-been, who slept so soundly there.

Long minutes he stood watching her, hoping the innocence might somehow invade her and stay, hating the necessity to wake her and knowing it would flee—especially with the tasks she must undertake for him between now and dawn. The sight of her almost turned his resolution. But at last he reached down his hand and stroked her cheek as gently as he could. "Nora," he whispered. She stirred. "Come on, lass!"

She awoke but did not open her eyes. The ease left her as she stiffened; a feline smile creased her face before she turned upon her back. The movement let the single blanket slide to the floor. She caught the hand that still caressed her cheek and carried it down to her breast. Only when it failed to play did she open her eyes. "Come on!" she said.

"Nay, lass," he replied, but with little conviction. He sat heavily beside her. It cost a lot of effort to go on. "There's more important work afoot." He ran one fingernail down her midline, from neck to navel, as if it had been long familiar there. "Fetch us some water," he commanded.

"Water!" She sat up.

Moonlight on her body . . . the closeness of her body . . . the smell of her body. . . . He compelled himself to look out through the window and speak with an edge of hardness. "Don't . . . question, lass. Just do as thou art bid. Fetch water."

Piqued, yet not daring to risk an open show of anger, she reached for her shimmy and the blue dress, now dry.

"There'll be no slumber—nay, nor naught else—this night. See thee, this'll be thy first big test. Thou must come through it."

Curiosity began to replace her annoyance. "Right, master! To be sure, master!"

She spoke with the same sarcasm she had given the words earlier that day but, unlike Walter, John chose to take them straight. "That's the cheese, lass," he said. "Jump!"

While she fetched the water he lit two candles. He washed face and hands with fastidious care, then bade her light two more candles and do the same.

When she returned from tipping out the water she found him lifting a writing case from the brassbound box. "What're thou at?" she asked.

He spoke as he worked, checking pens, paper, ink, and notebooks. "By daybreak tomorrow I need a letter of introduction from the Earl of . . ." He ruffled his moustache with his thumb and smoothed it again. "Nay, we'll make it Duke of Somerset. Aye! A letter from him and a note of hand from a London banker good for ten thousand quid. How's poor Pengilly? I should've asked."

"Sleeping now." Nora craned to see what was in the notebooks. "He come to hisself shouting, so they topped him up with gin. Eh—know what they call him now?"

"What?"

"Pegoleggy," she giggled. "Instead of Pengilly, see? Pegoleggy!"

"Not bad." He was relieved to see her resentment was quite gone.

"*He* didn't think it were anything to laugh at. They was howling their-selves daft, but he never even smiled."

"Nay—well, ye can see his point of view. Now . . ." He took the chair for himself and pointed for her to sit on the bedside, facing him across the table. "Get to work! Take pen and paper."

Intrigued, she obeyed. She dipped the pen, drained the excess against the neck of the well, and waited expectantly. "Aye?"

"Set this down then. Figure this. Ye knows yon tunnel, how it's shaped like an arch."

"Aye?"

"There's nigh on two hundred and fifty bricks reaches from the invert up to the soffit and down to the invert on the other side."

"Invert?"

"Bed. Floor."

She smiled. He asked her why.

"Bed?" she said, with a different intonation. "Floor?"

He grew exasperated. "Shape thyself, lass. No joking tonight. It's make or break, see thee. If there's five courses—nay, figure the cost per course. Allow nine inches to a brick—how many bricks in hundred yards? And what's the cost at four bricks a penny? And if a brickie can lay six hundred and forty to a day in the quadrant and takes three bob a day . . ."

"Three bob!"

"Aye. There's the *real* aristocracy for thee! If they get three bob a day, how long's it take 'em to lay hundred yards—and the cost? Got all that?"

Nora was scribbling furiously. "Aye, I think so."

"Think! Think's no good to me!" Though his words were hard their tone was jocular.

Her confidence was almost perfunctory. "Aye, I have then. Did ye say five courses to the arch? Ye want the answer five times up?"

His face creased in a slow smile, mainly of relief. "Thou'll do. And when thou has figured that there's timber, hardcore, ties, laying rail, stone . . . chippies, masons, navvies, Roman cement, gunpowder, coals, a thousand men, ninety horses, twelve—nay, ten—steam-winding whims . . . and more. All to be quantitied and priced by sunup."

"Oh ah," she said. Her hand, independent of her, was already jotting down calculations. "What're *thou* goin to do?"

"Help thee. But first, like I said—I must give meself some standing." He pulled a sheet of parchment from a shelf in the writing case. "See that?"

"Aye." She barely glanced up before she spoke; the calculations seemed entirely to absorb her, leaving an automaton in charge of all her other actions.

"Duke of Somerset's own crested paper. His grace is about to write us a recommendation. Here"—he held out another pen—"take thou this pen. Yon's mine. Me special."

She looked at him then; his words had just reached her. "It'll not be legal."

He smiled and made some practise flourishes on a blank page of the notebook. "Listen! Success makes all legal. And I'm going to succeed, see thee. Never mind 'legal.' No one'll talk of 'legal' when I'm made." Now he looked directly at her. "I've five thousand pound put by."

Her eyes grew wide. "Five thousand! Nay!"

"Aye. Not a penny—or not many—honestly come by. But I've *worked* for it, see thee! Have I not worked! And now I'll tell thee this. There's *legal* thieving, too. Industry's a golden turnpike to legal theft and extortion. For every pound I sweated for there's lords and baronets and men of middling sorts made thousands. And now I mean to join 'em."

"But a felony's still a felony—and that's what thou art at. Isn't it a hanging matter? Forgery?"

"If I fail. If I'm found out. Aye—it'll be a felony. But if I clear, as I expect . . ."—his voice fell as he beckoned her ear nearer—"if I clear thirty thousand on this and put it back to make hundred and that way on . . . if they catch me then, there may be one or two will think I were a touch naughty at the start. But if they say it aloud, they'll cry it in the bloody wilderness. Anyway, it isn't hanging now, forgery. Only for forging wills and power of attorney to transfer stock. Forgery's transportable now, see thee."

She had written £30,000 among her calculations, as if idly. "How can ye make that much profit on a job that's bankrupted another?" she asked.

He winked. "Because I got a factotum as *he* never had!"

"Nay. Bid off! How can thou do it?"

He was serious again. " 'Cause I got sense where he kept his brandy. I *know* what the navvy and craftsman can do. And I know how to encourage it. He slung money away, did Skelm."

"And shall I have a wage or a cut of the profits?"

Though her lips and glinting teeth smiled, as if she were really teasing, her eyes dwelled on his in a cold unhurried audit. This new depth of her excited him. He sensed a compulsion in her, and the compulsions of others always excited him. He understood them, those urges, as a musician understands an instrument or a craftsman his tools. And he could no more ignore it in her than a master carpenter could ignore a box of chisels found beneath a hedge. To recognize the power that gripped her was automatically to determine he would harness it and use it for himself.

"We'll see," he promised. "Tomorrow. See how ye take to the work."

"Eh! Isn't it exciting!"

Her delight was infectious. "Aye," he said fervently, "it is. It is. Ye've *just* hit it. I reckon a successful swindle's the most surpassing thing in this world!"

*     *     *

By morning even Nora's ardour for calculation was dimmed. She had worked through some parts of the contract six or seven times looking for savings—in the operations at the tunnel, in their sequence, and in delaying payment on the bills as they fell due. Time and again John had turned down her suggestions as "technically impossible" or "bad practice" or "not right by the lads"; but a few he had allowed—and not grudgingly but with admiration. So she had been encouraged to gather all these permissible economies together and calculate their total effect. The purpose had been to keep the cost below five thousand pounds, John's total capital, until payment was due on the contract on Boxing Day.

She could not conceal her disappointment. "There's no way I can trim it finer. It'll cost thee all of six thousand."

Strangely, though, his disappointment was more conventional than deep. "There *is* a way," he said. "I've not told thee yet . . ."

"Nay!" She choked a scream. "I can't. Not another. Me head's that zany with figuring! I couldn't!"

He waited patiently. "Have ye done?"

"*Have* I! Every bloody way! And I shan't—"

"Will ye listen!" She was silent. "Right. There's no figuring in it. No figuring to do. Plain reason is all. Ye say there's no way I can do it under six. Yet five's all I've got. Right?"

"Correct."

"So. I must find a scheme to let them pay us half what's due, half way twixt now and the end of the year. And then on, regular like, right through the contract."

"Oh aye—how'll thou do it?"

"I don't know. But something'll come to us. I'll find the way."

His daring and wholehearted acceptance of the impromptu left her wide-eyed. So did his mountainous breakfast of cold beef, hard eggs, potatoes, and beer. So, too, did the gentleman's suit and gaiters he put on for his visit to the directors of the Manchester & Leeds Railway in their smart new headquarters at Miles Platting.

# *Chapter* 8

The directors of the Manchester & Leeds Railway in their smart new head-quarters at Miles Platting were not in the best of humour. The whole railway world was still squirming at the memory of the Kilsby Tunnel, and the comparisons with Summit were uncomfortably resonant. Both were twin-track, brick-lined, with a horseshoe section and a twenty-six-foot span. Both had been surveyed by the Stephensons and both were originally estimated at about £100,000. And now, like Kilsby, Summit was running into trouble even before the driftway was through. The only difference was that Summit was 459 feet longer—hardly encouraging when one remembered that Kilsby had ended up at thrice its estimated cost. And every director there *did* remember it, only too well. Some at that hastily summoned meeting were seeking a scapegoat; others were praying for a saviour. The Reverend Doctor Prendergast was passing the sherry and Sir Sidney Rowbottom—sign of the seriousness of the occasion—was refusing it.

Edwin Payter, respected as one of the larger shareholders, was impatient; this day had many calls upon his time. "Sir Sidney," he asked, "may we not start? I'm to take luncheon with Bridgewater's agent. I daren't . . ."

"Quite. Quite. We'll finish this very quickly, I think. I take it all here have read Mr. Thornton's report?"

There were murmurs of assent. John Stevenson had not been alone in spending most of the night writing.

"I believe he's to be congratulated," the Reverend Doctor Prendergast suggested.

There were murmurs of assent to that, too.

"In that case," Sir Sidney went on, "I propose we see this fellow . . . er . . ." He searched among his papers.

"Stevenson," Thornton prompted.

"Yes. Not related is he?"

"No, Sir Sidney. Apparently not."

"Useful name, what!"

"But he spells it with a *v,* in any case."

"What's known about him?" Payter asked.

"Yes." Sir Sidney, not pleased to have the reins taken from him, looked at Payter, though it was Thornton he addressed. "Will he die in harness on us? Like this Skelm fella?"

"I think he'll satisfy you there, gentlemen. He *says* he can. I'd feel more competent to advise you as to his suitability to the contract. With your permission."

They approved; Sir Sidney nodded.

"I met with him last night. He was the ganger on the shift that had the explosion . . ." He paused. The Reverend Doctor Prendergast's mouth was an astonished O of black, inside which the tip of a large furry tongue was trying to wrap itself around a word . . . several words.

"Did you say *ganger?*" the tongue achieved at last.

"Yes, doctor."

"And this . . . *ganger* . . . is going to be able to satisfy us of his financial standing! Is he aware . . . are *you* aware, Mr. Thornton, that we are talking about ten thousand pounds?"

"Indeed, yes. I told him, in fact, that I thought you'd want to see more, since ten was what Skelm was broken on."

"Quite right," Payter said, nodding at everyone as if he had said it first.

"If Skelm ever had it," one of the others said darkly.

"Gentlemen!" Sir Sidney called. "I think *we* can satisfy ourselves of this Stevenson's standing. For goodness' sake, let Mr. Thornton appraise us of his other qualities."

Thornton waited for silence, and got it. "As I said, we discussed the contract last night and he says he's certain he can finish the driftway by Christmas, when the payment is due. He said we'd walk the entire tunnel together on Boxing Day."

"He'd be bound to tell you *that* . . ." someone started, but Thornton's cautionary finger, held aloft, silenced him.

"I must say"—he looked at each man there—"that, of all the people I know in any way fitted for this job, I'd trust most this fellow Stevenson. As a contractor."

"Not as a person?" Prendergast was quick to take up the qualification.

"I hardly know him as a person. But as a leader, a natural leader, an inspirer of men, he can have few equals."

"He becomes more interesting by the minute!" Prendergast's dilettante tone clearly annoyed Payter.

Thornton went on: "If you want your tunnel done on time and to specification—Stevenson's the one I'd back."

"And to price?"

"No man can guarantee that. I'll see he won't cheat or skimp, be assured."

"You've still told us nothing about him," Sir Sidney complained. "What's his background?"

"He may tell *you*, Sir Sidney. They call him Lord John, or Big Lord John, for he's well above six feet. Some have said he's the son of a peer, born the wrong side of the sheets, others that he's a felon gone to earth . . . er—so to speak—like so many of our navvies."

"But where's the fella from?" Sir Sidney was out of his depth among all this speculation.

"That's another curiosity. He talks like a north countryman. Yet Leeds men say he's from Sheffield. Sheffield men are sure he's from Barnsley . . . and so on. None will quite own him. And I once heard him speak as sweet as any gentleman."

"Sounds a thorough rogue!" Payter was anxious to end all this airy talk.

Thornton had no choice but to take each of them quite seriously. "Probably is," he agreed. "Probably is. Very probable. But he'll finish your tunnel on time and to the highest specification. And as close to the tendered price as man may get. Why should you want a saint into the bargain? Your pardon, reverend."

Prendergast waved magnanimous circles around him. "Not at all. Accurately stated. Quite agree."

Payter almost burst at every button. "D'ye think we might meet this . . . paragon!"

"Indeed, Payter," Sir Sidney soothed, "you're being very patient. Mr. Thornton, be so good." He nodded at the door.

Thornton quickly crossed the room and opened the door just wide enough to poke out his head and nod at John Stevenson, who sat there as unconcerned and smiling as if waiting to be called to a barber's chair.

If the directors had expected a ganger, a man in moleskins tied with twine below the knee and with a knotted kerchief at his throat, they were doubly surprised at what they saw. He had no cane or gloves, and his hat would have been passed from a true gentleman to his servant ten years since, but the clothes proclaimed a substantial tradesman at the very least. And the man himself had the bearing of a king. Stevenson was pleasantly aware of the impression he made. If he realized that this was to be the most important interview of his life, he gave no outward sign of it. "Your servant, gentlemen," was all he said.

"Now I place you!" Sir Sidney told him.

"Correct, Sir Sidney," the other said with a smile. "You were good enough to speak with me when last you inspected the driftway. So . . ." He pulled out a sealed parchment as soon as he reached the edge of their table. "I believe this is what you're expecting to see."

Thornton was most astonished of all in that room. Stevenson's manner and speech were so different here. Only the irony in his eyes, an occasional suggestion of something close to scorn, united the ganger of last night and this well-founded, handsome giant who now stood before them.

Sir Sidney ruptured the seal, opened the note, and began to read. "Do be seated, Stevenson." His eye scanned the note faster than he could read aloud. For the benefit of all he uttered only the key phrases: " 'Bolitho & Chambers . . . maintained regular deposits . . . government bonds . . . ten years . . . speak for ten thousand pounds.' Bolitho & Chambers? Who knows them? Payter?"

"Not I." Payter shrugged.

"I do, I believe," Prendergast said. "Bankers in Dowgate, are they not? Let me see." He looked closely at the paper and held it to the light before he turned to Stevenson. "Extraordinary," he added.

"Quite extraordinary," Sir Sidney agreed. "It prompts one to ask the . . . somewhat obvious question: Why, with the substance of a gentleman, have you felt it necessary to live as one of lower rank?"

Stevenson's heart danced. It was all going exactly as he had plotted. Now was the time to go on the offensive. "You force me to be blunt, Sir Sidney, gentlemen. I came here not to seek your approval for my conduct but to secure your nomination as contractor to the Manchester & Leeds for Summit Tunnel. My bankers have assured you of my standing and I trust Mr. Thornton here has told you of my competence. I cannot, with the greatest respect, see that you need more."

It was, as he well knew, more provocation than they would accept.

"Damn you!" Sir Sidney spoke for them all. "We mean to have it, sir—if you mean to have this nomination. It is altogether too extraordinary . . . you intend not to explain?"

"Very well!" Stevenson made it clear they had forced him to it. "Since you insist. Some years ago, like many others, like all here I daresay, I became convinced that the future lay with the railroads." That naturally brought a rumble of approval. "But not . . . your way. Not, at least, for me. The time will come when—and it will be soon, so you'll not find me a patient or complaisant man—the time will come when ye'll not be able to parcel out the lines to little men the likes of Skelm . . . furlongs here, fathoms there. Ye'll have to give the whole line—banks, bridges, drifts, stations, piles—the lot . . . ye'll hand it all to one man. And he'll set an army on: ten thousand men, and more. And he'll buy cheap. If any supplier swells the price, he'll go into that supplier's trade and bankrupt him. And the railway company that ignores him will . . . not prosper either. I mean to be such a man."

It was a far greater bid than anyone there had expected; and Stevenson had spoken with such quiet assurance, careful to meet each man there eye to eye, that for a moment no one spoke. The Reverend Doctor Prendergast cleared his throat delicately.

"I'm sure that's most laudable, Stevenson . . . but . . . er . . . with ten thousand pounds?"

Stevenson was ready for that. "No, sir! With something worth ten times that. If not more. Experience! That's the real wealth I've put by these many years. Experience. Which of you gentlemen here could lay a course of brick neat and true on a twenty-six-foot span? Or gauge the powder to blast a wall of compacted sandstone or millstone grit? Which of ye could look at a hill, cube a cutting through it, look at a valley beyond, dispose of the muck by way of embankment—all in the mind, mark ye—and then quantify out both jobs in men and days? Time and money?"

"But dammit, man"—Walter, representing the engineers, could not let this pass—"that's not your job, it's ours. We do all that long before we go to tender."

"And you're never wrong?" It was not really a question, but to underline the message for them Stevenson went on: "Last year—last summer, I was on part of the Maidenhead line. There was one cutting wouldn't hold. Too steep. They had to shave down four degrees more. Another thousand cubic yards of muck and nowhere to put it. Contractor, poor old Tom Essex, took a big loss on that. I'll tell Mr. Thornton this. Ye need only be two percent out in your estimate and in two furlongs that's a thousand yards of extra muck for a gang of twenty-five to waste four days dumping somewhere. Losses can soon mount. But not with me!"

"And *you're* never wrong?" Thornton sought to turn Stevenson's own question upon him.

"Not when it's my money says I'm right."

"This is no doubt all very interesting," Payter cut in. "But it's hardly to the point."

"Very true," Stevenson agreed. "My point, simply put, is this: I can now do every trade on the road—from surveying and quantities to plate-laying. What's more, the men know it. Skelm, I grant ye, knew cutting and embanking as well as any man. But platelayers, brickies, stonedressers, chippies, smiths . . . they walked circles round him even when he was sober. No man will do that to me. And there's no man in England, gentleman or labourer, can say that *and* put five thousand—" he cursed himself for his mistake—"er . . . let alone *ten* thousand pounds, where his mouth leads!"

Payter, unmoved by any rhetoric, put the one question that concerned him. "Ambitions apart, Mr. Stevenson, you're confident of finishing the driftway by this Christmas? It's only a hundred and twenty days."

It was time to work them to his plan. "Yes sir . . . ah . . . *with* the Board's co-operation." The traces of suspicion and even hostility he had read in their faces when he first joined them were gone. "At our present rate of working—never mind accidents—even at our normal rate, as Mr. Thornton will confirm, we shall be nigh on three hundred feet short of finishing at the end of the year."

The fact was clearly news to some of them, particularly Sir Sidney, who turned at once to Thornton. "That true?" he asked.

"It is, sir. Mr. Gooch has known for some time the—"

"Never mind that now," Payter interrupted again. "You have a plan to avoid that, Mr. Stevenson?"

"Yes. We're working the drift at twenty-six separate faces—twelve shafts and the two ends. Twenty-six gangs. All we want is a foot a week more progress from half of them and we'll more than make up the deficit. So, for each gang I'll estimate a good five days' progress, depending on whether they're in shale or grit, but let's say for discussion's sake it's five feet in five days. For every foot they do above the mark within each and any five-day period, I'll pay them a bonus day."

The Reverend Doctor Prendergast snorted. "Pay them more and they merely drink more. What's your plan for *that*? How'll you stop their drunken randies?"

"For every foot of *under*achievement they'll drop a day's pay. That's the other part of the bargain. There'll be no more randies this side Christmas—though ye may get little work out of em the first fortnight in 1840!"

"God help the countryside!" Prendergast said; but he was clearly pleased at Stevenson's answer.

"And if any man don't like it," Stevenson went on, "there's plenty of other work on the line. And plenty of sober navvy gangs abroad. There's three on the Bolton line I'd not mind . . ."

"Whoa!" Sir Sidney took the bait. "Some of us have an interest in that line, too! We don't want to buy progress at Summit at the expense of the Bolton line!"

Stevenson sat back in his chair for the first time, making himself something more of a partner, less of a supplicant. "Ye see, Sir Sidney. It makes *my* point. There's why ye need a big contractor. Ye're waging a campaign with a lot of good captains and no general."

"I do begin to follow." Sir Sidney was thoughtful, and others around the table nodded sagely. Only Prendergast looked puzzled.

"But see here, Stevenson, you're going to be badly out of pocket—paying out bonuses ahead of receipts, what?"

"Thank you, doctor," Stevenson said. It dawned on him there were depths to this man that belied his air of shallowness. "I was beginning to fear no one'd mention it. My proposal is that the Board adopt the same payment scheme with me as I intend to adopt with my lads. Payment by results instead of fixed dates. I daresay ye'd not be averse to paying the *full* sum if I gave ye your tunnel next week."

They laughed, of course.

Then, while the clerk jotted furiously, he outlined the payment scheme that had not completely formed in his own mind until he sat in the anteroom, less than a half hour earlier. There was still plenty of bargaining over the details, to be sure, but they had conceded the principle without a murmur. Stevenson was hard put to conceal his elation. The Reverend Doctor Prendergast had resumed his air of supercilious detachment but once or twice it was his interjection that allowed a concession to go to Stevenson.

So it was all the more surprising when, just as the meeting seemed wound up, and people were gathering papers and reaching again for the sherry, Prendergast dealt what might have been a body blow to Stevenson's acceptance by his fellow directors: "One moment, Sir Sidney. I would like to interpose one further condition. We have all met Mr. Stevenson and I'm sure I speak for all when I say we are most impressed. Most. It is an ending, I feel confident, to this nightmare of Summit Tunnel—the longest tunnel, and, in its potential at least, the longest nightmare, in the country."

"The world," Stevenson said.

"Quite. I say we are impressed because we have *met* Mr. Stevenson and recognized in him those qualities that, I am sure, will carry him to the very—"

"The point, man! What's the point?" Payter was angry again. He pulled out a fob watch, looked at it, and shook his head.

"The point, sir, is that our shareholders have not been so privileged." He smiled at Stevenson a smile of reptilian calm. "As far as they are concerned, viewing this affair entirely from the exterior, we have had one contractor default despite sureties for ten thousand pounds—and what do we do? Wonder of wonders, the very same day, we appoint another with sureties for . . . ? Ten thousand pounds! It looks ridiculous, don't ye see? It smacks of panic."

"But half the tunnel's done," Stevenson protested. He should have found a way of interrupting earlier; but Prendergast's helpfulness during the bargaining had allayed any fear of opposition from that quarter.

"And paid for! And paid for!" Prendergast countered. "So all should be equal. If, despite all his qualities, Mr. Stevenson should also default— which the heavens forefend; I merely say *if*—if he should default, it will be all our heads on the block!"

Sir Sidney cleared his throat to speak, but one of the others put the mind of the meeting in two words: "He's right."

Payter fiddled with his fob chain. "I'm sorry I was hasty, doctor. Once again we're in debt to your acumen."

Stevenson still fought but with little hope of winning now. "Will ye be asking for sureties against volcanic eruptions and a second universal flood? Where d'you stop once ye've set foot on this path? Faint hearts never yet built a railroad!"

Sir Sidney, true man of putty, wavered: "There *is* something to be said for that, too."

"But more to be said on Prendergast's side," Payter cut him short. "What were you about to propose, doctor?"

"We must make some extra requirement. Some token merely, but there must be some extra. I propose we require Mr. Stevenson to furnish sureties for an extra . . . what? . . . thousand pounds? No more than that. And I propose we appoint him contractor *pro tempore* for . . . fourteen days? And such appointment to be confirmed with no other new condition upon production of such extra surety. Shall we say a thousand?"

Stevenson forced himself to smile.

"At any subsequent inquisition," Prendergast concluded, "we could save our necks by pointing to this extra restriction. Not even the canal faction could say we had acted imprudently."

"That strikes me as eminently reasonable," Sir Sidney added. "Stevenson?"

Of course he had to put a bold face on it. "I'm considerably relieved, Sir Sidney. I thought Dr. Prendergast was about to suggest *doubling* my surety. But if your office can give me a note, on company paper, itemizing our agreement, I'll have no difficulty finding an extra thousand pounds. I'm confident of that."

"Excellent! I'm sure if you call by tomorrow you may pick it up. Yes?" Sir Sidney looked at the clerk, who nodded. "Yes. There! So, Mr. Stevenson, thank you for your attendance. May I say on behalf of the Manchester & Leeds that we look forward to a happy association."

"And mutually profitable!" Prendergast added.

"Indeed," Stevenson agreed. Then, because some kind of speech-in-reply seemed expected, he added: "I'll thank ye now, Sir Sidney, gentlemen. But, by your leave, I'll put off any speechifying until the day of the celebration run."

"Put a date to *that!*" Payter challenged.

Stevenson shot each a final glance before he spoke. "Aye. I'll put a date to it: Christmas 1840. Your servant, gentlemen."

It was a good exit, but even before the door had closed behind him he was wondering how on earth he'd get a genuine surety for a thousand pounds. His forged note of hand . . . he'd never dare take that to a banker. He was beginning to wish he'd risked more last night and told Thornton he had eleven rather than ten thousand. Yet there was something wrong with that, too. He felt sure that Prendergast would have found some pretext to raise the requirement still further. He'd badly underestimated that man. For some reason—and it had nothing to do with the Manchester & Leeds—Prendergast had wanted to get his extra condition carried; everything else had been subordinated to that one purpose.

He stood at the street entrance, wondering whether to go down Hulme Hall Lane to the pie shop or straight up to the station and wait for the one ten to Littleborough. The door at the head of the stair slammed and Thornton, like an excited schoolboy, came bounding down, three and four at a time. "Stevenson!"

Stevenson turned.

"Excellent man!" Thornton clapped him heartily on the back. "I'm so pleased. Let me be the first to shake your hand!"

"Until the good reverend doctor had his say!"

"*His* say? It was my suggestion! Didn't I tell you last night? Didn't I tell *them* this morning? That always happens to me. My suggestions are ignored; then someone else makes them."

"More eloquently," Stevenson suggested.

"With greater expenditure in wind and effort, and gets called a 'genius' for his theft!"

His complaint was too good-natured to need more than a wry smile from Stevenson. "But," Thornton went on, "that *is* principally what I wanted to discuss with you. Will you walk a little into Manchester as we talk? I must get there by one thirty for the Earlestown train; I'm off to London this afternoon."

"Are you?" Stevenson was surprised. "Am I to begin on Summit Tunnel on my own?"

Thornton shot him a crafty glance and smiled. "In a way. And in a way not. In a way I shall be there—or my support. This is my proposal. I have a

few savings and a small inheritance put by. I could stand a thousand on top
of your ten."

It cost Stevenson all his resolve to refuse the offer. Before he had started
on this venture he had decided that if ever his ambition were realized, he
would on no account contract a debt or an avoidable obligation—or at least
one that he could not repay and so discharge—to any engineer or company
servant. He had seen too many come to grief that way; the company must
seek and court the contractor or no good would come of their work together. Yet the opportunist in him forbade him to make an outright
refusal.

"Thank you, Mr. Thornton, very kind. But if ever I seek a loan, it'll be
from strength. Not weakness."

It sounded plausible. Noble even.

But Thornton laughed. "Ah! I didn't mean a loan. I meant it as equity.
I'll wager an oriental fortune you're going to come out nicely on this. It'll
make my four hundred a year look quite paltry. I think a thousand in your
hands would go far to supplement it."

In a flash Stevenson saw it was the answer to his dilemma. If Thornton's bankers could speak for the offer, he, Stevenson, could easily find a
local banker to use such an offer as basis for a further guarantee. That
would keep Thornton's name out of it as far as the Manchester & Leeds
was concerned. And if his stage-payments plan worked as expected, he
would never have to call on Thornton's cash and so—ostensibly—would
not be beholden to him. Stevenson succeeded in being nonchalant. "That'd
take some thinking on. I'm not saying no, mind you. But I couldn't yet say
yes, d'ye see? Why must you go south?"

"Oh! As to that you may congratulate me. I have a fortnight's leave of
absence. I'm to be married this Friday."

His boyish enthusiasm was infectious. Briefly and sentimentally,
Stevenson hankered for his own lost innocence. "Then I do congratulate
you," he said. "Heartily. I hope you may be very happy. Ye'll be bringing
Mrs. Thornton back here?"

He wondered what sort of a woman Thornton would take as a wife.
The thought of Nora came into his mind. He saw her face with its
equivocal share of guile and ingenuousness . . . her strong, lean hands
marshalling figures with a royal sense of command . . . her unsleeping
sense of self-interest. A long way after these he thought of her prettiness,
her body, the frankness of her lust. He wished he had caught the one
ten.

"We have rented a house at Todmorden," Thornton said. "But first
I'm taking advantage of the new line beyond Wigan to Preston to enjoy a
week by the seashore."

"The west coast."

"A village called Blackpool. It has quite a reputation among younger people of the better sort, you know. Mrs. Thornton—as she then will be—is of a romantic disposition and I considered that a brief spell on some remote shore that is both wild and deserted, yet not entirely devoid of civilized appointments, would please both her and myself."

"Most thoughtful . . . er . . ." Stevenson thought that perhaps enough time had gone by between Thornton's offer of the thousand and a casual closure on it. "When you're down there, you might ask your bankers to send a note of hand to my bankers here in Manchester—Hunter in Piccadilly—in case, while you're away . . ."

Thornton, as expected, looked dubious. "Well, now . . ." He was clearly embarrassed.

"Not a transfer of funds, you understand." Stevenson was all assurance. "That can await your return. Just a note. By way of precaution."

"In that case . . ." Thornton's relief was so open that Stevenson began to wonder whether he really had the money. Perhaps it was in trust until his marriage? ". . . in that case, no difficulty. But remember—*'nec quicquam acrius quam pecuniae damnum stimulat!'* "

He hardly expected Stevenson to understand, so it was with some shock that he heard the man—the contractor, as he now was—reply, with no trace of accent, not even that of the educated northerner the Board had met: "I have always thought Cicero wiser than Livy—*'Vitam regit fortuna, non sapientia.'* "

It stopped Thornton in his tracks; he stared at his companion open-jawed.

"You'll be late, if you stop."

"Yes." Thornton, jerked back into the present, began again to hurry. He shook his head in bewilderment as he said, "Ye're a damned odd fish, Stevenson. A *damned* odd fish!"

Stevenson gripped his arm, to take leave without hindering him. Now he spoke again in a deliberately broad West Riding dialect: "Fare tha well, Mr. Thornton, sir! We'll lewk aftert tunnel while tha comes back."

Thornton laughed aloud, frightening a horse out of his nosebag, as he drew ahead of Stevenson and strode purposefully out toward Liverpool Road. Stevenson sauntered on some way, watching him almost out of sight. What moved the engineer? What was his especial greed? Though they had worked closely for six months and would now spend most of every day practically in one another's pockets, Stevenson still had no idea of an answer to his questions.

As he turned to make his way back to the station a Stanhope drawn by a large bay cut across the road toward him. It was almost upon him before he recognized the Reverend Doctor Prendergast at the reins.

"Whoa!" he called, as much to Stevenson as to his horse. He saw the contractor eyeing the carriage. "What's your opinion?"

"Pray the horse doesn't fall to his knees," Stevenson answered, determined not to grease the cleric's vanity.

"Oh?" Prendergast was not amused.

"If the front cross spring yields on these, the back one offers no resistance, and the riders are pitched out. It's the same fault on all."

An urchin came up, hoping for the commission to hold the horse. He nodded wisely at Stevenson's criticism as if to say that he had always had that opinion of Stanhopes. Prendergast lowered his whip, resting it on the horse's flank.

"Climb aboard," he said. "See if we can oblige."

"I shall go back to Littleborough," Stevenson said, standing his ground.

"You shall take luncheon with me."

Stevenson inclined his head and stepped up into the carriage. The urchin turned away and walked on.

"I trust my . . . ah . . . little extra condition will not prove impossible to . . ." he said as he whipped up the bay.

"I think it will not, sir."

"I'm damn sure it will not. In fact, to make certain double certain, here is a note in my own hand—a genuine note. Take it to my bankers and they will furnish the necessary guarantees."

He passed Stevenson a folded slip of notepaper, unsealed. He took it, unfolded it, and read. It was an instruction to the banker to guarantee the thousand. Prendergast must have written it only moments earlier.

"A thousand pounds!" Stevenson feigned a different kind of astonishment. "That is most generous, doctor. Ye do me great honour . . ."

"Oh—" Prendergast's laugh was cold. "I doubt whether honour comes much into it!" He did not look at Stevenson; in all this time his eyes had been upon the road.

"But I have, in a way, already raised the sum, d'ye see?"

That made the cleric look. In fact, he pulled the horse up sharply, forcing a brewery dray to pull widely round them. He turned full face to Stevenson. "The devil you have!"

"Young Thornton . . ." Stevenson began, letting the rest hang delicately.

The other recovered his possession very quickly. "Well! He's either a lot more stupid or greatly more astute than I had imagined."

Stevenson laughed. "No, doctor. Not Thornton. I was about to say *he* had offered, too. And I turned him down."

It was about time to fire his second broadside—the one he had not needed at the meeting. He drew from an inside pocket the note on the Duke of Somerset's paper. It had lost the crispness of last night; already it looked as if he had carried it for years. With justifiable pride he handed it to the clergyman, pausing in sudden thought just as the other's hand closed upon it. "Before I let you have sight of this, sir, I'd welcome your assurance, as a gentleman of the cloth, that you'll never divulge what you're about to read."

"Ye have it!" Prendergast's smile was solid assurance. "There's my hand on it." He even took off his glove. "Ye have it."

Stevenson knew at once he had blundered, for Prendergast took no pains to conceal his skepticism. He peered closely at the broken seal, fitting its parts together and turning it this way and that. Then he uttered a loud "Hah!" and turned on Stevenson a radiant smile.

The horse must have thought he said Hup! for it started with a jolt that nearly unseated both men. Prendergast did not rein it in. He was too keen to press forward with what he had in mind. "It's your misfortune, Stevenson, not to have known . . ." He became absorbed in the contents of the letter. Dumbly, for he could only wait now, Stevenson took the reins. "I declare this is most excellently done! You have a worthy talent. . . . Yes!" He sighed. "The misfortune not to have known that I am related by marriage to the Duke of Somerset."

Stevenson was too practised a deceiver not to play his part with utter conviction still, though he knew well enough the game was up. "What luck, sir! Then as you see, we, too, are somewhat related!"

Prendergast, freed of the reins, never took his eyes from Stevenson's face. "I think not," he said at last. Stevenson made as if to speak but was cut short. "What is more to the point, I also happen to know that Robert Bolitho, of Bolitho & Chambers in Dowgate, has been dead these six months past and so could not have signed the note you showed us. A note dated a mere twenty days ago."

"Dead!" Now that the immediate panic was over, Stevenson, as always, found something to relish in his desperate corner. He coolly admired his own simulation of honest sincerity. For an instant the thought possessed him that winning or losing hardly mattered; the perfection of the act was worth pursuing for its own sake. It *was* the purpose of it all. He quickly shrugged off the notion. He had to shake Prendergast's confidence; *that* was the purpose of it all.

"Oh, but this is easily explained. I confess it is fully a year since I asked Bolitho & Chambers—and they were certainly both living then unless a pair of very substantial ghosts occupied my morning . . ." He laughed. Prendergast joined in, not pleasantly. "Fully a year that I asked them to prepare such a note and hold it against my immediate need. They must have signed it then and left the date until dispatch."

For some reason Prendergast was delighted. It was as if Stevenson were a pupil who had just done something exceptionally well. The clergyman reached for the reins, which Stevenson, disingenuous confidence outside, defeat within, yielded up to him.

"Good, good! But ye show lamentable ignorance of the ways of banks if ye say that."

The fact that Prendergast was obviously not going to drive him straight to the nearest lock-up was no encouragement. Stevenson wondered glumly what was to follow, though he continued to speak with that same honest conviction. "It cannot be, doctor. It is beyond *my* understanding. My London agent, you see, sent me that note not ten days since . . ." He paused in midflight as a new line of defence opened up. "Ah! But what if *he* is playing tricks with me. I was always warned for being too trustful! And what if he has . . . deceived me into deceiving you!"

Prendergast chuckled. "What'll ye do, man, eh? Fly posthaste to London? Seek him out? Drag him back here by the ears to explain?"

"Indeed. Indeed. We may still catch the connection to London . . ."

"And vanish forever from human ken! No, Stevenson. I had to see you under stress. I had to see if you were glass or diamond. But now to serious things. My club's just round here."

"But do let me assure you . . ." Stevenson began, determined to keep his end up to the last.

"You can drop all that, Mr. Stevenson. You've joined a bigger game than you thought. That's all."

They turned into Fennel Street and reined to a halt just before Hanging Ditch. Prendergast's "club" was a luncheon and supper house for merchants at the corner of Toad Lane.

They took luncheon in a private room. Throughout the meal, while the servants were present, Prendergast acted as if they were two casual business acquaintances with no very pressing reason to dine together. Stevenson was forced to admire the man's skill though he burned to know what kind of blackmail—and it could only be blackmail—was intended. But he did learn something from their seemingly idle talk: Prendergast was exceedingly well connected in the new world of railroads. There was hardly a director of any important line—and of *any* line north of Derby—whom he did not personally know. He knew their foibles and weaknesses. And he knew their strengths. Over salmon cutlets, during boiled sheep's head, tongue, and brains, and through the ginger creams, he made quite sure that Stevenson understood how intimate was his knowledge, how wide his connections.

By the time the port and cigars were set upon the table Stevenson had almost forgotten their true purpose here.

"Dear, dear, dear," Prendergast said. "I do hate to see a good cigar lit from the gas. It so spoils the flavour."

"My years below stairs have dulled my tastes," Stevenson admitted.

"You can withdraw," Prendergast said sharply by way of thanks to the servant who had waited on them through the meal. Impassively the man left them. Prendergast looked steadily at the door, as if he could see through it. "Damn servants! They grow more surly by the week."

"Unrest is widespread," Stevenson confirmed. "I see it at first hand."

Prendergast looked quickly back at him. "No trouble on Summit Tunnel—or the line? What?"

"Not so far," he said.

But Prendergast was hardly listening. Instead he was preparing once again to broach the subject the servant's presence had prevented them from discussing. He breathed in sharply several times as if about to speak, looked quizzically at Stevenson, rolled his cigar, puffed it, wheezed, and drained his glass.

"Port's with you," he said at last. And then, emboldened at the sound of his own voice, continued: "Now, see here, Stevenson . . ." It was going to be the friendly tack. "I have no real desire to know your true past—though I take you for a consummate forger. But I feel sure you have no ten thousand pounds." He waved away words that Stevenson had not been going to utter. His was now a waiting game. "Yet, now I know you somewhat better, I also believe you would not have embarked on this venture rashly. You truly think you can fulfill this contract? I see you're obviously not another Skelm, but there's many ways of coming to grief. Can you see it through?"

Stevenson paused before replying. He looked at Prendergast as if wondering whether to risk the truth. *"If,"* he stressed, "if the Board pay me as I propose." He knew well enough that going back on that undertaking was not in the other's mind; but he wanted to suggest an inability on his part to understand where all this was leading.

Prendergast chuckled, genuinely. Dinner had mellowed him; Stevenson noted the fact against future need. "Yes—that was one of the cleverest moves I've witnessed. I doubt they'll ever realize you walked a circle around them. Deftly done."

Still pretending to incomprehension, Stevenson tried a frontal assault. "What is your interest, doctor? Since you claim to be undeceived?"

Prendergast snorted a laugh into his glass. "Oh no—to be undeceived one must first be deceived—and *that* I never was. I *could* . . ." There was just the hint of a threat as he changed tack. "Let me put it differently. You have done well. Between the explosion yesterday (and how fortunate that was, too!) . . . between that and your appointment today, you have done marvels. Yet you have made two bad blunders. You signed a dead man's name—a capital offence if you knew him to be dead—and you forged a peer's signature and seal. Transportable, as I'm sure you know."

"Are you seeking to blackmail me, doctor? Let's be perfectly blunt."

Prendergast besought the heavens as if Stevenson had just made some unpardonable social blunder. "That is precisely what I wish to avoid. A blackmailer is a parasite. A leech. He takes his blood whether his host be healthy or not. For me it is quite the reverse. Let me suggest to you"—he was suddenly very earnest—"that if you are to avoid future blunders, you need a partner. You very *much* need a partner. One not as astute as yourself perhaps, but one who . . ." he sought for the exact phrasing, ". . . who has not been so long from the world of gentlemen and of wealth. One with position. One with connections."

"Your terms?" Stevenson was weary—though he hoped it didn't show. "I'm not saying you're wrong. But what terms?"

Again Prendergast looked pained and innocent. The effect would have been comical had the situation itself been otherwise. "Terms! Terms! Oh, this is so heavy. Not terms, dear fellow. A humble proposition. A partnership. A . . . "—he smiled to prepare for the word—"a *silent* partnership." He alone laughed. "I think I shall earn fully a third of your profit on Summit Tunnel." He laid no stress on the fraction; yet for Stevenson it was the only word that rang on into the ensuing silence. Then Prendergast said something that took Stevenson completely off guard: "And if I put two and a half thousand behind you, I daresay that would not be too far from a third of your *actual* capital? Eh? You see how determined I am to be fair to you?"

Stevenson's first thought was that Prendergast *must* know, or at least surmise, that there would never be any call on this offer. But did he? Prendergast, for all his railroad knowledge had not sat through those long calculations last night; he could not *know* the coming finances of the contract in such detail as he pretended. Perhaps he believed Stevenson really did need the extra moneys now offered. Intuitively, unable to say why, he knew he had to preserve that illusion—if it was there to preserve. "Damn you!" He laughed ruefully. "I've met my match all right! You sincerely mean it?" Everything about him hinted that the offer of extra finance had turned the scale.

Prendergast for once seemed sincere. "I've waited years to meet such a man as you. You're in the ascendant, Mr. Stevenson. You'll steam ahead now and there's no power in the land can pull you off the rails—save your own folly. Dammit man—ye *need* me! So let's have no more talk of black-mail or bloodsucking. What if my share *is* a third, ye'll always get twice that. Here's my hand on it."

"And mine!" They shook warmly; Stevenson had no way of telling if the other were as insincere as he. "May I have back my little joke—my letter from the Duke?"

Prendergast's smile was refusal enough. "Now that *is* a problem. D'ye see—there can be no written or formal agreement between us. And it will, by the by, be an aunt of mine who ostensibly lends you the money. So—until our partnership is working and thriving—I feel quite sure you'd not want to be associated with anyone who was so imprudent as to return such a document carte blanche. And while we're talking of it, ye'd better do another bank forgery signed only by Chambers. I'll find the opportunity to substitute it."

*"And* keep the original!" Stevenson outwardly conceded total defeat. "I've known many rogues in my time, doctor, but . . ."

"Oh, small fry, believe me!" Prendergast was delighted to accept his surrender. "Small fry beside the giants you're about to join. Good heavens, fellow, d'you think what you have done is in any way extraordinary! Some-what blatant, perhaps. But yours . . . uh, *ours* . . . is no case yet for finesse. There's no fortune to be made without chicanery, and all the world knows it."

He leaned back, puffed thick clouds from his cigar, and waxed expan-sive. "How easy matters would be if virtue were *more* than its own reward! After all, if mankind had never broken the rules we would all be living still in naked savagery—not to say *democracy*—in the Garden of Eden. No merchants' club *there!* No crusted port *there!"* He reached for the decanter and poured another liberal glass. "No fine cigars *there!* So—your health! Long may you thrive . . . and me with you!"

# Chapter 9

Stevenson's first act upon returning to his palace was to burn all the pur-loined crested papers in his possession save two from the bankers, Bolitho & Chambers. He was furious with himself for having fallen so totally into Prendergast's grip. It was no comfort to reflect that there had been no other choice. As soon as Thornton had told him that the Board, not the now-discredited Skelm, would reassign the contract, he had *had* to forge some evidence of credit. True, the letter of patronage had not been strictly necessary. That, in retrospect, had been a blunder. But the really damaging piece had been the letter on Bolitho & Chambers notepaper. If he could somehow—Lord alone knew how, but somehow—nullify that, the Duke-of-Somerset nonsense would immediately be less damaging. For one thing, no one had seen him hand it over. There was only Prendergast's word for it.

What was the flaw in that man? Arrogance? Vanity? Yes—vanity and overconfidence. But he was sharp, too. Never underestimate him. He was quite capable of working out that the "Duke's" letter was too thin to be of any real service on its own—especially without witnesses.

The girl, Nora, was a witness, of course.

But apart from that, it left the banker's letter and its replacement as the ace-and-all of trumps. If there were only some way to get the bank to adopt both of them as genuine . . . no, Prendergast would get there before him and prevent it.

Unless . . . unless he could play on the priest's vanity and feed his already fattened self-confidence. If he could get the man to believe that the firm of Stevenson was permanently stretched for money—until, say, Christmas—and if he could skim off all the profit before it went anywhere near a Manchester bank, and send it all up to Bolitho & Chambers . . .

Was that dangerous?

Yes, it was. Prendergast seemed to know a lot about that particular bank; he might have some way of getting the information out. Damnation! Of all the banks to have chosen!

Never mind. Risky or not, he had to do it. Chambers had to see fat and regular profits every month from now until as late next year as he could spin Prendergast's tolerance to accept. If he could tickle the banker's greed, he might get the forgery adopted.

He closed his mind to all estimates of how slim his chances were.

Instead he basked in the thought of taking the good news to Prendergast. Would he storm and curse? Would he take it on the chin? What *would* Prendergast do?

He might even make himself useful—as useful as he had promised to be. For there was no doubt that, if you took away the threat of blackmail, the cleric's suggestions and his offers of help had all been most sensible. Not thirty-three percent sensible; that was sheer greed. But . . . say, five percent? And five percent of Summit's expected profits was going to be something a great deal more than a sneeze.

He stood, suddenly erect above the dying fire, and breathed with deep contentment. *That* was his way forward—keep Prendergast feeling like cock-o-the-dunghill for the moment, then add enough to settle his greed, and finally break the good news to him in such a way that he'd want to make himself useful. No stick. Carrots all the way.

It sounded right. In fact, the best thing about it was that it didn't in any way cut across his main effort, which was to start organizing the working at Summit so as to yield the £25,000 to £30,000 profit he knew to be buried in there somewhere. He was really going to need that girl Nora now; what a find she had been!

The thought filled his day with a warmth and a radiance that made Prendergast and his blackmail suddenly remote and trivial. Rising, he stamped the last burned scraps to ashes as Meg, the old crone who looked after the shanty and served him his food, came out and watched.

"Why?" she asked. "What're thou burning it for?"

"For? 'Fore it hangs me," he said.

" 'Tis pretty."

"Go pack me things, Meg. I'm leaving this night."

"Leaving! Art thou in trouble?" She was alarmed.

"Trouble!" He laughed. "Nay! Thou'll never guess. Thou art lookin' at main contractor for Summit Tunnel. Name of John Stevenson!"

"Eee! Main contractor? Thou never are!"

Her delight brought back certain unconscious tricks her body had prac-tised in her youth—a certain coquetry. He saw that she must once have been more than attractive; and he regretted, now that he was leaving, never having got to know her better.

"Thou'd laugh," he told her, grasping her waist and doing a courtly little dance above the ashes. "This very day."

She grew younger still in delight as she danced with him.

"Skelm's bankrupt and they put us in. I shall stop at the Royal Oak in Littleborough—if they're still taking railroad folk."

"And the wench? Nora?"

"Mebbe," he said. "If she wants. Where is she?"

"Killing rabbits," Meg said. And then she reacted to the news all over again. "Eeee! Ye'd hardly give it credit! Lord John the main contractor! Eh!"

He stopped dancing and, his arm still encircling her waist, walked her back to the shanty. "Things'll change now, Meg. They'll get better. Thou'll see. Ye'll all see."

"They said the explosion would finish Skelm."

"He had but a narrow grasp on this contract from the start."

He felt her stiffen. "It were just by chance they give it thee, then? The contract? And thou wert on the shift as made the explosion?"

"Speak out, Meg. Never fear to speak thy mind with me."

"There's many'll say so."

"Many? When I stood there, too? Closest to the gunpowder for nigh on twenty minutes? Many?"

"Some, anyway."

He stopped short of the doorway and turned her to face him. Then he took her head between his hands, almost a lover's gesture, so that she blushed beneath the grime on her face. He spoke earnestly and low. "God save them if word of it comes to me! I'd take a terrible vengeance—and I'd not mind that widely known."

She grew uncomfortable at last. "What'll ye do with this palace?" she asked.

"I'm giving it to *thee,* Meg." He relinquished his hold.

"Me!" Now her delight was pure avarice, without a hint of the youth he had glimpsed earlier. "Nay! Me? Eh, but . . ."

"On condition," he added.

She was wary at once. "Oh ah?"

"Aye. What with living out, I'll not get to hear how the lads is talking. Not as I would if I was still here. I need ears, Meg. Eyes and ears."

There came a groan from inside the hut. Pengilly! Of course. He had forgotten.

"How is he?"

Meg shook her head dourly. "Bad today. Shivering, see thee. His brow's all dewed with sweating. I covered him well."

Stevenson went indoors and crossed the room to kneel beside the injured man.

"Well, Pengilly?" he asked.

The eyes, screwed up in pain, shivered open. "Boy," Pengilly said in a voice little more than a rasp.

"How is it?"

"Hurting some."

"Let's have a spy."

He threw off the blankets, which were alive with bugs. "Lay *them* out in the sun," he told Meg. Then he turned to undo the bandages he had put on the previous day. The cauterized stump had wept but there was no fresh bleeding.

"Cut to fletters, damn ye," Pengilly said. "Some old mess! Some sore, too!" He winced at the pain. Then, in a more philosophic tone, he added: "What'm I going to do now then, boy?"

A thought struck Stevenson. The steam engine! The one he had hired from the Board in that morning's negotiations. "Pengilly," he asked. "I'll just lift that . . ." He tugged gently at the cloth, stuck in the hardened rime on the stump. All the skin of the thigh moved with it. Pengilly bit hard and dug nails in palms to avoid crying out. "Good. Sorry 'bout that. But that'll heal well there. That dressing's as tight 'n dry as a bloody cheesecloth."

He pulled out a handkerchief and dabbed the sweat from the man's brow. "Did thou ever man a steam engine down in Cornwall?"

"Yes. When I were a boy. Tended . . ." He dissolved in pain. ". . . My dear soul!"

"Easy now! Easy! Meg," he shouted to the crone outside. "Some gin!"

But Pengilly's hand on his arm stopped him. "Nooo. Nooo. I'd sooner the pain!"

"Go on then. Steam engine."

"Yes. I tended the engineer over to Carleen District Wheal Vor."

"Big one?"

"Middling. Middling. Fifty-four inch, six-ten stroke. Working single."

Meg came over with a broken china cup near filled with gin.

"Whim or pump?"

Pain again racked Pengilly, making a reply impossible. Stevenson held the cup to his lips. "Come on," he said. "It'll still the pain." This time there was no protest.

"What for do ye ask?" he said when he had drained the cup and breathed out the fire.

"Whim or pump?" Stevenson insisted.

"Pump."

"Leave him be, Lord John," Meg said.

But Stevenson persisted. "Could'st thou man a whim engine?"

Pengilly pondered. "Yes. It isn't no different, really. Whim or pump."

"I mean, with thy leg gone?"

"Why, calculate I could." He even managed a chuckle. "Don't need a foot for it, damn ye. It isn't like a horse!"

"They'll be putting one more steam whim up on the tops. On the first shaft—number two, seeing as number one'll now be blind. Could'st thou tend it? If thou had a boy to help thee with the furnace?"

"Yes." Pengilly was confident. "Course, they won't pay I so much. Not with this here old leg gone."

Stevenson smiled. *"Me,* Pengilly. Not they. I'm the paymaster now, see thee. I'll pay thee what the job's worth. And ye'll get what bonus is going. And I'll damn that man who says I built on others' mishaps."

"Why thankee, boy, thankee." His eyes sparkled again. "I'll do it for ye. By God, I'll do it."

"There." Stevenson's relief was almost as great as the Cornishman's. "Rest easy now. Easy. Job's waiting for thee. We shall manage with horses while thy leg mends."

He stood and smiled at the man. The gin was working. The wrinkled eyes fell shut. "Thankee. You're some proper boy, you are. Proper handsome boy."

He and Meg tiptoed away as the man fell back into his stupor.

"Thou art a good man, Lord John," she said.

Stevenson shook his head. "Pengilly, too. He's too good a man to put on the parish. See thee, he can have my bed till he's mended; then it's thine, along with the rest."

They had reached the door and went outside again. "Now. The bargain twixt thee and me. Struck?"

"Thou'll give us this palace if I . . ."

"Hold thy tongue and shut the door." Stevenson was cautious of what Pengilly, drunk or no, might overhear. "Thou knows the rest. Thou knows what's what. Is it struck?"

For an answer she bared her toothless gums at him, spat drily at the palm of her hand, and held it forth to shake his.

"Struck," she said.

# Chapter 10

Nora was well spattered with blood and fur by the end of the day. As soon as she had heard of the breaking up of the rabbit warren she had run, still barefoot, across the fields to where the ploughmen, labourers, ferrets, and dogs were already beginning their work.

The warren was of some great age. At its heart was a mound enclosed by a once-stout stone wall in which there had been trapdoors for the warrender to let his conies in and out. But that had been in medieval days. Careful regulation of that sort had long since relapsed into chaos. The wall, now breached in dozens of places, had disgorged hundreds of rabbits into the country around, turning it into one vast unregulated warren—a plague of rabbits, intolerable to farmer and gamekeeper alike. Now every hole in that maze was to be dug out and obliterated. The rabbits were to be killed to the last, least one that could be caught. The mere thought of it set Nora's pulse racing.

For hunting was in her blood. Her grandfather had let their farm at Normanton go to ruin while he hunted and shot and fished anything smaller than himself that had fur, feather, or scales. Her father, too, would always leave his loom when the hunt was near enough to reach and follow on foot. Often he took Nora with him. She never forgot the day she had seen a fox cornered and torn apart. The look in its eyes as it faced the certainty of death had held her spellbound for weeks.

And now, as she pounded over the burrows, even before she saw the first rabbit of the day, she sensed the terror that thumped beneath her feet, through those hundreds upon hundreds of little hearts, and the shivering, furry bodies, waiting in bewilderment and panic as their world fell about them.

By sheer good fortune it was she who killed the first rabbit of the day. She stood with a stone poised over a hole that was being routed by a ferret. A young buck came out, too fearful of what was behind to be cautious of what lay ahead. Quicker than thought Nora brought the stone down; and her shriek of joy as the rabbit froze and was obliterated spread among the company like an infection.

By midmorning the rabbits were coming from earth as fast as men, women, youngsters, and dogs could kill them—faster at times, for several dozen escaped into the fields around. But hundreds more were caught and finished off.

Still the bloodlust was not sated. Always the next kill would be better, would have some especial quality to make it the kill of kills, to make the day live in memory forever. Such a joyous time effaced this whole last dreadful year. She would endure it all again if another such were promised at its end.

But by midafternoon the supply of victims had dwindled to a trickle. First ten, then twenty minutes would pass before a new shout went up and a new kill was made. And more and more it happened over in some other part of the warren. She became acutely aware that she had not slept the night before. Mentally she remained alert but her physical strength, already depleted by undernourishment, began to flag.

While waiting for new rabbits to bolt from ferret or plough she found her mind returning again and again to John's contract. The permutations of the work had absorbed her utterly—or, rather, she had absorbed them. So that she now had an intuitive grasp of its total pattern—something greater than the sum of all its parts. Within that pattern her mind began to practise a minor series of rearrangements, one following another. The way numbers could fall into patterns had often fascinated her, but this was something more than that. It was *real.* These were actual quantities and proportions that she ordered and reordered. The result was not meaninglessly beautiful, like arrangements of glass beads; it had the beauty of purpose, like a design for a weave. She wanted to *be* there when Lord John put it all to work. The one question that had not bothered her at all that day was whether he would get the contract or no. She knew he would.

Perhaps he would take her tonight. And then perhaps they would live together awhile. Then perhaps he would marry her, if she was very useful to him, and if she got with child that looked like going to term. Playing patterns with the contract was one thing, but when it came to her own life, the past had taught her to work from one perhaps to the next.

At last the warren lay utterly wasted. Evening was at hand. The men let her keep two dozen rabbits—practically all she had killed. She hung them on a pole, a dozen at each end, and yoked them over her shoulders. There'd be time to stew them well, with plenty of herbs to damp their wildness, before the navvies came down from the tunnel. She was almost in sight of the shanty when she saw John striding out toward her. He ran when he saw her. She shrugged off the yoke, dropping it in a ditch, and ran to meet him.

He almost stopped himself from hugging her when he saw how smeared she was with the blood; but, with a who-may-care shrug, he wrapped his huge arms about her and lifted her off the ground.

"Eh! Lass!" he said as he spun her round. At last he put her down. "I thought thou'd sleep today."

"Sleep? Me! How could I? Knowing what it meant?"

"After all thy work last night?"

"Nay. I could never sleep. I've been that pressed with worry all day. I went up to the warren they broke apart. Thou never saw that many cronies! I got two dozen back there. We'll eat ourselves sick tonight!" She paused. "Well? Tell us then."

He did not answer. He looked at her in a kind of wonder, as if he had forgotten and was suddenly rediscovering her. At last he spoke. "I hope I may always remember thee like this, Nora, my . . . most precious. Dusty. Loppered with blood. Bare of feet. Happy." He took her head between his great hands. "There's grand changes under way and they'll sweep up thee and me and carry us I know not where. I hope thou'll never lose this . . . sunshine in thy spirit."

His words brought her into a calm. She felt no need to say anything, and spoke only because his eyes still searched her face for some answer. "I don't know what to say. Thou art soft!"

He looked away, in something close to shame. "Nay, Nora. Hard. Too hard, I fear. A sight too hard."

"Did we get it?"

His eyes turned upon her again. "Before I tell thee, I want thee to answer me one question. I must know before I tell thee."

"Ask on." Her mind, in preparation, restocked itself with the quantities she had worked last night and played with for much of the day.

"Will thou take me to wed?"

Of all that he might have asked, *that* was the least expected. She became aware that she was smiling vacantly.

"Shall us not live together awhile?"

"What?"

"Thou hast not tried me. I may be barren."

"I want *thee*," he said. "To wife. Not a brood mare. Will thou?"

Trembling, feeling the blood drain from her face, she said more faintly than she intended: "Aye then. I'll take thee."

He kissed her with a devotion that quickly turned sensual as she grew warm.

"Now I can tell thee," he said when they broke at last. "We're on fortune's highway, Nora, thee and me. We're beset with enemies and ringed about with dangers—but we're away! And the Lord shall deliver us. See yon mountain?"

He turned her to face the brow of Summit, to the dark tunnel in the sunstruck rock.

"Aye," she said.

"The hole we punch through there may take cotton to wool and wool to cotton. But it'll lead thee and me to a land of milk and honey. So it will, love!"

Dumbly, tears brimming in her eyes and making the world swim, she fell to the earth and pulled him onto her. And there, hastily and without finesse, they obliterated the world that was soon to claim their every thought and action and dream.

It was several minutes before Nora realized consciously that her question "Shall I have a wage or a cut of the profits?" was answered. And it was several more minutes before John Stevenson realized consciously that in marrying Nora he was removing the only legal witness to his part in the two forgeries, for wife cannot bear witness against husband. Such thoughts did not in any way diminish or even stain their love. It is just that they were that kind of people.

# PART TWO

Blackpool

PART TWO

# Chapter 11

The day of her wedding—as Arabella later confided in girlish overstatement to her journal—had turned into one prolonged disaster. At the time she was so cowed by the sheer awfulness of everything that she had noted only its more obvious and, as she later realized, more trivial causes. Her grandmother had asked for gin and had told several stories of doubtful refinement—stories at which only the eldest Mr. Thornton had laughed. He, to be sure, was a long-haired, elderly reprobate (and much too free with his hands). The behaviour of both of them, she noted firmly, "can only serve to remind us of the great moral progress we have recently made—as well," she added, in case the lesson might later elude her, "as of the ever-present dangers of backsliding."

Other solecisms of that day provided no such moral texts to excuse their inclusion in her record, and she set them down from sheer habit of honesty, still transfigured with the shame of it. Her mother, for instance, had asked for sherry, though it was plainly a stand-up breakfast. And her sister had taken off her gloves—on the grounds that the day was too hot to require them! The fact that many of the ladies had come without gloves at all, even ladies of quality, was no mitigation. In less than an hour there had been half a dozen such incidents, each making her wish the earth would gulp her down.

She knew, too, that here was not the only journal in which the simple, honest gaucherie of her family would be set down in all its shaming detail. Letty, dear Walter's cousin, had seen and heard it all. And with unconcealed relish, too. "Her hot little tongue will cook a fine fat dish of chitbits to regale the countryside for months, I make no doubt," Arabella wrote. Absurdly (though the urge lay too deep within for her to see its absurdity) she felt that the mere spelling out of Letty's probable gossip in this way would blunt the cutting edge of its malice.

Still, as she realized the moment she had finished writing, these details, even taken together, could not account, not by half, for the profound unease of that day. There had been . . . something else. Some fleeting thought had crossed her mind at an unguarded moment. . . . But when? As they had cut the cake? Or when she had looked around the crowded ballroom and had been unable to find Walter, in that panic-filled moment before she at last saw him out on the lawns with his uncle, the elder Mr.

Thornton? No, it had been on some less obvious occasion—a moment when the now elusive thought had been too incongruous and disturbing to pursue. She had thrust it from her, forced herself on to other paths. And now the abandoned thought lurked in some almost discovered recess of her mind, challenging her to go in and fetch it out.

It had been an angry thought, she knew that much.

At least Walter, dear good kind Walter, had not noticed these blunders, she wrote. Then, deciding that this intended praise made him seem unobservant—as boorish in a different way as her own people—she added that he probably *had* noticed, but, being so kind and charitable, had forgot them in the same moment. It really was amazing that someone as good and dear as Walter could (God forgive her for judging) come from so unpleasant a family. True, he was only a first cousin of theirs, an orphan brought up by their charity. . . .

Idly, her pen at rest across the corner of her journal, she wondered what the Thorntons really thought of Walter's marriage to her. For most of their long engagement, she had felt repeated hints of scorn, a well-hidden conviction that Walter was marrying beneath him.

And that memory was the key which released her angry, unremembered, unforgotten thought: The truth was they *didn't care!* That was it! Walter could have married one of the sluts out in the back scullery for all the dent it would have made in the pride of his uncles and aunts and cousins. That was the truth she had learned on that frightful day as she had watched them, chatting and guzzling with such aloof assurance, patronizing her family, going perfunctorily through the motions of marrying off their poor orphan nephew and cousin.

At once the anger she had repressed that day reclaimed her. How dare they! *They,* mere jumped-up shopkeepers and tradesmen—and her father one of the most respected clergymen in Hertfordshire, and her mother the daughter of a bishop. It was insufferable. Walter was worth more than all of them together. His departure impoverished that grand house up on the hill, for all the wealth of the Thorntons who remained.

She turned back through the closely written pages, seeking comfort, and read for the fortieth time the words in which she had recorded the day's greatest moment:

"I spoke my vows in a clear, modest voice, almost as if I were speaking to dear father (who, after all, was only three feet away, and who, I am bound to say, was somewhat histrionic, as when he preached so finely at St. Alban's). Walter, with more sense of what was suited to our tiny church, spoke in a quiet, manly way with only the faintest tremor. And as the ring slid over my finger, it seemed that the many, many happy hours of devotion I have passed within those sanctified walls were as a preparation for this one instant of supreme and holy joy.

"I tried to pray that I would always be worthy of this new sacrament. I even had the thought that if I could complete the prayer before the ring came to rest, it would be most certainly answered. And I achieved this impossible feat in the most astonishing way. No *words* came into my mind. It was rather as if the whole of my body and soul *became* a prayer. I have often felt Christ enter me, but only passively, as a vessel. At that moment I underwent the complementary process. I was an offering, a self-offering, made truly vital for the first time in my life by that completely unexpected sense of dedication. A fearful joy filled me until I felt sure I had stretched to bursting. It seemed that I had already endured this ecstasy for an eternity.

"I was amazed then to see that the ring was still sliding down my finger. I grasped Walter's arm for support and he, smiling, returned a gentle squeeze of reassurance. My father, mistaking the sacred for the profane (a hazard, he has often said, of every clergyman's life), lowered a cautionary eyebrow at me. . . ."

She stopped there, regretting the honesty that forbade her to thresh and winnow this little part of history and remake her supreme moment into one that was quite, quite perfect. Even so, the memory of it had dispelled her anger at the behaviour of her in-laws during that wretched breakfast.

The disaster, she decided as she closed her journal, had, after all, been mitigated. But she shuddered at the thought of having to record the vile, horrid things which had happened that night—last night, already an unreal age away. And she looked unhappily out through the salt-stained windows at a rain-sodden Blackpool beach. Somewhere out there dear Walter was walking alone. Why did he not come back to her?

# Chapter 12

If Walter had noticed any of the undercurrents at his wedding, he gave no sign of it as he moved easily from one group of guests to another. A long and bitter childhood in that house had taught him well the arts of concealment. But lately he had used his independence to repay some of the ancient hurts he had suffered, and been forced to suffer, by his wealthy cousins—

especially from young Claude, or Claude George Thornton III, as the family Bible would record him. For railroad engineers were men of a new and exciting age. Theirs was a field where young men could quickly make their mark. And so Walter had an easy magnetism among people whose conversation rarely strayed beyond hunting, horses, the management of game coverts, the price of corn, and third-hand gossip about the strange goings-on at court. Despite their pretensions, the Thorntons of the second generation were only occasional (and obsequious) visitors at the great houses of Hertfordshire. Perhaps, now that Letty was engaged to one of the Desborough boys, the third generation might acquire the necessary veneer and so take the final step into acceptability—if their extravagance did not first bankrupt the family.

In such company Walter found it easy to claim attention with his tales of the romance of engineering on the line. One favourite was the story of how he and Mr. Gooch had surveyed the route of the Manchester & Leeds from Miles Platting to Normanton—wild transpennine country that grew wilder and more alien with every repetition.

"We finished the survey with only hours to spare," he said, nearing the end of the tale. "That was a tense night, I may tell you! If we had failed, you know, we would have lost the Act of Parliament and someone else would have built the line."

There was a shaking of heads and a sucking of teeth as his hearers mentally put the loss into terms of hard cash.

"So there we were, with three storm lanterns and a truckle table, taking our last levels beside the summit lock of the Rochdale Canal. After midnight. Imagine the fever! A chaise and two horses champing to be off. And two changes posted on the route. My, didn't they *fly!* They say the ink was still wet on the paper when it reached the Preston magistrates!"

The attentive little knot around him erupted into laughter. "Still wet!" one said. "Very likely!" said another, more literal soul.

"And what questions we had to ask!" Walter continued, seeing that he had them. "And the replies! We had to establish title as well as the physical survey, you see. I remember one place . . ." He chuckled. "This'll show you the sort of people—the sort of creatures—up there. We go to a rough row of cottages—rougher than anything in the village here. Knock on the first door. Great cart horse of a woman appears. 'Aaa?' 'Pray, who is the occupier of this house?' 'Why me 'usband to be sure.' 'And what is your husband's name?' 'Nay. I cannot tell ye that. He goes by the name of Bill o' Jack's.' 'But surely you must know your husband's name—his surname?' 'Nay, that I don't.' 'But I must have it to write down here.' 'Then ye must ask at Tom o' Dick's—he lives a bit higher yonder.' "

Walter's attempt at the Lancashire dialect was as lamentable as any southerner's, but it raised a hearty laugh in that southern company.

"What did you do then, Walter?" Dr. Paine, now his father-in-law, asked when the laughter had died. "What did you put?"

"Believe me, sir. That survey has gone up to Westminster with several dozen Toms o' Jack's and Bills o' Dick's scrawled across it!"

The laughter redoubled at that.

Then, sensing that they had had enough of levity, he went on in a more serious tone: "Mr. Gooch has calculated that if the railroad already existed, the five weeks' travelling we undertook in surveying its route would have taken, all in all, a mere four days."

Heads nodded sagely at this intelligence. The railways were, indeed, a wonderful thing; especially as they had not yet threatened this part of Hertfordshire.

Claude George III, who had stood sullen and irresolute at the fringe of the company throughout Walter's story, torn between the urge to walk ostentatiously away and the itch to stay and throw in a sarcastic comment if the occasion offered—Claude George III now spoke.

"You fill me with envy, Walter." His voice was almost a sneer. "Shipping is so slow and dull after the excitements of the railroad."

"Oh!" Walter was all solicitude. "Poor Cousin Claude!" He pronounced it as close to Clod as he dared. "Why not exchange with me? My life and prospects for yours."

Claude George III's features twisted in a salacious grin. "Now on the day you take such a tasty little morsel to wed, that is . . . a tantalizing suggestion!"

The slight laughter that joined his guffaw was strained and polite, supplied to spare him the embarrassment of laughing alone. Many turned to Dr. Paine to see how he would choose to respond to so studied an insult.

His was the soft answer: "You may regret that refusal, Mr. Thornton. There's a great deal of money being made in railroads."

The parson's unexpected mildness annoyed Claude George III, whose favourite gambit was to provoke anger and show his victim up as a humourless curmudgeon. Now he was unsettled enough to forget himself and to slip back into an earlier habit of open sarcasm: "I hardly think . . ." he began before he realized where he had been manoeuvred. He could not add, as he had intended, "Walter will be among them as are making it." Instead he finished lamely, ". . . I hardly think it is for me." And then, to fill the silence, he added: "No, by harry!"

Walter almost felt sorry for him. "No," he agreed. "Nor me. To make a fortune one must risk a deal. I'm afraid my small income will just eke out my salary to give starvation wages for a gentleman."

"What do they pay a young engineer nowadays?" asked Mr. Keating, the workhouse overseer and a man not noted for his tact. He was there as a tenant of the Thorntons, from whom he held a farm.

"Around four hundred," Walter said quickly, wanting to confine any embarrassment there to young Claude.

But raised eyebrows and amused smiles had already alerted Keating to his lapse. "Don't mind my asking," he said, turning redder than wind, sun, and rain had naturally made him. "Know a young fellow wants apprenticing in your line of country."

"Quite. Not at all—" Walter began before Claude George III cut in.

"Not bad!" he sneered. "Even a gentleman could live very tolerably on that—as long as he never stuck his nose outside the Lancashire Pennines!"

This time he laughed alone.

"Well may you laugh, sir!"

The company turned to see the young man's father, who had joined the group unnoticed, eyeing his son sternly. "And well may you talk! You lost more than that in two days at Newmarket this spring. So talk on! It's cheaper, by harry!"

The son's discomposure was now complete. If his father had hoped for such a humiliation, he now gave no sign of satisfaction. Disgust was more like it.

"Walter," he said in tones that were only a degree more kindly.

"Yes, Uncle Claude."

"Word with ye."

There was no smile, no nod, no "excuse me" to the company. He strode off, knowing that Walter would follow; a petty despot in his own small manor.

But for once Walter did not follow directly. Instead he walked across the room to Arabella and squeezed her elbow gently. "Time to change," he said, and basked in her answering smile. Its radiance would bear him up through whatever the elder man might say now; and in half an hour they'd be gone from here forever. How often had he thought this day would never come!

He turned to see Claude George II standing impatiently, stooped to pass beneath the sash window that led out, via the ballroom steps, to the gardens. It was typical of the Thorntons that, having added the ornate steps up to the windows and having found that the five-foot-eight-inch gap revealed by the sash window was *just* negotiable, if one stooped, they decided not to alter the fenestration to allow more generous passage between ballroom and lawns.

The bright sun had discouraged anyone from leaving the shade indoors, so that Walter and his uncle had the garden to themselves.

"Silly time to be tellin' you this," the elder said as they reached the gravel path. "But what with all this incompetence in the docks I've been so busy. Oh, I shall burst!" He undid the top buttons of his fly and breathed out with vast relief. "That's better. God's teeth, it's hot out here! May be a break on the way, though. Feels thundery. Are the women followin'? Anyone lookin'?"

Walter glanced about him casually. "No," he said after careless search. "Only those gardeners."

His words merged into the sound of a heavy piddle washing down on the gravel.

"That's better. I was drownin' inside!" He did up the lower four buttons again. "Talkin' of gardeners. Is the young un there? Wikes?"

"The one that lives up by the gatehouse?"

"That's him. Played a trick on him he'll not forget in a hurry."

From the moment the two of them had appeared on the steps, backs were bent inches lower and rakes and scythes flashed a little faster than human anatomy makes natural.

"Caught him mockin' me." They left the gravel to stroll over the lawns. "Imitatin' me to the other outdoor staff. Whole crowd of 'em hootin' with laughter in the pheasant run. Didn't say anything. Hah!" His sudden raucous shout made a peacock, which had just broken noisily through a yew hedge nearby, turn around and retrace its steps in feathery alarm. "Let the fella stew till Saturday. Last Saturday, talkin' about. Then said to him—end of the day it was—said to him, 'Come with me. Bring your turfin' spade.' Took him down the far end of the avenue."

His hand pointed over at the limes, matured a century earlier, that stretched in a long ride across the park, between the garden and the woodland away to the west. Fleetingly Walter thought of the countless fantasies of plague, holocaust, and divine justice that had made him master of this mansion and its acres so many times in these long years now past.

"Right to the very end. Hard against the woods. Made the fella cut a square foot of sod. Then brought him all the way back, past the house here, right up the long drive to the lodge."

The engineer in Walter automatically assessed this walk at ten furlongs.

"All the time, ye see, he's thinkin', 'Nearer home! Nearer home! Every step nearer home!' Ye know how it is when they leave off early on a Saturday. Six o'clock and perhaps a bit of meat waiting cooked. Heh heh!''

It suddenly occurred to Walter that his own presence was an excuse, a very flimsy excuse, for his uncle to relive whatever triumph he had wreaked on the wretched gardener.

"When we got there, I made him cut a square-foot sod from his own lawn and put the one from the avenue in its place. *Then . . .*" He dissolved in a cackling fit. "Then I told him to take the one from his own lawn all the way back down the drive and all along the avenue and put it where we'd dug the first one up! Should've seen the fella's face! 'We'll hear no more about Claude George Thornton II and his funny ways,' I told him.'' And now he hooted and brayed with laughter.

"He must have been relieved," Walter said when the other was calmer.

The word startled his uncle. "Relieved! I hope he was greatly put out!"

"No—I mean not to have been dismissed."

The bewilderment in the other's face showed that the very thought of dismissal was new. "Oh. Wouldn't dismiss him," he said. "He's one of me own. Been here from birth, young Wikes. Wouldn't dismiss him. Huh! Didn't even consider it. Too softhearted. Like you."

Inwardly Walter laughed at the comparison. Yet, ungrudgingly, he admitted that thoughts of dismissal (which would have occurred instantly to the third generation) probably had not entered his uncle's mind.

"I must be going soon, Uncle," he said.

They had reached the edge of the ha-ha, which separated the lower lawns from the park. Two young red deer, both males, broke from a small dingle of thorn about a hundred and fifty yards away. For a moment both men stood silent in admiration of their grace. Walter had time to observe that one was a two-year-old, a pricket (being a park deer), and the other a three-year-old, a brocket. And, he wondered wryly, what use was such knowledge to a penniless engineer on four hundred a year?

"Yes," his uncle said at last. "Well—can't put it off any longer. About your trust. Your father left, as you know, fifteen hundred. The interest, reinvested, and the increase in the value of the stock, has made it just over two thousand by now."

"Oh!" Walter was taken aback. "How splendid!"

He had known that his uncle had brought him out to talk about the trust; it was the only unfinished business between them. And he had expected that the moment would be postponed as long as possible, for he had been fully convinced that his relatives had found ways to plunder it over the years. He had expected to be about five hundred pounds poorer, not richer. He looked guardedly at his uncle, who seemed careful not to return the gaze.

"Point is, me boy—the trust ceases with your marriage. In my view it should have ceased four years ago when ye came of age. Still. There it is. It's yours now. If ye'll take my advice, ye'll leave it ·vhere it is—in consols. Good and safe."

"Very sound advice," Walter said, mentally reserving his offer of a thousand to John Stevenson. "I see I must thank you, Uncle, for your good stewardship."

The two young deer dropped behind a ridge far out in the park.

"And, too, for your care all these years," he added. Convention had urged him to say "care and kindness" but the words stuck in his throat, refusing to be uttered.

"Good of ye to put it that way." Embarrassment made his uncle distant, as if his mind dwelled on weightier matters elsewhere, making present conversation a double burden. "Been dashed difficult at times, of course. I know how badly mine have behaved to ye. But ye've come out of it a fine young man, so mebbe it's the tempering ye needed."

Twice in the one minute his uncle had shattered all expectation and gone against all precedent; first with the news of the swollen trust, and now with what came as close to an apology as the old tyrant could get. Walter felt the stirrings of something close to pity, almost to warmth; but it was the passing impulse of a generous heart. In cold truth, nothing the old man did now could roll back all those years of indifference and neglect.

"Well," Walter said noncommittally.

But the other had still more penance to do and Walter had no power to stop him.

"Did no more than simply family duty. Be honest. Which is what I really wanted to say. Having taken up the duty, bad to drop it half way."

"Drop it?" Walter wondered what he could mean.

"No no! Should treat ye fully as one of me own. Wish ye *were,* dammit. But ye see what a fine pickle I'm in."

Many a time in later life Walter was to suffer from—and see others suffer from—ruthless men who, having had their way and having sustained every crumb of advantage to themselves, would assuage what could only be the most rudimentary conscience with a frank, disarming confession. Thanks to his early exposure at the hands of his uncle, whom he knew and detested so deeply, he was never truly deceived—though, as now, it often paid to pretend as much. Always, he was to observe, the confession and apology would have carried more conviction half-way through the rape, instead of at its end.

"Really, Uncle," he said. "There's not the slightest need now to . . ."

"Me younger son's an amiable nincompoop and a prig. Me daughter's an empty-headed hoyden and another prig. And me eldest's a licentious spendthrift and ne'er-do-well . . ."

"Oh, come now—you're very hard. You take their very worst—"

"Plain truth, sir. Best or worst." Claude George II was determined to run his course. "Plain truth. Point is, if the business is to survive, it'll take all we've saved. Survive me own children, I mean."

Walter, recovering now from the shock of this unprecedented urge to apology, ventured a small experiment—confronting insincerity with its match. "Oh, Uncle!" he said, with a beatific smile that clearly alarmed the other. "I am *more* than content. You have given me both home and schooling these ten years. Never once, though the impulse to generosity must have been nigh overwhelming at times, never once did you encourage me into any false assessment of my future station. You gave me a good trade. The best of trades. And my inheritance you have raised by a third—five hundred pounds! Could any orphan nephew ask for more! He would be a monster of ingratitude who did so.'"

A crafty gleam of content (how transparent are the single-minded, Walter thought) stole into Claude George II's eye. It was dawning on him how glowing his stewardship could be made to appear—for every word that Walter had said was true.

"You're very good, me boy," he said as he put a hand to Walter's shoulder and turned back toward the house.

Then, to keep alive the illusion of this new-kindled warmth, he bumbled all the way with gratuitous advice—the sort that newlyweds must expect from those long initiated. "Don't ever buy land. Not ornamental land, ye follow. Worst thing me father ever did—buying this place off Macky. Gives the ladies ideas. Got ten gardeners here now. It's no good. Very bad for them. Help yourself—keep the money in gilt-edged and the women in a town house with a kerchief to water for a garden. The two worst diseases of womanhood? A big vista and a landscape architect . . ."

Anyone but Walter would have taken him for an affable eccentric.

\*     \*     \*

Arabella had looked conventionally beautiful in her wedding dress, for it had been her maternal grandmother's, the bishop's wife. How sad, everyone agreed, she had not lived to see her granddaughter wear it. Still, at the appropriate moments on that day, Arabella had brought conventional mist to the eyes, conventional gasps to the throats, and conventional flutters to the hearts of all the appropriate people. In a phrase which that same grandmother had often used to deflate many a proud parent of a newborn baby among her numerous offspring, it was "another little nonesuch" of a wedding.

During the endless fittings needed to adapt this heirloom to its latest wearer (though, for its size, *tenant* would have been an apter word), Arabella's misgivings hardened into a certainty that this gown would never make quite that stunning impression which all brides yearn for on their wedding day. It was unfashionable, heavy, well mended . . . and it would never hang about her properly, whatever skill was lavished upon it.

So the real impression, the memory that all would hold of that day of days, was to be reserved for her carriage costume. Never was a dress so designed, sketched, altered, redrawn, stitched, taken apart, and put together again . . . never were more bows, braids, lace patterns, rosettes, and tassels held against so many silks, cottons, paduasoys, taffetas, velvets, cords, and worsteds—and still deemed unsuitable. Tempers had frayed faster than any cloth in the months that led up to this great day; and more than once her mother, her dressmaker, and even the upstairs maid, had thrown up their hands in despair.

Nor had the problems ended at that; there was still the question of the proper staging of her entrance in this marvellous costume. Because of the crush of guests, most of them on the Thornton side, it had been agreed to hold the breakfast at Maran Hill, the Thorntons' large country house. As a changing room for Arabella, Mrs. Thornton had originally set aside the gun room, which communicated directly with the main hall via a small door beneath the bold, sweeping curve of the grand stair. It had taken months of diplomatic discussion (for one did not argue with a Thornton) to alter these arrangements so that Arabella would change in the second-floor boudoir and make her return *down* the stair.

But Arabella's quiet persistence had, in the end, worn through all opposition. And here she stood, in Mrs. Thornton's own pretty little boudoir, smoothing her perfectly smooth hair, puffing out the perfectly puffed-out lace, straightening the perfectly straight seams of the sleeves, and tightening once more the delicate silk gloves, which already fitted her better than an extra skin.

"Oh, miss!" the maid said, forgetting in her excitement—and for the first time since the wedding—to call her madam, "I never seen anybody look half so beautiful!"

"I thank you, Alice," Arabella said, surprised at the calm of her voice. "Well"—she turned to the dressmaker—"was it worth all the heart-aching?"

And the dressmaker had to allow that it would have been worth double the argufying to see such a picture.

Until that moment Arabella's mother and younger sisters, and Walter's cousin Letty, had all been barred from the room in the interests of calm and speed—an arrangement that only her monstrous persistence could have achieved. Now, by way of reward, they were let in for an especial preview.

Mrs. Paine had already prepared herself to sweep in with outstretched arms and a long tremolo of joyful surprise. In fact she began before the door was open half an inch, and she continued until her eyes fixed on Arabella. Unfortunately, the excitement she had prepared was several degrees too insipid for what she now saw. And what she now saw was—as she put it later—a vision of sheer loveliness. It left her standing, arms outstretched, wide-eyed and voiceless. Behind her the double doors swung fully open to reveal Arabella's sisters and Letty, equally transfixed in astonishment and admiration.

Their unfeigned cries of delight when they at last burst into the room and ran toward her told Arabella how right she had been to insist on her own ideas of style and material. With perfect countenance she stood and let them advance to fuss over her. And what strange fussing! Though longing to hug her, none dared even to touch for fear of ruffling some part of that perfectly composed ensemble.

Mrs. Paine, crying "Oh child! Oh child!", circled her as if she were a bone-china fortress, seeking some safe chink where they might make contact. At length, absurdly, she kissed the fingertips of her gloves and smeared them lightly on Arabella's rosy cheeks. Letty, at a greater distance, darted around her like a distraught fowl, eyes brimming with tears, hands clasping and unclasping in repeated transports. She was not as malicious as the comment in Arabella's journal made her seem—only lazy and rather empty-headed. She would always do the straightforward thing—be spiteful if spite were called for, or, as now, almost swoon with unaffected delight.

Louise, Arabella's youngest sister, was the first to regain some measure of composure. She came forward and nudged Arabella's arm. "Show a little happiness," she said. "How can you stay so calm!"

*How can they believe I'm calm?* Arabella wondered. Her heart, thrust high into her chest by the tightening of her corset, thumped like a forging engine, trembling through her soft flesh and making the lace upon it shiver. Could they not see? Still, she was glad it showed in no other way.

She took the first step across the boudoir and out to the stairhead, moving like a great and beautiful clipper in full sail on a calm sea.

The stairs were built to rise in a single central flight of thirteen steps to a halfpace, where they divided, curving around in two flanking runs, each also of thirteen steps, meeting at the landing outside the boudoir. The ballroom door being to the left of the stair, Arabella chose the flanking run to her right so that she was in full view of those below from the very first step of her majestic descent.

From those who saw her first a ripple of astonishment spread through all the company. In the cool light that filtered from the dome above, the ground below turned pale as face after face lifted upward and was held. In the silence she heard only the swish and creak of the women's clothing as they turned to see her. No queen ever made a finer entry; and if anyone had had the ill taste to applaud, there were many in that throng so lost to themselves that they would have joined in quite spontaneously.

Arabella gave no sign that she understood the impression she was making. When she reached the turn inward to the central flight, her eyes found Walter's as he waited by the foot of the stair, and never again left them until she had gained his side. And all that long, long while he basked in a whispered chorus of "by harrys!" and "I *says!*" Never had he felt such exultation of his spirit.

He was speechless until she touched his fingers. Then, "What a setting for my pearl!" he said quietly.

Her hand flew to the lace at her throat, for she thought he was referring to a little pearl he had given her at Christmas.

"I forgot it," she whispered, mortified. "I never thought!" Her eyes prepared to cry.

For a moment he was puzzled. "Oh no," he said at last. "I mean my pearl *beyond* price." He kissed her hand to reinforce his meaning.

Too close to tears to make any reply, she took his arm and together they walked among the guests to the portico, where the family coach already awaited. The crowd, animated again and buzzing with excitement at this beautiful climax, poured out behind them. Among them, prouder than she could ever remember, was Mrs. Paine, carrying the dark silken and worsted bombazine wrap that Arabella would need upon the train.

Two footmen came around from the courtyard, bearing the last of their trunks.

"Stow them firm, you fellas," Claude George II shouted. "The road at Harpenden is as rutted as Vauxhall Gardens."

Among the younger set only Claude George III and his flash crowd laughed.

"Father!" Letty called out. "That is disgraceful."

"There'll be rutting enough tonight, eh!" cackled old Mrs. Paine, Arabella's surviving grandmother. "Ye'll need no help from the roads! Eh, Walter?"

He did not even smile at her, but glanced in embarrassment at Arabella. She, however, was her usual calm self: "Grandmother, do be quiet or you'll vex us all."

Unrepentant, the old woman cackled on.

"Don't pretend you didn't hear," the younger Mrs. Paine told the older; then she arranged the cloak around her daughter's dress.

When she had done, there were handshakes and hugs all around until Walter, now stealing anxious glances at his watch, handed Araballa up into the coach. He followed as soon as she was seated.

Up to that moment Mrs. Claude George Thornton II had been somewhat remote. Now she appeared suddenly to realize that the younger folk really were going. "Your bouquet, child!" she cried, snatching up Letty's garland and thrusting it any old how through the still-open carriage door. "Oh!" She drew back from what she saw inside. "Such a picture! I shall weep!"

Letty, counting the bags on the roof of the coach, absently nudged her mother with a small bottle. "Your salts," she said.

There was a distant rumble of summer thunder.

"Said it," Uncle Claude called out. "Said so. Better hurry."

"One valise is missing!" Letty shouted and went back indoors to abuse the footmen.

Walter climbed out again, feeling guilty that he had not himself noticed the omission. He walked around the coach, looking with seeming purpose at the axle boxes, and came face to face with Claude George III. Both were embarrassed.

"Well, Walter," his cousin said. "Launched."

"I suppose so."

"And no ill feeling."

"I daresay not."

He walked back to the other side of the coach, where Letty had returned with the errant footmen and the missing valise. "One can rely on no one," she said with a victorious smile. "Be so happy, Walter dear!"

They embraced.

"And you, Letty. It won't be so long now for you."

"Don't!" she cried, flapping her hands in mock despair. "I daren't *think!* So much to do! How I wish it could all be as simple as this, today."

"And as cheap!" Claude George II chimed in.

There were some more casual exchanges and goodbyes before the coach bore them off, but it was these two remarks by Letty and her father that Walter chose to let ring in his ears. They were so characteristically *Thornton!*

It was like the dawning of a sweeter day to settle back in the coach beside Arabella. His rancour melted in the firm blue gaze of her eyes, and he fondled her new ring through the thin silk of her glove.

"It feels strange," he said.

"Not at all. It feels as if that hand had always lacked something—and not known what it was until today."

Her reply made him too happy even to speak, until he felt her shudder slightly.

"What?" he asked.

She did not at once answer.

"Are you cold?"

"It's the elder ones," she said. "How . . . uncouth and vulgar they seem."

"Yes," he agreed, uncertain that he wanted to open up this line of talk.

"How dreadful it must be to live so deficient of delicacy."

"We must always remember," he said, in tones that promised finality, "that they lived in very disturbed times. They had so few of *our* incentives to virtue."

"How right that is, dear!" A welcome admiration flashed in her eyes. "You are always so good and charitable. Father has always said it. In fact, it was he who pointed you out to me first as one to admire and aspire to."

"Really? Your father!"

The rector was, in fact, something of a womanizer—though, of course, his wife and daughters would be the last to hear of it.

"Oh, Walter!" Arabella clutched his arm. "Do please help me to be virtuous, too!"

And he, looking down at her trusting, adoring face, longed to behold and caress the untouched body beneath.

"Oh, but you are already such an example to everyone!" he said in jocular rejection of her plea. "I'm sure you will need no guidance from *me.*"

He wondered how prepared she was for the things they were to do that night. And while she leaned her bonnet on his shoulder and snuggled happily against his arm, his fantasy moved forward in time to the little room he had booked in the inn at Earlestown, way up there at the end of the line. Until they were married he had forbidden himself to imagine what would happen there; now he need have no such scruples.

"Tell me again about our house," she said, cutting across his picturing.

And for the tenth time he told her of the little house he had rented in the Vale of Todmorden, and how its front rooms looked up the valley to the Leeds mouth of Summit Tunnel, *his* tunnel. He told her of the long purple and blue shadows that stole across the fields at dawn and dusk. But as he had not yet lived there, he could tell her nothing of their new neighbours except that an acquaintance had said they were "respectable and God-fearing."

That was pleasing. "And factories?" she asked. "I meant several times to inquire and always forgot to."

Like most southerners she imagined the north had already vanished under brick and chimney. The desolate moors around Dotheboys Hall—a name added to the language that very year—were, somehow, set in the north of a different England.

He told her it was impossible to describe. No one who had not seen it could imagine that strange northern mixture of medieval-rural landscape and modern industry—of sheepfold and mill chimney. But she would see.

It sounded a fine, unfrivolous place, Arabella thought, seeking to reassure herself. The Maran valley and this part of Hertfordshire were undeniably beautiful, but it was all so manicured—so thick with park and covert and fine houses—that it seemed entirely given over to pleasure and sport. The thought that she and Walter would have to begin so frugally, with such a small house and only three servants (and only two of them living in), also pleased her—especially when she saw what wealth had done to the Thorntons.

"Oh, Walter," she said aloud. "We shall manage somehow. And we shall be so happy—I *know* it."

# Chapter 13

The clerk-in-charge at Boxmoor had been expecting Walter and his new bride, for Walter had bought their tickets north on his arrival earlier that week. He thought it something of an honour to have the young engineer make use of his station—the engineer in charge of the longest tunnel now building anywhere in the world. As the coach turned on the slope that led from the turnpike up to the station, he and the porter came out on the forecourt and—against all the rules—helped with carrying the luggage. This made Arabella positively glow with pride. She had seen Walter only as the poor cousin at Maran Hill; and here were these railway people, on such an important line as the London–Birmingham, treating him like a visiting duke! The dozen or so other passengers already waiting clearly thought, too, that he was someone of importance. Walter, aware of their attention, also glowed with pride, for he was sure that Arabella's beauty was the cause of it all.

They had come a good fifteen minutes ahead of the train, so there was plenty of time for the coachman and company servants to take the luggage across to the down platform. Then Mullins, the clerk-in-charge, came hurrying back, not so much to talk to Walter, for they had had a fair old yarn on that earlier visit, but to hover respectfully near by in case he was needed.

Dark clouds had blown up well clear of the northern skyline. To Arabella they looked like towering mountains wrenched from the soil and unleashed to wander overhead. It was a living tableau from a painting by John Martin. She was just about to turn to Walter to share this discovery with him when he hit his thigh excitedly and called out, "It's a Bury! Four-wheeler, two driven!"

He obviously meant the engine, now puffing into view up the line. How could he be so certain? To her it was still hardly more than a blur. She had seen but two trains in her life, both from the safe distance of the bridge at St. Alban's. It took all her courage to stand her ground as the great monster rumbled by. The *heat* it gave off! She had not expected that. And the strange, fishy smell of the steam. She was glad when it had passed and their carriage, comfortingly first-class, had stopped. Mullins leaped in to unlock it for them.

But Walter was not to be cheated. "Come and have a closer look," he said, making off down the platform. "This is a stroke of luck! We've just taken delivery of two Burys for the Manchester & Leeds. Let's see how well they're regarded."

Arabella meekly followed.

As soon as they arrived at the front he reached a hand up to the engineer. "Thornton. Engineer on Summit Tunnel for the Manchester & Leeds."

The other wiped his hands well before he took Walter's. "McConnell," he said.

"My dear, here is Mr. McConnell, our engineer"—he turned inquiringly back—". . . all the way to Earlestown?"

"All the way to Earlestown."

Arabella and the engineer nodded to each other. But this time Walter did not even notice the admiring glint in the Scotchman's eye; he himself was lost in admiration of the engine—a bright green creature with black bands around her boiler, a tall chimney, a great beehive firebox of burnished copper, and wheel splashers of gleaming brass.

"Manchester & Leeds," McConnell said. "I was to Bury's works at Liverpool last week for new spoke shoes for this. They tell me ye've bought two."

Walter looked at the number on the company plate. Number One, it said. "What's this, then? 1837? Ours are this year's, of course. Robert Stephenson's own design actually, not Bury's. Very like this to look at, but with four driven wheels. An improvement, I fancy."

"It's well enough," McConnell said. "But, mon, I cuid tell them a dozen improvements."

Walter smiled, seeing a kindred spirit. He, too, longed to design an engine—a Thornton eight-wheeler! "A longer boiler for a start," he said.

"Aye. Ye're right enough there! Feel the heat from this—mon, it's a terrible waste. And I'd anchor it up forrard only—put it on sliders to the frame back here. When it gets hot now, bolted both ends, ye should see the distortions to the frame!"

"Yes!" Walter began to grow excited. "And I'm sure we can now build crankshafts strong enough to let us do away with all these sandwich frames and inner frames that Stephenson and his father are so wedded to. Such a mess! We could manage with one single inside plate frame."

McConnell grinned and stepped down, beckoning Walter to come forward and peer under his boiler. "Bury's close to it here," he said. "It's a single inside bar frame."

"So it is. Yes—so it is. Well—that more or less proves my point."

"I'd go even further. I'd make a central common valve chest and drive the slide valves directly—do away with rocking valves and all that caper."

Walter looked puzzled.

"Put the slide valves on their sides, of course," McConnell added.

"Ah yes!" Walter said. "Yes. I see."

Arabella, looking from one to the other, both oblivious of her, felt the strongest urge to pinch herself. Plate . . . bar . . . slide . . . frame . . . tube. . . . She knew the meaning of every word. So how could they add together to make something so utterly incomprehensible!

Mullins came padding up the platform, embarrassed at having to interrupt. "The train must go, sir," he said diffidently.

Walter bade goodbye to McConnell. "One day they'll do it all," he said.

"Just you and I keep reminding them!" McConnell shouted back.

\*       \*       \*

They had not journeyed far before most of the sky grew black. The thunder that had rumbled so distantly at Maran Hill now roared above, shaking and tearing the sky apart. Some of the clouds were so dark as to merge with the dense smoke that poured ceaselessly from the engine. But no rain fell; and away to the west they could discern a hopeful band of clear yellow sky. As evening grew, an orange sun slipped down into this band, underlighting the dark hulls of the thunderclouds with the deepest hues of sulphur. The same infernal colour touched the leaves of willows and aspens as they whitened in the squalls that presaged rain.

Walter and Arabella, in facing window seats, sat spellbound, watching the long transformation from orange through carmine to the latest, deepest crimson of the sunset. Then, when the sun had gone and the heavens had returned to lead and charcoal, large oily drops of rain slid out of the sky. It was raining hard by the time they drew near to Birmingham.

Walter reached out a hand and, by a combination of luck and well-versed anatomical judgement, found and squeezed her knee. It was only a light, experimental squeeze, but she stiffened at once and he had to pretend that he had merely wanted to point out the passing scene to her. A solid wash of rain spouted down over the tossing trees and glistening roofs of Bordesley Green and Ashted.

The distant patch of clear sky had dwindled to a mere halo of smudged gray above the horizon. Arabella, reassured that he had meant nothing improper, pulled a theatrically glum face at this scene.

"Poor Mr. McConnell," she said.

"They dress for all weathers. And the fire soon dries and warms them. They're not like coachmen."

"When you and he make your own engine, contrive some shelter for your colleagues."

He laughed. "With portholes and chintz curtains!"

All the same, he thought, it was the basis of a sound notion. Later still he wondered why one never said "poor coachman" unless the weather was truly foul.

At New Street Station three clergymen and a stout lady, evidently a parishioner of one of them, were let into the compartment; but, as they were all Roman Catholics, Arabella was glad that no one attempted any conversation.

By Stafford the sky had cleared again and they sped on over Standon, through Crewe, and on to the Cheshire plains under a full harvest moon. In the darkening sky the first stars began to twinkle.

By the time they reached Earlestown, Arabella had had her fill of railway travel. She was disappointed at how routine it seemed after that first thrill at speeding so fast; very soon even thirty miles an hour seemed a snail's pace.

Most of their fellow passengers went on to wait for the last connection to Liverpool or Manchester, grumbling at the inability of the various companies to operate trains to a common schedule in the interests of the passengers. Only half a dozen or so—three commercial people, a lady so deeply veiled that none could see her face, and her servant, and, of course, Walter and Arabella—were staying at the nearby inn.

All their baggage was stowed on top of an almost derelict coach, which groaned menacingly under the weight. Walter put Arabella in the coach with the lady and her servant (pretty little thing, he noticed), while he walked warily ahead. The commercial gentlemen had taken one look at the ancient vehicle—or "ekkiparge" as they jocosely called it—and set off for the inn on foot. They already had a pint or two down by the time the rest arrived.

Walter and Arabella took dinner in their room. The maid, knowing they were newly wed, dissolved in giggles and simpering blushes, so that Arabella had to issue a sharp reprimand. Walter contrived that the claret flowed well, until her eyes were one tint brighter and her talk a shade faster and livelier than was usual. And when the maid had cleared away the remnants of the meal he made the excuse of seeing the landlord about breakfast and arrangements for their departure, leaving a tactful moment for her to undress.

He had hardly settled with his brandy before she appeared at the foot of the stairs, dressed for outdoors. He was already walking toward her by the time she noticed him.

"Oh dearest," she said. "I feel so restless. We were so long in the coach—and then locked in that train—and now sitting upstairs . . . I wish I could run a mile."

"Well . . ." He smiled archly. "If it's exercise ye want, I had something like that in mind—or its equivalent at least!"

"Oh good!" she exclaimed with all the innocent excitement of her eighteen years. "Out in the street? Are the streets safe here?"

"The streets!"

"Oh no—much better: the garden! See if they have a garden. Ask the man if we may stroll in his garden."

And that is what Walter, to his own considerable surprise, found himself doing, only moments later. He sent his brandy and bottle up to their room.

The garden was large and well kept, with gravel paths broad enough for them to walk on side by side. In an almost windless sky, thin veils of black and silver cloud drifted across the full moon. After the dim interior, lit only by candles and fishtail burners, it seemed as bright and blue as day, with the moon itself almost painful to look at. They could see every rain-drop where it hung from every twig or blade of grass. White roses shimmered with a fairy light, while red ones turned to deepest, wine-dark indigo. At a bend in the path stood a large hydrangea, like a shrub with a hundred pale-blue eyes. The cool air was heavy with honeysuckle and wet fern.

Arabella felt she must have entered paradise. To stand, her senses drowned amid such beauty, beside the man who of all men in the world was the kindest, noblest, and most dear, his hand clasping hers so lovingly and with such tender strength. . . . She breathed in, and in, and in, to cool the delight that coursed so wildly through her. Many and many a time before she had imagined that she knew the transports of love—when Walter had embraced her, or when his letters had arrived, or even when, on waking, she had brightened the new day with memories of him before she thanked God that they shared the same earth and time. But this was something so immeasurably more intense that it was almost a pain. It was so pure, and it so exceeded anything she had sensed before, that she knew it lay on the very frontiers of a love that could only be called divine. At last she understood how the love of two people could transcend time and space, speaking across centuries and generations, calling from beyond the grave, and surviving even the fall of civilizations. Theirs was such a love! It was a tiny portion of the same love that moved God (in fact, as she realized with some shock, *compelled* Him) to give His son for something so unworthy as mankind. It was truly awesome to have been drawn so close to an understanding of Him, there in that moonlit garden.

"Oh, Walter," she said, sighing out her long-pent-up breath, "I do love you so very much!"

His was a different mood. When they had stepped out of the door, once his eyes had grown accustomed to the light, he had looked up at the moon and realized that it was, in fact, past the full and a day or two into its wane. It was, he suddenly remembered, the same bright moon, then waxing, that had lighted up the cutting with the same sort of brilliance when he and John Stevenson had emerged from their inspection of the accident at Summit, only the week before. "Did ye tumble with her, sir?" Stevenson had asked. The question, and the memory of Molly (as he still believed Nora to be called), and the "glimpse of paradise" he had had with her, haunted him these last seven days like a tune that will not go away.

The possession of a virgin, he warned himself, would not be like that. He stole a glance at Arabella, who seemed lost in some inner rhapsody. It would be . . . gentler, more tender, more hesitant. With creatures like Molly you could throw aside all your caution; you could do anything. With Arabella he would have to be patient and understanding.

Again he looked at her, so young and lovely in the moonlight, picturing the warm, smooth body that moved with such supple grace beneath the outer ramparts of her clothes. His flesh, hungering for her, hung slack upon his bones.

And that was the moment she turned to him and, with that long, passionate sigh, declared her love.

It stopped him in his tracks. His flesh now cringed in self-disgust; and he resolved that they should pass that night at least in the purest embrace, expressing for each other only the noblest and sublimest kind of love.

He turned and took her in his arms. And before their kiss was three seconds old he knew how impossible such a resolve would be to fulfill. Besides, whichever course he took, he had no way of knowing now what she would think of him. Would she admire his forbearance and strength of mind? Or think him an unmanly sop? Worse—would she *say* she admired him but secretly believe him to be contemptible? How little he really knew her. Perhaps it would be best after all to be strong. Give her some brandy and be strong. He would have to see.

They walked on in silence, she in the seventh heaven of contentment, he in the seventh hell of indecision, both outwardly serene. By now they had completed their second tour of the garden.

"Well," he said, apropos of nothing. "Another long day tomorrow."

"But not such a day as this. Was it not perfect?" she lied.

"If every day were like it, we should soon die of bliss." Jocularity, he thought, offered the best way to be noncommittal. "Yet I venture to think we may find tomorrow . . . acceptable. I doubt we'll die of ennui."

She dug him in the ribs, pouted, and then hugged his arm in a sudden access of warmth.

"Bed," he said.

"Very well."

"You go on up. I shan't be long."

She looked puzzled and seemed about to question him; but then, with an inclination of her head, she turned and went indoors.

The air still seemed to cage something of the magic of her presence; yet, now that she was no longer there in person, he found it easier to imagine her as pliant and responsive. How odd, he thought, that flesh-and-blood Arabella was so saintly, while the ethereal wife of his daydreams was so much more a creature of the earth. He tried again to feel the disgust that had so overpowered him only minutes earlier. Nothing came! It must have been some sudden effect of her saintliness, or the way she had looked, or something like that. Besides, this wasn't a romance; it was a marriage. There were heirs to be gotten.

He went up to find Arabella sitting up in bed, writing in her journal. Of the brandy he saw no sign, and something restrained him from asking. Not cowardice, he told himself, just a certain prudence, a sense of what was fitting for the occasion. He would ask later. Her nightdress was, in fact, her innermost chemise, which she had shrugged back on after taking off her stays. Its only concession to adornment was a few ribbons sewn into the cuffs of the short sleeves.

He smiled at her shyly and patted the unruffled bedclothes on his side of the bed.

"Comfortable?" he asked.

She smiled, nodded, closed her eyes, and breathed in sharply to show that she was contented beyond words.

"Not knowing how you like your bed made," he said, "I told them to make it up my way—higher in the centre."

While he spoke he retreated into the partial concealment of the bed curtain on his side, only turning to her again when he had his nightgown on.

"We are quite isolated," he went on. "The haylofts are on the other side of that wall; there's the garden, there's the street. And the other side there is a cupboard and a staircase."

"Oh, Walter darling! You think of everything. You arranged this before you came back down south? This particular room?"

He beamed and nodded.

"So," she said, raising her arms like a priestess in a Roman print, "let them all snore or gossip through the night. We shall sleep at peace!"

He marvelled at her composure. His heart began to race as he looked down on her—the soft, blond skin of her arms. He raised a corner of his sheet and had just lifted a foot when Arabella, to his confusion, lifted the bedclothes on her side and slipped quickly from the bed. For one stunning moment he thought she was about to commence some little game in which he must chase and capture her. But her manner soon ended any such thought. She had not even appeared to notice the erection that thrust his nightshirt at her like medieval armour, or the prow of a somewhat flexible ship.

She knelt to pray.

"Oh yes," he said, chastened. "Of course."

He knelt at his side of the bed.

"Almighty God," she began, and then stopped. "Walter, dearest," she went on in more everyday tones, "do come around this side and kneel beside me. And," she went on while he complied, "listen to this most particularly. I have been composing and perfecting it for months of nights past."

He knelt beside her.

"Almighty God, here before Thee kneel two wretched sinners united this day in Thy house, dedicated this day in Thy service, strengthened this day in Thy ever-watchful care. Grant, dear Lord, that this work here begun shall daily prosper and grow more lovely in Thy sight. Prevent us in danger and chide us when we stray. And grant, too, most merciful Father, that in all we undertake we act with pure and contrite hearts, seeking no greater reward than the continuance of Thine abiding love. Strengthen our endeavour to become every day more godly, righteous, and sober in our lives, more pious, upright, and simple in our faith. And finally, Lord, we most impatiently beseech Thee, crown our marriage with the greatest of all Thy blessings: children. Quicken now, O Lord, my sinful body that our union may bear fruit, abundant fruit, for of such, Thou hast said, is the Kingdom of Heaven. Amen."

There was a short silence before she cleared her throat of no particular obstruction.

"Amen," Walter said, and shifted his weight to one knee, preparing to rise. His now unrisen flesh hung warm and flaccid on his thigh.

"Will you not also pray?" she asked.

"Ah . . . er . . . the blessing of God . . ." he began, using the words of the clerical benediction. Then he changed to: "Glory be to the Father, and to the Son, and to the Holy Ghost, amen." He stood as Arabella said amen.

Eager again he leaped across the bed and flung himself under the sheets with boyish energy. Desire began to rekindle a little as he watched her more deliberate entry, swinging her long blond hair back over her shoulders in a gesture that made her breasts tremble as she straightened and settled. He shivered with delight as he watched her move. *God make it last!* he prayed. *Sharpen all my awareness!*

"It was a very conventional prayer, dearest," he heard her say.

"What could I add? You said all that could have been thought of. It was beautiful." Then, remembering that the bitter Pennine winter lay not so far ahead, he asked if she knelt to pray every night.

"Of course!" she laughed, thinking he was jesting. Then, realizing that he might, after all, be serious, she asked with some primness: "Do you mean that you do not?"

"Only in summer. In winter I say them in bed."

"Then God will never hear you." She pouted. "He has nothing but sneers for such cheats. Unless they are truly bedridden, of course."

She made this one concession sound most magnanimous. But her tone was far too matter-of-fact; she was far too sober.

"I asked them to send up some brandy," he said, looking around the room.

"Oh? I told them it must be some mistake. I sent it back. They seemed to think it very funny goings on."

He should have snuffed the candle then. He should have swept her through one long bodily catechism from touch to kiss to caress to embrace to unity. But that was never his way. He must reason her to him; he must carry her mind as well.

"Did I not hear your grandmother tell you to drink plenty of wine tonight?" he asked.

"The old reprobate! She is a scandal!"

"Yes. But do you have no inkling of why she said it?"

Arabella smiled coyly. "Perhaps she thought I might recoil at the rough touch of a manly whisker!"

Come, he thought, this is better. "So you understand then?"

"Of course, dearest! It is only natural that the snatched kisses and hasty tendernesses of our courtship will give way to the more leisured sort of embrace now that we are man and wife. That is to be expected." And to show what she meant she lay full back upon the pillow and held out her arms to him. "Oh, dearest! We can take such *joy* in each other now."

Relief bubbled through his veins like lemonade. All along she had been teasing! It would all be easy and natural, even without the wine. He snuffed the candle and settled into the outermost reach of her embrace, intending to work his way in.

"That's a most becoming chemise," he said, fondling the ribbon in order to let his knuckles caress the skin beneath. "It makes this shirt of mine seem quite dowdy."

"Oh, no. Yours is very manly. It is like Papa's. I do not like to see a man all prettified. The frivolities of yesterday are not becoming nowadays."

He could not decide whether she spoke like a child repeating a lesson or more like a teacher urging a child to repeat a lesson.

"I wonder if it has started?" she mused in a different tone.

"What has started?" he asked, unconcerned. He was stroking her arm now from shoulder to elbow, pleased to see how catlike she was in her response.

"Our child," she said.

His eyes had grown accustomed to the dark, so that the moonlight flooding in made the room seem brighter than when the candle had shared the illumination. He saw that her brow had darkened in bewilderment. She was not teasing when she asked: "Walter—how shall we know when we are to be blessed with children? I mean—how shall we know the exact time when I am to come to term?"

His bewilderment was hardly less than hers. "I suppose the doctor will tell us. It'll be never, unless we make a start!" And with that he kissed her full and warmly on her lips.

When she began to respond, he moved a hand firmly on to her breast and squeezed. An inch away he saw her dark blue eyes open wide in panic, staring into his, flesh into uncomprehending flesh. Her whole body stiffened in rejection. She pulled her lips away and said to the wall, as if she could not bear to face him: "Walter!"

His body, caught in its own momentum and reluctant to be diverted yet again, impelled him to continue his massage, hoping for the miracle.

"Walter!" she repeated in outrage, still bouncing her words off the wall. "That is . . . it's private!"

"Not to a husband, my love." He tried to turn her face to his but she refused.

"To a . . . to an . . ." She stumbled as she sought for words. "To one who is honourable. An honourable man respects . . ."

"But how else," he interrupted, "are we to beget any children?"

Then she turned to him of her own free will; and her face held an open astonishment. "But you *heard* me! Could anyone have prayed more fervently?"

It took him a long moment to digest her words, for he could not believe their literal implication. "And . . . that is all?" he asked. "You really believe that is sufficient?" He searched her face in vain for some sign of understanding.

"Why . . . yes," was all she said. She looked warily into his eyes, like one who seeks for motive rather than for meaning.

He took away his hand. "And you have lived in a rural parish for eighteen years!" he marvelled. "How do you imagine gilts get in pig, or heifers in calf?"

She looked away again, this time in impatience.

"Do you not know?" he pressed.

Her impatience deepened. "Well, of course I do. But what, pray, has that to do with—"

"How?"

"The farmer puts them to a boar or a bull, of course!" She spoke with finality, as if to dismiss a red herring.

"And," he persisted, "what then?"

"The beasts copulate, to be sure." She spoke less petulantly now, for a terrible realization had begun to dawn on her.

"You leave me speechless!" He lay back, limp again, and searched among the cracks of the ceiling for inspiration.

"But, dearest," she said, shocked at his ignorance, "they are beasts. They have no souls. They cannot pray for—for offspring with souls. Piglets have no souls. Calves have no souls!"

"So," he said, not really believing that this was her conclusion, "humans do not copulate?"

"With humans, because they have souls, it is called fornication, and it is an abomination in God's sight. Papa has often said so. Many and many a time." Her self-assurance was boundless. "As to fornication—I wish it were true that humans did not fornicate, for I am sure the world would then be much happier. The poor, I am afraid, are very prone to it—which goes far to explain why most of them are so very wretched."

"I don't believe it!" He laughed feebly and sighed out his bafflement. "I cannot believe my ears. You . . . sincerely believe that prayer will bring you children? Prayer alone?"

"Us, dearest. Not just me. Yes, to be sure. Now that we are married."

"And no further action on our part is necessary?"

"Oh, Walter!" She laughed to raise her own courage. "I think you're teasing!" She devoutly hoped he was; she wanted him to edge back from those horrid things he seemed to hint at. "Of course *we* must act. We must strive in all ways to be pious and chaste and honourable."

Surely he would see that, she thought; how good and inviting it sounded when she said it with such joy.

Poor Walter was now in a turmoil. Her rejection of him and her serene piety had, if anything, refined his longing for her. He did not now want her as a man might want *any* pretty girl, but rather as a great connoisseur might sacrifice the whole world of beautiful things for the one treasure that surpassed them all. If by some magic he were transported to a garden of delight, waited on by a whole harem of beautiful wantons, his only thought would be to fight his way out and back to Arabella. But she had to accept him willingly—hesitantly, perhaps, but ready to be startled into joy. And how could he do that when she recoiled from him with such disgust at every little intimacy?

He felt no anger toward her, nor even impatience. It was her father who stirred his wrath. How dare that old lecher so warp his daughter's mind! To be sure—to be fair—it was difficult; these matters were difficult. Quite obviously the old man could not tell her the complete truth. In any case, it was a husband's task to complete a girl's education in these things, when the knowledge she gained would be less dangerous. But there had been no need for that old goat to bend her so far the other way. A girl left in partial ignorance, her fancies adorned by some charming myths and half truths, was like a fallow field ready to spring into joyful fruit. But a girl fed such claptrap as Arabella had been forced to devour—she was like a field of poisoned earth. Yes! That was cause enough for anger.

Arabella, at first puzzled by his silence, grew increasingly alarmed. She felt sure he was thinking of some other way to broach again those horrid thoughts. She had to stop him. *She* had to say it, to bring the nastiness out into the open, where he would see it and be disgusted, too.

"I thought . . . ," she managed before courage failed her. "It's impossible . . ." How her heart pounded! "Oh—I'm so confused—it must be the wine. . . . I thought you were suggesting that we should . . . behave like beasts!"

There! She had said it! She felt crimson with the shame.

"Beasts!" Walter's anger at her father now erupted. "Like man and wife! And I am not hinting it. I am *asserting* it. It is a fact of nature. And if you have thought otherwise all your life, you have been seriously de-luded. Misled. Sent a-straying. I tell you plainly—"

But he never told her. Shock and distress led her to do what she would otherwise never have done: she stopped his mouth with her fingers—an urgent, pleading gesture. All she could say was: "No—I'm sure it is wrong, I am sure, I am sure, I am *sure!*"

The touch of her fingers melted his anger. Gently he pulled her hand away and gently he squeezed it to reassure her. For a while he did not speak, and when at last he did, it was in the mildest tone.

"Dearest, you *are* deluded. How can I . . . ?" He sighed. Then an idea occurred to him. "You have heard of marriages that were annulled on the grounds that they were not consummated?"

"Yes." She was again wary.

"What do you think that means?"

"That they were childless, of course. Children are the consummation of a marriage."

Again he sighed, more heavily; she took it as a sign of exasperation. "But it is," she insisted. "It is so! I asked Papa when there was that couple two or three years ago . . . the . . . what were their names? In St. Alban's. Oh, what *were* they called? Papa told me then. It meant they had no children."

Papa again! Walter fought back the return of his anger. "But you were only fifteen then. He spoke euphemistically. He meant that they made no efforts to beget any children. Otherwise"—he thought now that he would make the argument unanswerable—"'why do not all childless couples annul their marriages?"

Panic began again to seize her, as with an animal at the moment it realizes it is being manoeuvred toward a trap. She knew that she must be guided by Walter. It was his place to correct her. But surely that was only in those areas where she was ignorant still—not in such a matter as this, where her certainties practically came from God. No, it was unthinkable.

"No, Walter, dearest Walter, you must be . . ." She caught herself almost saying *wrong*. "That cannot quite be so. The Parrys in the village are still childless and Papa says it is because God has not seen fit to bless them."

Again that man! "That's very bad luck for the Parrys . . .," Walter managed before she interrupted again.

"So it can have nothing to do with . . . whether they . . . you know . . . fornicate or not. So . . . that simply proves it. It must be divine and not . . . bestial." She felt so rash at contradicting her husband that her voice gained an unaccustomed tremble. Also perhaps within her an unconscious tactician was aware that her argument had not been the most brilliant. At all events she was very close to tears as she concluded: "The last thing I expected on my wedding night was to lie in bed, with my dearest husband at my side, and talk of annulment . . . and . . . beastly things!"

"Sentiments I may fervently echo," he answered, unmoved by her descent toward tears. "What you are saying is that all pious ladies have their children by virgin birth. Yes? Pray tell me then—why is the Virgin Mary considered so unique if the wife of every Bishop Backwater and Parson Limbo has done the same?"

What could she answer! She could frame no answer. Her panic mounted still further. Perhaps the unthinkable, the unimaginable, was true after all. Perhaps the noises from her parents' bedchamber were one and the same with the shivering, bronchitic breath of bulls and boars at stand. Of course it was impossible. Yet when Walter said that the alternative was as good as claiming to be the equal of the Blessed Virgin—one had to match one kind of impossibility against another.

And while she fought thus for her soul, Walter, creeping once more into her embrace, began a soft litany of encouragement: "Come now, dearest . . . I am right . . . you shall see . . . be easy . . . rest easy . . . it is no great calamity . . . no terror . . . there! It is the greatest, greatest joy. Come . . . I shall be gentle with you . . . there . . . there. . . ."

Again he touched her breast and again she stiffened; but now he did not stop. Instead, bathing her in that gentle rain of encouragement, he caressed her with ever greater fervour.

And, indeed, she found the strangest transformation overtaking her. A powerful languor, never felt before, consumed her muscles. And in the lower part of her stomach, below her navel, a warm thrill, almost a pain, began.

Her mind still recoiled at these events; but there was nothing it could do. It was a feeble, paralytic little thing, prisoner of a body whose functions had acquired a will and mastery of their own. And when Walter moved to raise her nightdress, she felt her astonished hands move in concert to assist. She felt them caress him, his arms, his waist, the strange hard stick of flesh that pressed upon her abdomen and that was hot and that beat like a second heart.

She felt her lips seek and close on his as if they had been fruit. The disgusted little censor in her mind lay unmoved by the fire and ice that surged through every vein. And it was silently dumbfounded that, when Walter moved upon her, her thighs parted wide and her hands went down to guide him home.

Walter had been well instructed. An old, fat woman, abbess of a brothel back in Manchester, had recently told him how to break a maiden-head with little or no pain. And that he now did, following the old crone's directions to the letter. So Arabella, not even knowing that it should be painful, was spared all but the lightest twinge. And what ecstasies followed! Heat like a living thing pressed itself upon her chest and thighs and the small of her back. Sweat poured from her. She wished more of him could unite with her and she clasped him with a passion whose very existence she had never suspected. Her heart beat as if it had developed resounding walls of oak. That, and the disorder of her innards, and the weight of him upon her, made her fight for breath.

And then, when she thought no pleasure could be more supreme, the whole of her erupted into a very storm of ecstasy. Waves of it rippled through her, sending her muscles into spasm quite at random. For an age she lay drowned in this floodtide liberation of her senses. Even the little censor was, at last, inundated and obscured. Even Walter had vanished— united in substance and person with her in one great carnal riot.

Nothing now could make it stop. Surely not. They were over the mountain and on to the uplands beyond. It was peace. It was the natural place for them to live. It was a land. A world. A new universe of peace. It was the purpose of life. It was a celestial harmony. It was the ultimate secret. It was . . . it was . . . *it was wrong!*

The little censor was back. Unmoved. Unpersuaded. It was eighteen years and unknown pious generations old. Arabella of the senses was but a newborn babe—strong and lusty, to be sure, and with an astonishing will of its own, but one to be tamed and crushed like any other baby. Next time the contest would be more equal.

# Chapter 14

Health is a negative sort of thing; one notices its absence more than its presence. But when Arabella awoke the following morning, she felt the profoundest sense of wellbeing—like a spirit in her veins. Through the lightly billowing curtains she could see the garden smiling in the sun. Apples hung green and heavy on their boughs. And nothing stirred. What was that land out there?

All this she perceived in an instant. The events of the previous night still lay beyond recall. Even the realization that, of course! they were in Earlestown—and, of course, Walter was beside her—did not at once bring them back. The Walter she remembered still had all his armour, gleaming with the prolonged purity of their courtship. She stretched and sighed, ready to turn to him with the smile she had lavished on that phantom every waking morning for the last two years.

Walter had awakened several minutes earlier; but, for fear of disturbing her, had lain still, exploring with his eyes the tangle of her golden hair, the pink, cherubic curve of her ear, and the soft nape of her neck, whose down was haloed in silver where it turned toward the window. Not since schooldays had he woken in a bed warmed by another body; he was aware of her now like a mild furnace, inches from him. He longed to reach out his hands and cradle parts of her again. *The very minute she stirs,* he promised himself, and the thought of it excited him. The moderate pain of his erection reminded him of all they had done the night before, and a great gladness filled him. His wife had proved to be a natural lover, responsive without being dissolute, inventive without being wanton. No man in all the kingdom could be happier.

So when Arabella moved, he moved even faster. Before she even began to turn he was at her back, his arms around her, once more flesh upon flesh. But the whores who had taught him all he knew had omitted the most basic lesson of all—the slower arousal of a real woman; so he felt rejected when she did not instantly respond. She would not move her thighs and he had to draw back for relief. And when he cupped her breasts they remained two dull, loose bits of softness, almost unconnected with her.

This time the shock did not last long in Arabella. She stiffened only momentarily and then fell into a state of total relaxation. Her mind, the little moral censor, was fascinated at this lack of response within her. The hard thing pressing at the back of her thighs might as well have been the muzzle of an importunate dog for all it meant to her. And the hands that caressed her could as well have been her own for all their power to arouse her. These remote things happened to her; and she observed them.

She was not so foolish as to imagine that the lusts of the night before would never again overwhelm her, but now she had the directest kind of proof that they were not invincible. So Walter's caresses filled her, after all, with pleasure—a vast moral delight. She welcomed his advances precisely because they had no effect upon her. Unwittingly he was forging the armour in which she would later vanquish him—or whatever it was that possessed him. She began to revel in her frigidity.

Disappointed, he stopped and pulled away his hands. Dismayed, she caught them and put them back, sighing with a satisfaction he did not understand. Now she tried something more daring. She raised her uppermost thigh to let him draw as close to her as he obviously wanted. Again . . . nothing! Not a ripple. Not a twinge. The Lord was speaking to her, she decided as her heart soared with joy. God moves in mysterious ways indeed, praised be His name!

"No?" he asked, baffled by the friendliness that she coupled with such total lack of response.

"Well then, breakfast!" He pulled away, patted her lightly through the bedclothes, and went across to wash.

She lay a good while longer, smiling at the new, miraculous power God had given her, just when she stood (as her prayer last night had said) in direst need.

*       *       *

During breakfast Arabella saw how people looked at her, stealing glances when they thought she wasn't looking, glancing hastily at distant windows and uninteresting ceilings when they found she was. Now that she knew what they were all imagining, she burned for shame: Imagine herself, in their minds, doing that!

But the shame evaporated when she and Walter left the place; within herself she was a fortress of calm. What had happened in bed last night, she decided, had been a challenge. The Lord was about to test her. Had the pleasure been but slight, the test would have been small and the profit to her soul insignificant. But by making the pleasure greater than anything she had ever known, greater than she had ever dreamed it possible for delight to reach, by overwhelming her in such ecstasy, He had left her no doubt of the size of the challenge He intended her to face.

Thus she repaired the damaged pages in her moral guidebook to the world. But one solitary rift stubbornly refused to mend: Walter's question about the Virgin Mary. She must write to ask her father about that. He would certainly be able to reconcile the conflict between faith and practicality.

# Chapter 15

"Dear, dirty Preston!"

The man Walter had been guessing to be a doctor spoke at last. He had come from the Liverpool train to Earlestown, and then had taken the same connection north as Walter and Arabella. For most of the journey he had read what, to judge by the illustrations, was a medical work. He was a short, rubicund man, powerfully built but running to fat. Seeing his squat hands gripping the book, fingering the page corners, turning the leaves, firming them down, Walter could easily imagine the scalpels, knives, and other weird implements of modern surgery in their unhesitant grasp.

Though he stole frequent glances at the stranger, Walter did not once catch his eye. Yet he formed the strongest conviction that the man was somehow assessing Arabella and himself. She, too, was plainly uneasy, for she made only the most desultory conversation and spent much of the journey gazing tensely out of the window.

"Dear, dirty Preston!" He spoke as if to himself; his manner did not challenge Walter to reply.

He looked at Walter, pursed his lips, smiled thinly, shook his head as if the two of them already shared some knowledge or opinion, and began to turn from the window. When he halted and looked back at Walter, it appeared to be in a spontaneous afterthought.

"Fisher," he added. "If I may make so bold as to introduce meself. Dr. Arbuthnot Fisher. I think we are all about to become temporary neighbours at Blackpool?"

"Why, yes!" Walter smiled and introduced himself before presenting the doctor to Arabella.

"You are from Preston?" he asked, picking up the older man's remark.

"No. From Manchester. But I have watched the towns of Lancashire—and Yorkshire—growing these last forty years and more. And the singularity of this"—he sighed and gestured at the Preston townscape—"never fails to surprise me."

"Oh?" Walter looked out at the town, wondering what the doctor could mean. It seemed much as any other northern town—a sea of slate over which tall chimneys poured an endless rain of soot.

"Indeed. Other towns, as they gain in numbers, wealth, and factories, gain also in civilized appointments, public cleanliness, and other material amelioration. Preston alone is as—" He stopped and looked at them in sudden thought. "Have you never visited here before?"

They shook their heads.

"Why, *then*," he laughed, "then you shall see a town as dirty and narrow and crooked as any your grandfathers ever trod in. The shops are as Hogarth might have sketched them. There are no public buildings—not even so much as a market. No public baths either, mark you; neither hot nor cold."

"No news rooms?" Walter asked.

"Two," he conceded. "But even the better of them is very unworthy of its subscribers. No"—he sighed again and spoke as a teacher might of children beyond salvation—"it is the citizens, the better citizens, who are to blame for this lamentable state of things. They seem intent only on gathering wealth. They give little thought to their town and its people. When I think what Manchester, Bradford, Wakefield, Halifax, and even Huddersfield have become, I shudder for Preston. Truly I tremble for it. Half a century of steady public spirit and expenditure would still leave it defective."

Walter wondered whether the doctor had at some time failed at a local Preston election. "I fancy we may soon see a like desertion of Manchester and other cities," he replied. "The railway will attract those who can afford the fares to move out of the centres. Preston may be in advance of the times. Other places may soon revert to Georgian barbarism at their hearts."

Though the doctor sighed and shook his head he did not, Walter noticed, seem overpleased to have his own pessimism outdimmed. His response was to clap his hands and, rubbing them vigorously together, beam at Walter over the tops of his half-moon spectacles. Then, still smiling, he turned to Arabella. "There!" he said. "No one comes to Blackpool to fret over the problems of our cities."

Arabella did not venture an opinion. The train had stopped and they waited to be unlocked from their coach. Walter searched out their tickets and the excess-luggage ticket that the clerk at Earlestown, not being as complaisant as the one at Boxmoor, had exacted.

"There's an iniquity," said the doctor, pointing to the excess ticket. "The rate has nearly doubled in only four years. What was it? A penny a pound, stated on the ticket. And now they cross it out and write twopence. I know. I read the prospectuses."

"Railways must live if railroads are to build," Walter said.

The porter unlocked them and both the men climbed out to hand Arabella down. The platform was wet and muddy and she had to pick her way with care.

"There are four or five public coaches at the gate," the doctor told them. "But if ye'll take my advice, ye'll wait out the hour and take Bamper's. He's only four inside and none out. It's the most comfortable doing the run from here to Blackpool."

"What d'you think, my dear?"

Arabella looked dubious. She was on the point of electing for an immediate departure when the doctor, with a knowing smile, added, "Unless ye've any pressing reason to get there sooner."

"No!" she said firmly. "Let us take the more comfortable coach, by all means."

Walter laughed as he turned to the doctor. "You have so praised this town that I greatly look forward to this delay."

"Ah," said the doctor, "but it boasts one jewel that no serious-minded young person should overlook."

"Oh?"

"Go to the corner of Church Street. Gilberton the chemist." Already he was walking away. "Ask him to show you his fossils."

\*     \*     \*

Gilberton looked more like a farmer than a tradesman. In fact he was no chemist but a mere retailer of drugs whose business had been greatly sacrificed to his geological mania. His face told of long exposure to wind and sun, and his hands always bore the mark of some recent digging. That the Thorntons were perfect strangers to him was of not the slightest consequence; they were interested enough in his work to delay here an hour—and that was a passport to his immediate confidence.

He took them through his shop to the back room, where stood three large mahogany cabinets each with two dozen drawers of various depths. Every drawer was labelled with zoological words in a barely decipherable hand.

"They're mostly of the mountain limestone formations," he said, opening one of them.

It was full of small mollusc-shaped stones and fragments. Many were tagged—and with more care than the drawers, for the names could actually be read. *Schizodus scholothemi* said a little thing like a lifeboatman's hat. *Terebratula digona* asserted a miniature miller's sack with a bullethole mouth; "That was from Bradford clay," Gilberton said. *Pleurophorus* claimed another hesitantly before offering in parentheses and a smaller hand (*Pleurorynchus* (?)). "It's so hard to come by information here," Gilberton explained. "One does what one can."

Many were unlabelled. There were snails with beautiful lightning strokes across their shells; ammonites with bands as sharp as the day they died; balls like giant, folded-up woodlice; coils like toy pagodas; shells like walnuts, like strange pastries, like well-tamed hair caught in a wind, like oak galls, like the gizzards of chickens.

"Such variety!" Arabella said.

"And each from its own stratum. Each to its own time. Not one in thirty of these can be found living today. These are from primary strata; these"—he opened another drawer in the neighbouring cabinet—"from secondary. Each to its time."

"Some are more than two thousand years old I shouldn't wonder," she mused.

He chuckled. "Twenty thousand . . . two hundred thousand . . . two million—who knows?"

"Oh," she said. "But the earth itself is only six thousand years old."

"We have only the word of a bishop for that. Here"—he pointed at his specimens—"here is the word of God. Written in his own handiwork."

"They really are that old?" Arabella asked, touching them with a new reverence. "Two million years?"

"That is a guess. It is all a guess. See. This"—he picked out a simple, nutlike shell labelled *Lingula Davisii*—"this is from the Silurian rocks of South Wales. Sir Roderick Murchison has this year published his analysis of the complete system. Do you know there are places where more than twelve thousand feet of aqueous rocks overlie the Silurian? Sandstone, carboniferous rocks, clays, grits, oolite . . . all formed by the slow, patient washing down and compression of river silt. How long do *you* think it might take to wash down twelve thousand feet of sand, or mud, or silt . . . for the seas to rise and fall and rise . . . for tropics to come . . . and deserts . . . and ice? And all to go again. Many times. Your bishop has strange notions of the laws God wrote for His earth to obey."

Arabella, who had never heard episcopal authority questioned before, was torn by this remark. On the one hand it was insolent of a mere tradesman to sneer so at a bishop; yet, on the other, the vision he offered of Creation was vaster and more sublime than the hazy notions she had been taught—a six-day frenzy a year or two before Abraham. Two *million* years! The idea of so much time, and so much happening!

"Two million years!" she repeated aloud.

"And all that time"—he held up the little shell again—"this little creature, or remnant of a creature, lay beneath that slowly gathering over-burden, waiting, waiting . . ."

"For you," Walter said.

Gilberton smiled. "For a good friend. William Smith. You may know him."

"I know *of* him, of course." Walter was impressed. "His geological maps are invaluable to us. A friend of yours!"

"I hear from Northampton he is very ill. He was sixty this March, you know."

"Dear me."

"Why is the history of South Wales so violent?" Arabella asked. "Or do you mean New South Wales?"

The two men laughed. "That was merely an example, my dear," Walter told her. "The history of everywhere else is just as varied."

While she absorbed this intelligence, Walter told the shopkeeper of his present work at Summit Tunnel.

They thanked the old man profusely for his kindness, and bought a small box of peppermints and some opium pills, so that he should not be entirely out of pocket, before they returned to the station.

"Do you think any of that is true, dearest?" Arabella asked.

"Not one quarter, not one hundredth, part of the truth," he told her. "So much yet remains to be discovered. But *that*"—he gestured back at the shop on the corner—"makes me feel very humble! We have no idea, no *idea,* of the wealth of treasures stored up by the labour of people in such humble classes. Up and down the country."

"One realizes," she agreed, "what progress there must have been in all grades of society—when shopkeepers can befriend professors and gain learning enough to mock bishops!"

The thought of it thrilled her, it was so *dangerous.*

"What do you think of my fossils man?" Dr. Fisher asked when they were in Bamper's coach and bowling along through the somewhat indifferent landscape between Preston and the sea. The fourth seat was vacant.

"Splendid fellow," Walter said, feeling the inadequacy of this judgement.

"Did he show you his bear's tooth?"

"No. Only his mineral remains."

"Pity. He has a splendid bear's tooth. Well, now. Where shall you stay at Blackpool?"

"We thought we'd get the coachman to drive around and let us pick the place we liked the look of best."

"Ah," the doctor said; his tone showed he thought little of the idea.

"Would that not be wise?" Arabella asked.

"There's two places ye'd pick that way—and only one of 'em ye ought to. Only one place in Blackpool for superior and cultivated persons. Dixon's. Out at the north end."

"Please don't hesitate to advise us," Walter pressed him. "The book I consulted is clearly somewhat out of date."

The doctor looked from one to the other, over his half spectacles. "Ye might imagine Blackpool is to Preston what Southport is to Manchester; but it ain't so. No. By no means. The superior classes of Preston go south to Brighton or St. Leonard's for their salt-water cures. I should think the highest in rank at Blackpool would be an ironfounder from Halifax or a Liverpool wine merchant."

"We hold no exaggerated opinion of ourselves, doctor," Arabella said, gathering her cape tightly about her.

"Then ye'll like Blackpool, for they're capital, friendly folk. They've good appetites for food—and laughter."

"But this hotel . . . Dixon's?" Walter prompted.

"Aye, there's two. Dixon's and Nixon's. Dixon's is five shillings a day, including at least five meals. And the accommodation is equal to any at Brighton."

"Is the north the better end?"

"The lodging houses and a great chaos of new building are all to the south. They say South Blackpool will soon eclipse the north. I think you will find Dixon's quieter and more select."

"You speak as if you shall not be staying there." Arabella put a polite degree of question into her voice.

"No. I shall stay nearby, at Nixon's. It is sixpence cheaper, and the whole company eats at a common board—which is more congenial to my northern way of thinking."

"Yes," said Arabella. "I noticed that in Preston. People here are much friendlier than we are in the south."

Her comment pleased the doctor. Walter later discovered that the real attraction of Nixon's was its total lack of male servants, so that the doctor could volunteer for the office of meat carver. And this, in turn, let him quickly rejoice in friendships with the ladies that would otherwise have taken days to foster.

The only remarkable feature of the whole tedious seventeen miles, as far as Walter was concerned, was the occasional sight of the new line to the Wyre, due to open next year. They had several glimpses of it, just outside Preston, again just outside Kirkham, and again between Weeton and Staining.

"If they put out a branch to Blackpool, that'll be the end of it," the doctor said.

Over the final mile, beyond Layton, the air grew steadily saltier and more invigorating; and when the coach finally gained the promenade, it was all Walter and Arabella could do to stop themselves leaping out and jumping down on to the long, almost deserted beach and running and running until they dropped.

\*     \*     \*

Dixon's was exactly to their taste. They were able to take a room with a private parlour at only a shilling extra, which Arabella thought would be useful, what with the weather so threatening. And there, after a good solid luncheon, they retired.

While Arabella went through the drawers and wardrobes, checking the maids' unpacking, Walter sat upon the bed and watched her. From time to time she looked at him and her heart sank to see that special excitement invading his face.

"Come here," he said and held out his arms.

"Oh!" She coloured and, seeking desperately for some distraction, ran away from him toward the window. "I do believe it may soon clear. Look! Is that not lighter over there?"

He chuckled as he strode across to her. "What's this? Coy? Come—we can bolt the door so that no one will disturb us."

She tried to swallow and could not. She tried to speak but could only croak and then had to turn it into a pretended cough. His arms went about her from behind. His breath was hot upon her neck. His hands cupped her breasts. And though she resisted, she felt again that warmth growing within her. Before she melted entirely, she made the still possible effort, tore herself away, ran half across the room, and turned to face him.

Not quite mistress of herself she repeated the one word "no" many times and with a firmness she had not believed she could muster. His face fell and darkened; the excitement vanished.

"I want there to be no more of that," she said. "I want to be chaste until we have guidance."

How he stared at her! And how unreadable was his face! What did that dark look mean—anger . . . shame . . . remorse?

"And last night?" he asked at length. "Do you not remember . . . ?"

"Oh, I remember," she blurted out. "And I burn for the shame still. We were beasts. We were worse than beasts. I mean there to be no more of it. Please? Dearest?"

There was no sound but his breathing.

When he finally broke silence, he was coldness itself. "There shall be no more of it," he promised. And, while she watched in misery too dumb to protest, he took his cloak and gloves and cane, and he left.

She saw him walk out into the rain and she watched him out of sight before she broke down and burst into tears. Until he vanished, she had been able to sustain the hope that he might turn and come back to her.

But she did not weep for long. Her whole upbringing was against such self-indulgence. Within ten minutes she was sitting at the bureau in the sitting room, preparing to record in her journal the events of her wedding and all that had happened since. And within twenty minutes only the most perceptive observer could have discerned the slightest redness in her eye.

# *Chapter 16*

Walter leaned into the rain, moving his head this way and that to let it sting his face. He bared his teeth at it, or opened his mouth to let the drops fall upon his tongue. Its astringent force, the roar of the wind, the dashing of the waves at the foot of the low clay bank known locally as "the cliffs," all combined to obliterate his thoughts.

But it did not last. His mood persisted, as dark and angry as the sky. And before long the thoughts came crowding back. Why was Arabella so contrary? She might have been two people: a dried-up old lemon of a spinster to greet the world and—sometimes—a *passionata* when her husband came to call. Perhaps it took longer for her desire to rekindle.

It was then that the idea occurred to him to let *her* make the next move. Let her entice him when she was ready! It might cost him something in self-control but he'd know right from the start of their marriage what her natural firing-up time was. There had to be a refractory period in these things; that was only reasonable. What a splendid idea. Also he'd be able to tell in a year or two if she were gaining on herself, as she matured. If she fired up quicker, it would be a measure of the goodness growing between them. A very difficult quantity to judge otherwise. Yes, it was an excellent idea.

Thus, warm with the enthusiasm of a new resolve, he put his worries from his mind and prepared to enjoy whatever Blackpool might have to offer—which, at the moment, was rain, a windy, wet, and deserted seaside path, and the distant prospect of even darker skies. The far-off sea was a flood of ink, relieved by dashing white horses, breaking and dying as far as the eye could discern. The showers were grey smudges, as if, in a picture, someone had smeared the paint while it was still wet. He counted six ships, all of them coastal vessels of various sizes.

The five that were close enough to make out in any detail had all shortened sail, not, he imagined, because the present wind was anything so very great, but in fear of squalls to come. One, a broad little lugger lying low in the water, came so close inshore that he could see the rain glistening on her dirty sails and falling in silver threads upon the decks below. The rain from the sternsail dropped in a steady gush from the sheets, which were lashed outboard of the after gunwhale. Thus the helmsman stood in the driest spot on deck. He and Walter waved at each other—two kindred souls amid the foulness of the elements.

He stood and watched the little vessel beating south, with the wind to starboard, until it was too small to be interesting. Just before he began walking again, he saw it almost run down by a two-masted brig, running north.

The newly paved promenade started just before he came to Nixon's. It looked a very inviting place, the doctor was right about that. Perhaps he would call in and see the old fellow—after all, both were on holiday and the doctor didn't seem a great one for formality. Or would it be better after tea? Tea! A warm cup of tea would be very welcome. He looked at his watch. If Dixon's and Nixon's had the same mealtimes, that would be in just over half an hour. Time to get to South Blackpool and back. Yes— teatime would be capital for calling.

But there was no need to call. For, as he passed by, an upstairs window was flung wide and the doctor, careless of ceremony, called "Thornton!" and beckoned him closer.

"Going for a walk?" he asked when Walter reached the lawn below the window.

"Yes."

"Alone?"

"Yes."

"May I join ye?"

"Be honoured."

"Two shakes of a donkey's tail," he promised and shut the window. Walter strolled out to the promenade again and, leaning his fingertips on the low stone breastwork, watched the sea boil and churn only feet below. It did not look a rich sort of water and he wondered if much fish were caught in it. No fishing vessels were anywhere in sight.

The brig was already much closer, running fast about three furlongs offshore. She carried only a fore and a foretop sail on her foremast and only a spanker on her mizzen; no jib or flying jib. Her martingale hung loose and several broken forestays trailed from her bowsprit into the water ahead of her.

"Some strange gypsies roam the sea these days," the doctor said behind him. "See the two figures by the bow?"

"Yes."

"One's a woman. Fat as a bladder of lard. Smoking a pipe."

Disbelief must have shown in Walter's glance as he looked from the doctor to the ship and back.

"Watching with me spyglass upstairs. Nearly ran down a lugger off the south shore."

"I saw that. Is there no fishing here?"

The doctor began to walk southward along the promenade. Walter fell in beside him, waiting for the reply. After twenty or so paces he had said nothing and Walter began to wonder if he'd heard at all.

"No trouble is there?" the doctor asked at last, staring ahead.

Walter looked at him, at the ship, at the churning waves, and back at him. "Trouble?"

"Not at all. Forgive me." He stepped out more briskly. "Surprised there's only two of us out. Country's going soft. It's not so very bad, would you say?"

"I surveyed through the Pennines, from Todmorden to Normanton, in the winter of '37. To me this is a balmy summer's day," he said. "I'm a railway engineer," he added by way of explanation.

"Then you'll know what cold is. It's mildness itself here." He raked his stick over the view of several dozen lodging houses straggling along the seafront, as if they enjoyed a special climatic dispensation. "Forgive me returning to the subject. You are on your honeymoon, I believe?"

"Yes," Walter admitted, but the other went on staring at him, so long and so anxiously that he grew uncomfortable. He only just stopped himself from volunteering further information.

"No. Not always the smoothest of times," the doctor said.

And Walter heard himself muttering: "Lot of stupid ideas to overcome . . ." before he regained control.

The doctor stopped, adding weight to his words: "Knock it out. Ride roughshod over it. Tolerate none of it. There can only be one helmsman."

Walter hoped that the smile he suppressed did not show even fleetingly. He walked again, letting the doctor fall in with him this time.

The promenade here turned a little inland, enclosing a short stretch of beach where the sand remained uncovered even at high tide. A bedraggled collection of wooden shelters and machines huddled beneath the wall.

"It's a dilemma," Walter said.

The doctor waited patiently, not prompting him.

"We each are responsible for our own salvation. No . . . I don't mean to put it that way. But if a wife meekly obeys her husband, not through her own inner conviction or moral will but through blind duty or even through fear, her own moral progress is . . ." He sighed. "D'you see?" He turned to the doctor.

At first he was affronted because he thought the doctor was laughing, but his annoyance turned to alarm when he realized that the doctor was, in fact, trembling with suppressed fury.

"Moral . . . balls!" he said at last, in what was probably the politest of all the expletives he had considered. "Women don't know *what* they are. Takes a man to show a woman she is one. Remove us and they'd spend a lifetime guzzling, gulping, gossiping, and snoozing. And never knowing the loss. Could you or I do that? Of course not. You young people—think we're all such reprobates. Hark now. There's wisdom here . . ." He stopped, turned, and held Walter's arm. "Go too far your way and before you're forty it's *you* will be singing all the soprano parts."

"I can assure you, sir . . . ," Walter began and then, having no notion of what he could assure the doctor, stopped.

His discomfiture seemed to galvanize the other, like one emerging from a trance. "My dear fellow! How unpardonable! What must you think of me! Most unwarranted! Dear, dear . . ." This effusion was more embarrassing than the outburst it was meant to repair and Walter was glad, at last, to see another soul. "Look," he pointed. "There's a lady to put *us* to shame."

She was standing in the surf, letting it knock her down and tumble her over until, just before the next breaker, she stood again and repeated the process.

"Damn!" the doctor said, pulling out his watch. "The ladies' hour. Didn't hear the bell, did you?"

"Ladies' hour?"

"One hour a day the beach is for the ladies. They ring a bell. If they rang it for her, we shouldn't be here."

"I heard no bell. What's the penalty?"

"Bottle of wine all round your hotel."

"Oh!" Walter feigned a vast relief. "Almost worth it, what?"

The doctor halted and looked hard at the bather. "I do believe it's Mrs. McKechnie!"

But Walter barely heard him for there, down by the hut from which the bather had come, was the veiled lady's pretty maidservant—the one he had helped into the decrepit coach at Earlestown. She looked up at the sound of their voices, recognized Walter, smiled, and then waved shyly. He smiled, delighted that she remembered him, and waved back.

"Oh!" The doctor was surprised. Then, recovering, he said "Oh!" again, this time in tones rich with insinuation.

Walter laughed. "They were at the Earlestown Inn last night—hardly the occasion to strike up *that* sort of acquaintance!"

They resumed their stroll. The rain had relented now to the merest reminder of itself.

"What did you call her?" Walter asked.

"McKechnie. She's the widow of a Scotchman. A Lanarkshire mill-owner he was. Left her well off, too. Two thousand a year, I'd be bound. She comes here every year. The maid's new, though."

"Fresh." Walter suggested a correction.

They both laughed, glad of that much common ground.

"She's coming out," Walter said. "It's probably not Spartan enough now it's stopped raining."

"We'll give her a minute or two and then go back. She stays down near Vauxhall. We'll escort them home."

The widow had put a voluminous cloak over her bathing clothes and was striding vigorously toward them; her maid trotted behind, laden with her clothing. When the lady recognized the doctor, she smiled—but not, Walter noted, with any great surprise; she either knew, or expected, him to be in Blackpool. He greeted her in the French manner, with a kiss on both cheeks, and presented Walter to her. She gave no sign of recognition.

But when the doctor suggested escorting her down to her lodgings, she said, "No, no—you'd be too slow," and strode off. "I'll come and play whist with you tonight, after supper," she shouted over her shoulder. "Bring your Mister . . ." She waved her hand airily instead of supplying Walter's name. The maid shrugged and made apologetic movements of her eyes as she bore up the rear.

By the time Walter returned to Dixon's, Arabella had finished her account of the wedding and, though solaced by it, was still miserable at Walter's hot departure and long absence. So when he came through the door she was overjoyed to see his spirits restored and his eyes smiling with their customary good nature.

They enjoyed a high tea of shrimps and sea trout taken from the nearby river Ribble. Walter recounted his meeting with the doctor and the Scotch widow and passed on their invitation. She thought it would be a very pleasant, *homely* way to end the day.

But her delight changed to horror when, on arriving at Nixon's and being introduced to Mrs. McKechnie, it became clear that they were expected to play for money—to *gamble!* It was only because Walter took the discovery so calmly and sat without an instant's hesitation that she was able to seat herself and play at all. The doctor must be a very skilled player, she thought, to judge by the way he could shuffle the pack.

After a while the fact of gambling did not seem quite so bad. The company was certainly enjoyable and both the doctor and the widow kept up a very civilized conversation. And they were only playing for pennies. And nobody seemed to win very much—or if they did, they soon lost some of it again. And there were several other parties in the room also playing for small stakes. And one had to admit that it did add a *little* excitement. And Walter seemed to see nothing wrong in it.

Even so, all these arguments only made it *seem* less wrong. There might be degrees of evil in gambling—just as there were degrees in anything else—but all of it, little wrong and big wrong, was still wrong; it offered no improvement for their souls.

The continual tension, as her mind wavered from one point of view to the other, soon brought about a headache; and its intensity grew as the evening wore on. She knew she was worse and worse company, and an ever poorer partner for poor Walter. Finally, toward nine o'clock, she could force herself no longer and had to make a truthful excuse of her headache and ask him to take her home.

"What brought this on?" he asked when they were out upon the road.

"My distaste for gambling, I imagine. I think you were marvellous to hide *your* dislike so well. I'm sure they did not notice."

He laughed. "Not a headache at all, eh!"

"But I did. I do."

"Oh." He gripped her arm to comfort her. "Why do you call it gambling? It's only for pennies. There's no harm in that."

He took her silence for acceptance. They walked almost all the remaining distance with only the roar of the sea and the crunch of the gravel underfoot to accompany them.

"Arabella," he began when they were almost arrived. "Are you distressed about what we . . . what happened last night?"

For the merest fraction of a second she imagined he was working out an apology, but the tone of his question, which lingered in her ear, told her that was not his aim. "Why?" she asked guardedly. She was glad, at least, he had chosen to speak in the dark.

"Would you . . . prefer it if we slept apart until you have discovered the . . . falsity of your present notions?"

For a moment she was too thrilled to speak; it was a kindness beyond the noblest dreams she had had of Walter.

"Since—for some reason—you choose to think I'm not telling you the truth," he added, throwing her into a confusion.

"Oh, it's not . . . it's just . . . well—everything I've ever been taught . . ." she faltered, unable to complete any sentence she began.

"Who *will* you believe? The local vicar here in Blackpool?"

"Oh, no! How could we possibly ask him!"

"Very easily, I should think. As we shall, in all probability, never meet him again in our lives. Who better?"

"I couldn't. *Couldn't.* Imagine asking him."

Walter, picturing precisely that scene, bit off a giggle. "Who, then? Doctor whatsit—Fisher?"

*"No!"* Her vehemence almost made her shriek the word.

"Where can one turn, then?"

"I shall have to ask my father. I don't know how. But I shall have to write to him. Would you like to see the letter?"

"I think it would make it easier to write if you knew I should not see it."

Again she was filled with gratitude; how considerate he was of her!

"It caps me, as they say in Yorkshire," he went on, ". . . it caps me why you take this attitude when you so patently enjoyed . . . last night."

It was quite a while, so that they were almost at the door, before she answered: "Enjoyment has nothing to do with it."

She was astonished to see him turn to leave her.

But he was not angry this time. "I shall come back soon," he said. "Just take a walk while you settle. Get them to throw a couple of blankets on the sofa in our sitting room. I'll sleep there tonight. You go on to sleep. Take one of your opium pills."

She was too overcome by the depth of his tenderness and consideration for her to reply. Smiling fondly, blinking, swallowing back the lump in her throat, she watched him move beyond the reach of the subdued light that struggled feebly from the curtained windows. What a paragon of a man he was.

And Walter, too, was smiling, pleased at the thoughts he had implanted and the memories he'd evoked. It was one thing to lie chaste in bed *before* one's sensual nature had awakened; but, as few knew better than himself, to do so afterwards, especially after such an awakening as they'd had last night . . . that was quite another thing. Quite another *impossible* thing! He smiled and sang lightly to himself—all the way back to Nixon's.

It was the doctor who suggested that they play for higher stakes, an insistence that he must later—several hours later—have regretted, for he ended the night almost three pounds down. He cheerfully refused Walter's offer of a quick game to recover part of the loss. And widow McKechnie politely declined his offer of an escort home. So that was that. A very successful evening.

The night had transformed itself while he had been indoors. A watery, waning moon stood almost overhead, clear of the clouds whose rearguard was now dropping away over the Pennines, far to the east. For the first time since he had left the workings he felt a tug within himself to return—part curiosity, part the itch of any professional to be at work. In a curious way he felt jealous of Stevenson, having Summit Tunnel all to himself for the next week. The ragged edge of cloud must be somewhere above there at this moment. He pictured himself standing in the cutting and seeing the moon break free and ride out into the clear sky. His nose strained to catch that special smell of a tunnel—a compound of broken stone and water and the imported smells of gunpowder, candlesmoke, and excretion; but its precise quality eluded him. He turned his face toward the sea and walked across the promenade to the wall. A pleasant, cooling breeze tugged at his hair, and he took off his hat to give it more scope.

The tide was out, laying bare the miles of smooth firm sand for which the village was so popular. Away in the distance he could see the Penny Stone; they said it was all that remained of an inn and that travellers' horses had once been tied to a ring let into it.

Well—it was still a capital place for riding. In fact, there was someone out there now. Going fast, too. But, as the dark shape of the horse drew near, he saw that it was riderless. His first thought was that it had thrown its rider, but then he saw it was not even saddled. In any case, now that the creature was almost below him, it was clearly just a young colt, escaped from its field and out for a run. What a lark it would be if he could get on its back and go for a gallop!

He looked for the steps, but they were far away to his left—too far. He let himself over the wall and slid ungracefully down to the beach. The colt threw up its head, turned, showed a pair of flying heels, and bolted. But it ran only a hundred yards or so, almost to the steps, and turned again to watch him. That was when he saw the two dogs, far out on the beach, running toward the colt. Swiftly but warily he ran along the foot of the wall, hoping to reach the colt before the dogs could alarm it.

The jolting he gave himself as he ran prevented him from seeing earlier than he did that these two dark running shapes were not dogs but only yearling calves. They all arrived at the same spot at almost the same time. And there they stood in a breathless, impromptu group. The three beasts looked so like truant boys that Walter almost laughed aloud; they stared at him just as if they waited to see if he were angry or no. To think of riding the colt was suddenly absurd. Walter stooped and lifted a handful of damp sand. He lobbed it high above and beyond them and the soft smack it made as it fell galvanized them once more into flight. They ran straight as an arrow to the very brink of the sea—where, no doubt, they scanned *its* face for the same signs of anger or menace.

He turned and began to make his way up to the promenade. At the third step Dixon's came into view over the top; Nixon's was still hidden behind the wall. He paused, trying to work out which light might come from their room. None, he decided. So Arabella was asleep. He imagined her lying there, warm and drowsy . . . so lovely . . . and so very desirable. He yearned to be beside her now; to waken again those fires that had burned so fierce last night. He almost formed the intention before his wiser self prevailed. Let her work to it gently. Let the thoughts he had implanted germinate and grow. Let *her* come to *him* with this same degree of yearning, and he would never need look back.

He had just taken the next upward step, bound by this cooler philosophy, when he heard an urgent conference, part whispered, part voiced, somewhere nearby. Slowly he moved to the shadow of the wall and crept up, step by step, until his eyes could just peep over the parapet and take in the promenade beyond.

It was Mrs. McKechnie and her young maid. They whispered heatedly yet did not quite seem to be arguing. Shortly, as if making a concession, the widow took her fob watch from her pocketbook and gave it to the girl, tapping it several times to emphasize whatever she was saying. The girl shrugged and turned toward the sea, but not quite full face to Walter. The other looked at her undecidedly for a moment and then turned and walked back in the direction of Nixon's.

Walter immediately saw the danger he was in. If the girl now came to the wall, he could hide in the moonshadow where he was. But if, for some reason, she took it into her head to stroll down onto the sands. . . . As swift as the thought, he crept surefooted backward down the steps to the beach; without pause he put twenty yards between himself and the foot of the steps; and then he strolled out into the light and stood with his hat off, facing the sea, as if he had been there ten minutes or more. Only moments later he thanked the sense that had warned him away from the steps; the girl was, indeed, coming down.

At the foot of the steps she walked straight toward the sea, ignoring him. Surely she saw him.

"Good evening!" he called.

She halted and turned in his direction. She had to wipe her eyes before she saw him. That was why she had failed to notice him.

"Mr. Thornton?" she asked in a voice almost sure.

"Yes. Miss . . . er, I ought to know your name—you're Mrs. Mc-Kechnie's companion."

She shrugged. "You'd better just call me Sanders. I'm her maid, not a companion."

Was she Welsh? There was a slight trace of something there. A very appealing voice, in fact. The way she had suppressed her tears was astonishing.

"Miss Sanders, then."

He was sure she blushed. She stood irresolute, the way girls do when they blush.

"There's a dashed odd thing." He pointed out to sea. The colt and yearlings had gone.

"What?" she asked. "I can't see clearly. Not that far."

"A young colt and two yearling calves straying. Galloping round here like puppies."

She giggled. It was a *very* appealing voice.

"Look," he said. "Here are their tracks."

Following them brought him closer to her—not alarmingly close but close enough to avoid having to raise their voices that slight degree.

"Do please put up your hat, sir. I'm not used to such courtesies," she said.

"Well." He complied. "If you'll permit me no courtesies, at least you'll allow me to do plain gentleman's duty. Let me escort you back to your lodging."

"But you are staying in the other direction."

"That's no answer."

"I thank you very kindly, sir, but I'm not going home just now."

Walter looked at the clear sky, and breathed deep draughts of the fresh salt breeze. "No," he said at last, as if in total agreement with her. "It's too fine a night."

"Fine for some," she said glumly.

He looked at her. For a moment they stared at one another. He sensed that she had something to tell; as she looked at him she was trying to frame the right words. Hers was a mobile, feline sort of face, with a little chin, precise, firm lips, wine-dark in the moonlight, a straight nose, and large, watchful eyes. If he had not been here with Arabella, oh, what efforts he would make to get her!

"Is Mrs. McKechnie still at Nixon's?" he asked.

"You might say so. She came out with me, but she's gone back."

"Ah. No doubt she will emerge in a moment and you can escort each other back."

"She will emerge"—the girl pulled out the watch Mrs. McKechnie had passed to her—"in seventy minutes. Give or take thirty."

"I say!" Walter said as understanding began to dawn. "The doctor, eh!"

The girl said nothing. And when she did speak, it was as if to change the subject: "Did he let you win at cards tonight?"

"I won. I don't know about *let*."

She snorted. "I do. About three pounds? And he took it very calm?"

"You must have heard. Mrs. McKechnie must have told you."

"I've heard, all right. Many and many a time. If you're wise, you'll go back to pennies and halfpennies. If you're wiser still, you'll pocket your winnings, and call it a day."

"He's not like that," Walter assured her. "He's too kindly. Too good a companion."

"I make no doubt of it." She spoke with complete conviction. "A kindly man. And a good man. But it's his vice. Something . . . compels him to it."

Walter was too astonished to make an immediate reply. And it was true that the doctor had made some very surprising blunders in his play. Then, feeling that some comment was called for, he observed, "All of us have *some* compulsion or other, I suppose."

"Yes."

"But to get back to the point," he went on, "I thought his room was on the first floor up. I saw him up there this afternoon."

"That's the upstairs parlour. He spies on the ladies bathing from there with his glass. His room's around the side. With its own stair to the garden. Oh, he's well in with Nixon!"

"But what a hard go for you!" Walter exclaimed. "Having to cool your heels for an hour. What are you supposed to do? Keep out of sight?"

"I shouldn't tell you any of this."

"You mean two wrongs don't make a right? Well—maybe not, but the second one can often take a lot of the sting out of the first."

"I'm supposed to go and hide myself in her bathing hut until she comes and drops pebbles on the roof. She's put a chaise longue inside where I can sleep if I want."

"How very . . . considerate of her," Walter said. The pause he made was involuntary; it was to suppress the tremble that overtook him as the dizzying prospect of the girl, the hour, the location, *and* the cause all dropped into place. But his hesitation had the effect of adding an insinuation he had not been bold enough to intend.

It evidently startled her. "Oh!" she said. Not "There'll be none of *that,* sir!'' Not ''I'm a good girl, sir.'' Not an affronted drawing in of skirts and an offended gliding away. Not, as far as he could tell, a blush. Just a speculative, almost empty ''oh''—as if the idea had not until then occurred to her. How could one ever tell what women were thinking?

Anyway, what did it matter what she thought? As she herself said, she was only a servant girl. At the very worst she could say ''no'' and that would be an end to it. There'd be no wider reverberations.

''What's sauce for the goose is sauce for the gander,'' he said.

She walked toward him, speaking as she came. ''You're an odd one for a honeymooning man!'' She held something in her hand. ''Here's the key—see if you remember which hut it is.''

He took the key but held on to her hand. ''I'd know it from above,'' he said. ''It's the one whose roof is almost worn through with dropping pebbles.''

She elbowed him gently in the ribs and giggled. But when he unlocked the door and held it for her, she paused.

''You're not going all the way with me,'' she said. ''I want that understood. I'm not going to let you inside me.''

He nodded impatiently toward the interior. ''How dull for you,'' he answered as she passed.

Inside it was so dark that he could make out no part of her. ''Come on. Shut the door,'' she told him. He heard her cloak and bonnet drop to the floor; she was over in the corner. Buttons were popping energetically and the small room seemed filled with the rustle and swish of her clothing.

''I'm not going to be left with a sprained ankle,'' she said. ''Especially by the sort of fella as'd sooner double the height of the hedge than help a lame bitch over the stile.''

''How do you know I'm that sort of man?'' he asked, wondering why her insolence and hardness were so exciting to him. ''You're a very unromantic young girl.''

''What has this to do with *romance?*'' He saw her teeth flash dimly as she smiled; he was just beginning to make out shapes in the dark.

''Do shut the door,'' she ordered coming across to do it herself. ''Are you still clothed? And here's me moulted!''

He felt the heat from her body, still warm from her clothes. In the second before she shut out all the light he saw there was little more for him to do.

''What's still on me remains on me,'' she said, guessing the direction of his thought. ''It'll take long enough to struggle back into what's already shed.'' Her nimble little fingers were busy with his buttons.

''Delicious'' was the word he applied to that night whenever he recalled it in later years. In a life of unflagging obsession with the delights of women, that encounter always retained a quality of its own. The difference began with his knowing, from the very start, that it was going to be a dry old night up in Hornington Crescent. It was the first such occasion in his life, so he had no idea what was in store. If not *that,* then what? he wondered. Every previous experience amounted to an assuaging of a lust— a gluttonous satisfaction of a hunger that merely swelled itself in consequence. But compared to those ravenous feasts this was like an evening in the hands of a great chef—one with a matchless skill at preparing an endless bounty of hors d'oeuvres.

Quite obviously Miss Sanders had been there many times before. It was she who led Walter from delicacy to delicacy, giving him the taste of delights he had known of in the abstract but had never experienced in the flesh. Yet whatever peaks of ecstasy they assailed together, the conscious mind was always partner to the act. This engagement was the least muscular, least hurried, most languid he had ever enjoyed with any girl. Nothing they did was a mere subordinate part of some headlong rush to a remote and all-important summit of delight. Each moment was itself, each act its own reward. And when his climax came it was just another among many delectations. Not an end, not a beginning. Remotely surprised, he observed his body continuing afterward as before.

In the end it was she who stopped them. Some internal night watchman awakened her broader self-interest. She lowered her thigh onto his ear and nudged him, already half asleep, away. Then she sat up and breathed in and out, profoundly replete.

"Sauce for the gander!" she said with a soft laugh. "I should think Mrs. McKechnie's had the dryer evening—from one look at her old doctor."

He found her mouth and kissed her, full and soft and long. "Don't talk, please," he begged in a whisper. As always at such moments, he felt only the deepest gratitude. This time it was keener than ever because of all the unsuspected joys she had led him to. Something of his mood communicated to her for she pulled him back into one last gentle kiss and then dressed in silence as he had asked.

He was dressed before her and pushed open the door, letting in the fresh salt air and the splash and knock of the surf—now noticeably nearer. After the dark it was alarmingly bright out there; the waves, especially, gleamed with a supernatural light.

"Don't go up these steps, please," she said. "If you walk along the beach to the end of the wall there's a little path goes up to the road."

He nodded. "I don't suppose we'll get another chance," he said.

"I hadn't even thought of the possibility." She laughed. "If we do, are you laying odds we *wouldn't* take it?"

He looked from her to the sky and then at the long, northward stretch of beach. A great sadness, broad rather than deep, a sense of something lost, something . . . perhaps unattainable, filled him. "I don't want to go," he said.

She snorted, not unkindly. "No purpose served talking like that," she told him. "Go you must, kind sir." And she nudged him out and shut the door.

Dispirited, he walked along the foot of the wall. The moon, now in the western sky, left no shadow for him to hug. When he reached the path he was startled by the sudden appearance of a short, powerful man, holding a lantern.

"A colt and three calves?" the man asked, out of breath. "Seen them?"

"Two calves."

"Buggery! They've split. Colt's a mealy bay with a pink snip."

"I tried to corner them but they were too frisky. Halfway to Lytham, I'd think, by now."

"Buggery," the man said again. "I best go mounted after them."

He strode back inland. Walter could still see the lantern swinging as he let himself quietly in by Dixon's never-locked front door.

# *Chapter 17*

By next day the bad weather had returned. Low clouds scudded across the sky, seeming to boil downward, toward the land. And the turbulent sea rose and fell in tongues of deep green fire. It was "blowing marlinspikes," an elderly guest, a retired sea captain, told them at breakfast after they returned from communion.

A vessel must have foundered somewhere offshore the day before or in the night, for a vast mass of timbers and other flotsam had been stranded by the ebbing tide. Already it had attracted a crowd of sightseers and wreckers, as well as two men from the excise department. Three adventurous souls wrestled with a barrel out in the heaving surf.

When Walter and Arabella returned from matins the wind had eased, though it occasionally blew in strong, squally gusts. There was still no rain, but the sea, now nearly at full ebb again, thundered mightily, throwing up a spray that could sting as hard as any driven rain.

"Let us go down near the waves," Arabella begged. "I have not been on the sands at all yet."

A few dozen others had the same idea and the beach was quite crowded. Most were out walking, but several were mounted and one or two had come out in carriages to drive up and down the smooth hard sand.

"Did you see all the building-up they are doing down beyond the church?" Walter asked. "If this place gets any more popular, its wildness will be all spoiled."

"It was wild last night," she said. "I wondered you stayed out in it at all."

"Not *wild,*" he said, smiling as his eyes lingered on one distant bathing hut. "The moon was out."

Her brow creased. "But that was much later," she said. "About eleven o'clock."

"Well, I went back to the doctor, feeling we had made an inadequate parting. And they prevailed upon me for another hand or two. That's why I was late." He found it distasteful to lie to her, precisely because she was so easily deceived. It was like cheating a trustful child.

"Walter!" She was deeply disapproving.

They had arrived at the Penny Stone—a "venerable antique" his guide-book called it. To them it looked like any barnacle-bitten, weed-strewn rock. They could find no sign of the iron hooks or rings that horses might have tied to.

"Between thee and me and this stone," Walter said, "I think our doctor is by way of being an amateur at cardsharping."

"Indeed!"

"I believe he allowed me to win last night, when I had returned. It is their trick, you know. To let you win a little and then take ten times back on the next occasion."

"Oh, Walter! Thank heavens you perceived it!"

"Well, that's not quite so," he said, emboldened by her gullibility. "It was little Miss Sanders, Mrs. McKechnie's maid. I left the hotel with them, intending to escort them home, when Mrs. McKechnie want back for something. Miss Sanders took the chance to stay briefly behind and warn me against the doctor."

"Oh, but how generous of her."

"Yes. I am so inexperienced in these things, I was very grateful." He could have gone on in this vein for a long time but he forced himself to stop. It was so unfair.

A seagull blew past them, its rigid wings tilted at a crazy angle. Farther up the beach some people were scattering crusts; a small flock of gulls had already crowded them, pecking and retreating. Their plaintive mewing carried far across the sand.

"There aren't many gulls here," Arabella said. "It isn't like St. Leonard's."

"Not much fish," he told her.

They walked on in silence for a moment. When he looked back he saw the sharp dint of his footsteps beside the broad swath from her skirts.

She stopped and looked out to sea. "Such power!" she said. "I once thought the most powerful thing on earth was a horse. Until I saw the sea. Those waves! They could lift you as easily as a cork. And crush you like a puffball. I wonder how it would feel to drown?" She raised her eyebrows to him as if he must already know. He shrugged but said nothing, studying her face intently. "Imagine—wading without flinching into . . . all that majesty! To *submit* to it! Oh, Walter—think of that! To feel your utter helplessness! To know you are as close to death as any living mortal may come!" She looked at him again and spoke so low her voice seemed to merge with the wind and the sea. "I have often thought it would be our nearest earthly intimation of paradise."

She held out an arm for him to take. "Hold my hand," she begged. "Tight."

They strolled along the sand again. "Oh, husband dearest, promise you will never let me drown!"

Once more her voice washed in and out of the wind. "Let you *down!?*" he asked.

"*Drown!* Drowning is such an heroic and tragic death. I often dream of waves rising and falling. Do you think perhaps it is my fate to drown someday?"

"Such nonsense!" he said, squeezing her hand again.

An especially large wave broke and threw up a mass of spray. Some of it, caught in the wind, rained down upon them with a stinging force.

"Wheee!" they cried, and set about dabbing their faces dry. Arabella had to pull her wet bodice from her skin.

"I suppose," she said, "one day—ooh, doesn't it *cut* when your clothes are wet!" They turned from the sea and walked obliquely up the beach toward Dixon's. "That's better with the wind behind," she said.

"And what was it you were about to suppose—one day?"

"Ah—one day I suppose all you engineers will tame the seas and all these dashing waves will be set to turning great engines."

"How extraordinary," he said. "During the sermon just now I was mentally calculating the power of the sea, just in this one bay, between here and Furness. Do you know, if—"

"During the sermon?" she asked.

"Yes. Well—I ask you: what a text for August! 'Let us go now, even unto Bethlehem'! Anyway. If we take it as seventy square miles and if we take the useful tidal extremes as ten feet apart—"

"Ten feet!" she broke in again. "The tide goes out half a mile!"

"No," he laughed. "I mean vertically. Ten feet up and down."

"Oh." She did not understand at all.

"Seventy square miles, rising and falling ten vertical feet, requires at flow and dissipates at ebb over a thousand million horsepower daily!"

"Good gracious! Surely there aren't so many horses in all the world!"

"Inconceivable, is it not!" He was swept up in his vision of it. "All the work performed by all the men and all the machines and all the beasts in England in a whole year does not require one fraction of the power that is quietly applied and expended in moving this body of water up and down twice every day. Here in this remote corner of the kingdom!"

Now she, too, was entangled in his vision. "Oh, Walter—how romantic! It is the power of Nature that Mr. Martin captures so well in his salon pictures."

"Yes," he sighed. "What a puny thing is man. We take such pride in the wondrous changes we are making, and the power we exert over Nature. But they are as nothing when set beside the forces *she* commands, in even the most casual and unremarkable process. Do you know, in the whole of Manchester and Salford, according to the Statistical Society's latest report, there is only nine thousand nine hundred twenty-four horsepower applied."

Back at Dixon's, Arabella went into the bedroom to change out of her wet promenade dress. Walter said he might as well stay damp until the evening. If they went out again after dinner, he might only get wet once more. He stood at the window watching the angry sea consume the sand. Every last shred of the wreckage had vanished. Occasional large drops of rain began to fall. "What an August!" he said; and his breath actually clouded the windowpane.

At last she returned. She stood in the door and waited for his approval.

For a moment her loveliness took his breath away. "Say!" he cried when he found his voice. "What a beautiful dress! Is it new?"

"I have worn it before, but the ribbons and bodice are new. As a matter of fact, your cousin gave them to me. Papa said—"

"My cousin? Which cousin?"

She settled on the sofa, which was now back in the middle of the room. He leaned against the mantelpiece and looked proudly down at her.

"Clod Three. Papa said it was not seemly and desired me to return them, but Mama said that the gentry must be permitted some licence."

"Hah!" Walter's harsh laugh split the air. "Gentry! The Thorntons gentry! They're tradesmen."

"Shipowners, dear. And in the Russian trade, which is very select."

"The shipowning is quite ancillary to—"

"In any case," she interrupted, "with Letty soon marrying into the Desboroughs and with their connections through the Kents to her Majesty, my goodness—if that isn't better than Lord Tomnoddy going bankrupt in Radnorshire—if they aren't accepted among the quality soon . . ."

"*And* they'll go bankrupt themselves soon after. You'll see. What the older aristocracy took centuries to achieve—the long hard road from wealth to poverty—Clod Three will do in ten years. That's progress for you!"

She looked disappointed. "You are so charitable about everything—except your family."

"Plain justice. They taught me all I know of charity! Let me ring for some chocolate."

He pulled the bell cord.

"No. Tea," she said. "Let us have tea. It'll be dinner in twenty minutes. The bodice is not quite new. It used to be cut in the style that was such an enthusiasm in 1835. How mawkish it looks now!"

"Mawkish?" He looked in astonishment at her bodice. "Mawkish is the last word I'd use about that."

"No, no. Not this. The style of 1835, I meant. It looked dreadful."

"Oh." He lost interest. "I can't say I had noticed any change."

The maid came in. "Ah, Sally," he said, brightening. "Be so good as to bring tea for Mrs. Thornton and chocolate for me."

"That'll warm ye, after yon blow," she said as she left, not even noticing his disapproval.

"I *like* their friendliness," she said, smiling at his petulance. "And how typical of you Thorntons—chocolate *and* tea! Most married people accommodate to one another, but with the Thorntons, *he* must have brandy, she tea, and the young ones everything from vodka to ginger cordial."

He snorted, wishing he'd ordered tea. "They probably think it most aristocratic. *Très bon ton!* Yes, there's nothing the Thorntons would dislike more than to rest at the level of mere gentry. Jove, how they ape the Desboroughs and old Cowper! And Melbourne over at Brockett Hall! They're like . . . *schoolchildren!*"

She sat silent, looking out of the window, not wanting to reopen the subject of the Thorntons.

"Still," he concluded, "they put me out to a good trade."

"Surely, dearest, it is almost a profession to be an engineer."

"There's nothing undignified in labour. Trade'll do me."

The maid returned with their tray. She handed Walter his chocolate and left Arabella to make her tea.

"Thank you, Sally," Arabella said.

"It's a champion supper tonight. Always is, Sundays, like," Sally told them as she left.

Walter waited until the door was shut. "I wish you would not thank the servants as though they had done you some personal service. You will regret it. It is her *duty* to bring what we ask. Not a favour needing a thank you."

"I'll try to remember." She spoke absentmindedly, preoccupied with the tea ritual.

"Look at that!" He thrust his cocoa under her gaze and then crossed back to the fireplace with it. "They must be using bobbin grease instead of cocoa butter." And he spooned the melted fat off the surface into the empty hearth.

He had barely finished before the girl returned. She had a letter in her hand. "This was to be left for you in the post office, sir," she said, passing it to him. "Only Bamper, who brought you here by coach, knew you was here and so come on special like to drop it."

It was from John Stevenson. "Oh, *thank* you, Sally," he said in his excitement, before he saw Arabella's look of amused accusation.

"Bamper'll want something," the maid said bluntly.

"How far's he had to come—extra, I mean?"

"All the way from south shore. Coach and horse and all."

He gave her a shilling.

Arabella was still smiling, catlike, at him when the maid left.

"All right!" he said. "Point taken." And he fell to reading the letter. She sipped her tea and watched him.

"How is our money invested, dear?" she asked when he finished.

"That's a damn funny question for a pretty young lady to ponder!"

"Please don't swear. People are making fortunes in railways."

He laughed knowingly. "And losing 'em!"

"Not everyone," she persisted. "The Wilkinses were very humble people five years ago, and, Papa says, they turned two hundred pounds into two thousand in one year. And now everyone talks about their being wealthier than Lady Cathcart . . ."

"Don't say 'wealthy,' " he corrected. "Say 'rich.' "

"And that was all through railways. Surely, as you know so much about the railways, you could avoid the risky lines and do even better?"

He felt greatly uncomfortable to be discussing their money with her— almost as if she imagined he was accountable to her. "If it were as simple as that, pigs could choose their palaces," he said, hoping it would stop her. She never asked for engineering technicalities to be explained; why should she begin to fuss her head about money?

"You think it better I know nothing of our affairs?" she asked. Then, seeing that he was trying to find a kindly way of agreeing, she added: "Like poor widow Carter, Lawyer Carter's wife, who thought her husband had the back-door key to the Bank of England?"

"No . . ." he said. What else could he say? "No . . . no . . . I— er—obviously you should—yes." He looked again at the letter from John Stevenson. "As a matter of fact, funny thing, you talking about railways. I *am* thinking of one investment. Or *was*. I don't know now. Let me read you this. See what you think. This is from the contractor at Summit."

She patted the sofa beside her. He sat there, took a sip of cocoa, and began to read: " 'My dear Thornton' . . . Hm! It used to be 'Mr. Thornton sir'! 'My dear Thornton, I'm mightily obliged to you for the note from your bankers. In the meantime, I've managed to lay my hands on an extra thousand and so have no immediate need to translate your kind offer into equity. However, you have my word that, should the opportunity of investment in my contract arise (as I doubt not it will soon enough) and should you then still desire to take it, yours shall be the first offer on which I shall call. Work on the tunnel is proceeding at the accelerated pace I predicted when I introduced my bonus scheme. Indeed, one of the gangs will draw *two* days' bonus in this first week; but they will no doubt soon moderate to a more sensible pace. I now have no qualms but that you and I shall walk the entire driftway this Boxing Day 1839. I have taken lodging at the Royal Oak in Littleborough till then. When the driftway is complete, I presume it will be more convenient to move to Todmorden. The young girl—' " He stopped there. "And so on," he said.

She was smiling at him. "It sounded as if it was about to become a very masculine letter!"

"Oh," he chuckled. "Not at all." He looked again at the letter and then, speculatively, back at Arabella. "I'll tell you about it. The week before last I walked over near Littleborough, which is this side of our tunnel. To catch the mails. On the way back I passed a young labouring girl. Tramping over the hills to Leeds with her toes sticking out of her boots . . ." He stopped, realizing that he was spoiling the point he wanted to make. "I can't tell you more at the moment. You'll soon see why. Tell me first what you make of this letter? Of the writer of it?"

"It is very direct," she said. "Quite to the point. He is educated, clearly . . ."

That wasn't quite what Walter had meant. "How can I put it," he mused. "Suppose . . . if the making of a railroad were a military operation, what do you think the writer of this letter would be? What rank?"

"My background is hardly military!"

"No . . . but . . . just guess."

"A major? A colonel?"

Walter grinned broadly. "Exactly! So he is! He, that is, John Stevenson, the writer of this letter, is the contractor for Summit Tunnel, as I said—and the contract is let for over one hundred thousand pounds."

Arabella drew a deep breath in a near whistle.

"Yet last week," Walter went on, "this same man was a mere ganger! The equivalent, I suppose, of a sergeant. From sergeant to colonel in a week!"

"Good gracious!"

"He is, I say, a most extraordinary man. A most . . ." Words failed. "When you see him among the men—'the lads,' he calls them—well, he's not exactly one of them, but he's not one of *us* either. He's a natural—I was about to say 'commander' but he doesn't command. He's a natural *leader*. He can tell the most drunken, surly, disorderly, rebellious bunch of navvies to do something and, by the powers, they do it! But he doesn't command them, as if from a distance. He leads them, from among them. He gives them pride, I suppose . . ."

"He sounds dangerously radical!"

"I believe he could sound anything he wished. He could *be* anything he wished. I saw him talking the Board of Directors into giving him the contract that broke the previous man. Until then I knew him only as a ganger—so you may imagine what I expected to walk through the door. But not a bit of it. There he was—every inch the provincial businessman. With a banker's letter good for ten thousand! A *ganger!* And when they asked him to find surety for a thousand more—no worry—no furrowed brows—nothing but smiles all round. I decided, on the moment, that he was the man. Offered him a thousand. But"—Walter sighed and patted the letter in his pocket—"he's found it somewhere else."

"Wasn't it a risk, dear?" Arabella had the vaguest of feelings, a mere presentiment which she could never have articulated in words, that this Stevenson was some kind of threat. It was unlike Walter to show such uncritical enthusiasm.

"It was—on the face of it. But I have the strongest notion that this man is . . . nothing will stop him. If anybody is going to make a fortune at the railways, it'll be Lord John."

*"Lord* John?" she asked. That was different; Walter had not said he was a peer . . . but how could a peer be a ganger?

"Oh—that's just a nickname. Every navvy has a nickname. Though they say he *is* related to the peerage; on the wrong side of the sheets, you know. In fact, he's hinted as much to me."

"How exciting!" Arabella's eyes gleamed. "And how romantic! Perhaps he's only waiting to prove his claim and to cast out some dastardly usurper . . . perhaps he was stolen away as . . ."

"I hardly think so!" Walter laughed. "They *also* say he is a felon, a master of some nefarious trade, on the run. If every runaway felon in England were taken back into fetters, half our navvies would vanish overnight."

"Oh." She was crestfallen.

"Well, even *that,*" he teased, "viewed through glass of the proper tint, could be made to *appear* romantic."

She pouted and gave him a self-deprecating smile. Then, seeing him eye the teapot, she rang again for Sally and asked for an extra cup and more hot water.

"Curious thing," Walter said, suddenly remembering the incident. "When I offered the money, I said, *'Nec quicquam acrius quam pecuniae damnum stimulat'*—'Nothing stings more sharply than to lose money.' And without even pausing to think, this man, who had lived two years among navvies, men who can't write even their names, this man replied that he had always thought Cicero to be a better guide than Livy. And he quoted, *'Vitam regit fortuna, non sapientia'*—'It is fortune, not wisdom, that rules men's lives.' What does one make of it?"

"I can hardly wait to see this man of mystery."

Sally returned and set down the extra cup and the fresh water. Arabella said nothing, but, turning her face from Walter, gave the girl a warm smile. When the door was closed, she chilled her expression and turned back to Walter. "Was that better?" she asked. "More to your liking?"

"Much," he said.

She poured his tea. "And what of the girl?"

"Girl?"

"The one with her 'toes sticking out of her boots'? Walking to Leeds?"

Walter sipped his cup and breathed out his appreciation. "To be sure. Yes—it was late afternoon and I knew she'd have a hard job to get over to Todmorden by dark. She looked exhausted already. So I told her to seek a night's shelter with Lord John's gang. He'd never see anyone go hungry. Which she did. And now . . ." He took the letter from his pocket. "He writes that she is to have permanent shelter. In short, he is to marry her, this coming week. It's dashed quick—and dashed odd! And another thing: She gave her name to me as Molly. He says it's Nora."

Arabella gave a suspicious snort.

"He writes that she is 'a genius at calculations and, from selling produce off their own few acres, has developed an amazing faculty at bargaining.' And I took her for no more than a simple farm servant." He turned to Arabella. "That is what I most admire in him. I see no more than a ragged little waif—she dresses like a field girl and talks like a field girl. Ergo she *is* a field girl to me. But not to Lord John. He is not like that. He is not, as it were, held back by the assumptions and prejudices that cloud my assessment—and most people's assessment. He sees through all that and finds some *essential* quality—something I would never have dreamed . . ."

"Oh, dearest . . ." Arabella was beginning to weary of Lord John and Lord John and Lord John. "You are so charitable! He is probably putting the best face on it! That's the simple truth."

"Best face? On *it?* On what?"

She tutted and lowered her voice. "He's probably got her into trouble. That's what it is."

He threw back his head and laughed, slopping tea into his saucer. "How well we insist on knowing those we have never met! No," he went on more seriously, "it's too quick for that. This happened less than a fortnight ago; just over a week, in fact. The way among the inferior orders is to wait for months, until the fact is well established. He wouldn't marry her until . . . November, if *that* were his game."

"Oh," she sighed. "Why can they not put more trust in God!"

He set down his cup and drew himself to her side. He stroked her under the chin, shaking his head in smiling disbelief. "Dear, sweet Arabella!" he said.

She drew in her lips to a stubborn slit.

"So wrong—and so convinced!"

"Very well, Walter." She spoke to the ceiling. "I know it is not *you* who mocks."

He brought his hand down to her arm, rubbing the silk of her blouse gently with his knuckles. "Now what fancy is this?"

"Fancy!" she said with a strange, cold bitterness. "Yes, in my fancy you were a Christian knight. Ready to battle any evil." She turned to him and spoke more warmly, as if desperate to encourage him. "Well, take heart. When the Devil seizes you again—as he did at Earlestown—I shall be there to see your lance does not droop!"

He tried valiantly to keep a straight face. And, of course, his laughter was all the stronger when it came. He could see the shock and the hurt in her face but it did nothing to halt him.

"Well may you laugh, sir," she said when it had died its natural death. She was deeply offended.

"I'm sorry!" he said, wondering how to soothe her.

"It is no laughing matter."

"Oh, come!" He hoped to appeal to her sense of fun. "I know at least *one* young bride who would have been mightily downcast that night at Earlestown if my *lance*—as you put it—had drooped prematurely! Once, that is, her natural coyness had been . . . over*ridden!*"

He watched her eyes go wide. He laughed again, to encourage her.

"Walter! I did not mean *that!* When I said 'lance' . . ."

"I know! I know!" He nodded and laughed yet again.

"Oh, now I am all flustered." She *was* smiling—or trying hard not to. She had to look away. "How *could* you! How *could* you think it." She was saved further embarrassment because he moved close to her and kissed her long and tenderly. He felt the seriousness grow within her as she surrendered.

"I love you," she said, touching their noses together.

"And I love you."

She rested his forehead on hers. For a long while they stayed thus, staring into one another, dark eyes into dark eyes. He breathed in her sweetness and yearned for her.

When they moved apart, a little frown creased her brow. She was trying to say something. "I wish. . . ." She rose and strolled away to the bureau, where she stood irresolutely.

"What do you wish?"

She picked up her fan from one of the shelves. The leading aile was damaged. "I wish I had not broken this fan."

"What were you really going to say?" He motioned to her to come back to the sofa beside him.

"I wish you would not gamble."

"Oh, come," he said. "It is only on holiday. I don't gamble at all in normal—Well, I *hardly* ever do. In any case, even your father is not above a little gaming."

She fretted with her broken fan. "I think each generation should strive to outdo the one before it. Otherwise, how may we ever hope for moral progress?"

"The logic of that is impeccable," he sighed.

"In fact, Walter dearest, I do not really approve of Blackpool. It seems so—"

He interrupted. "But you are having such fun—or so I thought."

"I *am*," she said, growing more agitated. "But not . . . I do not . . . it is not the *best* side of me. It is my lower nature. I agree there must be some occasions—holidays and feasts and ceremonies—perhaps four or five or even six days a year when we should put aside our more solemn striving and unbend a little. A *little*. But *ten days!* All at once! Try as I may I can find no sanction for that. It seems to me the sheerest licence."

His heart melted as he watched her serious little face, frowning at her own laxity of moral spirit. Such an earnest young girl!

"Understand me, please," she went on. "I'm glad we came to Blackpool. I'm glad to have experienced it. But all this idle jollification seems . . . I don't know, somehow so *antique*. It is an archaic mode of pleasure. It is shallow. And certainly it is unworthy of you and me."

"What would you prefer?" he asked.

But she looked guilty again. "And now you are going to be good to me and pamper me. I would not press this upon you. I know how hard you have worked on your tunnel. And I'm sure you'll work the harder when we return if you have enjoyed your break from it. So . . ."

He squeezed her shoulder again. "What . . . would you prefer?"

She looked up at him to gauge his reaction. "To be completely honest . . . I want to see our new home." She was delighted to see his face light up. "You too?" she asked.

"Well—it's a fairly tense time at Summit. New contractor. Hint of labour unrest. I must admit . . ."

"Tomorrow?" she suggested.

He chuckled. "We'll go tomorrow."

"How will you tell Dixon?"

"Oh—I'll tell him the letter I got today contained some news, which, now I've slept on it, leaves me too uneasy to enjoy the rest of the holiday."

She sank her head on his shoulder again. "Oh, Walter! How can I ever be as good to you as you are to me."

Thinking of a dozen ways, he held his peace.

*          *          *

When they went to bed Arabella undressed skillfully, without revelation of herself, even though he was in the room and watching closely. The question of where he would sleep tonight still lay delicately undecided—the blankets he had used last night still lay folded in the cupboard. In fact, he assumed that Arabella's unnatural resolve had melted; she, for her part, assumed he had conquered the Devil within and was ready to enter the chaste and continent Christian marriage bed she had always wanted for them. Each was brought to realize how wrong these assumptions were even before they had lifted the sheets. Walter's turn came first, as Arabella prayed for them.

"O God, Who hast ordained the holy state of matrimony that it be not enterprised unadvisedly, lightly, or wantonly, to satisfy men's carnal lusts and appetites, like brute beasts that have no understanding, stretch forth now Thine almighty arm and touch with understanding Thy two servants who kneel here in sore perplexity and direst need of Thy guidance. Grant us, O Lord, the gift of continency that we may keep ourselves undefiled members of Christ's body. Teach us to draw our pitchers at the deep and everlasting wells of Thy pure love, most especially when our frailty prompts us to renew them at the shallower springs of lust and carnal pleasure. Help us . . ."

"*Amen!*" he said, unable to contain his disappointment longer.

". . . when we are most like to stumble . . ." she faltered.

"Amen!" he repeated and rose stiffly, not looking at her.

Meekly she got into bed. "I had not finished, Walter dear," she said in mild reproof.

"I believe you had," he told her. "At all events you had said quite enough."

"If you tell me so." Her only thought now was to pacify him; he was angrier than she had ever seen him.

"I do, ma'am. I do." He breathed deeply, several times. Then, rubbing his eyes and shaking his head, he went on more gently, "And 'sore perplexed' is the word, right enough. Yes. Sore perplexed. Which way do I turn? To whom do *we* turn?"

"Oh, dearest!" she cried out, wishing he could talk to her instead of to the empty air.

"Oh, dearest—oh, dearest!" he mocked. "I say, if I had married a Hottentot or . . . a Mandarin maiden . . . I could not have met with a more . . . foreign . . . a more unfamiliar mode of thought."

Arabella was shocked. "How can you say it? It is a *Christian* mode."

"It has that appearance." He looked at her like a hunted animal. "You make me doubt myself."

"No," she whispered, wanting to hold him and quieten him.

But he persisted. "You make me feel . . . unclean . . . unworthy . . ."

"Oh no!" The hot tears that had trembled at the rims of her eyes began to fall uncontrollably. How she longed for control—to be able to tell him it was not *he* that was unworthy, not *he* that was unclean . . . only the Devil within him.

"Oh, yes!" he said. "A week ago I felt for you the greatest . . . the most stirring love that any man could feel. In every . . . in every . . . *fibre* of me. My heart would not dance twice upon the same spot in here. I was all fired and steaming within. Every minute of my day sang for you. You were all. You were *my* all. You were my world . . ."

Why did he talk about it in the past? "But that—" she began.

"Wait! Let me finish. Please. That world . . . that whole . . . that all . . . that allness . . . was *all* loves and all kinds and conditions of love. Carnal—yes, it was carnal. But spiritual, too. Of the purest. *And* affectionate as well. As brother and sister, as old friends . . ."

"And I too, dearest," she stammered in a voice that wandered recklessly up and down the scales. "You feel me tremble when you . . . touch . . . and you see how I melt when we . . . when . . . but it is our *lower* natures. It is the Devil . . ."

"Then it is *not* for you as it is for me, whatever you may think. To speak of different kinds of love is a mere convenience. It is not like an apple with core, flesh, and rind—eat what you will, discard what you will. It is a living thing fed by three arteries. Pinch one off and some region it irrigates must wither. And from it a gangrene must spread that may rot the rest. Entirely."

He made it sound so right when he spoke. As she listened, bathed in his words, she could only think how noble he was in his suffering. Her lower nature, too, was urging her strongly, at levels far below the reach of words, to join with him as they had joined at Earlestown. To comfort him! Her entrails lurched in delight at the thought. And, as she felt again all that she thought she had conquered—the melting lassitude of her limbs, the shallow breath, the tingle in her bosom, the heat in the pit of her back, the riot of her heartbeat—as this ocean of sensuality rose to drown her and obliterate the wreckage of her conscience, something within her was singing an anthem of purest joy. And to its swelling volume she surrendered herself entirely.

Walter was lying on his back, exhausted with all this talk; his eyes were shut. Dumbly, slowly she leaned over him to pinch out the candle. Before its light fled she saw his eyes open wide in astonishment and then fill with half-believing rapture.

"Arabella?" he began before she placed her palm flat across his mouth and bore down hard. When he struggled she relaxed and kissed him there softly.

He lay motionless. She knew he was excited. She could *feel* that—down there. But he did nothing to advance her. She itched for his hands to caress, for his nails to scratch, his tongue to melt, his lips to graze, his breath to winnow her body. But he did nothing. If she lowered her lips to his, he kissed. But if she took them away, he did not follow.

At last she threw off her chemise and lowered her breasts to him. In her solemnest, innermost, unreachable heart, she knew, she *still* knew, that this was wrong. But for the rest of her, the sense of wickedness and shame merely added a spice. So that, even as she surrendered herself so utterly and wholly, feeding and swelling his lust and hers, she learned a deep-etched lesson on the tyranny of sin and of the subtle powers wielded by the Prince of that dark land.

*     *     *

The coach called at half past nine. Dixon was sad they had to . . . quite understood . . . wouldn't dream of keeping the money, returned the unused portion . . . had capital fun. Yes—*very* sad they had to go.

They stopped at Nixon's to bid adieu to the doctor, but he was out.

When they drew near to Vauxhall, Arabella tapped the bodywork for the coachman to stop.

"Why?" Walter asked.

"There's that Miss Sanders. We can leave a message if her Mrs. McWhatsit is so friendly with the doctor. Yoo hoo!" she called as she pushed open the door.

Miss Sanders came across and curtseyed when she saw who it was.

"Will you see the doctor?" Arabella asked.

"Doctor Fisher has gone with Mrs. McKechnie for a boating trip, madam."

"And left you?"

"I'm no sailor, ma'am!"

Arabella explained why they had to leave so suddenly and asked to be remembered kindly to both absentees. Not once did the girl look in at Walter. Then Arabella, remembering how this girl had, in fact, warned Walter of gambling further with the doctor, felt she would like to give her some little reward.

"My dear," she said, turning to Walter, "do you have a box of those peppermints we purchased at Preston?"

Mystified, Walter produced a box and gave it to her.

"Here," Arabella said, passing the sweets to an equally puzzled Miss Sanders. "These are for you."

"Thank you." Miss Sanders took them. "I'm sure I don't know what for."

Arabella smiled, as if to chide her. "I'm sure you do. It's for the little service you did my husband on Saturday night."

No landed fish ever gaped as wide or stared with such unblinking glassy eyes as Miss Sanders.

"As he told me himself," Arabella prattled on, "he's *so* inexperienced in these things, it would never have occurred to him on his own. I'm very grateful. We *both* are."

She was slightly put out by the girl's total lack of response—the way she stood and just stared so, even after the door was shut and the coach moved off.

Unseen by her, Walter opened his eyes at last, let go his breath, and eased his fingernails from the trenches they had dug in his palms.

"Please don't tell me I was too effusive, dear. I know she's only a servant. But she's so ladylike and demure—I can't help thinking of her as something more."

"That's strange," he told her solemnly. "Nor can I."

# *Chapter 18*

Summit Tunnel is a 2,885-yard hole through the spine of England. From Oldham Road, Manchester, through Mills Hill, Blue Pits, and Rochdale the line rises steadily until it is 250 feet above its origin. Between Rochdale and Littleborough it levels off, but this is a mere breathing spell before the effort ahead. From Littleborough to the farthermost end of the tunnel is a steady climb to a summit point 331 feet (and three inches) above the Oldham Road terminus. Like the canal and the turnpike before it, the line deviates from its general easterly course to run northward through a great fold amid the rolling moors. Beyond the summit the line, still following the northward fold, drops to Todmorden, a mile and a half away and seventy feet nearer sea level.

These are daunting gradients, even for a stout little Bury with its four driven wheels. But they are as nothing compared to the inclines faced by travellers on the road and canal; their summits are fully a hundred feet above that of the railroad—with more than forty lock gates to open and close between Littleborough and Rochdale. Yet the traveller on these open highways is always surprised to be told how high up he is—more than six hundred feet above the sea. He looks about him and sees only the mighty moors rising a further seven hundred feet within a mile of where he stands. And beyond them are hills of even greater eminence—range upon range of wild fell and moor receding in the blue-grey distance. To the immediate

west of the turnpike the land rises steeply for over a hundred feet to a
bluff, or "scout" as Pennine folk call it. In places it is broken by dashing
streams, but elsewhere it rises sheer for a further hundred feet or more.
Here, in earlier days, ran the packhorse trail, still the only free passage
across the countryside. The turnpikes want a shilling for your journey; the
canals will take up to three halfpence a mile and twopence a lock for every
ton you send.

The country is rough sheep moor where mat grass, tormentilla, common bent, ladies bedstraw, and tall fescue are the chief fodder, and blue
flax, purple molinia grass, and greenweed the chief decoration—with a
sprinkling of petty whin and four-leaved heath in the damper hollows. No
farmer ever made a fortune up on these tops. The money here is all
assembled in the bottoms.

The new age stands down there, filling the air with soot and steam and
vitriol and strange new gasworks smells, banishing the night with a thousand lighted windows, bringing the valleys alive with the muted thunder of
many thousand looms. There is a place near Butcher Hill, they say, where
you may feel the ground in ceaseless vibration from Fielden Brothers' mill
at Water Side, a quarter of a mile away; and on a windless night, when
canal traffic is all moored, you may see the face of the water so agitated
that a net of standing ripples is formed, making it seem one long ribbon
of shattered glass.

And Fieldens', with its single room *one acre* in extent, where five
hundred operatives tend as many pairs of looms, is only the largest among
dozens. Every village and hamlet between the mouth of Summit and Todmorden—places like Strines Gate, Ramsden Wood, Walsden, Hollins
Bottom, Gawks Holm, Dobroyd, and Salford—has its power mills, iron
foundries, vitriol work, or forges. They stand strung out along the artery
that carries their raw materials in and their products out: the Rochdale
Canal—their link with far-off America to the west, and the Baltic ports and
Russia to the east. From it and into it they presently draw and pour their
wealth.

But in terms of time they stand poised at the dawn of an incomparably
brighter era. For with the coming of the railroad, these remote and rustic
valleys are at last brought into *instantaneous* communication with the
world's great centres of trade and capital. People can only guess at the
wealth this newer and mightier artery will induce in these once sleepy
hollows and unreachable vales.

Already the physical effect is profound. Along the foot of Reddish
Scout, which looms above the turnpike, runs a string of shafts, fourteen in
all. To the casual visitor they would appear like a rank of slow, cold

volcanoes. From the mouth of each a great mass of rock spoil tumbles in an ever broader cascade, down the steep banks to the road below. In years to come these banks may grass themselves over and round themselves off to blend with the vaster natural piles around; but now they form massive barren spills of white-grey millstone, whose long, pale fingers already reach down to the valley floor.

And every ounce of this great letting of the living rock is hacked and blasted and loaded by human hand, hauled by steam to the top—at one place over three hundred feet above—and tipped down wooden chutes to tumble as deep as gravity will take it. But that is still far above the heads of the thousand-strong army of navvies and bricklayers and masons and sinkers working below.

Their method is first to sink these vertical shafts along the proposed route of the track, the foot of each shaft reaching exactly to the floor, or invert, of the tunnel. The engineer then lowers two plumb lines down each shaft, their points of anchorage at the top lying precisely along the midline of the tunnel. When all pendulum motion has ceased, the assistants below can be sure that the bobs now delineate the direction of the tunnel at its proper level. From this they can set two marks in the invert, from which, like the fore- and back-sight of a gun, the true course of the tunnel can be aimed in either direction. In this way two tunnels may be driven toward each other through several hundred feet of intervening rock and meet with an error of less than an inch at their centre lines.

When Walter Thornton and his bride returned from their shortened honeymoon, that lining-up of plumb bobs was many months in the past. And from the inverts of each of the fourteen shafts an eight-foot driftway had been drilled and blasted out toward its neighbour on either side. In places where the rock was dry and solid the going was ahead of the time-table, and they had already begun the enlargement of the driftway to the full twenty-six feet of the tunnel itself. The spoil from these shafts was fine and dry and often blew up the valley in a cloud of dust. In other places, where the rock was fractured and intermittent underground streams ran through, the spoil came up as a grey slurry that oozed down the hillside and drained away in muddy rivulets. From these shafts the going was poorer than predicted, and it was they that gave rise to the fear that the driftway would not be complete by the end of 1839.

All of this Walter explained to Arabella as they stood high on Moorhey Flat and looked down at the line of shafts below Reddish Scout. They had not even gone to their new home yet, so impatient was he to see his tunnel and to show it off to her. She stared at the wastage of the moorside and felt a surge of pride that Walter had done all that. His hand

had ruled a line across a map in 1837 and here, two years later, an army of
little ants, several of which she could see scurrying around the shaftheads,
had spilled out all this muck and re-formed the valley side. Above each
shaft a standing engine was at work, pouring black smoke and venting
waste steam into the air; a steady breeze carried it northward up the valley,
obscuring the canal and turnpike immediately below them.

She turned around, putting the wind behind her, and looked back over
the steep path by which they had climbed.

"Which is our house?" she asked.

He peered north through the thick pall of smoke, product of almost
two dozen chimneys scattered up the intervening mile and a half, and
shook his head.

"That hill—it's somewhere halfway up that hill at the head of the
valley. Pigs Hill. Or Pex Hill, some call it."

"We shall call it Pex Hill. The *pigs,* it seems to me, are all down in the
valley, belching out this foul smoke."

"I said you can't get far from a factory in the progressive parts of the
north."

She continued to look glum.

"Don't fret so," Walter told her. "We are well up the hill and it
deflects the worst of the smoke when the wind is southerly. And when it
blows any other way, it passes us by altogether. You'll find I chose carefully when you see it."

Still she did not smile.

"Do you not like it?" he asked, disappointed.

"It is certainly very different from the Maran Valley." She looked at
him and smiled at last. "Yes," she added and took his hand. "I like it. It is
our life. And I like these wild and windswept moors and their vast open
skies."

For several minutes she had been aware of a tall gentleman with a low-
crowned, wide-brimmed hat climbing toward them. The path threaded its
way up to where the scout was crumbled and eroded away, just north of
where they stood. So, when they turned to retrace their steps to the turnpike
at Deanroyd, they came almost face to face with the tall man as he gained
the brow.

"Stevenson!" Walter cried out with delight. "My dear fellow! All is
well?"

"All is well."

They shook hands warmly. He was huge, she thought, like a man
magnified. Even at arm's length—*two* arms' length—he seemed too close.
It made her nervous.

"My dear, this is John Stevenson—Lord John, as they call him."

She nodded shyly but did not offer her hand. How deep his eyes were—and how they pierced!

"Your servant, ma'am. Word of your grace and beauty preceded you here. But it pales beside its true example," he said. And, indeed, he thought, up here on this wild moor she looked as pale and lovely as a piece of fine porcelain.

Arabella drew herself primly together. "I should prefer," she said, "to be known for modesty and piety."

Stevenson laughed. "That's easy work in these godless parts! Still—a becoming sentiment." He wondered how unassailable she really was.

"A *resolve,* Mr. Stevenson," she said. "No mere sentiment, I assure you."

Why did he stare at her with such amused superiority?

"My dear!" Walter chided. "Mr. Stevenson spoke lightly. I'm sure he had no intention to unbridle your evangelical fervour!"

To her horror, Stevenson winked at her! Fortunately Walter, turning from her to him, saw neither his gesture nor the consternation it aroused in her. As soon as Walter turned, Stevenson said: "Lord John was a well enough name for a ganger but a touch presumptuous for a contractor."

"Point taken. How are we steaming?"

Stevenson looked back over the line of engines and the tumbled heaps of muck—a sight that brought him evident satisfaction. "We're well on course," he said, turning back to Walter. "The usual harvest of crisis and mishap. But we're well on course."

"Anything particular? Shall we walk down?—we are making for Deanroyd. I sent our baggage on by Chaffer's coach. He's coming back to collect us at Deanroyd."

"You know Chaffer has tendered for the contract to meet the Todmorden trains? Tell him you have influence and he might take a bit off," Stevenson suggested.

"I'd never dream of using my position in that way!"

Arabella felt proud of the indignation in Walter's voice.

Stevenson shrugged and set off down the hill. Walter came behind to help Arabella over the rougher parts. Stevenson was careful not to turn round, in case Arabella had to lift her skirts above her ankles to negotiate some of the obstacles.

"We shall be settling in at Pigs Hill—I mean, Pex Hill—between now and Friday, so I don't think you'll see me until next Monday, unless the business is urgent."

"There's only one thing worries me," Stevenson called over his shoulder. "On the Leeds face of number twelve—where we had the invert failure."

"Oh?"

"It's too wet for my liking. I want to suggest driving an adit in from . . . it would be about where you see those three oaks. To relieve it."

"But there's no point in the valley we can get *below* the tunnel invert. I tell you what: as I'm here, I'll have a quick look at it now, and then again on Monday. Often the water we strike proves to drain from some primeval cistern that, once emptied, never refills. We give them all time to prove themselves."

"Ooh! May I come below with you?" Arabella asked, delighted at the thought of seeing the working at its very heart.

Stevenson halted and almost looked around.

"I'm afraid not, my dear," Walter said. "The men will tolerate no woman in a drift. They'd rather tramp fifty miles to another site than go back to a tunnel where a woman has been."

"What superstitious nonsense!" she retorted. "Who gives them their religion?"

"You raise a very pertinent point, Mrs. Thornton," Stevenson said, but elaborated no further. "Be careful here," he added. "This is where the steps begin."

The trail fell so steeply that the limestone slabs were butted one to another in the form of steps. It took all their concentration to negotiate, and no one spoke until they came to more level ground, where Moorhey Clough, swollen by the unseasonable rains, gurgled beneath the pathway. Here Stevenson pointed to a house about a furlong distant, halfway up the hillside and overlooking the northern end of the tunnel.

"What d'you say to it?" he asked.

"Hello, house?" Walter suggested.

"Forgive my provincialism," Stevenson said, not pleased at this gentle ribbing. "I mean, what do you think of it?"

"For what purpose—for you?"

Stevenson nodded. "It may fall vacant January next. Old Hartley up the top, who farms Higher Allescholes, thinks his son could take on this farm. But he'd not want the house for a year or two. Till he marries."

They started on the final leg of the descent, a cart track that led all the way down to the turnpike. Here the three of them could walk side by side.

"Suit you ideally," Walter said.

"I think I'll take it. Twenty-eight shillings a month." They passed the farm gate. *Rough Stones* said the legend.

"Pity you can't improve the name."

"Ah!" Stevenson said. "There's something appeals to us in the idea of starting from such a home. You've a far grander place up at Pigs Hill—despite the name."

Walter cleared his throat. "We call it Pex Hill," he said.

Stevenson laughed.

"So you have seen our house, Mr. Stevenson?" Arabella asked with interest.

"Mrs. Stevenson and I went up there yesterday to keep the servants on their toes—not knowing you were coming back so soon. I hope they have the rooms aired for you."

"I'm sure we're very much obliged. Do tell me what it's like." She spoke more warmly than she felt, for she was still shocked at the effrontery of his wink; but, for Walter's sake, she thought she ought to be friendly.

"Mrs. Thornton, my dear!" Walter gently rebuked her. "We shall see it soon enough." She managed to both smile and pout at him. *"You* should move over here now, Stevenson. Stop at the Golden Lion or Queens in Todmorden. I'm sure we should all enjoy some capital evenings together."

"January will be time enough. The drift will be through by then and it won't signify which side we live. Until then, though . . . I fear we do too much purchasing in Manchester to move very far from Littleborough."

This bluff rejection of Walter's kindly suggestion seemed rude to Arabella. She decided not to get on social terms with these uncouth Stevensons unless Walter insisted on it. The decision brought with it an unexpectedly powerful sense of relief.

They were almost down on the road by now.

"Ah, well," Walter said. "You know your own affairs best, I daresay." He looked up the highway, which was empty except for some flocks of chickens, and some distant riders. "The coach hasn't come back yet, I see. Stevenson, would you very kindly shepherd Mrs. Thornton around the exterior workings while I go quickly—"

"Oh no, Walter!" Arabella cried out involuntarily as soon as his intention struck her. "That would be—"

"My dear!" Walter spoke with the faintest trace of anger, discernible at once to her. "I must look at the workings. You may *not,* as you have heard. Mr. Stevenson is as good as the yeomen of the guard."

"Walter!" she pleaded at his departing back, knowing how rude her tone must seem to Stevenson. But Walter marched on without a pause.

Stevenson was smiling broadly at her evident consternation. "I know I'm a poor deputy, ma'am."

"Oh, I don't mean to be churlish, Mr. Stevenson. But it does not seem proper to me."

"Nay, there's naught amiss. Our northern way is more direct, ye'll find. What may pass for proper reticence in Hertfordshire—if I may presume to advise—will likely give offence in these more friendly latitudes."

Again she found his insolence insupportable. "It is latitude we must beware of, Mr. Stevenson," she said with a frosty precision in her diction.

Nothing, it seemed, would wipe that superior smile from his face. "Why, ma'am, if the railway people don't know their station—what'll the country come to!"

He knew she would laugh. He knew that if he fixed her—just so—with his eyes, and worked his mouth in that invitingly humorous way, he would make her laugh. That was what frightened her about him. He knew what to do and how to make her response inevitable. Yet, intellectually, she was delighted with him and to that extent her laughter was unforced. He had so quick and ready a wit.

"Well," he said. "Mr. Thornton would not be pleased to return and find you knowing as little about the outside workings as you did when he left. So . . . to school we go."

They crossed the turnpike and continued on down a shallow bank with a two-foot drop at the bottom. He offered his forearm and she leaned hard against it as she jumped. It amazed her to see how little he moved; she felt she could have swung on that outstretched arm and it would have given no more than if it were a steel spring. He must have the strength of an ox in that great frame of his; she could imagine him digging the tunnel single-handed. There was something both repellent and attractive in the thought of so much power compressed into one body.

But he was turned from her as she swung down and as soon as she landed he walked on—greatly to her relief, for, if he was going to attempt an impropriety, it would be in such a situation, where it could easily be passed off as an accident.

"Here's one of the prettiest things your husband has done," he said over his shoulder as he led her to a great hole in the ground immediately ahead. It was not until they stood at its edge and peered down that the beauty of its shape became apparent, for the bricklayers were just beginning to line it, from the base up. The wall they were building was an elegant oval, about forty by twenty feet, with the long axis spanning the track and laying bare the tunnel a mere two chains from its northern end. The invert was less than six fathoms below them at this point.

"It is beautiful," she agreed. "But if he meant it for ventilation he ordered it several sizes too big."

Stevenson laughed. There was a rumbling from below. Two great cart horses lurched into view, led by a man and a boy, and passed quickly across the gap; behind them they dragged a line of tubs filled with muck from the driftway working.

"I wasn't in charge when this was designed but I understand they had a right old game of high jinks between here and Deanroyd." He pointed to another tunnel about two furlongs farther north, and then swept his hand in a circle to include all the land around. "This was a vast natural basin of silt. Before they started the cutting, it was a marsh. They said you could make the land quake for two chains around you, merely by jumping on it."

Arabella looked nervously at the floor of the cutting. "How will they be able to run great trains over it?" she asked.

"Come and see," he said, and led her around the oval shaft to a clearer view of the cutting beyond. "They have driven dozens of piles hundreds of feet into the earth. And I don't know how many tar barrels they have buried. But there's the result."

And, indeed, the cutting looked as firm and dry as if it had been made through solid rock. It was also a scene of the most amazing industry.

The horses had come to a halt about half a furlong out into the cutting. The man and boy, helped by two navvies, were tipping the tubs, spilling their contents alternately on each side of the track. From near the piles a precarious-looking runway of planks and boards led up the walls of the cutting.

"What is that?" she asked.

"Runnings," he told her and then, seeing her still puzzled, added, "Have ye never seen navvies at work?" She shook her head. "Then let's go closer."

They started to pick their way carefully along the top of the western bank, toward the chattering little Walsden Water, still fresh and cold from the moor above.

"Where do you get them from? Your navvies?" she asked.

"We make 'em, ma'am. For they're not to be had elsewhere. They say a coal miner'll make a navvy in two month, a farm labourer from clay country'll take six, a domestic a year, a renegade clerk two year, a gentleman never." He looked up and held out a hand to stop her. "Watch this. Here's a navvy at work, now."

They were close to the plank "running," as he had called it, and she could now see that a rope ran down its full length. At the top it passed over a roller and was hitched to a horse. At the bottom a tall fair navvy, with a red bandanna, a crushed and ancient silk hat, and trousers tied with twine below his knees, was testing the knot that tied it to a large wheelbarrow, which he had just filled with the muck the cart horses had brought out. They and their driver were already going, pulling the line of tubs back into the maw of the tunnel.

"Now!" Stevenson said.

The fair navvy lifted the handles of the barrow and blew a piercing whistle. The horse at the top of the bank did not need the touch of its driver's switch to set it off at a frantic near gallop. The slack in the rope took up and the barrow lurched with a jerk that must have torn at the navvy's shoulders even as it slowed the horse to a labouring trot. Pulled from before and guided from behind, the barrow flew up the plank as if it had been shot from a spring. When it reached the top, the navvy adroitly turned it to one side of the roller and, when it was past and on the level, threw it over on its back so that it disgorged its payload in one well-conserved pile.

"Four hundredweight or more in that," Stevenson said. Then, just as the navvy righted the barrow and prepared to return to the foot of the cutting, he called out, "Yorky! Yorky Slen!"

The navvy halted, turned, and then ran quickly to them.

"Aye?" he asked.

Now that he was close she could see that he was almost too drunk to stand. His bloodshot eyes crept slowly west and shot back east with a mechanical regularity; they could fix on nothing they saw—if, indeed, they could *see* anything. His laboured breath filled the air with juniper, aniseed, and gin. She shuddered to imagine the mixture—and the quantities—that must have slid down the furry gullet he now bared at them.

"How long have ye navvied, Yorky?" Stevenson asked.

"Eight year. Nine come January. Began on the Manchester–Liverpool."

Stevenson turned to her with pride. "He's been on as many railroads as any man in the kingdom. An aristocrat of the line is our Yorky."

"How many times a day do you do that—what you just did?" she asked.

"Make the running," Stevenson interposed.

"Eee—twenty, thirty, forty. Depends, see, on the height of the cutting and the rate the muck loads."

"Have you never slipped?"

Yorky looked fuddled.

"Has he never!" Stevenson exclaimed. "A week or more back. Yorky here lay trapped on yon far bank with four ton of rock on him. He were back at work next day." He smiled and nodded at Yorky. "Look at him. Forgotten already, he has!"

"Oh—ah!" Yorky said, though, to judge from the thin degree of confidence in his voice, only the dimmest memory filtered through.

"How extraordinary," Arabella said. "Do you like this work?"

"S'all right. For a labouring man it's the king of trades. I must go now."

"Aye, Yorky lad," Stevenson agreed. "Off ye go."

He looked at her and said "Ma'am" before he lurched away and, picking up his barrow, ran unerringly backward down the running.

"They're on bonus, ye understand," Stevenson explained the haste. "Keen not to lose on the day's measure."

"He was *intoxicated!*" she said, hoping to convey not only her shock but her disapproval that Stevenson would present a man in that condition to her.

The lad who had been with the horses came back into the light, stooped to pick up something, and ran again into the tunnel.

"See where that young fellow bent down? That's the very summit of the line. Stand a penny on edge there and it would split in two trying to decide whether to roll back down to Manchester or on to Normanton."

Arabella, not liking this change of subject, made a little throat-clearing noise. Stevenson turned and looked steadily at her. After only a few seconds of this inspection her instinct was to look away; but a stubbornness within impulsively set her to stare him out. He broke slowly into a smile.

"Intoxicated, eh?" he said at length. "Does it worry you?"

"Very much. Very particularly." She bridled.

He became serious again. "Good," he said. "I hope that's a fact."

"I am not in the habit of lying."

"What if I tell you that every mile of railroad costs a thousand pounds in beer and spirits alone."

"I'd question your . . ." she began, and faltered.

"*My* veracity," he said, to spare her the embarrassment of finishing. "I wouldn't blame ye. It's an astonishing figure. Yet I've known lines where it would be an underestimate. Here's a case." He pointed at the tunnel. "There's seven hundred pound a week goes in wages on this contract. At least a third goes out again to the jerry shops and public houses." Arabella's incredulous stare encouraged him. "There's thirty pubs and eighteen jerry shops—to my knowledge—in Todmorden alone."

"Gracious! And we have taken a house there! I must tell Mr. Thornton at once."

He shook his head. "Ye'll not find a less drunken town, I promise. These places here"—he pointed at the succession of hamlets strung out up the valley—"they're far worse. Far and away. There's no quality to set an example." He looked at her sharply as he spoke these last words.

"How truly dreadful!" she said.

"If I was to take you along these workings and give you a guinea for every completely sober man we met, ye'd come out a pauper."

"Why don't you simply forbid it?"

He laughed at her naïvety. "After the . . . accident, I forbade gin and other spirits anywhere there's shotfiring. That near caused a riot. But if I forbade beer and cider, they'd walk off to some other contract."

"Then you must pay them less. It is quite patent they receive too much if they can spend a third of it in liquor."

He merely shook his head at that. "No answer," he said.

She looked across the cutting, near to where an aqueduct carried a stream above the line. "Why, there are two over there in a dead stupor," she said.

He followed her gaze and frowned. Then his brow cleared. "Oh, no. That's something else entirely," he told her. "Ye were asking where we get our navvies—and I said we make em." He nodded at the two ragged, supine figures. "There's two in the making. Come and see."

"You are certain they are not intoxicated?" she asked; but she was already following. They walked over the thin earth vault of Deanroyd tunnel to the eastern bank of the cutting.

When they were closer, and she could see the pitiable condition of the two men, her heart softened.

"On yer feet, lads," Stevenson shouted, firmly rather than harshly.

"Oh—poor fellows! Please don't get up!"

They paid no attention to her, but got up as Stevenson had ordered. "There," he said. "Not as much fat on them as would grease a gimlet!"

"They seem at death's door," she said, staring at them in horrified fascination. Their clothing was ragged enough to border on the indecent.

"They'll not die," Stevenson said confidently. "Will ye, lads?"

"No, sir," they said together.

"No, sir," he echoed and then turned to the taller, a young labourer with few teeth, mostly rotten. "Well, Darbishire—still set on navvying?"

"Yessir!" he said anxiously.

"And you, Walsh?" Stevenson turned to the other.

"Aye, sir." He blinked continuously; one eye was almost crusted over with malignant skin.

"And when ye draw down yer first wage, what'll be the first thing ye buy with it?"

"Steel shovels, sir," Walsh said, looking ruefully at his own poor wooden shovel, still lying in the grass.

"And steel-shod boots," Darbishire added.

Stevenson nodded approval and turned to Arabella. "Look at this, ma'am." He bent and picked up Walsh's shovel, handling it with contemptuous care. "They come off their farms with these . . . *toys,* and their soft boots. Lift up yer feet, Darbishire. Show the lady." Darbishire obliged; his feet were shod in soft, torn, almost shapeless patches of leather. "See? And they hope to match the steel of men like Yorky Slen there. Drunk or sober it'd take eight of these starvelings to meet him." He looked sadly at them; they smiled hopefully back. "Back to work!" he ordered.

They obeyed without demur.

"Oh, but they can't," Arabella protested. "They're shivering with fatigue."

"Ye may consider me hard, ma'am. But 'tis the navvy's catechism. They'll work till they drop. And tomorrow. And the next day. And the next. And so on—every day for a week. And if after that they *still* want to navvy, they'll be taken into the brotherhood. It's *spirit* makes a navvy. Long before he builds the muscle to support it."

"How dreadful!" she said, her eyes still fixed on the bent, exhausted shapes of the two labourers.

Stevenson raked his gaze over the hills around. "Blame the farmers who paid them starvation wages—and the parish unions that drove them on and out."

She bit her lip. "Oh dear," she said. "One does not think. One just does not think. I heard my own father lately praise our parish beadle for sending so many mendicants on and saving the poor rate."

"For saving coin," he said and, pointing at the two scarecrows, now going on all fours down the bank, added: "Well—here's the other side of that same coin. Tarnished, as ye see, to some depth."

She nodded in sad agreement.

"Yet," he said, brightening, "here is where they earn back their self-respect. So, if ye've any pity, save it for those who never reach us. Come next Easter and ye'll not recognize those two starvelings. And they'll crack the heads of any dozen parish beadles. And none but another navvy'll restrain them!"

"You're proud of them!" she said in surprise; and immediately she wondered why he should not be. She hastened to explain: "For us, the navvy is a creature of—"

He interrupted. "I am one of them, ma'am. I've endured that same terrible baptism. Believe me, I know how muscles feel when tortured beyond their natural stretch, the stupidity that builds out of habitual starvation, the despair that's fed on rotten victuals . . ." He vanished into a private reverie; she dared not break the silence between them. When he returned he looked momentarily lost. "Aye—I'm one of them," he repeated. "And to me they're the salt of the earth. And if there's wealth to come from their weal, I'll see they have their share."

His materialism shocked her, moving though his sentiments were. "Wealth without the light and love of God," she said, "is as dust and ashes. Besides—what if they just drink more heavily?"

He took no offence. "I'm glad we've come back to that," he said. "The drink is a problem—"

But further words were cut short by her sudden cry of pain. In the rough grass of the bank she had turned her ankle. She all but fainted, the hurt was so intense.

"Your ankle?" he asked, grasping her elbow.

She nodded and bit her lip; his firm grip calmed her. A light sweat started on her brow.

"Can you hop, if I hold your elbow?"

She tried. "Yes."

"Then try and make it to the top of the bank. There's cold running water there. Get your foot in that."

She did as he suggested and found it quite easy. The lift he gave her to boost each hop was like flying. The stream ran only a few yards away from the top of the cutting and she was soon sitting on its bank. Gingerly, she eased off her shoe and then realized she would get her stocking wet. "My stocking!" she said.

"Get cold," he ordered. "Every moment's delay makes it worse."

The throbbing pain was, indeed, getting worse. Reluctantly she obeyed.

"I'll send for Mr. Thornton," he said but made no actual move to do so.

The cold water brought an immense relief. Soon she could jog her foot up and down without provoking extra pain.

"Does that hurt?" he asked.

She shook her head, and held out a hand for him to help her up.

"I'd better have a look at it," he said when her foot was clear of the water.

She looked around to see if this was just another piece of his tasteless humour and realized with horror that all this time they had been—and were still—out of view of the workings and, in fact, of any nearby house. Her mounting panic was not helped by the realization that he was perfectly serious in his intention. "No!" she said. "Oh, please!"

He let his arm fall, so that she sat involuntarily. "Be still!" he said. "I've tended more sprains and fractures than you've had vapours."

"Fractures!" she cried out in even greater alarm. "Oh—please send for Mr. Thornton. Oh, Mr. Stevenson! Please no! Oh, who can see us?"

But he already had her foot in his strong, competent hands. "Does that"—he flexed it—"hurt more than that?" He pointed her toes inward.

"Ouch!"

"We're out of sight, so calm your fears. Can you move your toes?"

Dumbly, beginning to feel just a little ashamed of the fuss she was making, she obeyed.

"Hurt?" He watched her face.

She shook her head. He was very like a doctor in his manner. Very distant.

"Good. Now make as if to clench your foot." Still he kept his eyes on her face, though he held her foot firmly in his hand. "Excellent," he said. "And what if I stretch it . . . so?" He pulled gently on her heel until he saw her wince. "Sorry." He let the foot return to its natural position. "Well, ma'am, nothing broken. Just a strain on that side. The ligament, you see"—still his eyes fixed hers—"runs from there all the way . . . up . . ."

"Mr. Stevenson!" She broke the spell when his caress reached beyond her calf. "I'll thank you to confine your anatomy lesson to . . . in fact, to conclude it entirely."

Later he regretted having taken such a liberty. But she was such a green little saint that only another green little saint could have resisted the chance to tease her.

All injured innocence, he froze—conveniently leaving his hand where it was. Beneath her anger, which was only superficial, she felt a calm contempt: the superhuman Mr. Stevenson was very human after all—as human as the elderly men she and her mother used to take scraps to in the parish. They used to stroke her situpon whenever they got the chance. He was as human and as harmless as they. "You poor old gentleman!" she said.

She was instantly rewarded to see him blush; no other words of hers could have reduced and humbled him so swiftly. He snatched his hand away and stood awkwardly, looking down at her, and measuring her with a new respect in his eyes. Or so she thought—but he spoiled it by breaking just as suddenly into a shameless grin.

"I see nothing to smirk at!" she said.

He walked away a pace or two to retrieve her shoe. When he bent to put it on her she snatched it from him and pulled it on by herself.

He went to the top of the bank. "Yorky Slen! Bacca! Look brisk, lads!" he called.

She stood unaided, tested the ankle, and winced. Her being shrank at the thought of asking his help.

"A bloom off a pruned bush is seldom missed," he said, as if to the air.

Fortunately for both of them she did not grasp his meaning—then or later.

"Aye?" Yorky's voice came up from below, out of sight to her.

Stevenson jerked his head in her direction. "Mrs. Thornton's hurt her ankle. Fetch the litter and bring my—"

"The what?" Yorky interrupted.

"Dead man's phaeton," Stevenson translated. "And bring me cloak from the linesman's hut."

She heard them run off.

"And send one of them others for the gaffer. Gaffer Thornton."

"Aye!" Yorky Slen's voice drifted back from a fair distance off.

For a while they stood in silence, Stevenson looking up the line, Arabella trying to make it appear that she stood still by choice and could easily walk away if it became expedient. Then she realized that this would be a good moment to disabuse this man of any ideas he may have developed. "Mr. Stevenson," she said, "I do not know the class of person you are accustomed to mingle with. But I wish you to understand that I neither welcome nor enjoy such advances. As you are so close a—an associate of my husband's, we cannot avoid occasionally meeting in such a small place as this, but I . . ." She began to falter; how she wished he would not stare so! "I would be obliged . . ." His eyes! Really it was most disconcerting—just when she wanted *him* to feel uncomfortable. "I must ask you not to stare so. . . . Please!"

But he was not laughing. There was no mirth in his eyes, no sardonic twist at the corners of his mouth. "I owe you an apology." He spoke clearly and with every appearance of deep conviction. "A very sincere, very humble apology."

This was almost worse than his insolence. "Well," she said, firm again. "Let's say no more."

"I took you for a . . ." He looked away. "Well—no matter." Then he turned suddenly back to her and said with great urgency: "There's a power in you that's . . . waiting. Held in check as yet. God help whatever you choose to unleash it on."

His intensity was very disturbing. "Whatever meagre power I have," she said, "I intend to 'unleash' it, as you put it, on my husband, my home, and any family the Lord may see fit to bless us with."

"It's too great for that," he said with the same intensity.

"What *did* you take me for?" she asked, to change this embarrassing topic.

At last he smiled. "One of these modern young misses, whose empty-headed prudery is as easily turned as a pair of Liverpool sheets," he said. "I was wrong."

He spoke so engagingly that she laughed aloud. He was quick to join her. And for some odd reason all her animosity vanished and she found herself liking him more than at any time since they had met.

"Mr. Thornton says you do not command your men so much as lead them," she told him. "And it is quite true. Having watched you, I believe you could lead them to anything."

He, too, was glad to change the subject and he came down, eager to help her to the top of the bank. When they were in view of the world again she felt greatly relieved. "Aye," he said. "So I could. Would ye know the secret?"

"What?"

"It's so easy a dame-school zany could learn it."

"Ah—there's Mr. Thornton," she cried as Walter came hurrying from the tunnel. "Do tell me." She turned back to Stevenson.

"Care," he answered. "Fellow feeling."

"Oh? In what way?"

Yorky Slen and Bacca emerged, hard on Thornton's heels, bearing the litter between them. "For example," he said, "if any man here is maimed past working, there's a pension for him from me. Or for his wife and children if he's dead. And there's no other navvy working now in England can say as much."

She warmed to him even more. He really was a very *good* man underneath it all. "You may be sure," she told him, "that, whatever it may cost you, your charity is building a far greater store of treasure in heaven—"

But the word seemed to have stung him. "Charity!" he said. "There's no charity in it, ma'am. It's a regular insurance through Lloyd's of London. Fourpence per man per week. I stop it off their wage. I'm no buttermilk-hearted philanthropist."

"Oh," she said. The way he put it made the arrangement sound even more virtuous.

Walter was close enough to call out now. "Arabella!"

"Slow down!" she called. "All's well!"

But he scrambled up toward them without slackening his pace. "Oh, my darling!" he was saying. "Oh, my dear. I should not have left you!" It was almost as if he wanted her hurt.

"A sprained ankle; that is all, dear. It was greatly painful but fortunately it was soon past." She smiled to reassure him that it really was so.

He pulled out his handkerchief and mopped his brow. "Are you sure? How do you know it is not broken?"

"I took the liberty of examining it." Stevenson said, with the greatest casualness, as he took two steps down the bank to help with the litter, which Bacca and Yorky Slen brought at that minute. "Good lads," he said to them.

Arabella saw the handkerchief pause for a fraction of a second as Walter took in Stevenson's words. She could have kicked the man for blurting it out like that, bad ankle or no.

"Oh . . ." Walter said uncertainly.

"Aye," Stevenson went on, still as unconcerned as before. "A strain. No more . . ."

He arranged the litter where she could stretch herself out upon it. "Put a cold compress on it when ye get home and keep all weight off it for a day or two and it'll carry you to church this Sunday."

At that Walter smiled—to Arabella's relief. He bent to help her down onto the litter.

"I see you've had quite some conversation with my wife," he said, taking up Stevenson's cloak and laying it to cover her feet from view.

"Yes," she said. "We had quite some conversation. Shall we see *you* at church on Sunday, Mr. Stevenson?"

Yorky Slen and Bacca bent to lift her.

"No!" she called out. "They're too drunk. I don't trust them."

The two navvies laughed and would have lifted her if Stevenson had not told them to get back to work. "This'll reckon as two runnings for bonus," he called after them. They slapped each other on the back and danced up the track to their horse and barrow.

Walter took the front, Stevenson the back.

"Shall we?" she repeated. "Church?"

He smiled tolerantly. "Mrs. Stevenson and I have the rent of a pew at Paul Row Wesleyan Providence. I hope you may find the sermons of the Right Honourable and Reverend Mouncey to your taste."

He winked again but this time she looked coldly away. She did not ask him to elaborate his comment on the vicar of Todmorden.


# *Chapter 19*

By the time they reached Pigs Hill, the pain in her ankle had receded to a dull ache and the swelling was completely subsided. How wise Stevenson had been to get it into cold water so quickly. She found that if she walked on her heel and put as little weight as possible on the ball of her foot, there was no discomfort at all—except at the resulting inelegance of her walk.

The house on Pigs Hill was a triumph of ingenuity rather than of elegance. Even so, its first impression was much grander than Arabella had dared to hope. It had a gabled porch crowned by a little wooden spire, and this, coupled with the mansarded gable over the master bedroom, justified its name of *Two Gables.* Inside, too, it was furnished and appointed on a scale far better than she had anticipated. The three servants, kitchen maid, housemaid, and living-out cook, warned by the advance arrival of the baggage, had hastily spruced and dusted and polished every visible object, knickknack, and surface, and now stood at the hall door in nervous welcome; for, although Walter had engaged them, he had made it clear that their appointment depended on Mrs. Thornton's approval.

"Mrs. Bates, madam."

"Sweeney, mum."

"Horsfall, mum."

They curtseyed in order of their rank. Arabella smiled at each and looked approvingly at their neat dress and the spotless hall. "Mrs. Bates," she said, "as you no doubt have the supper to prepare, I shall speak with you first."

"I have tea all ready to brew for you, madam."

Arabella looked at Walter.

"It would suit me," he said. "I can read our mail."

"Very well. I shall have a quick look over the house and then we shall take tea in the drawing room in ten minutes." She took a little notebook from her pocketbook and went upstairs with Sweeney.

They began in the maids' rooms, on the third floor—two small, plainly furnished rooms squeezed in below the mansard roof at the back, where they would catch the first of the morning sun. She looked at the sheets and found the little scullery girl Horsfall's grey with grime.

"How often does she bath?" she asked Sweeney.

"*Bath,* mum?"

"She's to bath every morning, winter and summer. As is everybody in this house."

The maid breathed deeply but said nothing.

Opposite was a large box room whose floor lay at the bend of the mansard, so that it was not so much low-ceilinged as high-floored. It lay empty except for their own luggage. She counted. "There's a wooden box to come."

"That would be the linen, mum?"

"Yes." Arabella smiled at her. "I expect you thought the linen cupboard looked empty."

"I hope it's soon, mum. Else we'll be trying to wash, dry, press, and air within the one day."

They went down to the second floor. "I think we must carpet these stairs, at least up to your landing," she said as she made a note in her little book.

On this floor was an empty, bare-boarded room at the back, an earth closet, a linen cupboard, the master bedroom—below the gable end—and two other rooms furnished as bedrooms. Now she understood why the box room had been so pinched, for the ceiling of the master bedroom was lifted up into the space that the mansard created. She cried out in delight when she saw it, for the effect was very elegant; the walls rose to a normal ceiling height of about ten feet and then sloped inward on all four sides making a total height of fourteen feet. Two oval fastlights were let into the longer outside face and the whole sloping part was decorated with plasterwork mouldings and swags. On the inner face, corresponding to the windows, were cartouches representing Peace and Plenty. Of the decorations on the shorter walls she was less certain; they demanded much closer inspection. Their titles were, respectively, "Sacred Love" and "Profane Love."

"Why is there no water in the pitcher?" she asked.

"I bring it up hot when you and master retire, mum."

"Hot?"

"Yes, mum. The new range they've put in has a side boiler with a brass tap. There's hot water a-plenty all day."

For a moment Arabella felt herself tempted. The luxury of washing in hot water twice a day! But she soon rejected the idea. Hot water was so enervating. "We shall wash and bath in cold," she said. "And you'd better let it stand all day so the sediments may settle."

The maid smiled. "We've no sediments, mum. It's crystal clear, fresh from Watty Spring every morn."

"Good. That's understood then. You and Horsfall will bath at quarter to six, when you rise. Then you'll scour out the bath and bring it to our bedroom at seven. The master will have his hot shaving water at a quarter past and we shall breakfast at half past."

"Very well, mum."

The ground floor had a drawing room and parlour at the front and a dining room at the side. The kitchen, in the fourth corner, was down three steps. "I'll see that when I instruct Mrs. Bates," Arabella said. "Then I shall go through all your duties with you."

The other rooms struck her as being rather too *plainly* furnished. They lacked pictures, and plants, and other kinds of ornament. Of course, she told herself, it was only natural. One couldn't expect a furnished house to come complete with one's personal ornaments.

"We must start filling these shelves, Sweeney, or you'll die of boredom!"

Sweeney smiled wanly.

"In fact," Arabella continued, as if she were thinking aloud, "it is hard to understand why a house this small, and with only two people to serve, needs three servants." She saw the alarm she hoped for in Sweeney's eyes. "Can you sew?" she asked quickly.

"Yes indeed, mum," the girl assured her.

"Good."

At tea she read a letter from her father. It so delighted her that she almost read it aloud to Walter at once. The gist of it was that conjugal relations were permissible if there was a clear intention to beget children. If only someone, her mother or someone, had told her before! What miseries she and Walter would have been spared. And poor Walter! He had been right—or partly right—whereas she had been wholly wrong. She had a lot to make up to him. Well, so she would! Tonight. They could go to bed straight after supper. She stole a glance at him. The powerful lust that she had feared washed through her, unrestrained—now that it was no longer lust. She would read out her father's letter for Walter to hear just before . . . just before they started. It would be like a licence.

She saw Mrs. Bates and little Horsfall together and went through their duties minutely. Horsfall was to rise at quarter to six, bath (that was a shock, she could see), and come down to light the open range. This was a splendid new monster of iron and brass, completely fitted out with an oven, side boiler, sliding cheek, revolving shelves, wrought-iron bars, and a warming cupboard. Then she was to clean the hearth, fill the boiler and kettle, and go to the spring to draw fresh water. Then there were the kitchen and larder to sweep, the hall to clean, the front steps and kitchen steps to scrub, and the oil lamps to prepare. Then she and Sweeney could take their breakfast, which would be porridge, one slice of bread and dripping, and allowable scraps from the previous day.

Mrs. Bates would have arrived at quarter to seven and would at once make the breakfast rolls and then cook the rest of the breakfast, to be ready at seven thirty. She would serve the breakfast herself and answer the bells and single knocks until luncheon. When the breakfast bell rang, Sweeney would go up to empty the bath and begin the upstairs work. Until then she would prepare the breakfast room, light the fire—in winter, of course— sweep the hearth, and do the other tasks that Arabella had already described.

After breakfast, when the master had left, they would all assemble in the parlour and she would lead them in a brief prayer before they began (and she used the word without irony) their daily round. Their main prayers for the day would be said before evening dinner, when the master returned. The night, she reminded them, was a time of temptation; it was then that they most needed spiritual cheer. During the day, they had their tasks to keep them from devilment. After her full catechism of their chores, from larkrise to owlhoot, every hour filled as meticulously as the first, none could doubt it. And none could doubt who was—and intended to remain—the mistress of the household.

And in case they did, a little incident occurred to resolve the matter. When Arabella was leaving the kitchen, the butcher's boy called with some meat. She made him unfold it upon the table and show it.

"Is this satisfactory to *you*, Mrs. Bates?" Arabella asked.

The older woman looked at her, at the meat, and at the boy in bewilderment. "I think so, mum. Loin of pork and shin of beef. It's what's ordered."

The boy nodded to confirm it.

"Then I tell you, this will not do for *me*. Look—the shin is bruised here along the bone. And this pipe, running through the loin here, should be removed before the joint is hung." She sniffed close to it. "You see. It is already putrid and the rest is barely hung. Who is your master, boy?"

"Me dad, mum."

"And does 'me dad' have a name?"

"Roberts, mum."

"Well, young master Roberts, you're to take these back and get your father to cut the pipe from the loin and supply some unbruised shin. Is his the shop on the corner, by the livery stables?"

"Yes, mum."

"Then half an hour should suffice. If he wishes to retain the custom of this house, you're to return within half an hour."

The boy picked up the meat and ran; the servants laughed as they heard his handcart go rolling off down the hill.

"He's not run that fast since the bull got out from Carr Laithe!" Mrs. Bates said.

But Arabella was not laughing. "Go and fill that coal scuttle, Horsfall," she said. And while the girl was gone, she told the cook that she herself would keep the pantry key and do all the purchasing.

"After all," she said, smiling to sweeten the news, "a mistress must have her tasks and duties, too!"

But Mrs. Bates was not pleased; there was a percentage on dealings with tradesfolk, and money to be made from dripping, candle ends, and so on. Still, at twelve pounds a year, plus five pounds for living out, the job was the best any woman in her row could claim. And she appreciated the way the mistress had sent the girl out before she broke the ill tidings. One couldn't have everything one wanted.

Horsfall looked very worried on her return. "I'll never remember it all, mum," she sighed. "I just know that."

"Then you must look to Mrs. Bates. She is your immediate mistress. You must attend to all her needs. And if you are nimble and diligent, and finish your own work quickly, why I expect it won't be long before Mrs. Bates trusts you with some little cooking tasks and tells you a secret or two. And in that way you may in time rise to a post in another house where you will be as important as Mrs. Bates is here. Then your eight pounds a year, which I'm sure seems very handsome now, will seem very little."

The child grinned at such an impossible thought. And Arabella was glad at the self-satisfaction that glowed on the face of the cook. Her whole intention, after breaking the bad news to Mrs. Bates, was to build her up again. A disgruntled cook was worse than an empty kitchen.

"Eee!" the child said when Arabella had left. "She's hard, she is!"

"Hold thy tongue and be thankful for a firm lady with a Christian soul. There's dozens of places thou'd do worser than here," the cook told her.

Sweeney waylaid Arabella in the hall. "If ye please, mum, and what about followers?"

Here Arabella had her grandmother to thank. Among her own generation it was the growing custom to forbid followers absolutely and on principle. But her grandmother had warned: "If ye do that, they have followers anyway, because it's against Nature not to and ye've lost all control, and ye send them off to clandestine assignations, and ye reward their habit of deception. For the better they deceive ye, the more pleased ye are with their seeming obedience."

And so, in her grandmother's words, she said to Sweeney, "You may have followers if they call by invitation, if you first introduce them to the master and me, and if they neither smoke nor drink spirituous liquor while on the premises."

Sweeney, when she joined the others in the kitchen, said they surely had a pearl of a mistress. And they all set about working their one-month-on-approval with a will.

The new master and mistress retired shortly after dinner. Arabella washed behind the screen and came out in her chemise, ready for bed. Walter, who had been waiting for this moment, now pointed to the plaster decorations on the themes of Love.

"What do you think . . ." He paused. ". . . Or, as Stevenson would put it: What do you 'say to' them?"

She looked first at the Sacred, then at Profane. "Hail . . . and Farewell?" she suggested. It was a little too sharp for Walter and his face darkened.

She giggled.

"You are somewhat skittish tonight," he said.

"I have every reason for it," she answered. "And *you* should be pleased."

"Oh, *I* should?" He took up her mood.

"Yes. You remember I told you guidance was at hand in this business of . . ." and she flapped her hand from the one decoration to the other.

"Of hallo and goodbye?"

"Well, see!" She poked her fingers in at the top of her chemise and pulled out her father's letter. "A letter from dear Papa—in which he sets everything straight."

"Does he now!" Walter was instantly wary. "Well—he *is* something of an expert, you might say. I shall be interested to see how he . . . er . . . contrives to distill his . . . er . . . experience, for your eyes and ears."

She held the letter for him to take.

"No, no!" He went to the washstand and took off his shirt. "You read it to me."

" 'My dear child,' " she read. " 'The matters you raise are of vast moment in the lives of people. Yet, to our shame, they have been so little written of or talked of by the pure and reverent that we have abandoned them to the impure and vile—amongst whom exaggeration and misinformation rule unchecked.' " She paused. "No—that wasn't the part. . . ." Her eyes rapidly scanned the lines. "Ah! Here: 'There is a wise eastern proverb: To satisfy the appetite is not always good. Man alone can say: *I shall fast.* Appetite thus conquered maketh man king over the beasts. Every . . . ' this is Papa writing again now . . . 'Every young person should be taught before marriage—as your mother, I believe, should have taught you—that the closest conjugal relations should never be allowed without a willingness in both partners that parenthood should follow.' "

She wondered how much Walter had heard, he was washing himself so loudly. He said, with the faintest edge of sarcasm, "Oh! He does allow it *then!*"

"Yes!" she laughed. "You see! You were right! What a goose I have been—and what pleasure we may take now!"

He was not as pleased as she had expected. "Is there no more?" he asked.

"Oh, yes! He is so wise. You will see. He says: 'In this there should be

*no* pandering to or indulgence of the lower nature while there is an unwill-
ingness to bear as many children as a proper, manly' . . . I think he
might have added 'womanly,' " she complained.

"No doubt he wrote to encourage *himself,*" Walter said and chuckled
—as if it had been a funny remark.

" ' . . . as many children as a proper, manly, Christian temperance
will allow. There is a higher plane of loving than the animal plane.' Shall I
go on?"

"By all means! If we can procure enough of his lines and his planes, we
may be able to construct a whole *geometry* of love."

She knew something was going very wrong. He was not taking it at all
as she had hoped and expected. Still, she now had no other course but to
read the letter through: " 'There is a higher plane of loving than the
animal plane. And nowhere in life is self-control so needed as here. For
where the lower nature is indulged at the expense of the higher, the *man* is
dwarfed to the precise degree that the *animal* is gorged and swells.' "

She looked up at his expressionless face before she read on. " 'I have
known many couples, here in my own parish, in whom failure to obey
these simple precepts has led to the most piteous ruin. At the start, over-
indulgence may lead to no more than simple irritability, backache, headache, nervousness, and lassitude. In every case, I weep to tell you, it has
ended by encompassing their total moral and physical ruin.' "

Walter sat at the foot of her bed, staring with a disconcerting intensity
into her face. "Such a pity he does not name them," he said. "One could
judge for oneself then."

"Oh, but he explains it," she hastened on, increasingly desperate to
convince him. " 'The man expends a vast quantity of vital force—enough,
after all, to sustain a child through nine long months of gestation. When
this force is wasted in the simple gratification of the flesh, its loss can only
weaken and deprave him who loses it. But when it is conserved, as Christian control demands, it adds so much and more to the mental and moral
force of a man, because it raises him up to a higher plane of being.' "

Still he fixed her with that steady stare. She raised her eyebrows.
"Please continue," he said.

With heavy heart she read on. " 'The happiest married people are those
who live in strictest continence, and who call the lower being into existence
only for the begetting of children. With one joyful voice they assert that
they thereby enjoy not only better health and greater strength—but supreme happiness also.' " She refolded the letter and looked at him. "Oh,
Walter! Is that not *beautiful?* What a noble ideal we now have set before
us!"

It had been a failure. Her father's thoughts, which had so inspired her
and filled her with such hope for their future, had somehow left unsaid
those words that might work a similar miracle in Walter. He looked at her
so . . . emptily.

"Walter?" She hesitated.

"Your father wrote that?"

"Yes."

"Your father."

"Why?" she asked. "It is very much in his style."

He smiled wearily, as if she had made an unintentional joke.

"In fact . . ." She opened the letter again. "There's a postscript for
you. I thought the part I read was so inspiring you would not need it . . .
but . . ." She read again: " 'To Walter I say: a strong lower nature is
not a curse but a blessing. God made no mistake in making man what he is;
but He never intended the lower nature to rule the higher. The struggle is
worth it at all costs.' He's underlined that three times. 'The struggle is
worth it at all costs, and the man who gains mastery grows only *more*
manly and more noble. But if lust be given the sway, the man becomes
increasingly beastly. Take heart: If you gain and keep the mastery, your
struggle will not be endless. When, in middle life, the reproductive urge
begins to hush, you will find a growing peacefulness and manly poise
which will be marked by increasing intellectual and moral strength.
Acquisitions and achievements will then be possible that were quite *im*possible in your earlier days.' "

With a trembling heart she looked up to see how he responded; surely
he could not now remain so churlish. He must respond to so fair a vision
and so eloquent a promise.

"You see, dear!" she prompted.

He looked, unseeing, at her, at the bed, at the wall. "Hip hip hip
huzza!" he said tonelessly.

"Walter?"

"We may take delight in each other now?" he asked.

"Yes! Oh yes!" She put all the invitation she could manage into the
words.

Walter picked up the letter. "This . . . permits it."

"Yes." She was less certain now.

"And when we are assured that a child is on its way?"

"Then we . . . oh, let me read it to you again."

He pulled the letter beyond her reach. "In your own words."

"Then we live in the greater joy of God's sublime ordinance. In Christian continence. Gaining daily in the power and achievements of our higher natures."

He looked at her most strangely, half sad, half sardonic. "Then we have not a moment to lose." He smiled, grinned, bared his teeth; his eyes flashed.

Relief surged through her—and lust. He was such a tease! And he was so . . . desirable. She wriggled her toes, trembling with the hungers she had repressed. And, then, before she could stop herself, she pulled off her chemise and sat watching him hasten out of his own clothing. She burned with embarrassment at her impulsiveness but kept saying to herself, again and again, that it was all right now. Intellectual knowledge fought with a lifetime of implanted modesty.

Perhaps that was what threw a pall over them that night and damped, in her, the fires that had cracked and rejoiced so merrily in anticipation. Perhaps it was that they had not snuffed the candle—with the result that Walter did not turn into the dark, fluid, powerful phantasm of her ecstasy, but remained everyday-sized, sweating Walter, with the blue shadow ready for shaving off his jowls and the white spittle at the corners of his lips. And the light revealed, too, an unexpected aloofness in his eyes. And she, because no deep emotion had transported her away, watched him . . . how could one characterize it? . . . *sample* her. This way and that, he used her as if she were a component, or a piece of equipment, or a fruit to be wormed from an awkward shell. He made no *partner* of her in his own heedless delirium. To be sure, she still enjoyed it. It was pleasant—like eating a little delicacy, or washing dirt away, or coming in out of the cold. But that great, overpowering, sensual alchemy was missing. Some ingredient had vanished from the mixture.

Walter, too, was not the way he had been at Earlestown. When he had finished his convulsions, he withdrew from her, blew out the light, and lay upon his back, breathing regularly, for a long time. She knew he was not sleeping though.

"You will be replying to your father?" he said at last.

"Yes," she said, startled.

"Then let me suggest the general lines of what you will write."

She did not at once reply.

"Well?" he said.

"Would . . . would you like to dictate it? I will take it down word for word. I'm sure it would please dear Papa to—"

"No, no." He cut her short. "Your turn of phrase in these things is so much more felicitous."

"Very well, dear." He did not make it sound complimentary.

"You will of course begin by thanking him for the trouble he has taken to answer your questions so fully. Say that I at least can imagine the effort it must have cost to divert his mind from its everyday paths on to the unaccustomed—not to say alien—byways opened up by your inquiry."

"Yes indeed!"

He let the echoes of her enthusiasm die before he continued, speaking in those same flat tones. "Yes indeed. Then you will say that one of the glories of the Church of England is that her clergy do not—like the papists—pursue their better class of parishioners into their homes and rant at them with homilies and tracts."

The true drift of his words reached her through his level delivery. "Oh, Walter! . . ." she began.

"You will further add that a daughter who marries must no longer look to her parents for instruction and must, moreover, strive ceaselessly to remember her vow—her freely given vow—of obedience to her husband."

Wounded tears filled her eyes and fell from her cheeks. In all their long courtship she had never seen him cold and indifferent to her. Angry, disappointed, disapproving, chiding . . . yes, he had, though rarely, been all of these. But never so cool. It frightened her.

But his voice went on, in the same distant vein that seemed so menacing. "Add that it is henceforth he, the captain of her soul, who must sustain her from weakness to strength, guide her from ignorance into the light, and—should the painful need arise—*chastise* her from disaffection into submission. And your Walter, you may truthfully say, is not the man to shrink from any such duty, however personally repugnant."

She wept now uncontrollably.

Still he did not stop: "And in conclusion, Mrs. Thornton, you may tell him that it is no fault of yours or mine that you now face the necessity both to write these truths in your letter and apply them in your life. And that is one letter I'd be obliged ye'd show me before ye send it."

He turned over and, at once, composed himself to sleep.

She wept on as silently as she could. She was never one for uncontrolled abandonment to any of her senses. And it was not long before thought began to reassert itself, at first in random notions that strayed in and out of her misery, then in longer packages of reason. It occurred to her that Walter did not extemporize that reply to her father; he had composed it earlier. And the only time available had been between the reading of the letter and his time of convulsion. All the time he had been . . . doing that to her—no, not *to* her, *upon* her—all that time, he had been stringing together his sneering, insulting reply to her father's wonderful letter. He had not loved her; he had violated her love.

When she turned on her side, she felt the sticky slime he had voided into her and her soul was nauseated.

The Arabella who finally went to sleep was no longer tearful; she was calm and determined. No matter how terrible the struggle, no matter what the cost in all those shallow and trivial expressions of tenderness and affection between them, she would steer her husband from his viciousness and bring him to her way, to God's way. The thought filled her with a righteous joy far more sustaining and enriching than the meretricious passions her lower nature had served up. The light of God's purpose now shone so clear on the path ahead that she would never again stumble, never more stray.

*       *       *

Walter was pleased to see her so radiant when they rose on the following day. The quiet intensity of her weeping had filled him with doubt and he had lain long awake, wondering whether or not to make more gentle love to her. He wanted to show that playing the stern, biblical patriarch was not a role he relished. He pictured in imagination the wonder of that orgy of reconciliation; but by the time he made the first move she was soundly sleeping.

That morning, reading *The Vicar of Wakefield,* Arabella came across a passage so remarkably apt that she copied it, word for word into her journal:

The modest virgin, the prudent wife, and the careful matron, are much more serviceable in life than petticoated philosophers, blustering heroines, or virago queens. She who makes her husband and her children happy, who reclaims the one from vice and trains the others up to virtue, is a much greater character than ladies described in romances, whose sole occupation is to murder mankind with shafts from their quiver, or their eyes.

She underlined the words *who reclaims the one from vice.* And she added: "What directed my eyes to this passage? Surely these are the ways God chooses to speak to those with ears to hear, and eyes to behold."

Increasingly in the days that followed, Walter was impelled to wonder where her fire had gone. He tried everything in his limited, juvenile repertoire to bring back the glory that had come against her will at Earlestown and Blackpool. He even tried some of the things little Miss Sanders had shown him—only to earn Arabella's sharp rebuke. In bed she was merely sociable. Their almost nightly exercises were like agreeable diversions—

like a picnic, or some amusing conversation between their bodies. Increasingly he thought of that time in the graveyard with Nora. He began to fear the obsessional, mocking return of that memory. Once or twice he wept uncomprehendingly at the sense of loss that now pervaded the marriage of which he had once held such great, impossible hopes.

Naturally it was not long before these little bagatelles to fill the minutes between waking and sleeping became something less than nightly. It was not long before Walter, to Arabella's proud approbation, began to think of his duties in the world at large—meetings of Manchester engineers and Manchester societies dedicated to the advancement of science, visits to consult works of reference available only in Manchester, trips to the Manchester & Leeds headquarters, and so on. And it was not long before she noticed how these visits greatly diminished the impulses of his lower nature. Often when he returned, he would go three or more days without lurching across the bed and satisfying himself upon her; and sometimes another cause for visiting Manchester would intervene, and the interval before his next assault was even longer.

It proved how right her father had been. The activities that so engaged dear Walter in Manchester were all of an improving nature and all belonged to the higher being. To the degree the higher being was thus nurtured, the lower withered and died.

By the time winter fell she was able to record great progress in her journal. "I look back," she wrote, "on these first months of my marriage—and what a journey I have come! The ignorant, credulous child has endured the most searing temptations of the flesh and has emerged, I devoutly hope, a mature and Christian woman. Last night Walter did another of his convulsions on me, which, fortunately, are increasingly rare. This time I can truly say I felt but the faintest and most distant twinge of pleasure—no more than would be occasioned by a casual scratching of one's scalp. My passage has become no greater source of delight than my toenails—and this by the devout and assiduous application of Christian principles. How I wish it were none of it necessary! If only we could propagate as modestly and chastely as trees!! And as effectively—O Lord, quicken me soon!!!

"Now I gather strength to inspire Walter to similar heights of Christian achievement. Poor dear man! I know it will be harder for him than for me. And I must try not to feel superior. I must remember that God has made us the weaker vessels and so given us less to conquer. But men He has endowed with such aggression and such a fierce animal nature—and, to be sure, with the greater strength and intellect to overcome it. So I know Walter's nobility will, at last, be even greater, because he will have triumphed over so much more than I.

"Be patient and loving, o heart! Shine as a beacon to him, o soul! And let us prove to all the world that perfect marriages are not made in a bed, nor in the passionate congress of our vile bodies, but—oh, most true and wonderful—in *Heaven!*"

By the end of November, her prayer was answered and her body was quickened—though it was April 1840 before that fact was confirmed to her. Then Walter was given added inducement to neglect his lower being—at least on her side of the bed.

# PART THREE

Chartists

# Chapter 20

The winning of the Summit contract had wrought subtle changes in John Stevenson. Aspects of his character whose very existence he had not once suspected were suddenly revealed to him; they had, as it were, lain dormant, waiting for this event to bring them into play. In the first place, to find himself suddenly respectable was more irksome than he had feared. And it was made worse by his determination to play the thing so straight that his word would be as good as a contract and a guarantee in one—the very opposite of what most understood by the word "contractor." He wanted to know that when people told one another "Stevenson has agreed" or "Stevenson promised it" they moved from the shadowy realm of uncertainty to a world of accomplished fact. But, as he was finding, it was one thing to specify the end and quite another to establish the means.

His attitude toward the men, his lads, had also changed. It showed in small ways. As ganger, working on a shift all day, he could see a navvy sweat his guts out and idle by turns, if that was the man's nature; if he did the day's measure, that was good enough. But as main contractor, paying out seven hundred pounds a week in wages alone, he would chafe in fury at the sight of an idle man, and often had to check himself and remember the reasonable accommodations he had once been able to make. He knew that many in that little army of his were only too ready to test the mettle of the new commander, so he was on the lookout for challenge, often where none was offered.

The change showed in big ways, too; and there it was less easily dismissed. For instance, he knew that to put navvies on bonus and leave the craftsmen on the old flat-piece rate was asking for trouble. In fact, when he first decided on the plan—that day he gained the contract—it did not enter his mind to exclude the trades. Yet in the first few days, after he had put the scheme to one enthusiastic navvy gang after another, he found it almost impossible to formulate a like arrangement for each of the trades. He would half-think one out for the masons when some potential problem with the blacksmiths would intrude, followed by a related difficulty with the bricklayers . . . and so on in a circle. And for all his obsessional toying with the principles and practicalities of a trades-bonus scheme, nothing of any definite shape would emerge.

Soon he could no longer blink the fact that something within him was blocking the thought. Something was unwilling to make any kind of solution. That something had an unpalatable thought of its own to suggest. For years afterward he wondered when that thought first gained his conscious recognition—though he never doubted its power and influence before it took such shape. Was it before or after he heard of the first rumblings of trouble among the craftsmen—especially the bricklayers? He never was able to remember.

But there was such a moment. And the thought, when it finally crept out into the light, ran further: If he could provoke a head-on collision with one of the trades, and if he could win in some overwhelming way, so that folk would talk of it far and wide, he'd never lack for contracts, he'd get closer to becoming independent of the Reverend Doctor Prendergast, he'd have no trouble with his labour for years ahead, and—a lesser consideration in the long view, but no less important when he had to conserve every penny he had—he'd save paying bonuses to craftsmen until he absolutely had to.

Small wonder he had hidden these arguments, even from himself, in that first generous flush of his triumph! And even when he did articulate them, he fought a long rearguard against their conclusion. And when, finally and reluctantly, he accepted them, he realized with a deep sadness the truth it revealed about himself: John Stevenson's great ideals might still stand, but they came a poor second to a much more commonplace ideal —the preservation and advancement of self.

Still, there it was. The sealed orders had been opened, the course set. It was no use sailing backward into battle and protesting later that one had been looking at other things. If you had to kill a pig, you didn't make the blow less cruel by bungling the job and weeping at the creature's anguish. So he buttoned his lip, kept his counsel, and prepared for the storm to come. And when the gangers and the clerk of works and Walter Thornton told him he really must harmonize the bonuses, he would sigh and scratch his head and look harassed and agree. They, for their part, would say to one another that John Stevenson was as good a man as ever at practical things—there was no workaday problem in the tunnel to which he did not have a ready answer—but he had a lot to learn about the trade of employer. That opinion would have won his grim agreement, for he was about to test his small learning in that field to its very limit.

For Nora, too, these were difficult days. Even before she married him she knew that a man so afire with ambition and so determined to compete was not the man to offer a life of obscure and petty struggle—which was the most for which she had ever dared to hope. She had had her dreams, naturally, but dreams were toys to make reality acceptable—and God help those who tried swelling them into hallucinations to banish the real world entirely. John Stevenson offered to abolish this division, and her hopes of obscure and petty struggle seemed suddenly tawdry. The change, to be precise, happened when her mind's eye ceased to dwell on servants in powdered wigs feeding pretty little deer in an infinite parkland, and instead settled on a kitchen with an indoor water pump.

Just as the contract had awoken in Stevenson aspects of his character that had long lain dormant, so his marriage to her, and the prospect of unscalable heights suddenly brought within grasp, revealed elements within her that were both novel and fascinating. The first thing that struck her was her inward *un*surprise at her change in fortune. It was the same with her love for John. In hindsight she knew that she had fallen under his spell the very moment they met, but it was not until he spoke of marriage that she had dared admit it to herself. Hopes were safe and comforting until you put them into words; then they gained an independence that threw them on the mercy of the world—and she'd had eighteen years of that brand of mercy. So that when she at last consciously acknowledged her love for him, there was a part of her, deep within, that had known it long before.

The acknowledgement of her good fortune, too, found that same cool acceptance; part of her had long known that she was worthy of it. Though she had lived a whole life in poverty, only in the last few months had she passed over into out-and-out destitution—the months before she landed the market job. Of her earlier times, when she lived with her father and family, she had only the happiest memories. And her father's memories were all of days impossibly grand. Times without number she and her brothers had sat in their own cottage in Hunslet, passing the warp through the heddles or retying the rinks and marches with their nimble little fingers, while their father, at the other loom, would tell them of their grandfather the farmer and their great-grandfather the squire. On the road to market, too, when they carried in the meagre produce of the five acres that still survived from those days of glory, he lightened each weary step with memories of the hunt, of harvest fairs and sheepshearing, of poaching trout and raiding orchards. So she knew, and always had known, that she was of finer clay than the poor around her, who had never been other than poor. She had never felt like one of them, and her stepping up with John was like inheriting a state that, though she had never owned it, had long been intended for her use.

The first marks of her change were in her clothing. They had to be. The shabby blue dress, purloined from a drunkard in Manchester, soaked by filthy water from rotten sacking, spattered with blood from that orgy of death up at the warrens, and marled with earth when she and John sealed their love together on the banks below—that dress was hardly fit to smuggle her in by the back door of the Royal Oak at Littleborough.

"Eh! What'll thou do with it?" Nancy Spur, the innkeeper's wife, asked. "Shall I burn it for thee? It's not fit for paupers." She had lent Nora one of her dresses until she could come by some of her own.

"I'll keep it," Nora said. "Just as it is—blood, mud, and all. If we get too proud in times to come, it'll find its uses."

Nora's fitting up was the first cause of disagreement between herself and John. He had wanted her to get a whole wardrobe of pretty dresses, all ribbons and flounces. She, remembering that dead lilies smell worse than dead weeds, thought it not at all fitting to the risks ahead. She saw, more clearly than he, how ill-organized they were to accept the contract and what a mountain of humdrum work was needed to keep it running smoothly. All the lace and silk in the world wouldn't move a single ounce of hardcore or lay half a brick.

He conceded the logic of her argument long before he consented to its conclusion.

"What dost thou fancy thou'll be doing?" he asked.

"Nay, lad! Dost think I'll sit here all day in me finery? Taking tea and paying me morning calls?"

He hadn't thought.

"I'm a working girl and I'll be a working wife to thee. I'll stick by thee like a leech, see thee. Till I know every supplier and his competitor, every price and the cause of its augmentations and reductions, every carrier, every porter—"

"I'll be damned if thou does!" he said, divided between anger and laughter at her presumption.

"And bankrupted if I don't. Take thy choice."

"Bankrupted?" Anger began to dominate.

"Aye. I'm not looking for trouble, but God helps them as meet it ready—and God help them as doesn't!"

"Bloody riddles, woman. Speak plain!" he ordered.

"Thou art a bloody one-man circus: John Stevenson, ringmaster, trick rider, singer, dancing bear, ticket seller, crystal reader. What if thou art sick? Who deals with suppliers? Who knows who they are till they send a bill? Who's to check it?"

"Jack Whitaker'd manage—or Fernley, me clerk of works," he said. His look was that of a man who had just produced the argument stopper— but his tone was less certain.

She knew enough not to press him further; just let the doubt nourish itself and grow. But she could not help adding, just to have the last word: "Oh ah! One of them's thy new factotum then?" And to show it didn't worry her if it didn't worry him, she changed the subject by asking his opinion of the cloth samples the dressmaker had left. She showed great interest in his choice, for there were only good, plain, serviceable materials in single, dark colours to pick among.

The following morning, at breakfast, he had smiled at her and said: "Thou had best get thy bonnet and cloak. Mebbe there's something in what thou says."

And so she had gone with him to Manchester—the first of many visits in the course of which she grew to know every supplier and the ins and outs of his trade as well as Stevenson himself.

For both of them it was Summit and Summit every waking hour—and many sleeping ones, too. They had no social life that did not arise directly out of their business. One evening Arabella Thornton, pressed no doubt by Walter, had invited them over for songs and games and a little supper, but it had been a limping fiasco. Nora was embarrassed at the memories Walter inevitably awakened; he, for the same reason, had been ill at ease and overgallant by turns. Arabella, though hostess, behaved as if some law of the universe decreed that a permanent one-fathom divide must always separate her from John Stevenson. And John, in Nora's view, had been worst of all. For instead of helping the evening along, which would have been child's play to a man of his gifts, he had watched them all like a tolerant old hound among puppies. At least he afterward agreed with her that neither of them should ever consider social engagements until Christmas. By then they'd know whether they were to sink or to swim. Meanwhile she was glad that the best part of five miles separated them from Pigs Hill; and it did not worry her in the least that Arabella Thornton almost certainly shared the sentiment.

Yet, despite her wholehearted dedication to their business, she was never certain whether John was patronizing her, or tolerating her, or whether he really saw the force of her argument and actively wanted her along. So it was no easy time for her; she constantly felt she ought to prove her point and justify her presence. She managed it in little ways. For instance, she could always remember prices and quotations and little details that the day-to-day press of affairs at the tunnel had obscured in his mind. And everywhere they went she would manage a rapid stocktaking of everything visible and if some item that John might need was running low, she would point it out and get an order in, or even make a purchase.

"She has a sharp little eye, that lady of yours," he was told by more than one of his suppliers.

"Thou'll soon be coming to Manchester by thyself," John said jokingly to her once; but he never actually let her go.

Then came the day when she proved herself beyond all possibility of doubt. They had gone to Manchester for, among other things, timber—for templates for the arches, for scaffolding, and for shoring up where the driftway ran through fractured overburden. They needed almost a thousand cubes. But it was one of those occasions when a sudden rush on the heavier timber had emptied every yard in the city, taking the merchants themselves by surprise.

"I think someone's found a way of turning it into gin," one of them told John.

"It's all these extensions to the Bridgewater canal," another explained.

At the last yard they tried—that of the aptly named Ossie Oakshaw—they could get the promise of five hundred cubes for the morrow.

"But it'll cost," Oakshaw said, sighing with a ready sympathy, as though the rise in price would hit him just as hard.

"How much?" John asked.

Oakshaw sized him up with a frankness intended to disarm. The autumn sun danced on little flecks of sawdust held lightly in the furrows on his brow and on the luxuriant thickets of bristle that sprouted over his eyes. "Tell you what I'll do, Mr. Stevenson. We've not dealt before, much to my sorrow, for I'd welcome your custom. To show good faith and let ye see what a plain-dealing man I am, I'll take no profit on this load. I can't take a loss—but, as ye'd well imagine, I *could* take a sizable profit, things being as they are this week. But, to establish what I hope will be a long association, I'll forgo the immediate advantage. Can't say fairer, can I?"

"If . . . ?" John prompted.

"If?" the other repeated in seeming bewilderment.

"Aye, Oakshaw. You're no fool, for I see the legend 'Established 1805' above your gate."

"There's no *if*." Oakshaw winked so violently that a small cataract of sawdust fell sparkling in the sun. He looked different after, plainer and less interesting.

"What does 'cost' cost?" John asked.

"Eighteen pence."

They both whistled. "But that's threepence over last week's going rate!"

Oakshaw looked sad again. "I object as much as you. But what with bad weather in the North Sea, the timber ships from the Baltic all put back. There's been but four loads through Hull all week. The price to all is up. Let me assure you—eighteen pence is cost."

Mention of Hull unlocked a recent memory for Nora. Some weeks earlier she had been standing in the square at Littleborough, watching a train laden with goods steam up to the working at Summit. Within minutes it was out of sight; but on the canal, just beyond the line, a barge still glided north at its snail's pace, hardly seeming to have moved.

"There's an omen," she had said to Spur, the landlord, out to sun himself before the evening rush began.

"Don't you believe it," he said. "I don't hold with all these folk as say the railways'll kill the canals. Look at yon narrow boat—laden with coal for Todmorden. And there he'll get grit from the quarries at Knowl, or vitriol from Gawks Holm, or iron . . . and so on, working back to Hull. And there he'll pick up Baltic timber and bring it all the way back to Manchester. At rates they charge, the railways are never going to get *that* trade."

He had continued in this way for some considerable time, prompted by Nora's careful questioning. She had learned what sort of goods moved up and down and what sort of rate and profit and contract the narrow-boat men looked for. And it was that memory, and all the carefully stored information it invoked, which she now recalled.

John was asking Oakshaw about delivery when Nora, looking idly around the yard, was suddenly struck by its most singular feature—no heavy timber, of the kind they were after, was anywhere to be seen! It could only mean that the timber was still on the barge and the barge still on the canal. She fervently hoped it could only mean that.

"I think we might as well leave it for a day or two," she said aloud. She was as astonished at her audacity as the two men, but she did not show it.

"You what?" John asked.

"Let's go and find somewhere to eat," she said and casually walked away.

Within moments he was at her side. "Are ye ailing?" he asked.

"Will ye trust me?" she replied urgently.

"Mebbe."

"Say goodbye to Mr. Oakshaw," she said.

John turned. "I'll think it over!" he called. "The lady's ailing."

"Don't linger," Oakshaw called, and, as they left the yard, added lamely: "Hope she improves."

"I'll improve *his* bloody price," she said, with more confidence than she felt.

"Will ye?" he asked, amused and bewildered.

"Aye. What did ye agree on with yon Oakshaw?"

"A thousand at eighteen, what's that?"

"Seventy-five pounds," she said without thought. "If I get it for last week's price—sixty-two pound ten—what then?"

He considered briefly. "I'll split every pound with thee that's under seventy-five."

Her eyes opened wide; it was clear he didn't believe she could do it. He nodded back the way they had come.

"Are ye going back to badger him down then?" he asked.

"Never mind! Ye've seen the last of yon Oakshaw."

"Until four this afternoon," he said. "If ye've not done it by four o'clock, I'll be back there and seventy-five poorer."

"Come on," she said. "Time's short."

Oakshaw's yard was hard by the canal bank off Shooters Brow. They skirted quickly round through a number of back lanes and alleys to Ancoats, where they could safely rejoin the canal towpath without being seen from the timberyard. They walked northeast for just over a mile before they met the boat she was looking for. At the Naylor Street wharves two canal officials looked at them with hostility but, seeing John Stevenson's size and build, let them pass in sour silence.

Her interest in the contents of each barge that went by quickly alerted him to her scheme.

"Eh, I'm jiggered!" he chuckled.

"What?" she asked, for his tone seemed to hold some accusation.

"Thou'rt ready enough to go at us for taking chances and mixing opportunity with certainty. . . ."

She halted and looked at him in astonishment. "Do ye fancy I'm *happy* with this day's work? As I'm proud of meself?" She saw she was right and that he, for his part, could not comprehend her astonishment. "Ye bloody would!" she went on. "If ye'd thought up this work, ye'd be like cock of the dung heap!" He laughed, unable to deny it. "I tell thee," she said in a voice of great certainty. "I'm standing here kicking meself for a fool." She began to walk again. "I've seen yon boats laden with timber bound off for Manchester. I've stood on Littleborough platform and watched them. And it's never struck me!"

"Eh but . . . what if boatman's contracted to Oakshaw's?"

"Nay—give us *some* credit!" She could elaborate no further because at that moment, just as they reached Varley Street Wharf, she saw the boat that was bringing the timber. "This is *my* fox," she said. "I got the scent of him first. Right?"

He nodded. They strolled up to where the boatman stood talking with two other canal men. Though aware of John and Nora, he did not break off his talk with his friends.

"How do," Nora interrupted.

They stared incuriously at her, and then slightly more carefully at John.

She nodded at the barge. "Timber," she said.

The two canal men laughed. The boatman looked at his cargo in pretended astonishment and then at her. "Tim-ber!" he said as if it were a new word. "Eh, all the way from Hull I've been wondering what it were— I were fair puzzled to remember it. Timber!"

She joined their laughter at herself. "I'm in the market for wood," she said.

It was clear they did not even think her serious.

"A thousand cube," she added quietly.

That stopped them. They turned and looked very hard at her. The boatman cocked his ears into a better hearing position. "Yer what?" he asked.

"A thousand cube now. Five hundred every third week. I'm offering a contract." A heavy sniff from John, behind, did not deter her. "To deliver at Calderbrook lock and Deanroyd."

John began to stroll aimlessly away, as if he had lost interest.

"Yer offering?" the boatman repeated.

"Aye," she said, as one talks to a child. "And yon's still timber. And I still want a thousand cubes."

The man sniffed. "Calderbrook and Deanroyd."

She looked at the skies.

"What's it for?" he asked.

She pointed behind her, where John, twenty yards away, was turning round to saunter back. "For me man."

"And why's he not buying?"

"Because he says ye'll not sell."

"Oh aye. He does, does he?"

"Aye. He's contractor to the railways." She saw the hostility come down upon them like a cloud over the sun. "He says canal folk'll not deal with railroad folk—even when it's to their own advantage. He says ye'd sooner let dealers in Manchester take the profit than deal direct with railroad folk."

She saw the boatman hesitate. "Advantage?" he asked.

She ignored it. "I told him. I said, 'Canal folks is the same as others. If they saw advantage they'd be as quick to take it as railway men'd be.' But he'll not have it."

One of the other men spoke. "And what do you know of canal folk?" He spat at the water.

"I know Tom Spur," she said, not knowing whether she was playing an ace or a deuce. "He's told us . . ."

"Not Tom Spur at Littleborough?" the canal man asked. He looked interested suddenly.

"Aye."

"Who keeps the Royal Oak?"

"The same."

"Who's Tom Spur?" the boatman asked.

The canal man turned to him. "His dad worked for thy gaffer. Old Sandy Spur. He were bare-knuckle champion of Lancashire."

The other one spoke for the first time. "Aye. Thou wants to stop off at Littleborough. There's always a pint for navigation folk at the Royal Oak."

The boatman turned back to her. "Then thou knows Tom Spur?"

"Aye."

"What . . . advantage was thou talking about?"

She took a deep breath, looked back at John, smiled weakly at the men—in short, did everything to foster the illusion that she was a silly young female who had just realized how far out of her depth she had strayed. Seeing no apparent help or escape she plunged in. "We'll give fifteen pence a cube for yon load and we guarantee fourteen pence on future deliveries."

The man's face was a battlefield of emotions. His tongue flickered across his lips in nervous greed. His brow furrowed with anxiety in case there was a hidden catch. His eyes darted from Nora to John and back, frightened he would not support her offer. John uprooted a pebble with the toe of his boot and flicked it into the water. The canal men glared at him.

"There's the return cargo," the man said. "It's a catch cargo from Manchester but there's never any lack. What'll I catch at Castleton or Deanroyd?"

"I'll guarantee all the stone ye want. Millstone grit. Any grade ye want."

"Grit?" the man said dubiously.

John gave Nora's arm a surreptitious squeeze to alert her he was joining the game. "Come away, love. It's as I told thee. There's railroad contractors down the line quarrying stone for lack of it in the cuttings. There's turnpikes can never get too much grit for hardcore. But I told thee—canal folk'll not see it. They'd cut their own throats first."

The boatman, seeing the best offer he'd ever had evaporate before him, suddenly darted forward and grasped Nora's hand. "Done!" He shook it vigorously and spat.

She smiled, pretending a dazed bewilderment.

"Hundred and thirty-five quid," he said.

Her look changed to one of scorn. "What's that?" she said. "French-man's reckoning? A thousand cube at fifteen pence—I make it sixty-two ten."

"Who said a thousand?" His cunning leer told her something had gone wrong.

"Him." She pointed at the nearby narrow boat.

"And him?" He pointed to the boat behind. "And him?" And to the boat behind that.

An explosion behind her spun her round, fearful of John's anger. But he was not angry. He was howling with laughter, slapping himself on the knee, dancing like a lad took short.

At once she felt angry; angry and also contemptuous. He must have known, or guessed, there was more than one boat—and yet he had let her go on with the deal. What did he intend now? Repudiate the bargain, pay the man a pound or two compensation for the fun and step in and buy just the thousand cube at—say—sixteen pence? Teach her a lesson? Was that it? The humiliation would be more than she could bear; she had to dig her own way out. And quickly.

The worry left her. It was extraordinary how, when you got in a really tight corner, you grew suddenly calm and clear-headed. She stood silent and upright, watching him coolly until his mirth died.

"Right, John," she said. "Thou had best stop here and sort out the best for us. I've gotten a thousand, a hundred and sixty cubes to sell."

His mirth really died then. She saw his face fall as he quickly tested her idea for loopholes and found none. She turned to the boatman. "I'll need your cargo manifest or bill of lading," she said.

"Ye can have bill of lading when I've got the cash," he answered. "Ye can take the manifest." He looked at Stevenson for consent.

John nodded, not altogether happily.

She smiled, her confidence completely restored. "I'll split profit with thee if I may trade in thy name." The potential reward, she knew, would outweigh the risk; she saw the same thought winning him over.

"Done," he said. "Shall I come with thee?"

"Nay. Look out the best for us."

She was so proud and fierce that the two canal servants who had almost turned them off on the upward journey now let her pass with even less hesitation. Several times she began to play the imaginary scene of her forthcoming encounter with Ossie Oakshaw through her mind, but a streak of superstition told her not to. She feared that if the real encounter took an unexpected turn, she'd spend so much time trying to force it back to its imagined lines that she would let genuine opportunities pass her by. She emptied her mind of all fantasy and forced it to concentrate on the physical world around, playing a game whose rules held that if she could remember each succeeding detail with a painter's accuracy, the coming business would go well.

Before long she was amazed at the number of sights she would have missed but for this act of concentration. There was a bloated dead cat, grey-skinned and hairless, floating in a miniature lagoon of broken rainbows. There was a midden heap behind one of the new terraces and already it towered over the rooftops; her nose wrinkled at the putrefying stench it gave off. Wryly she remembered that her old lodging had looked out on just such a stinking heap of rotting garbage and night soil and she had never given it a second thought. She realized what a change only a few weeks among the civilized amenities of the Royal Oak had wrought in her.

The only preparation she made, just before she went through Oakshaw's gate, was to glance down the cargo manifest and memorize the major quantities.

When she saw Oakshaw's wide and condescending smile, she knew at once how she would manage him. And she blessed the caution that had stopped her from imagining this encounter; for her mind would have cast him in her own mould—fierce and predatory. It would have been a real old ding-dong set-to up there behind her eyes; but here in the timberyard by the canal backwater, it was not going to be like that at all. It was going to be very quiet and sweet.

"Are ye better, ma'am?" he asked.

She thought, *Better than you!* but she said, "Well nigh, thank you, Mr. Oakshaw."

"He's sent ye back to close the deal, has he?"

"I intend to make a deal, aye."

His eyes narrowed. "It's eighteen pence," he warned.

"And that's *cost?*"

"Aye."

She looked puzzled and a little dazed. "Ye sure?"

"Cross me heart, hope to die. Show us a Bible, I'll swear it."

She smiled in vast relief. "Then I've news to crown your week for ye, Mr. Oakshaw. I've gotten it for seventeen pence, and I'll let *you* have it 'at cost'!"

He frowned; the first stirrings of alarm showed in his face. "Let me have what?"

She thrust the manifest into his hand. He took it in a bewilderment that rapidly changed to alarm as he ran his eyes up and down the items listed.

"What's up?" she asked. "Seventeen pence—I've saved ye nine pound on that lot."

"Seventeen pence!" he began scornfully before he realized he couldn't pursue that line very far. "But this is mine," he said. "My cargo."

"Oh—he never told me you paid for it."

"Well, of course, I haven't *paid* for it. Not yet."

"He never said it were contracted to ye."

"Nay, but it's a regular delivery, like. There's no need for contracts."

She smiled sweetly. "Until today," she said.

He looked at her, then at the manifest, then back at her. A younger man would have grown angry; but he was survivor of almost forty years of trading, a lifetime of win-a-little, lose-a-little, the sort of man who would rather salvage cash than pride, any day of the week. He snorted, shook his head ruefully, and said, "Seventeen pence!"

Now it was her turn to face internal conflict. She knew beyond doubt that she could hold him to the price; the predator within urged her to do so—tempted her with the profit she'd gloat over as she split it proudly with John. But a wiser Nora forced her to consider her broader interest. She wanted a triumph to take to John. True. But she also wanted a good story about herself and her skill to get passed around the Manchester taverns where the traders and suppliers met. And she didn't want an enemy in Oakshaw. A hard price would not win her that. The time to be really hard was when she was inviolate and her position unassailable. And that was a long, long way off yet.

"Tell ye what, Mr. Oakshaw," she said. "I've just made a regular contract for timber for us at Summit, so we'll do no more trade for it here in Manchester. But there'll be other contracts soon enough, I daresay. And we shall need a good regular supplier here then. I'd not look to make an enemy of ye where I might have a good friend in the course of time. So I tell ye what I'll do. I'll knock a farthing off if ye pay by bill of exchange. And I'll knock a halfpenny off if ye pay cash. But I can't stand a bigger loss than that."

Of course, he no more believed she was taking a loss than she had believed his "cost" of eighteen pence. He looked away, no doubt wondering whether he could drop her more.

"It's just that if we are to deal together," she continued, "it's as well we neither take the other for a fool. You took us for fools—I got so mad when I heard you call eighteen pence 'cost,' ye drove me to this. Trouble is . . ." she laughed richly, forcing him to smile. "I were too mad—I went and bought the lot!"

He knew he was beaten and that she was making acceptance easy for him, but he had one last try. "Hundred and thirty pound ten!" he said. "I've never kept that much in cash."

She laughed again. "Nay! We're keeping our thousand cube. There's only a thousand, a hundred and sixty to sell. So I'm only asking for seventy-nine pound fifteen."

"Only!" he cried, but he was smiling. Now that the bargaining was over, he looked at her appraisingly. "Are ye partial to a drop of sherry, Mrs. Stevenson?" he asked.

"I am that, Mr. Oakshaw."

"I've never done business with a lady before, so I don't know whether the customary courtesies'd be a bit forward, like."

The way to his office led beside a long line of sawpits. When they passed by, the work slackened and halted as one bottom and top sawyer after the other took in the unfamiliar sight of the guvnor with a female.

His office must once have been quite imposing but there was now so thick a pall of sawdust over everything that it might as well have been a corridor in a flour miller's. The glass into which he poured her sherry, though, was clean and sparkling; he held it up to the dusty window. Rich and golden, it was the brightest colour there. He poured himself one and toasted her silently. Gravely she responded. It made her glow within as it slipped smoothly down.

After he had paid her, he said: "I'll send one of me men with ye. All that cash. D'ye carry no pistol?"

"Nay." It had never occurred to her.

He saw her to the gate. "I shall need the bill of lading," he said, waving the manifest loosely. "This grants no title."

The workman-escort walked a dozen paces behind her. His presence alerted John to her success. When they had less than a furlong to go, he left the boats and came to meet them.

"Thou may send thy bulldog home," he said. She looked at the pride in his eyes, and she luxuriated in it. His pleasure and his approval were the real profit on her day.

"Nay," she said. "He's to stop. He can take back the bill of lading."

"It's all ready—waiting for the cash."

She counted out seven pound ten, held it up and winked at him, and dropped it in her pocketbook. His response was ambivalent, but he took the pouch with the rest of the money, counted his own contribution into it, and went to complete the sale.

As they watched Oakshaw's man go off with the boatman and two of the boats, she said, "By rights I should go meself, but that'd only rub his nose in it."

"Bad, was it?"

"Not in the end, as it fell out."

He sniffed. "Seven ten? I thought ye might of gotten nine."

"I might," she said airily. "I might very easily. But I had better reason not to press Ossie Oakshaw. I left him in good cheer. Laughing at hisself. Mebbe that's worth more to us than fifty bob."

He stopped and turned to her, taking her face between his great hands. She saw his head come down, down, out of the sky, growing larger and larger until it filled her universe. It *became* her universe when he kissed her, tenderly, briefly. "What've I gotten meself?" he asked, the wonder of it still in his gaze.

She blinked and swallowed. "A peck of trouble?" she suggested.

He laughed then and began to walk again. "Mebbe," he chuckled. "Aye, mebbe." He looked up at the clear blue sky above the haze of smoke and tasted the cool sulphurous air. "Eh! Autumn's a grand season, though ye'd never think it here in Manchester."

She gazed in disgust at the belching chimneys, the filthy, reeking canal, the stinking middens, and the mean, cramped dwellings all around. "Aye," she sighed, "the threat is ever near."

"Nay!" he said, becoming cheerful again. "This'll never do! What's next?"

She took the half sovereign from her pocketbook. "Dinner," she said. "I'm taking thee to the best in Manchester. The Mitre!"

He whistled. "I can't afford that!"

"I said, *I'll* pay."

And, of course, she did not need to ask if she could be trusted with some of the purchasing in future.


# *Chapter 21*


John Stevenson still had to go into Manchester from time to time, for the gaining of supplies was only a part of his business there. When it was done, he would withdraw to the luncheon houses or taverns where businessmen met. And there he would keep his eyes open and his ear close to the ground, learning of the movements of trade, who was building what and where, how the canals were being extended, where the new mills and warehouses were—always on the lookout for future contracting work.

On these visits he often ran across members of the Board of the

Manchester & Leeds, most of whom would find an occasion to buy him a drink and nudge him in the ribs while they congratulated him on the shrewd bargain he had driven against them. He always managed an astonished, pained look in reply—which made them chuckle the harder. Within weeks the news of his adroitness had become a byword among the fraternity. A younger man would have had his head turned by such attention and might then have made a bad blunder. But Stevenson was old enough to know that his future depended on gaining a reputation for performance to match the one based on his astuteness. Smooth Jacks came and went; astute men who kept their word were as gold.

Sometimes on these visits he would meet the Reverend Doctor Prendergast. More than once he was sure it was no accident, though the cleric was always careful to show the greatest surprise and delight at the chance that brought them together. For his part, Stevenson conveyed the impression of a worried man putting a bold face on his problems.

"I think we'll pull through," he would say. "But we're not that far off the back end. It's bread-and-scrape for a week or two yet, I'd say."

And once, when Prendergast seemed to be getting a little short of trust, he added: "I fancy I may be calling on your offer of capital soon, reverend. We're nigh broke for a bit of ballast." (That was the week when his net profit first topped the thousand mark.) His suggestion induced in Prendergast a sudden interest in his watch and in the distant horizon. Nevertheless, the threat was always there, always dimming his and Nora's pleasure at the success they were making of Summit. He'd have to do something more positive soon.

Jack Whitaker, his assistant, said of Stevenson at this time that he was "greedy" for work, but there was a whiff of sour grapes in the judgement. Whitaker had failed, through no fault of his own, on the Bolton line. Stevenson, never one to see a good man wasted, had taken him on as an assistant at £120; Whitaker, though glad of the rescue and duly grateful, nevertheless remained a trifle resentful of the contrast in their fortunes.

He admired Stevenson for the deal with the company, which he estimated to be worth £2.15.0 a yard for the driftway and a further £43.10.0 a yard for the tunnel. At these rates—though they were geared to performance—he could hardly fail; and his contract ensured that the cash flowed from the very outset. That was a feature which Whitaker especially noted; he himself had failed not because the ultimate profit was insecure but because he ran out of cash along the way to it.

He therefore could not understand why Stevenson was not content to bank the profit, see the contract out, and then begin another somewhere else. Why this endless ferreting around in Manchester for work he was in no position yet to undertake? The time it cost—and the effort! To Whitaker it seemed obsessive to the point of monomania.

Stevenson worked a gruelling eighteen-hour day, seven days a week, except for service each Sunday. He was out at five each day and had toured all the workings before any of the gangs came on at six. Within weeks he knew the name and face of every one of his thousand lads. He measured every inch of progress himself, and he learned every square foot of rock face as it was exposed. Though he had never worked through millstone strata before, he soon learned its nature and its quirks. Before long his mind knew the geology below Reddish as well as a cattle drover knows a long, tortuous trail. Often he would say to Whitaker something like: "Make a note that when we're enlarging the drift, the northward party must cease at the fourteen-twenty-yard mark until the southward party come through to meet them." Or, "There's a chain's length to shore north of the two thousand fifteen mark when we come to line it." Nothing that could be charted was left to chance.

For most of the day Stevenson was up and down the workings like a jack-in-the-box, and many gangs and gangers must have thought he harboured an exclusive concern for their particular section of the face. There were those who said he had "too much go in him" and they'd "thank God when he got other contracts to bleed off some of his interest," adding that "it couldn't happen too soon."

But, as Walter Thornton said when Whitaker passed on some of this complaining gossip: "We've lost not a single life here since John Stevenson took over. When you think there's close on a thousand men, most of them half drunk, working over twenty faces, up to three hundred feet below ground, with powder lying around in open barrels—a lot of credit *has* to go to Stevenson." And he told of other contractors up the line who spent seven days a week never more than two feet from a gin bottle, with men in the shallowest of cuttings and on the smallest of embankments, where at least one life a month was lost. You couldn't gainsay figures like that.

Thornton himself was boundless in his admiration of Stevenson. It was quite possible for a young railroad engineer, especially one with an income and pretentions to being a gentleman, to spend much of the day hunting the country bordering the line he was supposed to supervise, or paying so-called morning visits around the neighbourhood each afternoon. But Stevenson, by his conduct, shamed Thornton into becoming the sort of professional he might have slightly despised only a year earlier. Like the contractor, Thornton now rose early—sometimes as early as six o'clock—and worked late several nights a week.

Even when the whistles blew at seven in the evening and the gangs went off to sup, Stevenson, though he went back to the Royal Oak himself at that time, usually returned to some part of the workings for several more hours. There were always stores to check, engine parts to maintain, and changes in the deployment of the gangs to be prepared against tomorrow.

Though he was too intuitive, too natural an organizer, to see it in the terms of an accountant, he knew that the same man working with the same effort might be worth ten times more in one place than another—and that those profitable and profitless places changed from week to week. He knew that a ton of muck brought out by steam cost much more than a ton brought out by gravity, but that against this there was an equilibrium to be struck in speed of working, congestion of the face and line, and the ease of disposing of the spoil. Poor Skelm, now jailed for debt and fraud, had never begun to grasp such notions; to Stevenson it was second nature from his very first day.

On top of all his other work, he had two further chores that few other contractors might face. Every midday dinner hour, fair weather or foul, he would personally inspect every foot of rope on the windings of two and sometimes three of the shafts, so that every shaft winding was checked in rotation every week. He did not, as many do, get the engineer to turn the winding drum slowly and hope to spot a defect as it turned. He actually spanned each shaft with a portable catwalk and would make the engineer pay out every yard, as slowly as possible, while he watched it pass him and run through his fingers on its way into the bowels of the pit.

There were those who—behind his back, to be sure—mocked him for this caution; but they were few. Most of his people were glad enough that such a man was in charge of the contract and reckoned him the best contractor they'd ever worked for. Craftsmen as well as navvies shared this opinion, which must go far to explain why the trouble among them took all of three months to come to its head. Men accustomed to taking a lot of rough with very little smooth were not quick to ignite—not when personal insult or threat was absent.

The other chore was more immediately profitable. It went back in origin to Nora's inspired suggestion to the boatman on that unforgettable day at the Varley Street Wharf. When he had spoken of other contractors up the line quarrying stone for lack of it in the cuttings, and turnpikes crying out for hardcore, his words had been no hot flannel; and it was not long before he had a regular and very paying trade in stone and grit, with boats plying both west and east. The notion of selling unwanted spoil to other contractors, who might be desperate for muck for embankments, though it was very simple and obvious, was then quite novel in railroad working. Within five years it had become commonplace and before the decade was out it was the rule. By then contracts were awarded at rates that discounted the profit from selling the excess. Until that time, however, Stevenson had the profit of the idea, for he took care always to bid for sections where there would be a surplus. At Summit the total profit on these sales was a respectable £873, as near as Nora could reckon it. In later years Stevenson himself often claimed that the scheme was the saving of his neck at the time, and he always credited her with the devising of it. In a contract that, when all the accounts were in, netted a little over £30,000 (just as he had forecast), this claim was obviously more than exaggeration. However, the scheme did bring a welcome inflow of hard cash in that grim November of 1839, when the great dispute threatened to slow the working, and the bonuses from the Manchester & Leeds might cease, temporarily, to flow.

In an industry where tempers are generally strong and violence never very far below the surface, the trouble on Summit must have established some kind of precedent for the length of its gestation and the frequency with which all and sundry, right down to the lad who brought the ale up to the site office, predicted its eruption. Indeed, those closest to Stevenson, who had predicted it earliest of all, were so discomfited by the middle of November that they had begun to shake their heads in pained surprise and to say that perhaps he would get away with it after all.

Stevenson himself had a special set of nerves for these things. On Sunday, 17 November, he knew that the unrest among the tradesmen—among the bricklayers, to be precise—would come to its head the following day. Accordingly, by ten o'clock he was off the site and on his way to Manchester, where he took care to stay until gone six o'clock that evening.

Most other mortals, after so many months of unremitting labour, would have seized the chance of this enforced absence to make it a day of rest. But Stevenson put it to better account. What was left of the morning he used for small tidying-up errands. He had his hair cut and got himself measured for a suit, a riding habit, and some waterproof boots. He also got his fob watch oiled and a new, unscratched glass put in it.

Then he had lunch with Sir Sidney Rowbottom, whom he "happened" to run across at the house he was known to frequent almost every day. Without revealing his strategy, he left the chairman feeling assured that he, Stevenson, knew what he was doing and was well able to deal with the troubles now about to break out.

Only a fortnight earlier, to that very day, the Welsh magistrate John Frost had led the Chartist riot in Newport. With seven thousand men, and more waiting in the hills, he had mounted an armed assault upon the

Westgate Hotel to secure the release of his fellow Chartist Henry Vincent, then under trial for sedition. The hotel was guarded by no more than thirty soldiers. The mob discharged their guns into the building, wounding the mayor and several others. The thirty soldiers fired back. Whereupon the seven thousand, displaying the undiluted self-interest that has kept England safe from revolution ever since it forgot what Cromwell taught, took to their heels and the hills, and left poor Frost to the law.

Yet this sad little incident now had respectable England agog with tales of rebellion and unrest. Manchester, like all the northern towns, was deeply divided. Until 1832 the archaic system of apportioning the parliamentary constituencies had left them virtually disenfranchised. The towns and manufacturing valleys had bristled with Parliamentary Reform Associations whose list of demands had closely foreshadowed those of the Chartists. Now with the high price of corn, the depression of wages, and the long and fruitless wrangle to establish a fifty-eight- instead of a seventy-two-hour week, the centre of discontent had shifted from the newly enfranchised millowner and townsman to the disgruntled labourer and factory hand.

But in that winter of 1839 the shift was incomplete. And though the millowner and burgher neither saw nor felt a common interest with the farmer and landowner, memories were long—certainly long enough to reach back to Peterloo, when for an unguarded moment the old order of aristocracy and gentry had shown its naked contempt for the new. So industrial Lancashire met the disorders of that year with mind and heart at odds. There were enough of the older "moral force" Chartists left to give silent and uncomfortable acquiescence to their newer "physical force" brethren.

Stevenson found the town alive with rumour and innuendo. The agitation gave him a certain melancholy satisfaction; he could not have wished for a better backdrop against which to stage-manage his own approaching drama—*if* he wanted to take things that way. It was still a big "if."

In the afternoon he called at Payter's offices and asked him to put in a good word to the Duke of Bridgewater's agent for the next major works on the canal. If he was to get the better of Prendergast, he needed more money than Summit was yielding. And that meant more work.

"I don't know!" Payter said. "If they go on like this we'll have more miles of canal than Venice. Do what I can, dear fellow."

And finally he went to his bank in Piccadilly and asked them to open an account for him at Bolitho & Chambers, bankers of Dowgate in the City of London—his supposed guarantors. To them he transferred a modest one hundred pounds. It was the other thrust in his campaign to rid himself of the Reverend Doctor Prendergast.

He spent the afternoon nosing around the canals and mills to the east of the city. There, where shanties and hovels pockmarked the wasteland between factory and wharf, it took little foresight to conjure up rows of neatly built back-to-backs, and the shops and chapels and pubs to go with them. Buildings. Hundreds of acres of buildings. Fistfuls of contracts.

To a man with only one eye it was plain that railroads weren't the half of it—not the tenth of it. Even if John Stevenson grew as big as ambition had already made him, there'd be work for a hundred more like him. If things went on this way.

He must have walked a circuitous eight or ten miles before it grew too dark to see and too cold for comfort. But by then his inner eye had formed the sharpest possible vision of the future—and of what he was now staking in his gamble up at Summit.

He arrived back at Littleborough at seven that evening, prepared— though not really expecting—to see a knot of angry workers picketing his lodging. But in that chill wind no one stood anywhere for long. Passers-by hurried from work to home or home to shop or shop to pub. Only two dogs, larking around in the light from the bakery window—each trying vainly to make the other take the unnatural part—watched him pass. They panted hard and stared up with guilty, bloodshot gaze until he had gone by. Then they returned to their fun.

Nora took his coat, kissed him hard and long, and shivered by proxy at the cold that seemed to radiate from him.

"Eh," she said. "One day they'll find a way of conducting the waste steam from the engine back along pipes through the coaches."

"There's no heat in waste steam," he said.

"Nay—nor in the bloody coaches, neither."

As his senses thawed he became aware of a certain edge to her behaviour; it was so excessively normal as to be odd.

"Whitaker been here?" he asked. He knew she did not like him and that whenever he called at the Royal Oak it left her uneasy.

Nora maintained that there was an unreliable streak at the core of Jack Whitaker, that one day he would let John down. John, for his part, would tell her she was a better judge of figures than she was of men. "That must flatter *thee!*" she said.

He knew, from the careless way she turned to face him and the synthetic effort she put into trying to remember who might have called that day, that Whitaker had indeed come a-calling.

"There's trouble," he said.

She smiled confidently. "When is there not!" She turned him to the door and gave a playful push. "Come and sup. Broth'll warm thee and beef'll fill thee."

He obeyed. "Whitaker'll be back," he said.

"Mebbe."

Whitaker was back, very soon. He must have guessed at Stevenson's hour of return. They had barely swallowed their broth when they saw his rubicund face and curly hair peering this way and that through the smoke of the four-ale. At last he saw them and threaded his way among the crowd until he stood at their table.

"Bring our beef pies," Nora told the potboy who was then clearing away their bowls. She could see that John was tense and excited, as if he could not wait for Whitaker to begin.

And Whitaker certainly was biding his time. He stood looking down at John as if he had eight things to say and couldn't decide their proper order. John swallowed his impatience.

"Sit down, Whitaker," he said, pointing to a vacant stool. "Sup with us? Have ye supped?"

"That I have not. Nor do I think *you* will when you hear what I have to say." He paused.

"Am I to hear it then?" John asked. She could see he was becoming desperate for Whitaker to speak.

"There's trouble at the workings. Ye'd best come."

John looked at him coolly. "The brickies?" he asked, almost gleefully.

"Aye." Whitaker's brow furrowed.

"I thought ye'd never come!"

"I came this dinnertime," he protested. "It started this morning."

John laughed. "Nay! Lad—I mean five weeks back. I've been ready for this five weeks now. Five and more." He stood, eager to leave, rubbing his hands. Time for battle.

Nora leaned over the table and plucked his sleeve. "Ye'd best eat," she said.

With a delight that was near feverish he looked from her to him; his hand absently reduced a slice of bread to crumbs. "I'm ready for this fight," he said. Excitement slurred his voice.

"Are ye drunk?" Whitaker asked.

Nora looked sharply at him; she did not know John permitted such familiarity.

John merely laughed.

"If thou can swallow thy glee," she said, "thou'll think how it may look if word gets out."

John frowned. "Word? What word?"

"He comes in here"—she nodded at Whitaker—"with glum news and thou art out like a shot off a shovel. It'd look like he'd put the wind up thee."

John looked undecided.

"Who were that ship's captain," she asked, "went on playing skittles when the Frenchy fleet were due?"

John laughed at that. "Mebbe thou art right," he said and sat again. "Come on, Whitaker. Sit and sup."

Glad to have the decision taken from him, Whitaker did as he was bid, and ate and supped his fill.

"Do you *want* a fight?" he asked unbelievingly.

John grinned but made no other reply. Whitaker looked at Nora and she at him; they raised their eyebrows and shrugged, but the subject was not raised again.

Nora inclined her head toward John. "I pity the poor, ill-thriven sods who think they could beat yon man of mine!"

Six beef pies and a gallon of ale later the two men strode out through the door, buttoned their coats against the flurries of sleet that howled around the deserted square, and set off for the works, whose southern end was just over a mile distant.

"We'll go up the track," Stevenson said.

They went along the Ripponden road, under the new railroad bridge, and, climbing through the still uncompleted fence, scrambled up the eastern embankment to the track.

"I can see nothing," Whitaker said. "It's a blind man's holiday all right. Let's at least get a lantern from the station."

"They'll be shut."

"We can wake him up."

"Nay," Stevenson said firmly, and set off northward. "I can see just grand with these two ears." And after a minute of steady walking, with only the moaning of the wind to accompany the soft fall of their feet on the wet ties, he stopped. "Someone coming," he said. "One man. On his own."

In a little while the sound of approaching feet was plain even to Whitaker. "Don't frighten him off," Stevenson said and coughed.

The footsteps fell silent.

"Who's that?" Stevenson called out.

After a silence a voice asked, "Why?"

"I'm John Stevenson, contractor to this line. I ask—have you a right to be on these premises?"

"Oh!" The voice was relieved. "Lord John!"

"Aye. Mr. Stevenson to you, if that's Peter Etheridge."

Silence. The other walked closer.

"Is it? Peter Etheridge?"

"Aye, sir." He came right up to them. "I'm not meant to talk with ye. Is this Mr. Whitaker and all?"

"Yes," Whitaker said.

"Not talk?" John said, scornfully. "No. Of course not. Took an oath, didn't ye!" It was frustrating to talk to someone he couldn't see and yet whom he so desperately needed to see. He strained his ears for every scrap of information they could glean.

Etheridge merely breathed. Was it indecision? Or stubbornness?

"I hope *thou's* taken no oath," Stevenson prompted.

"I'll not join their bloody oaths."

Silence.

"The stupid fools," Stevenson said, hopefully.

Sniff. "Aye." Long pause. "But I'll join in their demand."

"Oh ah," Stevenson agreed. "Mebbe I'll know what that is soon enough."

"Aye."

Another silence.

"So there'd be no great damage like if I know now?"

Still Etheridge did not speak. The sleet had stopped falling and the wind was dropping a little.

"Does this bonus run through all the trades?"

"There's . . ." Etheridge began and then halted.

Stevenson played his last card. His voice rich with understanding and sympathy, he reached out, patted the other on the arm, and said, "Never thou fret, lad. I thought as thou were out of the conspiracy. Or I'd not have pressed thee."

He felt Etheridge stiffen at the word "conspiracy." He heard him breathe in to speak. He turned to leave just as Etheridge blurted out, "No bonus!"

Stevenson halted, his breath stopped in midflow. "No bonus," he said at length in as neutral a voice as he could muster.

Etheridge walked quickly away. "We want three and six a day, flat rate."

"That's not too bad, guvnor," Whitaker said when they heard the last of Etheridge's footsteps. "Forty-two pence."

Stevenson did not at once reply. At last he said, with what sounded like wonder in his voice, "They've sworn a combination!"

"You don't mind?"

Stevenson turned to him in the dark. "Mind? I came out tonight to meet a demand for bonus that I thought would be fair, and difficult to fight. And instead it's *me* that's given the bonus. *Two* bonuses. One—flat rate demand. Two—they swore a combination. Stupid fools! It's like stealing sugar off a sleeping bairn." He stamped his feet to restart the circulation. "I've got 'em, Jack. I don't want 'em—or I do and I don't—but I've got 'em, see thee."

"You sound as if you don't want them."

Stevenson thought before replying. "I don't," he said. "As God is my witness, I'd as soon forgo this fight. But . . . we are as He made us in a world as He made it. If I shirk this contest now, I'll live to fight it more bitterly and win it to someone's greater hurt hereafter." He sighed. "Aye. Well then. Set to!"

"Are you going up to the works?"

"Nay. The meeting'll be squandered now." He turned and shook Whitaker's arm warmly. "Nay, Jack. Go on home now. There's no more work this night."

"And you?"

"Now I'm come out I'd as well take a look at yon new winding engine. We'll assemble that tomorrow."

He left Whitaker standing in the dark. But he did not, as he had said, go up to the works at all; in fact, he went no farther than the old wooden shanty, Meg's palace as it now was.

Going through that door was like a homecoming. It was a furnace heat that pressed onto his face and reached up his cuffs and down his neck; it was laden with the steam of drying clothes and boiling beef, the aroma of spirits, the acrid smoke of tobacco and candlewicks, and the pungent stink of thirty or more bodies that bathed in nothing but their own sweat. As a fisherman might sniff the salt-laden winds, or a farmer the breeze off a new-ploughed field, Stevenson breathed his lungs full of that rich reek.

"Shut yon door!" several called before he was halfway in and they could see who it was.

A cheer went up from a card school almost at his feet. Yorky Slen was there, and Bacca Barra.

"Come and join us, Lord John," Yorky said; and the cry was taken up by others.

"Aye—let's win some more money off thee," Bacca said.

He grinned down at them and then at the rest of the room; these were the only men he'd ever understand. The only folk he'd be proud to own. The only ones who knew what it meant to call him Lord John. Navvies'd never form a combination. They might use their fists, they might do a mischief to the guvnor with the sharp end of a steel shovel and leg it fast to the next works, but they'd never do anything so daft as surrender themselves to a union.

"Nay, lads," he said. "It's the brickies' turn now." They roared at that. "Where's Meg?"

Bacca pointed to his old corner. As he went across to the curtain he heard the laughter spread with the repetition of his joke from group to group.

Old Meg sat alone staring into a cracked jug with a little gin at the bottom. His heart sank; he needed her sober. He pushed the jug to one side, sat down facing her, and pulled the candle between them. She looked very sinister with the light coming from below her face.

"Lonely, isn't it," he said. "In here."

She looked up at him. Her eye was steady and his heart rose as he realized she might not be so drunk as the nearly empty jug suggested. "Have a drop," she said.

He took a sip from the jug. The raw spirit burned his lips and tongue; its subtler flavour of juniper hit him only when he breathed out its fire. "Cold out," he said.

"Was it snow I seed?"

"It's not laying." He looked around approvingly. She was keeping it all neat—and she was ruling the men well. "Aye, Meg. It's quarter day. I've come for me rent."

Her eyes narrowed until he laid a finger up the side of his nose and winked. "Oh ah!" she said, suddenly recalling their bargain.

"Art sober?"

She giggled hoarsely. "Nay, I can't say."

"Sober enough I fancy. Have ye heard?"

"Heard what?"

He showed his impatience. "I didn't give thee this shanty to bandy words with me."

"Com-bi-na-tion?" Her lips mimed the words and her brow framed the question that his ears barely heard.

He nodded. "What are the lads saying? Speak up. Don't be afraid."

"They say brickies is bloody fools. They say as Lord John'll make soup and two veg of them and swallow them for his supper."

He breathed easier. "There's no sympathy?" The word meant nothing to her. "No fellow feeling?" he corrected.

Her lips curled in scorn over the black gaps in her teeth. "Fellow feeling! They've no feeling for theirselves. Nor one for the other. Fellow feeling!"

But he persisted. "It's important to me, Meg. There's none said . . . brickies isn't daft . . . or . . . it isn't all wrong on the one side . . . or anything of that sort?"

"When navvies take side with brickies ye'll hear the last trump!" she said; but he sensed she was holding something back—not out of cunning but because she had remembered it and dismissed it as trivial at the same moment.

"Not one?" he urged.

She said it at last. "There's Catsmeat and Steam Punch."

He was surprised. "Steam Punch? Who were on *my* gang this August?"

She shook her head. "Nay. New ones. Started with Banner's gang this morn. They said . . ." She fell silent and her eyes grew vacant.

"What'd they say?"

He moved the candle to one side; the reek from it stung his eyes. She came back to him. Again, for a fleeting instant, he saw the young girl she must have been as her soft grey eyes came to rest on his. "Shut thy gob and I'll tell thee. They said, or Catsmeat said—they're in the corner, if ye want them. Sharing a wench."

"I'll get to know them. What'd they say?"

"Catsmeat said brickies on the Great Western Railway are getting five and three a day on bonus."

He shrugged. It meant nothing—threatened nothing. "Were that afore our brickies met this evening? To form their combination?"

"Nay," she assured him. "They never said anything till Bacca come in with the news of the combination."

"Catsmeat and Steam Punch," he repeated, more to himself than to her.

"Sup more." She pushed the jug at him.

He shook his head. "How's yon Pengilly? Pegoleggy Pengilly?"

"Sleeping," she said and drained the jug. She looked deep into it and added: "Strange thing. Since he lost his leg I've not seen him touch a drop of spirit. He'll sup a drop of beer to wash down his meat, but he's never drunk now."

Stevenson nodded.

"And he's taking good money as winding engineer." She reached across and patted Stevenson's forearm. "Ye done him a right good turn there."

"Does *he* say so?" Stevenson did not smile.

"He never stops singing Lord John's praises. To hear him talk, Lord John's the risen Lord and new Messiah in one."

Stevenson shook his head sadly. "That's blasphemy," he said without making it a reprimand. For a while he looked down and closed his eyes, seeming to fall into prayer. When he opened them again he thrust his hand in his pocket and pulled out all his loose change: a sixpence, a groat, a penny, and a farthing. He made a neat pile of the coins and passed them across to her. "I'll need *thy* help, Meg. I'll need all me friends."

He left without looking to see what her response might be.

# Chapter 22

Combination or no combination, the ordinary work—even the ordinary bricklaying—went on. In fact, the works ran more smoothly and tightly that next day than it had during all the preceding weeks of slowly building tension. Those whose knowledge of John Stevenson was only superficial expected him to come like a fury through the works and seek out the instigators of the combination. But those who knew him well were not in the least surprised to see him behaving as though this day were like any other.

He began, as usual, with the mile-long walk up to Summit for his early tour of the whole works. He left Littleborough soon after five. The skies had cleared in the small hours and the wind fell to the merest breeze, which often died to a complete stillness. Yesterday's rain now lay in frosty pools that groaned and shrieked at each footfall. A gibbous moon stood at its zenith, showing the path well enough for him to take the turnpike instead of the longer way by the railroad. Near the rising to Summit he joined the throng of mill hands who daily at this hour, when trade was brisk, came streaming down from the hovels and cottages at Sally Street, Smithy Nook, Mawrode, Calderbrook, and other hamlets. The air was heavy with a fatigue that no sleep, short of eternal sleep, could lift from their wasted frames. They were women and children mostly—huddled, silent creatures clutching their thin rags about them as they dragged their way over the rail bridge to the steam works by the canal. Smoke already rolled in greasy billows from its tall chimneys. Yellow gaslight reached feebly out through its lint-shrouded windows, illuminating nothing.

Hot porridge, cold bacon, hard eggs, wheaten bread, and stewed coffee swelled him comfortably. The memory of it was still between his teeth and on his tongue. He looked around him at this wretched human stream and wondered how many dozen of their stomachs it would take to outweigh his. Despite the law, there were children among them of eight and nine, barely awake; one carried on his back a child of five or six, fast asleep still. But they none of them looked like children—more like a new race of stunted men. Bow-legged, crook-backed, two teeth in every three already shed, cheeks hollow, skin shrivelled and sallow, they stared up at him from great incurious eyes, anxious only not to stand in his way.

His iron-shod boots rang loud amid the shuffle of their bare feet and tattered slippers. He was glad to leave them and take his own customary path to the works. This daily meeting distressed him. He had once tried leaving Littleborough earlier to avoid it but then had only met the men, women, and children going to the Rakewood coal pits—and compared with them the mill hands were an aristocracy. He turned and looked back at the stragglers, running half-heartedly to catch up. In the pale moonlight their blue breath hung above them, almost as substantial as the wraiths that breathed it out.

An industry that created and then relied on such starvelings, he thought, was pernicious—a danger to good order. If revolution ever came, here was the wasteland in which it first would breed. Why were people so blind to their own best interests? The well-paid craftsman, who had least to gain from it, formed unions as readily as good soap forms useless scum; these poor mill hands, who had everything to gain and precious little to lose, would fight one another tooth and claw at the mill gate rather than organize. And the employers were the worst of all; for the misery and resentment they fostered day by day was surely a corrosion that would eat the country into two halves, each renouncing all kinship with the other. At the end of their road stood two Englishmen sustained only by their implacable ignorance of and hostility to each other. Why could they not see that? If men like Fielden over at Todmorden could keep the hours down to fifty-eight, and give two hours' schooling a day to every child at the mill—*and* turn in a better profit—how could the rest be so blind?

At six o'clock, the first of his own boozy, guzzling, randy aristocrats came on. Light was scattered all along the line of the workings. Men with lanterns streamed out along the path or struggled up the slope from the trail below. One after another the engine fires were kindled, throwing out red, flickering light that drowned the first hints of dawn in the east and restored an infernal kind of night in the valley. Men caught in its glow looked strong and full of cheer. They moved with purpose and gusto. He heard singing and laughter.

Now as every morning he inhaled deeply to catch the pungent smell of burning wood and kindling coal. Logs spat and cracked. Boilerplates groaned with the enforced expansion. Cold water began to trill and whistle as it heated. Running water from the cloughs gurgled in the conduits as the trappers diverted the day's quota to the engine reservoirs. As this sleeping giant of his stirred into power and life, the whole of his spirit lifted and he went to watch the assembly of the new and more powerful winding engine at number seven shaft.

Progress had been slow here, largely because of the 321 feet of shaft up which the muck had to be lifted. The old engine had not really been man enough; this new one, the engineers all said, would move the same loads twice as fast.

The Manchester & Leeds engineers had not been too happy at the casual way their engine had been hired out to John Stevenson. It was an almost new one of their own design and they wanted to see it work longer under their own immediate supervision before they let it out. Which was why Stevenson had had to wait until November to get it from Miles Platting to where it now lay, above Stanor Bottom Farm at the foot of Reddish Scout. Even so they had insisted on sending one of their own senior steam engineers out to supervise its reconstruction.

A band of cold ultramarine hung above the eastern horizon, heralding the day to the Vale of Todmorden. In the growing light the long, rolling moors of Blackstone Edge stretched in a perspective that deepened with every passing minute. Below, the canal and turnpike lay like two pale streaks along the valley floor.

He told the men to kindle the boiler for number seven because they'd need it to steam the new engine; and, in any case, it would take three or four hours to assemble and test, so they might as well use the existing engine until then.

"Shall I start, sir?" his own engineer, a Scot called McKinnon, asked, nodding at the knocked-down components set out on the moorside.

"Best wait for their man. Ye could assure yourself it's all there."

"I might like to trial-fit their frame to our stone base. Just to be sure the bolts will marry."

"Aye, ye could do that right enough."

While the gang gingerly lifted the cast-iron frame onto the stone base, he walked away to the outer edge of the spoil heap and looked down at the turnpike. In the dawn twilight he heard the horse long before he saw the horseman; and so, too, did the keeper of the toll bar, who came hurrying out with his lantern to halt the rider. Stevenson chuckled, imagining the keeper's chagrin as he saw the rider turn uphill at Stanor Bottom, a few yards short of the bar. It must be the company's engineer. Stevenson ran helter-skelter down the side of the heap to meet him.

The way up was steep and stony, and the rider had wisely dismounted. He and his horse were no more than shadows against the dark hills beyond.

"Stephenson," the rider said.

Stevenson laughed genially. "Aye." He shook hands. "Ye have the advantage, I fear."

"Stephenson," the other repeated, a little bewildered. "Robert Stephenson. Engineer."

"Aah! . . ."

Each realized simultaneously where the confusion lay.

"So you are John Stevenson!"

"Aye. With a *v*. Indeed. I'm greatly honoured, sir. Greatly. We have, in fact, met. Once you came up with your father. In July. I was ganger on the number one face, then. Ye'd not remember, though."

"I do indeed, Mr. Stevenson. You've not shrunk, I see."

They walked up the track. After a short distance they left it to join the path that linked the line of shafts.

"I expect today part of you is wishing you were back at number one face," Stephenson said.

"How?"

"This trouble with your brickies."

John chuckled. "When you build an engine to steam a hundred miles an hour, you've a name ready made."

"Oh. What would that be?"

*"Bad news!"*

The engineer threw back his head and laughed with a sudden violence that made his horse shy.

They tethered it on a long rope and left it to graze around the clough. By the time they reached the engine site the first touch of gold was lighting up the east.

"What a country!" Stephenson said. "How can we plan for anything! Yesterday—the depths of a wet midwinter. Today—apologies to one and all—we're to be given a bit of autumn the clerk of the weather forgot!"

For the next few hours Stephenson and McKinnon—and Thornton, who joined them soon after Stephenson had arrived—patiently assembled the engine, joining piston to crosshead, crosshead to crank, crank to fly-wheel, and lavishing oil and grease and tallow over every moving or sliding part.

John watched them carefully, though a thicket of engineers' heads often obscured the view and he was left to infer the wonders of this new machine from Stephenson's proud grunts of self-congratulation and the answering whistles and cries of admiration from Thornton and McKinnon. From time to time Stephenson included him in the explanation of the engine, whose novelty lay in the ingenious way they had been able to raise the operating pressure (and thus the temperature gradient—and thus the power delivered) without adding extra piston rings of hemp.

"So we keep the friction of the rings down to acceptable levels, you see," Stephenson said.

John nodded. "If that's another way of saying my coalyard bill for number seven shaft is going to drop, I'm greatly in favour of it."

Stephenson chuckled and looked at the other two. *"There's* a man who knows what we're all about." He jerked his thumb at John over his shoulder. "A beautiful piece of mechanics like that, a beautiful little construction, all the excitement . . . and what is it to him? A lower figure on the coalyard bill at the end of the month!"

They laughed.

"I'm right, though," John said. "Ye'd not do it if it put the bills up."

Stephenson agreed. "There has to be a division somewhere between engineering and architecture, and I daresay that's it. Architects put the cost up. Engineers down."

It took a further hour to sweat the brass bushes onto the crank and crosshead and to get it perfectly lined. Then there was the boiler-feed pump to connect to the crosshead slide, and the flywheel to bolt to the shaft. Then after some minor adjustments to the eccentric shaft and rocker, and after lavishing pints more oil over every moving surface, the engine was ready to steam.

They first turned the flywheel several dozen revolutions by hand, and the sweat that poured from the navvies who did the turning was a handsome testimonial to the power the machine would deliver even when idling. Then they cautiously opened the steam valve on the new feed line. The paint in the threads at the junctions bubbled and wheezed until the pressure made the seal firm. For a while nothing happened. The hot steam, rushing through the tubes, dropping in pressure and meeting the cold metal, condensed uselessly in the cylinder. And when the engine did finally make its first trembling revolution—to a rousing cheer from the whole company—the waste-steam pipe spat and spluttered like a bull with a loose bowel.

Soon it was turning, slow and smoothly, at about 50 rpm. Stephenson and the two other engineers listened carefully, checked oil-galley levels, squatted on sight lines with moving parts, accelerated the engine, decelerated it, started it slowly, started it with a jolt, tested the flywheel brake, and all the while exchanged private glances of worry or approval or relief.

"Works like a free pardon," John said.

Stephenson agreed. "Very well, McKinnon," he said. "She's all yours for the next hour. Take her slowly up to about 200 rpm. We'll get that hemp nicely bedded in before we set her to work."

The boilerman brought a pail of warm water and some soap. Within minutes the engineers were gentlemen again.

"Well, Stevenson-with-a-*v*," Stephenson said, "my father wants me to look over these works while I'm here."

"Gladly, sir. If I may, I'll join ye at number three in half an hour.

Thornton'll show ye the first two. There's a little matter I must attend to."

"Do you know who the ringleaders are?" Thornton asked, implying by his tone that he did.

"I've not been informed. But I'll guess as to three of em. I'll guess Thomas Metcalfe, number one. And I'll guess Arthur Burroughs and Wilfred Hope. Hundred to one—are ye on?"

Thornton gave a shrug of resignation. "It's useless," he said to Stephenson. "You can't tell that man a thing he doesn't know about this works."

"I hope he knows what he's doing with it," Stephenson said. The serious threat in his voice was only partly masked by humour.

John plucked a straw of dead grass. "So do I." He sighed lugubriously and put the grass in his mouth. "Aye—so do I and all."

But Robert Stephenson had other ideas. "Where are your brickies—these three leaders you mentioned?"

"They'll be working—if that's the right word—on the oval shaft at the summit of the line."

"We'll come with you then. I don't mind which end we begin." They started walking. "In fact, I'd prefer that end, so that we can all go and take luncheon in Littleborough."

The path was the same as the one John had taken when he first met Arabella Thornton standing up on the scout with her husband—indeed it was the only path between the scout and Deanroyd.

The sun was now well up in a sky of clear cerulean blue. It shone in an autumnal thinness, barely warming to the skin; but it struck the moorland with dazzling clarity, picking out such colour and detail that you felt you had suddenly gained new powers of vision. There was now no wind at all and the smoke from the engine boilers, and from all the factories and mills up the valley, rose straight and black, not dispersed until the columns topped a thousand feet.

"On such a day," Robert Stephenson said, "you can really see and feel the power of man." He spoke with a pride which they, by their agreement, shared. They gained the brow of the scout in silence.

"Who will you put to tend that new engine?" Thornton asked.

"Pengilly, I think," John said. "He's shaping well."

It was a moment or two before Thornton connected. "Ah yes! Your discovery!" He turned to his senior. "This Stevenson is a most amazing man, you know, sir, at discovering people. He's an explorer in the land of human skill. Pengilly, this new engine minder, was an ordinary navvy on Stevenson's own gang. Now he's a full-blown steam engineer!"

"How so?" Stephenson asked.

Thornton wet his lips with relish. "Thereby hangs a tale. There was an accident and he lost a leg—"

"Only a foot," John insisted. "It wasn't a leg. Only a foot."

"Well . . ." Thornton waved a dismissive circle, though he knew perfectly well it had been a whole leg to the knee, "a foot then. Anyway—there's a man who's a fit object for parish relief; but Stevenson here . . . what was it you did?"

John reached inside his cravat and scratched his neck uncomfortably. "I learned he'd tended an engineer on a big Cornish engine, when he was younger. So I told him I'd give him a trial at one of these engines. Now . . . ye'd think he'd never done anything else all his life."

"You see! A discoverer."

Stephenson looked at the contractor with a new interest. "And there's Mrs. Stevenson, too, I hear," he said. "I hope we may meet at luncheon. If she hasn't gone sowing fear and terror among the merchants of Manchester!"

John laughed then. As before, he led the way down the stepped part of the trail.

"I may claim a little credit there," Thornton said, bringing up the rear. "For it was I discovered her first. May I tell it, Stevenson?" he asked.

"I find it all an acute embarrassment," John said. "But I daresay that'll not deter ye. Thereby hangs a different tail, eh?"

"Oh come! It's too good not to tell. Stevenson's wife, you know, sir, comes from an old landowning family near Leeds. The Tellings of Normanton. But they fell on hard times and this August, with her father dead and the two younger children dead as well, she was left alone and as good as destitute. Over in Manchester. And she was tramping this way, intending to take this very track we're on now, when she met me. Or I met her. Anyway, our paths crossed." He turned to look behind. "No, you can't see it from here. But there's an ancient cemetery just the far side of Calderbrook. That's where we met. She was so exhausted I told her she'd not make it over here to Todmorden before nightfall—and in any case the Todmorden Union has refused to build a workhouse."

"Still?" Stephenson asked, in surprise.

"Oh—*that* is going to be a long, bitter fight," Thornton said. "But that's another story. The long and short of it was, I sent her to seek a night's shelter with Stevenson's gang, knowing he'd not see her starve—"

"Your reputation for charity may now be your undoing, Mr. Stevenson," the engineer said.

"I have no charity, sir, as ye'll hear when Thornton drags out the ending of this interminable tale. But even if I had, it would not extend to bricklayers and other highly overpaid tradesmen!"

They all laughed at that. By now they had gained the broader path, below the house called Rough Stones, and they could stride out side by side.

"The point of this story," Thornton said, "is that . . . you must remember I did not know her then. I did not know her background or history. All I saw was a destitute girl in a torn dress, exhausted. A field girl, I thought, for a field girl she looked. But Stevenson here . . ." He glanced across at the contractor and met his level, sardonic, almost mocking gaze. "Stevenson, within twenty-four hours, finds that this same girl has some kind of genius for figures, numbers. Not just adding up and simple operations like that but. . . . What did you write to me when I was in Blackpool? You put it very succinctly, I remember. You said she could see oddities and discrepancies in figures the way you or I could see, without any calculation, that a boiler was too big for an engine. Isn't that it?"

"You put it better than I did."

"It's very good," Stephenson said, looking at John with renewed admiration. "I see exactly what you mean. To have such an ability . . . that is a real gift. And you really saw it at once! That is an equal gift."

John laughed with embarrassment. "Thornton exaggerates. In the beginning all I saw was that she was good at sums and products and dividends. To be honest, I was *slow* to see her real powers." He halted briefly and surveyed the open part of the workings. "Aye. I shudder to think I once considered meself fit to run this contract on me own! I'd never have gotten out of the sidings." He turned to Thornton. "Ye sent her on to me in the very nick of time."

Robert Stephenson nodded thoughtfully. "The chances our life may depend on! It does not do to dwell on them too deeply!" He looked at John and said, more briskly, "And now she's the scourge of Manchester, I hear!"

John shook his head. "It's just the unfamiliarity of dealing with a lady makes them say it. There's many men her equals." He looked again at the cutting, where Walker, one of his gangers, had just blown a blast on a horn. "Watch out!" he warned.

"A shilling says it's a blank," Thornton said.

John just managed to get in "You're on!" before the bank of the cutting lifted and dissolved in smoke. Thornton said "Damn!" just as the roar of the explosion reached them.

"Never bet against Walker's shotfiring," John advised.

Thornton counted out a shilling. "They stand so close," he said. "The wonder is no one's hurt!"

John pulled a grimly resigned face. "I've done telling them. You could talk a blue month. It'll take a death to bring sense into their behaviour.

Mutilation means nothing. A stone pierced Bacca's cheek last week—he swallowed it, he was so surprised. Now he sips gin through the hole for a laugh! That was him standing closest just now!"

Stephenson, who had turned round a moment earlier, drew John's attention to a young lad running down the track behind them. "Probably wants you."

They stopped to wait for him to catch them up.

"There'll be trouble up the line tomorrow," Thornton said, merely making casual conversation.

John pricked up his ears at once. "What trouble?"

"Calley," Thornton said. "Doing the Todmorden–Hebden Bridge section. He's having a payout. First for seven weeks."

John whistled. "Irish navvies, too," he said. "The gentle, abstemious people!"

Stephenson chuckled grimly. "That'll start something!"

"I don't hold with it," John said. "I'm starting to pay out weekly here. From next Saturday."

The two others looked to see if he was joking. "Isn't that asking for trouble?" Stephenson suggested.

"I don't know." John smiled. "But I think not."

"He's up to something," Thornton said.

"Mebbe."

The running lad caught up with them at that moment. "Lord John! Sir! Trouble at number seven shaft, sir." He struggled for breath.

"They are coming by battalions!" Thornton quipped.

His levity startled Robert Stephenson. "The new engine?" he asked anxiously.

"Nay—this lad's come from off the face. What trouble?"

"We're into fractures. Like buggery. It's nothing but powder in places."

"Damnation!" John swore. "And thou art on the Manchester face?"

The lad's eyes rolled as he worked out which face he was on. "Aye," he confirmed at last.

"Double damnation!" Thornton said.

"Why?" Robert Stephenson asked.

"We struck fractures on the Leeds face of number six on Saturday," John said. "They're two chains apart still—so there's probably a month working in fractured grit. Thank God we've got your new engine! We'd not make Boxing Day without it. Not with this."

"Got enough carpenters?" Thornton asked.

"Ye spend so much time shoring up," John said.

"Mr. Stephenson knows something of tunnelling . . ." Thornton gently pointed out. John, who had intended to refer to cost, not to offer an explanation (for he had worked at Kilsby Tunnel under Robert Stephenson), was fleetingly annoyed at this correction.

"Thank God, I've little to do with it these days," Stephenson said. "What's their worry over bonus?"

"We're afraid of losing it," the lad interjected.

John was still deep in thought. "Ye'll not lose bonus," he said. And though he spoke offhandedly, as if dismissing the least of his problems, Robert Stephenson noticed at once that the lad was instantly reassured. It was only a little incident but to an observant man it revealed much of John Stevenson's power with his own people.

"Go back to number seven," John told the lad. "Tell them they'll not lose bonus. And tell Chalky I'll send two chippies directly."

The lad began to lope back up the moorland track. The three men started the final descent to Deanroyd. "Welcome to Summit, Mr. Stephenson!" John said. "It is, as ye see, a very ordinary day!"

When they reached the turnpike, John led them to the mouth of the big oval shaft—the same route by which he had taken Arabella three months earlier. The wall was only slightly advanced from the state it had been in then, mainly because the bricklayers had meanwhile been at work lining the southern end, which now ran at full diameter for over a furlong. Now they were back, bringing the oval wall up to ground level. The more muck that came out southward, the better, for that way gravity did the work of steam.

"There's my man," John said, indicating a bricklayer on some scaffolding opposite. "Thomas Metcalfe."

"That one?" Robert Stephenson asked in such surprise that John turned to him and laughed.

"What d'ye expect?" he said. "Cloven feet, horns, tail, and a stink of brimstone?" He looked back at Metcalfe. "No," he said, "he's a good man. The best brickie I have and a man with a brain to fit him for great places if he took the notion."

"You admire him!" Stephenson said.

"I've a lot of time for Tom Metcalfe. Aye."

He spoke too quietly for his voice to carry across the shaft, but Metcalfe's apprentice, a lad named Baxandall, spotted them and reached up through the scaffolding to tug his master's trousers. Metcalfe looked down and followed Baxandall's eyes up to where the contractor, flanked by the two engineers, stood silhouetted against the sky. For a long moment they stared thus in open assessment of each other. Then John said to the engineers, without taking his eyes from Metcalfe, "I'll catch up with you at

number twelve or eleven. Don't let any man go down number seven by the
new engine yet. I mean to be first man down."

Stephenson looked at him, puzzled.

"It's my way," John said. "I never ask any man to take risks I've not
faced."

The engineer's doubt turned to admiration. "By God," he said.
"You're the man, all right! I'll go down with ye."

As the two men left, Thornton gave his arm a reassuring squeeze.

Stevenson walked around to the eastern edge, directly above the bricklayer. From there a knotted rope, tied to a stake, led down to the scaffolding. With an agility that brought gasps of surprise from the bricklayers—
and a cheer from a passing horseman, whose empty dram rang like thunder
in that great oval sounding box—Stevenson let himself down the rock face
to the scaffolding.

Metcalfe must have thought Stevenson was falling, for he strode
swiftly across the platform to catch him. "You all right, Mr. Stevenson,
sir?" he asked in his strange, half-Hampshire, half-Lancashire tongue.

"Thankee," Stevenson said, delicately leaving open the question of
whether he had needed help or not. He looked about him and raised an
appreciative eyebrow. "Ye're doing well."

Metcalfe, his calm returning, stretched to his full height and gazed at
Stevenson through narrowed eyelids. *"How* well?" he asked. A little smile
pulled down the corners of his mouth. He was tall, square, well built—a
good physical match to Stevenson. But he was ten years younger, ten years
less crafty—a poorer match there by a decade. For a moment Stevenson
pictured this fair youngster in jail. He shuddered at—indeed, shrank
from—the necessity of it. But he chased the thought from his mind and
faced the man he was going to have to risk putting to the treadmill.

"Well enough," he said casually. "That's what we're to talk over. Isn't
it?"

Metcalfe merely smiled. Stevenson had come to *him.* He felt he could
claim round one.

"Tell the truth," Stevenson went on. "I'm amazed to see all the brickies
here. All at work."

"Oh?" Metcalfe said, feeling his strength. "How's that?"

Stevenson dug him in the ribs. "Someone whispered to me ye was all
off to a better contract with Calley up the line."

Metcalfe smiled at that, for Calley was a notorious master. "Ye'd soon
come to grief," he said, "believing all what's whispered hereabouts."

"That's what *I* said," Stevenson answered. "I *told* them that. I said—if
they'd had better terms offered, any man of 'em, he'd come straightway to
me afore he *did* anything."

Metcalfe, unnerved by this almost sycophantic agreement, did not know how to answer.

Stevenson went on: "Even if he were only seeking better terms—never mind no offer from elsewhere—even a man *seeking* terms'd come first to me afore *doing* anything. Aren't I right, Metcalfe?"

Metcalfe licked his lips. The sycophantic note had melted to reveal an edge of menace. He searched Stevenson's face for some plain meaning.

Stevenson pressed him further still: "There's other whispers, too, Metcalfe. I hear many vile and ugly whispers up on them moors. They say the brickies is formed in combination and will act in concert to restrain working on this contract."

Now that it was openly said, Metcalfe's confidence began to return. This was ground he had prepared to fight over. "I shall say nothing as to that." He looked at his pile of unlaid bricks and the position of the sun in the sky.

"I see," Stevenson said.

The bricklayer's lip curled almost imperceptibly. "Make what ye like of it."

Now Stevenson leaned toward him and spoke urgently. "I hope, Metcalfe . . . I devoutly hope, that if any brickie here, or any other man, navvy or tradesman, wanted better terms, and could show just cause, *good* cause, I hope he'd come direct to me."

Metcalfe took the bait. "What would ye say were good cause, Mr. Stevenson?"

Stevenson drew back and spoke in more measured tones, no longer seeming to care if the other believed or not. "Just at this very moment, Metcalfe, I know a sight more about *bad* causes than good ones. And I'd say it's a bad cause that stops any man from dealing direct with his master. I'd say it's a bad cause that seeks to . . ."

He had done it! How easy! He had drawn Metcalfe out into anger. Anger was going to be this man's Achilles heel. "There's many masters *think* so," Metcalfe sputtered. "And there's many and many a man here it fills with sadness, Lord John, to find thee among that other camp. When not three month back thou were one among us."

Stevenson shook his head sadly, patronizingly. "I'm one among thee still, see thee. But . . . lad! There's ways of getting forward and there's ways of getting bogged in the mire. And if . . ." Metcalfe's anger was again at a boiling point. ". . . Listen!" Stevenson persisted, dominating him. "If Tom Metcalfe wants a bigger wage, let Tom Metcalfe talk with Lord John. Man to man."

"Servant to master!" The venom in that reply shocked Stevenson profoundly. He had reached into wells of bitterness and anger whose existence he had never suspected—and he had known Tom Metcalfe well for the best part of a year.

"Flesh and blood all," he soothed. "And free men. It's the same for Arthur Burroughs. If he wants more, he can ask. And Wilfred Hope." He wanted Metcalfe to know he knew the names. "But when the *three* of ye set up shop as a committee to ask on behalf of Peter Etheridge, and young Baxandall, and Bennett, and Webster, and XYZ-and-parcel, I tell thee—I smell fire and brimstone!"

The bitterness still lay heavy upon Metcalfe. "Ye talk as if me or Wilf or Arthur coming to ask you was like equal met with equal!" Spittle showered from his lips.

Stevenson's mood changed again. Now he was sad, remote, magisterial. "I've thought same as thee. Many a time. I've thought, 'Let's act in concert.' And I've been against right villains—not fair men the likes of me. But men who've buggered off to America, owing thousands to me and mine. Subcontractors who underbid and went bankrupt, leaving navvies and tradesmen to starve . . ."

"Aye. Aye—I've met it too, and all," Metcalfe said.

"So it's easy work saying, 'Let's all join together. Act as one. Make a union.' " He shook his head at the folly of it. "But thou should'st look at the destination afore thou buys a ticket."

"Destination?" The idea puzzled Metcalfe. "What's wrong with it, then?"

"What's wrong with it! I'll tell thee what's bloody wrong. At far end of thy road is a fat clerk with white hands who ye've never met, calls hisself 'union negotiator,' with an address the likes of thee'd never visit; and puts on an old-pals-together act with a great fat toad *I* never met, calling hisself 'master's negotiator' in a house *I* never visited. And every time *they* hiccup, *we* dance. I'll tell thee, too"—he made it a bald statement rather than a threat—". . . I'll have none of it. Not here. Not while I live and breathe."

He saw the shutters falling across Metcalfe's mind as he spoke and he knew how, if need arose, he could always cut off further communication between them.

"It doesn't sound that bad to me," Metcalfe said confidently. "At least it sounds like thy 'fat toad' and our 'fat white clerk' is equal."

"Aye!" Stevenson's disgust was total. "Equal! Equal in villainy, equal in love of comfort, equal in hatred of all enterprise, equal alike in their hatred of thee and me."

Metcalfe, though he understood the meaning of the words, lacked the experience of the world that could turn them into whole, meaningful statements. He waved his hand dismissively. "We're all entitled to an opinion. . . ." He made it sound a generous concession. Stevenson, listening glumly, watching dourly, felt suddenly old. "I'll not get drawn on . . . all that," Metcalfe continued. "All those . . . it's too vague, all that. Too far in the future. It's here and now for me. For *us*. For the likes of us. Here and now."

He paused, as if he expected an interruption from Stevenson. But the contractor merely nodded, unconvinced, and said, "I've said my say. It's thy turn."

Metcalfe stood straighter, a little awkwardly. "I'm speaking . . . we are speaking on behalf of—"

"Hold hard! Just a minute! Hang on!" Stevenson cut in. "What was that word? *We?*"

Metcalfe smiled, like a magician before the climax of a trick. He leaned over the scaffolding. "Burroughs! Hope!" he called.

Stevenson acted at once. "I'm having no meeting here," he said and swung himself out on to the ladder and quickly clambered down to the track. Metcalfe had no choice but to surrender his initiative and follow.

Burroughs and Hope came nervously over.

"Committee, is it?" Stevenson asked.

"Officially appointed," Metcalfe said primly.

Stevenson looked at each in turn. "My God!" he said vehemently. "Ye'll build your own gallows! And splice the hangman's rope for him!"

Metcalfe, seeing the others flinch, quickly went on the offensive. "What are you threatening, Mr. Stevenson?"

Stevenson turned slowly and spoke in a low key. "Statement of fact, man." He shook his head again, more in sorrow than in anger. "Statement of fact. This game's got rules, see thee. And I'll play by 'em. Burroughs. Hope." He looked at each.

"Sir?" they said.

But he merely shook his head again. Metcalfe leaped in once more: "On behalf of the bricklayers at this working we are asking for an increase in the rate."

"Ye've let us down," Burroughs said, emboldened by Metcalfe's firmness.

"I'm still listening," Stevenson said, turning inquiringly to Hope.

"Ye put navvies on bonus two month back," Hope said.

"Aye. That's true," Stevenson said flatly.

"Well then!" Hope spread the palms of his hands to show that their point was made.

"Well what?" Stevenson asked. "What's that to do with it? I put navvies on bonus because I needed their output. If this driftway's not through by first of January next—that's it. I'm as good as dead. Off the contract! Duffed! Dominoed! And the likes of you lot are standing cap in hand before the next contractor. Ye want that?" He looked searchingly from one to the other. "Ye want a man like Skelm back?"

"Nay!" they chorused.

"Or go and work for Calley up Todmorden?"

Their denials were even more vociferous this time.

"So! Aye—I put navvies on bonus. But I've not got money to chuck around. I've no need yet for extra bricklaying. I'd not fart no louder if ye laid twenty or two hundred cubic yard. Ye may all piss off tomorrow for all I care. Good bloody riddance."

"That's not what we understood," Metcalfe said, his confidence unshaken.

Stevenson looked contemptuously at the three of them. "Oh? Who's the great teacher then?" he asked. "Who's been broadening yer understanding?"

Hope began, "Mr. Thornton said . . ."

"Shut up!" Metcalfe snapped.

"Well, he's wrong," Stevenson said. "But if ye're still seeking understanding, I'll tell ye: If I was another contractor likes of Skelm, likes of Calley, likes of a dozen others we've all met and could name, if I was like them, I'd bounce the three of ye off this site clear across Yorkshire. But I'm not like them. Ye *know* what I'm like—soft as poor Will. Mebbe that's why ye'll try this on. So I'll tell ye."

"Tell us what?" Metcalfe sneered.

Stevenson turned to him and looked him up and down. "The whole truth, Metcalfe. All of it. Do ye know how many bricks'll be required for the whole Summit Tunnel—including all twelve shafts we're leaving?" He looked around to invite the others to answer. Several of the bricklayers had walked over to stand within earshot.

"Ten million?" Hope suggested.

Burroughs looked at him in scorn. "Never!" he said.

"Listen then," Stevenson said. And now *he* was the magician about to climax a trick. "Twenty . . . three . . . million!"

Incredulous whistles rose around him but Stevenson was interested only in Metcalfe's response. This was the crucial moment. The bricklayer looked around at the satisfaction and glee on the faces of his brothers and his whole expression turned to open scorn. From then on Stevenson lost all compunction about the possibility of running the man into jail, for Metcalfe was, at heart, not interested in the welfare, security, or wages of the Summit tradesmen; he was out to fight some remoter, more abstract battle.

"Twenty-three million," Stevenson repeated when the commotion died. "Aye—and eight thousand ton of Roman cement. And the last one—the very lastest brick—*must* be laid December twelvemonth. One year! And ye think there's no bonus coming! Someone's head wants looking at." He carefully avoided turning his eyes on Metcalfe, but the others all did.

"We'd want details. We've gone too far to—" Metcalfe began.

"Gone too far!" Stevenson mocked. "Ye've gone nowhere. Ye've gone to the threshold of the jailhouse door, that's where ye've gone. But I'll tell ye. I said I would and so I will. From this twenty-eight December, when the driftway's finished and the main working can start, I'll pay two shilling and threepence—twenty-seven pence—a yard for clean brickwork up to spess." He turned abruptly, taking them by surprise, and left. At the edge of the oval shaft he paused and turned back. "Ye may think it over. I'll come back at knocking off tonight."

After he had gone, Hope looked at Metcalfe. "Well!" he said. "*There's* something what don't run square and true with what Mr. Thornton—"

"Shut up!" Metcalfe said. "He's coming back!"

And indeed Stevenson stood again at the edge of the oval. "I'll tell ye one thing that's fast now," he shouted, walking to rejoin them. "If ye've any notion of forming any kind or degree of combination or union, ye'll put all such thought from ye." He smiled and looked at each in turn. "I'll tolerate papists, Jews, devil worshippers, and Irishmen. If ye twist me arm, I'll even put Lancashire men on." He grinned and pointed to James Moffat of Littleborough. "Like old buggerlugs here! But I'll never, never, never make terms with a union. Never!" He left again, this time for good.

"Yes, *master!*" Metcalfe called after him.

Stevenson arranged with Fernley, his clerk of works, to take on extra carpenters for shoring up through the fractures. He was about to start out on the path over Summit when he saw Metcalfe waiting for him at the edge of the turnpike. He stopped about five paces short, forcing the bricklayer to walk to him. As Metcalfe came, he began to speak, trying to regain the initiative: "I don't know what your game may be, Mr. Stevenson . . ."

"Then I have the advantage of you, Metcalfe. For I know yours—from foundation to toppin' out." He halted, wondering if it was even worth trying to talk to Metcalfe. When he spoke again it was as if he were merely making a test of the other's ability to follow. "There's only two really dangerous sorts of men in this life. One is the villain that lacks all principle and all regard for his fellow man. I'm bound to say I've never met such a villain—and I've mixed with some right desperate folks. The other is the very opposite. Some may even call him saint. He's the man that's so full of principle, so full of regard for his fellow man in general, that he's no time left for the neighbour folk around him."

Metcalfe smiled sarcastically. "And you have met such a man, of course. You think that's me."

Stevenson changed his position on the highway, showing that half his mind was no longer eager to be away up the path. "I'd be glad to be shown up for wrong," he said. "But thou'rt a born believer. Thou'll find a cause —mebbe it's Chartism or working man's rights or anything of that nature— and thou'll crucify thyself for it."

"How can you possibly say the like of that?"

"I've watched thee."

"Huh!"

"I have. I've forgotten more about men than thou'll ever learn. It's my trade."

"You may imagine so. But if it's teachin' and learnin' time, I fancy it's thee that's got the lessons comin'. The middle classes got their demands, their *just* demands, in '32. We didn't. Now we're goin' to get 'em too. Thou'll see."

Metcalfe paused for breath but Stevenson cut across him. "If I truly thought thou were after betterment for these lads of thine, I'd tread soft with thee and deal with thee to the best of my ability. But if, as I truly suspect, I find thou art willing to trample over my lads' better interests in pursuit of this bloody union, I'll not scruple to smash thee. That's me last word to thee—play fair and thou need fear naught. But try coming it with unions and conspiracies and ye'd best wear armour double indemnified and triple proof."

Metcalfe drew himself up to full height, looking at Stevenson eye to eye. "Thy threats hold no fear for me, Lord John. The interests of my men and of their union are one and the same. Fight for one and ye fight for all. We'll get our rights our own way. No thanks to thee."

Stevenson smiled, not the least put out. "Thou'll find soon enough thou'st picked wrong battleground, wrong tactics, wrong master."

He walked off across the turnpike without waiting for any answer. Nevertheless, answer came before he reached the other verge. "But the right *principles!* And in the long run that's all that counts," Metcalfe called.

"The long run?" Stevenson called back. "In the long run we're all dead!"

# Chapter 23

Luncheon was long and heavy, for Robert Stephenson was a champion eater. "Not as athletic as his father" was the kindly way of putting it. Nora was glad that Thornton, who still was incapable of behaving normally with her, stood in such awe of the great man, for he hardly looked her way all the meal. Stephenson was also a champion storyteller and kept them amused with his account of his days in South America, when he had worked as a mining engineer in Colombia. At one point he looked around at them and said: "Truth to tell, there is a direct connection between my time out there and the work that brought me here today." He smiled. "The man who can tell me shall have the privilege of buying the next bottle of wine. For a special toast."

No one could guess. Nora, looking at their faces, could see that Jack Whitaker thought he was on to it, but he was being cautious.

"I'll prompt you," Stephenson said. "High-pressure steam."

"Your father?" Walter asked.

Stephenson shook his head.

"Watt?" John suggested, with even less confidence.

Nora nodded at Whitaker. "He knows."

"Perhaps . . . no, I'd rather not."

"He's too mean to buy the bottle!" Nora teased.

"He has a son called Francis, also in the business?" Whitaker asked.

"You've got him," Stephenson confirmed.

"Trevithick," Whitaker said at last.

Stephenson grinned and nodded. "Make it this same claret," he said. "We'll toast the memory of one of the greatest."

"Trevithick?" Walter said dubiously.

"Cornishman, was he?" John asked.

Stephenson looked sadly from one to the other. "How quickly history gets lost! And how fickle is reputation! Trevithick was a greater man than all of them—greater than Watt. Far greater. And than my father—which I say in no disparagement, for he's said as much himself many a time. A genius. The kind that comes along once in a century—if our luck holds. Yet you've never heard of him . . ."—he nodded at John. "You're doubtful of his achievement . . ."—he turned to Walter. And then he asked of Whitaker: "And you—what do you know of him?"

"I know nothing of his recent activity."

"His 'recent activity' is rotting in a pauper's grave in Dartford. Six years he's been at it there."

No one spoke; Robert Stephenson was not the sort of storyteller you prompted with questions at every pause.

"I met him in Peru in 1827—or perhaps it was Colombia. No one knew. He was penniless, of course. It was a very characteristic Trevithick sort of tale. He'd gone out to install steam in their mines in Peru and walked"—he smacked his hands together—"like *that* into civil war. One side presses him as fortifications engineer, then the other side takes him and turns him into surgeon! He hadn't a brass button left when I met up with him."

The potboy came across with the new wine bottle and Whitaker indicated he should pour all round. John stopped Nora's glass. "I've work for thee," he said. She pouted in pretended annoyance.

"Yes." Stephenson lifted his glass to look at the colour. The others, thinking he was about to make the promised toast, reached for theirs, but he rested his again, and looked around at them. "I remembered my father telling me how when he was a lad, not yet twenty, he went to Wylam Colliery in Newcastle on his day off—he walked all the way—just to see a new steam locomotive. The first they'd ever had up there. They were trying to run it on rails of wood! In fact they never gave it a chance. I don't believe it ever ran. But that engine was what put the gleam in my father's eye—and the steam in his veins. That is where the Stephensons began. And it was Trevithick who built it. So you may imagine my thoughts as I stood out there in that God-forsaken place and saw Trevithick himself, in the most straitened circumstances. It was a chance at last to repay a twenty-year debt."

There was a ruminative silence before Walter said, "I had no idea he was so important."

"Nor did his country. Nor . . ."—Stephenson laughed—"nor even his wife. When he returned from Peru, he landed at Falmouth and they'd not let him ashore, because he was destitute again—having lost what I gave him. They threw him in jail and sent for his wife, who kept a pub, the White Hart, I think, over near Penzance." He chuckled again, preparing them for the point of the tale. "She came over, bailed him out, and then drove back in her carriage without even seeing him—left him to walk!"

They all laughed at that.

Stephenson looked serious again. "Yet *there* was the man who built the first practical high-pressure steam engine, built the first railroad, ran a steam-carriage service in London, built a steam dredger, a steam shovel, a steam threshing engine . . . and all these iron ships, you know—they

owe more to Trevithick than anyone will admit. More than the Admiralty
would admit, for they never granted him a bean on his petition."

They looked down in silence at their glasses.

"And he died in a pauper's grave, eh!" John said.

Stephenson sighed. "I heard of it too late. Yes. Too late." He looked
up. "Curious thing, you know. When it became known down there in
Dartford that poor old Trevithick hadn't left enough for a proper burial,
the workpeople—not the masters, the workpeople—at the Hall Engineering Works got up a subscription to give him a decent grave. But they failed
to gather enough. Think of that, eh? Think of the fortunes people were
making in railways! By the time I learned of it and went down there . . .
they couldn't even find the spot where he lay."

John, thinking of the pauper's grave where Nora's father lay, looked
across at her and pulled a glum face. But she glanced from him to Walter
Thornton, then immediately lowered her eyes and coloured. It cost some
effort, but she avoided catching Thornton's eye. Stephenson, unaware of
these exchanges, proposed a toast to the memory of Trevithick.

Shortly after that he returned to Manchester by train, having sent his
hired mount back to the livery stable before the luncheon began.

Walter Thornton, when the train had gone, suddenly remembered that
Nora had, in fact, been their hostess.

"I quite overlooked it—being in a tavern," he said greatly agitated. "I
must thank her properly."

Stevenson grinned broadly. "Never fear. There's no ceremony with her!
I'll say your thanks for you," he assured him.

But Thornton would hear none of it; he must thank her himself. When
they arrived back at the Royal Oak, Stevenson went up to tell her of
Thornton's mortification and how he wished to make amends.

She was changing from her best plain dress, which she had put on
especially for the lunch, into her everyday plain dress. All she said was
"Huh!" in a tone of deep scorn.

"What'll I go down and tell him?" he asked.

"Send him about his business." She formed a curl around her little
finger and released it.

"No kind word? Poor bugger's smitten with thee."

She turned to him, shocked that he could say such a thing.

"Desperate bad," he added.

"Tskoh!" She turned away again, losing her patience. "I'll discuss it no
further. Thou should die of shame sooner than say such things."

He smiled indulgently. "See it from his point of view. Think what it's
like being married with yon tender angel."

Nora's laugh rang across the room.

"Not," he went on, "as I've got anything against her. In fact . . ." He grew thoughtful. "If you ask my opinion, I believe there's a strength in that one as'll rock young Mr. Walter on his heels one day. I fancied her for temperance work among my lads but she's not come round to it."

"Temperance!" Nora's surprise quickly turned to scorn. "That Arabella! And our lads!"

"She's got the makings of that sort of person. She lacks a fit purpose. But when she finds it, or it finds her . . ."

"Thou!" She smiled at him softly. "Thou never sees a dirty grey goose but thou art shouting what a lovely swan!" Her face fell then. "But I'll tell thee this for nothing: The thought of going over Summit to live at Rough Stones—it fills me with dread. We'll have *him* living in our pockets. And *her,* likely."

"Oh?"

"He's not comfortably wed, I'll tell thee that. He's like a man what's fed on nothing but curry from birth."

There was a knock at the door.

"Seems normal to me. He were behaving normal up there, today."

"Normal to thee." She smiled. "Thou'rt no woman."

He stood behind her; she spoke to him via her looking glass. He leaned forward, dropping his hands in front of her, and slipped one of them into the V of her blouse and under her shift. "Art complaining?" he asked.

The knock was repeated.

"See who that is," she said.

He did not move for a moment. Then, caressing her breast more fervently, he leaned down to kiss her. She leaned back upon him and closed her eyes, surrendering to him.

In the glass John saw the door soundlessly open to frame Walter Thornton. As his eyes took in the scene his jaw fell open and he stood transfixed in horror and shame at his intrusion. Only then did he notice Stevenson's mocking gaze fixed on him in the looking glass. He closed his eyes and turned to leave, pale and shaken.

Nora, feeling John's lips smile, opened her eyes, expecting to meet his; instead she met two pools of white. Quickly she followed his gaze to the glass—just in time to see a hand slip from between the door and jamb so as to ease the door silently closed.

"The new maid," John told her, and she pretended to believe him. But she knew *that* hand.

He pulled himself away and, readjusting his trousers, crossed to the door. "I'll go down and tell Thornton to take his appetites home where they belong."

He arrived downstairs in time to see Thornton hurrying over the square; Nora must surely see him, too. Chuckling to himself, he returned to her. "Must have gone already," he said.

Her eyes fixed on him. She bit a little sliver of skin from her lip.

"To work," he said.

She remained silent, not taking her eyes from him. In the end her steady gaze discomfited him and he had to take her by the shoulders, steer her to the table, and lift their business ledgers himself from the chest. While he did so she smiled a little smile of secret triumph.

"What I want—" he began.

"John," she said, "why would Mr. Thornton be bound off now for Manchester? What d'ye think he forgot to thank Robert Stephenson for?"

John paused. "Manchester," he said.

"He went direct to Littleborough station. There's no company train for Summit, is there?"

"Nay," he said. Then in a more distant and altogether softer voice he added: "Poor young bugger."

Nora, having felt excluded by John's pretence about the maid and Thornton, was suddenly and deeply touched by this unexpected sadness. In the same instant she divined Thornton through John's tenderness. She saw the man's true poverty with John's insight and measured his hunger by John's compassion.

She stretched her hand across the table and squeezed his where it lay loosely on the ledger. He caught it up and held it tight between his. She moved her other hand across to wrap around his, and for a while they sat thus, locked in awe of each other and of the moment.

"I've none but thee," he said simply.

She, not fully understanding, was suddenly impelled to ask, "Hast thou no family? Thou hast never said."

He continued to look at her. And through his gaze something seemed to leap from him to her as if from the very heart of loneliness and isolation; she was filled with an urge to cradle and comfort him, though she did not stir from where she sat.

"I've none but thee I may share with," he said, leaving her uncertain as to whether he was answering her question or amplifying his own statement. "None I may talk with. Explain meself to."

She squeezed his hand until her arm muscles ached.

"Not even on Summit," he said. "There's not a man there'd understand. Not Whitaker. Not . . . yon poor bugger, Thornton."

"Not Whitaker?" she asked. "He seems an educated sort of man." She knew very well that that was not what he meant; she hoped to draw it out of him.

"I sometimes ask meself why I chose Whitaker. Mebbe it's to keep before us a living picture of where straight thinking'll bring ye. He thinks right for an employee—he's the same kind as Thornton—but . . ." He shook his head. "He'd never manage a business. Not our thrusting sort. I mean—take thee and me. We see a crow fly hundred feet overhead and we say, 'How can I put that crow to my advantage?' That's our nature, thee and me. But not Jack Whitaker. He'd lend ye his arse and shit through his ribs if he could think how it was to be managed."

"Aye. He's soft as a suckin' duck. I'll grant that." Her expression changed quickly. "One thing puzzled me when we ate. There was none of 'em talked of striking or combination."

"Why do'st thou ask?" His eyes narrowed.

She thought a while, still looking at him, before she answered. "I think thou wants one," she said.

He sighed and shrugged. His fingers teased the edge of the leather quarterings on the ledger. "I don't know," he confessed. "We may need one." He sat down again.

"Need! How do'st thou make that out?"

"But if I manage it wrong . . . eh—it's a perilous way."

"I'd say we need a strike like we need twins."

"Still," he said, with something close to conviction, "where the rewards are great . . . the risks are great in like measure."

She realized he was quite serious, not—as he sometimes did—just saying things to hear how they sounded.

"Which trade?" she asked. She was all sharpness now; a casual eavesdropper would have thought it her contract, not his. For a fraction of a second she saw him wondering whether to allow himself to understand her or whether to pretend incomprehension. She smiled—their minds were wonderfully alike; when concentrated by the pursuit of profit, they could leap instantaneously for the identical point. There was something about this strike—or nonstrike—that he could not share with Whitaker or Thornton; and it was something that left him undecided. If only he would share that thinking, she knew they would not quarrel in the decision.

The sight of the ledger, which he had opened casually, without particular aim, seemed to determine him. "There's a weakness in our contract I should've seen and didn't," he said, not quite managing to look her in the eye.

"Bricklayers?" she suggested.

He raised his hands in a gesture of resignation. "I can tell thee nothing." He stood again and turned from her while he spoke.

She, thinking he was now bitter, ran to him, cursing herself for being so forward. "Eh, love. I'm sorry, I'm sorry!"

But he was not the least annoyed. "Nay," he said, taking her in his arms and hugging her like a bear. "No cause. There's no cause for that. I'm . . . it's just I'm puzzled how thou art always ahead of me. It's thy nimbleness of mind."

Happy again, she leaned into him and said, "I had nothing to do all morning, 'cepting think about the contract."

He let her go and held her chair for her to sit again.

There was a knock at the door. This time it really was the maid, come to make up the fire.

"And what did thou think of it?" he asked.

"I think I know what weakness thou may be on about," she answered, indicating the maid with her eyes.

"Nay, talk on," he said.

She shook her head. He smiled at her caution but waited quietly until the maid had gone.

"That one's a gossip," Nora said. "The weakness, or so I believe, is that we get our bonus only on a finished yard of drift or a finished yard of tunnel. Unlined tunnel pays us nothing—but we've got to pay navvies on their work, bonus and all."

"Aye," he sighed. "Good lass. Question is, does Tom Metcalfe know that?"

"How would *he* know?" Nora asked.

"It seems like Thornton's been gassing on to 'em." She looked shocked. "Not with malice aforethought, see thee," he assured her.

"Nay, mebbe not. But the end result is no different." Her face hardened. "Poor bugger thou called him. I know what I'd call him! To his face if he were here. I'd tell him his name for nothing."

John was not to be diverted. "Never thou mind all that now. If the cream be spilled, it's spilled. What I want thee to do is to work from our weakest position. . . . Let's think of all the worst possibilities and see where it leaves us. Hast thou stomach for it?"

"Aye," she said bravely—even a touch scornfully. "It'd not be the first time"—she tapped the side of her head—"up here."

"Then let's suppose Metcalfe and the brickies know. Suppose they strike and we don't get bonus. Suppose the navvies go on at full steam, and all the other trades, and we pay out full bonus to all, weekly like I've said. And suppose every supplier gets frightened and wants cash-with-order. . . ."

"And suppose thee and me just goes out and hangs ourselves!" she said; but her tone was light and she spoke with a smile. "I'm sure the Manchester & Leeds'd stake thee," she added seriously. "It's not their interest to have a strike succeed."

"Course!" he agreed. "If it comes to a strike, I tell thee, if they start at knocking-on time, I'd have the ringleaders away and the rest o' the lads back by knocking-off time. On my terms."

The calm that came over him as he spoke frightened her. It was a side of him his men knew well, but he did not often show it at home. She was glad never to have to face him in opposition and she pitied the led, though not the leaders, among the bricklayers.

"But," he went on, "I must know the very worst. I must know how long we could last if all went against us. If all income ceased and all outgoin's went on."

She opened his writing case and took out his pens and set to work. Now that the question was out in the open, he, of course, wanted an immediate answer. Having pondered it silently for over a week, he now found it unbearable to have it hanging between them for a minute.

"Thou must have some idea," he hinted.

She merely smiled and continued with her preparations, scraping the dried ink from the nibs and firming down the blank paper.

"If thou has done all the thinking thou lays claim to."

"Nay!" she said. "Shut up. Thou never employed me to guess."

"Me employ *thee!*" he exclaimed with ironic astonishment.

She looked at him seriously. "I'll say this much," she said. "Thou knows these books as well as me. Thou knows we've more cash now—by several thousand pound—than we had three month back when we started. And it's *thee* that's done it. I couldn't say how, but Skelm lost his coin by the bucketful, and thou hast never dipped under three thousand. Like I say, I don't rightly know how—but the only difference is thee and him. So—I'll go far enough to say that the answer thou wants'll be better than what thou supposes now."

"But how *much* better?" he persisted, tantalized rather than satisfied by this answer.

She shook her head, sadly and pityingly, to herself and returned to the work. "Piss off," she told him, not looking up. "Go and hire yon screw that Stephenson had this morning. Go and ride somewhere."

"Nay," he laughed. "I'll go to the works." He paused at the door and added: "When I've got thy answer I'll tell thee all."

*     *     *

Impatience brought him home again by five. He had the bricklayers' meeting to attend at seven in the oval shaft at the far end of the tunnel; he decided for once to go by horse, though he was not the world's best or most willing rider. He had tried Robert Stephenson's hack that morning for a short stretch of the road back and had found it docile enough. So, as he turned the corner by the church, he left his usual path up to the town square and crossed instead to the livery stables.

Just as he entered their gateway a voice behind him called his name; it was a voice he knew, yet he could not at once place it. The street, when he turned, was deserted except for a cat who stalked a small flock of poultry while keeping a wary sideways eye on two geese. Then he saw the man who had called him, and instantly he placed the voice: the Reverend Doctor Prendergast.

His sly black shape erupted self-importantly from the churchyard gate. Stevenson waited and held a smile of welcome until he drew close enough to discern clearly in the failing daylight. Prendergast was not pleased.

"Have ye quelled this mutiny?" were his first words.

"Welcome, reverend," Stevenson said.

"I don't like it. Not a bit. Don't like it a bit."

"I'm about to hire a hack here to take me up to the strike meeting tonight."

Clifford, the ostler, relieving himself against the tack-room wall near by, shouted over his shoulder, "Which one?"

"Yon ye hired the other Mr. Stephenson this morning."

"Stephenson?" Prendergast asked. "Robert?"

"Right away?" Clifford asked, shaking a burst of golden droplets from a member of equine dimensions before he buttoned up the front flap of his breeches.

"Six o'clock will do."

"What was Robert doing here?" Prendergast asked.

"He'll be up the Royal Oak, ready for you, at six, Mr. Stevenson, sir. Never fear."

"Very good."

"On the same business as me I'll be bound," the cleric answered himself.

Stevenson turned to him. "What business would that be, doctor?" he asked. "Come to tell me how to manage my affairs?"

As soon as he said it, the thought seized him that Prendergast had come out to look at his books. His heart began to race with fear. Of course that was it. There was this strike in the offing, and Prendergast, whipped to a frenzy by all these wild rumours in Manchester, was out here to seize what he could before this Chartist blood tide washed it all into oblivion.

"I'll tell ye one thing," Prendergast said. "Ye'd best move from those two wretched rooms at the Royal Oak."

Stevenson's mind almost burst at the thoughts that now came crowding in. And there was one that ran, leaping, darting, showering pure gold through . . . over . . . upon, all the rest: A frightened man is as a man of clay; skillful hands may mould him to any shape they please.

"Indeed?" He spoke as if Prendergast's command had been mere small talk.

It would be wrong to say that Stevenson formed a strategy there and then; but he certainly got an intuition of the totality of this new situation. Here was the first real chance to play Prendergast in a more positive way—the old way: from fear to salvation. But had the cleric yet stoked up enough fear within himself? Find that out first.

"Dammit!" Prendergast thundered. "You're a man of substance now. Stopping at an inn makes ye look—"

"Man of substance!" Stevenson echoed sarcastically. "My bricklayers seem to share that opinion. Well—they're in for a surprise! Is that what you've come to hear, old partner in crime?"

Prendergast, catching the ambiguity of this interruption, shot him a suspicious look. "I've not come to *hear* anything," he said darkly. "Certainly no more pleas of poverty. No sir! By no means, sir!"

"Ah! Then you've come to put your two and a half thousand pounds where your tongue is?" Stevenson made it sound only remotely like a question; but it stopped the priest in midstride. Indeed, he almost stumbled as he turned his astonished gaze upon the other.

Stevenson halted a little way ahead and turned back. "You take that for a jest?" he asked mildly. "Or plain impudence? I tell you, doctor: If you still cherish hopes of this contract, I shall now need every last penny of your pledge." Then, without waiting for Prendergast, and without much outward interest in his reaction, he resumed his stroll toward the inn.

"Will you dine with Mrs. Stevenson and myself?" he asked when the other had once more drawn level.

"No, I thank you." His politeness was that of an automaton. "I shall dine later tonight in Manchester."

"Dine twice. That is quite within the hallowed traditions of your church."

Even this insolence provoked nothing. Prendergast still walked—and looked—as if all the blood had drained out of him. All the way across the square he said nothing.

When they reached the Royal Oak the priest went out the back to relieve himself. Stevenson called for a pie and a bottle of sherry and then, when he was sure the cleric was well away, he raced upstairs to Nora. She must have noticed them crossing the square, for she was already half out of their door.

"Where is he?" she asked.

"Coming." He gripped her arm to show her how important this was. "Listen! We need his two thousand five hundred."

"Do we?" Her tone was sarcastic.

"I'm telling thee. If he doesn't go from here with that belief firm and fixed, I can do naught with him."

She grinned and nodded, taking his meaning at once.

He was already on his way back downstairs, ready to stand where the reverend doctor had last seen him.

The sherry and pie arrived upstairs immediately behind Prendergast.

"Ye'll not change your mind, doctor?" Stevenson asked when the introductions were over.

"No, thank you." He looked at his watch. "I shall take the six o'clock." He stared at Nora, evidently thinking she ought to leave them to their affairs. But she took her glass and went over to sit at the dark end of the room, lit only by the glow of the fire.

Stevenson, seated by the room's single lamp, tucked heartily into his pie. "Mrs. Stevenson is privy to all our affairs," he said.

Prendergast, on hearing that, sat opposite, but with ill grace.

"If that's so," he said, "she will know how well you've done for yourselves this last month or two."

Stevenson chewed his mouth empty and swilled down the shreds with sherry before he replied. "For all of us, doctor." He smiled. "I look upon you as a partner." He chuckled. "And never more so than now!" There was just the faintest menace in his laughter—enough for Prendergast to catch the whiff of it.

"I don't understand," he said. In fact, he said it twice.

Stevenson paused, a steaming lump of ox kidney halfway to his waiting jaws. "Very simple," he said. "Your two-and-a-half will float me ten further days at worst, twenty at best." He trapped the meat and shredded it. "Either way I'm going to need it—old silent partner!" He smiled a long smile at the other. "And you *are* silent!" he added at length.

He enjoyed Prendergast's quandary; but the priest recovered swiftly. "Very well, Stevenson," he said, with something like his former aplomb. "Let us suspend our disbelief. You prove to me you need it, and you shall have it."

He sipped his sherry and waited. Not once did his eyes stray from Stevenson's.

"You can do your sums as well as the next man, reverend," Stevenson began.

"Ah!" Prendergast cut in. "I hoped we'd get to that. You've been earning bonus on driftway and on finished tunnel. Yet you've been paying bonus only to navvies. With two hundred tradesmen on flat rate, you must have been doing nicely!"

Stevenson leaned his head to one side in provisional agreement.

"In fact, by my reckoning of the payments we have made to you from the Manchester & Leeds account, and guessing at your outgoings, I estimate that you have never dropped below two thousand pounds reserve. . . ." He paused. Stevenson discovered a piece of meat stuck between his teeth; it interested him more than this revelation. "And even if your purchasing has been"—here Prendergast looked across the room toward the fire, where Nora was sitting—"grossly inept, you must still have at least that sum put by. And probably double!" He folded his arms and smiled at the ceiling a smile of deep satisfaction.

In fishing for the piece of meat, Stevenson's eyes happened to settle briefly on Nora—where they dwelled long enough to catch the faintest shake of her head and the merest hint of a pitying grin. Fortified, he turned again to the priest. "Not bad," he confessed. "In point of fact, we have four thousand two hundred and something-odd." Then, filled with admiration, he turned to Nora, openly this time, and added: "Astute gentleman! Didn't I always say it!"

She nodded, trying to look defeated.

"And ye've come for what? Fourteen hundred? Your third share? First dividend?"

"Is that so unreasonable?"

Stevenson gave a conciliatory nod and waited.

"You've not been straight with me, Stevenson. You've pleaded poverty and desperation . . . you—you come to Manchester and I see you eat pies off street sellers . . . you live in these wretched rooms . . . you send your wife shopping for iron and timber like any tin-pot village tradesman. And yet I find you've been making money at the rate of a thousand pounds a month over these last few weeks—"

"Oh, more than that!" Stevenson interrupted cheerfully.

Both Prendergast and Nora looked at him in astonishment—Nora with some alarm, as well.

"At least double that," he went on. "The total profit, I estimate, will be within spitting distance of thirty thousand. Ten of them"—he turned a beatific smile on the priest—"for you, reverend doctor. Not a bad return on an outlay of two and a half, eh?"

"Hm! Words!" Prendergast said. But he was very calm suddenly; his annoyance had vanished and once again he settled to watch Stevenson's every gesture.

"Words so far. I agree," Stevenson said. "That's what I'm saying. You must now put your purse where your tongue has led you. My four thousand-odd will see me safely through two-to-three weeks, as I say. I need to see four-to-five weeks' clear backing if I'm to weather this storm that's now brewing. That'll see the driftway completed. Then we move into a different ocean. But first, d'ye see, I must weather the storm."

"This strike?"

"This strike. Another glass of sherry?"

Prendergast lifted the bottle but did not at once pour.

"The strike," Stevenson repeated. "Yes. I intend to provoke a strike—now that I know I can count on your backing."

He took the last bite of pie as Prendergast thumped the bottle down and exploded. A thin spout of golden sherry leaped at the ceiling from the neck of the bottle and fell upon him. Fortunately his redoubled shout of annoyance masked Nora's sudden, incontinent fit of giggles, which she stayed in midflight by holding her mouth in the sort of grip one might be driven to try on a savage dog. Then she prevented its return by busying herself wiping the doctor down and fetching cloths dampened in the ewer by the door.

Stevenson cleaned off his plate with crusts of bread. "A brief strike now," he said, as if thinking aloud, "lasting a day, say, with the ring-leaders resoundingly crushed, then given the maximum sentence—three months, I believe—yes, such a strike would do nothing but good."

Prendergast, now plainly regretting his intemperate outburst, nodded. "Well, that sounds more reasonable," he conceded. "But can you win?"

Stevenson looked at him a long, uncomfortable time before he answered. "It's risky," he admitted. "But then, the stakes are big. We'll never reach that profit if I can't rely on the labour. I have to show them now who's master—especially as I've just come up from among them. It's a choice between a pitched battle now or a running skirmish from this day until the opening ceremony."

Prendergast nodded.

"I've chosen to stand and fight . . ."

"But can you win? I ask it again."

"Are you with me, reverend? Let's cease this sparring, you and I. There's a much bigger struggle afoot and I need to know who I may count on."

Now it was Prendergast's turn for a long silence.

"I'll tell you," Stevenson continued, just before he judged that the other was about to speak. "If you want your fourteen hundred, you may have it. This very hour. I'd write you a bill of exchange now. But if you take it, then it's all Lombard Street to a china orange that we can both kiss

goodbye to any profit on this contract. On the other hand, if you support
me now, you'll get your due. Every last penny."

Prendergast had to think again. He wheezed and groaned with indecision. He looked at the windows, the floor, the door handle, the ceiling, as
if he hoped each might hold some augury. "I'll go this far," he said at last.
"I've had no part in planning this battle of yours. I've not been consulted—
if anything, I've been downright misled. So it's your decision. It's your way
of doing things. I am bound to say it would not be mine—but, when all's
said and done, it's your contract and your labour. So I'll go this far: You
deliver these men up to me, have your strike, crush it, deliver the leaders to
me, get the rest of them back on your terms, and I promise you—*then*—
that you shall have my two thousand."

"And the five hundred?" Stevenson pushed it.

Prendergast smiled, not joyfully. "Contingency reserve," he said.

Stevenson accepted with a nod. "Why d'you say deliver them to you?"
he asked.

"Have you not heard?" The priest swelled with sudden vanity. "I am
now chairman of Rochdale magistrates. Your strikers will come up before
me. And it'll be no three months, I can tell you! I'll have them transported.
Twelve years. I promise you that."

"For a one-day strike?" Stevenson said. "That would reek of vengeance, not justice. No—if you want to see your profit out of that tunnel,
you'll not help by giving our enemies a martyr. Three months is the very
*most* we need."

Prendergast was not pleased but he offered no argument. Nora could see
that something still worried John, something that had struck him as soon
as he had learned of Prendergast's chairmanship of the bench at Rochdale.

"Well . . ." Prendergast stood suddenly. "It's not what I came here
expecting. It's not something I like. But"—he looked hard at Stevenson—
"ye leave a man no choice."

Stevenson spread his hands wide, to stress his plain-dealing honesty.
"I'll write you a bill of exchange now, doctor," he offered.

Prendergast chuckled grimly. "As I say: no choice."

He took his leave of Nora curtly and went below with Stevenson. "I
must also tell you this," he added on the stair. "You can look for no
support to the Manchester & Leeds in any of this. You're only an agent of
theirs. Legally. You're an appointee, not an independent contractor. We'd
have no power to back you with cash. That must be understood."

Tom Spur, the landlord, came out of a room at the foot of the stair,
embarrassed at having been forced to overhear this threat, and trying to
show by his surprise at seeing them that he had in fact overheard nothing.

He would have been genuinely surprised if he had seen the relief and then the delight on Stevenson's face as he returned to Nora.

She scanned his eyes anxiously for some sign of how she was to behave. "Thou art a master," she said. "With men. Thou knows just what may be done with them; and thou knows how to do it. A master."

He jerked his head toward the square, where the dark shape of the priest could just be seen as it merged among the shades of night. "We've not won the war," he said. "It's not even settled yet that we've won the battle. But if yon bloody Church of England gets the better of us, I'll never hold me head up again."

It surprised her that he spoke these depressing words with such a hopeful smile. She kissed him on the nose lightly. "You'll beat him," she said.

He stood off and looked at her in surprise. " 'You'll beat him'!" he quoted in even fancier accents than hers. "What's up with thee? Swallowed Dr. Johnson?"

"Speak proper to me," she asked. "Like thou does—like you do to yon Church of England and to Mr. Thornton and them engineers. Those engineers."

He laughed.

"Nay," she persisted. "We must talk proper now."

But when he looked her in the eyes she plucked up her apron and hid her face in it giggling.

"Thou art serious?" he asked.

She nodded, still hiding her face. Then, blushing, she lowered the apron and said: "When we're at Rough Stones, we'll have three or four servants. I can't talk to them like what we talk now."

He saw her point, yet thought it strange that he retained his dialect for better communication with his lads while she, for the equivalent purpose, would have to lose hers. "We'll start tomorrow," he said.

But there was an element of sadness in the decision. Nora talking like Arabella Thornton would be . . . well, she wouldn't be Nora any longer.

"I must go soon," he said. "Tell us what's what."

He knew from the glint in her eyes that the results were going to be as good as she had promised. "If we're paid only for the finished driftway," she said, speaking carefully, then, seeing him trying to suppress a smile, she punched him hard in the stomach and reverted to her thickest dialect. "I'll be reet out o' consait wi' thee, thou slape bloody eel! If thou don't gi' over, I'll put all Yorkshire on thee! Now frame thissen!"

He composed himself, as she commanded. Only when she was quite sure of him did she begin once more. "If we're paid only for finished driftway, and nothing beside, and if we must pay out all but bricklayers, we shall be back where we began—where *I* began anyway—in eleven weeks five days."

"Eleven!" He began a spontaneous little dance of joy that shook the room. She watched him, smiling with pride as if she had created, instead of merely calculated, the situation.

"Eh!" he said when he came to rest at last. "I thought eight. But eleven!"

"That's if we go on as *now,*" she said. "I've ways to push it farther yet."

"No need, no need, lass," he said. "Eleven's all the edge I want. Nay—it's more than I could possibly want."

"For what?" she asked. "What'll we do?"

"We'll have our strike and be done. And then we'll turn to face our *real* enemy." He picked up Prendergast's sherry glass. "See to it that this is smashed," he said.

After he had gone she began to worry at what he had said. She hoped that hatred was not going to warp his judgement.

# *Chapter 24*

It was almost totally dark by the time he dismounted on the turnpike above the large oval shaft. Even from a distance, as he rounded the bend at Stone House bridge, he could see this was to be no casually arranged, last-minute meeting. Metcalfe's people must have been busy the last few hours making and staking the torches, which burned in a cheerful circle around the rim of the shaft but far enough away to prevent any spills from dropping into the hole. When he drew close, he could see that they had also built a low dais at the eastern rim, above the scaffolding where he had talked to Metcalfe that morning; it was obvious Metcalfe intended to speak from there to the men who were presumably gathered in the shaft below. He began to worry as the realization dawned on him that Metcalfe had stolen the initiative. This was no meeting of twenty-eight bricklayers; something much bigger was afoot. Metcalfe knew what; and he, John Stevenson, didn't.

Metcalfe waited for him at the edge of the road. "Evening, Mr. Stevenson, sir," he said.

"Somewhat grand to my taste," Stevenson said. "All I come for were a simple yes-no." He dismounted and gave his horse to Baxandall, Metcalfe's apprentice. "Thanks, lad." He turned back to Metcalfe. "What is it? Yea or nay?"

"Full meeting'll tell ye," he answered.

Stevenson chuckled. "There y'are! The poison already!"

"Poison?"

"Aye, lad. The union. I said—it's a poison to come between employer and workman."

"A shield more like."

"Where's *my* union?" Stevenson asked. "Can thou see me and Calley or any other master on this line—can thou see us in the same union? I'd snatch the very bread from his mouth afore I'd even sup at the same board."

Metcalfe shook his head pityingly, pretending to regret Stevenson's inability to comprehend. "The likes of you and Calley need no union," he explained. "Your union is everywhere. All around. It's the law. It's the established Church. It's property. It's the fabric we live in. That's your union. I know I'm risking jail by this. But if I go, it's your union'll put me there, whatever you may call it."

To Stevenson it seemed a very feeble line of argument. "It's thine as much as mine," he pointed out. "Every bit as much. Diligence, thrift, honesty, and luck—they'll get thee inside. It's open to all men on them terms." He faced Metcalfe with every sign of sincerity and, gripping his arm, added: "And I'll tell *thee,* Tom Metcalfe—I've had this contract long enough to say it'll make no great fortune, but if we do naught daft, it'll pay well enough. Then we'll be on to bigger and better work. That's when I'll need good men. I don't speak idly now—thou knows I'm a man of my word. And I say I've gotten *thee* marked for a brisk future." He stood back a little and gave the man's arm an encouraging shake. "What dost thou say?"

He turned so as to bring Metcalfe's face into full light. As he expected, it formed a perfect mask of contempt and anger. "I'd say," he responded coldly, "that ye've told me everything I wanted to know."

"Thou'll not join me?" Stevenson began a slow stroll toward the amphitheatre of the oval shaft.

Walking seemed to mellow Tom Metcalfe, for he answered with none of the contempt Stevenson had just noticed. "You are a good man, Lord John. And a good master as masters go. But the union's my lodestar and the only salvation I see for the working class. This isn't Metcalfe versus Stevenson. There's none of that in it. This is the working class versus capital and privilege."

Stevenson shook his head. "Eh—poor old working class! Send us a ticket for the funeral."

They were now at the western edge of the shaft, skirting around it to the dais at the far end. As soon as they were seen from below, the foot of the shaft was transformed into a sea of bobbing faces. A great, ironic cheer went up—with, Stevenson noted in some shock, a good mixture of jeers and catcalls. He looked sharply down. His heart gave a lurch. There must be over a hundred people down there—more than he had ever addressed in his life!

His immediate urge was to run.

Angry at his cowardice, he wanted to vent that anger on Metcalfe. And then, like the sudden lifting of a mist, he felt the resurgence of his own unbounded confidence. He looked back at that sea of faces, still cheering, and booing, and thought, *How can I put all that to my advantage?* And though he could spell out no immediate plan, he knew that Tom Metcalfe was going to regret this day's work. The jeering, he had time to notice, came mainly from the bricklayers at the back of the crowd, farthest from the dais.

"Ye've gotten them all," he said lightly.

Metcalfe smiled in triumph. "Every last man. They've all come to listen and learn. I hope I may have gotten them, too."

"Ye'll press this to the end, then?"

"To the bitter end." Metcalfe mounted the dais and threw up his hands in a dramatic gesture that quickly brought silence. "Brothers!" His voice rang across the shaft.

*And you,* Stevenson thought to himself, *have told me just what I needed to know.*

"Brothers! Mr. Stevenson, as ye know, has agreed to come here tonight like, and put this latest offer of his to us."

While Metcalfe spoke a simple introduction, Stevenson searched around in the mud and grass tussocks behind the dais for the rope. He soon found it, still tied to its stake. He picked it up, came to the edge of the dais, and squatted to feed the rope over the wall of the shaft.

"I've put the offer," he said loudly but conversationally. "What I come ere for was the reply." He stood and dusted his hands.

"I wanted them to hear it from you," Metcalfe answered, not realizing what Stevenson had been doing.

"You wanted? Then you shall get," Stevenson promised. And with the same agility he had shown that morning, he grasped the rope and, plummeting down the side of the shaft, landed lightly on the scaffold. It brought a chorus of gasps, laughter, and cheers.

Now that he was closer to it, the crowd looked much larger. He felt the blood hammering in his throat. He had no idea what quality of noise was going to issue when he opened his mouth.

But he lifted his head and said, in a voice that, to his relief, rang without a tremor in those brick confines, "I'll force no man to look up to me!" And the great roar of laughter and applause it brought made him almost feel sorry for the young would-be leader, now standing marooned above him in the torchlight. But the bricklayers at the back, he noticed, still for the most part wore grim faces.

"Well, lads—" he began.

"Shut your legs, your breath smells," came a voice from the back. It prompted a ripple of light laughter; but that, in turn, was soon drowned in shocked and angry cries of *"Hush!"* and *"Silence!"*

"I've been on this contract three month," he said. "Until then I was, as ye know, ganger on number one face down Littleborough end. I've made some bad mistakes since I started. I'm the first to say it. Bad mistakes. But the worst was to put navvies on bonus and leave craftsmen likes of you all here on the same old flat rate as Skelm was paying."

Calls of "Aye" and ironic cries of "Hear him! Hear him!" rose. He let them die before he went on.

"Aye indeed! I can't now say how I was so daft as not to think of it. But I didn't. Not till Tom Metcalfe"—he cleared his throat meaningfully— *"drew my attention to it!"*

The murmuring turned to laughter, and heads lifted to Metcalfe, still standing in his unlooked-for solitude above. He was either too cowardly or had too overweening a sense of his own dignity to descend by the rope. And to go round by Deanroyd cutting and come back through the tunnel would not only bring him in at the fringe of the crowd but would put him too long out of contact with events.

"As soon's I heard," Stevenson continued, "I saw he were right and I were wrong. So I come to him straight. No pride. No stiff neck. No pretending I meant to do it all along . . . I fully confess it took Tom Metcalfe and his band of 'brothers' to teach me what I should of . . ."—with an orator's instinct he dropped his voice to the limit of audibility, forcing them to total silence—"what I should've *felt* for meself. I come straight to him with an offer this very morning." His voice now rang out again: "It lets brickies earn on bonus three shilling—likely three'n six—more than what they take home now."

He expected someone to object that they'd have to work harder for it, but the only response was an appreciative stir.

"What of us chippies?" a carpenter asked.

"Aye—and the smiths?"

Stevenson nodded. "Aye. I'm glad the other tradesmen are here and all. For I've similar bonus plans for every one. Any man on this contract can now earn at least, *at least* three shilling more than what he gets flat rate."

Again he waited for the objection and this time it came. Peter Etheridge, the bricklayer, called out, "Aye, but we'll work a bloody sight harder for it!"

Stevenson looked at him coolly. "Mebbe building tunnels is man's work, Mr. Etheridge. Any man afraid of hard work has got no business on a railroad. There's all the *easy* bricklaying ye want in Manchester at fourteen bob a week."

When he saw the nods of agreement all around and heard their low-voiced murmurs of assent, he knew he was over the summit and on the downhill run. He realized, too, how much he was enjoying the sense of power that came with talking directly to so large a gathering of men. The fear, that twist in the guts inspired by the sight of so many faces, so many pairs of eyes, staring so relentlessly . . . that fear was still there; but above it lay a joy that, while it was on you, transcended all other public joys. He was talking to many, yet he spoke as if to one; and it was *he* who made them one!

He wanted to play them then, as an angler would play a fish. What could he do with them? he wondered. How far might he go?

"When?" a voice called.

He pointed in its direction. "Fair question. You craftsmen come into your own the day the driftway's through. When the tunnel starts a-building. Bonus starts the first of January next."

"Five bloody weeks!" one of the smiths called.

Stevenson smiled but said no more. The grumble grew to a loud buzz with an angry edge as they saw nothing in the offing before Christmas. I'll push them further, he thought.

He spread his hands and adopted a take-it-or-leave-it stance. "I've no *need* of any extra effort from you lot until then. Ye're all goin' along very nicely thanks." He heard their rumbling grow angrier still. "I've not got money to chuck about. Ye all know that well enough."

Strangely, that assertion moderated their anger; if he'd been among them, he thought, it would have made him even angrier. A master who took on a contract without enough to do the thing properly was cause enough for any workman's fury, he'd have thought. He almost decided not to make the offer he had been about to disclose; fortunately a wiser instinct made him continue.

"But there's one thing I *do* need from ye . . ."

"Aye! Blood!" a bricklayer called.

He knew it was meant as a joke but he decided to take it seriously. "Blood!" he cried, and his face twisted in a terrible anger. "Blood?" he repeated in even more towering fury. "Who's the man as says John Stevenson looks for blood?" He glared over their heads, fighting to master a rage that had swiftly become genuine—such is the intoxication of a mob. A chilled silence fell. Men stared at him open-mouthed and held their breathing. "He's no man as I know, nor as knows me," he said quietly into the face of that great quiet. "Since I took this contract, there's not one man has given his blood beneath these rocks. I'm pained . . ."—he fought to control himself as his voice choked to a whispering tremble—"pained . . . as any man of mine'd think I ask for blood."

He breathed deeply and hauled himself erect. "I was saying . . ." he continued crisply but his warmth toward them was now openly withdrawn, "I was saying there's one thing I need from ye. *Attendance.* Accordingly I propose to pay to every man—to every tradesman—as attends every working day from now to January first a bonus of twenty-four shilling." There was a gasp of delight at that but he spoke on through it, still tight-lipped and remote. "To be paid on Christmas Eve—on which day knocking-off will come an hour early at six." Their delight raised itself as far as a cheer. He sensed that they were trying to win back his humour; but he remained implacable. "For every day's absence for which no leave was sought nor good account rendered, the twenty-four shilling is to be reduced by four. The same applying to the days between Boxing Day and New Year as before. Them among ye as is conversant with figures, 'up to Cocker' as the saying is . . ."

Feeble though the humour was, it gave them their first opportunity to laugh since his rage and they took it immoderately, trying to woo him back. But not a flicker of a smile split his lips. "Them as can do their sums'll soon find out it puts ye on level footing with the navvies." He took the first step from the scaffold and then paused to add a footnote. "Oh aye! Proportional bonus for apprentices," he said.

He took one more step and remembered a further footnote. "Aye, an one more thing. This bonus is part of a private contract betwixt me and thee, and thee, and thee . . ."—he pointed randomly at faces in the crowd— "and thee, and thee . . ."

"No!" Metcalfe's roar of anger fell down on them from above. The torchlight painted him a hellish orange against the deep purple of the sky beyond.

"A contract sealed on a handshake twixt me and each man singly . . ."

"No! No! No!" Metcalfe stamped and stormed with rage.

". . . twixt me and each man singly," Stevenson continued relentlessly. "And one clause in that contract binds each such man to join no union . . ." He paused to let it sink in, scanning the faces before him anxiously.

"No!" Metcalfe called again from above. But he had shot his bolt too soon. This third outburst had a strident edge that made him seem petulant.

Nevertheless his cry was taken up by his brother bricklayers and one or two of the other craftsmen. Stevenson waited to see if it would become general.

It did not.

From the overall calm and the nodding of heads and the slowly rising buzz of talk, it was obvious that the refusals were in a small minority—mainly among the bricklayers.

"You bastard!" Metcalfe called down with all the bitterness and venom Stevenson had noted in him earlier that day.

He could not have made a greater blunder. To a southerner the word was merely one of strong contempt, as in politer society a man might say "you cad!" But to that northern assembly, where it was taken in its literal sense, no word bore greater insult; if Stevenson had shinned back up that rope and personally dismembered Metcalfe, not a man there would have blamed him.

A terrible hush descended. Metcalfe must have sensed at once that he had said something a great deal more than he had meant. Everyone waited to see what Stevenson might do in his wrath.

But he had done with the use of anger for that evening. He watched that sea of stunned faces until all had turned from Metcalfe back to him. Then, slowly, slowly, as if his arm moved through invisible beds of clay, he raised a single pointing finger. And such was the majesty of his gesture that if a bolt of lightning had leaped from its tip and struck down the unhappy man above, it would have seemed a fitting conclusion to most who watched. When his arm was at full stretch he jabbed his finger once, twice, at Metcalfe. "Thou'll pay for that word! By God, and as these men are my witness—thou'll pay." Metcalfe stood and took it.

He snatched his arm down and turned to face them again. A deep sigh went up. "I'll say no more," he said quietly. "But from five o'clock tomorrow I'll be standing by the clerk's office to shake hands on a contract with any man among ye as wants to better hisself. Sleep on it! And sleep well."

He swung himself down from the scaffold and walked out among them to the short tunnel that led north into Deanroyd cutting. No emperor ever had a way cleared before him so swiftly; but he looked neither to one side nor to the other. Every man in that assembly knew that he, personally, had to make anew his compact with Lord John and earn his favour afresh. This night's work had cleaned the slate of all goodwill.

When he came to where his horse had been tethered he saw it was Metcalfe who held its bridle ready. It was an act of courage he had to admire.

"I owe you an apology, Lord John," Metcalfe began.

"Accepted and forgotten." Stevenson took the reins. "I know the way ye meant it, Tom. I've worked in the south. Ye weren't to know how it'd get took up here. I bear thee no malice—not for that anyway." He mounted and pulled the hack's head toward the turnpike. "What I said . . . well, I couldn't let the lads think as I was . . ."

"I know," Metcalfe said. "I understand."

"Then I'll see thee at work in the morning," Stevenson said carelessly, spurring his mount forward.

"No!" Metcalfe called. And, when Stevenson had reined in again and half turned in his saddle, he added, "Bricklayers will be on strike from tomorrow. That was to be thy answer. It still stands."

"But I've met thy terms."

"Thou may think so."

"Then ye may all go to Hades!" Stevenson spurred the horse to a canter and set his face southerly for fear that by some unguarded look or word he would reveal to Metcalfe his delight.

He was so elated that he wanted to ride straight back to Nora and tell her of all that had happened. He had not simply talked to a crowd of a hundred men—he had pressed them into an almost united band, he had taken them to the verge of mutiny, and then he had brought them back until they were ready to eat out of his hand. He wanted to be with Nora at once and to relive every moment of it again, and then again. Triumph! It was triumph made incarnate. He wanted to cry it aloud, to shout it at all the hills around and into every corner of the blackened sky above.

When he reached Littleborough, he leaped down and hammered on the stable door.

"Open it thyself," Clifford's voice came from some distance inside.

He pulled open the tall door and led his mount into the dimly lit stable. It was warm with the humid reek of dung and ammonia.

"Is he lathered?" Clifford asked. The words fell from the hayloft above.

Stevenson looked up to see the man's face peering down through an open trap.

"Nay," he answered. "Not sweated at all. We never done more than a trot."

"Aye, well—put him in yon third stall where there's a pail of water and

just loosen the girth and bridle. It'll be a while afore I can come down."
He winked and vanished.

Stevenson hadn't needed the wink to tell him what was happening. The
loose, flushed face he had seen and the by-no-means furtive rustlings he
heard as he put the horse to its stall, told him exactly what was detaining
the ostler. And having seen the size of it limp, his mind boggled at the
thought of it proud! Who among the girls in Littleborough, he wondered,
could manage it?

His mind, picturing the lascivious scene above and peopling it with a
whole row of pretty Littleborough maids, quickened with the thought of
Nora, now waiting for him at the inn. Hunched against the cold, he trotted
all the furlong that lay between them. And when he burst breathless into
their parlour, and she came swiftly to him, he threw his arms around her
and, lifting her to the ceiling, whirled her around above him.

"Eh!" she cried in great delight. "I know what thou wants of me
tonight!" She reached her head forward, trying to kiss him, but he held her
off. "For a change!" she added.

Slightly sobered by the tone in her voice, he lowered her to the ground.
She parted his cloak and crept inside.

"Have I been remiss?" he asked, thinking backward day to day. "Aye,"
he had to confess. "Mebbe I have."

"There's been a lot on thy mind."

The smell from her warm body was heady in his nostrils. He began to
tremble with desire for her, and the sudden force of his lust robbed him of
words. He lifted her face and covered it with hot kisses.

She reached out a hand and slipped the snib on the door before she
surrendered totally to him. They left a trail of discarded clothing in their
slow, delirious progress from the door to the couch beside the hearth. At
last he stood in only a hoisted shirt, she in her corset and a torn chemise.
The cheerful orange light from the glowing coals made her lovelier than at
any time since they had first met.

"No hurry, John," she soothed as his hands fiddled urgently with the
drawstring of her corset; and she opened his shirt, button by slow button.

When her corset eased itself from around her waist, the bone of its
stays seemed to sigh with the relaxation. It slithered to her ankles and she
stepped lightly from it into his embrace. Lightly, too, his fingertips
caressed the folds its grip had piled in the flesh around her waist and
hips.

The delicious freedom of his fingers brought her almost to an ecstasy,
so that she stood on tiptoe and raised a thigh to curl it round him. But even
on tiptoe she was still too short for him and he had to tighten his grip on
her waist and lift her on to him.

There was no labour in it. He relaxed his hands to take a different grip and the torn chemise fell between them.

"Tear it off me," she whispered in his ear.

He hesitated; the puritan in him was shocked.

"It's torn anyway," she added. "I'll patch it tomorrow." More than anything she longed to feel his great, powerful hands wrench the cloth in two and burst her from it, flesh to his flesh.

Slightly astonished at himself, he gripped the cloth and took a half turn on it as he would on a rope. She felt his muscles ripple and harden as he took the strain. It held more firmly than either of them expected. Her excitement intensified as he braced himself for a greater effort. Bands of iron thrust out the skin of his torso; his arms shivered, sending her into a delirium. Hot flushes billowed through her body. And then, with an explosive violence, the cloth parted. Its tucks and ragged edges seemed to score her stomach as they raced past; and then she was all skin to his skin, surge to his surge, cry of bliss to his deep-voiced sigh.

Peeled, it seemed, to her very insides, impaled upon him, she clasped him with her arms and thighs while he, brought to his extremity by her sudden writhing and clamping, charged by seven nights of unintended continence, filled her till he thought he'd never stop.

At length, when their hearts had ceased to race, and their breathing returned to near normal, and the sweat that bathed them turned a little chill on the side farthest from the fire, she eased her grip, lowered her thighs, and slid gently from him.

Drained and sated, they fell drowsily to the couch and lounged side by side in the fireglow. She reached out a toe and raised the torn, sweat-stained chemise.

"Ow—*how* do gentlefolk do it?" she asked. "D'ye think they mebbe wear gloves and say please and thankee for everything?"

And when he laughed, she, having no apron to hide her face in, turned to him and buried herself in his chest. He laid his arm on her back and caressed the pale skin of it. She was so strong an individual in herself that it was only at times like this—when she was girlish and impulsive—that he remembered she was only eighteen. In a curious way she had grown both younger and older these last three months. Her body was younger; the starved flesh that had creased her skin with lines of toil and care had plumped out and filled each crevice, making her as full and firm and supple as a girl could grow. Her dark hair, too, had turned more lustrous as she gained in health. She looked at the world with a brighter eye, a firmer jaw, and a head held proud.

Of course she had been born destined for a certain beauty. Even in the rags she had worn when first she passed this way, her hair unkempt, her face grimy—even then men had renewed their hunger as she passed. But now, when she stood tall and almost arrogant in the self-imposed plainness and severity of her dresses, there was something compelling about her.

That was what John meant when he thought of her as having grown older. From that very first night, as he had watched and helped her work through the small hours, marshalling figures with a nimbleness of mind that outstripped his at times, displaying an inventiveness that soared far beyond any ethical constraint, from then on he had never considered her anything other than a full partner in his business. In fact, her grasp of it sometimes frightened him.

At such moments he shallowly envied those of his contemporaries who kept pet wives at home like sweet toys or private playthings; men like Thornton—though, considering the panting little doggie he had turned into this lunchtime, rushing off with the Irish toothache like that, it made one wonder what sort of plaything the fair Arabella had turned out to be.

His life with Nora had such a rightness that he rarely thought of these comparisons. Only at such infrequent moments as this, when her eyes were hid and her girlish body lay curled across him, the perfect counterfeit of the toy wife, did they strike him.

There was a sudden stab of heat on his stomach; it turned cool and quickly slithered away down a fold of his skin. Wet! A tear?

Nora weeping?

She was not moving as a sobbing person moves. Her breathing was regular.

He put one hand upon her hip and fondled her hair with the other.

One more tear fell; now he was certain of it. He tightened his grip, but she did not stir.

"Nay," he said gently. "What's made thee miserable then?"

She shook her head and still more tears fell upon his skin. He leaned forward to see her face but she turned farther from him and buried herself again. She was like a small furnace upon him.

When he lay back once more she resumed her former place. She sniffed back an ocean of salt and said in a voice choked to a whisper: "I'm happy, thou soft fool." And then, her voice growing steadily more reedy and disobedient, she added: "Oh John! Thou art such a marvel of a man. I think there's none like thee in all the world . . . and how I had the luck to meet thy notice and gain thy . . . regard . . . I'll never . . . never . . . understand."

And with those last, halting, straying, whispered words she burst into sobs and wormed her face into his chest in a soup of tears and streaming nose.

He, unable to speak through the tightness of his throat, unable to see her clearly through his brimming eyes, unable to hold and cherish her where she lay, grasped her and lifted her onto his lap, and held her.

Still not letting him glimpse her face, she threw her arms about his neck and sobbed without remission onto his neck and shoulder, and into his hair and ear.

At last her passion spent itself and her tears ceased to flow. His single deep sniff, clearing his nose of its blockage, alerted her to his condition. So, too, when he spoke, did the hoarse edge to his voice.

"Now see what thou hast done! Lord John weeping!" he said.

She laughed, stoking up the furnace at his ear. But still she did not pull away to see his face. He felt her whisper, secret and tickling, in his ear, "I can *feel* another effect I've had on thee and all. Thou ram!"

He found her ear with his lips. "A bit more?" he asked.

She pulled her head away from him then. "Nay," she said, a surprising degree of normality back in her voice. "I must hear about this strike we've gotten."

Laughing, he poked the tip of his finger delicately into her umbilicus. "Spoken like Mrs. Stevenson!" He walked his fingers lower down, tempting her. "Sure?" he whispered.

"Sure," she said, smiling unblinking at him.

"Then bloody shift!" he said aloud. "It hurts!"

Laughing, she changed position but did not rise. She laid her arm across his chest. "Eh!" she said. "We're disgusting dirty, thee and me. See that. Could grow potatoes there on you."

"It all wears off," he said.

"Nay. We'll have a bath tonight."

"Ee, I'll fall down dead of weakness tomorrow! Anyway I had a bath when we wed."

"We'll have another tonight."

She stood and tried unsuccessfully to piece her torn shift around her; in the end she pulled a face of theatrical complicity at him. Then she shrugged on her corset and backed up to him to have the strings drawn tight.

He began to itch for her again. "What is it?" he asked. "When your body's had all it needs and has given all it's got, what is it makes you still . . . *yearn?* That must be love, mustn't it!"

"Aye! I've torn this petticoat, too," she giggled.

During dinner he told her of his triumph at the oval shaft by Dean-royd, and her eyes shone greedily as she lived and shared his joy in the telling.

Then they took their bath, by the same fire that warmed their earlier labours. If she curled her legs carefully she could get all of them under water; and then, if she lay like a stuck turtle, she could submerge from neck to loin while he poured hot water over her.

"When we get to Rough Stones," she said, "we'll have a big bath like this and we'll bath by the fire every evening. Look at this water! It's plain disgusting."

They went, renewed, to bed.

But instead of pinching out the candle, Nora put her proposal to him. "When I sweated in the mill down Stockport," she said, "foreman there made us spend a third part of the wage at the tommy shop. It were mildewed flour and meat with no fat on it—all lean and gristle—and cheese with mites for lodgers. They'd not of dared offer it elsewhere. But they must of made a fortune. . . ." His astonished gaze halted her. "What's up?"

He shook his head in wonder. "Thou want us to do *that!* Thou, that's suffered from it thyself!"

"Aye," she said. She could not fathom his objection. "We're in the position to do it now, aren't we! Get our own back."

"I'd as soon see us transported."

She relapsed into baffled silence, watching him fall deep in thought.

"See if I can make thee understand," he said at last. "This is what I learned in three year with the navvy. There's folk as is afraid of him. Thou! Thou were afraid. Dost recall? Yon day?"

"Aye—and I'd still be afraid if it weren't for thee. They're like . . . different men."

"Well, I'd say there's no better worker nor more loyal servant than the English navvy. To them who treats him right. I been under bad masters. Men who'd cheat ye afore yer back's half-turned, who'd keep the lads in debt on piss-poor ale and tommy rot, who'd welsh on payday. But I'll tell thee: They make no profit in it, not in the end. They make naught but trouble. What do they get? They get bad work finished late by sullen lads. I'm not preaching Chartist rubbish now. What I'm saying is common sense. A good master—by which I mean a fair one, not a soft one—a good master'll always make more profit than a bad one. And I'll tell thee for naught: I'll never cheat on any lad as works for me. I'll pay best. I'll demand best. And I'll *get* best. I'll look after 'em through lean times and they'll stay by me when labour's short and they could walk on to any site in the land. Because, lass, we're not here to make a few thousand today and skip to America tomorrow. This is our trade for *life*. Hundred years from now, old navvies'll meet on the highway and they'll look at each other with that certain special glint in their eye, and they'll say, 'I started as a lad with Stevenson's lads!' And they'll be *that* proud!"

She was tense with the grandeur of this vision. "Meet on the highway?" she said. "Nay—on the *rail*way."

He laughed. "Mebbe! And I'd like to say as one mile in every five they travel were put there by them and *us*."

She sighed. "Aye . . . well, then—no truck. No tommy."

"Nay!" he said. "I never said no truck. I've naught against selling *good* grub and beer. But no tommy rot. There's farmers hereabouts, see thee, paying eight shilling to labourers with families, all nigh starving. And them same farmers come to me—there was one there last week by Stone House watching my lads, on fourteen or fifteen shilling before bonus, and he was grumbling saying why couldn't his labourers work as willing! And they can't *see* it. They're blind. Porridge and bacon rinds—what can any labourer do on that! It's so plain they can't see it."

Silence fell.

"Eh, love, forgive us!" He dropped a hand on the outer cover, over her thigh, and gave a squeeze. "I know I rabbit on. I do."

"I was going to ask thee one other thing," she said.

"Ask on."

"Shall us . . . shall us rear bairns? Shall us start?"

He looked puzzled. "Do ye mean we've not?"

"Not yet."

His eyes narrowed. "What hast thou done?"

"I been drinking tea of sweet basil," she said and pulled a face. "Tastes like bloody ditch water."

"Oh aye?"

"Don't always work, Mrs. Hampton said, but—"

"Who's she?" he interrupted.

"She were next down to us in Stockport. When me dad died. She had thirteen bairns. . . ."

He laughed. "Aye! I see what she means and all: 'Don't always work!' Thirteen bairns. I should think not!"

She joined his laughter at the confusion but then sought to explain. "Ah, no. But wait, see thee. There was only four reared. And the youngest was eight year old. And she had none after him, and her man was always at it. He was one like yon Thornton. And that was when her auntie put her on to sweet basil. Because she could've had . . . oh, she could've had dozens, see. She started so young. . . ."

He reached over her to pinch out the candle—an act that brought him to straddle her. He saw her eyes gleam with fresh promise in the moment before the light failed and he stopped her monologue with a kiss.

"Aye," he said softly. "Mebbe we'll share this bed with sweet basil while we see this contract out."

# Chapter 25

The frost was so sharp that when he rose at three thirty—early for this day of days—there was ice on the water in the ewer. Its chill sharpness shrivelled his skin but brought a fiery afterglow that made him ready for whatever might follow. Nora always rose at the same hour as he and took breakfast with him, though, unless it was a day for going to Manchester, she usually then returned to bed.

Today they ate porridge, cold smoked trout, veal and egg pie, and a slice of tart, washed down with sweet coffee. It was as well, for when he opened the door he stepped out into a white world far below freezing temperature. The snowclouds had passed over, and the waning moon was still rising in the eastern limb of the sky. The wind swirled in madcap eddies, lifting storms of powdered snow that spun like ghostly dancers over the deserted square and collapsed silently in the lee of one or other of the walls that framed the area.

Behind him Nora shivered and clutched her shawl to her. "Poor John," she said as she kissed him her warmest goodbye. "Good luck."

He shivered, too. "Shouldn't never ought to've bathed," he said.

She pushed him playfully out and shut the door. The church clock struck the hour, four o'clock, as he stamped by on his silent way. And in all that long journey he passed not one other soul. Snug in their beds or shivering in their hovels, the whole world lay drowned asleep beneath a new white shroud. He was glad for once not to join that pathetic throng of paupers on their way to the mill; he was even too early for the miners today. To see children as thin as fishbones walking barefoot through this icy waste would be more than he could bear. The mill loomed dark and silent as he passed. The moon, picking out the cotton dust on its panes, lent the windows a spurious and eldritch light, as if a host of phantom weavers tended the hushed looms and silent spindles.

A little way beyond the mill he entered the Blackstone gap. Here the hills banked sharply up on either side, towering white over the black, turgid ribbon of the unfrozen canal. Water from its summit reservoir gurgled down the clough and dashed, cold and complaining, over the spillways of every lock. He startled a stray sheep upon the turnpike, making it turn and hasten back up the sides of Reddish Scout—the first living thing he had encountered since leaving Nora at the inn.

A doubt began to nag somewhere in the cellars of his mind. There was a wrongness. Something was wrong. In the landscape ahead. It was . . . too red. The red cast was alien to this wintry night. Filled with a growing doubt, he quickened his pace. Was it the jolting of his walk or did the glow truly flicker? He stopped; the flickering did not. *Fire!* Something ahead was on fire. He broke into a run.

The strikers had fired the site office!

Or perhaps Fernley, his clerk of works, who had come early to copy out the terms of his offer and put them up on display, had knocked over a lantern and set the hut ablaze?

Or was it a conflagration in one of the houses—nothing to do with his site?

Every possibility flashed through his mind as he ran to the bend at Stone Bridge, from where the whole of Deanroyd would come into view. But when he reached that vantage, the scene spread before him was one whose possibility would never in a thousand miles of running have entered his mind.

The firelight glow came from the torches that last night had lined the rim of the oval shaft; now they stood in a random grouping, refilled and relighted, on the gentle slope between the site offices and the canal. And around each there was gathered a knot of men, stamping their feet, warming their hands, joking, horseplaying, laughing, passing flasks of spirit . . . waiting. He estimated their numbers at eighty.

Two hours before knocking-on time? It could not be his lads. Moreover there were no footsteps in the snow—had they been there all night? No, it could not be his men.

Well—a contingent of out-of-work bricklayers come to break the strike? Or special constables? Would they just turn up without reference to him?

"He's there!"

That was Martin Carter, one of his masons. So some of his lads were there anyway. The cry galvanized the rest. They turned as one man and peered out along the dark turnpike, seeking him. Then, like a face of broken rock coming adrift, the whole solid phalanx of men erupted toward him.

Still he did not understand. *They're out for my blood,* he thought. What had gone wrong? What had Metcalfe said or done after his departure last night?

Even so he did not falter in his stride. Against the glowing torches he could read no expression on the faces—he could not even see the faces—of the silhouettes that bore down upon him . . . *cheering.*

Finally it was their cheering that alerted him to their mood: It was warm; it was not the chilling vengeful howl of an angry mob. Among the earliest arrivals there was a scuffle to be the very first to shake his hand and clap him on the shoulders. And all the way to the hutments he walked a gauntlet of proffered hands and a barrage of greetings, some profuse, some mumbled.

The mumbling was curious; there was in much of it a suggestion of shame or guilt that jarred oddly with this hearty—and quite uncharacteristic—enthusiasm. Too mystified to remember his public face, he passed unsmiling among them, noticing their growing anxiety, yet failing to connect it with his own apparent severity.

Blacksmith, mason, carpenter, engineer, mason, carpenter, carpenter, smith . . . not one bricklayer. Yes there was—one. Bennett, born to be different.

"Where's the brickies?" he asked.

No one answered. They looked away when his eyes met theirs. One spat in disgust.

"I see." He looked around. The inconceivable truth was beginning to reach him; this was some kind of atonement. At last he smiled, and the relief he saw spreading among them was beyond all proportion.

"Another question: How long have you lot stood here? I thought I were early enough but I saw no mark in the snow of any foot."

Now they grinned, and some laughed, like men who have played a warm, unwounding joke on one of their number. Martin Carter, the man who had seen him first, nodded up toward the scout and said: "We come over the brow."

"Knowing thou always come by the bottoms," Trevor Wood, a smith, added.

"We determined that last night," Carter said.

Now the full extent of their purpose—and their unity of spirit—was borne in upon him. He was suddenly too moved to speak . . . to trust himself to speak. Then he saw that his emotion embarrassed them; it was not what they expected of him.

"Right!" he called, standing taller and taking a firmer grasp of himself. "Ye're wasting good working time! Get about then, lads! Set to!"

That was more in the expected spirit. No one moved in obedience but, with broadly smiling faces, cheerful in the torchlight glow, they groaned and jeered and catcalled.

He pretended to be insulted, withstanding their onslaught; the shock on his face soon turned to stoic severity. "An hour's working wasted now is an hour's drinking wasted at the far end."

Their hubbub renewed itself but with a new edge of anticipation.

"Every man that starts on now is to be let off at five this afternoon." He had to raise his voice then, to shout above their cheers. "And them as isn't too tired and can drag themselves home and can come back in drinking rags is bidden to a hotpot supper in Summit Tunnel East at seven o'clock."

Their cheering rose to a deafening crescendo; but all his instincts told him that this was not the mood in which they should disperse. So he added: "And if any man attends drunk, he shall be suffered to turn about and go back home." Though none believed him, it let them boo and hiss and jeer again, and so disperse laughing to their anvils, benches, and frame saws.

As he watched them go he realized that he had never, even when he was one among them, felt closer to them in spirit. For the first time he saw that a master could actually be closer to his men than they might be to one another. He also began to appreciate something that, until then, he had known only instinctively: If some natural talent or quality set you above your fellows, you had to give them the chance once in a while to jeer or mock. Do that, and there was no enterprise you might not undertake with them.

Soon the valley rang with the hammering, sawing, and shaping of stone, iron, and wood. Now that the site was deserted the flaming torches seemed extravagant.

"Shall I dowse them lights?" Fernley asked.

"Aye. Leave just this nearest one to light up the terms of the new contract. Pin it there."

In a curious way it seemed quieter when the light was diminished. The silence was broken by a plaintive yapping, some way away.

"Is that a dog in a trap?" Stevenson asked.

Fernley took out a flask. "Vixen," he said. "They spread her cubs yesterday. Up in Henshaw wood. She's been doing that on and off all night."

"Do they hunt them much? Mrs. Stevenson's an eager one for hunting."

"Not much. Hares mostly." He took a swig, then, remembering himself, apologized and offered it to Stevenson.

"No thanks."

"Go on. Keep thee warm. It's rum!"

"I can smell that from here."

Fernley corked the flask and returned it to his inner pocket. "There'll be a long, cold wait now," he said.

"Think so?"

"Stands to reason. Them as was coming early have come. It looks like we'll not get the brickies. . . ."

"Bennett's there."

"Aye—well—Bennett's Bennett, isn't he. There's no law nor no regularity for that man. Ye've got all but eight of the remaining craftsmen—and four of them is sick, to my knowledge."

"Mebbe."

Fernley pulled out the flask again and took another swig. This time, too, he offered it to Stevenson, who once more refused it.

"I've seen navvies of twenty-nine broken down," Stevenson said. "Like old men of sixty. Broken with boozing."

"Aye!" Fernley swigged deeply and breathed out a pungent and fiery satisfaction. "Aye—it'll ruin ye right enough." And he rammed the cork home to emphasize his agreement.

"I were on a stretch of the Great Northern last year," Stevenson continued. "This side Wakefield. . . ." He snapped his fingers and sought as if to pluck the name from the air around him. "Ossett!" he said at last. "Near Ossett! There were one navvy there were drunk for a month. Least, I never saw the bugger sober."

Fernley laughed grimly and jerked his thumb up the valley toward Todmorden. "Oh aye! There's one here and all. Up the valley. Irishman. One of Calley's mob. Irish fella. 'Swimmer Dandy' they call him. They say as he's been dead drunk all the week." He sniffed and looked up over Walsden Moor, where the dimmest band of green suffused the sky. "Day's breaking," he said.

"I don't understand the Irish," Fernley went on after a silence. "I reckon of all the different kinds of Englishmen, the Irish is the worst. I'd sooner have a Scot than an Irish. A Scotchman's not a bad sort of Englishman."

"Still—when they're not boozing, the Irish make the hardest-working navvy of all, I'll say that." Stevenson laughed. "They'll all be off boozing today. Calley's paying out."

"First time in seven weeks. Aye, they say they'll carry Swimmer Dandy round Todmorden as a mascot. He can't stand straight no more."

"Swimmer Dandy!" Stevenson relished the name.

They heard the rattle of tools in his canvas bag before they saw the next man walk down off the turnpike to the site office.

"That's William Shortis, carpenter," Stevenson said as soon as the first glimmer of a reflection showed him up.

Fernley looked down his list and placed a mark against the name.

"Morning, Lord John."

"Cold enough for thee?"

"I'd of come sooner but our Mary's got a croup—coughing and barking all night."

"I hope she may mend soon. Read that." He pointed to the sheet where the offer was set forth for each trade and grade.

While Shortis read, Stevenson took Fernley's list into the light and, scanning it quickly, pointed to five names that ought to have a mark beside them. "Tom Upjohn was there, and his brother Wilf; George Burnett . . . Noah Ashroyd . . . Jethro Carr—they was all there."

Fernley snorted in admiration. "Mr. Whitaker always says there's no need for paper where Lord John goes. I reckon if every man on this works was to file past a gap in a hedge half a mile off, thou'd call out their names as they went by."

"Nay!" Stevenson said, perfectly seriously. "Not more'n half of them." And he did not really understand why Fernley—and Shortis, who had finished reading—both laughed.

"Well. And ye've seen the offer, Shortis?"

"Aye. I have."

"On a good drift thou'll make twenty-one shilling and sixpence."

"Aye."

"And it's understood there's no shifting twixt thee and any union other than friendly societies, public house benefit societies, and that sort of thing?"

"Aye. I can't abide 'em anyway. There's me hand on it."

Stevenson shook it. "Set on now and ye may knock off at five with the others. They'll tell thee why."

"That's all the carpenters now," Fernley said when Shortis had gone. "Still naught but one brickie."

A sudden memory struck Stevenson. "Yesterday—when I come about two more chippies for shoring fractures in six and seven."

"Aye."

"Wasn't that two brickies wanting work was stood here?"

"Aye. They said if they never found aught they'd likely come back today."

"If they do, take 'em on. New bonus terms after one week, seventeen shilling till then. But tell 'em . . ." He paused.

"Aye?" Fernley prompted.

"If our brickies form a picket line, tell 'em not to cross it. These new ones, and any others. Tell 'em not to cross it."

"*Not* to cross it?"

"Aye."

Fernley was so astonished he broke into weak laughter. "I can't believe me ears."

"Thou'rt not paid to believe thy ears. They're not to cross it. If they do, they're dismissed."

"What—just stand here?"

"Just stand here."

"Drawing wages?"

"Aye." He laughed at Fernley's deep skepticism. "Never fret, lad! I'm not gone daft. Thou'll see—things'll move fast now."

But the sun was almost up before there was fresh movement of any kind. A figure—and even though it was no more than a moving speck against the pale, snowclad moor, Stevenson knew it was Metcalfe—came over the crest of Moorhey Flat and began the precipitous descent of the northern slopes. The time was a quarter to seven, fifteen minutes before the regular knocking-on time. Metcalfe, surefooted despite the snow, made good speed down the trail and soon arrived on the turnpike. He looked at Stevenson, fifty yards off, but neither man made any gesture of recognition or movement toward the other.

Stevenson watched calmly, as he had watched the man every inch of the descent. Metcalfe stood in the turnpike and looked—a little anxiously— north and south. Before long he was joined from the north by Hope, leading a party of eight brickies. They all stood and stared, now with fixed and open anxiety, southward. While this was happening Jack Whitaker came around the bend at Stone Bridge and began walking over the broken ground between there and the huts. The sight of him reminded Stevenson that this was the first day since he had gained the contract on which he had not started by visiting each, or most, of the workings.

He quickly brought his assistant up to date and then took him aside to a place where they could not be overheard.

"I want ye to go from here, Jack," he said, "as if ye're doing an ordinary everyday inspection. But when ye get over yon brow, out of sight, like, I want ye to get down to Littleborough and go to Rochdale—by horse or train, it's of no consequence to me—and fetch the constabulary back here. They'll need at least a dozen—more if they can manage."

"A dozen!" Whitaker was surprised.

"If things go as I believe. But listen—this is the most important. They're to come after noon. Between noon and one o'clock."

"Ye play a hand damn close to your chest, Stevenson, I'll say that."

"Not before noon, now." Stevenson patted his arm. "Good man. Off you go."

During this time, Burroughs made his belated appearance with a larger band of fourteen men.

"Eh, I'm buggered!" Fernley said. "Every fookin' brickie."

"Except Bennett." Stevenson shook his head. "Loyalty's an odd piece of goods. No doubt of it."

They watched the brickies gather for a brief conference in the middle
of the turnpike. Then they broke into two parties, each of about a dozen
men. Burroughs and Hope led one to picket the pathways leading down to
the site offices. The other, led by Metcalfe, went a hundred yards or so
north, picketing the entries to Summit East, the short reach of tunnel that
lay north of the oval shaft.

Fernley was aghast at this behaviour. "They're standing on your contract, Lord John!"

Stevenson clapped him on the shoulder. "Where I want 'em, lad," he
said. And as he went up the path to the nearest picket he turned round and
shouted back: "I want thy timber and stone orders for next week. See
they're done before knocking-off today."

The pickets, alerted by his voice, shuffled nervously and looked at one
another for support. Hope and Burroughs, alone, did not look around.

Stevenson walked among them and out onto the turnpike without so
much as a sideways glance. Once on the turnpike he looked both ways, as if
expecting someone—but without anxiety—and then, glancing knowingly
at his watch, set off for Metcalfe's pickets. Every step of the way he held
his eyes fastened on Metcalfe's; Metcalfe fixed him with the same unblinking stare.

As he came within a few yards—apparently walking straight up to
Metcalfe—he saw the man rearrange his features and breathe in, preparing
to speak. But at the last minute he changed course and walked immediately
to the man's left, passing within inches of him.

"Morning!" he said, without a break in rhythm and without even a
sideways glance.

Metcalfe said nothing.

Stevenson walked quickly into the northern works.

Summit below ground was to have its excitement that day, too, for it
was the day on which the driftway in from the north broke through to meet
the drift from number twelve; and since that drift had, in turn, met with
the one from number eleven a week earlier, there was now almost half a
mile of continuous passage opened to the north. Within the week, he
estimated, they would have broken right through to number seven and
more than half the tunnel would be open drift.

The moment of breakthrough is one of immense excitement in the
making of a driftway. For months your boring bar or pick rings and jars at
the stubborn, unyielding wall of living rock. By the end of each day, when
you swing your sledgehammer against the head of the bar for the ten
thousandth time and its tip leaps a sixteenth of an inch farther into the
rock, you feel that the task of driving forward even one foot more through

that passive, adamantine face is beyond human power—or human frailty, as it then seems. Day by day, with your endurance renewed, you stand by the light of a guttering candle, wreathed in clouds of the dust your efforts raise, breathing air that grows steadily more fetid, and you gain, inch by weary inch, on that least yielding of all substances.

But then comes that moment, long predicted, daily measured, known to the precise hour—often to the minute—yet not one whit the less surprising: the moment when the very rock changes character. It rings hollow. The distant tapping from the opposing drift magnifies to an echo of your own insistent hammering. Your bar lurches from you as if the rock had suddenly degenerated into clay. And the face in front of you dissolves and shatters as your opposite number hammers through into the air space you have spent so long creating. And then you can hear each others' cheers and can reach your hands through to shake theirs. And then it seems only the work of moments to break down the yielding fragments that still divide you. And so you turn the two driftways into one.

Stevenson, who had not missed this moment on any of the other drifts, saw it right through now on number twelve. The cheers and excitement were over and they were beginning the final breakdown before he turned to the exit and met Walter Thornton on his way in.

"Stevenson!" he said. "I thought you might like to know. Some time ago three gentlemen joined up with your bricklayers. Or your erstwhile bricklayers."

"Oh, no. They're still mine," Stevenson said. "They'll all be back at work tomorrow. All except the ringleaders."

*     *     *

The three gentlemen Thornton mentioned had descended from the coach and stood uncertainly in the centre of the roadway looking about them like the beleaguered rump of a vanished army. By chance they stood between the two pickets.

"Stand firm, brothers!" shouted Metcalfe, to their left. "No disorder. Here's the magistrates."

"Never!" Hope's scornful shout swung all three to their right. "That's no magistrates. One of them's that Methodist from Smallbridge."

The minister thus identified smiled and raised his hand. "Good morning, brothers!" he called. Still none of them moved, being undecided between the two groups of pickets.

"Good morning." Metcalfe's guarded welcome decided them for his party.

"Mr. Metcalfe?" the minister asked.

"Who wants 'im?"

"I'm Thomas Findlater, the Methodist minister of—"

Metcalfe's suspicions vanished beneath a sudden, broad smile. "Tom Findlater the Chartist?"

"The same."

They stepped toward one another and shook hands warmly. "We've met," Metcalfe said. "On the moors behind Mr. Fielden's place. When Feargus O'Connor spoke."

"I remember it. But not you, I fear."

Metcalfe shrugged. "Who remembers anyone else that day but Mr. O'Connor!"

"Indeed," Findlater answered, giving Metcalfe's hand, which he still grasped firmly, one final shake. Then he turned to his companions. "These two gentlemen are also of our cause. Mr. Spencer Fox, attorney, and Mr. Stuart McLeish, gentleman."

Metcalfe beckoned his two committeemen. "I'm Tom Metcalfe," he said while they walked up to join them. "This is Wilfred Hope and Thomas Burroughs . . ." he completed the introductions.

Findlater lowered his voice. "It occurred to us, when we heard of your action, that you might need witnesses of standing."

It had obviously not occurred to Metcalfe for he brightened visibly at the offer. "Well thought!" he said.

Fox was then careful to discourage any foolish optimism. "It may do little good at the magistrates courts, but should there be any subsequent inquiry or any need for agitation in the press . . ." He left the implications delicately unspoken.

It certainly sobered Metcalfe. He glanced nervously at the other two to see how they took it; but they were so impassive they might not even have followed. He turned back to the three visitors with his warmest smile. "Well, gentlemen! Ye are all royally welcome!"

But several hours later, when Thornton walked past them with no more than a sardonic smile and, like Stevenson, vanished into the drift, they were all a good deal less cheerful. They were simply being ignored. The whole working, except for the bricklaying, went on exactly as before. People walked past them as if they were not there. They felt cold. They felt superfluous. The three gentlemen were now almost continually blowing on their fingernails and stamping their feet.

Metcalfe called Burroughs and Hope up for a conference. They decided to give it fifteen minutes more and then let half of each picket go off for half an hour of refreshment.

"This is quite extraordinary," Findlater complained.

"Does he think," Fox added, "that if he ignores you, you'll go away?"

Metcalfe gave a short, bitter laugh. "Oh—he's no man's fool, Lord John. Just look at our pickets. They're not the men they were at seven this morning. Nothing's worse than being ignored."

"You told us what your grievance is," Findlater said. "But you didn't say what sort of an employer he is."

Again came that short, bitter laugh. "It may sound . . . funny, you know, like, for me to be saying this. He's not been master here for more than . . . what? Three month. Until then he was a navvy ganger."

Fox cleared his throat and nodded knowingly. "They're the worst. These lower-deck commissions. Tartars."

"On the contrary," Metcalfe said. "You couldn't work for a better man. And it's me who says it. I've said it to his face. I said: 'This fight's not me against *you*. It's the working classes against the ancient regime and privilege!' "

"That is put so exactly!" Fox said, wanting to make up for his earlier error.

Findlater looked speculatively at Metcalfe, as if discovering depths he had not suspected. "What . . . first stirred you to the cause of union- ism?" he asked. "Your struggle here is more than just wages, I feel."

"Our struggle here is about the right and dignity of the working man," Metcalfe agreed. "As to what first moved me that way, I can't say. I've often wondered. Often and often. Trying to think back to that moment when . . . the first moment when that . . . that *rage* heaped up in me." His eyes raked over the snowswept hills around, as if they held the secret. "I think it was in the village where I was born. Whitchurch in Hamp- shire—do any of you gentlemen know it?"

All shook their heads.

"My father was stockman there to the Earl of Portsmouth at Hurst- bourne Park. It was a Sunday and we children had gone out of the church while the confirmed people stayed on to take communion. For some reason—on account of the heat, I suppose—they had left the door open. And I crept back alone to watch. I shall never forget that. I saw my father and the other labourers wait their turn while the peerage and gentry and the village worthies swigged and guzzled the blood and body of One who in life would have stood there lower even than the labourers. That had its effect on me. A very powerful effect. My anger . . . I think it grew me up. My father had been as a god to me until I saw him there, taking part in his own humiliation—aiding and abetting it. But it wasn't his fault. It's what the working classes are taught from birth—to aid and abet their own humiliation." He looked at his small dispirited army, and said with little heat: "Aye. It's a holy war for me!"

For a while no one spoke. Hope and Burroughs looked at him with a kind of reverence. At last Findlater said: "How very humble you make me feel." His companions muttered their fervent agreement. "You see, Fox—here is the book where we must learn to read."

"Indeed," Fox said. "The true true abstract of our life and times. What of you, Brother Hope?"

Hope had no intention of competing with Metcalfe. "Haw! 'Tweren't like that for me!" His strong Northumberland dialect gave his words an incongruous edge of cheerful surprise. The upward lift at the ends of his sentences seemed to his southern—and even his northern—hearers to turn every statement into a question.

"Even so," Fox said, "I'm sure we'd feel privileged to hear it from you."

"I've never heard you talk of it," Metcalfe said.

Reluctantly Hope began. "I started work as a mining brickie in Northumberland. And that was when the miner was gettin' thrippence a ton. For hewing the coal and stacking it and all. And firing his own shot and making his own fuses with the straw in the fields after harvest and all, ye know. Thrippence a ton! And the Duke of Northumberland, who did fook-all but sit up there on his fat arse all day, was gettin' a farthing a ton for every ton of coal that come up out the ground. And he's still getting it and all! By! I says it's scandalous. If they'd count the true cost of all they have and what they take! One damask tablecloth costs two families starving for a week. A fine new carriage—and there's four wee bairns dead of ratbites. If our struggle makes—"

"Here comes someone, surely," Fox interrupted.

They all turned, to see Stevenson standing in the cutting, talking earnestly with Thornton.

"That's John Stevenson," Metcalfe said. "The taller one."

"And the other's Mr. Walter Thornton, engineer to the railway board for this tunnel," Burroughs added.

"I'm sorry." Fox turned back to Hope. "I believe I interrupted."

Hope, looking directly at Stevenson, now approaching them up the path between cutting and turnpike, said: "Aye. I says, if our struggle makes it just that mite better for folks and their families and all in years to come, then we'll struggle gladly whatever the cost."

Fox just had time to say "Well spoken!" before Stevenson arrived.

He stopped on the turnpike edge—as if he were one of the pickets—and, scrutinizing the three visitors, turned to the leader. "Well, Metcalfe. Your union secretary, I take it. See how wrong I was—a thin white cleric and I promised thee a fat white clerk!"

Metcalfe did not rise to it. "This is the Reverend Mr. Findlater . . .

Mr. Spencer Fox . . . and . . ." He had forgotten the name of the silent third man, who stepped forward to introduce himself.

"Mc—Mc—Mc—" he tried.

"McLeish?" Stevenson asked. "Stuart McLeish? The Chartist?"

"—Leish!" McLeish exploded.

Understanding appeared to dawn on Stevenson's face as he looked again at the group. "Mr. Spencer Fox, attorney and Chartist. Reverend Thomas Findlater, Methodist and Chartist. Chartists all." He smiled.

"You're well-informed, sir," Findlater said. They crossed the road to join him among the pickets.

Stevenson turned to Metcalfe. "A minister, an attorney, and a gentleman! You're prepared for all chances."

"They've come of their own will," Metcalfe said.

"I wonder how they'll go!"

"We'll g—g—go when j—j—justice is d— is done," McLeish interjected.

"Then ye've a long wait. There'll be no justice done here this day," Stevenson said. "I've warned him of that." He nodded toward Metcalfe. "He chose to enter against me after I told him. Now it's his affair."

"So!" Fox said triumphantly. "You already admit injustice will be done here today!"

"Not the least bit," Stevenson said to him calmly. "These bricklayers are fighting their employer for the mastery of this working. It's a fight they have no possible method of winning. They are bound to lose. *How* they lose is not of our choosing. Chance will determine it. And whether justice enters the matter in any way is also a chance determination."

Metcalfe, controlling his anger, but only just, leaped in. "That's not what this struggle is about. . . ."

"Ye're trespassing, gentlemen," Stevenson told the two who were standing on the grass. His words cut across Metcalfe's flow.

The two joined McLeish on the turnpike and turned back to face Stevenson and the pickets. Stevenson continued. "There's no right to loiter on a turnpike. I'll get them to remove ye if ye stop there." Findlater looked at the field on the far side of the road. "I know the farmer," Stevenson said, anticipating his movement.

"As I said"—Metcalfe's voice came from behind—"your union's all around us!"

Fox now spoke: "Will you kindly point out to us the nearest common land?"

"Aye," Stevenson said with all the kindly good nature of a man directing a stranger. "They'd have a problem trying to turn ye off the old packhorse trail up there. . . ." He pointed up the hill and then directed their eyes down the turnpike toward the north. "And yon bridge, Deanroyd Bridge, is part of the former highway. Ye might stand there, I daresay."

Findlater skipped backward across the road, looking at both pickets as he did so. "Brothers!" he called. "Can ye hear me?"

"Aye," came the response from the two groups of men.

Thornton nudged Stevenson. "Got to stop this." But Stevenson merely shook his head, implying that they should wait.

"Brothers!" Findlater shouted in his grandest, field-meeting voice. "We are deeply sorry but we have no course other than to withdraw a short distance. But—anticipating some such turn of events, we have come prepared." He darted a hand inside his coat and drew forth a ship's spyglass. "See! Be assured—we shall be watching your and their every move through this from the bridge yonder. Remember only this: Offer no violence or obstruction and do not let them entice you from our view!"

"What's all this?" Stevenson asked him. "Your view? What's this spyglass for?"

"Witnesses, sir," Fox answered triumphantly. "We are witnesses. We are here in that capacity."

Stevenson looked at him narrowly. "Ye mean—ye'll make no speeches?"

"In view of our purpose here," Findlater said loftily, "that would hardly be to the point."

To Stevenson's quick mind it seemed too good to be true. "Ye'll take no part, no active part whatsoever, in the events, such as they are, at this working? Though unevents would be a better word."

Fox was an elaborate parody of courtesy and patience. "That, sir, would confound our aims entirely."

Stevenson saw his chance. He had to get Metcalfe to accept the presence of these witnesses, unquestioningly and long enough for his own purpose. He turned to the strike leader and, with a sarcastic snort, said: "God spare *me* such friends in my hour of need, Tom! They come here knowing not a scrap of what may befall ye. But one thing they have already determined is they'll lift no finger to aid ye!"

Both Findlater and Fox protested loudly that this was a most scurrilous interpretation of their purpose but Stevenson turned laughingly to them, spread wide his hands, and said: "Gentlemen! Gentlemen—ye may stay. And welcome!"

"Stevenson!" Only Thornton's voice broke the astonished silence. "Is that wise?"

"I think so," Stevenson answered, turning to him calmly. "There's nothing'll happen here as *we*'ll have to answer for." And then, before the mood could evaporate, he beckoned the three back to nearer the pickets. "Gentlemen," he said, turning to Metcalfe, "I call on ye to witness. Thomas Metcalfe, as contractor on this site and your master, I require you to go at once to your appointed place of work on the oval shaft and so fulfill your agreement with me."

Metcalfe answered in a ritualistic formula that had clearly been well drilled: "I have no desire other than to work. And so I will when our terms are met."

Had Fox drilled them in this phrase? Stevenson wondered. He'd had most of the morning to do it in. If so, had Fox anticipated the full ritual? "Ye wanted three and six a day and ye got it. Terms *are* met," he said.

Metcalfe licked his lips and looked nervously at Fox. That was it then! "Not . . . in an acceptable form," he said, hesitantly.

Stevenson now went straight into his other broadside. "Then I must further tell you I propose to put on another in your place. To avoid a breach of the peace, I require you to tell me your intention toward such a man. . . ."

"Do not answer that!" Fox blurted out.

Stevenson rounded on him at once, triumphantly. "Aye. I thought ye would! Witness indeed!"

"Fox," Findlater said in annoyance. "You jeopardize our whole position."

Stevenson again addressed Metcalfe. "I require you, Tom Metcalfe, to give me assurance that you will let such man or men pass without—"

"Blacklegs!" Metcalfe exploded. "Men! They'll be no true workingmen."

"To let such man or men pass without let or hinder," Stevenson, the model of patient calm, repeated.

Metcalfe turned sideways to him and folded his arms. "That we cannot do," he said firmly.

"That we cannot do?" Stevenson quoted with a hint of surprise. "*We!* Ye'll note that royal word, gentlemen: 'We.'" He turned rapidly on Burroughs. "Thomas Burroughs, as contractor on this site and your master I require you to . . ." He repeated the whole formula, not pausing, even when Fox, who had become increasingly agitated, finally burst out again.

"Look, Findlater," Fox said. "I can't let this happen. Metcalfe's walking into a trap. If this goes on, Stevenson's going to be able to call us as witnesses for the Crown. Against these men."

"Surely not!"

"Don't say it!" Metcalfe and Findlater cried together.

Stevenson continued relentlessly with his catechism of Burroughs.

"What've we done wrong?" Metcalfe asked urgently. "Picketing's our right."

"Mr. Fox! What do I say, sir?" Burroughs in an agony of indecision cried out to the attorney when Stevenson pressed him.

"You must give Mr. Stevenson the assurance he seeks," Fox said unhappily.

"No!" Metcalfe roared. "No! No! Never! We'll never stand idly here and let blacklegs by."

"Fourth George IV, chapter ninety-five," Stevenson said.

Fox nodded dourly.

Metcalfe looked from Stevenson's assured, smiling face to Fox's mask of worry. "What's all that?" he asked.

Stevenson responded cheerfully, "It says ye may meet to discuss and determine your wage; but any of ye who should 'by violence, threats or intimidation, molestation, or obstruction, do, or endeavour to do' . . ."—and here he turned to the gentlemen—" 'or aid, abet, or assist in doing' . . ."—smilingly back to Metcalfe—"and there follows a list as long as short speech by Feargus O'Connor of all the things ye may not do—like interfering with a contract between man and master—anyone as does any of them things shall be subject to a maximum of three months with hard labour."

"That true?" Metcalfe asked Fox.

Fox nodded glumly.

Stevenson, speaking over Metcalfe's head to the pickets—all of whom had wandered up to the group—said, "In my opinion, any leader who'd take his men into this sort of pickle ignorant of the law is worse than a general who'd send soldiers into battle ignorant of the terrain and country."

"No one's interested in your bloody opinion," Hope said, but it was the only support for Metcalfe that anyone offered.

"And what games have you been playing, Mr. Fox, attorney-at-law?" Stevenson continued. "I gave ye all the best part of the morning for them to cool off and you to talk some sense to 'em. D'ye imagine I want trouble for these men? What sort of master d'ye think me to be? If you gentlemen will go quietly back to your books and flocks now, and these men here return to their appointed tasks, I'll forget the whole thing ever happened." Fox looked uncomfortably down and stirred the snow with his boot.

"Wait now," Metcalfe said, feeling every initiative drain away. "What was it thou said in yon list—not by violence . . . molestation—what was it?"

"Violence, threats or intimidation, molestation, or obstruction," Stevenson said.

"We'll offer no violence, no threat, we'll not intimidate or molest. . . . What constitutes 'obstruction'?" he asked Fox.

The attorney grew even more uncomfortable. "It is not determined," he said.

"It means whatever the magistrate wants it to mean," Stevenson said.

"If we don't block the way of the blacklegs? If we just . . . reason with them?"

"That . . . might be considered obstruction," Fox said.

"If we just hold up . . . I don't know . . . placards or papers or some such thing with our demands and grievances listed?"

"That, too, might be held to be obstruction," Fox was forced to say. "It depends on the magistrate. Where are we here, Lancashire or Yorkshire?"

"This highway's Lancashire; the railroad is Lancashire. . . ." Thornton pointed out the succession of features on the valley floor to their east. "The canal is in Yorkshire. The boundary is a little stream in between. Not visible from here."

"Lancashire." Fox's pessimism deepened still further. "Ye'd come up in Rochdale, before Reverend Prendergast . . ."

"But he's a director of the railway," Metcalfe protested. "I've seen him out here inspecting these works. He'd have to disqualify hisself."

"It's not a railway dispute," Stevenson said.

"Not—" Metcalfe began to shout.

"It's between an independent contractor and his servants. Me and thee."

Fox, shaking his head, concluded: "If you were simply to breathe in the path of these . . . 'blacklegs' . . . as you call them, I fear that Reverend Prendergast would consider it obstruction."

"If thy breath stank as bad as thy planning of this lamentable occasion," Stevenson added, "it bloody would be and all! Can't ye see, man—it's the kind of law that forbids treason, murder, rape, arson, and breathing."

Metcalfe looked from one to the other of them in anguish. "What may the working classes do?" he asked. "Where may we turn? You say we may meet to determine a wage, yet you also say we may not lift a finger—we may not even breathe, you say—to make that determination real. We may speak to none, communicate with none. Such rights as we may have are *worthless.* While you may do all you wish. There is no law to harass and imprison you!" He turned to his men. "Brothers!" he said. "If we must fight iniquity we must fight it *now.* If we must smash oppression, we must smash it *now!* If we must cast off the yoke of our slavery, we must do it *now!* Now is the hour of our struggle. If we fail, if we let this chance slip by, if we surrender, having taken up the burden, we strengthen not ourselves but them. We hand them swords to wound us with, irons to brand us with, chains to bind us with. We lie down before them and ask to have our faces ground in the dust like whipped curs. We should end like those wretched souls as shuffle into the mills each morn. Without hope. Without pride. Without future. Brothers! I say to you and I say it most solemnly: Your future starts here and it starts now. Your pride in your craft . . . your future as craftsmen . . . your place—your honoured place—at the spearhead of the great working-class struggle, starts here and it starts now. And I say they shall not pass. Whatever the cost! Whatever the sacrifice!"

"Fine words butter no parsnips—" Stevenson began. But Metcalfe burst into the song "Bold Robinson the Fighter"—putting Stevenson's name wherever Robinson's stood and substituting "brickies" for Tiley. Laughing, all his pickets joined in and soon the valley rang with their song. Connected speech was hopeless.

"Gentlemen! Witness, my three fine witnesses . . ." Stevenson shouted to them. "I ask you to note who prevented me from addressing my men."

"You'd best let him speak," Fox advised Metcalfe, but the only reply was a triumphant shake of the head and an even louder burst of song.

Stevenson walked a dozen paces away and turned. Raising his voice to the highest and loudest pitch he could muster, he pointed at Metcalfe and shouted: "Obstruction . . . arrest . . . disgrace . . . treadmill!" And then, pointing to the workings: "A guinea and more a week! The best-paid bricklaying in Lancashire!"

The volume of the singing fell noticeably away. Stevenson leaped in, stabbing a finger at one of the group. "Thou—Ephraim Webster—what'll thy Ann do, how'll she fend for them four bairns of thine while thou art sweating the flesh off of thy bones at the treadmill?"

The volume fell below the level at which the singing could easily sustain itself. Stevenson lowered his voice further and turned the screw yet tighter. "You, Reverend Findlater, there's twenty wives and nigh on eighty bairns stood behind these men. You may not see them, but I do. You may not think of them but I do. You may join in Metcalfe's way of thinking and consider them part of the necessary sacrifice, part of the unavoidable cost, but I don't. Will you fine gentlemen dig into your purses and support the hundred unprovided-for victims of Mr. Metcalfe's great working-class struggle?"

"I feel sure a subscription would be raised," Findlater said.

Stevenson pulled out his watch. "I'll speak no further," he said crisply as he snapped its cover shut and returned it to his pocket. "I'll allow two minutes for thought. Any man as wants to throw himself on Tom Metcalfe's treadmill, and his wife and bairns on the Reverend Findlater's subscriptions, may stop where he is. Any man as wants a share of the best-paid bricklaying in the whole county may take that path and re-engage with Mr. Fernley. There's two minutes to choose."

He turned and walked slowly up the road, removing himself as a nearby presence, a focus for the uniting of their opposition. Metcalfe's despairing and repeated cries of "No!" and his appeals of "Brother!" told all he needed to know. When he turned again to begin the short walk back, he counted ten remaining, including all three committee members. Ephraim Webster had chosen to stay, though he looked distinctly unhappy about it. Just before he returned to the fringe of the group, Stevenson said, "Time's up."

At that moment Webster turned to go. "Thou art too late, Ephraim," Stevenson called after him. "This race goes to the swift." Miserably the man returned to his brothers.

A horse with a woman rider came around the corner beyond Deanroyd, going at a slow canter. Stevenson, seeing that Metcalfe was about to shout in anger at him, said: "Ten!" He put surprise and disappointment in his voice. "That's seven more than I thought thou'd muster, Tom." And of course Metcalfe had to respond as if the loss of more than half his pickets were indeed the triumph that Stevenson appeared to concede.

"Ten's enough," he said. "Three would suffice."

Stevenson addressed them all. "I've asked ye to return to the works. I've asked ye to give assurance ye'll let others pass unhindered. Ye've done neither. Ye are all to be dismissed forthwith. Such tools and belongings as ye left on the site have been gathered and may be got at the site office. From this minute on, ye're trespassers all. Which"—he turned to Thornton—"is a railway company matter."

But Thornton was looking in astonishment at the fast-approaching horsewoman. It was Arabella. And her face and manner showed every sign of extreme alarm.

"Mrs. Thornton!" Walter called. "What are you doing here?"

She reined in. All the men removed their hats. "Oh, Walter!" she said in breathless distress. "It's so dreadful. . . ."

Thornton looked around in embarrassment. "My dear—this is no place to come tattling to me—"

"No tattle," she interrupted. "Believe me. No tattle. Those *dreadful* men! They'll murder us all!"

"Be calm!" he said. "What are you trying to say? *Who* will murder us?"

"The Irish, is it?" Stevenson asked coolly. "Calley's navvies—all got drunk?"

"Drunk!" Arabella cried, as if the word did not describe one tenth of it. "They are like beasts! Worse! It is a riot. They have put the whole of Todmorden in a siege." She glanced around at her bareheaded hearers and added, lamely inconsequential: "Put up your hats, please, gentlemen."

Stevenson looked suddenly worried. "Has Calley vanished without paying?" he asked.

"I only wish he had! They've bought up every last drop of liquor in the town."

"Oh, ye're all right then." Stevenson's concern turned to relief. "That's a plain honest randy. No great harm'll come of it."

"No harm! They've broken every window in four public houses. No harm! Mr. Thornton, can you not *do* something?"

Thornton's patience was on the verge of breaking. "My dear! I am not engineer for that section. But even if I were, it's not company business. We have enough company business here to contend with. It is for the justices and their constables. Besides, Mr. Stevenson is right—there's no real harm in a randy. They'll brawl and make a shindy and break a few things—but no harm. Do go home now."

"Oh, no!" she cried in terror. "I dare not."

Thornton's small stock of patience was now exhausted. "Madam. You may not stay. . . ."

"But they are coming this way!" she said.

Stevenson was suddenly very interested.

"They are now between here and home. They mean to walk to Littleborough for fresh liquor."

"Oh . . . very well," Thornton said with ill grace. "I shall escort you."

"You'll excuse me, Mr. Thornton," Stevenson said. He took the engineer aside and spoke for his ears alone. "I've no wish to determine your affairs but . . . this is company property and a company matter now. . . ."

"What—your bricklayers?" Thornton asked.

"They're none of mine. They're trespassers. The Board might think it strange if ye left at such a moment."

They had come close to Arabella. "You're right," Thornton said reluctantly. "I may not leave."

"I'll see Mrs. Thornton home. I have business to arrange in Todmorden."

Thornton did not immediately reply.

Arabella, who shook her head the moment Stevenson made his offer, now burst out, "Oh, Walter—no!" just as she had on the day they had first met.

"Dearest," Thornton said, in a voice empty of all warmth, "that is churlish. Mr. Stevenson is quite right. Besides—there is no man in England better fit than he is to get you through *any* mob of navvies, drunk, sober, whatever their mood."

"Come on," Stevenson said—whether to her or to the horse she was not certain—and, taking the bridle, turned the creature and pulled it to start for home.

"Mr. Stevenson!" Metcalfe called after him. "We mean to stay and mount picket."

"It's out of my hands now. Ye've all had warning enough, and more." He called a lad over from the top of the cutting. "Go and tell Mr. Fernley I'm off to Todmorden to arrange the supper. I'll be back near two o'clock."

The lad, his thoughts already on that supper, ran off with delight.

"Is that those wretched strikers?" Arabella asked.

"Aye. Is this your gelding?" He patted its gleaming, well-groomed coat admiringly.

"No!" she said. *"We* couldn't afford a horse yet. I hire him an hour each day from the livery stables behind the Golden Lion."

"I mean to get a horse. I spend too long on foot each day. It'll be worse when we move over here to Rough Stones."

She looked back up the hill to the house itself. "That's certain now, is it?"

"As certain as anything in this life can be. I have it in mind to walk through the driftway on Boxing Day—as promised—with your husband and make our transition from Littleborough that way."

She laughed, a pretty, ringing peal of laughter. "You have a romantic soul, Mr. Stevenson," she said.

"Aye. Belike I have. But, remembering your interest in seeing the works, I thought you and Mrs. Stevenson might care to make up the party?"

"You're certain it will be completed? What of all these strikers?"

"They'll not hinder the drift."

"Why don't you simply order them back to their work? If you are their master, they have to obey you, surely?"

"That's what a strike means." He patted the horse again, admiringly. "What's the rent?"

"Of the horse? As I take one out every day and am not too particular on always having the same, they charge threepence for the hour."

His laughter carried an edge of irony. "In a day this gelding could earn more than a farm labourer!"

She was puzzled by that. "What is the connection?" she asked.

They stopped. The horse pawed the ground and bent to breathe wreaths of steam toward its feet. "Still!" Stevenson called at it.

In the silence they heard a distant murmur—so distant it might have been mistaken for a vast rookery settling prematurely for the night, or a steady avalanche of rock; but, because they were expecting it, they could both identify it unmistakably as a great, raucous, rambling, randy mob.

"See anything?" he asked.

"Yes," she said. And though she spoke almost in a whisper he could hear the dread in her voice. But the sound of them and the knowledge that they were coming filled him with delight. They started to walk again.

"I can't see why you're so complacent," she said; her voice was stronger now but no less alarmed. "They've done some dreadful things. There is one man—I heard this from the servants—this one man they are carrying around in a sedan chair, dead drunk—"

"Swimmer Dandy!" Stevenson said.

"What?"

"Swimmer Dandy. That's his name. His fame has spread down here before him. They say he's been dead drunk all week and has now lost the power to stand erect."

"How disgraceful!" She tossed her head in a fury that made the horse half shy. "What wretched creatures!"

"Do you remember," Stevenson asked, "when we first met? That day in early September?"

She looked briefly around at the workings, just before they passed from view. "I meant to ask," she said. "Those men you showed me. The two new ones, half dead with fatigue."

"Darbishire and Walsh," he said without hesitation. "Aye—two useful lads. Another three months and they'll both make fine navvies. I told you."

"I remember."

"But I was not thinking of that," he said. "You remember that . . . misunderstanding between us?"

He had never seen a face turn redder quicker. "I have no idea what you can mean," she said in a would-be casual tone. "I have entirely forgotten *that* incident."

"You must remember," he persisted wickedly. "I told you I thought you lacked a purpose."

"Did you now?" Her eyes strayed pointedly over the hillsides, as if they—or anything—would offer more interest than this conversation. "I really don't remember. I can't think what you might have meant by it."

"I believe there is work here for you, Mrs. Thornton," he said. And now he was no longer teasing. "I believe you may find a purpose here—and one severe enough to daunt Medusa herself. Keep your eyes skinned and your wits sharp now. You may come to agree."

Responding to his solemnity she looked long at him. "How strange you are!" she said at last. "What to make of you? I'm sure I don't know."

She was glad she could look him in the eyes at last. He seemed to have lost that old power to confuse her and make her tremble. Or had *she* changed? She felt stronger with him now. And he never made her feel like a goose—he never had done that. Yet in a curious way it was as if that new confidence came partly from him. He seemed to expect her to be . . . different. Walter was always saying that Stevenson could get people to do things they couldn't have done on their own. In a way, that was rather disquieting, because to her Stevenson usually behaved as if he knew she was going to do something grand. And whenever she tried to show him how ridiculous that was, he just brushed it all aside. In her journal she had called this insistence "enervating" and then "tedious"—but she had had to cross out both words because neither was true. As yet she had found no word to put in their place.

"Can you still see them?" he asked breezily, yet again changing the mood and pace. "One can certainly *hear* them."

They were close enough now for individual voices to be distinguished —shouting, cheering, laughing, singing, brawling.

"Yes!" she said. "They're just coming over that new bridge, Skew Bridge." She looked around in alarm and pointed to the side road leading up to Ramsden Wood. "Oh, please! Let us withdraw a little way up there until they pass."

He glanced up at her, his face offering some obscure kind of challenge. "We'll go on as we are. And we'll meet them somewhere here in Strines Bottom."

"*Meet* them?" she cried. "Oh no! Please no! Please turn off at once. I cannot meet them."

"There's nothing to fear," he said. And certainly the calm in his voice was reassuring.

He pulled the horse to the right of the road, placing himself between her and the highway where they would have to pass.

They were in sight now. A wild, ragged, bedraggled caterpillar of drunken men. Drunken *giants* of men. If anyone had told Arabella that the other recreations of these creatures included straightening out horseshoes barehanded, she would have found no difficulty in believing it. She looked at Stevenson. His broad back and unruffled stance were all that stopped her fluttering heart from thumping itself right out of her body.

"Look at their eyes," he said. "Do not be afraid. Observe them closely—especially their eyes. Look keenly at their eyes." The horse grew restive. "Ho!" he said quietly and it, too, fell still.

He spoke first. "Top o' the mornin' to ye, lads!"

The clannish suspicion that had grown in their faces with each approaching step did not at once vanish. Then one, near the front, gave a whoop of pure joy. "Good Christ!" he called. "It's Lord John hisself!" The mood changed then as word and recognition spread. She heard the words "Lord John . . . Lord John . . . " pass like a watchword down the throng.

Inertia carried the leaders past and brought the rear crushing forward so that soon she and Stevenson were hemmed in on all sides by the jostling, cackling, rowdy mob. She did not believe that even he would bring them through it unscathed. Yet curiously enough, now that she was actually among them, she found herself surveying them with more curiosity than fear.

She had never seen so much blood. Fully one man in three was bleeding from somewhere; and she did not see one who was not marked by a large bloody scab or by a staining of fresh-dried blood or at least by bloodstains on his clothes. And the stench! If all the liquor in a large public house had been tipped with all the clothes from a workhouse mortuary into the foulest sewer and there churned to boiling point it would barely compete with this.

Yet there was, too, a kind of joy about them that she found strangely compelling—a childlike, unmalicious liberation of their spirit that took her unawares. And she saw that Stevenson was quite right when he had said there was no harm in them. She could imagine that, had she been born a man, she would have enjoyed a day of their carefree company. The two or three nearest her horse's head patted and fondled it and bared its teeth and opened its eyes with expert nods and shakes of the head. "That's a grand horse now!" one said, and she found herself returning his smile.

"Well!" Stevenson called. "Yorkshire beaten ye, has it? Going to put the fear on Lancashire!"

"Arra! Lord John!" called an older man with blackened teeth and a ringworm the size of a skullcap. "When'll ye bomb Calley off the line, Lord John, and squeeze us on yer pay roster!"

A great gale of laughter went up, and, though she did not understand the joke or its reference, she joined in. Stevenson turned around and looked at her strangely then, as if her laughter—but not theirs—had wounded him.

He faced them again. "When the kings come down from Tara," he said. "And Swimmer Dandy takes the form of Finn McCool!"

They loved that. It was the greatest joke of the day.

"Anyway," he went on, "why should I take such a drunken, dissolute lot of randy rebels on my payroll?"

This, too, raised a storm of laughter and some applause. She heard cries of "He's the lad!" and "That's the man himself!" The older, ringwormy one, who was taller than most, looked around and called: "Swimmer Dandy! Show him Swimmer Dandy now. Fetch the man!"

The cry was taken up and passed to the tail end. There an object was hoisted up above their heads and carried from hand to hand toward the front. It was almost level with them before she realized it was not an unconscious man but a corpse, already quite stiff. "Don't let them drop it!" she said involuntarily.

As he had died in the depths of alcoholic poisoning, death had laid him out in caricature of every drunken Irish yokel that never lived. The skin of his face stretched in a ghastly grimace, baring great splayed teeth below a potato nose that sprouted between unblinking eyes that stared every which way, one down, one up. When he was brought level they struggled to hold him upright; but even in death the feat eluded him and he swayed above them, like a candle with a broken stem.

"There, sir," said the tall one. "Good Christ, wasn't he the little darling!"

Stevenson looked at it with distaste. "Eh!" he said. "If I pulled it out on a fishhook, I'd cast it back for pity."

That brought renewed laughter.

"Where are ye bound for, lads?" he asked.

"Sure they've no liquor in Todmorden. We're away to Littleborough for a daycent Christian wake to bid farewell to poor old Swimmer here."

"That's a long way," Stevenson said, and there was a note of promise in his voice that many of them were quick to catch.

"Ah it is, sir!" The tall one smiled. "It is. It is indeed. A long, thirsty way! Indeed!"

"Aye!" Stevenson surveyed the sky. "It'd be champion if a man could stop halfway like and wet his whistle!"

"That's the truth! The God's own truth, that is."

He looked at them and smiling broadly, said: "Now that I think of it—I might have seen some casks of ale in the cutting beyond Deanroyd Bridge. Aye. . . ." He rubbed his chin speculatively. "Mebbe there might of been a drop of brandy there and all."

They gave out one bloodcurdling whoop that brought sudden shivers to her spine and then poured southward, like river ice in a thaw. By chance they passed Swimmer Dandy back to his "sedan chair"—in reality a simple litter of branches and rope—at just about the same rate as they streamed forward, with the result that he pitched and yawed and rolled, now prone, now supine, before them, as a log, trapped at some point on a river bed by a submerged branch, might dance on broken water. And his wild eyes and grinning mask made it seem that this lunatic seesawing and spinning conveyed more true sense to him than anything else in that whole, final, stupefying week.

"You're the Christian, sir!" they shouted as they trotted and stumbled past Stevenson. As he watched them go he rubbed his hands in a glee that was itself a kind of intoxication.

When they had gone, the air, now burdened only with the faint aroma of vitriol and—more pungently—with stray coal gas and the decaying water of the canal, smelled sweet indeed. The passage of so many feet had obliterated the snow, giving the Todmorden turnpike the character of a mid-city street.

"I suppose there's little real harm in them," she said as they resumed their walk. "Certainly not when one can handle them as you did."

"Aye," he replied. "It's easy to detest the Irish if ye merely hear of their doings. They're not like other Englishmen at all. But when ye meet them . . ." He shook his head. "There's no denying they've a way about them."

"Even that corpse they were carrying . . ." she said. "I don't know . . . it had a sort of romance. It seemed to be enjoying the fun, if that doesn't sound stupid."

"I know exactly what you mean," he said.

They passed a small group of cottages, new ones, built for the mill at Walsden. A woman, hearing them pass, came hesitantly out of her door and stood on her step, looking nervously up and down. "Are they gone?" she asked.

"Aye," he told her. "They'll not come back today."

She lifted her apron and fanned her face with it. "Eee!" she said. "I were that ruined with worry!"

"You? Why?"

She lowered her voice. "I've a licence to brew ale," she said. "There's sixty gallons in here. I thought they'd smash the place to bits."

He stopped when he heard that and introduced himself. "Mebbe I'll need sixty gallons, tonight," he said. "Bring us a cup; I'll see the taste of it."

The taste was to his satisfaction and he offered sevenpence a gallon. She couldn't let it go under a shilling. He'd have to join the Anti-Corn-Law League if he wanted prices down. In the end they settled at ninepence, and him to collect and return. She didn't know anyone who had killed a bullock or any other kine recently.

"I do," Arabella said proudly when they were moving again.

"You?"

"Yes. The clerk stands by the churchyard gate and announces all the slaughterings after matins each Sunday. I used to get our meat from Roberts the butcher. But now I go round the farms where they're slaughtering. And I do much better for us that way."

"And who is it today?"

"I'll only tell you if I may have the rump, one of the kidneys, and a pound of the liver."

"Done," he said.

"I've forgotten the name but I've had the farm pointed out to me. It's over at Swineshead Clough."

That was only a stone's throw from the turnpike, about two furlongs ahead, at Gawks Holm. The stretch between there and Walsden village, which they were just leaving, was—as yet—the least built-upon part of the valley.

"I was watching you," he said, "among that mob. I thought their drunkenness would appall you more than it seemed to."

"Yes," she said distantly. "I thought so, too."

"They need someone to work among them. A . . . a sort of missionary. An example. Men are no good. We've had ministers here from time to time. It's useless. It needs the gentler persuasion and more spiritual example of a woman."

She was so surprised that, involuntarily, she reined in her horse. Then she laughed in sheer embarrassment and shook her head. "Oh no!" she said. "You are not thinking of me! Certainly not *me!*"

"Don't," he implored and pulled a punch on her knee to make her look up and stop this silliness.

It did that all right! She sat up, eyes wide, nostrils flaring.

"How dare you!" she cried.

"Don't," he said again, quietly and deliberately. Curiosity got the better of her. "Don't what?" she asked fretfully, as if reserving the right to return to her anger.

"Don't underesteem yourself! You may find this laughable—but I tell you, I've watched you since you've come up here. There is a power in you, a moral power, that will one day astonish you. When it finds a worthy object on which to bend its force it will sweep you along with it. There will be none to match you—if you set your mind to it."

She laughed in the same embarrassment as before but did not this time hide her eyes. "Gee up!" she spurred her horse.

"I don't know why you think it of *me,*" she said when they were walking again. "I'm no abstainer."

"No!" he said fervently. "Abstentionists are no good. They replace one kind of licentiousness by another."

"I don't follow."

"Abstention . . . any of these enthusiasms . . . they're all a kind of superabundant indulgence of the moral spirit. As bad for the soul as an excess of liquor for the body."

She was shocked. "One cannot have too much morality," she said.

He laughed, cheerfully and a little patronizingly. "One must be very young to think that. The young bricklayers' leader back there has an excess of moral zeal—about class and wealth. He drank his fill of it yesterday; he's drunk on it today; tomorrow he'll have a thick head from it—three months thick. Avoid these fanatics and enthusiasts. Temperance—not abstinence. Temperance in all things. Cut the cloth to the pocket and the sail to the wind."

A devil in him, amused at the intensity of her anger when he had punched her kneecap, now moved him to reach a hand up there and gently squeeze it.

But now no anger flowed. She looked steadily at the sky and then lowered her eyes to him with weary asperity. "Please, Mr. Stevenson . . ." Her voice was flat, the way one might talk to a child too old to be spoken to as a child. "Do not always be so . . . infantile. Kindly remove your hand."

He sighed in disappointment. "At least," he said, "you do not shriek to the heavens and slap my face this time."

"Nor did I last time!" She almost shouted in her astonishment.

"Ha haa!" He turned. "You said you had forgotten! Now you smile . . . yes, you should smile more often. Tight lips do not become you."

She obeyed resignedly, implying that he was incorrigible but harmless. "When I was sixteen," she told him, "I used to go around the parish with my mother, taking broth and scraps to the sick and the poor. There was one old man I remember who was crippled while felling trees—on Mr. Thornton's uncle's estate, in fact—and he was then completely destitute. Well, whenever my mother's back was turned he used to reach out—just like you, then—and squeeze my situpon. I tolerated it, I think, because I realized there was not an ounce of harm in the poor old fellow."

Stevenson inclined his head, ruefully accepting defeat. "I must take care not to earn your pity in future."

"Yes. You must take great care."

They rode on a short way in silence, with only a hundred yards or so remaining before they reached the turning to the farm. The man-made landscape at this point might have been especially prepared as an illustration for some popular treatise on communications. The river, following the contours, swung sharply left and then more slowly right in a great arc before swinging left again to resume its northward course. The old road followed the same pattern, though, being higher up the hill to their right, its twists were less extreme. The canal, built by more confident engineers, followed even straighter lines that carried it clear over the river at two points. Then the new turnpike, less careful of gradient, arched over the canal and cut straight through a shoulder of the hill, making a small cliff between itself and the old road, higher up. And finally, on its long viaduct of flying arches, soaring majestically over river, canal, and road, cutting the straightest swath of all, ran the new railroad, now almost complete. When they reached the junction where the Bacup road runs west from the turnpike, they could see all four levels at once—railroad over road over canal over river.

"Look," Stevenson said. "I doubt there's much we do would impress the ancient Romans. But I fancy that would."

She looked at it and nodded. "My husband tells me you're quite the classical scholar, Mr. Stevenson."

He shook his head and led her horse forward again. "Slip o' the tongue, ma'am, no more." He spoke in a way that did not invite further pursuit of the subject, so she returned to a point she had meant to raise earlier and had forgotten.

"You talk of temperance and suppressing drunkenness among your men," she said. "Yet what of you? You're a fine one!"

"Oh?"

"Yes. Who told those Irish navvies about the liquor at Deanroyd?"

He stared at her, wide-eyed in his innocence. "What liquor?"

"The beer, and the brandy . . ." She paused. "You mean there is none?"

"Nary a drop!"

"But . . . goodness! Will that not simply provoke them?"

"Greatly, I hope. Clubs will be trumps then all right!" He laughed and pulled out his watch. "It is . . . ten minutes past midday. At any moment the Rochdale constabulary will arrive to suppress a strike. I am hoping they find a riot."

She was shocked. And she could tell that, despite his truculence, he was not as happy as he tried to make himself seem. "What have you done?" she asked.

"I have put an Irish cat among some Lancashire pigeons." He spoke with no humour now, and they continued in silence.

Just before they reached to turn to Swineshead Clough she asked: "Mr.

Stevenson, when did you first conceive the idea of putting this 'Irish cat' among your 'Lancashire pigeons'?"

"First?" He had to think. "Of course I knew I must crush the strike the minute I heard of it. Then . . . I knew I might somehow use the turmoil of Calley's pay-out. But it was no more than an idea at the back of my head until you brought the news they were headed south."

She was too scandalized at his use of her to speak. And he felt her silence as keenly as any accusation, for he then added: "The constabulary was sent for much earlier—before you came." She did not respond. "I gave them every chance," he continued. "Until just before you came, I was offering every man his old place back."

She bitterly regretted now that she had opened the subject. These were things she did not understand: but everything she heard merely strengthened her feeling that a wrong had been done—which his succession of excuses only confirmed.

"Please," she said unhappily. "Don't think yourself accountable to me."

"But I am," he said flatly. "We are all accountable to those whose friendship we value and whose opinions we therefore esteem."

"Well . . ." She looked unhappily around. There was more life stirring here, now that the Irish had gone well past; the bruised and fearful town was returning anxiously to its usual ways. "I think I would rather go to the farm alone," she said. "I shall tell him you will call later today." He nodded. "I'll wish you good day," she concluded.

She had turned before he replied. "The best thing I may wish you, ma'am, is a life so comfortable you need never make a choice such as I have faced today."

This appeal struck her as so unworthy that she could not hold her anger as she turned back to face him. "You may think to ask yourself—you who so detest extremism as you claim—who has been the extremist today? Who has sacrificed *all* to one particular end? The defeat of these men was already ensured. The constabulary was already sent for. What do you gain by blackening them as violent? What gain was worth that devious sacrifice of your honour? And as for wishing me comfort—I seek no comfort. I tell you frankly: I would sooner a bed of nails than your feather mattress of a conscience."

She realized that the longer she spoke the angrier she was growing. So, making short of her farewell, she turned for the last time and spurred her horse away up the hill.

He smiled as he watched her out of sight. What if that fervour could find a worthy cause!

# Chapter 26

"Yon fookin' pig! When I fookin' catch it, I'll fookin' kill it!" Eph Ackroyd said aloud. He spoke—for want of a better hearer—to Emily Ann, who had been put out into the porch at Stone House, to sun herself. She turned her pretty, idiot face toward his voice and cackled and nodded, cackled and nodded—just as, minutes earlier, she had cackled and nodded at the squealing pig as it rushed by and made for the bridge—and just as, minutes before that, she had turned her head toward the turnpike and cackled and nodded at the Rochdale constabulary, hurrying past. Emily Ann's was a laughing, affirmative world, although she spent most of her time in it lashed hand and foot to the rocking chair in which she now was seated. At night she was manacled to her bedroom wall; at mealtimes her padlocked leather waistband was chained through the back of her chair to a ring in the floor.

For whenever she escaped these fetters—as happened several times a year—Emily Ann would streak up the valley like a cat that's sat in pepper. And word would ripple among the menfolk that Emily Ann was loose. And Emily Ann would be passed from shed to woodland to coalhouse to loft to storeroom to cellar. And men would stand in surreptitious, sniggering lines and wait their turn at Emily Ann. Always the women would find her in the end and take her, exhausted and bleeding, back to Stone House.

Sometimes, a few months later, she would drop a small, cold, formless thing like a wreckling piglet; more often there was no issue. The men said she laughed the way she did in memory of her past escapes; to the women it seemed more likely to be in heartless anticipation of her next.

Eph paused and looked closely at the knots which bound her, as he always did when he came this way and she was put out to sun. Once he had been the first to find her—or to be found by her—when she had broken loose; and for ten delirious minutes, longer than he had ever spent in congress with his wife or any other woman, he had moaned with her among the reeds by the canal bank.

With falling spirit, he surveyed the new, resilient cords that bound each slender limb. He mopped the sweat from his brow and neck. Mrs. Cobb, her mother, came out and tested the bindings with a vicious tug. Finding them to her satisfaction, she snubbed Eph with a nod and returned indoors. Emily Ann nodded and cackled. Moments later Mrs. Cobb raised the downstairs sash and called to him: "Yon pig'll be half-way up Summit Tunnel, the way thou art loitering, Eph."

"Aye," he grumbled, "or Todmorden pound, more like." And, with a last regretful look at Emily Ann—who cackled and nodded yet again—he ran heavily, sweatily off toward the turnpike and the errant pig. He met it "half-way there but comin' back," as he later had to explain. On reflection he knew he ought to have tried to drive it off, back toward Deanroyd, for it would then have made a bolt for home between his legs and all would have been well. But memories and thoughts of Emily Ann were still confusing him and, seeing the pig already headed for home, he foolishly stepped aside to let it pass. To the pig there could be no plainer sign that something underhand was intended and it naturally turned and made for Deanroyd as fast as it could scuffle, leading Eph—though he did not yet know it—into the deepest trouble of his life.

The sight that met his eyes when he reached the bend was as startling as the one John Stevenson had seen from that same spot about eight hours earlier. Now a battle was raging across the cutting, from canal bank to turnpike, the like of which the valley had never seen. He had been dimly aware of some commotion or other as he had chased the pig down over the fields, but only when he came as close to it as this did he see how serious it really was. For one thing the constabulary was there, and they had never been seen in the valley before—certainly not in such numbers. And most serious of all, his pig—or his master's pig, Mr. Randall's pig—was darting in and out among the fighters like a creature demented.

It was one thing to bring an animal home from the pound and face a tongue-lashing from Mr. Randall; it was quite another to take that pig home dead, a full month before Christmas—even if he were lucky enough to extract a whole corpse from that embattled mob. He could, with very little imagination, easily picture Mr. Randall's response to that. With a cry of torment, and heedless of his personal safety, he hurled himself along the turnpike toward the heart of the storm in a do-or-die effort to save himself from that intolerable fate.

As civilian onlookers are often known to wander miraculously unscathed across a field of war, while men in uniform are falling and dying all around, so Eph was somehow enabled to chase Farmer Randall's pig once, twice, and then thrice around and among that bloody melee. Single images, seen at haphazard during the chase, etched themselves into his mind—a man with a steel shovel splitting another's scalp from crown to neck; another hopping to safety with half his calf muscle hanging free; two men holding a corpse already stiff and using it as a ram to batter down a constable; two more alternately punching each other and sharing a bottle of spirits; another too drunk to know that his punches found no mark at all, yelling imprecations at the air he battered with such want of mercy; another stopping his fight by pinning his opponent to the wall with a hand and a boot while he fished in his own mouth with the other hand for the stump of a broken tooth; another pinching into place a severed lip so that he could drink with greater facility.

But these were mere lightning images caught—literally—in passing while he doggedly chased "yon fookin' pig" in and out among the legs and fallen bodies. His excitement grew as he noticed that the creature, already fat for Christmas, and already winded by its long run, was visibly tiring. At last came the supreme moment—the moment when he leaped on its back and grasped its ears, ready to throw it and tie its feet. The pig, however, made one last great effort and bolted—straight between the legs of Police Captain Starr.

On its own the pig would have made it. If Eph had let go, no great harm would have followed. But this long hour of frustration and peril now past urged him at all costs to hold what he had and take the world with him. He certainly took Police Captain Starr with him, towering backward hopelessly off balance, with the rippling face of Walsden Water rushing up to swallow him. Eph swears he will remember to the day he dies the horror and disbelief frozen on the Captain's face as he lay supine in the curtains of white water his impact flung out in all directions—moments before he himself landed on the policeman and thrust him hard upon the shallow bed.

The next thing he remembers, after some moments of pardonable confusion, was being marched in a catch-as-catch-can hold to a waiting cart. It cannot have been long since his tumble in the icy stream, for across the canal he saw the pig, pink and black against the snow, limping slowly back across the fields to its sty.

# *Chapter 27*

By the following morning the police had had more than they could take of the Irish. If there's anything worse than a drunken band of Irish navvies in a fighting mood, it's that same band sobering up the following day. Captain Starr asked for a special court of summary justice to be held that same morning.

The usual upstairs room at the Dog and Duck being too small for such a crowd, the bar parlour and public bar downstairs were cleared. Twenty-eight of the Irish were charged; none of the English had been held, they being the defenders rather than aggressors—or so it was said. The proceedings were simple and very quick. All twenty-eight pleaded guilty in unison to a charge of riotous assembly and making an affray. Then a constable led them forward one by one to let the magistrates, the Reverend Doctor Prendergast and a Mr. Cyrus Love, get a good look at them. If a man was badly wounded he was fined only threepence, on the ground that he probably got worse than he gave. If he was unmarked he might be fined as high as thirty pence, on the opposite ground. In between they operated to a sliding scale.

The penalties were made deliberately nugatory, for heavier ones would imply that the troubles had been serious and so would have supported a petition for special constables to be appointed at the expense of the directors of the railway under an act of 1838. Prendergast was having none of that.

At last, to the grateful relief of all, the Irish were released into the street and left to make their way back to Todmorden. As they looked around, one of them noticed John Stevenson standing by the gate to the inn yard, beckoning them over. In a mixed mood of anger and surprise—for, of course, they considered him to be the author of all their misfortunes—they hastened to where he stood.

"That was a poor fookin' joke, Lord John," one cried.

"Ye're a man so mean as'd take the turf, let alone the bread, from an honest man's mouth," said his neighbour.

Another dashed forward and bared his flaming gums at Stevenson. "Look at that!" he shouted, pointing to where two teeth had been—as if whatever their loss demonstrated were too obvious to state.

"You lot look at that," Stevenson said, pointing to a pair of dray horses, harnessed to a large cart, ready to go.

Gingerly they approached it, looking back at him every second step, fearing another trick.

"I made a mistake when I told ye where that ale and spirits were," he said disingenuously. "It were in this cart all the time! I'm right sorry about that."

When they found that this time he was speaking the truth and that the floor of the cart was, indeed, lined with kegs and barrels, they forgave all and, crowding around him, clapped him on the back, clasped his hand, told him he was the Christian and the darling, and if ever he was short of labour to send for them, and may his prick and his purse never fail his honour.

The driver, a Todmorden man, came from the inn kitchens, buttoning his coat against the cold.

"Ye'll go round via Bacup," Stevenson reminded him. "We'd not want another misunderstanding at Deanroyd!"

They laughed and piled in, eager to broach the spirit kegs and get this terrible day back on its normal keel. Before they were all aboard a policeman threw open one of the ground-floor windows and shouted: "Oy! Mick! Don't ye want this corpse?"

Guilty at having forgotten poor Swimmer in their own misfortune and excitement, they slunk back across the yard. Two policemen inside, not wanting to touch the cadaver, took the table on which it lay to the window and tilted it, as for a burial at sea. At a certain critical angle it shot downward with a speed that almost foxed them, but they caught it just before the head took a further battering on the cobblestoned yard. The rigor had gone and Swimmer lay limp in their arms. His role as bludgeon and ram had not improved him, for his head was now flat and his lower jaw was wedged inside the top of his ribs.

"Best get yon underground quick," the constable said. "He'll not last out the day—his balls and guts is already green."

When they got him on the cart, back, so to speak, in his element, one of the navvies shouted across to the constable, who was on the point of closing the window again: "Hey you! Where's his fookin' hand?"

The policeman held up his finger. "Oh ah! I forgot." He rummaged among the papers on the captain's desk and found an old ten-pound sugar sack with its drawstring pulled tight. He brought this to the window and swung it out to them. "It come off this morning," he said. "We tied it up in that."

"Sure he'd be a lost man without it," said the one who had noticed its absence. "It's the hand he boxed the Jesuit with."

Stevenson did not understand the reference, though the ensuing laughter told him it could only be sexual.

About an hour later, when the world was rosy again, and the cart had reached Bacup, they decided to do their best to tidy poor Swimmer before his interment. It was only then they discovered that the sugar bag, in fact, contained three slices of a very tasty game pie. At almost the identical moment Police Captain Starr opened an almost identical sugar bag and discovered, in somewhat nauseous circumstances, that he was not, after all, going to enjoy any game pie that lunchtime. It did not improve his temper for the more serious proceedings of that afternoon.

# Chapter 28

Metcalfe, Burroughs, and Hope were all unmarked, for Whitaker had been able to point them out to Captain Starr the moment the constabulary had arrived. Their case was heard separately, after the charge against Eph Ackroyd had been dealt with.

Stevenson and Nora, attending the afternoon proceedings, met John Randall, the owner of the pig, going in.

"Come to get your man?" Stevenson asked.

"Have-I-buggery-yer-pardon-ma'am," he said in one word. "I've told yon. If I've told him once I've told him a thousand times—'Get yon bloody sty mended-yer-pardon-ma'am.' And he's done naught. I'll teach him a lesson the way he'll remember it, this time, see thee." And he went gleefully upstairs to the regular courtroom to await his moment for revenge. They followed him and took seats near the back. On the way they passed the three bricklayers, wedged between two constables, their eyes fixed ahead of them, recognizing nothing. McLeish was not there but Fox and Findlater sat nearby.

It was unfortunate for Eph that Captain Starr, cheated of his pie, had gone from the Dog and Duck in search of a substitute lunch. For though many could swear that a pig had been loose among the rioters, and that Eph had been chasing it, only the Captain could give it as certain evidence that Eph had not so much charged him as been pulled onto him by the pig.

Prendergast made several scathing references to the absence of the Captain, for, of course, there was little affection to spare between the magistracy and these newfangled usurpers of the magistrate's power, the police. "Perhaps if Captain *Starr* could be prevailed upon at least to bring his *tea* to the Dog and Duck we could all *Starr-t!*" he said amid howls of sycophantic laughter.

But in the event he did not let the absence hold up proceedings. Eph was bundled forward to the chair that served as a dock, and the charges—joining an affray and assaulting an officer of police—were read.

"What d'you say to those charges, Ackroyd?" Prendergast asked him.

"I say I were only there chasing yon pig."

"Yes, but do you plead guilty or not guilty?"

"Nay, I know naught about it, sir."

"Come—you must know something."

"I know that when I pushed yon captain into the water I had hold of yon pig and couldn't help meself."

Love turned to Prendergast. "Must be a plea of guilty with mitigating circumstances," he said.

Prendergast looked back at Eph. "Is it? Come, you're wasting time."

"Is it what, sir?"

With the thinnest of patience Prendergast interpreted: "Are you saying you were there, you *did* strike or push Captain Starr, but it was all because of some . . . pig or other?"

Eph's face glowed with relief that his case was understood so quickly, and he was full of admiration for the magistrate who had pieced it together so exactly. "Aye!" he said happily. "That's *just* hit it. It were just like that!"

Prendergast, with a thin-lipped smile, said to his clerk, "Guilty." He looked up again. "The only element of doubt would seem to be this pig. Did the pig push this unfortunate fellow into our gallant, gourmetizing head of police? Is there any man present who witnessed the incident?"

One of the policemen had. At least, he had turned to see Ackroyd falling into the stream on top of the captain and in such a way that it could have been none other who pushed the captain. He saw no pig but could not swear that none had been there.

The farmer, John Randall, with undisguised satisfaction, swore the pig had been in its sty when he had done his last round before retiring for the night. He had no personal knowledge of any escape.

"So," Prendergast turned back to Eph, who could now see the world falling around him and was wondering what he would say to his Mary that night, "your story evaporates beneath the hot searching light of inquiry. It turns into a tissue of lies!"

"No, sir!" Eph cried. "It were—"

"Silence!" Prendergast thundered. "You struck down Captain Starr and threw him into the canal."

"I never seen him, sir—being so intent upon the pig!"

"If you do not hold your tongue, I shall have you gagged and placed in irons." Eph squirmed. "You struck him down, I say. And moreover I tell you that you may consider yourself fortunate to have escaped with your life. If Captain Starr had drawn his sword on that dreadful night, I cannot answer for—"

"Sir! It were broad daylight! In the middle of the afternoon!" Eph could not restrain himself.

"Will you be quiet, sir!" Prendergast roared. "I warn you for the third and final time!" Then, in a voice only slightly moderated, he continued. "Afternoon, eh! Broad daylight, eh! So much the worse for you, my man. It makes your story even less credible. You understand? We do not believe this . . . this farrago of falsehood . . . this pack of prevarication . . . this mountain of mendacity . . . this cock-and-pig story. . . ."

The laughter in the court drowned his conclusion: "Guilty, fined two pounds."

"What, your Honour?" Eph had to call. "I never heard."

"Guilty!" Prendergast shouted. "Fined two pounds."

"Two pounds!" Eph's cry brought a momentary lull in the laughter. "Your worships, that's five weeks' wages. I'll never find two pounds."

"Then you may go to jail for five weeks instead—as you have been good enough to place an exact value on your own time. What could be fairer?"

The renewed laughter drowned Eph's last agonized cry. "But sirs! Oh please, sirs! What of me wife and bairns?"

But Prendergast, Love, and the clerk were already conferring on the next and far more serious case.

Nora looked up at John beside her. "What is it?" she asked.

"I've no love for magistrates nor courts," he answered.

"Metcalfe asked for it," she reminded him. "We warned him every way." She looked at the back of the strike leader's head, two rows in front; all the stubbornness for which he now had to pay was carried there.

"He'll get a fairer hearing than Eph Ackroyd," Stevenson said. "Fox is representing 'em."

"Fair hearing, aye," Nora said. "But in the end it'll be the same brand of justice they give Ackroyd. *Gave* Ackroyd."

The charge was the single one Stevenson had predicted—one of obstruction, brought under Fourth George IV, chapter 95. Captain Starr, back again, gave evidence of the arrest—to fulsome praise from Prendergast, who, judging by the "snug fit of the prefectorial paunch within its pantaloons," predicted an uninterrupted trial of possibly as long as an hour.

Fox's questioning elicited that the three defendants had stood apart from the fray that was also in progress when the constables arrived.

"What made you pick these three?" Fox asked. "Out of all the hundreds assembled there, some of them behaving with extreme violence, these three were the very first to be taken into your custody."

"That is correct. . . ."

Starr would have continued but Fox turned to the bench and said: "I make this point to explain my clients' lack of wounds or bloodstains, which lack—or so I understand from this morning's proceedings—goes hard against defendants in this court."

Prendergast waited until the laughter died. "Mr. Fox," he said. "If any humour be lacking in this court, you may firmly rely upon *me* to provide it. But you shall not provoke me to anger, sir! Oh no! Don't imagine that."

Fox nodded, satisfied, and returned to Starr. "You were about to say what was *so* especial about these three men that you selected them from among all the remainder as your first and most urgent responsibility."

"They were nearest," Starr said.

"No other reason?"

"Not as comes to mind."

"Then it was presumably your intention to arrest everyone in sight, beginning with the nearest, whether fighting or no."

"No. That was not in my mind."

"Then you return us to the puzzle, captain. Why these three? They were not fighting. They offered no resistance. They were merely the nearest."

"That's it, sir. The nearest."

"Did you feel that your men needed a little *practise* after their long journey? Two or three easy arrests before they waded in to the *real* affray?"

Starr looked unhappily about him.

"For God's sake," Stevenson said, ostensibly to Nora but loud enough for all to hear, "why doesn't he just tell the truth—Jack Whitaker pointed them out."

Everyone turned to him and he looked around, shocked to have been overheard. He stood up and apologized humbly for his unintentional interruption.

"Far be it from me to cavil at any interruption that may hasten these proceedings," Prendergast said as he turned to Starr. "Did Mr. Whitaker point these three out to you?"

"He did, sir."

"Then you should have said so."

Fox, who had been staring uncertainly at Stevenson ever since his interjection, turned back to Starr. "In what words?"

"He said: 'Those are the three behind all this.' "

A great deal of irrelevant testimony followed, which, though it was clearly unrelated to the charge of obstruction, Prendergast permitted over Fox's repeated and increasingly strenuous objections. In fact, the police were making so bad a case of it that there was a growing likelihood of the verdict going on to an inquiry and being thrown out on at least a dozen technicalities. Stevenson shook his head in growing disgust at the incompetence, and Prendergast, noticing the gesture and interpreting it correctly, pulled himself together and began to run an entirely tighter trial. Finally, when a policeman who had had an ear severed was produced, and Fox had quickly established that the prisoners were, by then, well on their way to the lock-up, Prendergast commanded the unfortunate police solicitor to economize on their case "so strictly that only evidence relevant to the charge" was brought.

Not long after that Stevenson was called. There was an expectant coughing and whispering and a general crossing and uncrossing of legs. Nora filled with pride at the simple, confident way he stood, facing the two solicitors.

For the best part of thirty minutes, largely unprompted by questions from the prosecution, he gave a plain man's account of the week's events. He spoke without notes and in a low, almost monotonous key, avoiding any suggestion of drama. It was a modest and well-received performance—overmodest perhaps, in that it credited fate with certain achievements that more properly lay at John Stevenson's own door.

And when, half shamefaced at his own weakness, he outlined the extraordinary lengths to which he had gone in order to reconcile the men to his offer, even after they formed their picket, Prendergast, indigo with rage, thundered at him: "It seems to me you bent yourself dangerously far to accommodate them."

"And it seems to me," Stevenson snapped back, "that I did no more than a just man should ask of himself. I'm not the sort of master to relish the thought of seeing his men led off in fetters."

The sudden fire in his voice, after his long and monotonous account, was especially effective and Prendergast had to quell the applause before Stevenson could continue. His story left no doubt among his hearers that he was a good if somewhat simple master driven to unwanted measures by three dangerous and violent malcontents who had infiltrated and unsettled a formerly happy working force. Once they had been removed, the seven remaining pickets had come voluntarily to him and confessed their error—and had even asked to be taken back on. And so he had agreed, on condition that—by way of forfeit—they remain on their former rate for three months before they earned the right to bonus.

Now there was tumultuous applause and some people even wept openly to see such goodness and charity and forbearance so quietly and manfully displayed. But, looking around the crowded room, he noticed Arabella Thornton sitting inconspicuously in the corner. Her level, unblinking gaze held his in steady contempt. He was glad he had not noticed her earlier. Thornton, beside her, nodded his heartiest approval.

Mr. Fox, who had made surprisingly few notes during the course of this evidence, rose to cross-examine.

"Mr. Stevenson. Why, on the evening of Tuesday last, the eve of these unhappy events, did you receive a visit from the chairman of this bench of magistrates, the Reverend Doctor Prendergast?"

For less than a second there was utter silence; then uproar broke loose.

"What are you implying, sir?" Prendergast roared.

"I imply nothing, doctor," Fox said smoothly, when the room was again quiet enough for him to be heard. "But I think we may be left to infer that a director of the Manchester & Leeds railway and a contractor to that railway have, in part at least, a common cause. Against the working man."

"Then you're *wrong!*" Stevenson's shout was loud enough to drown the rest and to silence even Prendergast. "I have no cause against any working man. On the contrary. It's his very opposite—the *non*-working man—as brings me grief!"

Above the laughter Fox shouted, "Clever! Clever! But you shall not slide out so easily."

"I do not seek to slide out at all. It is perfectly true that his Honour visited me last Tuesday—not as magistrate but as railway director. But I warn you, Mr. Fox, not to press too hard to hear what passed between us. For it goes quite contrary to your inference."

"Indeed!" Fox's confidence was unshaken. "We shall let the public be the judge of that."

Prendergast, catching Stevenson's eye, had the sense to keep quiet.

"He came to warn me," Stevenson said, "that I was alone in any dispute between myself and my men. I could expect no help from the Manchester & Leeds, no financial support, no accommodation of timetable. He reminded me it had taken but an hour to appoint me and to unseat me would take even less time."

Fox began to sneer.

"Indeed," Stevenson went on, as if the memory had just returned to him, "I believe the landlord can corroborate me, for he overheard part of our talk."

"Oh." Fox was nonplussed. Then, playing for time, he added: "Did you believe in this warning?"

"In principle, yes, though not in detail. I could see why he felt constrained to tell me as he did."

Fox, having started the hare, could not abandon it there, but he knew he was now gambling on being nimble enough to spot a chink in whatever Stevenson might say. "Perhaps you will enlighten us," he said.

"I could see that to the Board of the Manchester & Leeds I must have appeared to be vacillating. To that degree it made sense to send an emissary with some such message of encouragement to stiffen my backbone."

The renewed laughter would surely, he thought, force the attorney to abandon this line, which must have looked so promising when he had stood up to begin his cross-examination. Stevenson felt himself relax and immediately had to force himself to remain vigilant, for he was not yet out of the forest.

Fox made one last effort to gain some advantage from this meeting between magistrate and contractor. "Do you mean you did not discuss the strike in any detail? You did not, for instance, discuss the type of sentence a striker might face?"

"Of course we did, ye daft pennyworth!" Stevenson said, provoking gales of laughter.

"Mr. Stevenson!" Prendergast shouted, and though Stevenson knew it to be a shout of alarm he chose to take it as one of outrage.

"I apologize, your Honour," he said. "But really! These attorneys seem to imagine that we men of business go about our work as carelessly as they go about preparing a case!"

For the first time the laughter unnerved Fox. "We shall see," he said automatically, before it seemed to penetrate to him that Stevenson had actually made a serious confession. "What sentence did the pair of you decide would be appropriate for these three men?" It came too late to have any real force but it was, even so, a telling question.

"Naturally we discussed sentences in relation to no particular man or group of men—only in relation to the offence committed and the state of the law with regard to such offences. Again I would warn you not to press me, for once more the answers would run contrary to points you may wish to establish."

It was still bait that Fox could not resist, though he alone, in all that room, thought benefit might come of it. Metcalfe sunk his head in his hands and there remained. "So—after these terrible threats are delivered you turn at once to an abstract consideration of the law! That is somewhat hard to believe."

"I care not a fig what you believe, sir. I'm sworn here to tell the truth. And the truth is that there had been talk at Summit Tunnel of secret oaths being sworn—for which, as his Honour then told me, the penalty may be transportation for life. I told him I'd take no active part in bringing or supporting proceedings that led to such a savage sentence. I said further that I thought three months with hard labour severe enough. And I think I know at least three men in this room who, if they are sensible of the way their case is being conducted, will be glad such a conversation occurred!"

In the buzz of approval that followed, Metcalfe tugged at the attorney's cloak and whispered something in his ear.

"Very well, Mr. Stevenson. Let us set that aside for a moment and come to the day itself. You say you sent your assistant, Mr. Whitaker, for the constabulary. At what time would that be?"

"At about ten minutes before seven o'clock."

"So it was *before* the arrival of the bricklayers?"

"During. Half had arrived and were standing awaiting the arrival of the other half."

"But before they—the bricklayers—formed what you choose to call 'pickets'?"

"Yes. It was before that."

"So yours was, in fact, the first hostile act."

"Only by the perverted logic that calls the constabulary enemies and makes brothers of lawbreakers."

At this point Metcalfe stood and said to Prendergast: "Sir, I wish to dissociate myself from this defence and conduct my own."

Fox glanced briefly at him and then looked down.

"Very well." Prendergast sighed and consulted his watch. "You shall have your chance later. You two others . . ." They stood up, too. "Do you wish to do the same?"

Hope and Burrroughs looked miserably at one another and then at Metcalfe. "We could never talk like what you can, Tom," Hope said. They shook their heads and sat again.

"You have a vote of confidence, Mr. Fox," Prendergast said.

Fox, his voice almost obliterated by the embarrassment, said: "At least, Mr. Stevenson, you cannot deny you left the works before the trouble began?"

"Speak up!" several voices urged.

Fox had to repeat the question.

"Mrs. Thornton had arrived on horseback with news of the approach of the Irish. Mr. Thornton could not leave the works, with the trespassers being on it. I had business in Todmorden. . . ."

Fox recovered sufficiently to say: "You are simply repeating your main testimony. I wish to hear about one specific offer you made to the Irish. And I would remind you that Mrs. Thornton is in the court and could be called."

Stevenson laughed. "Really, Mr. Fox, ye spend half the afternoon protesting that every mention of the Irish is irrelevant (in which, I may say, I heartily agree)—and now it is you who is most eager to parade them before us yet again."

"And you who is least so," Fox said above the chuckling and laughter.

"Not at all. If you called Mrs. Thornton she'd probably tell you—as I do, too—that the band we met was not a vicious, rioting mob, but a cheerful, roistering motley—"

"Yet they had smashed the windows out of four houses in Tod-morden!"

"Quite! The very point I was about to make. Your Irish are as volatile as your Latins. And though they were cheerful and carefree when we met them, there was no telling what another dry mile or two might not do. So I offered them my hospitality."

"Yet there was no liquor to offer."

"So I later learned."

"There was no question of a collusive agreement between you and the Irish."

"None whatever."

Though he gave no outward sign of it, Stevenson was, for the first time, worried. There were a dozen questions Fox could ask in this area that would dent his case. He could see that Fox was winding up to a knock-out—or what he imagined would be a knock-out.

"Then kindly tell us, Mr. Stevenson"—he looked around, wagging one finger heavenward—"why you were seen this very morning escorting the Irish prisoners to a cart laden with ale and spirits for a free ride home to Todmorden—*all* paid for by you!"

It produced the sensation he expected. Stevenson could see the gleam in people's eyes as they scented blood.

When he had the silence he wanted, he said: "I must ask you, Mr. Fox, if you really wish to pursue that question. Again I warn you—"

"Oh, come!" Fox laughed. "You don't catch me that way three times."

"Answer!" someone in the crowd shouted.

"Yes, sir," Prendergast leaped from what he must have seen as a sinking ship. "Answer the question."

Even Metcalfe betrayed a slight hope. Nora alone smiled, serenely sure of him.

Stevenson sighed. "I paid for their beer and spirits and ride home out of self-interest," he said, speaking slowly as one would to a dim but good-hearted servant. "The Irish are no more subtle than you, Mr. Fox." There was a titter at that. "They are every bit as capable as you, Mr. Fox, of assuming that by telling them there *was* liquor where it later proved there was *not,* I had stood them up as a row of skittles." The laughter was stronger. "And then, Mr. Fox, it would be the work of moments or at least the work of one dark night—for them to come down and do several thousand pounds' worth of damage to my works. So, Mr. Fox, I paid what you might think of as insurance, and cheap at the price, I'd say. And that, Mr. Fox, is a fact so self-evident, that only an attorney, Mr. Fox, or some other spinner of wild and fantastical tissues, Mr. Fox, would need to have it explained to him. Mr. Fox."

The titters rose to a chuckling and continued to swell until they almost drowned the end of his reply. Fox, unheard save by those beside him, said: "No more questions," and sat abruptly down.

Stevenson felt no pity for the advocate; his defeat was self-inflicted. He had stood up with at least four supposedly lethal questions to ask: Why had magistrate and contractor met before the strike? Why had the constabulary been summoned even before the men's intentions were clear? Why had the contractor left the site and met with the rioters only moments before the riot started? Why had he given liquor to the rioters the following day and provided free transport home for them? Taken together, they framed a devastating and beautifully consistent theory of conspiracy. It must have seemed that no further work for the defence was necessary. Yet it would have taken only the slightest degree of caution—or the slightest ability to stand in another's shoes—to see how easily the case might fall apart. As, indeed, it had.

The police solicitor stood again. "To return to the points at issue, Mr. Stevenson. You required these men to work and they would not?"

"Yes."

"You sought an assurance that they would peaceably let pass any others you might hire in their stead?"

"Yes."

"And this assurance they refused to give?"

"Yes."

"Whereupon you, fearing a breach of the peace, were obstructed from taking new employees on?"

"Yes. Not only new employees but also those who had abandoned their attempts to strike. I felt able to take on no bricklayer yesterday."

"That, your Honour, is the basis of the case against the prisoners."

"Well"—Prendergast smiled coldly—"you led us quite a dance getting to it. Now, Metcalfe. Your defence."

"*What* defence!" Metcalfe stood morosely. "Mr. Stevenson. At the start of your evidence ye stated there was no personal element, no grudge, in any of your actions."

"Aye. I did."

"I believe I made the same point in different words, to you, the evening before our strike."

"Did ye? Ye said it wasn't thee versus me but the working classes versus privilege and the ancient regime."

Prendergast shuffled his papers impatiently. "I suppose you have some purpose in these questions, Metcalfe?"

"I am trying to establish my motive, your Honour."

"We don't give a brass farthing for your motive, my man. We are here to determine whether or not you broke the law."

Resignedly Metcalfe nodded and returned to Stevenson. "Do you remember the occasion when you first mentioned the statute under which we now stand charged?"

"I do."

"You recited a list of actions forbidden under it. Could you now repeat that list and say what my response to each of them was?"

Stevenson was filled with admiration for the mind at work behind these questions. Metcalfe already knew that jail was a certainty for himself and the other two; the case he was now laying down was for trial before a much wider court—the ultimate court of public opinion. "It forbids violence . . . threats . . ." he began.

"Wait! What did I say to violence?"

"You said you would not use it."

"And to threats?"

"You said you would make no threats."

"Go on."

"It further forbids intimidation. You said you would offer no intimidation. It also proscribes molestation. You said you would molest no one. Finally it forbids obstruction. You suggested you might speak to new bricklayers without physically obstructing them. You suggested silently holding up some kind of written statement of your grievance—again without offering physical obstruction. Your own attorney then warned you that such actions might, in this court, be held to be obstruction."

"In this court particularly."

"That was his opinion."

"And insofar as you cautioned me about the state of the law, what did you say?"

"I told you you hadn't a hope. You were setting yourselves against the kind of law that forbids treason, rape, arson, murder, and breathing—or some such phrase."

"Thank you." Metcalfe sat down, letting the laughter at Stevenson's quip do its work.

"I should add," Stevenson went on wickedly, "that your two fellow prisoners shared your rejection of violence, threat, intimidation, and molestation."

Metcalfe, knowing he should have made the point himself, nodded awkwardly and looked at the floor.

Prendergast, seeing that his ship had not sunk after all, climbed back aboard: "Well, Mr. Stevenson. Your enemies must learn to fear you most when you offer the greatest advice, assistance, and other apparent concessions."

"We should all be wary of unsolicited gifts, your Honour."

Prendergast stared at him long and hard after that.

Other evidence followed but the case against the three was already proven. An unhappy Reverend Findlater corroborated part of Stevenson's testimony; and Thornton gave evidence of trespass—to corroborate the intention to obstruct—after the men had been dismissed.

The prisoners then standing, Prendergast, after only the briefest consultation with Love at his side, delivered judgement. "We find you, all three of you, guilty of the charge of obstruction. There has been a lot of wild and dangerous talk at this trial. Just as there are wild and dangerous and desperate men at large in this country. All this talk of secret oaths . . . we mean to stamp out this secrecy. No greater threat could be levelled at our English traditions of liberty and security than all this secrecy. . . ."

There was a great deal more in this vein, very little of it relevant to the present case. It ended with the traditional fulminations of magistrate against police. "There was a riot," he said, "and the police were attacked with great ferocity. One even lost an ear. There was a suggestion that your actions were at the bottom of this riot; but we find that not proven. As far as this court is concerned, the wounding of a constable or two—even the severing of an ear—is neither 'ear' nor there. . . ." Yells of laughter forced him to halt and hold up his hand for silence, though he was not too insistent about it. "The police must be well aware by now that they can look to this court for no more than the coolest tolerance. But"—he leaned forward, speaking fiercely and jabbing his forefinger repeatedly toward the prisoners—"by that same token, you three troublemakers and other ranters and traitors like you can look for even less. It is agitators of your sort and kidney who make the police a necessity. The old parish constables could have dealt with nuisances like the rioters who came before us this morning. It is you dangerous subversives who make the police such a loathsome necessity. Without your kind we could abolish the police and all breathe free men again."

Murmurs of approval swelled into cheers and it was some time before he could continue. The police in court, well used to such attacks, looked on with calm equanimity. "The one extenuating circumstance," he said when it was quiet again, "is the manly forbearance of your master, Mr. Stevenson. He is indeed a prince among employers, and you have treated him scurvily." Looking pointedly at Fox and the Reverend Findlater, he continued: "Indeed, there have been times in this whole wretched affair when he was your only true friend—just as there were times in this court when he was your best advocate. By speaking for you he has mitigated what would be a far severer sentence. You will go to prison, all three of you, for three months. With hard labour."

It was, as everyone knew, the maximum sentence. Fearing demonstrations, the police bundled the three prisoners smartly toward the door behind the bench, where a stair led straight to the yard.

"Lord John!" Metcalfe called just before he reached this door.

"Aye, Metcalfe?"

"Thou has not been dealt the last card yet!"

Wishing he could let Metcalfe have this petty triumph unalloyed, Stevenson nevertheless answered: "Come—take it like a man! Thou lost. I won. I had *the better combination!*"

Even Metcalfe joined the laughter—though his mirth was, understandably, not the loudest or longest. The three words "the better combination" were passed around as those who had heard the reply shared it with those who had not, who then shared it with those on the stair, and so on to bar and parlour.

Only a disconsolate Fox and an aggrieved Findlater were left behind when Captain Starr made an application for the release of Eph Ackroyd on the grounds that his story about the pig had been true. In his pocket a half-sovereign from Farmer Randall—"for the prisoner's keep" to be sure—ensured that the good news would somehow fail to reach Eph himself until the following morning. And at half a sov Farmer Randall had just purchased a chastened, fearful, and willing servant right cheap.

Stevenson was the hero of the hour. Friends and men he'd never met gathered round to shake his hand and pummel his back. The very frenzy of their congratulation showed him how intensely the Chartist violence had made them fear for their property and lives; it also confirmed—to his satisfaction, at least—his wisdom in introducing the Irish and their violence. A peaceable strike quietly overcome would have passed without notice, and he would have had to find some other way to gain his end. Briefly, as the cheers rained upon him, he wondered if folk would congratulate him quite so fervently if the full tale were known. Among them he saw Arabella Thornton, who, with a meaning that leaped straight from her to him, told him he had made "an excellent showing."

With Nora he walked the three miles back to Littleborough, glad of the exercise and air after the stifling atmosphere of the court.

"What do ye think of yon Arabella Thornton?" he asked when they were well away from the Dog and Duck.

His directness puzzled her. "Not much either way. I've not seen her but twice since we had yon jollification. And back there at court. She looked at thee a bit . . . afternoonified."

He laughed but did not explain.

"She rides well," Nora allowed. "I've seen her come through Little-borough a time or two."

"Thou'd like to ride?" he asked.

"Eh!" Her eyes gleamed.

"Mebbe we'll buy a horse when we get to Rough Stones. Mebbe thou could go riding with Mistress T."

She hugged his arm in delight at the thought of having a horse. "We shall have to live more friendly with the pair of them, when we're over there," she said—adding coldly: "Won't that be merry!"

He nodded abstractedly and stared glumly ahead, so that she wondered whether he had meant his promise of a horse or had just been speaking idly.

"What ails?" she asked. "It'll not be that bad."

"I was thinking of Prendergast," he said.

"Dean of the Dog and Duck!" she laughed.

But he did not share her amusement. "Don't ever think yon's just easy quarry," he warned. "Today, I did what I had to do. But from one point of view, it were rank folly."

"Oh?" She, too, was serious.

"Aye." He sighed and looked impatiently about them. "Until this day I've taken every care to see that our dear reverend doctor thinks of me as just plain, honest, straightforward . . . well, not *honest* . . . but *simple.* Easy to manage. No challenge to him, like. Not when it comes to devious and underhand dealing. Well . . ." He laughed sourly. "He knows different now, doesn't he?"

They went on a short way in silence before she said: "Even if we got Chambers to own that forgery, there's still yon Duke-of-Somerset letter."

"Nay," he told her. "He'd never use that on its own. There was no witness to it, see thee. Nay, it's Chambers holds our fortune now."

"Do you know him?"

"I know *of* him. He's a Jew. Not one of—"

"A Jew!" she said in a voice full of alarm.

"Aye."

"Not . . ." she began fearfully, "not . . . a *moneylender!?*"

He stopped and looked at her in amazement. "Well of course he's a moneylender, thou soft duck! He's a bloody banker! What do thou think a banker may be if he's no moneylender?"

"Eh!" She approached the new thought as one might approach a bomb. "Aye . . . it never struck me."

"Anyway," he went on. "He's a Jew. He's on the outside looking in, for London's never been warm for the tribe of Abraham. If we put, as I expect, over a hundred thousand pounds through our Manchester account and transfer a profit on it of thirty thousand to Mr. Chambers, I think we shall kindle a gleam in his eyes bright enough to blind him to the fact that I took his name in vain."

"Any banker would," she said.

But he shook his head. "Not any. There's lots are still very old-fashioned. Especially the big London ones."

"That's why you chose him!" she said, suddenly realizing it and looking at him with renewed admiration.

He sighed. "I just don't know."

"Don't *know?*"

He tapped his cranium. "I'm beginning to suspect there's something in here lays deep plots unknown to me and only tells me when it's too late to reverse."

She laughed, not believing a word.

"I *must* get Chambers to own both them letters," he said. "Then . . ."

"Then Prendergast can kiss our royal Yorkshire arse!"

"Nay," he laughed. "He can start *earning* his keep. There's no doubt but what he could be very useful to us. He knows the railway fraternity. None better. That's where he's daft, see thee. If he'd just bide a while, he could earn hisself a fortune putting work our way, when we're ready for it. A fortune. Open and above board, like. I'd not stint him."

"Why not tell him?" she suggested hopefully.

He laughed at the irony of it. "He might of believed it once. But not now. He'd never believe it now, would he! Nay. I must force him to it."

"Aye," she said, glad it was settled one way or the other. "That's best."

"Only question is: Will he force me to bend to his way first? It's a race. As we get richer over this next six month, we'll be better and better placed to beat him; but he's better and better likely to start skinning us. It's a race, see thee. And he knows I'm no simpleton now. He'll not trust us."

"We'll win," she said. "There's none else could do it but thee."

"Me and thee."

"As a matter of fact," she said in a different tone, "there is a notion I've had. For making more money. Or making our present money work better. I'll tell thee how it first came to me."

She took his arm and hugged herself tightly to him as she talked.

"Ye know the Todmorden turnpike, about two furlongs out from Littleborough, where there's a little brook comes down from Gorsey Hill across the field?"

"The one they've just straightened and fenced?"

"Aye—yes."

"Town House Brook it's called."

"If ye look where they've straightened it, and ye look at any one place, it's just water moving"—she moved her free hand smoothly across their path—"steady . . . one way. Then you cross the road and look at the natural brook and it doesn't flow like that at all. It goes"—she swirled with both hands to mime eddies and miniature creeks of slow-moving water—"like that. The natural course, d'ye see, is not to rush the water by as fast as may be, but to delay it."

"The flow is the same though," he said, not yet grasping her argument. "The same quantity of water flows in both systems."

"Yes," she said, "but if you were an animal and had to depend on water, which side of the turnpike would ye choose?"

"Below," he said. "The unimproved reach. Though I can't say why. It seems right even without thought."

"That's just it," she said. "If we were them animals and water was money and the river opposite to one yard of riverbank was our bank account . . . it's the same, isn't it! I can't say it the way a lawyer could but I know, I know it in me bones, I know it from doing the books, from seeing the cash come in and go out, in and out, in and out, same day often enough, I *know* we're like being beside the new artificial section and we *should* be down below. We need a way to make money. . . ." Her hands described the same eddies and stagnant creeks as before.

"Aye, I see that," he said. "Not a bigger flow. Same flow. Just delay it on its way."

"Yes. Make use of it."

Looking at her bright eyes and earnest little face he knew she had more to say than that. "How?" he asked.

"Well . . ." She took his arm again. "I agree with all you said about truck and tommy rot . . . but . . . supposing we was to sell *good* tommy, at a little profit but not great in proportion. . . . We'd fetch back between five and six hundred of the weekly wages. If our profit on that was only four per cent, it'd be twenty to thirty pound a week. And that's a good cure for sneezing, any day."

She had expected him to raise objections but even before he spoke she could feel he had accepted the basic idea. Her heart began to dance in anticipation; it had irked her all these months to play no active part in making money, except for the routine of purchasing. Somehow purchasing for *use* lacked the excitement of purchasing for resale.

"What sort of tommy?" he asked.

"Only basics," she said—adding, mentally, *to start with.* "It'd be meat, flour, salt, sugar, potatoes and one other vegetable according to season, and tea and ale. Them seven items covers nine-tenths of your navvies' necessary spending."

His laugh was tinged with disbelief. "How can you possibly know that?"

"Because I went and asked among the wives. I asked twenty of them. And then I give up—gave up—because I kept getting the same story. Would ye like to know?"

He shook his head in wonder. "Thou art a bloody marvel! Asked the womenfolk. I'd never have thought of doing that."

"Do you want to hear?"

"Aye."

"Your navvies—this is just the navvy now, forget the family for a minute. Your navvy puts down in a week nine pound of meat at fivepence, ten pound of bread at twopence, twenty of potatoes at about three pound a penny, a quarter of tea at a shilling, a pound of sugar at eightpence. It comes to twelve and ninepence in all. Eight hundred navvies at twelve and nine is five hundred and ten pound."

"They'll not all buy from you."

She noticed that "you," not "us." "I've not counted any craftsman—nor spending on any wife and bairn. I'd say five hundred pound or sixty percent of the wages'd come back through us."

He walked on in silence for so long that she had to prompt him: "Well? What do you say?"

"I say let's see what prices we can get in Manchester."

She noted that "we" and rejoiced quietly in her victory. "I know someone who'll give us a very good price," she said. "But there's no hurry. I'd not start before we've moved to Rough Stones. I'll need one of your offices for a shop."

"Hah!" He gave a single, sharp laugh and raised his hands to heaven as if to blame Providence for her deception.

That evening, when he returned from the workings, he found a letter from Prendergast waiting for him. He took it upstairs and opened it with Nora looking on. "See how quick he can move when he wants," he said.

The envelope contained a cheque for two thousand pounds and a letter.

"Who's Ermyntrude Prendergast?" She pointed to the signature on the cheque.

"His aunt, I think. A nominee. He'd never associate himself directly. Too cautious." He read the letter quickly. "He doesn't even mention it here—see."

He passed it to her and she read:

"Dear Stevenson,

I write on behalf of the Board of the Manchester & Leeds Railway Company, who have appointed me to conduct a preliminary Audit of your Books. This we are bound to do, as you are an Appointee and Agent of the Company. I cannot see my way clear until the New Year, but would be grateful, if you would be ready to present yourself and your Books at the Company's Offices at a mutually agreeable Date in the second Week in January. Yours . . . etc."

Nora laughed in delight. "At least we can forget our Church-of-England until after Christmas. And we can easily do a false set of books by January!"

But he was not cheered. "Nay—he must know that. There's more in this than floats to the top." He sighed. "It's no case for false books. Our biggest outgoing is wages, and we can't falsify the wage bill. And if we doubled every other receipt, we'd still show four times the profit we want Prendergast to see. Nay . . ." He shook his head. "This is a case for spinning and weaving, see thee. I must play him like a pike on shoddy thread." He turned more cheerfully to the cheque. "As to this—I think he means us to understand he's a man of his word. Of *all* his words."

"What'll we do with it?"

"Send it straight to Bolitho & Chambers!" He laughed. "That's justice. And when we draw the double line on Summit's books, he shall have this back, plus interest, plus five hundred for his silence—it's worth that. But as for ten thousand . . . he can kiss me royal Yorkshire arse, as one of the great financial geniuses of the age put it to me."

\*      \*      \*

After supper, she could see he was still uneasy in mind. She tried to distract him by talking of the arrangements to be made for their removal to Rough Stones—the servants and furniture to be hired, the linen and cutlery and utensils they would have to buy, and so on—but it seemed to distract him very little.

"What is it?" she asked at length. "What bothers thee?"

He breathed in, as if preparing for an ordeal. "You mentioned Gorsey Wood this afternoon—where Town House Brook rises."

"Yes?" she said guardedly.

"That would be . . . uh . . ." He looked away, staring deep into the fire. "The old cemetery up there . . . that was . . ."

"Our dad's buried there," she said, feeling even greater misgiving.

He said nothing more.

"What of it?" she had to ask.

"Do you not want him properly interred? Thinking of what Robert Stephenson said about Trevithick's grave. How they couldn't find it."

She knew he was seeking to head her off—that this was not what concerned him. "Nay," she said. "We'll let him rest."

"I hoped not to distress you with mentioning it."

"If I lived away from here a hundred years, I'd find the place again."

"Aye. Of course," he said to soothe her. "And your brothers? Do ye want to get the sentence on Daniel reviewed? And the other that's in service—d'ye want us to find him a post?"

Now it was her turn to be silent so long that he had to prompt. "I'd not mention it, only I thought you'd have said something before this."

"I've thought," she said. "I think . . . let's not raise any hopes until we're sure. I'll write to Mr. Sugden in Leeds, who was always a good neighbour to us, to see if he may find Sam's whereabouts." She leaned across the table and squeezed his arm.

Later, when he pulled off his boots and sprawled with his stockinged feet steaming before the fire, picking his teeth with a goose quill, she came and curled herself up beside him, leaning on his shoulder and reaching her arms around his huge torso. "There's something still on your mind," she said. "You'll fret all night unless you tell it. I know you."

"And I know you!" he said. "That is my problem."

She squeezed him; with her ear on his shoulder, and only his shirt between them, she could hear the swish of his blood and the gurgle of his bowels. It almost distracted her but she squeezed again in case he might think he could let the matter slide.

Once more he breathed in, facing that imagined ordeal. "I wish to propose something," he said. "Something we should do. And I fear—I *know*—it will disgust you to the very depth of your soul."

She neither moved nor spoke.

"What are your feelings toward . . . Metcalfe?" he asked.

It so astonished her that she sat upright, pulling her hands away. "Metcalfe!" she cried. *"Toward* him?"

"About him, then," he corrected himself. "What's your opinion of him? You saw him in court today."

"Aye," she said. "He's me brother Daniel all over again. I don't understand them. His sort. Bigots. They always want the impossible *now*. And every benefit they gain, they turn to dust and ashes before they sample it. Daniel's strike were a dead copy of this one. He got the demand for a limitation of hours granted but they'd not acknowledge the union. And, of course, he stuck out for acknowledgement. I told him he were daft. I said: 'If the *threat* to combine is enough to achieve the demands, then ye need no actual combination. Threat'll serve well enough every time. Bloody sight cheaper and all.' But he'd not see it. It's how they're made, men of that sort. Eh! Hark at me!"

"What would you say then . . . more important, what'd you *think* . . . if I said I want to see Metcalfe's wife and children don't suffer? He's two bairns. I want to give 'em ten bob a week while he's away."

She was scandalized at the thought. "Disgusted to the very depth of her soul" was not too far off the mark. "I'd say—*and* I'd think—thou had gone addled in the brains." She sighed and forced herself to speak more calmly. "He'd not thank you, you know. He wants them to suffer."

"No!" he cried.

"Take it from one as knows. There was a certain . . . satisfaction . . . in Daniel, seeing me left with young Sam and the two little bairns and no money and the fields gone. It suited all he said about injustice and the need for revolution. You could see satisfaction painted all over him."

Her bitterness took him by surprise. But he quickly recovered. "You mean to say," he asked innocently, "if we helped his family, it'd be like a kick in the bowels to him?"

Not having thought of it that way she suppressed a smile and replied with equal innocence: "I'm not one to kick a man that's down."

He pulled a punch on the point of her chin. "I'm right to fear thee," he said. "Thou art slick as a bloody eel."

"*Fear* me?" she asked in astonishment. It had never crossed her mind that Lord John would fear any man or any thing, much less any woman, much less her.

"Aye. I've pondered all day how to ask it of thee. I want it to seem as I know nothing of it. I want it to seem as *thy* notion, and *thy* action, kept secret from me. I want thee to go weekly to Tom Metcalfe's place in Caldermoor and give his wife ten bob. Knowing how thou would feel, I want to ask that of thee! Of course I fear thee."

Swifter than thought she reached a hand under his jaw and turned his face to her. "Who does thou think I am?" she asked.

He stirred uncomfortably and tried to look away but she turned him to her again. "I'm Nora Stevenson," she went on. "Thy wife. Fear to ask me? Thou may ask *any*thing of me. There's one master in this marriage, one master on this contract—on any contract. I'll discuss anything with thee and give thee my honest view. I'll argue with thee and all. But in the end it's thy will to rule. . . ."

Relief and gratitude lighting his face, he pulled her into his arms and settled her head once more on his shoulder. But it did not stop her speaking. "I may argue with thee," she added. "I may disagree. But I'll never cross thee, and I'll never work contrary when thy back's turned." He hugged her and patted her back and hugged her again. Still she spoke on, with even greater urgency to convince him. "How can you go out on yon works—how can you plan anything—if you're never sure what you may bid me to?"

"Will ye take this money each week?" he asked, still not quite believing that she would.

"I'll still think it good money wasted. Let them three Chartists look after the prisoners—they can take one apiece. But I'll do it because you ask it. And in all the world there's no better judge of men and actions than you."

He lifted her from him a little, to bring her face close to his, and to see her dark eyes, softened in the candlelight, and to see her lips, full and warm, and to kiss them, long and tenderly.

"I'll tell you," he said when they broke apart and there was no tension between them. "It's nine chances in ten that you've got the right of it. Metcalfe may have become a fanatic beyond cure. But there is still that chance, d'ye see, that one-in-ten chance he could be a useful man to us. Did ye see when he questioned me in court today?" She nodded. "He wasn't even trying to prove his innocence. He'd abandoned all that. He was laying claim to a wider hearing. He just *used* that court. . . ."

"I thought he was using you, too. The answers you were giving him!" She chuckled. "I should've known."

"He was. Or I let him. I wanted to see his mind at work. And I kept thinking, 'If I could get that mind to work for *us!*' He's young as yet. He's still too rash. But three month on the treadmill can do a lot to steady a man—if he's stopped from becoming bitter. Young Metcalfe could be everything Jack Whitaker ought to be. Whitaker's had education, Metcalfe's had next to none. But Metcalfe could walk circles round him if he got the right experience. I believe that one-in-ten chance is worth the outlay of six, seven pound."

"It's not that I grudge the money—" she began.

"Bloody liar," he interrupted.

She laughed ruefully and lay back on him. "Aye. You're right. I know. I grudge every last farthing. But even so, that's not my objection. It's the loss of pride. I walked from the Dog and Duck, *proud.* I was proud of you. And proud of the justice that had been done. Now to go and hand over ten hard-earned shillings each week—and pretend I do it of my own will and contrary to thy wish. . . . It tarnishes that pride."

"You young people!" he said loftily. "When you get to my age, you'll understand that pride is a commodity like any other. And—like any other—it has its price."

She hissed like a cat in his ear and then put out her tongue to lick it. He shivered. "I'll say one thing," she said softly, almost whispering. "You taste a lot sweeter since we took to bathing!"

He made a deep, relaxed growl and eased a hand inside her bodice.

"No," she said. "Come to bed."

Later, after he had fallen asleep, she cursed herself for letting a chance go by. How easy it would have been to say, as they had sat on the sofa, "There's something I've been feared to tell *thee,* and all." Why had she shirked it? Was it the memory of all those past stillbirths? Did she want to get into the fourth month—which would be about February—and so be sure before she spoke? How would he take the news?

With all these doubts still unresolved, she fell into a shallow sleep— only to dream that every room in Rough Stones was tenanted by mendicants and depredators, all claiming to be Lord and Lady So-and-so and the Duke of Somewhere.

# *Chapter 29*

When he left at five the next morning, the snow had gone, swept away by a rain that felt almost warm. He came round from the stables, where his mackintosh coat had to be kept on account of its stink, and kissed her goodbye. "We'll have another breakthrough today," he said. "Four and five." The thought of it appeared to put an extra jauntiness into his walk as he vanished into the dark and rain.

She was glad to go back to their still-warm bed and listen to the steady downpour on the road and watch the sky grow slowly pale. But she could not get back to sleep. Thoughts of Metcalfe's wife and two children kept crossing her mind. What were they like? she wondered. The woman was probably the demanding kind—a bigot, just like her husband. Soon find out. She'd go and visit them this afternoon.

But she hadn't been up half an hour before she knew she'd have to make the visit at once and have done with it; she couldn't let the thought of it hang like a pall over the day.

Soon after eight the rain eased off and she went out of Littleborough on the Caldermoor road, which, by chance, happened to be the short cut she had taken on her way to Summit that fateful August day . . . was it only three months ago! She tried to remember this particular stretch of it, but the whole journey had been such a weariness that all its parts had, as it were, coalesced into a single nightmare road from which no one element could now be retrieved; it was as if she had never been this way before.

Finding the Metcalfes was less easy than she had expected. No one seemed to want to admit to knowing them or where they lived or anything of them. But at last one brave soul, defying her neighbours, pointed to the alehouse, where, she said, the Metcalfes had rented an outhouse from the landlord, a man called Sutcliffe. "But he's kicked 'em out," she said. "Yesterday. When the news come through about him."

Nora's face darkened. "Were they behind with the rent?" she asked.

"They paid up the month," the woman said. "It's a shame, I say."

According to her, the place was called the Acorn, though no sign proclaimed the fact. And the landlord, as if to underline this indifference to trade, proved to be still abed.

"What?" he shouted down from an upstairs window when Nora's insistent battering on the door at last dislodged him.

"Mrs. Metcalfe and the two bairns."

"Gone!" He slammed the window shut.

She hammered again on the door until he returned.

"What now?"

"Where?"

He looked extremely angry. "How should I know? Try Rochdale workhouse at Wardleworth!" He was on the point of slamming the window again when the sight of her stopped him. She stood shivering with rage, pointing up at him with a single accusatory finger.

"Now hark here, Sutcliffe . . ."—a tigress gifted with speech would have had such tones—"I shall come back to this place at two o'clock this afternoon. If they are not here by then, I shall go myself and seek them and return with a constable and have you put in charge."

He stared at her, open-mouthed, too astounded to reply.

"When you take rent, Sutcliffe, you make a contract. If you break that contract, you go to jail."

Her voice still ringing in the dumbfounded street, she turned and stumped away, back down the hillside to Littleborough.

The intensity of her anger astonished her. It could not be—it could not possibly be—that Sutcliffe's action had discovered and unleashed in her a hitherto unsuspected love of abstract justice. She asked John about it at lunchtime. "It's daft," she said. "I went up there with little taste for the meeting and so you'd think I'd be glad Sutcliffe had saved us the trouble. Instead of that I stood beside meself with fury."

He laughed. "I've had that happen. On the London-Birmingham, when

I was a navvy. There was one place we went through a cesspit. Someone had to go in and clear it. Me, as it happened. So we go off that night and I get all ready—in my mind, like—to do the job next morn. And when we get there we find the disturbance to the soil has cracked it and it's all drained away. Nothing left for me to do. And they all clapped me on the back and laughed and called it 'Lord John's luck.' But d'ye know—I was *disappointed!* Same thing, isn't it."

She returned at two o'clock to find that her words, and her fury, had proved effective. A fire burned in the outhouse hearth (for it had formerly been a washhouse) and two bonny children, a girl of nine and a boy of seven, were playing a counting game with stones.

"Mama!" the elder one called.

"We never stopped in the workhouse," the boy told Nora while she waited.

"I know you didn't," Nora said.

A plain, tall woman with dark hair and eyes red from weeping came to the door. Incessantly she wiped her hands in her apron and on her thighs. "Aye?" she asked. From her appearance one would have put her in her late thirties, though she could not have been much over twenty-seven. Nora wondered briefly whether the girl was Metcalfe's, since he was only twenty-five.

"Mrs. Metcalfe?"

"Aye."

Nora summed her up. She was no bigot—just a simple, frightened soul, unable to understand what wrong her husband had done and why the punishment had extended to them.

"I had little sleep last night on account of you."

She had hoped to arouse the woman's curiosity, but the poor creature took it that she was in some way to blame for Nora's insomnia and so faced her accuser with weary resignation.

"I mean," Nora said, "that last winter I were left with two bairns of four and three—me young brother and sister—and a brother of fourteen to look after. When me other brother, the elder one, got transported for swearing oaths of combination."

All light fled from the woman's face. "Oh," she said tonelessly. "You're one of them politicals. One of his."

"Am I!" Nora said derisively. "Nay. He went off to glory and martyrdom—I were left behind in a pigsty."

For the first time she saw a glimmer of warmth in those apathetic eyes.

"Ye did well then," the woman said.

Nora looked down. "Nay. I lost both bairns, and me brother went into service. So I *know,* Mrs. Metcalfe. I know what it's like. That's why I slept so little last night. Thinking of you. And I determined that since my fortune's changed I'd do what I can to aid you and these two bairns."

The woman leaned against the door and began a long keening whine, the tears streaming down her face. She rolled her forehead on the doorpost seeking some frantic kind of relief and finding none. Nora saw the young boy standing rigid in a strange posture, with his little pointed elbows bent and poking out, as if he had been frozen while imitating a chicken. He shivered and stared at his mother with eyes that begged her to cease. The girl bit her lip and by her glance implored Nora to help. "She can't stop once she's started out," she said.

A long, agonized monologue poured wetly from the woman's lips. "I don't know what's happened, nor what to do, nor where to turn. First he sends us to the workhouse, then he brings us back but he says we must go, end of the month, and Tom never told us, and now they took him and I can't see him and they won't say where he is, and I got *nothing.* He ain't left us nothing. What can a body do? Oh, what can a body *do?"*

"You can take this." Nora held out ten shillings, hoping her disgust did not show too plainly. She was disgusted that a woman could so let herself go in front of her children.

The woman stared uncomprehendingly at the money. Nora turned to the children. They boy was still locked, shivering, in his awkward position. With her free hand she thrust him forward. "Comfort your mother, son. You're the man of the house now. Summer's gone—you'll catch no flies in that great open mouth." The boy gingerly began to obey. "Go on!" Nora urged. "Hug her! You too, girl. Can't you see she needs you?"

The girl looked at her mother and then at the money still in Nora's hand. "I could take that until she's calmer," she said.

Nora broke into a great smile of approval. At least there was one person around here with a head on her shoulders. She counted the coins one by one into the child's dirty clutch. "Ten shillings," she said to the mother. The woman, calm again, but now almost vacant, nodded and gave a wan smile.

Nora looked at the outhouse. "What rent does he ask?"

It was as if the woman did not hear. The girl held up one finger.

"A shilling?" Nora asked. The child nodded. "What's it like?" She walked past the woman and looked inside. It was dry. The walls were rendered smooth. There was a stone floor. The fire kept it warm. For a shilling it was not a bad bargain; in Manchester you'd not get its like under eighteen pence. A bit dark. That was the only real drawback. She turned and looked at the woman, still framed in the doorway facing out across the courtyard. She had a good, broad back and strong legs. She could easily get work at one of the mills if only she pulled herself together. There was no need for a great strong thing like her to go to the workhouse. Unless there was trouble on account of her husband's politics. Even so, she could go to Fieldens' in Todmorden. He'd take them, and that was only a fifty-eight-hour week. And the girl would work only forty-eight hours and get two hours' instruction a day, free. The boy could go to dame school in Little-borough—that would be only twopence a week and in the afternoons he could keep house and get a good supper ready. The mother could earn eight shillings a week on two ordinary looms, the child three or three and sixpence. If they were nimble, or lucky, they'd get sheeting looms and that would be an extra four shillings. So their earnings would be at least eleven and possibly fifteen and sixpence! There was no need for charity here. All that was wanting in this little household was spirit.

"Can you read, girl?" Nora asked.

The girl nodded proudly. "Dad taught us. And young Tommy. He can read too. Better'n me."

"Can you, Tommy?"

The boy nodded.

"Show me."

He darted into the room and came out with a small, battered cloth-bound book. Nora had expected some little children's verses or a fable; but the boy read without faltering:

"The doctrines which fanaticism preaches, and which teach men to be content with poverty, have a very pernicious tendency, and are calculated to favour tyrants by giving them passive slaves. To live well, to enjoy all things that make life pleasant, is the right of every man who constantly uses his strength judici-ously and lawfully. It is to blaspheme God to suppose that He created men to be miserable, to hunger, to thirst, and perish with cold in the midst of that abun-dance, which is the fruit of their own labour."

"That's a jawbreaking book to be sure," Nora said.

"Don't blame the child, missis," the woman told her. "It's his father who teaches him. All them pernicious books as have brought us so low. I hope he sees now where such books have put us."

"Do you understand it, Tommy?" Nora asked.

The boy nodded and gave a knowing little smile, as if he wanted her to understand he had not merely picked a passage at random.

"Show me the book," she said.

The little girl, watching this, swelled with pride, even more than her brother. Indeed, it seemed he considered her admiration was sufficient for both of them, for he handed over the book without affectation. Nora looked at the title. *Cottage Economy,* she read, by William Cobbett. The contents page promised information on Brewing Beer, Making Bread, Keeping Cows, Keeping Pigs, and so on. She looked through the pages and found them filled with practical hints on how a rural labourer might reduce the cost of his domestic economy while actually increasing the quantity and amenity of his food and home. One passage caught her eye for no particular reason: "Rye, and even barley, especially when mixed with wheat, make very good bread. Few people upon the face of the earth live better than the Long Islanders. Yet nine families out of ten seldom eat wheaten bread." She remembered the shape of the map of England framed in the bar parlour of the pub in Littleborough. There was a long island up at the top left of that.

To test the boy she let the book fall open at another page and passed it back to him. "Read a passage from there," she said.

The boy rapidly scanned the page and smiled. " 'This, therefore, is a matter of far greater moment to the father of a family,' " he read, " 'than whether the Parson of the parish or the Methodist Priest be the most "evangelical" of the two; for it is here a question of the daughter's happiness or misery for life. And I have no hesitation to say that if I were a labouring man, I should prefer teaching my daughters to bake, brew, milk, make butter and cheese, to teaching them to read the Bible till they had got every word of it by heart; and I should think, too, nay, I should know, that in the former case I was doing my duty towards God as well as towards my children.' "

He closed the book and looked up at Nora with that same knowing innocence. She could not help smiling back. "You may return the book, Tom. You're that sharp, you'll cut yourself one day."

His precocity was a problem. No dame school was going to take him, that was certain; but a lad that sharp should not be left at home in idleness all day. She turned back to the woman, who had watched these exchanges in listless silence.

"Well, Mrs. Metcalfe," she said cheerfully, hoping to rouse her, "I see a kettle singing there. Do you have any tea?"

Mrs. Metcalfe brightened at this return to everyday things. "Aye," she sighed. "I could just do with that."

Nora followed her inside; the two children went back to their stone-counting game.

"When I was left to fend for a family," Nora said, "I lacked for more than you, but one thing I never lacked for was good neighbours to talk to. It seems you want that very thing and I mean to supply it."

"They're not that bad hereabouts." Mrs. Metcalfe spoke more easily now that she could busy her hands; but her voice still hung low in bewilderment and grief. "It's just they're frightened, like. Police frightens them. You never said what they call you, Mrs. . . .?"

"Nay," Nora spoke with reluctance. "I've been dreading telling you. But I must tell you, I can see that," she faltered.

"I'll save you the trouble," Mrs. Metcalfe said. "Mr. Sutcliffe said he thought it was you when he come for us at the workhouse, because folk here told him it was. Eh!" For the first time she smiled and put some warmth into her words. "You put the fear of God on Sutcliffe!" She nodded at the fire. "Them's *his* coals burning there, not ours. He lit that for us."

"I'm glad," she said, embarrassed to be thought of as the sort of hussy who ordered people about in such a fashion. "I lost me temper. It's not me usual way."

"Mebbe not," Mrs. Metcalfe said. "Still, it's handy to know it's there if ye need it." She placed a cup of tea on the plain deal table below the foot-square fastlight in the back wall. "Sit you down, Mrs. Stevenson," she said.

"I should've said it straight out," Nora admitted. "When I was stood out there."

"I'm that glad ye didn't." She almost chuckled. "I were too frightened to think, even."

"Frightened!" Nora was astounded. For the second time in less than twenty-four hours someone had claimed to fear her! Why was the world's Nora Stevenson so different from the one she knew?

"Aye," the woman assured her. "Course I know it's only a joke, but even so . . ."

"A joke?" Nora was now completely bewildered. "What's only a joke?"

"Well . . . about *you*. You know." She was now afraid again.

Nora tried to be her very warmest and most assuring. "Please tell me," she said. "I really have no notion of any of this."

The woman sipped her tea miserably, committed now to revealing what she had meant. "Well," she said, "it was last Tuesday night. After that meeting." She sighed. "Seems a blue month since. Metcalfe was sat there where you are. Burroughs was here. Hope was there. And they was all discussing the strike and picketing and that. And Tom Upjohn and Jethro Carr and some of them others what live round here, they come in and said . . . mind, I know they was only jokin', but they said that brickies should take care Lord John didn't . . ." She swallowed. "Didn't turn his wife loose on 'em. But, like I say, they was jokin'. I know they was only jokin'."

Nora's silvery peal of laughter rang out through the door and around the courtyard, fetching the children eagerly to the door. "Mrs. Metcalfe!" she said, still laughing. "Have you any notion what I was doing while these warnings were flying around in here?"

"Nay."

"I was walking up and down, up and down in our room in Little-borough, which"—she looked around—"isn't much bigger than this, trembling with *fear* . . . aye, Mrs. Metcalfe, *fear,* fear and anxiety, for Lord John's safety and our possible ruin."

Mrs. Metcalfe blew on her tea and shook her head in bewilderment. "Well, I'll go around the houses!" she said. "Is that a fact?"

"I'd take my Bible oath."

"Well . . . is that a fact."

Both of them sipped their tea.

"Where can such a notion have come from?" Nora asked.

"Well," Mrs. Metcalfe said, wondering if she dare point it out, "people in this row of houses, and Sutcliffe, they don't need to get it from outside. They seen it happen. And heard it."

"But that was today. And anyway I lost my temper. I never thought he'd believe me. I was dreading having to carry out that threat. But Tuesday last. They'd no ground then."

"Well. That engineer on the line . . ."

"Mr. Thornton?"

"Aye, that's what they call him. He's told tales of you turning back barges on the navigation and doin' I don't know what to Manchester merchants."

"Mr. Thornton has a way of telling fancy tales." She drained her cup and spat the tea leaves back into it before accepting the offer of a second.

Mrs. Metcalfe said: "Ye'll not think me ungrateful. That I said naught nor did naught with them ten shillings. . . ." She jerked her head toward the door.

"I'll think you idle if I ever have to come back with more," Nora said. "A strong woman like you—*two* strong people, for yon girl's a strapper—should find work well enough to fetch in eleven bob a week."

Mrs. Metcalfe was on the point of replying when they heard footsteps on the cobbles outside. Fearing that it might be Sutcliffe, she leaped up and peeped around the edge of the door. At once she straightened herself and began that incessant wiping of her hands which Nora now recognized as her sign of anxiety.

She turned back to Nora. "It's a priest," she said.

A moment later Nora heard the footsteps stop and the voice of the priest who had given evidence yesterday—Reverend Findlater. "Are you Thomas Metcalfe's little ones?" The children ran indoors without answering. Nora, watching Mrs. Metcalfe, was astonished to see her once again polishing her fingers in her apron. She breathed in short fits and repeatedly whispered "Oh dear," to herself, as if it were a kind of prayer.

Findlater knocked and said: "Anyone at home?"

Nora inclined her head toward the door and nodded encouragement to the woman, but she merely bit her lip and retreated even farther into herself.

"Reverend Findlater," Nora was forced to call. "Come in."

Puzzled both by the children's retreat and by an invitation from—or so he supposed—a woman he had never met, who still had not seen him, yet who knew his name, he entered as if he feared each flagstone he trod on were a trap door. And when he saw Nora sitting in the small patch of light by the window, his bewilderment was total. "Mrs. Stevenson!" he said and bowed awkwardly.

Nora turned to the shadows behind the door, where Mrs. Metcalfe and the children had withdrawn. "Mrs. Metcalfe. Here is the Reverend Findlater, Methodist minister at the Wesleyan church in Smallbridge. He was a supporter of your husband."

Findlater bowed at the shadows; his eyes, growing accustomed to the dark, could just make out the shapes of the mother and her children. "I still am his supporter, ma'am. You shall find him not without friends. Since yesterday until this noon we have been at work to organize a petition—"

"While his wife and children were sent to Wardleworth workhouse!" Nora sneered. "Aye—you have the same values as him! Agitation first, people second."

Mrs. Metcalfe was sufficiently emboldened by Nora's hostility to come from the shadows and stand nearer the table.

"Your pardon, ma'am," he said stiffly. "But that is unfair. Mr. Metcalfe assured me that his rent was paid until the end of the month, so I had no ground to apprehend any distress to them."

"Then ye've a lot to learn of human nature. Do ye think she needed no comfort? While you and Fox organized your grand petition, did ye think this poor woman sat up here singing her head off with joy because the rent was paid to the end of the month?"

"Mrs. Stevenson!" he began, but the protest expired in his throat.

"If you've any impulse to civil behaviour with me, reverend," she said, "you may ignore it. You've strayed too far from your study and your hymnbooks. You've meddled with commerce. You must expect nothing but hard talk from me. Hard, plain talk."

"A cup of tea, reverend?" Mrs. Metcalfe asked with cold hospitality. "I can soon freshen it." She sent the children out to draw another pail of water at the pump across the yard.

He accepted the offer and sat on a stool, the other side of the table from Nora. "Since frankness is the thing, Mrs. Stevenson," he said, "I must ask you frankly why I find you here. Only yesterday Mr. Stevenson gave the evidence that put Mr. Metcalfe in jail. And now . . ."

"It was not my husband's evidence alone," Nora said sweetly and, turning to Mrs. Metcalfe, added: "Perhaps you do not know that this reverend gentleman gave testimony against your husband yesterday?"

It said a great deal for Mrs. Metcalfe's self-control that she not only held the teacup in her hand but continued to carry it steadily across the room and placed it before the gentleman.

"That, too, is unfair, ma'am. I was forced to it. I was not a willing witness. But what Mr. Stevenson may hope to gain by—"

"My presence here has nothing to do with Mr. Stevenson's hopes," Nora said. "I am here by my own wish. Mr. Stevenson has no notion I am here at this moment, talking to you." Mrs. Metcalfe sat down between them so that they made three sides of a square with the window on the fourth. "I know nothing of politics and have no sympathy for those whose meddling with politics brings them afoul of the law."

Findlater opened his mouth to speak but Nora pressed on: "I was telling Mrs. Metcalfe. Earlier this year my own brother led a group of workmen against their master. Just like Tom Metcalfe, they got their demands accepted but no acknowledgement of their union. Just like Tom Metcalfe, he held out his plate for more. Only *he* didn't have an employer like John Stevenson. Everyone knows Tom Metcalfe and the others swore secret oaths. Everyone knows they could have been put in prison for years—or transported. But who was it stood up in open court and told that magistrate to his face that he thought as three months' prison was harsh enough and he'd play no part in furtherance of more serious charges?"

She waited for a reply, but Findlater had taken her question as merely rhetorical.

"Who?" she repeated. "You know and I know, but Mrs. Metcalfe doesn't."

"Mr. Stevenson," Findlater admitted reluctantly.

"And I think Mrs. Metcalfe should know it. She should know what sort of man Mr. Stevenson is. My brother had no such employer and he is now in Van Diemen's Land. He left me without money or house or any support for two children, younger than these two, and a young brother. It is memory of those days brings me here. Not Mr. Stevenson's bidding.''

Defeat was in the very way he nodded. "I owe you an apology, ma'am. I was too hasty—and too ignorant. . . . I knew nothing of all this, of course.''

"Of course," Nora echoed, enjoying his humility. Gentlefolk could be very harsh when they were the high and mighty ones; but they had weaknesses so great as to be potentially fatal. Their sense of honesty and of fairness, for instance—that was an area always soft enough to let the knife slip through.

"Then may I ask not why you are here but whether you had reached any decision and whether or not you or Mrs. Metcalfe would welcome help from Mr. Metcalfe's other friends?''

Nora pondered before answering. Mrs. Metcalfe looked at her in growing anxiety and was on the point of speaking when Nora said: "I'll tell you. I *had* come here prepared to support Mrs. Metcalfe and the children. But I find a strong, healthy woman and a fine, strapping young daughter, who'll have no difficulty getting work—at Fieldens', if nowhere else. And a boy able to look after himself well enough, I daresay. It's encouragement and cheer they'll need—not money.''

"The boy . . .'' Mrs. Metcalfe sighed and shook her head. "It's young Tom's the problem for me. He's that lively no one's willin' to . . .''

Nora patted her arm encouragingly. "We can solve all that when the gentleman's gone," she said. "There's nothing to detain him here when he's finished that cup.''

Findlater, by now a little accustomed to Nora's extreme bluntness, merely looked at her and smiled slightly. "I'd heard tales about you, Mrs. Stevenson, but until today I did not believe them.''

"Now there you are the very opposite of Mrs. Metcalfe," Nora said calmly. "She had heard the most stupid tales—and believed them, too, until today. Now she no longer believes them—do you, my dear?''

"No!" Mrs. Metcalfe said with alarmed eagerness, as if any other answer would carry the death sentence. "No. I'm sure I don't. No.''

"Perhaps in the few moments he can still spare us, Mr. Findlater will tell us what hope for an early release his petition may hold out for us.''

And poor Findlater had to admit there was no hope of curtailing the sentence but that this work would keep alive the issues for which Tom Metcalfe had been martyred.

"I'm sure that will be a great comfort to Mrs. Metcalfe," Nora said. And Findlater was now so embarrassed that he had to rise and take his leave. Even then Nora did not pull the hook from his gills. When his hand

touched the latch she added: "At least we all have one thing in common—
we are all helping to keep *some*thing alive."

And with a nod he was gone, almost falling over the water pail, which
the children had placed by the door before returning to their twice-inter-
rupted game.

The two women heard him say: "Hello. You are Beth and you are
young Tom. Your father has talked to me of you. I am the Methodist
minister of Smallbridge."

They heard Tommy's serious little voice: "And are you more evangelical than the parson, sir?"

"Bless my soul!" the minister said. "What a very strange question, to
be sure!"

But, having had enough of solving puzzles and finding no answers to
his satisfaction, he left without pursuing his inquiries further.

The problem, Mrs. Metcalfe explained, was young Tommy. The dame
school in Littleborough wouldn't have him for he could already read better
than Elizabeth Ede, who taught there. He was too lively just to leave at
home, for he only got into mischief. She had tried getting neighbours to
take him and had even offered fourpence a week, but one by one they tried
and withdrew. He was too much of a handful.

"We must think about this," Nora said. "You have enough by you to
keep body and soul together, so we have a few days in hand to solve this
problem."

She already knew the solution she was going to propose but she would
have to talk it over with John. Before she left she noted down the title of
the little book with all the good ideas for saving money: *Cottage Economy*
by William Cobbett. "That's going to be very useful, is that," she said.

# *Chapter 30*

"You see, in much of December I'll be over at Rough Stones at least part
of the day. I want to wash everything through and get all the furniture in
and everything properly set before we go over on Boxing Day," she explained to John. "And there's a thousand things the boy could do—clean
windows, scrub floors, paint, sweep. And he could do his studies for part of
each day, for though he reads so forward, I doubt he writes well. I could

give him hooks and links to copy. . . . What do you say, dearest?" He opened his mouth to speak but she went on: "And when I start the tommy shop . . ." She laughed. *"Tommy* shop! I hadn't thought of that. He could help there, weighing out things and adding and keeping things tidy and sweeping. He could make himself useful there, too. And learn in practical things—as I did when I was seven. He might earn thirty pence a week. And I'd only charge his mother fourpence to look after him. . . ."

John laughed. "You'd charge her!"

"Of course I will." Nora was surprised at his laughter. "She's no call to look for charity from us. And fourpence is what widow Ede charges at her dame school, because I asked. I'd not want to take more than that. And if the three of them are bringing home over thirteen shillings a week, what do you say?"

"What do *I* say?"

"Aye."

"You mean it's my turn now?"

She grinned and leaned her forehead on his chest. "I'll be silent," she promised.

"I say it's a topsy-turvy world. When a mother and two children can go out and in fifty-eight hours earn more than a farm labourer in seventy. The age of the independent female is at hand."

"Be serious," she said to his buttons, still not lifting her head from his chest.

"It's not what I had in mind. Not by any manner of means."

She stood upright again. "They'll thank us more for this. If Metcalfe has any sense they'll stop at work and put the children to it in their time. In ten years they could save the best part of five hundred pounds. He'd not need no bloody union then. He could have a business of his own."

"Or partner us in some small contract and add a hundred or two in a month. Eh—I hope he learns sense in yon penitentiary."

"So you think we may—I may."

"We'll give it a try."

"Eh!" She hugged him hard in her delight. "He's a lovely little lad," she said. "You'll see."

Since she had left the little outhouse behind the anonymous Acorn she had pictured young Tommy again and again, reading so fluently—and that knowing little look of his when she asked him if he understood what he read. There was something in him of Sam, her younger brother. That same impishness.

She had missed Sam this year. He was so good at observing people and could imitate them so that you had to laugh—not just the way they talked but how they stood or stroked their chins or wagged their fingers or scratched their hair. He could do it all. And he could always see the funny side of things; you never saw him coming but you made a welcome for him in you. She hoped Mr. Sugden would soon write back with news of his whereabouts.

Next day Nora was just about to leave for the Acorn when she saw Arabella Thornton come riding up from the direction of the church; she must have come from Todmorden by the turnpike. They had met no more than a handful of times over the last few months and Nora had still taken no particular liking to the engineer's wife. She envied the way she spoke, though she also thought it effete. John had talked of her strength of character but Nora saw no sign of it; more likely it was her pretty blond curls and dark blue, almost violet eyes that softened his judgement. She also envied her that horse, and again she wondered if John had meant his promise.

Arabella, too, had her own private reservations about Nora. The way she meddled in her husband's affairs and—by all accounts—ordered people about was very unbecoming. Walter went on about how well connected the family had been but really she was no more than a servant girl. Bright— almost too bright, but . . . jumped up. Still, there was no choice but to ride this way today and talk with her. Mr. Stevenson had asked Walter if she, Arabella, would be kind enough to take Mrs. Stevenson under her wing and teach her some of the duties and graces fitting her new-found station, and Walter, in passing on the request, had made it clear that Stevenson was destined to a position of some importance in the world— and one of great importance in the career of any rising engineer.

Their greetings were superficially warm but brittle.

"Mrs. Stevenson! Good morning. I hope I find you well," Arabella called.

"Ye do," said Nora. She held the horse's head while the other slipped to the ground. "Will you come in for a glass of ale?"

"No. I thank you." Arabella smiled. "I don't wish to detain you. Were you walking? May I go with you a little of your way?"

"Gladly," Nora said, wondering what had prompted this sudden interest. "I was on my way up the Calderbrook road. I'd be glad of a little company to lighten the walk."

"How delightful. I was intending to return by that road myself." She took the bridle as Nora released it and together they walked up the street.

They made an odd pair. There was fashionable Arabella with her striking black beaver hat trimmed with ostrich feathers and a free-flowing veil of green gauze, and her dark-green zephyr-cloth habit embellished with wine-coloured buttons whose curved rows accentuated her tiny waist and swelling bosom. And there beside her walked Nora, in the plainest brown dress, covered with a mantle of dark blue Botany worsted and crowned with a cottage bonnet of the same material.

Arabella thought: *We must look like a lady and her maid.*

"It's not often we see you riding over this way," Nora said.

"No. To be candid, I have come here of a purpose."

"Oh?"

"Yes. I have been thinking over your and Mr. Stevenson's kind invitation to spend Boxing Day with you. In our delight and eagerness, Mr. Thornton and I overlooked the inconvenience to you. . . ."

"You must put such thought from you. I'm sure our walk through the tunnel, and our afternoon and evening together afterwards, will complete this year very nicely."

"You are very kind to say so, Mrs. Stevenson. Yet I am sure you would find it more convenient—and Mr. Thornton and I would be doubly delighted—if you and Mr. Stevenson would spend the night of Christmas Eve and all of Christmas Day and night at Pex Hill. In short, from Christmas Eve to Boxing Day morning."

"Oh, yes," Nora said. "That would be champion, Mrs. Thornton. We'd do that with pleasure. Thank you indeed."

Arabella was taken back. "You mean you can say so now? Without first asking Mr. Stevenson?"

"Oh, of course. As to his business, I'm sure it's indifferent to him. But as to our preference—to spend Christmas at an inn or with two such good friends—I'm sure there's no comparing them. And"—she brightened still further—"you are in Yorkshire. I could never feel easy, spending Christmas in Lancashire, not with Yorkshire in full view."

That made Arabella laugh. "Well, that's settled then. I am glad."

"Do you like our northern ways better now? Last time we met I fancy you were uncertain."

They had to pause here and pull into the side of the lane to let a wagonload of big square-cut timber take the bend into the gate of Hare Hill house. Nora watched with admiration as Harper the carter managed his four pairs of drayhorses without rein, trace, or whip—entirely by variations in his calls to them. "That's Romany talk," she said.

"Is he a gypsy?" Arabella asked.

"I don't know. They call him Master Harper hereabouts. I know a travelling bootseller who says he'll never buy one of this man's horses. They've only got to hear his voice, however distantly, and there's no controlling them."

When the timber swung through the gateway they resumed their walk.

"How are you settling then?" Nora repeated.

"It's very hard for a southerner. When I first came I was sure people didn't know how to behave at all. Now it is quite clear they know full well what ought to be done but are determined not to do it."

"Aye, that's very possible—" Nora began.

"My neighbour, for instance—there is a field between us and their place—he is the office senior at Lovenden's mills, and very well connected. Skellhorne, their name is. I believe they are a cadet branch of the Duke of Ripon's family. Well only yesterday, when I was leaving home to go down to the stables, I was in the drive and I heard her shouting up to me: Yoo hoo! Yoo hoo! Could she send a girl up for a jug of sugar because they had run short and the Misses Dawson were coming within minutes? And so I, of course, have to shout to all the neighbourhood that I've only the red dirty kind of sugar left because it's my day for provisioning. And she shouts that'll do for the Misses Dawson and why don't I join them and forget my riding for a day because they always have such champion fun! Really—I almost swooned with embarrassment at it. I dare not describe such goings on in my letters home."

They had reached the corner of the Calderwood road. A squall of wind, heralding a shower already over Rochdale, ruffed the puddles on the road and spread the tails of a flock of chickens as it bowled them along. Nora, who had kept one eye on the dark cloud, estimated she would reach the Acorn just as it broke overhead.

"Does no one behave in such ways where you come from?" she asked.

"No one. Well—perhaps one or two elderly and eccentric members of the aristocracy—but only those with no position to keep."

"I suppose," Nora said idly, "taking a sensible view of our likely future, Mr. Stevenson's and mine, I should know these southern ways. There's no chance to learn them here."

Arabella's eyes shone with her eagerness. "May I tell them to you?" she asked. "It would be such a kindness if you let me. I am afraid I shall quite forget them unless I have at least some cause to remember."

As soon as she heard these words Nora guessed with fair certainty that Arabella had come this way with the express purpose of suggesting such an arrangement. Which meant that Thornton must have asked her. Which meant that John must have asked him. It must all go back to her casual remark to John the other evening. She looked at Arabella, smiling so eagerly, waiting for an answer. One would think for all the world that the idea had just that very minute occurred to her. Nora realized that she was, in a way, getting her first lesson in finer behaviour, and she felt warmer toward Arabella than she would ever have thought possible.

"I'd be very glad of that, Mrs. Thornton, and more than grateful."

"Good," Arabella said. "Good."

Both stood smiling at each other, uncertain what to say next.

"Do you not think . . ." Arabella began diffidently but Nora had turned, involuntarily, at the sound of an approaching horseman—if that was quite the word for what now hove into view.

A morose man, dressed in an outfit that had seen its best days in the years before Waterloo, and a wig of the same vintage, sat awkwardly astride a spavined nag, which trotted with an uncertain lurch and at a pace slower than most horses manage to walk at. Only the man's long nose and grim mouth were visible beneath his broad-brimmed, low-crowned hat. Nora, when she had first seen him some weeks earlier, had taken him for a Quaker preacher.

When he drew level with them his mouth split in a smile even grimmer than it had seemed in repose. He lifted his hat and said, without appearing even to see them, "Good morrow, ladies."

His wig sprang from his head as if forced away by some magnetic repulsion; instantaneously his skull seemed to shrink and to rattle inside the wig like a ripe nut in its shell.

They nodded graciously in response, neither daring to trust her voice, and he dawdled past in that same unhappy trot.

When he was well out of earshot the two girls, hidden behind Arabella's horse, fell laughing upon each other for support.

"Who could it *be!*" Arabella asked as she caught her breath.

Nora, dabbing her eyes and standing straight again, said: "It's that lawyer from Rochdale . . . his name'll come to me in a minute . . . *Huxtable*. Lawyer Huxtable. He goes over to see a Lady . . . someone, over Todmorden way. You've never seen him?"

"Never!" She laughed again, and then, new light breaking on her, added: "Not Lady Henshaw of Henshaw Park?"

"I believe it is. Yes—that was the name."

Arabella began to laugh again. "He would!" she said. "I can just see it!"

"See what?"

But Arabella shook her head and began to lead her horse again along the road. "I won't spoil it for you by even *attempting* a description. But I'll say that if you thought the lawyer a comedy, wait until you see the Lady. And you can't miss seeing her, for she's just around the corner from you at Rough Stones."

Nora, content with the promise, returned to their earlier talk. "What were you about to say when he came by, Mrs. Thornton?"

"Oh yes," Arabella said, and this time there was no diffidence; the intimacy of their shared laughter now made it easy. "Do you not feel that as we are neither of us yet twenty and are soon to become much closer neighbours, all this Mrs.-Thornton-Mrs.-Stevenson is a trifle stiff? I would be so happy if you would call me Arabella."

Nora was suddenly too shy to speak. She could merely nod and smile and hope this would be taken for consent.

"Come," Arabella said, slipping her arm through Nora's and giving it a warm squeeze, "and may I not call you Nora?"

"Oh yes!" Nora spoke at last. "It will be so champion to have a friend . . . Arabella. I think you are my only friend up here. Apart from John."

Arabella's laugh carried overtones of bewilderment. "But Mr. Stevenson is your husband," she said. "That is different."

Nora agreed that it was and they walked on a little way in happy silence, still arm in arm. Yes, it *was* different. The friendship of another woman was different. Nora hadn't realized how true her words were until she heard herself speak them.

"But . . ." Arabella added in a while, her voice delicately poised between thought and speech, "it is quite one thing for *us,* as we are still so young. But as Mr. Thornton and Mr. Stevenson are already quite the greybeards"—she giggled and Nora joined her—"it would be Most Improper for them to share in such intimacies. That is agreed, I hope."

"I think," Nora said timidly, "that I should still sometimes like to call him John."

She spoke so solemnly that Arabella had to stare at her for some time, and with growing embarrassment, before she realized that Nora was not being serious. "You tease!" she laughed and shook Nora's arm, which Nora let go limp so that no other part of her was moved. "You tease! I see I shall have to keep my eyes and ears sharp with you!"

Until this moment Nora had not realized how far she had grown into womanhood since her father's death. It had been all that time since she had enjoyed a laugh with another girl her age, or talked of inconsequential things—things of *absolutely* no consequence, things you forgot the minute you'd spoken them because they were not really information, or opinion, or even gossip; they were . . . like singing.

She looked down at her dress, so plain it might have been chosen to express the sole idea of poverty—and poverty not just of pocket but of spirit, too. And there was Arabella's, so dashing and elegant—it was another of the things she had been missing without properly realizing it. Well, she was going to Manchester tomorrow—she could choose the materials and get a good day dress and a good evening dress made up in time for Christmas. And she could surprise them all on Christmas Eve and again on Christmas Day.

At that moment the first drops of rain began to fall. They had by now reached the courtyard gate of the Acorn, where Nora had intended to make her excuses and leave Arabella to the weather. Instead, she suggested that Arabella come inside and shelter while the shower passed.

In that way Arabella came to learn of the help Nora was giving to the Metcalfes. But she also saw the other side to Nora's character when Nora lay down what were virtually orders governing Mrs. Metcalfe's next few days. Tomorrow, Sunday, after chapel, she could try the mills toward Rochdale for work. If that were fruitless, she could spend Monday looking in the other direction, toward Todmorden. Once they had work, Tommy was to come down to her at the Royal Oak each morning at six. Mrs. Metcalfe could spend today and tomorrow teaching him one or two simple meals to make so that if Nora had to send him home midafternoon he'd have employment to keep him from mischief.

Mrs. Metcalfe was tongue-tied with her gratitude, which seemed to annoy Nora. The two youngsters were greatly in awe of the beautiful lady in her fine clothes, for they stood and gaped at her from the moment she came in until the moment she and Nora left.

"Do you think it fitting," Arabella asked when they were back by the gate, "to send her seeking work on the Sabbath?"

Nora appeared not greatly interested. "I'm sure the Lord would think less of her for sitting at home using up another's charity when she might be busying herself abroad. All the mills hereabouts do some work on Sundays—as we do at Summit."

The broken roadway glistened brightly in the rain. A woman in the house immediately opposite took the chance of a letup in the weather to hang a pair of very soiled sheets out to air. Arabella, shirking an honest rebuke to Nora's laxity, now felt acutely embarrassed at this display a few yards from them.

"I must return," she said, "or I'll outrun the hire on this hack."

Nora arranged that anytime between now and Christmas when she was at Rough Stones she'd hang a pillowslip in an upper window—"a clean one," she said pointedly, having noticed Arabella's reaction to the sheets. They embraced and parted.

Arabella, as she rode away, wondered how she could ever have considered Nora to be at heart a servant girl. While Nora, remembering Arabella's fine colour and smoothness of skin, wondered whether she, too, was pregnant.

# PART FOUR

Henshaw
Park

# Chapter 31

In the days following the trial, John, seeking to trade on his new fame as "Better Combination" Stevenson, had put in a tender to build a small factory wharf on the Duke of Bridgewater's canal. Despite Payter's good offices, the company had refused to take his bid seriously, thinking him far too big to give proper supervision to a contract worth a mere £950. The job went to a navvy gang acting as its own contractor.

"And where will *they* be when the wharf begins to leak!" he asked. But he had to swallow his disappointment and nurse the wound to his pride—and turn, exclusively again, to Summit.

The drama of Metcalfe's strike meeting, of the strike itself as well as Stevenson's counterstrike supper in Summit East, all of it topped off by the trial, had drained down every vestige of ill will at the site, and the work began to go forward with a better spirit than ever. The rapid succession of the breakthroughs also helped, as blind caves, where the air grew quickly foul, became one open tunnel between a succession of ventilation shafts.

Nevertheless, the fractures between six and seven were a cause of great and increasing concern. For, with the best will in the world, there is nothing you can do if, when you have drilled out a foot of what is intended as a fifteen-inch powder hole, the overburden cracks and shifts, turning your neatly bored hole into a nutcracker vise clamped together by forces unimaginably great. You must simply stay calm, take up another boring bar, and begin again. And even when it happens three times in a row you must, with that same equanimity, take up your fourth boring bar and start once more—knowing that, for all the progress you have made, you might as well have had another ninety minutes abed today. Progress between six and seven was running at a quarter of its predicted rate.

Stevenson tried every possible expedient to overcome this problem. He found that a trapped boring bar often came loose when a second was inserted and he tried the experiment of driving a softwood peg in the hole the first had made and dowsing it with hot water. The swelling of the wood had the effect then of locking the fractured rock and making further drilling a little less risky.

They all said what a master Stevenson was to have hit on the idea—except Thornton, who said: "I should have thought of that. It's the way the Romans used to quarry stone, without powder, you know."

But still the progress did not satisfy Stevenson. He elaborated the technique further by getting the drifters to cut wedge-shaped holes into the face along the lines of the fractures. Into these he drove softwood wedges that, when wet, served the same purpose. In a day or two he was satisfied that a wedge angle of thirty-five degrees was sufficient and the shallow cut it permitted was easily and quickly made in the rock. He had the smiths make up iron templates to this angle so that the carpenters above and the drifters below were working to a common standard, and every wedge made above fitted every niche cut below. His reward came by the end of the first week in December, when progress, despite the difficult nature of the rock, was actually a little faster than predicted. Nevertheless, so much way had been lost earlier that it was still doubtful that the faster rate would consume the backlog by Christmas.

On the tenth of the month he put a nightshift of eight men on each face, using ladders to avoid steaming the engines round the clock. Their bonus was eightpence a shift, and there was no shortage of volunteers.

At this time, too, he began his practice of paying out weekly, which was then virtually unheard-of in navvying trades. It was a risk, to be sure, but with everyone concentrated on the performance and attendance bonuses he thought he'd not lose too many men to the brewers. Events proved him right and by the third weekly payout, in mid-December, there wasn't a contractor on the line who wouldn't have envied his daily roster of absences.

By Sunday the fifteenth the driftway was complete from south and north with only the troublesome fractured burden between six and seven to break. It was down to thirty feet, which, if no further problems intervened, was within—just within—their present capacity to drift through in the ten remaining days. Of course, the financial penalty for finishing on, say, New Year's Eve instead of Christmas Eve was trivial—three days' pay, no more; but the cost to his pride and to the men's spirit would be incalculable. Come tempest, come hell, he was going to walk Nora and the Thorntons from Calderbrook to Rough Stones on Boxing Day.

During these weeks Nora, too, was busy. She knew how much Arabella was doing at Pigs Hill by way of preparation, and she was determined not to let Rough Stones show any less brilliantly on its special day. So what she had intended as simple preparations for their move grew daily more elaborate. Extra help had to be brought up from the cottages along the bottoms and the house was cleaned and polished from threshold to attic trap.

These chores were greatly enlivened by young Tommy Metcalfe. Whatever he did—whether scrubbing floors, colouring the walls, washing down the paintwork and windows, or grubbing out docks and nettles from a disgracefully neglected path—his cheerful voice and endless patter seemed to fill each room or the whole garden. Nora could easily understand why widow Ede would not have him at the price of ten and why, left alone, he would get into endless mischief. His curiosity was insatiable. He wanted to know whether an engine was stronger than a horse, and then—when that was clear—why they had to work so hard making the slope easier for the engine when the horses could take the much steeper slope by the road, and why Mrs. Thornton's horse could come up the very severe slope to Rough Stones. To Nora's mind John did not acquit himself too well explaining that one.

The funny ideas his mind leaped to also fascinated her. Once she had come into the room upstairs that was to become their bedroom, where he was supposed to be scraping and washing the glass in the windows. Instead she found him looking solemnly out at the hillside.

"Come, come, Tommy—that's not what you're paid for," she said.

He sighed and returned to his work. "Wouldn't it be champion if we could find the engine as makes all the clouds!"

Looking over his shoulder she could see the engine of number ten shaft and from it came great fleecy billows of steam that lingered long in the chill December air. She laughed, making him look around sharply, full of suspicion that she was mocking him. So she turned him to face the window and put her arms around him from behind to hug him. "What'd you do with it if you found it?" she asked.

"I'd make rain when folk wanted and I'd tell them when I wasn't so they could enjoy the sun."

Often, when Nora was doing quiet things, such as fitting the curtains, or patching clothes, she would ask him to come and sit by her and read from the book on *Cottage Economy*. She grew very tired of Mr. Cobbett's social and political prejudices—especially his endless tirades against paper money —and told Tommy to skip those passages. But whenever he gave a recipe or quoted some prices, she would stop what she was doing and, taking pen and notebook, make Tommy repeat it all at dictation speed, always substituting today's prices for the ones Tommy read out and then checking that the argument still held.

Once she made an elementary slip in her addition, making seven and five add to eleven. She felt Tommy stiffen at once and was about to correct herself when she saw his fingers hard at work under the table. He re-checked three times before he plucked up the courage to point out her error.

"I'm terrible at adding," she confessed. "One day I'm sure Mr. Stevenson's going to find me out and then he'll give me the sack."

"You must bring all your reckonings to me, ma'am."

"You promise you'll help me?" Nora was just as solemn.

"Yes. If you went away, where could I go?"

She laughed and hugged him all the more firmly. And often after that, she would make little errors in her reckoning and always he would check and recheck, three times, on his fingers before he corrected her openly.

Even when she went to Manchester she took him with her, like a page boy. She was astonished at how little the idea of a shop conveyed to him, apart from provisions shops; he wandered in and out of them as if they were museums or menageries. But, of course, once he had seen Nora make some purchases and had grasped the idea, he wanted her to buy everything he set his eyes on.

"Oh, you could get *that*," he would say of a large clothes boiler or a set of glazier's tools or a corn shaver. And when he had said it for the tenth time—about a large bolt of broche taffeta, in this case—she asked: "But what would we do with it, Tommy?"

"We could *keep* it," he said.

Then, passing a saddler's in Portland Street, his eyes fell on a set of hearse feathers. This time he said nothing, but she felt the tug of his hand as he halted. She waited for him to say, yet again, that she could buy *that*, but still he was silent. "What is it?" she asked.

But he only smiled, and looked shyly up at her with those deep brown eyes, and prepared to walk again at her side.

"Do you know what they are?" she asked.

He shook his head.

"Hearse feathers." It meant nothing to him. "When people die they go to the cemetery in a special carriage called a hearse, and it has feathers like those at each corner. And the horses, too, wear them—like a crown."

He looked back at them in even deeper wonder. "When I grow up," he said, "I'm going to die and have feathers like that on my hearse."

She laughed at his fancy. "Time enough yet to think of dying," she said. "You've a long, hard road in front of *you*."

But while they stood there talking, she had suddenly noticed a riding crop with a silver handle, and the question that had plagued her for days— What do I get John for Christmas?—was answered.

She went inside and arranged with the shopkeeper the rather special design she required for the knob, several times reminding Tommy that this was secret, a surprise, that Mr. Stevenson was not to know of until he opened the box on Christmas Day. "In fact," she said, as one conspirator to another, "I'd be obliged, young man, if you'd go to the door this minute and look carefully both ways, up and down the street, and make sure Mr. Stevenson hasn't followed us to town. So that our secret will be safe."

And while he went to the door she quickly arranged for one of the hearse feathers to be wrapped and sent as well.

They had a little over half an hour before they needed to hurry for their train, so she took him around by the street where her lodgings stood, the ones from which she had fled, leaving six gold sovereigns hidden in the wall. For a moment she thought she must have picked the wrong street, it was so unfamiliar. Then, aghast, she realized that the whole row of tenements, including her lodgings, had been demolished. Already the first tender shoots of grass sprouted from the rubble; somewhere under there—unless someone had made a very lucky find—lay buried the wealth whose extortion, and then whose loss, had led to her present altered fortune. She stood and shook her head in amused chagrin at the devastation before them.

"What's that?" Tommy asked.

"That . . . is all that now remains of the house I lived in until this summer."

He looked at the rubble with new interest. "Does it make you sad, ma'am?" he asked.

She laughed. "One thing makes me sad—I saved up a little money and hid it in one of the rooms and forgot it. Now it's hidden forever, somewhere in there."

Without pausing to hear more he dashed across the road. "I'll find it," he shouted with all the confidence in the world.

Scolding him half-heartedly, she followed across, telling him not to get dirty. But even before she reached the opposite gutter he gave a cry of triumph and came racing back to her holding two coins. They were not gold and they were not hers, she could see that at once. But he was so overjoyed and proud that when he said: "I told you. I said I would," and gave them over to her, she had not the heart to disown them.

"But," she said, after thanking him and going through a parade of her joy to be at last reunited with her savings, "but, I don't really need them now, for I have Mr. Stevenson to see me well. I think that as you found them, you shall have them."

His eyes almost popped in a joy that, for once, left him speechless. She looked at the coins to see what value she was giving away but did not recognize them. "Let's see which ones you've found," she said and took him to wash them at the pump, two streets away. But even when they were clean the coins were still unfamiliar to her. Both were silver, of the time of George III. One, dated 1811, said five shillings—one dollar. The other, dated 1816, had the unusual face value of eighteen pence. Whoever in that house had collected them had done so for their oddity.

"I remember those," she said. "I kept them because I'd never heard of such a thing as an English dollar or a one-and-sixpenny piece. They say he was mad, that George the Third, you know. . . ." She looked again at the coins and shook her head. "I think, before I give these to you, I must ask Mr. Stevenson about them. If they're the money of a madman . . . we'd not want that, I'm sure."

But Tommy got his coins in the end, for, although neither John nor Thornton had any idea what they were, the vicar of Christ Church, to whom Arabella applied with them, said they were safe currency. The dollar had started life as a Spanish-American coin and had been restruck as English currency during the Bonaparte crisis; the eighteen-penny piece was simply valid currency. So Nora scoured them up bright and clean and gave them to the boy.

Thornton, who heard of this growing attachment between Nora and Tommy at second hand from the tales Arabella brought back to Pigs Hill, told Stevenson he didn't think it all that good. But Stevenson merely said that Nora would start their own family soon enough and there would be the end of it. He did not add that he had worries enough at Summit without adding the burden of a disgruntled wife.

And over it all, casting his dark shadow forward on every success and every hope of success, loomed the Reverend Doctor Prendergast.

# *Chapter 32*

At eleven in the morning of Christmas Eve, to the most tumultuous cheer that Summit had yet heard, the last stubborn barrier between Lancashire and Yorkshire crumbled, tottered, and spilled before a rain of blows from a dozen eager drifters, each taking his turn. Moments later Stevenson, on the Yorkshire side, reached his hand through the gap and grasped that of Thornton. "What did I tell ye!" he crowed, beside himself with relief and delight. "What did I tell ye!"

Now that there was a space for fractured rock to fall into, the remaining breakthrough, ironically, went at almost lightning pace, and several hunks of more than a hundredweight apiece came away at a single heave of pick or bar.

"You want to keep one of those," Thornton said. "Get it trimmed. When you build your own place, use it for a foundation stone."

Stevenson thought that a capital idea, and had one large chunk sent out for the masons to dress. Later he sent out another, on which the arms of the Manchester & Leeds Railway were to be cut. "We could set it over the keystone of the southern portal," he said.

He had some of his men bring in two dozen of champagne, kept in the store against this hour. And the corks began to pop as soon as the carpenters hammered the last nail into the last length of shoring. Only those who had worked the two driftways on the two shifts shared this particular treat; but everyone knew that two hundred and fifty gallons of beer were waiting up at Deanroyd. Beyond the immediate circle of celebrants, in the dim light that fell down the shafts, or the fitful glow of torches and lanterns, eager hopefuls could be glimpsed open-mouthed and waiting.

"The minute yon rail track is made continuous from Deanroyd to Calderbrook . . . *and* has carried a tub of muck all its length . . . we may send for the beer," he said.

The thirty-foot length still unmetalled was the scene of the quickest bit of tracklaying Thornton had ever witnessed. And all along the line men checked bolts and rivets, ties and ballast—even the track width and camber; nothing must delay the arrival of the beer. When they had finished, it was safe enough for the queen herself to have trusted.

"Shall we walk it?" Thornton asked.

"I suppose we ought," Stevenson answered. "Yet I wanted to save it for Boxing Day. Tell you what—you go south, I'll go north."

Thornton considered it odd that Stevenson should want to keep his pledge so literally; it was a relic of navvylike superstition, strange in so practical a man.

By four o'clock the beer train had reached Calderbrook and, as most of the men already had their back teeth well afloat by noon, there wasn't a sober navvy left underground by knocking-off time at five.

Nora, still in her plainest clothes, had left Littleborough with the carter and all their belongings at midday. They called first at Rough Stones, where they dropped most of the load—together with a long list of tasks for the two servants, Bess and Tabitha, to carry out before Boxing Day morning was very far advanced. There were at least two mice who were not going to play while *this* cat was away. Then she gave Tommy three parcels—not to open until he, his mother, and his sister had helped carry them home. One, with *T* for Tommy in a corner, held a small tin whistle and a plume of hearse feathers; one, with *B* for Beth on it, had a little Sunday pinafore with a border of pretty blue and purple and yellow flowers; and the third, with *F* for family, held a mince tart and a pound of beef jelly and dripping. As she was on the point of leaving he tugged at

her dress and, when she turned, he handed her, in an agony of embarrassment and joy, a small flat paper packet.

"For me?" Her surprise was quite unfeigned.

He nodded and squirmed. She could see he was longing for her to open
it so she said: "If it's something very precious, I don't want to take it to
Todmorden where all the robbers live; I'll leave it safely here. Shall I just
have a peep at it and see?"

He giggled and crammed all ten fingers in his mouth. She opened the
packet, which was really just one piece of paper folded inside another. The
outside one said: "Mrs. Nora Stevinson." "Only I'm not a widow, you
know," Nora said, remembering the social conventions Arabella had been
teaching her. The address ran: "Rough Stones, More Hay Wood, Rochdale
Road, Wallsden, Lancashere, near Yorkshere, England, The World,
Creation."

The paper inside was a drawing, or four drawings, in Tommy's
childish hand, of the two coins she had let him keep, front and back. They
were not well done, for his draughtmanship was no match for his skill at
reading and talking, and there were several errors of spelling; but to Nora
they changed the tarnished silver of the originals to purest gold. She turned
to see him staring up at her, the very picture of anxiety. His elbows were in
that same cramped, awkward posture as when his mother had broken down
and he had not known how to respond. Only when she stooped and lifted
him and hugged him and swirled him around did he relax and laugh.
"There's nothing you could give me I'd want more than this," she said,
and ran upstairs to put it in a place of absolute safety. She took the outer
wrapping, though, to show the others. Then she went outside to the cart
and left for Pigs Hill, taking an excited Bess along to help with her
dressing.

From midday onward Arabella, who was a great deal more girlish since
her friendship with Nora, had gone to the window at least once every five
minutes and out to the gate at least every fifteen. Her excitement was
nearly a fever by the time Nora and her maid actually arrived, shortly after
two. Throwing all decorum to the wind, gloveless, hatless, cloakless, she
dashed out into the roadway and jogged impatiently up and down. As soon
as the cart came into view around the bend, Nora leaped from it and,
hitching up her skirts, ran the forty paces between them in equal delight.
They kissed and hugged and held each other at arm's length and hugged
again.

"Oh Nora! Such doings! I don't know what to tell you first!"

"You have some boxes came for me, I hope," Nora said.

Arabella's hand flew to her mouth and her jaw fell open. "Oh, no!" she
breathed.

"What?" Alarm seized Nora. "Two boxes—at *least* two boxes—from Costillio's of Moseley Street!"

"Oh, my dear, my dear! They were quite right then!"

"They? Who? What . . . ?"

"I have done the most dreadful thing! I have sent them to Rough Stones. . . ." But she could maintain the pretence no longer and her eyes, brimming with mirth, gave the game away to Nora.

Ever since Nora had deceived Arabella, the time when they dropped their surnames, the two had played such practical jokes on each other.

"You!" Nora cried and made a throttling movement with her hands. The cart passed them and turned into the drive, where Sweeney and Horsfall stood ready to take the baggage indoors.

"What are they?" Arabella asked. "Costumes? From Costillio's!"

"I have kept it a secret. John does not know, even now. And he's not to know either—let's go in, you must be perishing without even a shawl—he's not to know until I'm completely dressed and ready."

Arm in arm they turned from the lane and swept along the drive toward the house. A fine mist condensed on the bare twigs and boughs of the trees and glistened coldly in the gray daylight. Every stray breeze shook them by the dozen to the ground, but soon other droplets hung in place, ready, in their turn, to fall.

"It's not the sort of Christmas we usually offer up in these parts," Nora said.

"I don't care two straws about your Christmases! I want to know about these costumes. You young slyboots! You've said nothing."

But "In good time," was all Nora would add. So Arabella had to turn to her next piece of news. "What do you think—this morning a footman came up from Mrs. Redmayne of Todmorden Hall with such a charming note." She shut the front door behind them. Nora heard the three maids already gossiping and giggling upstairs. "It was to say we should all be welcome down at the Hall for their celebrations this evening."

"An invitation!"

"Not quite," Arabella said. "That's what was so good about it. She says she quite realizes we may already have made unalterable arrangements for this evening but if we have not, then, as newcomers to the district, we may not understand that they keep a sort of open house for his tenants and the families of his staff. And as he's a director of the railway, he'd be pleased to see us there and any of our guests, too. So that includes you, you see! There's a servants' ball, and a young people's ball, and my maid says they have a large oak buffet at the side of the main hall with mince puddings and every kind of meat on it, so I sent back to say we should all be very pleased to come down there—what do you think?"

For Nora it was the best and the worst of news in one. She understood well enough that if their business prospered, she would have to learn to move at ease in respectable society, but she had hoped to arrive there by degrees, beginning with this short stay *en famille* with the Thorntons. And now . . . here she was, going to Todmorden Hall her very first time out!

Arabella divined at once the cause of her hesitation. "It sounds very informal and jolly. We come when we may, eat what we want, dance or not—without programme—and leave when we please."

In the end Nora rose to the challenge of it—helped, to be sure, by the excitement it would be. "We must start getting ready at once," she said and, taking Arabella firmly by the arm, went eagerly upstairs.

"Your maid can sleep with Horsfall," Arabella said. "She's such a tiny thing there'll be plenty of room in her bed."

First Nora and Bess unpacked the two boxes and checked their contents carefully—though it was more likely that a day of the week would go missing than that Costillio's would pack a delivery wrongly. Bess had never seen or handled such fine and beautiful clothes before, and Nora had to call her to her work more than once.

She had bathed and washed her hair the night before so she needed only a wash before she started to dress. She started with a strapless chemise of fine cotton, over which went a voluminous horsehair petticoat, followed by six more of cotton, the outermost one being black. Bess alone could not pull the lace of her stays tight enough, and had to go and fetch Sweeney to help. She was away rather a long time, but came back explaining that she first had to help Sweeney with Mrs. Thornton's corset—"And ma'am! She's gotten down to twenty-one inches!"

"Has she!" Nora said. "Then twenty it is for me! So come up, you two good strong wenches—pull on it!"

She held herself to the foot of the bed while the two maids, each with a foot on her kidneys, strained at the strings. She breathed out and sucked her vitals up into her ribs to make it easier for them. Then, when the string would draw no tighter, Sweeney took both ends while Bess dashed forward to secure them. Nora was almost apoplectic with lack of breath by the time Bess said, "Done!"

"Quick, what is it?" she asked.

They stretched the tape around her and measured.

"Twenty and a half," Sweeney said.

"It'll do," Nora told her with a grimly satisfied smile of self-immolation.

From the start Nora had known that her skin was not and probably never would be of the fashionably pale and sickly cast, so she had chosen dark colours to make it appear as light as possible—against the protests of Madam Costillio, who thought only of the very latest fashion and its demand for pale and delicate colours.

For the bodice Nora had chosen a silk pekin woven with fine black and wine-red stripes. It was cut pointed at the waist and very décolleté at the shoulder, so that she could not raise her arms above the horizontal. She was determined that this dress should in every way be the very opposite of those she usually wore.

It was now dark enough to light the lamps. "And I think, on this day of all days, Mrs. Thornton'll not grudge us the luxury of those two candles as well," Nora said. She looked critically at her lace bertha. "It's too white," she complained. "It shows up the darkness of my skin."

"It's never this bright in Todmorden Hall, ma'am," Bess comforted. "You step back from the light and you'll see the effect better."

Nora obeyed and, seeing how the contrast narrowed once the light was reduced, felt a little happier about the choice.

The bertha completely covered her short, tight sleeves, revealing only their lace cuffs, which hung loosely below the elbows at the back but, at the front, were gathered up to smaller rosettes of the same crimson silk as the dress.

"Look at these hands," she said. "I doubt they'll ever grow ladylike."

And Bess, being an honest girl, could this time offer no comfort. Nora tried on the gloves she had bought for the especial purpose of masking her hands; they were of flesh-coloured silk, trimmed at half-arm's length, just below the elbow, with orange ruffs. The transformation was almost complete.

"Now," Nora said, "for the hair."

"Before that, shall I fetch you a pot of tea, ma'am?" Bess asked.

"Yes. Very nice. And a cup for yourself, too. We could both do with it, I think."

But as she opened the door, Horsfall, in her best tucker and pinafore, being honoured to wait above stairs, came in with a tray of tea and two cups, along with a little plate of Christmas savouries and fancies.

After she had made up the fire, Horsfall peeped quickly out of the window—the third time she had done so since entering.

"It's all still there, is it? Outside?" Nora asked.

Horsfall blushed. "It's the gentlemen. I must keep a eye—*an* eye—skinned. I'm to let them in," she added proudly.

"And you can show Mr. Stevenson to the little room at the back," Nora said. "He can dress there. He's not to come in here."

When Bess had shot the snib again and they were safe from interruption, it was time to begin on Nora's hair.

Bess parted it in a double parting, meeting centrally at the forehead. With her nimble little fingers she began to plait a broad band of hair to cover Nora's ear on the right; the loose ends she took back and tied temporarily to the back hair. She was about to repeat this on Nora's left when John knocked at the door, calling: "What's all this?"

"Go away!" Nora laughed. "You'll not get in here before I'm finished."

She heard him go to the other spare room, grumbling that he'd never known such fussing and faddle.

"He'll fall down in wonder when he sees thee, ma'am," Bess promised.

It took her a lot longer to plait the left-hand side, for she had to keep checking that it was properly symmetrical with the right. But she managed at last to make a perfect match of the two, and very soon she plaited all the loose ends and the back hair into a low knot at the neckline. This she spiked into place by an ebony comb set with artificial gems. All that then remained was to place a row of gaily coloured feather-flowers in the form of a diadem right up and over the crown of her head. Above and behind her right ear she put three bigger flowers, set in a spray of green feathers cut to imitate leaves. Over her left ear, to prevent a totally deadening symmetry, she put only two.

Bess stood back, her eyes glistening. "Oh madam! . . ." she began before Nora, waving a monitory finger, stopped her in mid-flow. *"You've* got no time to waste," she said.

Bess had no idea what she meant. "Me, ma'am?"

"Yes. You come from just below here in Gawks Holm, don't you?"

"Yes, ma'am."

"Well—you'd best get home and put on your first-best dress and bonnet and pinny—you want to look your grandest at the servants' ball tonight, I fancy."

Bess had obviously not understood that she was to come to the Hall as well. "But of course you are, you soft pennyworth! Who's to take off my boots and put on my shoes when we get there?" She heard John step noisily from his bath in the room across the passage. "Before you dash off," she added, "you should give that little Horsfall a helping hand to empty Mr. Stevenson's bath. Take this tray down."

No chore could even dim Bess's sudden transport of delight. "Eh!" she said. "Thank the Lord I never knew till now. Me hands would of diddered so much I'd not've managed aught. Eh! *Me*—at Todmorden Hall servants' ball! Eh!"

Nora smiled as the girl left. Not four months earlier, she herself would have thought the servants' ball elevation enough. But to be a guest of the squire . . . ! She went to the door, barred it again, and walked out to the centre of the room to stand where she could see herself full length.

Even now she could not believe that clothes could do *so* much to change one. That the rich and patrician-looking young woman in the mirror was the same as the girl who had once bargained away ten minutes of her body for four shillings and sixpence—and to the master of this house. She remembered John's words that same night out on the banks, about how there were riches now to be made by ordinary folks as would turn the kings and queens of past ages green with envy. Well, here was the proof, if proof were needed.

She moved closer to the mirror and subjected what she saw to a more critical, other-womanly scrutiny. Something was missing. Yes—the little pendant she had bought. It was a single unfaceted but polished ruby encircled by minute pearls, all set in a silver-filigree mount. She had bought it because it came with two fastenings. One was a silver-braid band that enabled it to fit around her head as a ferronière, with the pendant high on her brow, just below where the twin partings met. The other was a silver-link chain that converted it to a simple necklace, with the pendant at the pit of her throat. She tried it both ways and found it impossible to decide between them. She would leave it to John. Not that he had any especial taste in such matters, but both places were good and it would please him to be their final arbiter.

She pulled back the snib and opened the door—only to find herself face to face with Walter Thornton, ready changed. He might easily have been passing by, yet there was about him a suggestion of guilt, as if he had been at the keyhole. Was that why there was no key? She had no time to think further just then; it was obvious that he did not instantly recognize her.

"I'm Mrs. Stevenson," she prepared to say, but just before she uttered the words, he blurted out "Nora!" so that "I'm Mrs. Stevenson," following immediately after, sounded like the swiftest of rebukes. He coloured and his eyes fell.

The air in the unheated passage was suddenly very cold to her naked shoulders. The temperature outside must have dropped to freezing.

"You flatterer! Pretending not to recognize me!" she said, realizing the futility of an explanation and wanting to make light of it all.

But he looked up with what she called his sheep's eyes and said lugubriously: "I recognized you. How can I forget! But you have never appeared so lovely. That I must confess."

"Thank you kindly, sir," she said briskly and squeezed past him in a

rustling of silk and petticoats to knock at John's door. She did not see that
Thornton stood behind with his head bowed and eyes fast shut; John
Stevenson's exasperated "Come in!" woke him from his reverie and stirred
him to move away. Nora felt suddenly afraid to open the door and Stevenson had to repeat his call.

He had, of course, known that she was up to something with a dressmaker in Manchester, but he had never imagined the result would be
anything so exquisite as this. He dropped the neckcloth he had been failing
to tie and stared at her in a bewilderment that slowly turned to adoration.

The room was chill. She shivered and turned back toward the passage.
"I need your advice on this one thing," she said. "Come into our room."

In his stocking feet and shirt sleeves, with his neckcloth hanging loose,
he padded after her, closing the door behind him.

"Which do you think . . ." she began, picking up the ruby and pearl
pendant. But he had his two great hands on her shoulders and moved her
gently a pace or so forward to where he could talk from behind her to his
own image in the looking glass.

"Who's that?" he asked his own reflection.

"That? That is the most beautiful lady in this kingdom. Belike in the
world," he answered.

"I thought so the minute I saw her."

"D'ye know what I'm goin to do with her?"

He chuckled. "I can guess!"

She lowered her eyes and blushed.

"You can *not*. I'm going to kill her—that's what."

She looked up in bewilderment at his image. Her reflection looked up
at him.

"Three months back . . . think now," he said directly to her, "what
did I tell thee? It were clothes like this I had in me mind, but—eh! I never
thought it'd . . . I never thought . . ." Slowly he lowered his head and
kissed her shoulder, first one, then the other, then her neck. She shivered,
not with cold this time, and turned to embrace him. But she could not lift
her arms, because of the décolletage.

She snorted her contempt for the fashion. "It's well enough for one
grand evening, I daresay, but if I faced a lifetime of lacing to this degree
and such exposure and"—she tried again to lift her arms—"such confine-
ment, I'd sooner live savage."

He raised her hand and kissed it. "Wear what you will, you're always
this lovely to me. But tonight even the purblind will see it."

He decided she should wear the pendant at her throat. He had to kneel
while she helped him with his neckcloth, which he tied with an osbaldeston
knot. His evening dress harmonized perfectly with hers. The coat, worn

open, was of a rich dark brown, with purple silk facings to the lapels. His waistcoat was of crimson velvet embroidered with black, crimson, and purple braid. His white shirt was frilled and ruffled, and his pantaloons, of black kerseymere, were drawn high enough to show off his black silk stockings and elegant pumps with their ornamental silver buckles.

When all was done, she took her red velvet shawl about her shoulders and gave herself, and him, one last inspection.

"Frightened?" he asked.

She put her hand on her stomach. "Eh," she said. "I've got the north wind blowing through here."

He shook his head reassuringly. "Just . . . be yourself," he said. "When you walk in through that door, think: Which of these folk is going to be of use to us?"

"Not tonight!" she began, chidingly.

But he was quite serious. "Especially tonight."

And she suddenly understood what a chance it meant for him—for *them;* she saw, too, how much she had been influenced by Arabella's view of the world over these last weeks, so that the sudden springing upon her of this invitation had seemed no more than a chance to exercise the social graces that Arabella had been teaching her. But for John—and, she now understood, for her, too—it was something far more vital.

The understanding brought its own regret, though. Her innocent evening of Christmas fun would have been doubly enjoyable because the year's work was so well done. But now, the simple fun was over before it had even started. And Nora, newly young and free of care, was not invited; Mrs. Stevenson, cofounder of a great enterprise in the making, would go in her stead.

The thought then struck her that she would *never* be young. If she lived a century, she would die without ever having tasted real youth. She had gone from childhood to poverty and unremitting toil, to destitution. And now, when her fortune had changed so dramatically, an equally pitiless and demanding code had taken the place of the iron laws of poverty. Had there been a magic moment in between? When the one had been lifted and the other not yet imposed? Indeed there had, she realized: that day they destroyed the rabbit warren—that gorgeous day. That had been her youth and all of it. For the first and only time she envied Mrs. £400-a-year Arabella Thornton—not just this or that aspect of her . . . her smooth hands, or her knowledge of the social graces . . . but her whole, entire state.

"You'll never guess," John said when they were downstairs in the drawing room, waiting for Walter and Arabella. "I had to bath in cold. They bath in cold water here."

"What—with that lovely kitchen range that makes so much hot? They don't use it?"

"Not for baths they don't."

"I'm not bathing in cold," she said and walked directly out to the kitchen.

As there was no meal to be taken in the house that night, both cook and scullery maid were hard at work scouring the knives and polishing the plate for tomorrow.

"Oh ma'am, ye do look that lovely!" Horsfall said.

Nora smiled and shut the door behind her. "What are the arrangements for bathing tomorrow morning?" she asked.

Mrs. Briggs looked at Horsfall, who brightened at once. "Please ma'am, Sweeney and me is excused a bath tomorrow, and we are to bring you and Mr. Stevenson's at half past six."

"Straight from the spring?"

"Aye, ma'am."

"I tell you what, then. Save you making two journeys in the morning. Fetch ours tonight and store it in that thing." She pointed at the stove.

Horsfall grinned. Mrs. Briggs coughed with ironic grimness. "Same as usual," she said. "Them two maids hold their water in yon boiler all night."

As she came back along the passage, she heard Arabella coming downstairs. "Nora? No trouble, is there?"

"No," Nora answered lightly. "I just wanted them to be sure to tell us the moment Bess gets back."

Her words trailed off as soon as she caught sight of Arabella, who stood in the full light of the hall lamps. It was clear now why she had taken longer to dress. "Oh, Arabella," she gasped. "That's lovely! That is lovely! Don't stir from there. John! Come out and see!"

Arabella, laughing with delight, stood as bid and waited. "And you," she said to Nora. "Come into the light. I can't see you there." Walter, coming down behind her, paused one or two steps up from where she stood. He peered over at Nora, shading his eyes to accustom them more quickly to the dark. Self-consciously she fiddled with the lace of her tucker and bertha.

"Eh, what a picture!" John said from the drawing room door. "We have two princesses for company tonight, Thornton."

Arabella, rewarded, completed the descent of the stairs. She went straight to John and offered a cheek for a kiss, which he, not showing his surprise, gave her.

"Merry Christmas!" she said.

And "Merry Christmas!" they all repeated as they, too, exchanged kisses or shook hands—in which Walter, to Nora's taste, lingered rather too long and squeezed her fingers rather too fervidly. And, of course, Arabella admired Nora's dress rapturously, once she could see it properly in the light.

She herself, being already as pale as fashion could dictate in an age that shunned cosmetics, had chosen the lighter colours that were then coming in. Her bodice was of pale blue watered silk, very pointed at the front, stiffened by three bones. She, too, wore it very décolleté, à la Grecque. Hidden between her breasts was a little phial of water to nourish the real violets she wore at her bosom.

And violet was the theme of her dress, which was even fuller and more voluminous than Nora's. It was of a broche silk, printed with broad vertical bands of pale blue and white, edged with narrow stripes of violet. The blue bands had little violets, very naturalistic though only half their proper size, printed on them. The hem was gathered up into four stiff swags of silk at front and back, pinned by dark-blue terry-velvet ribbons.

But the real masterpiece was her hair. Sweeney, whose fingers had learned their dexterity in long childhood years down at the mills, had braided and woven its golden tresses with a perfection no machine could match and with an artistry beyond any mechanical contriving. Flat oval chaplets covered her ears; but the braids themselves were intertwined at the back with delicate silken ribbons of pale ultramarine; and among the braids of the front Sweeney had woven a string of hollow glass balls, each the size of a small walnut and opalescent green in colour. This string ran twice over her head, once vertically, as a sort of diadem, once horizontally forward, like a ferronière worn rather high, just above the start of her single central parting. At the back the loops and tresses of her naturally curly hair were gathered up with some of the silken ribbons from the sides and plaited at their ends into a delicate little knot that was held in a small net of silver.

Walter watched her float from hall to drawing room, and later from drawing room to car, with fierce but hopeless pride. *How like an iceberg,* he thought. And, mourning her vanished ardour, he quenched—as he had so often done this autumn now past—the upwelling of self-pity he felt within. He reminded himself that Arabella was beautiful, that she ran their home like a well-engineered machine, that she adored him and deferred to him in almost everything, that whenever he needed to express his lower nature she would lie still and let him, registering nothing more than the most silent and resigned of protests. What more could a reasonable man ask of a wife?

In fact, as they jogged along in the car, he listened to the chatter of the two girls, missing most of it whenever the wood blocks of the brakes were pulled hard on, for the way down was steep. And he wondered whether his envy of Stevenson wasn't misplaced. Nora was a terrible one for having her way; they all said that. Stevenson had to argue everything through with her and she had much too big a hand in their finances. And look how, the day after the trial, she'd gone to the aid of the Metcalfes—after all that man had done to ruin her husband. Yes, even Stevenson, even the great Lord John, could have taken on more coals than he could haul. No doubt he got all his oats at home; but the price was high. All in all, he decided, his life with Arabella was preferable by far.

It was dark when he made this decision; but shortly after, as the car went past Fieldens' at Waterside, where they kept three street gaslights burning, he saw Nora buried warmly in the dark brown burnoose borrowed from Arabella, and his logic and resolve were almost undone. It brought him no joy; for the ten thousandth time he groaned inwardly at his thralldom to a bright eye, a swelling bosom, a neat ankle—and to the bodily images they unfailingly conjured of soft buttocks, yielding thighs, and a warm pudendum.

For some time he had been aware that little Bess, Nora's maid, had been jolting beside him with the movement of the car over the rougher stretches of the turnpike. And just as they passed into gloom again, beyond the reach of Fieldens' three lights, the car went down and up a wide pothole. The down brought the girl against him with a shriek of apologetic laughter; the up removed her torso to at least a few inches distance, but it somehow left her hip and thighs firmly against his. And it was now very dark. Dark enough to show the stars, twinkling in a clear, moonless sky, but very little besides.

Looking innocently ahead—knowing full well how fatuous it was to seek to misdirect others in this way, yet nevertheless looking innocently ahead with all the intensity of a harbour pilot—he slipped a hand around her and squeezed what he was delighted to find was not corset but hip. How deliciously she wriggled against him. Quietly, in the dark, he had to ease his dropfront, which she took as an invitation to more daring play. He soon had to stop her or she'd have spoiled the evening before it began. How and when could he get to her? Quickly during this ball? Or just feel his way to heaven now and arrange something for later that night? They could meet in the kitchen. Or in the old wash house across the yard. His heart and all his civilized parts sank at the prospect. It was going to be cold, dirty, and uncomfortable. It was going to rob him of sleep. It would expose him to the danger of discovery. Why, oh why, could he simply not say no and have done!

But his hand went on caressing and fondling that girlish little hip, and straining past it for a touch of that restless, slender thigh.

Damn all women!

". . . Thornton?" he heard Stevenson say.

"Walter!" That was Arabella, sounding a little scandalized.

His hand froze on that hip. Ridiculous, of course. They couldn't see him. "What?" he asked, hoping it did not sound as guilty to them as it did to him.

"I said—what d'ye think are the chances tonight of snow?" John repeated.

"Twice!" Arabella laughed.

"Sorry." Walter laughed and eased away his hand. "I was lost among the constellations. Which is Cassiopeia? That W shape, is it? They say it makes the initials WS, and William Shakespeare was born under it, you know."

"It's certainly cold enough for snow," Arabella said.

"Oh . . . yes," Walter said. "Snow. A white world for Christmas. It would be good."

After a little silence Arabella began again. "I think it so quaint the way streets keep changing names here every ten yards. That's Salford Brig we've just come by. Here it's changed to Pavement. In a dozen paces it's Neddy Brig, then it's New Brig, then it's Church Street—and that's all less than a hundred paces along the same street."

"It's the Lancashire–Yorkshire boundary," John said. "Perhaps that's why it's in such a muddle."

Nora almost cried out in disappointment: "You mean Pigs Hill's in Lancs?" But, being on her best behaviour, she held her peace, feeling it would be discourteous to the Thorntons to draw attention to this deficiency in their home.

The joyful strains of music came through the quiet night and moments later the car braked before the unpretentious wrought-iron gate of the Hall. Its windows were a blaze of lights—every one uncurtained and several hinged open. The building was one of those rambling Elizabethan stone houses whose exteriors frankly confess the failure of the interior floors to meet on the same level; so much so that three storeys on the left gable became two by the time the eye travelled across to the right gable, and the windows of the three false gables in between showed how the transition took place.

Though it stood in the centre of Todmorden, the "lawns" that sloped down to the main road were, in fact, a cow pasture; and twice a day the maidservants came down to drive the cows across the road to the river for a drink.

"Hope they've swept the drive!" Walter said.

When they reached the door Bess and Sweeney stooped to replace the two ladies' boots with indoor shoes and then set off for the back of the premises. Nora followed Bess part of the way. Both maids stopped. "You go on, Miss Sweeney," Nora said, and when she was alone with Bess, she continued urgently: "You just listen here, young miss! I don't know what was going on just now and I don't want to, but if you break your ankle with any man, you'll be out of Rough Stones faster than you can pack—and your belongings with you. You know what I mean now?"

"Yes, madam." Bess barely breathed the words.

"Enjoy your evening then," Nora said and returned to the others. "I'm sorry," she apologized. "Bess is so young though, I didn't want her getting up to anything reckless tonight." She avoided looking at Thornton.

"You haven't kept us," Arabella said. "No one's answered yet. Ring again, Walter dear." She alone did not realize the meaning of what Nora had just said.

A fat silhouette of a man darkened a window to their right. "Just push in!" he shouted with a gruff heartiness.

"Is that Redmayne?" John asked as they obeyed and shuffled hesitantly into the hallway.

"I have no idea," Walter answered. "I've never met him. It seems we just pile our clothes here and wander in."

Arabella invoked the heavens with her eyes and looked at Nora, smiling and shaking her head.

But John, hearing the players—a catch group of three fiddlers, a bass fiddle, a concertina, and a flute—strike up a tune he knew, began to sing in a bell-like baritone that startled Nora, who had never heard him sing in any voice: "Now Christmas is come, let us beat up the drum . . ."

At that moment the fat man, whose cravat badly needed retying already, opened the door from the large hall, and, hearing John, said: "My dear sir! You mustn't keep such a voice to yourself. Especially if you know the words—which not one man in a hundred does these days!"

"John Stevenson, sir, contractor at Summit Tunnel," he introduced himself. "And Mr. Walter Thornton, engineer in charge. Er . . . Mr. . . . ?"

"Redmayne," the fat man said and then, with a chuckle as they became deferential, added, "but not the squire. Know what you're thinking. I'm his uncle. But he tolerates me, don't you see. I make meself useful."

Since he had joined them he had hardly taken his eyes off the two women. John introduced him to them and he kissed their hands. "Ah!" he sighed heavily. "If there had been such prettiness in the world when I was young! Things would have been very different! This is indeed an age of progress."

He took them into the brilliantly lighted hall and presented them to his nephew, the squire. Upwards of a hundred people of all ages and conditions were gathered there, from moppets of six years right up to one old lady who later claimed to Nora that she remembered as a child hearing of something called Culloden—a great battle, as far as Nora could understand it—and of the escape of someone nicknamed "Pretender." Nora's heart fell at how much there was for Mrs. Stevenson to learn that plain Nora Telling had done so well without.

The squire received them affably and invited them to join in the amusements of the hall. His humour seemed a little forced, John thought. And he said afterwards to the uncle: "Something's on his mind."

"Last year! That's what's on his mind. That's why he was so glad to see you, I'll be bound."

"What happened last year?" Nora asked.

"Young Lionel"—that was the squire, who was all of fifty!—"he likes these old-fashioned Christmases. It's all we can do to stop him electing a Lord of Misrule and waiting on the servants on Christmas Eve—as it is, you see how we must fend for ourselves, while the servants have high jinks in the back. Well, anyway, last year he had all this open-yer-doors nonsense and every idle vagrant and mendicant in the district—"

"Oh!" John said. "The railway! Just beginning! I see it. You needn't tell me."

"So, with yourself here, there'll be none of that."

The organization, or disposition of forces, in the big hall had slowly become apparent to them, though it seemed chaos itself when they had first entered. Up near the "orchestra" were those who wanted to dance—and they ranged from farmers' sons and daughters up to a smart young ensign from the King's Own Yorkshire Light Infantry. Nora did not decipher the acronym until the next day—when she sat in church, to be precise—and she wondered why people kept referring to the youth as the "young coyly man" for "coy" was the very last word she would apply to his behaviour.

Around the dancers were groups of mainly young people who from time to time joined in, some clapping to the music or whistling or singing, some dancing for brief spells if they knew the steps. But in order to dance, a young man had to leave the company of his fellows with all its jokes, chaff, and buffoonery and cross a gulf to ask a girl to leave the gossip and confidences of her group. It did not often happen; so most of the dancers were youngsters and those already married.

Between them and the window, looking very territorial, was a dangerous group of young bloods. Sons of the masters and the local gentry, these were clearly only beginning their evening here, waiting for the doors to the inner hall to open and the free drink to flow. Later they'd be out to terrorize the neighbourhood and strew wild oats in common country—those not robbed of the faculty by liquor. To Walter it was Clod Three and his cronies all over again and he regarded them with a special contempt.

"That's the Ule Clog, you know," Uncle Redmayne said, rejoining them after ushering in a party very familiar to the house and so needing no escorting. "There's not one in a hundred knows the old customs now. But that"—he pointed to a giant tree root burning in the hearth—"is a real Ule Clog, lighted from a brand saved from last year's. Of course, you youngsters think it's all nonsense, you railway folk!"

They protested that they did not. Nora said, "We've had a Ule Clog every Christmas I've memory for." It pleased the old man inordinately.

Between fireplace and door were mostly youngsters, children, and a sprinkling of old folk. On the other side of the door, farthest from the dancing, stood the respectable and fashionable elite, toward whom the Stevensons and Thorntons were slowly working their way.

But they never quite reached it, for the inner doors were thrown open and everyone, voluntarily or not, was swept toward them in a vortex that mingled the careful assortment of grade, age, sex, and inclination in one human tide moved by one appetite toward one goal: the buffets.

They were long, oaken, and very plainly decorated; but they groaned with Christmas fare. Because of the servants' absence it was all of the serve-yourself variety: pork pies, every kind of cold meat and cheese, mince tartlets, frumenty cakes in hot milk, and gingerbreads. Milk and punch were kept warm over spirit lamps on a separate table.

Here gathered the bloods, wanting to cram down as much of the free liquor as they could hold before they began their evening's revels. When John and Walter, who had stood patiently waiting a turn at the bowl and ladle, came near the front, a tall, thin, curly-headed youth, leaning against the panelling with a well-studied air of indifference, said to a friend: "Really, Rupert, ain't it a blister! One was used to the servant classes holding their revels and neglecting their betters on Christmas Eve, but when they start joining us . . ." And Rupert said: "I blame the railways. They'll soon carry bastards to court, I'll lay."

Walter, colouring hotly, said, "Stevenson! They mean us."

But John was not the least bit roused. He looked calmly at the two and, without taking his eyes off them, said: "I think not. I agree they seem to be two very simple whisks—but I doubt they're quite that foolish."

The one who had spoken first, holding and returning John's gaze, said in a languid voice: "How well we fine apples swim—says the horse dung!"

There was a sharp intake of breath from the half-dozen bystanders who had heard, and the two young men and their friends dissolved in laughter, guffawing and punching each other's shoulders.

John took a quick step forward to the serving table and picked up a heavy pewter tankard. From there it needed only two more steps to bring him face to face with the one who had delivered the insult.

"No!" several voices cried. "Outside!"

"Stevenson!" Thornton called. "They are not worth it."

But they all fell silent when it became clear that John intended no violence. Smiling, he lifted the tankard, dangling it on his little finger like a cup on a hook. When he had roused their curiosity sufficiently he changed grip with a lightning speed, like a juggler; so that one minute the cup swung idly and the next it was firmly in the grip of that huge fist. The young man, still the very picture of arrogance, had not yet looked at the mug; in fact, he had not taken his eyes from John's face, which he examined as a naturalist might look at a specimen.

For a while John was so motionless that people—even Thornton—began to wonder if he'd lost his nerve. But then someone said, "Look!" and the gasps that followed made even the young man tear his eyes from John's face and look at the fist that held the mug. And then his eyes went wide with alarm as John moved his hand to a point uncomfortably close, much as to warn the other not to let his attention wander from it.

The fist and arm did not tremble. What they were accomplishing seemed no effort. Yet slowly, silently, with a smoothness that was almost graceful, the fingers were folding and rippling and crushing the tankard to a simple ball. After that first gasp of astonishment the entire company of bystanders stood transfixed in silence, hardly breathing. And when the tankard was reduced to as near a ball as it would go, there was only a great collective sigh. The youth and most of the onlookers were now certain that he would use the metal ball as some kind of fist strengthener, and the young man's face for the first time registered fear.

But John, with another of those rapid flicks of the wrist, changed his grip so that he was suddenly holding it as a magician might hold an egg.

"And now, young whisk," he asked. "Your opinion of this, if you please. Is it an apple, would ye say? Is it horse dung, would ye say?"

People began to chuckle, realizing that there was to be no open violence done.

The youth, alarmed yet stubborn, pursed his lips and shook his head.

"Come. Ye were so free with your opinions just now. Apple or horse dung?"

There was such an edge of menace in his voice that the young man, his wit deserting him, was forced to say: "Pewter, sir." He looked to see if John would be satisfied and would let him go.

But John was by no means finished. "Ye were right in one thing, though," he said, conversationally. "There *is* a decided odour of horse dung in here. I think it was you brought it in under your shoes. Let us see."

The youth stared at him blankly.

"Lift up your foot," John said, and again the menace was there.

Slowly and reluctantly the other obeyed. Quicker than sight John reached down his other hand and ripped off the young man's spur. The wrench twisted his ankle and he only just prevented himself from crying out in pain. When he looked again at John he found the hand that had held the pewter ball now waved the spur mockingly before his eyes. All around them people were openly laughing—even, such is loyalty, some of the youth's own crowd. He made a snatch at the spur—but not nearly fast enough; before he had reached the end of his swipe the spur again danced tantalizingly before him. The action brought only renewed laughter.

When silence returned, John said: "It won't be *that* easy. I must give you the chance to win it back. Do you box?"

The other looked in dismay at John's size and at the fist that had mashed the mug to a ball. Not daring to risk the disgrace of a refusal, he simply repeated the word—"Box?"

"It's that—or an apology," John offered.

The young man licked his lips. "I apologize," he said, with no grace.

John sniffed the spur, which, being a dress spur, had of course never been near the side of a horse. "Ye were right," he said. "It *is* horse dung." And he dropped it neatly in the V of the man's embroidered waistcoat.

And then, bathed in laughter and a scattering of applause, he turned to the serving table and calmly helped himself and Walter to their punch, as though his turn had come and nothing untoward had occurred.

The whole episode had lasted little over a minute and had happened with such lack of commotion that most of the company, busy talking and helping one another to food, were unaware that anything had taken place. Even the final laughter and applause appeared to indicate no more than that someone had said or done something fairly sharp. The young man, followed by the others of his set, stalked angrily from the room.

"That was well done, sir," said an eminent-looking man in his mid-fifties when John and Walter had returned with the punch for the ladies. He introduced himself as John Fielden of Dawson Weir. Stevenson eagerly presented Walter and the two ladies. This was exactly the sort of luck he had hoped for. Fielden was not only the biggest employer in the district, he was also Member of Parliament for Rochdale. To be in with Fielden was to be *in*. Also his brother or cousin, Thomas, was a director of the Manchester & Leeds.

"You're not 'Better Combination' Stevenson?" Fielden said.

"Is that what they're saying?" John laughed.

"Oh, it's the talk of Manchester. And seeing you handle those young rips, I now believe every word. You know who that was, I suppose?"

"I've never seen him in my life."

"Young Dicky Redmayne, our host's son!" He laughed at the shock and dismay in John's face. "I shouldn't worry. His father will thank you. Dick's a thorn in his flesh."

John and Fielden talked for the best part of an hour—about labour, unions, despotism, unrest, progress in the north and the possible eclipse of London by the new money-making centres that reach from Liverpool through Manchester to Leeds and Hull; they talked of people—of Hudson the Railway King, as folk were beginning to call him; of Prendergast; of Brunel, whose *Great Britain* had that year crossed the Atlantic; of Frost, the Chartist who led the Newport riot; of Metcalfe and the local Chartists; and of the local millowners, whose heartless exploitation of their workers contrasted so strongly with Fielden's and Stevenson's practice as masters. And then, looking at his watch, and saying he had intended merely to cry in for a few minutes, Fielden took his leave, saying that they must meet again.

It was a good start; for so busy and important a man as Fielden to spare John a whole hour on this festive evening was an achievement that would not go unmarked and unreported. But that, too, was a worry. What would Prendergast do when the news reached his ears? Prendergast could have helped him much more than he had. His failure to do so could only be explained away as a kind of caution—waiting to see how Stevenson performed. If it now turned out that Stevenson was openly reaching above Prendergast's head, the cleric might start presenting one or two bills. It was time to consider whether or not to advance his visit to London, to Bolitho & Chambers, despite the dangers of such a course.

John went back to the large hall in search of the others, who had left him and Fielden fairly early. He found Nora standing watching Walter and Arabella dancing the quadrille. "Come on!" she said as soon as she saw him.

"Can you?" he asked as they took the floor.

"I can do the lancers and it's very like," she said. "Arabella taught me. And that young ensign's taught me the waltz except the band can't do three-four, they keep getting into six-eight."

"You *have* been busy!"

They started to dance and Nora showed no hesitation.

"I've learned a lot," she said, her eyes shining.

"So have I," he told her, and threw himself wholeheartedly into the fun.

Later there were games, mainly for the younger people—fool plough, hoodman blind, hot cockles, steal the loaf, and shoe the wild mare. The youngsters, too, made good use of the mistletoe bough—as did Walter, though, by the time he had plucked enough courage to include Nora, the last of the berries had been picked and he had to hop around the room on one foot by way of forfeit.

Then Uncle Redmayne, remembering John's singing of "Christmas Is Come" out in the entrance hall, asked him to sing it for the company. John took little persuading and his mellow baritone stilled the entire room as he sang:

> "Now Christmas is come
> Let us beat on the drum
> And draw all the neighbours together.
> And when they are here
> Let us all make such cheer
> As will drive off the wind and the weather . . ."

And so on, through the half-dozen verses. Nora was, of course, as proud of him as a hen with one chick.

The band claimed they were "blowed and scraped dry" and left their little stand. But the entertainment continued. One of the daughters of the house recited Southey's "Holly Tree," whose uplifting final stanzas, comparing the holly's modesty to the speaker's own virtuous ambitions, came oddly from one whose behaviour had, only moments earlier, been so wildly hoydenish.

Then the young ensign recited Thomas Campbell's "Men of England." Not a Whig heart there that did not beat a little faster; nor a Whig head that was not held a little higher as that stirring panegyric to English liberty unfolded. . . . The cheers were so great that he had to repeat it before they would let him go. Then another young man recited Wordsworth's "A Perfect Woman," not so much to the company as *at* one of the young girls.

"Say, he's going it a bit," Walter muttered when the man reached the line about "steps of virgin liberty." The girl clearly thought so too, to judge by the way she turned from the man and stood presenting him with the shoulder farthest from the fire.

The company, wanting more of this sort of fun, cheered him even more tumultuously than they had the ensign; but the young man, being something of an opportunist—"apprenticed to a Rochdale solicitor," a neighbour told John—and having noticed how well the ensign's patriotic jingle had done, capped it with Cowper's "Boadicea."

The oracular promise of the druids to the doomed British queen—that the Roman Empire would crumble and that a greater British one would arise—stirred everyone there. And the final insult, hurled proudly from her dying lips at the advancing Romans . . .

> Ruffians, pitiless as proud,
>   Heaven awards the vengeance due;
> Empire is on us bestowed,
>   Shame and ruin wait for you.

. . . was for most of them the climax of the evening, despite the many pretty, comic, and tragic recitations that followed.

Looking at the glow of pride that lighted up the eyes of every listener—especially of the young folk—Nora became aware of the existence of an England she had never known: an England of the spirit. England to her had been a motley collection of houses, streets, mills, fields, highways, and hills, a place that stretched beyond sight and ken. But here, to these young people, growing in an age of boundless progress and opportunity, it was something so much grander—an idea, an ideal. And as that ideal seized her, she filled with this pride she had never sensed before, feeling a new kinship with all the unknown people of Kent and Cornwall and Dorset and Oxford, and all the places that until now had been, quite simply, "foreign parts."

To be English was something stupendous; but even more it was to be *young* in England at such a time and to know that as one grew, England's greatness would grow in step. She wished that someone else would speak more patriotic verse; and she was obviously not alone in this desire, for when the band returned, the first song that everyone demanded, once someone had suggested it, was "Rule Britannia."

Unfortunately she did not know the words, but those of the second verse . . .

> The nations not so blest as thee
>   Must in their turn to tyrants fall,
> Whilst thou shalt flourish great and free,
>   The dread and envy of them all.

. . . so moved her that she would have been unable to continue even if she had.

When the last stirring strains of the chorus died away, Sweeney came deferentially in to say that the car driver was now waiting and had three other calls to make, so if they didn't go with him now they'd be past midnight for getting home.

As they took their leave, Redmayne coldly thanked John for his adroit coupling of tact and manliness in dealing with young Dicky.

Walter, remembering Bess and still, despite Nora's interference, eager for adroit coupling of a different sort, led the way out—into a world dismayingly bathed in brilliant moonshine.

"I think it's snowed," Arabella said. But the powdering was so thin they had a job deciding whether it really was snow or just a trick of the moonlight. Walter found himself seated between John and Arabella, forced almost knee to knee and eye to eye with little Bess, who did not once turn her eyes to his. He comforted himself with the thought that at least there'd be no unseemly scrabbling in frostbitten outhouses tonight. And there was always Arabella. . . .

Arabella lay in bed, later that night, listening to the way Walter washed and shed his clothes. She had become especially tuned to these things—his breathing, his pauses, his scratching, even the way he folded his inexpressibles—and she knew that tonight he was going to assert his rights on her. It did not weary or depress her; she was now past all that. Much as one might look out on a gray day and, seeing an approaching shower, say, "I hope it will soon be over," without meaning it deeply or even thinking much more about it, she heard these telltale sounds and automatically thought, *I hope it'll soon be over.* At least Walter no longer seemed to want any active response from her; in fact, quite the reverse, for if she so much as moved to get in a more comfortable position or just responded to one of his passionate kisses—and he *knew* she had no objection to kissing, in moderation—or if she even breathed noticeably, he would stop in annoyance, just as he would if she interrupted with a question when he read to her from the papers. He would stop and freeze, as if gathering together something she had shattered, and then, often with a heavy sigh, would begin again.

She lay supine, seeking a position that would have to remain comfortable for ten or fifteen minutes, and waited.

Walter, having tried in the months past to provoke a response from Arabella, with steadily diminishing success, had accommodated himself to her indifference in the only way possible: He had made it part of the act. Indeed, he had made it the *point* of the act. The moment the light was blown out he lay still beside her and imagined a scene in which a beautiful, and outwardly healthy, young girl was despaired of by doctor, nurse, father, mother, and quite often, for good measure, by a faithful dog, too. The girl expired—she was never Arabella, of course, but was blond, auburn, honey gold, red, russet, brown, black . . . everything by turns, and anything from a well-developed fourteen to a sweet sixteen years old. One by one her tearful family and attendants left and then he, concealed nearby throughout these touching scenes of bereavement and farewell, would emerge, steal across the room to lock the door, and walk luxuriously back to the bed; every step of the way he savoured the uninterrupted and unprotested intimacies that were about to ensue.

Slowly, tenderly, gloatingly he would lay aside the sheet that shrouded her glorious, still warm body, raise the nightdress in which she had just expired, and explore every virgin, unprotesting inch, with hands, with fingers, with fingertips, with fingernails, with eyes, with lips, with tongue, with teeth, with breath. He would twine her arms in great silken ropes and hang her from the tester of the bed . . . drape her over furniture . . . put her kneeling . . . arch her backwards . . . impale her on his tree of life and waltz her into his delirium. . . . And then, then, taking her to the bed, he would lay her on her back—and this was the moment when Arabella entered the drama, and he, her.

It was not very satisfactory. He knew that. It was squeezing out the best of a dull show. But tonight Arabella spoiled it for him. He had barely begun when she coughed and whispered, "I hate to interrupt you, dearest, but can you not be a little calmer about it? I'm sure the Stevensons next door can hear every one of your grunts and cries."

"Not the night for it, eh?" he said good-naturedly and, pulling away, kissed her and seemingly fell at once into a soundless sleep. To him the sacrifice was small compared with any loss of her affection and goodwill.

About five minutes earlier Nora had nudged John, then just getting into bed, and said: "You'll never believe it—listen!" They did; and there was no mistaking the noise. "Talk about 'born with a horn'!" John said.

She slipped her hand out from under the sheets to lift his shirt. "Here?" he said.

"If you're quick, they'll never know."

He pulled a face. "Let's save it. Night after next we'll be alone at Rough Stones. Save it, eh?"

"Oh, you poor old fellow!" she said.

Which was how she got her way with him.

Fully two hours later, Arabella turned in her sleep and fitfully woke. Next morning she was no longer sure that she had not dreamed it. For, in that half-waking state, she could have sworn she saw Walter sleeping against the wall.

What she had not seen was the tumbler that he pressed—indeed almost mashed—between his ear and the wall. Nor did she see the excitement in his eye. For, through the agency of that empty glass, he could magnify every idle breath into a passionate flutter, every chance creak of the bed-frame into a four-quarters thrust, and every sleeping sigh into a moan of ecstasy.

And there, alone, in the chill of his bedroom, in that sleeping house, in the small hours of a Christmas morning, while fine drifts of snow fell all around, Walter lent his lonely ear to his illusions and finished, alone, the solo drama Arabella had let him start alone.

Two days later, the first chance he got, he took the train to Manchester to report the splendid progress out at Summit. After lunch he went to one of the big-number houses over in Salford, chose their most innocent-looking little bobtail, and took her upstairs.

"What do you usually ask, Polly?" he inquired.

"A pound, sir, for I curtail nothing." She smiled.

"Well, listen, sweet, here's what I want. I want you to make me feel you're my bride. A young virgin, you see—yet eager once she gets warmed to it. A young bride."

Polly nodded brightly, but he knew she would have made the same response whatever he had asked.

"You do that—make me believe it—and there's *two* pounds for you. Pretend this is the first night of our honeymoon. Remember—be chaste. Be modest."

Again she flashed that eager, uncomprehending smile-of-all-nations at him.

But though her greed was great, her wit would not stretch; her idea of chastity was to be slowly—instead of quickly—lascivious and then to burst into a most unconvincing whimper the moment his shots fell between wind and water.

In fact the charade was not as grisly as he had at first feared. Her acting was so atrocious that there was something quite appealing, indeed stimulating, about it. He even toyed briefly with the notion of returning regularly and subjecting her to increasingly impossible demands—read her the story of Dante and Beatrice and get her to play Beatrice while he had her—or she could do the balcony scene from Romeo and Juliet. . . .

Even she knew how bad she'd been, and was pleased enough with the extra three bob he gave her—"for trying your best," as he said with that nice little smile of his; he was quite a nice young fellow, really.

On the train home he looked out at the snowclad but already sullied landscape and decided it hadn't been such a bad year, all things considered. Thank God he had Stevenson in charge at Summit, and doing it so well there was no problem keeping inside the budget. If it finished on time and within the negotiated price, he'd become an engineer to note. And that couldn't be bad.

Arabella must surely start to carry soon, and that would relieve him of the depressing sense of waste that assailed him every time he went to sleep beside her without first having used her. Apart, of course, from the positive side—the joys of being a father, and so on.

And his rise in salary would make it easier to slip away to Manchester two or three times a week. You could get quite a good girl for less than five bob.

All in all it was a good year, a good beginning. Things were getting sorted out and settled down, everything in its proper compartment.

# *Chapter 33*

After the excitements of the Hall the previous evening, Christmas Day passed very quietly. Nora wore her new day dress, an afternoonified version of the modest costumes she habitually wore. For it she laced in to only twenty-three inches and put on two fewer petticoats. It was a full-skirted dress in tartan wool—dark green and blue with fine red and yellow lines. She wore the bodice open over a sleeved chemisette buttoned up to the base of her neck. The frills at the neckline fell in such a way as to make her shoulders seem weaker and more sloping than they really were—an effect enhanced by the broad, frilly bands of braid that trimmed the bodice and skirt en tablier.

Arabella wore the dress in which she went away from her wedding breakfast, with the addition of a flounce at knee height and some new trimming to suggest—falsely—that it opened down the front.

Except for their more sober shirts and more everyday shoes, the men had on the same costumes they had worn the previous evening.

After a light breakfast of porridge, ham, herrings in oatmeal, baked rolls, and Christmas ale they set off on an invigorating walk of a mile or so, around Dobroyd Hill and above the new railway station, to Christ Church.

Several inches of snow had fallen overnight and the two girls had to hold their skirts slightly lifted at the front to avoid ploughing it into ridges that would have buckled their skirts and petticoats under them and sent them tumbling. With all the factories silent and only the faintest whisps of smoke ascending from the banked-down fires, the Vale of Todmorden had returned to its ancient rural calm. A light breeze carried away the sulphurous outpouring of several hundred domestic chimneys before it could blot out the opposite hills; occasionally it would waft to them the ghostly bleat of sheep that were no more than dark specks on the distant moorland.

Low cloud drifted above them, dark enough in places to threaten more snow. But far away, over toward Oldham and Manchester, hung a brighter light that might have been sunshine. The soot and smoke from those distant chimneys lent a murky amber tone to the clouds now overhead, for everyone who could afford a Christmas dinner (and many who could not) would be cooking it at that moment. The yellowed light that scattered through this canopy seemed to muffle sound as well as sight and to make the Vale close in upon itself, becoming at once more remote and intimate.

Arabella expressed the hope that Todmorden would soon grow enough to force them to reopen St. Mary's, the old church, near the Hall. Christ Church was well enough but there was a world of difference between worshipping in a new building and one that was centuries old.

For Nora, Sunday worship was like washing—an act whose necessity it would be foolish to deny but one worth little comment or notice. She could remember back eleven years to when her father had gone with other Methodist levellers to the Wesleyan chapel up at Brunswick in Leeds, near the cattle market, to riot against the new organ the trustees had put in, but the enthusiasm behind such acts remained incomprehensible to her. Just as there were those who would argue the merits of washing the skin in hard water and soft water, so there were those who got excited over the merits of high, low, moderate, primitive, evangelical, New Connexion, and all the other one, true, and only churches; all such enthusiasts were far beyond her understanding. For her, water was water and if it was at least moderately pure, you could wash in it; and churches were churches and if they were at least moderately respectable, you could worship in them. Nevertheless, she found the Right Honourable and Reverend Mouncey's sermon tedious—a long, private ramble through Christmas customs back to the days of the druids, with a heated little tirade against the Puritan levellers to enliven its most barren stretch. Walter was fairly certain that it was the first draft—or even the finished draft—of a paper for some antiquarian journal.

When they returned to Pigs Hill, they exchanged their presents. Walter gave Arabella a pair of wrought-iron five-light candelabra, cunningly worked to look like roses growing up a narrow, ruined classical column; and she gave him a japanned iron coalbox, equally ornate.

Nora shyly produced a little present she had bought for the Thorntons and was alarmed to see Arabella's face fall. "But I have nothing in return for *you*," she said. "It is not the custom, you know, outside the family."

But Nora, warmly squeezing Arabella's arm, reassured her. "You have already given. The most wonderful present. This Christmas with you . . . sharing your home . . . your invitation to the Hall. . . ."

"Yes," John added, "it's just a little trinket to express our thanks in more lasting form."

The "little trinket," a white porcelain cameo, of a pretty maid in profile encrusted in a blob of clear glass, was, Arabella said, "just what we have always needed."

"I chose it because the girl looks so like Arabella, you see," Nora said, as she pushed it toward Walter. "It'll make a paperweight."

Nora's present to John was the special riding crop she had commissioned. At the top of its silver knob *John Stevenson Christmas 1839* was engraved in a circle around the image of a train wheel. The side had low-relief representations of the south and north portals of Summit Tunnel as they would appear when finished; she had had to take Jack Whitaker into the secret so that he could sneak out copies of the final designs. The tunnel between them was, of course, the channel for the wrist thong. The lower border was finished with a formal, repeated motif of crossed picks, shovels, and boring bars. Everyone was impressed by the ingenuity and realism of the design, and John, who had had no idea that anything of this kind was in the offing, was delighted.

"That'll be something I'll never tire of," he said. "My two little things are very dull after this."

His presents were in a parcel labelled *Nora—To Ease Rough Stones*. She opened it with trembling fingers and found the two things she wanted most. One she already knew she wanted—her own copy of *Cottage Economy;* but she had not known that John was even aware of her interest in it. The other was something she would never have thought of in a lifetime—a telescope. But as soon as her mind's eye pictured the view from the upstairs windows of Rough Stones, looking down the steep hillside to the workings, and the men just too far away to be easily identifiable, she knew it was *exactly* what she would have asked for if she'd had the wit.

"You couldn't have done better," she told John.

And Walter and Arabella agreed they were a wonderful set of

presents; though later, privately, they reached a different conclusion. Nora's was very good; but what would Stevenson give her next year, Arabella wondered—"a ready reckoner and a set of survey instruments?"

John and Nora, too, privately agreed that the Thorntons were a rum couple when it came to present giving. "I suppose next time," John said, "he'll give her the dog cart and she'll give him the wheels!"

Nora wondered how Tommy had liked his little whistle and the plume of hearse feathers.

In the evening, after family prayers, they played whist, in which John and Nora finished up three mother-of-pearl buttons, a domino, and two draughts poorer.

Later, when she and John lay in bed, with the moonshine spilling upward into the room off the fresh snow, Nora listened to the faint grinding of his molars and leaned across to put an arm around him. "Never fret," she said. "You'll see the tunnel again tomorrow and be back at work the day after."

He snorted a gentle laugh. "Plain as that, is it?"

"You're twitching like the devil in a gale of wind. You must in some way learn to ease yourself from work."

"That I'll never do," he said. He spoke not challengingly nor with pride but with a weary resignation.

"I know," she said soothingly. "I know. It's the same with me. There's not ten minutes in any day, taken at haphazard, when I've not had me mind dwell on us and our affairs."

"Aye." He tapped her arm with a fingertip. "Are you all set now for starting with the tommy shop?"

"Yes," she said, a little surprised at his sudden change of subject.

"When you said you knew where to get a good price, was it Charley Eade ye had in mind—him who tried to kill you?"

"Yes." She felt him shake his head. "What?" she asked. "Why?"

"I hope our bairns get their courage from thee—whatever they may take from me. . . ."

"Strength, goodness of heart, cunning . . ." she began.

He chuckled. "I think I may set all three of those at your service when we face Charley Eade this Friday, day after tomorrow. If there's a produce mart."

No question of hers could wring more from him than that.

The following morning she found herself ready so quickly that there was a full hour to spare before breakfast, so, eating a bit of cold plum pudding from yesterday and washing it down with a cup of beer, she left John to his shaving and went out for a walk. She followed the path they had taken to church the day before.

The temperature had moderated and now stood only a degree or two below freezing, so the snow no longer blew in a light powder but packed crisp and firm underfoot. A few light clouds hung almost motionless in an ultramarine sky, and the pale sun of an early winter's morn stood a finger above Turley Holes Edge, high over the town, which still slumbered in a deep blue lake of shadow. It was the sort of day that filled you with a zest for life.

She had walked more than a mile, right around to the north side of the hill, and, not wanting to go on into its shade, was about to return when she heard a sound to kindle ecstasy and electrify every nerve—the winding of a huntsman's horn. He was playing the recheat, three strokes and a blast, to gather straying hounds. The sound carried clear up the valley through the frosty air and turned her eyes unerringly upon a stretch of parkland opposite, landscaped around a large country house with a stone-columned portico. Though it was almost half a mile away, she could just discern the master and the huntsman among the two dozen riders at the meet. The pack was a russet swarm that spilled restlessly this way and that upon the snow.

With every fibre of her being she yearned to be among them. And when at last the moment came for them to turn, and the huntsman blew the single blast for move to covert, she actually took three steps in their direction before she realized the futility of it and danced on the spot in her vexation. They were headed north, too, away from Todmorden, away up to Stansfield Moors. She could have cried with frustration.

"Eh oop, lass! Thou'll bust a vessel."

It was John's voice. She turned, like a child caught stealing apples. He came to where she stood and sought whatever it was that angered her so.

"Todmorden Hare Hounds?" he asked incredulously.

"I don't care what they hunt—hares, stags, otters, foxes—I'd give . . ." She was going to say *everything* but she was too practical for that— ". . . a lot, I'd give a lot, to be there."

"Can you ride? Horseback?"

"Never mind that—I'd find a way."

"No, but can you?"

She lowered her eyes. "I mean to learn. If ye had to run to the moon and back to qualify, I'd do it. Did you mean it about getting a horse? I've been feared to ask."

He laughed. "Every word!"

But she bridled, for she thought he was simply patronizing her. "I'm not jesting. You think of yon Thornton with his Irish toothache—well, that's me with any sort of hunting. It's my blood. I can't help it."

He took her arm and turned her for home. "I'll not stand in your path," he assured her. "There's no sense making money if ye can't do the one thing you want."

When they came to the point where the northern arm of the valley would pass from view, she stopped and turned for one last look. And he, watching her eyes seek and scan for the pack and its followers, recognized again the burning girl who had walked down from the wasted rabbit warren last August and entered and filled his life.

Lime trees raised their bare boughs on either side of the lane, arching overhead to mingle with one an ther. The sun, now higher in the sky— high enough for it to begin to feel warm—struck among the trees, laying sharp blue shadows on the untouched snow.

Nora, turning from the view of the hunt, breathed a deep sigh of repletion and, looking up among the branches and along the vaulted canopy they stretched overhead, said: "Eh! It's like an open cathedral here. I fancy hunting'd be my best way to worship the Almighty. If worship is an exaltation, as the ministers all say, that's my worship."

He sniffed. "Make an interesting new church. The Connexion of Sabbath Hunters . . . the True Church of the Lord's Day Chase. . . . You'd get half England joining you!"

But she did not laugh. And when he squeezed her arm and said "Eh?" all she would answer was: "I hope you don't think that's funny."

"Dear God!" he complained. "I hope you don't think me serious."

She laughed a little then, but only a little.

After lunch they all four went down to Gawks Holm to take the regular two o'clock stage operated by Outhwaite & Co. between Leeds and Manchester. They descended at Calderbrook but they still had to pay the full-stage fare from Todmorden to Littleborough, which annoyed Nora, even though, as John pointed out, it was less than half the price of hiring the car again. He and Walter had to ride outside. When they got off at Calderbrook bridge a gentleman, walking toward Littleborough, blessed his luck and took one of their outside seats. Nora, seeing this, shouted to him that the seat was paid for to Littleborough and he was welcome to it and was to make sure they only charged him from Littleborough onward. The man smiled gallantly and tipped his hat and several of the other passengers laughed. The driver glowered at her but waited until he set off before he cared—or dared—to shout that tickets were not transferable.

"It's their way of charging," John chided.

"An excellent trick," she said grimly. "We must learn it."

He wondered what was troubling her. Was she still feeling frustrated by the memory of the hunt? Or was it nervousness at taking the Thorntons up to Rough Stones now?

They had to walk south for a furlong or so before they came to a place where the ladies could easily reach the track. This was just south of Meg's palace, so Nora was, in effect, tracing in reverse her first stroll along this way with Lord John. On the fairly level ground behind the palace most of its inhabitants were playing a game of football with occupants of the huts and smaller shanties up the line. It was the usual hundred-in-one-team-ten-in-the-other sort of game where dogs and children changed sides quicker than generals in a civil war and where no referee spoiled the play.

In front of the palace a few nonsporting navvies sat sunning themselves. Most were asleep, but two were reading—one of them being Pengilly, who scratched his stump incessantly and mechanically. Verminous bedding and workclothes, partially laundered, festooned every bush and hedge or hung draped from lengths of perished winding rope good for no stronger purpose.

Pengilly and the other reader, a navvy called George Hartley, known as Letterman since he had taught himself to write as well as read, stood up as soon as they saw the party approach. John, seeing Pengilly, hesitated in whatever he had been going to say. So much so that Walter eventually had to ask what the trouble was.

"I wanted two men to light us, but . . ." He pointed to Pengilly's leg.

"Wake one of the others," Walter suggested.

But Pengilly, hearing this, volunteered himself. "I aren't no damn cripple," he said angrily, making Walter tell him quite sharply to control his tongue.

"Two shilling each to see us through," John offered.

It seemed an outrageous fee to the other three but they all kept their counsel. And to be sure, Pengilly and Letterman were delighted to oblige. All six set off up the line, walking on the continuous stone tie under each rail, Walter and Arabella, followed by John and Nora, followed by the two navvies.

"It seems more huts and shanties here than last summer," Nora said.

"Lots more," John answered. "Wintertime. They've all come down off the tops."

Indeed it seemed that every level inch beside the line was occupied by a shack, turf hut, or some other kind of temporary structure. Their sole purpose was to provide shelter to hard-working men after a twelve-hour day; when, as now, they had to serve, too, for the recreation of those men and their families, their woeful inadequacy was apparent even to the least discerning eye. Arabella, looking out over this squalor from the vantage of the embarkment, hoped Stevenson would not start again with his suggestions that she should undertake some kind of work among these unfortunate creatures.

In any case, it was stretching things to call them unfortunate; they were paid double the wage of the best of the labourers she knew in her father's parish. If they chose to live in this way, it was an interference in their liberty to try to force them to better themselves. One had a duty to assist those in sin, to bring them back into God's grace; but to live in squalor was no actual sin—however much sin it might cause or lead to. And one's duty to alleviate poverty did not extend to harrying and interfering with those who, though far from destitute, chose to live like the lowest of the low. At heart she wanted a world like the one she had grown up in, where every labourer had his hovel, where the deserving poor were known from the wretches whose poverty was self-inflicted, where charity could tread a regular and orderly weekly course. The idea of working like some kind of missionary in this shiftless, squalid world they were now walking through was revolting to her soul.

She turned and saw Stevenson's eyes fixed upon her with that dreadful sardonic gaze, and she had to ask Walter to explain some detail about the track's construction to mask her disquiet.

The arch of the southern portal was almost complete, with only the keystone and a few of its neighbours still to be inserted. Around it the design provided for radiating fins of dressed stone, capped by two massive rounded ledges. When complete it would all appear to be carved from the living rock, which reared in a conical peak a hundred feet or so above the tunnel mouth.

Arabella, gazing into that black hole, gave an involuntary shudder. "It looks so dark," she said.

"Your eyes soon grow accustomed to it," Nora reassured her.

"Why—have *you* been in there?" Arabella asked, startled, for she remembered the brusque way she had been refused entry on her first visit to the workings.

Walter described the drama of that day to her, turning several times to Pengilly for confirmation.

"We'll see if I can even recognize the place now," Nora said. "It was nothing like so brave as Mr. Thornton claims. All danger was past by the time I went into the working."

"Will they not object now to our entry?" Arabella asked.

"Not now the drift is finished. From this moment forth it's Summit Tunnel to us, not Summit drift."

Nora had made two burnooses of a coarse woolen waterproof cloth lined with cotton for Arabella and herself to wear during the tour. These, together with the two torches, were stored in the linesman's hut at the mouth of the tunnel. They tied the garments on while the men got the torches well alight. Then, with Letterman ten paces ahead and Pengilly stumping ten behind, they entered the drift. The curves at each end made it impossible to see daylight through the length.

The first section, already completed and lined with brick to the full twenty-six-foot diameter when Nora had last come this way, was much as she had remembered it, though now it ran considerably farther in.

"We're more advanced this end because gravity has done most of our work for us," Walter explained.

They were well round the entry curve, and almost beyond the reach of daylight, when John stopped.

"What is it?" Walter asked.

"Do you not recognize it?"

Nora saw that he was asking her. She looked around. But it was tunnel very much like all the rest they had walked through. "Was it here?" she asked.

"Aye."

"How can you possibly tell?" Walter laughed.

John walked to the side wall on their left and pointed to an X scratched in one of the bricks. "That marks the transverse centreline of the blind number one shaft above us here."

"So—the rails ended here," Nora said. "The powder barrels were over there and some burned timber. And, Pengilly, you were"—she walked to a point a little to the left of the midline—"here, I think."

"No," John said, walking to a point only two feet away from her. "It was here."

They all laughed at his pedantry. Pengilly came forward to the point John had marked, looked at it, looked at the roof, from where the overburden had fallen and crushed his foot, and then, to the surprise of all, threw back his head and roared with laughter.

A few chains farther and they came to the long straight run—over twenty-five hundred yards. Here the scaffolding for the bricklayers was still in place and the brick courses were only partially complete. Walter demonstrated how they married each lining ring of brick with its counterpart in the brick invert. "Where we have a brick invert, which is about eighteen hundred yards all together, we build it immediately behind the advancing face of the drift, so that we can lay this track for carrying out the muck. Where we leave the living stone as a natural invert, it's three feet, almost three feet, above this. Later, we can confine the ballast below the road in sections, where we expose the rings of the brick invert and marry the tunnel rings to them."

"Oh yes?" Arabella said.

"Letterman," John called, "come behind a moment. You and Pengilly go back a bit. Let it get dark here."

Arabella looked inquiringly at Nora, who shrugged back her own incomprehension.

"What's this?" Walter asked.

"You'll see," John said. "I hope."

When the two torches were far enough away he turned to face up the tunnel and said "Look!" They strained their eyes and then saw what he meant as gradually, one after another, the faint pools of light that fell down the ventilation shafts came just within the limits of visibility. The dark around was so intense that the first glimmer, from the nearest shaft, had no anchorage and seemed to float away, the merest ghost of a gleam, as their eyes strained to hold it. Then came their gasps of wonder and delight as the next pool came, as if by magic, into view, then the next, then the next, in slow succession. By the time the most distant one hovered on the threshold, the nearest pool was almost bright; the gradation between them stretched the perspective to a depth that seemed infinite. It was an infinite line of pale to darkest grey, aimed at them—at each one of them—lost in an infinity of blackest black.

Walter was the first to speak, and in a voice almost as faint as the light. "I would never have imagined it," he said. "Never. When did you first notice it?"

"The same time as you," John answered. "I wasn't sure . . . I thought with almost two days and no working, it might have cleared enough. . . ."

"Do you mean . . ." Arabella began but was unable to frame the question.

"We may . . .," Walter said, not struck with the full meaning of his words until he actually spoke them, "we may be the first people—the first people *ever,* d'you realize that, *ever,* ever to see such a sight."

Sobered still further by the thought they looked back, but the increasing adaptation of their vision was now revealing facets of the rock face, and the drift itself was growing visible. That eerie floating of grey phantoms in a void was gone.

"Why?" Nora asked. "Why d'you say the first?"

"Well," John said, "where is there another . . . where has there ever *been* another drift eight foot wide and more than a mile long, with ten shafts in a dead straight line, only a hundred to three hundred odd feet below ground? And one where people walk in the dark, with the air clear from two days' idleness . . . the chances against all that are so enormous,

I'd say Thornton's almost certainly correct. No one's ever seen that before."

"Well!" Walter stirred them all back to life. "It's gone now. The effect. For me, anyway. I must say that is a sight I shall remember for a long time. A very long time."

"A sight?" Arabella said more gently, as if to compensate for his rumbumptiousness. "A vision."

"Yes," Nora whispered, still treasuring it.

"Righty-oh Pengilly, Letterman!" John called.

And when they brought their torches into view again the light was painful. But at least now they could see every detail as they passed.

"Did you really imagine *that,* before we entered?" Walter asked John.

"Something like it—I had no idea it would be so beautiful."

Walter shook his head. "That's a faculty I envy. To imagine how things might seem in unknown conditions."

"No great art, surely," John scoffed.

"I don't know about art, but I say it could save you thousands of pounds in the years ahead."

And Nora, proudly listening, thought there were times when Thornton's mind showed real flashes of insight.

And Arabella, listening too, and remembering a time when that very faculty had led Stevenson into error, wondered whether or not to point out that even the best and sharpest faculties without divine and moral guidance are a snare and a delusion; she thought better of it and decided to find or make some quiet occasion in which to remind Mr. Stevenson of it privately.

Although both men had started by explaining every detail of the drift to the ladies in the most considerate way, it was not long before they vanished, in spirit at least, into their own technical world. After all, this was the first time both of them had walked every foot of the drift, from portal to portal. Behind them Nora and Arabella picked what crumbs they could and walked as if through a foreign museum of the underworld.

"Look!" John would say. "We had thought of five rings of brick here. This is the seven-sixty-eight-yard mark. But having taken—"

"Wait!" Walter would protest, laughingly. "Are you counting each yard?"

"No. But that formation there, where the cracks make the shape of a giraffe—that is the seven-hundred-seventy-yard mark."

"How do you know?"

"I know the wall patterns at ten-yard intervals throughout the drift. As I was saying—having taken a closer look, I think we want to begin the six-ring course here . . ."

And so on. In the end, Nora and Arabella had to remind them that *tomorrow* was the next true working day. Thornton ruefully agreed with Stevenson that the provisional specification for the rings would need revising all the length of the drift, in the light of the experience gained on bricking the southern curve. And, to avoid any imputation that Stevenson, who was already clear in his own mind what was needed, had unduly influenced the engineer, Thornton would make his own survey independently and the two would compare notes on New Year's Day.

By this time they were approaching number seven, the deepest shaft of all. John, who had hurried them past the other shafts, now made them halt. "And you two, Pengilly and Letterman, rest those lights over there and come and see this, too."

When Pengilly was close, John said to him: "This is thy shaft, lad. Thou hast never seen it from the bottom, I'll warrant."

"I haven't neither, that's a fact," Pengilly said.

"Look!" Arabella cried. "A star! I can see a star!"

"Oh yes!" Nora was equally excited. "So can I! Look, dear! Two stars."

And their enthusiasm was so warm that the men, though they had seen the effect often enough before, pretended to share the discovery, admiring the two stars of whatever constellation happened to be in a position at that time to shine directly down the shaft.

"But they are moving," Nora said. "They must be shooting stars."

"That is the motion of the earth," John told her. And the idea made her so giddy that she automatically reached out for his support.

Despite this and the earlier vision, their dusty, uncomfortable walk—so long anticipated, so soon over—was a disappointment for Nora and Arabella. Each yard of rock had spoken volumes to John and Walter; yet, try as she might, neither wife could see anything other than long torchlight vistas of rough, dull, grey rock, interrupted here and there by stretches of timber shoring and of brick—for two thousand eight hundred and eighty-five yards. Both privately concluded that any ten yards of drift, taken at haphazard, was very much like any other ten yards of drift. Their relief as they negotiated the final curve, leading to the oval shaft and out into Deanroyd cutting, was almost palpable. Only two men so totally absorbed in their vocation as John and Walter could have failed to notice it.

Before they left the railroad, John paid off the two men, who set off at once into the tunnel, the way they had just come, both delighted. They took the two protective burnooses with them.

"Easiest money they've ever earned," Walter said.

But John let his words die and then told the other three, all of them still looking at the north portal: "We four have just walked down the centre line of what, this day twelvemonth, will be the longest man-made tunnel in the modern world—and the ancient world, too, for all I know."

"Aren't there canal tunnels longer?" Arabella asked.

"Moleholes!" John said contemptuously. "Look at that! *That* is a tunnel. And this man here and me will have built it."

"*Si monumentum requiris* . . ." Walter began.

But John clapped him on the back and cried, "No! I don't want it to be one tunnel; not just one tunnel. I want folk to stand in the middle of *England* and say that!"

And the impudence, the hubris, of his words took Walter's breath away. But Arabella, thinking he must be joking, merely laughed.

Then they all went up to the turnpike.

"This is the first time we've had snow here since the day of the strike," Walter said, and he looked around as if he still expected to see some trace of that day's events.

"How is young Tommy coming along?" Arabella asked.

"Oh!" Nora cried, suddenly remembering the wrapping in which Tommy had sealed his drawings for her. "Look!" She dug the paper from the bottom of her pocketbook. "He made me a drawing of those quaint silver coins for a present, but see what he wrapped it in."

They all read the address and laughed. " 'Lancashere, *near* Yorkshere'! I like that very much," John said. "He's not so daft, that Tommy."

"He's not daft at all," Nora said.

At that moment, as they were about to take the lane up to Rough Stones, they heard a sound that made them turn and stare at one another in open bewilderment. Arabella's face was the first to light in recognition, quickly followed by John's and Walter's.

"She's back, then," Walter said.

"Who? What is it? Who is back?" Nora looked from one to the other.

"This is what I mentioned," Arabella said. "Lady Henshaw." She turned to the men. "Don't tell her. See if she can guess."

Nora listened. "A circus?"

They laughed. "Better than that," John said.

"It's goats," Nora said next. "If you told me it's a travelling goat slaughterer, I'd believe you."

"You could go the length and breadth of England and not see this," Walter said.

"Oh, what *is* it!" Nora almost screamed, straining her eyes along the road.

"Here it comes," John said.

And around the corner at Stone House came a string of about two dozen goats, black, white, piebald, and one roan sport, bleating, trotting, walking, stumbling, gasping, panting, as they lurched and strained at the traces of a very handsome town chariot. It was the elegant sort of closed carriage one would expect to see drawn by a pair of greys at the very least.

"I don't *believe* it!" Nora laughed.

"A unique sight," Walter agreed. "And so is she."

They watched this extraordinary troupe all the way along the turnpike until it drew level, by which time the noise and the smell were both fairly powerful. The coachman looked fixedly ahead with a disdainful air almost superior enough to compensate for his motley twenty-four-in-hand. The four watchers expected the coach to sweep by in all its bizarre majesty, but a voice from within suddenly shrieked "Stop!" The goats took this as a command to them and came slewing to a halt, leaving the coachman no office other than to apply the brake as fast as he could. The animals nearest the coach flattened themselves to the road, well aware that it could be a second or so before the brake operated. As a result the coach actually slid to rest above at least half of its draft. Near the head of the line a billy mounted a nanny immediately in front of him; he had been trying to get aboard her for most of the journey and his efforts alone must have accounted for half the motion of the vehicle.

This frank little drama helped the four of them to concentrate on the carriage, whose dark interior still concealed its occupant. The postillion leaped down and, poking his head under the back of the coach, began to shout, in a strong Welsh accent: "Out from under there, you wretched little artists! Get out! Come on!"

As he merely spoke to them without attempting to hit or kick, they paid no attention, but continued to sit there, panting, scratching, wagging their ears, and bleating.

As if in obedience to his command a middle-aged lady with a round almost nut-brown face peered out of the open carriage window. "Madoc!" she bawled in a cracked and very unmusical voice.

"My lady?" he said, coming around to where she could see him.

"What are you doing? Who are you talking to?"

He shrugged with weary resignation and pointed lamely at the road under the carriage.

"Who?" she insisted even louder.

"I know you never believe it," he said defensively. "But they've got under there again."

"You're talking rubbish, man."

"Well, listen!" Madoc almost out-bellowed her. "Where d'you think that noise is coming from?"

"You are as confused as ever," she said with all the considerable patrician calm she could muster. "Drunk I shouldn't wonder. Get back on the coach this minute."

He shrugged once more, with the same weariness, and returned to the back of the coach. As a parting shot, before hoisting himself aboard, he stooped and shrieked at the goats, pointing at them with one finger outstretched: "I hope you all get run over!" The goat nearest to him, almost between his legs, tried to bite his finger, but that was the full extent of the attention they paid him.

Hearing him, Lady Henshaw now poked her head out of the window. "Be silent!" she bawled.

He, now seated again, and pulling the coach rug around him, looked heavenward.

"You are dismissed!" she went on. He mouthed the rest of her words, silently, in time with her: "The moment I find someone to replace you. You are dismissed."

The four astonished onlookers had to rearrange their faces very quickly as she turned to them. For one lunatic moment it seemed she was about to offer Madoc's post to them as she peered from one to the other through her lorgnettes.

"You're all too far away," she said. And her voice, after the shrieking she had given the postillion, was so soft and gentle and her smile so warm that they all involuntarily moved toward her.

"Is one of you Mrs. Stevenson?" she asked. "Do put up your hats, thank you, gentlemen."

John quickly stepped forward. "Allow me, my lady. Mrs. Thornton . . . Mrs. Stevenson . . ." The two ladies curtseyed in response to a gracious nod from the carriage window.

"Mr. Walter Thornton, engineer to the Manchester & Leeds, and I am John Stevenson, contractor on that works."

Lady Henshaw's eyes lit up with satisfaction. "I have shares in all of you," she said. But then a sudden doubt invaded her. "You do *eat* properly, I hope," she asked sternly. They nodded their assurance. "Plenty of goat's meat?" she said.

"All we want," John confirmed.

"Can't have too much," she said. "I'll send you some. It's the next best thing to venison, you know." She looked up the line of goats in front of the coach, where the copulating billy was just reaching the deep pelvic thrusts of his extremis. "It's easily come by." She sniffed as she turned back to them.

They stood in various degrees of embarrassment.

"Mrs. Stevenson," she said, "I'd be grateful if you'd call on me. Any day next week."

"Gladly, my lady." Nora curtseyed.

"Benham," Lady Henshaw called to her coachman. "If Monty has finished with Pamela, you may proceed."

They stood in silence, wanting to laugh, yet fearing to be thought indelicate, while the coachman shouted strange oaths, and the goats at the head scrabbled in the snow, and those under the coach crawled, slid, or let themselves be dragged into the open air. At last, by some miracle, they were all brought standing and facing approximately forward—and only two had to be rescued by Madoc from death by strangulation. They took so long to sort out that Monty was beginning to sniff again at the delights of Pamela never more than a foot from his nostrils. But just as he got his beard upon her haunches Benham gave a final explosive "Hapaaaoi!" and the ragged motley jerked its antic way down the turnpike, the bleating and the stench fading quickly on the winter air.

Nora turned to Arabella. "A newcomer to a district should wait until her neighbours have visited her before she attempts to visit them," she quoted.

It gave them a respectable focus for their laughter.

"I resign," Arabella said. "The north of England is a law unto itself!"

# *Chapter 34*

At half past five the following morning Tommy descended from his fiery Arabian steed, sheathed his faithful scimitar, rebottled the genie, and threw handsful of golden coins at a grateful populace, before he reached up for the kitchen door latch at Rough Stones and let himself in. The household was already long awake. The fire burned brightly in the dining room, where, by the light of a single candle, John and Nora were eating their breakfast and going over the day's arrangements.

"Please, ma'am," Bess said when she came in to collect their plates. "Young Tommy's come."

"You can set him to peel the potatoes until I come out," Nora said. And then, turning back to John, added: "And while we're away in Manchester he can clean out the shed down at Deanroyd. For the tommy shop. Will Whitaker be around?"

"Whitaker or Fernley."

"They can see to him. And I'll set him some reading. And some letters to do a hundred of. Keep him out of mischief until his mother comes."

Tommy was overjoyed when, at nine o'clock, he was taken down to spend the rest of the day cleaning and scrubbing and whitewashing "his" store. And Nora, watching the solemn, professional way he set out the cloths and brushes, feeling their bristles and marshalling the soap and pails before he began, yearned to stoop and kiss him farewell, knowing that she and John might not return until after he had gone home again; but she never displayed such tenderness when others were present, so she contented herself with tousling his thick shock of hair. It seemed to embarrass him even more than a kiss would have done. He was a man down here; a man among the other men. He refused to respond, pretending to be more than ever busy with his various bits of cleaning equipment.

The coachman was the same as yesterday's. He was very stiff with them, saying pointedly before he let them board that it would be the *full* fare for the stage. Nora knew that, had she been alone, the man would have driven on by, pretending not to see her.

"I must have been a bit fierce yesterday," she said when they had paid their fare and were safe inside. They were the only inside passengers.

"Slightly."

"It was nerves," she confessed. "The Thorntons, Rough Stones, first day, everything."

"It went very well," John assured her—for the tenth time.

"I think she liked the furniture we've hired."

"More than that," John said, and there was a cautionary note in his voice. "I thought I detected just a faint trace of envy there. She knows that in terms of income we've steamed far ahead of them and will always be so. . . ."

"That or bankrupt." Nora laughed. "Anyway, our move will at least delight his Reverence, the Church of England."

"Yes," John sighed. "His Reverence. For two whole days I had almost forgotten his Reverence."

"What do we do about him?" she asked more seriously.

He shook his head. "Play him on . . . make excuses . . . dare him to bring it all down in ruin about us—not in so many words, to be sure, not an open challenge. I think come March, come April, we may *just* have enough to tempt Mr. Chambers. It's a thin hope, I know . . ."

She said nothing for a long while; it did not have the sound or the feel of a winning strategy. For the first time she glimpsed a real possibility that Prendergast might be driven beyond the borders of his tolerance; wounded vanity might outrun even his monstrous sense of self-interest. For the first time she seriously contemplated the prospect of ruin and jail for them both.

She shivered. "A lot depends on our shop," she said, thinking aloud.

"Aye," he agreed. "If profit on it is good, it might tip the balance up in London. And anyway, it's a good reason to give Prendergast as to why our capital's shrunk and why we've not had time to do the books up to date. That's what I mean. We must play him week by week."

\*     \*     \*

The Wholesale Produce Mart behind St. John's had had one of the busiest mornings of its year, what with the two idle days of Christmas behind it and the weekend to come. Charley Eade was in the middle of a gigantic stretch and a yawn when, through the watering of his eyes, he saw what looked like the girl whose disappearance had plagued his nights and frayed his days until well into the autumn. He shook his head and wiped the yawn-water away; it was a *lady*. But dammit, it was the girl, too! It was that girl . . . Nora!

"Nora!" he said.

"Mrs. Stevenson to you, Charley."

"Oh! Hark at you!" he sneered.

She was as cocky as ever. Well, she'd not escape so easily this time. He looked around. No one with her. Where the hell was that boy? Send him for the Connally brothers. . . .

She stared at him as if she read his every thought.

"You've found some fancy man," he said.

Young Tony came back carrying a pail he had just filled at the pump outside. "Look who's here," Charley said to him, adding out of the side of his mouth: "Get the Connallys."

"Hello, luv," Tony called to her and, grinning as broad as Judas, left to do Charley's bidding.

Nora's continued smile made Charley increasingly uneasy. She picked over the fruit and vegetables that remained on the stall, leaving them in disarray. He fussed after her, straightening out the display. She was doing it deliberately; she knew enough of the business to realize that. Thank God, trade was virtually over for the day; this time he could deal with her properly.

"You're asking for trouble," he said.

"No I'm not, Charley," she told him brightly. "I'm asking for ten percent."

He snorted.

"You still milking Coulter & Co. for six and two-thirds?" she asked in the same light tone.

He laughed in astonishment. "You must be mad," he said. "You . . . this is . . ." His voice tailed off as he saw John join her.

"John," she said. "This is Mr. Charley Eade I've told you so much about."

John nodded; Eade stared at him open-mouthed.

"Charley, I want you to meet my husband, John Stevenson. Contractor for Summit Tunnel to the Manchester & Leeds Railway."

Charley swallowed and licked his lips, looking nervously from one to the other of them.

"That's what we want to talk about, Mr. Eade," John said. "We've got a thousand men and their families out there and we're not satisfied about the food they're getting and the money they have to pay for it."

"We think we can supply better and cheaper," Nora said. "We can manage the better. And we're looking to you to manage the cheaper."

By now Charley was totally confused. Feeding a thousand men . . . that he understood. At that point he had prepared his mind to consider a plain business proposal. Now there was this word "cheaper" and the sweet smile on the face of that young bitch. And the big fellow. He looked a bloody sight too useful. By God those Connallys should hurry.

Nora, too, was feeling nervous. This was the moment she ought to hand over a bit of paper to Charley Eade. She and John had composed its contents the previous night, after the Thorntons had left. It read as follows:

9,000 lb. of beef, viz: aitchbone, mouse round,
   hock, thick flank and udder fat, thin flank,
   brisket, clod, shin—to average not above 4d.

| | |
|---|---|
| a pound and maximum . . . . . . . . . . . . . . . | £150 |
| 21,200 lb. of potatoes, to cost maximum . . . . . . . . . | £ 24. 10s. |
| 250 lb. of tea, to cost maximum . . . . . . . . . . . | £ 43 |
| 1,000 lb. of sugar (red), to cost maximum . . . . . . . . | £ 27. 10s. |
| 500 savoy cabbages, to cost maximum . . . . . . . . . | £ 3. 12s.6d. |

| | | |
|---|---|---|
| | | £248. 12s.6d. |
| advance 10% | | £ 24. 17s.3d. |
| balance (in 7 days) | | £223. 15s.3d. |

Prices to include delivery to Oldham Road Station and loading on Stevenson's wagons.

In her view, to hand this over to Charley Eade was like asking him to cheat them. Suppose he could get the meat at 3⅝d. but persuaded the wholesale butcher to invoice at 4d.—it would leave them £14.1.3 to split. Even a difference of ⅛d. was £4.13.9—tempting enough for anybody.

But John pointed out that whether Charley Eade cheated them was neither here nor there. Nora would be coming to market once a week—twice, sometimes—and she'd see the prices being asked. It would soon become clear whether there was a pattern of deception. That was the important thing, not the occasional light-finger exercise. They had to remember their own main interest: bringing back most of the wage to delay the cash on its natural course. They knew the price they could get. They knew the profit they wanted—part of it in well-fed, contented workers rather than in cash. They knew their costs, more or less. And so they knew the maximum they could pay for each item. To have *any* kind of an agent was asking to be swindled; all they had to do was to encourage him to keep the final prices below the maximum.

"Cheaper?" Charley said. "How d'ye mean—cheaper?"

"We're starting a tommy shop, Charley," Nora said. "Only it's not for tommy rot. This is our own workers and we've no interest in a man with bellyache or the squits or too starved to toil hard. This is best-quality tommy. And to get the keenest price, we, Mr. Stevenson and myself, have determined to come to Manchester, to Charley Eade. My old friend, who'd have good cause to see us well."

"Good cause?" Charley laughed nervously, looking at John, who seemed to be losing interest; he stood a little way off and picked out some apples with care.

"A thousand pound a month, Charley. Twelve thousand pound between now and this time twelvemonth. That's what we aim to put through this market—with your help. You see, Charley, there's no way I can get in here early enough, and I'd not want to stop overnight just so's I could be here first covers off. So we need a purchasing agent. That's when I thought of you."

Charley, beginning to relax now, beginning to feel less threatened, took a step or two in John's direction, picked up an apple for himself and returned to her. Narrowing his eyes in the hope of seeming more astute, he bit the apple and, while his teeth mashed its wet, crisp, flesh, said: "What's there for me?"

"Before I tell you that, you must know it's only five commodities we're seeking here—two of them off this stall. So you've only meat, tea, and sugar to seek elsewhere. For that little service we'll guarantee you forty-six shilling a week, *but*"—and here she produced the paper—"here's me first shopping list. Look at those limits, Charley. Every penny you save, every penny you get under those limits you may keep seven-eighths of—*if* the total exceeds the guarantee. D'ye follow?"

"Ye mean I may have forty-six shilling or seven-eighths of the savin' on these figures, whichever's the greater."

Nora smiled and turned to John. "Didn't I say? Where understanding of his own best interest is concerned, there's no man in Manchester quicker than Charley Eade!"

"It's beginning to seem that way," John answered.

Charley, evidently deciding it could do no harm to go further into the offer, now threw his arms open in a widely expansive gesture. "Meself," he said, "I was just goin' to the Duke of Bridgewater. There's a good tally of private bars there where we may conclude any business. What do you say to that? Some hot toddy on such a raw day, eh?"

Nora nodded. "Lead on," John said.

Charley took his cashbox and locked the little cubicle that served as his office. He left a porter to repack his displays. "You like apples, sir?" he asked John.

"I like these," John said.

So Charley told the porter to take a box up to Oldham Road Station for the gentleman. "A good Kentish pippin that," he said. "You never saw them up here before the railway." He left a card, saying *Duke,* hanging from a nail on his door.

When they were settled in the private bar, warming their hands around cups of toddy, Charley did not quite know how to reopen the subject. He fished out the paper she had given him. "Well," he said. "These prices now."

But Nora cut in. Speaking to John, she said: "Remember I told you how quick this Charley is?"

He nodded, watching Charley intently and much to Charley's discomfort. In the smoke-filled gloom, the pale light that filtered through the cheap glazing of the narrow window did not let one read John's face; in fact, he might almost not be there, sprawled back like that in the darkest corner.

"All the way over here," Nora went on, "he's been juggling four thoughts. One—How can he argufy us into raising these maximums? Two —Is the seven-eighths likely to exceed forty-six shilling frequently and by much? Three—What's to stop him making private business with butchers and grocers, copping the difference, or half of it, himself *and* our guaranteed forty-six?"

She stopped there, seeming to have finished.

Charley laughed and waved his hands as a lead-up to his protested innocence of all such thoughts. "You said four," he reminded her.

She sipped her toddy and looked intently at him. "Number four, Charley, is the answer to the other three. You're wondering why we've come to you. Especially when I *know* you to be as black a rogue as ever got hisself double-dyed. Why you of all people?"

Again Charley prepared his protest, but she went straight on: "We've come to you, Charley, because you know something about me, too. You know how long it took me to discover the true extent of your swindle against Coulter's. . . ." Charley tried to bank down her voice with his hands, while he looked nervously around at the door, the tops of the partition walls, and other places through which sound might travel.

"How long was it, Charley?" Nora persisted. "One hour? A little less, I think. Well, I've chosen you because that little discovery has taught you how stupid it would be to try to deceive me. There's no blackmail in this, you'll agree. We're offering a very fair proposal, very advantageous to you without the need to cheat us." She paused. "I'm asking your agreement to that statement, Charley. That we are being fair?"

"Yes," he said calmly, almost judiciously. "I have to agree to that. These prices and your offer is very fair."

"Even so, people being what they are," Nora went on, "there would always be the temptation, in anyone else, to seek even greater advantage. That could lead to some very painful lessons, Charley. Very humiliating lessons. Very *hard* lessons in personal cost. But you already know better than to try cheating us, you see. There's no need for you to learn that lesson."

Charley held up a hand to stop her. Now that her intention was plain, and now she had denied wanting to blackmail him and given convincing reasons for her denial, he could feel the ground firm beneath him once more. It was, as she had said, straight business, regular business, profitable business, and money as good as guaranteed. Unless some little loophole struck him, it looked as if she was right, too, about the folly of trying to cheat her. It was neat. You had to admire it. He could not really believe that the honest course was actually the most profitable one as well—that would be flying in the face of nature. But, for the moment, it seemed so. And, for the moment, he'd tread that path. Her only weakness, as far as he could see, was the lack of muscle behind her threat—or, since she had not actually made a threat, behind any that she *might* make.

"I see your meaning clearly," he said and rubbed his hands. "There have been few moments in my life when I could put my hand on my heart and say the honest way pays, but it really looks like this is one. Nora—shake on it. Bargain's struck."

Nora did not take his hand. "Mrs. Stevenson to you, Charley." He waved a circle of good-natured apology. "Mrs. Stevenson. Struck?" She took his hand then and shook it warmly. "Struck!" Then, with a slow smile, her eyes not leaving his, she added: "What'll ye tell the Connallys?"

"Connallys?" His surprise was very convincing.

"Pat and Paddy. If I'm not mistaken, it's them outside now."

"Eee!" He appeared to search his memory. "I've not seen them since . . . eee!" But he did not specify the term. "Do you know Pat and Paddy then?"

She was about to say that John did—as John had told her to—when the Connallys burst in. They were dressed exactly as they had been in August, right down to the spotted blue bandanna. Charley was about to call the pair of them off but they, eager to earn back their reputation with him, and whatever fee was offered, crowded Nora at once. Pat, the elder, grasped her chin between thumb and forefinger and jerked her face up. "Oh—lay*dee!*" he said with smiling menace.

But he went no further. His brother nudged him hard in the kidneys; he spun round to see what the problem might be, and then, following Paddy's alarmed and frozen gaze, turned toward the corner and the slouching figure there in the dark. "What?" he asked angrily.

"Well look!" Paddy said.

"Hello, Pat. Hello, Paddy," John said, still not moving into the light.

Nora felt Pat's hand tighten. She jerked her jaw away but the hand hung there, just where it had been, empty and petrified.

"Big John?" Pat asked.

"Ye old idiot!" Paddy swore. "Who else'd it be?"

"Offer your guests some toddy, Mr. Eade," John said. "I'm sure they'd not mind supping with three potatoes the likes of us." There was no humour in his voice. As he finished speaking he sat forward into the light. The effect on the two brothers was galvanic.

"Good Christ—ye never said about Big John!" Pat turned to Charley.

"Said? Big John? I have no notion what ye may mean," Charley protested. "I'm sitting quietly here. Drinkin' with two friends. And the pair of ye come bursting in . . ."

"Ah—bad 'cess to ye!" Paddy said, and plucked his brother's sleeve. He looked shiftily at John as they left. "No harm intended," he said.

John's coldly malevolent stare sped them on their way.

"Believe me," Charley said after they had gone, "I had no notion that would happen."

Nora and John laughed heartily and long. "No, Charley," Nora said. "I believe that! Indeed I do!"

Later, when they were on their way to the printer, she said: "You must have been a hard sort of man in your youth."

He was not pleased. "Not so much of the 'have been,' if you don't mind," he said.

She accepted his rebuke with an inclination of her head and thought ruefully of how, only a month or two earlier, he would have congratulated her for the way she had handled Charley.

"Anyway," she said, "if Charley Eade tries to screw us now, he's a bigger fool than I take him to be."

"Aye." He brightened—though it was plainly a deliberate effort. "Ye did well there."

They walked on in silence under his umbrella. Heat rising through poorly insulated houses was melting the snow on the roofs all over Manchester and causing minor avalanches to slide down the slates and fall on the pavements—and often on their unwary pedestrians, too. The air temperature was still below freezing, though, and very quickly the slush that fell grew a skin of ice, which crunched underfoot. Nora's toes were so perished with the cold that when they stood at the New Bridge crossing she had to wriggle them furiously just to make sure they were still there.

"Looks like there'll be a hanging tomorrow," John said, nodding over the river toward the yard by New Bailey prison. There a gang of workmen were busy erecting stands. "D'ye want to come back and watch it?"

She shook her head. "I'd as soon watch dogs tear a caged fox. No fun in a hanging, to my taste."

"I'm glad ye feel like that," he said.

A little waif, a girl of about nine, shuffled barefoot from a nearby doorway. She was so thin her head seemed perched only very precariously on her shoulders and quite out of proportion to the rest of her shrivelled little frame. It was a sight so common that Nora saw her and looked away without interest. Only when the child tugged her cape did she turn again. "What?" she asked.

The girl's lips barely moved as she muttered a few inaudible words in a hoarse croak; when she finished she stared up with her listless eyes, so heavy-lidded that she seemed to lack the energy to open them more than half way. Even to look at her in her threadbare cotton rags made Nora shiver.

"Well, what do we do with this?" John asked.

"Little bag-of-nails," Nora said, feeling the child's arm through her cotton sleeve. If the child had been dead it could have been no colder.

"I know this lay." He shook his head.

The child was so unsteady, she rocked dangerously on her legs. Nora wondered for a moment if she were drunk.

"D'you say you know her?" she asked John.

"I know the lay. 'Grafting with charvies' it's called—sending bairns out in pitiable rags to beg."

Nora put her fingers under the almost transparent material of the girl's bodice. "This bairn's near dead. Where's the sense of a dead child for a beggar?"

John shook his head. "As Lady Henshaw says, they're 'easily come by.' I imagine there's eight or nine others at home and if they bring in less than two pound on a day like this, there'd be a dozen or more of the strap for them."

"I'd say this child's dying now. You just feel."

John looked up and down both streets. "There's a pieseller. I'll go and get a hot pie," he said. "You stay with her."

Nora, though cold herself by now, pulled her shawl out from under her cape, and, wrapping the child in it, tried rubbing some warmth into her shrivelled limbs. "Going to get you some food," she said. It raised no light, no sign of expectation, in those listless grey eyes.

Just before John set off on the return journey from the pieseller's cart, a woman who had been standing a little way off came forward. "What may you be doin, ma'am?" she asked in a curious mixture of belligerence and sycophancy.

"Are you her mother? This bairn's mother?" Nora ignored the woman's question.

"And if I am?" The woman tossed her head. "What've ye got, Emmy?" she asked the child roughly. Mechanically Emmy held out her left hand, which until now she had kept tightly clenched. She opened it to reveal about seven coppers, as close as Nora could estimate before the mother snatched it.

"What's this?" the woman said quietly, menacingly. The child at last looked up at her with that same battered resignation. "Five and a half pence!" She lashed out with her fist and felled the child to the pavement. The child did not rise.

"How dare you!" Nora cried, standing up so as to strike the woman for this outrage. But before she could even raise a fist John, arriving at the double, grasped her arm and pulled her away.

"You're playing into her hands," he said. "There's nothing she'd like more than if you struck her."

A small crowd began to form, asking each other what was afoot and sharing their misinformation avidly.

Once he was sure Nora was not going to be stupid, John turned round to see to the child. The woman was unwrapping her from Nora's shawl. He gripped her arm to stop her; she was about to protest when her eye caught his. "Ye'll not lose by it," he said quietly. "Leave it to me."

He lifted the child and helped her to the doorway in which she had earlier been sheltering, wrapping her again in the shawl. He took the pie from his pocket and put it in her hands. Still the child did not really believe it was for her. "Eat!" he said, and he waited to see that she obeyed before he returned to the woman. Most of the bystanders, seeing there was no fight in the offing, went their ways. Those that remained found reason to leave when John looked at them.

"Yon bairn'll die," John said to the woman.

She shrugged. "There's no other lay for the brass. If I send her out properly clad and in boots . . ."

"Nay!" John was scornful. "But there's *ways*. Dost thou not know?"

Nora went across to Emmy. The woman looked at him blankly, keeping a suspicious watch on Nora out of the corner of her eye.

"There's ways to dress a charvey as looks bad without risking death."

"Eee!" the woman said in wonder.

He took out a silver shilling and held it where she could see it. "D'ye know Ma Lock?" he asked.

"Ma Lock?"

"Over Germany Street, off Newton Lane?"

The woman shook her head.

"Here's a shilling," he said, though he still did not give it to her. "Take this bairn home now. Get her covered up and warm. If thou don't, she'll die on thee. That'd be no service to thee. Tomorrow, thou art to take the bairn to Ma Lock, Germany Street, over Ancoats way. Say to her, to Ma Lock, Big ı sent thee, and she's to show thee how to dress a charvey for this raw ·. Say if she does that, all is quit. She'll understand."

The woman nodded at each instruction and he made her repeat them until he was satisfied she had it perfect. Only then did he give her the coin, saying as he did so, "If thou does not do those things, I'll seek thee down and drive thee out of this town." The woman nodded, gaping at him again. "Take the bairn home then," he said.

Emmy had finished the pie and was sucking the spots in her clothing where the gravy had fallen. Every now and then she sat upright suddenly, as a bird repeatedly rears its head when drinking from a pool; unlike a bird, she swayed in confusion, her eyes taking in nothing.

"Keep that shawl round her," Nora said coldly. The woman helped the child up and, looking very motherly in the way she stooped over her—a kindly, well-dressed lady helping a poor little ragged waif to sanctuary—set their course for home.

John turned at once to Nora, a few fences to mend. "She'd have taken us for pounds if ye'd laid half a finger on her." They resumed their stroll up toward the collegiate church.

"But the way she hit that child," Nora protested, even though she knew John spoke the truth.

"It would've been intervening between parent and child. Even the law can't do that."

"Poor little bunch of dog's meat."

"But what if she sent the child out warmly clad and well shod? How deep would that make you dig in your purse?"

Nora was silent.

John pointed to a well-dressed young boy who at that moment was leaving a bookshop just across the street. "If yon lad was to come up to ye, begging, how much'd you give?"

"A box on the ear," she agreed. Then, after only a moment's thought, she added: "But it's terrible, what we just did."

"Aye," he said.

"We just rewarded that . . . that old . . ." Her rage found no word strong enough.

"I told her where she may learn to clad the child fitly for this harsh wind."

"But she'll still have to go barefoot."

"Oh, aye. She can't have everything."

Nora crushed the ice on a snowpile nearby and shivered. "Eh," she said. "What's the answer?"

"We're engaged upon it now: work. Employment. The sooner we build a railroad, the more we hasten the day when things like that become impossible. Bad dreams. Bad memories."

"Meanwhile. . . ?"

"Meanwhile? We see as any man who works for us gets a fair crack."

"No—I mean . . ." She nodded back toward where Emmy had stood. "Likes of her, Emmy?"

He sighed. "For them, we cheat; break the rule. Our tomorrow'll come too late for them."

Again they walked in silence. "Well . . ." he said, as if she had accused him of something. "If we'd left her there, she might already be dead."

"Still," she said, reluctantly voicing the thought he had been afraid to meet, "if every charitable person in Manchester stopped giving, that . . . evil . . . that, using a child in such a way, it'd soon stop."

"Bairns'd die before then."

"They die anyway. But every penny given to that child is rewarding the cruelty practised on her."

The faint strains of an anthem reached them from the church across the road, where the devout were celebrating matins. He gave a short, bitter laugh, quite unlike any laugh she had ever heard him give before. "It's enough to make God turn in his grave," he said.

It struck her as such a shocking statement that even to protest, even to gasp the astonishment she felt at hearing it, would perpetuate it and, to that extent, lend it dignity. She wanted it unsaid. She wanted it effaced. It was to be forgotten.

She grasped his arm and led him forward, quickening their pace considerably. "Well," she said, "we've done what *we* can. Which is more than the thousand other folk who've walked past that young waif today."

And he, sensing the shock that engendered this sudden briskness, smiled back, patted her arm, and said, "Sorry!"

The printers were in Long Gate, the far side of the cathedral. He took her a little way beyond their shop to where there was a small gap between the houses opposite. "See that bridge there, over the Irwell?"

"I know yon bridge!" she said. "That's Strangeways workhouse beyond there."

"Well, that's Hunt's Bank. This bank of the Irwell. And that's where the Manchester & Leeds are going to build their main Manchester station."

Nora was surprised. "Not Oldham Road?" she asked.

"Hunt's Bank," he repeated. "The Act went through Parliament this first of July and that was two days before the Manchester & Leeds opened the service from Oldham Road to Littleborough. So Oldham Road had its fate sealed even before it opened."

"Eh! Money's like water to railways!"

"But look . . ." He pointed again at the site. "There's two places where, if you want to go by train right across England, coastline to coastline, Liverpool to Hull, there's two places where you have to get out and proceed by coach. One is here in Manchester: Liverpool Road Station to Oldham Road. Hunt's Bank is on the line they'll build to link those two. The other place is between . . ."

"Between Littleborough and Todmorden!" she chorused with him. "Eh! What if we got the Hunt's Bank contract!"

"You're there!" he said. "You and me . . . we're like *that*." And he held out two crossed fingers. "To be known as the man who put Liverpool and Hull in communion!"

She was still excited at the thought, feeling it to be hers as much as his. "D'you think we'll get it?"

"There's a story going round that the Liverpool & Manchester want a different route going south round the city on arches all the way."

"Which'd be best? For us?"

"Difficult . . ." He shook his head. "Southern route's about £700,000; Hunt's Bank's about £450,000. But which would show us most profit, I'd not say. The southern route has more engineering than I can estimate. I'd need a good engineer—with bigger experience than McKinnon. . . ."

"Not Thornton!" she said hastily.

He laughed, in a way that underlined her judgement. "Not Thornton. Though he's a good man for tunnelling and other railroad work."

She relaxed. "Mind you," she said, "we'd never be short of a laugh with him about us."

"Come on," he said. "We've a busy day."

# Chapter 35

STEVENSON'S SHOP the handbill was headed in a bold, black face. They had discussed many alternatives—Summit Stores, Site Shop, Railroad Shop, and so on—but had decided that if the venture was successful, they would repeat it elsewhere and so would want a general name whose goodwill would transfer.

"I want lads or their wives to say 'I got it at XYZ,' or whatever we call it, and to mean they got a right bargain," John said.

"Stevenson's Shop" had just the quality they desired.

Beneath the heading was a simple list of the victuals sold and their prices, with the date 1st January 1840.

Well-hung beef with no gursley or impure matter @ 5d. the pound for boiling and stewing.
Potatoes good and firm with no rotters or bungs @ 3 lb. the penny.

"What's a bung?" Nora had asked when they composed it.

"A joke," he said. "The lads'll understand it. When ye get a little potato they say it'd do to bung a London whore." Still she looked mystified. "There's a lot of little bairns are whores in London," he added.

Savoys, good hearted and well headed @ 2d. each.
India tea, best ordinary with little dust @ 1s. the quarter.
Cheap red sugar @ 8d. the pound.
Beer, best local brew @ 10s. the 10-gallon cask (2s. returnable deposit).
Bread in two- and four-pound loaves mainly of wheat @ 2d. the pound.

For beer they had organized the woman who had supplied the feast in
Summit East and a dozen other licensed beer brewers like her to provide,
between them, about five hundred ten-gallon casks of beer each week to an
agreed standard. Each had signed an affidavit agreeing to use nothing but
malt, hops, water, and yeast, and especially to refrain from stretching the
beer with treacle, colour, sliced root of liquorice, salt of tartar, capsicum,
Spanish liquorice, or logwood. "We can conduct tests for all these adulter-
ations," Nora assured them—wondering privately how long it would be
before one of them tried it.

The bread they got from two bakers, one in Littleborough, one at
Gawks Holm, both of whom had their own retail shops adjoining the
bakery. Nora had foreseen, quite rightly as it turned out, that other shopkeepers beside the line—who had been making small fortunes out of
cheating and short-weighting the navvies whenever they could—were going
to be furious to see the bulk of their trade vanish overnight. And they
would probably combine to refuse to supply the navvies with coffee, spices,
butter, gin, and the dozens of other commodities not on the Stevenson's
basic list. She therefore made it a condition of the bread contract, which
was worth seventy pounds a week gross to each shop, to undertake the
supply of any such commodity thus refused.

"What, even pork?" Allinson, the Gawks Holm baker had asked.

"Even pork."

He scratched his head. "I don't know about that," he said.

"Only to order," she said. "They'd have to order one day, collect the
next."

"Even so . . ."

"You mean to tell me," she chided, "you could not go out now and
stand in your shop doorway and cast your eyes on a dozen farms where they
keep pigs? And you mean to say Wally Fadden wouldn't go and kill one
for you, and deliver it ready butchered down to joints? All you do is take
the order, tell Fadden, put the joint on the shelf, and take the money."

But still he sighed. "What if they give the order and don't come
back?"

"Get a deposit, threepence in the shilling down. They'll come back."

"Deposit!" His eyes were wide in surprise.

"Aye. They've got money, our navvies, do ye know. They're not like your farm labourers and mill hands—every Saturday black with repaying loans."

"Deposit!" he repeated.

At length, after a great deal more persuasion and cajolery of this kind, he agreed. She had never had much of an opinion of shopkeepers and this sort of encounter merely deepened her contempt. *One day,* she thought, *I shall use their petty-minded cupidity to my own much greater advantage.* John was right; there were so many fools with money around that a clever person could build fortunes that would make the monarchs of history seem mere paupers.

Thus she closed the loopholes and insured against the dangers their new venture seemed to offer. Now they could only wait. The six wagons they had rented from the Manchester & Leeds were already being painted over with the name Stevenson. They bought two large, used tents to do duty as storehouses. The shop, clean and spruce inside and out, had a new sign, STEVENSON'S SHOP, painted over its doorway. All that could be made ready was ready.

Then on the Monday, the thirtieth of December, the handbills came, in time for distribution up and down the line before the shop opened. Tommy helped unpack them. First, of course, he took them out to read.

"You learn those prices well, Tommy," Nora said. "You're going to have to help me add them up when we start to sell."

She saw his fingers rubbing the backs of the sheets idly as he read; they had felt the indentations of the letterpress and were tracing around the shapes thus embossed on the back. He had got no farther than the potato prices when his interest in the shapes dominated him. He turned the sheet over and, noticing at once that the indentation read ꟻOHꙄ ꙅ'ИOꙄИƎVƎTꙄ, said: "If they printed it with letters the wrong way, blind people could follow it properly."

Nora laughed. "No one else could read it then," she said.

Only later, when he had read the notice and returned to his copying, did it strike her that the idea had been quite a good one and she told him so. "Keep it for when you grow up. There may be some money in it," she said.

He was pleased. "Even if there isn't," he said, "it could be a great help to them. The blind."

And his generosity of spirit, though she knew he did not intend it that way, seemed to her like a rebuke.

There were on the printed bills some further lines, which, Nora hoped, would copper-bottom guarantee the success of this venture.

When she and John had finished drafting the price list, John looked at it and said: "That should bring them." But he saw that she seemed unhappy still.

"We need . . . I feel something's missing. Something that'll *force* them to come and again," she said.

"Why?" He looked at the list in puzzled disbelief. "They look all right to me."

"They're the same prices as the shops around here . . ."

"But the quality! Better quality all round."

"I doubt that's enough," she said. "It's a woman's feeling I have. There's all the other things they can get up the shops." She looked at the list again. "It needs . . . something to make folk take notice. To make them talk."

He relaxed and looked at her in good-humoured accusation. "Come on," he said. "Let's have it. There's something on your mind. You've already thought something out. I know thee."

She refused to smile back, still playing her previous game. "I want them to say 'Have ye seen? . . . Did ye hear? . . . The Stevensons have gone mad up there, but while it lasts I'm using yon shop of theirs.' Something of that sort."

"You might as well say it straight out," he told her.

"What if . . ." She looked at him and slowly bit and released her lip. "What if we were to *give* food away?"

Jokingly he appeared to consider the idea. "Give food away," he mused. Then he delivered his judgement: "I think we may fairly say that would bring folk flocking to the shop and that they'd say we'd gone mad. It would do all of that."

She smiled secretively and pulled out another bit of paper. "Suppose this was how we gave it away," she said and handed it to him. It read:

For every 5s. spent at the shop this week you may have with next week's purchase, free of charge:—6 lb. potatoes

For every 10s. so spent, you may have with next week's purchase, free of charge:— 1 lb. beef and 3 lb. potatoes

For every 15s. so spent, you may have with next week's purchase, free of charge:— 2 lb. beef and 3 lb. potatoes

She watched him read it. Of course his skepticism had been playful; he knew her too well by now to think any scheme of hers could be even slightly harebrained. He tested it. Read it again. Smiled. Thought again.

Looked at her. Smiled again. And then he said, "It's too good. That"—he tapped the paper—"that is sheer genius." He looked at the fire. "We're in the wrong business. When I see this, I think we're in the wrong business."

"We'll use it?" she affirmed anxiously.

He looked at her. "No doubt on it. We'll use it. Eh! But to waste it on yon . . . shanty-shop!" He read through it yet again. "But, for this hand-bill now, ye've got to think how it'll look in print. I fancy it needs a name. When Mrs. Slen comes in, she's going to say, 'And I want me . . . me . . . whatsit, from last week.' We need a name they know. Instead of whatsit."

"A name they must have heard these weeks past till they're sick of it is *bonus*," Nora said.

His eyes lit up at once. "That's it. Lads get their bonus at the working—wives get theirs at shop. 'Wives' bonus' call it."

She shook her head. "Men'll think it's not for them. There's a lot of single men. 'Shoppers' bonus'? No—we'll just call it bonus, and have done. Bonus."

"Write it at the top," he said. "We'll get it put in thick black letters, at the top: 'Bonus—free food to loyal customers.' And if that doesn't bring them and keep them, we may as well go to America."

"And at the bottom," she said, "I'll put 'Shop open every Friday and Saturday from 8:00 to 8:00.' And in thick black letters again, under all, 'No credit.'"

"Aye," he said. "That's very important."

* * *

The following Wednesday, the first day of the new decade, she returned to the produce mart, scarcely able to contain her excitement. It was almost noon when she arrived and she found only Tony on duty at Coulter's stall.

"Where's Charley?" she asked.

"Over the Duke I should think," Tony said. He went on sweeping.

"Then you'll go and fetch him here."

"Oh, will I!" Tony still did not stop.

"If you value your job, Tony."

He gave a scornful snort.

"Listen, lad," she said. "I know you saved my life last summer, though you probably had no such intention. I don't forget that. But Charley Eade works for me now. Can you find some room for that fact to lodge in that block of wood on your shoulders? Charley Eade is my agent. And if you don't run, *run,* and fetch him there, toot sweep, today is your very last in this market."

Tony ran.

Charley was all goodwill and cloying gallantry; he kept emphasizing whatever he said by opening his arms, as if he were on the point of embracing Nora. She sobered him, however, by saying she hoped all the weights were full. "They've a new German steelyard for the weighbridge at Oldham Road," she said. "It can tell you the weight of a laden wagon to the nearest pound." His face fell.

Shortly after, while she was checking the quality of the merchandise, she saw Charley sidle off for a word with the butcher, who came up later with another tub of joints.

"Right," he said. "That's the lot."

She smiled, too, to see that when she returned from lunch four bags of potatoes had been added to the pile. Later, when the wagons were weighed, the meat proved to be 430 pounds overweight and the potatoes almost five imperial hundredweights up. The sloppiness annoyed her. So did the fact that Charley had obviously no idea of how much he had originally intended to cheat her by.

"Well, Charley," she said. "You invoice me for nine thousand twenty-six pounds of meat—which looks, on paper, very nicely measured, I must say—and you deliver nine thousand four hundred and thirty. And the same story with the potatoes. It's not good enough."

"I'll amend the invoice," he said miserably.

"You will not. You may unload sooner."

"I can't do that. That's the half of an ox extra."

"Well, I'm not paying. If we hadn't weighed them here, you'd have been happy to see me steam off with them."

"Would I buggery! I'd not've . . ." He stopped, realizing he had already said more than was wise.

"Aye!" she sneered. "Ye'd not've topped up the meat and potatoes. If I'd not mentioned this weighbridge." She moved close to him and poked her face to within inches of his. "You disgust me!" she shouted. "The one place ye thought ye could still manage to diddle me—the weight. Ye think yourself the king of diddlers and ye don't know B from a bull's balls!"

Unable to withstand this close-up assault he pulled away from her. "We can't weigh properly down there at St. John's."

"That's your problem. And ye've seven whole days in which to solve it. So let's have this determined now. I will accept and pay for a variation of one percent either way, two percent in all. To me that seems generous." He snorted. "But every pound weight above that I'll take as a free gift from you. And every one percent ye go below the allowed variation I'll take it as attempted fraud on your part, Charley, and I'll knock five bob off what I'm due to pay you."

He looked at her in unconcealed hatred, and she saw him forcing himself not to utter any of the dozen insults that must have been passing through his mind. At length he said: "I pity yon bloody man of thine, Mrs. Stevenson. And I should want to meet whoever put a woman in business. I'd tell him his name for naught."

"Business!" she sneered. "Ye think what you do could be called 'business'? Petty theft? And bungled, at that! Business? It's not worth the dignity of the name."

"Ah—go back to your kitchen!" he shouted and walked away.

"The day the likes of you can pull it over me, I shall and all!" she shouted after him.

So she started trade with a good margin—a quarter ton of potatoes and four hundredweights of beef free.

The supplies came up the following morning and were hauled on from Littleborough by a horse team, making the transit of the tunnel during the break for lunch. After knocking-off time a gang of navvies earned a few shillings bonus between them by carrying everything except the meat up to the store tents. The meat, securely padlocked in the wagon, was left overnight.

"We'll make a little siding here," John said. "Temporary like. So the wagons may stand without hindering the working."

"We should've thought of it earlier," she said. "We could have sold straight from the wagons. Put a siding the other end and we could sell down there, too. Friday there, Saturday here." She warmed to it as she spoke. "Why not? We'd do a lot more trade. In fact . . ." She was so excited now that she seized both arms and shook him as she spoke. "In fact—why not sell as we go, all the way up from Littleborough? Get all the shanty women . . . *listen!*" She had to stop him from laughing. "Get all the shanty women to make up a bulk order, for even if they've only twenty men, there's at least a hundredweight of beef there; get them to make up bulk orders and drop them off into the shanties as we pass by! Eh!" She hit her forehead repeatedly with her fist. "We've not been thinking. We've just not been thinking! We could offer them . . . threepence or threepence-halfpenny in the pound. They'd jump at the chance."

Tommy, who had watched and listened with growing dismay, plucked at her sleeve and said: "You're not going to close my shop, ma'am? Please!"

"Oh, be quiet!" she said, brushing a handful of air at him crossly. "We're talking business."

John shrugged free of her and, clasping her shoulders, held her four-square to him. "Suppose," he suggested, "that we just sell this week's supplies exactly as we planned. And next week, when we shall know everything there is to know about keeping shop and could quite easily retire if we wished, next week, try something different—even this tinker-on-rails notion if ye haven't had a hundred others by then."

"D'you think it foolish?"

"I do not. But I believe we must first touch ground beneath our feet."

She nodded. "You're right." She smiled at him. "We've work enough to move this."

"Shall I have any supper tonight?" he asked.

"Oh, you are hard done by, poor man!" she mocked. "I'll lock up now. Where's Tommy? His mother'll be here soon."

"Back in the shop."

She found him lying on a bag of potatoes, sobbing his heart out. The sight of it mortified her, for she remembered how sharp she had been. Yet it was also puzzling, for she had often been severe with him before—when he had copied letter shapes badly, or done some job in a slovenly way—and he had always taken it well. He did not usually smart under a rebuke or turn resentful; indeed, she had often wondered whether anything would ever discourage him or dim his seemingly irrepressible spirit.

One jocular remark after another rose to her throat and refused to be uttered. In the end she simply leaned forward, picked him up—glad to see he did not protest or struggle—and hugged him to her. His sorrow quickly subsided and soon he was shaking himself and her with convulsive gasps as he tried to breathe smoothly.

"Now, listen," she said, almost whispering into his ear as he lay with his head hard pressed into her shoulder. "Be calm and listen. As long as we are working at this site, and as long as there's a Tommy Metcalfe living in Lancashere-near-Yorkshere, there will be a shop here."

"Tommy shop," he said.

"A tommy shop," she agreed.

"This one," he pressed.

She put him down but he clung at once to her with his arm about her hips and his face buried in her petticoats. "Very likely," she said.

"Yes, yes," he insisted. "It must be."

Now she was in a quandary. She wanted to pacify him and get him all quiet to go home. But she wasn't going to lie about something so important. She pulled a glum face at John, who shrugged good-naturedly as if to say, take your time.

"There's no must about it, Tommy," she said as gently as she could. "A shop, any kind of shop, whatever you may believe, is not just a place—walls, doors, roof, and windows." She took him to the door and pointed uphill to the crown of Moorhey Flat. He, not wanting to be given any reason for abandoning the idea that "his" shop was a permanent feature of the universe, if not, indeed, its actual hub, came only with reluctance. "Look," she persisted. "If we did a very foolish thing; if we built this shop up there, how many folk do you think would take the trouble to clamber all that way up and buy there?"

He smiled, thinking that argument a very easy one to overcome. "But we built it here," he said proudly.

She nodded. "So we did. And we think we're right. We think. But we don't know. And if we're wrong, we shall move it. We shall take the shop where folk want it. Because—and listen to this, Tommy, because I don't ever want you to make this mistake again—a shop is, first and above all, its customers. If a shop's got no customers, ye might as well break the rest up for kindling. That's why I want you back here tomorrow wearing your best smile and boots blacked ready to put the best one forward. And every customer goes out this door is going to say, 'I must do me shoppin there again next time.' Because *they* are the shop. Now there's your mother and sister so you'd best be off."

And she gave him a little dusting on his bottom to send him off and spare him the indignity of being forced to agree with her. She was glad she had explained it to him, though, for even in her own mind the thoughts had never been set out quite so explicitly.

As she and John walked homeward up the hill she said: "I suppose it was a waste of time to tell the little fellow. He's got that other idea so fixed, about 'his' shop, he can't see anything else."

"He'll come to it," John reassured her.

"No, but the idea was beyond him. The thought was too . . . you know."

"I believe you must always stretch a young mind with thoughts beyond it. There's no learning without bewilderment. I hope when we rear bairns, ye'll not be too busy with affairs to talk like you did to Tommy down there. Me and all."

Again she found herself on the point of telling him that she was quickened, and by now could be almost certain of holding the child; but, again, the memory of earlier miscarriages held the words bottled within her. For the moment.

The following morning Tommy slipped down to the shop on his own, before seven o'clock, when it was time for Nora to go down and start moving up the meat. She meant to scold him when she arrived, for he had left her to carry down the ledger and the bonus book by herself; but as she drew near the doorway she saw him standing at the threshold with his arms folded, looking very proprietorial, wearing a folded paper hat. And its cockade was composed of a magnificent black plume of hearse feathers. He tried to look solemn but the excitement within kept bubbling up and forcing him to grin. Just as she came to the door he stood aside with a flourish and revealed, pinned to the door, a scrap of paper bearing the words "Tommy Shop."

She shook her head in mock despair. "Is that what it was all about!" He grinned. "I don't know, Thomas M. What do we do with you?"

But she soon showed him once they were inside. He was to manage the bonus book, sitting next to her at the pay desk by the door. She would tell him how many tickets to give each customer, and he was to tear them off and note down their numbers and the name of the customer in the bonus book. At half past seven her four women assistants came up from Walsden. She ran through their duties once more: one was to serve meat, another potatoes and cabbage, another tea, sugar, and bread, and the fourth was to keep their stocks replenished and to serve out the ale casks as Nora directed. She herself kept the ale book, where she recorded the deposit each customer paid and noted whether the cask was at once removed or left for a husband to collect on his way home in the evening.

To start with, trade was not at all brisk, and by midmorning Nora, with a heart that sank lower into her boots each idle moment that passed, was contemplating the ruin of the whole scheme. John had come in several times and on the last occasion had left looking very thoughtful.

Tommy drew a palatial shop, with its wares displayed in the air all around it, thronged with customers.

"I wish it was like that," Nora said when he showed it her. She was just toying with the idea of giving away a pound of beef to each of the first four hundred customers, thus passing on most of Charley Eade's unintentional bonus, when half a dozen wives entered in one hesitant group, as if they needed the mutual support. Ten minutes later they left, staring at their bonus tickets and looking a lot more cheerful. Never in their lives can they have had such swift and willing service. Even before they had left, more had arrived, then more, and still more. By noon there were actually lines of people waiting.

With a bit of insight, as Nora later cursed herself, she might have worked it out. Of course, most of the women would hang fire, waiting for one or two brave, or foolhardy, souls to return. Then they'd compare the quality, drink a cup of tea, have a gossip, and finally make up their minds to give it a try. If she had worked all that out for herself, she could have let her assistants off for an early lunch and have taken some herself. As it was, with the line growing longer by the minute, there'd be no lunch today for any of them.

The line worried her. By one o'clock it was taking thirty minutes between joining the line and even reaching the door. Had *she* been a newcomer she was sure she'd have turned around and gone elsewhere; but it seemed to have the opposite effect on these women—as soon as they saw the long caterpillar of people stretching back from the door, they actually broke into a run. And the noise of their chatter and laughter blotted out all other sound; it even brought the menfolk to the mouth of the tunnel to stare in wonder. As she watched the women come inside, their eyes shining and replete as if from a feast, she realized that, far from seeming irksome, this enforced wait and the chance it gave for a chat and a laugh was a welcome element in the day.

Soon there was such a crush that she had to halt the entries and, later, to resume only on a one-out-one-in basis. John came over then, filled with relief. "Want help?" he asked. She shook her head. He watched the operation for a while. "Ye want a bigger door," he said. "Or another door over there. Every body and every thing is coming in and out by the one place." But she refused his suggestion. "If ye want," she said, "ye could put me in a door at the back, where Mrs. Cattermole can bring fresh stock in and out." By three o'clock one of the carpenters was sawing a hole in the back wall to take the door he had made. "I've no lock furniture," he said, "but I'll come back at eight this evenin and screw it fast the jamb for thee."

Then there was a lull and she was able to let the women go, one by one, for a late lunch. Tommy took his bread and cheese and a pot of small beer up to the turnpike. He liked to watch the horsemen and cattle go by and the coaches made him jump up and down in excitement. A flock of chickens gathered around the milestone where he sat, and fretted at him for crumbs. Before he returned he played "Three Blind Mice" for them on his whistle.

The next rush was at six, when the single men came off work and the husbands called to collect the casks their wives had paid for earlier. A lot of men, she noticed, bought nothing, but watched their mates being served, or searched thoroughly through the produce on offer and left. At first this puzzled her until one said as he left: "I'll send the missis tomorrow."

"Victims of past tommy shops," John said later. "You can't blame the buggers."

At the end of the day, they carried over £276 up the hill to the new iron safe at Rough Stones. John was delighted, and not a little relieved. But all Nora would say was: "We must do better tomorrow."

\*     \*     \*

The first day was no guide to the second. The rush began only fifteen minutes after the door opened; and though they were as gossipy and jovial as the earlier crowd, they were also more critical. A lot of talking must have been going on around the fires last night. If she didn't lack for trade, Nora also had her fill of good advice. She should open Mondays, too; or Tuesdays; or every day; she should stock carrots, turnips, pork, coffee, leeks, onions, Scotch kale, mutton, salt. And though she gave no outward sign of it, she grew tired of saying they intended to expand their lines as soon as they had experience of the trade, and of giving out the two addresses where supplies were guaranteed if the other shopkeepers took offence.

She found it a great comfort to have Tommy at her side most of the time, for he read to her when trade was down, and did drawings, and wrote little stories, and copied his letters. She supervised his work in the bonus book several times and found not a single mistake. Many of the women thought it a marvel that a boy so young could do a grown man's work; and this, for reasons she could not fully explain, made Nora feel very proud. When lunchtime came, they shut the shop for half an hour and she and Tommy went up to the turnpike.

She sat on the milestone while he sat on her lap. And when they had finished their pies he reached guiltily into his pocket, pulled out a potato, and offered it to her.

"For me?" she asked. He nodded. She felt it. "But it's raw," she said. "I can't eat potatoes raw."

He laughed then. "Not you," he said. "My chickens."

She looked at the poultry, fretting around them in the roadway, and at the potato in her hand. "I just give it them?"

He shook his head, and, with a look of even deeper guilt, took another potato from his pocket. Before she could speak he made a tiny bite in its flesh and spat the morsel at his feet. At once the chickens made a dart for it. Nora giggled. Emboldened, he took another bite and spat it, this time, into the middle of the highway. The flock darted there and harried the one who got it first. Nora laughed. "Go on, ma'am. You too," Tommy said as he took his third bite and spat it as far over the road as he could manage.

Nora took a bite and followed suit. It was amusing to see how the stupid, demented birds flocked around, running this way and that, mobbing the successful, driving off the weak, grabbing, losing, looking stupidly north when one more astute than they ran stealthily south with a full beak—they were very human, really. And soon the air was full of bits of potato, feathers, laughter, and hysterical birds.

"Which is your favourite, ma'am?" Tommy asked when neither of them had any potato left to chew and spit.

"The one with a black patch over the eye—that one. The cock."

"But he gets all the bits. Hannibal, he's called. He's the greedy one."

"How d'you know he's called that?"

"Only by me. I've given them all names."

"Oh! Have you? And I suppose you've been spitting my potatoes at them, too. Is that what you were up to yesterday?"

He looked at her fearfully. "I'll pay," he said. "I've not had more than I could pay for."

She laughed and tousled his hair. "You may have three," she said. "Three like that." He grinned weakly in his relief.

"Which do you prefer?" she asked.

"Biddy," he said, pointing to one whose tail feathers had been mostly pecked out by the others. "I'm the only one who likes Biddy."

She shook her head sadly. "You're your father's boy all right. You love all the weaklings."

He looked at her, to see her mood, before he said: "My father calls them the meek and the poor in spirit. Jesus loved them."

She did not know how to answer. But at that moment the northbound stage came hurtling round the corner in a flurry of gravel and flying hooves. If there had been cows or sheep in the road, it would never have managed to stop in time. Tommy, shouting, "My chickees!" stood up and was about to leap in the road to save them when she grabbed his belt and hauled him back. It was not a moment too soon for in the next second the road immediately in front was a thunderous, rumbling, shuddering cavalcade of pounding hooves, foam-mottled mouths, sweating flanks, and rolling iron-tyred wheels. The noise was so colossal that she not only heard it but *felt* it, shuddering at the very pit of her lungs. She hugged him, shivering, his elbows locked in that familiar, awkward stance while he shouted at the coachman, a wordless, shrill cry of hate. When the noise had dropped and the coach was swaying and jolting away down the road, her mind held the image of the coachman, his fierce grin, his weather-browned cheeks, his flashing eyes, as he had been in the instant he swept past them.

Tommy was still rigid, making an unnatural gurgle in his throat, and pointing at a bedraggled little bundle of dirty feathers in the road, just where the coach had passed. Like him, Nora, when she saw it, thought at once it was a dead chicken. But it was only the weakling hen, Biddy, squatting down the way they do for a cockerel on the tread. Something in her pea-sized little brain must have taken the coach for a juggernaut-cockerel; only now, when it was almost out of sight down by Deanroyd bridge, was she stretching her wings and standing her full height again. Tommy laughed to see she was still alive and would have run into the road if Nora had not grabbed him again.

"You see!" she said. "They can take care of themselves. Unlike *you*. That was very stupid. Even they've got more sense. You might have been killed. D'you know that?" He stood sullenly looking down. "Do you understand that?"

"Yes."

"If I thought you'd do a stupid thing like that again, I'd stop you coming up here. I'd forbid it."

"No!" he pleaded.

"I would. You promise you won't?"

"Yes."

"Promise?"

"Promise."

"Never again?"

"Never. Never."

"If I see you, I'll stop it for good. So you be cautious." She could see he took her seriously. "Now you go on back to the shop. Here comes someone I know."

He ran eagerly back to his shop.

The "someone" was Lady Henshaw, on a fat sorrel mare with a white face. Behind, though she took not the slightest notice of it, trotted a single goat.

"Mrs. Stevenson," she called. "Was that boy wearing hearse feathers in his cap?"

"Yes, my lady," Nora replied.

It was only then that Lady Henshaw allowed astonishment to show in her face, as if the fact needed confirmation before the reaction could properly be registered. She stared after Tommy's vanishing, fleet-footed little shade until her horse halted beside Nora. "How eccentric," she said absently and then, turning to Nora, added with much greater intensity: "And so young, too."

"I've not been to call," Nora said, "because I've been too busy."

"The devil you have!"

"I fancied I might come round after midday this Sunday."

Lady Henshaw was too astounded to make any sort of a reply to that.

"Well"—Nora was now even more defensive—"I've a living to make. I've not got leisure like some folks. Sunday's all I can spare." She wondered if Lady Henshaw had heard.

"D'ye like me horse?" was all she said.

"Looks a good hack in need of a sweating. That's something I'd like to know more about. Horses. Horseriding . . . hunting."

At last there was a reaction: Lady Henshaw's face lit up like a beacon.

"Capital!" she said. "Champion. I knew there'd be something *you* needed. Till Sunday then. Don't bring Mr. Stevenson, mind. No discourtesy meant, but this isn't idle social fan dangling."

Nora shrugged. "Can you give me any idea, madam?"

Lady Henshaw turned the mare for home. "Oh . . ." she called airily as she ambled away. "I'm writing a book. Need your help."

The goat ran before the horse all the way home.

That Saturday evening Nora was able to strike a balance in her book.

|  |  | From sales | £621- 3-3 |
|---|---|---|---|
|  |  | less cost | 485-13-6 |
|  |  | Gross profit | 135- 9-9 |
| Rent of wagons . . . . | £ 4-10-0 |  |  |
| Rail haulage . . . . . | 1- 8-0 |  |  |
| Other haulage . . . . | 2- 0-0 |  |  |
| Wages . . . . . . . | 10-0 |  |  |
| Apportionment of costs (buildings, sidings, equipment, working capital) say . . | 10- 0-0 |  |  |
|  | £18- 8-0 |  | 18- 8-0 |
|  |  | NET PROFIT | £117- 1-9 |
|  |  | free from C. Eade(!) | 9-14-0 |
|  |  |  | £126-15-9 |

She passed it to John. "Not too rusty," she said self-deprecatingly, "for our first week's trading."

He looked at the figures and whistled.

"Mind," she said, "we handed out just under eleven pounds' worth of bonus tickets against next week. And we can't expect Charley Eade to be so generous next time either! It'll be down by twenty pounds or so."

"I think I might just manage to fight back my tears," he said.

\*     \*     \*

They had further cause for joy at this time, too: The Reverend Doctor Prendergast was almost killed by an attack of bronchitis that had turned to pneumonia. They did not actually pray for his death, but they earnestly entreated Providence to forgive him his sins so that he might be more fit for judgement. Word reached them that it would be at least a month before he put a foot to the floor.

John wrote a hypocritical note wishing him a speedy and complete recovery. Nora sent it over to his house with a jar of goat's milk cheese—a gift to her from Lady Henshaw.

# *Chapter 36*

Once Nora grew used to the stink of goats and dogs she found Lady Henshaw's place quite agreeable. Henshaw Park was a smallish country house of about twenty principal rooms and upstairs provision only for the above-stairs staff. Below-stairs servants slept in an annex that linked the house to its stables and cowsheds, so that they were topologically *in* without being architecturally *of* the main house. The style of building was the dull, insipid, fake-classical mode of the previous century. Inside, however, the rooms were pleasantly airy and well lit—as she discovered when Madoc showed her in.

"Her ladyship may be ten minutes or more, madam," he said. "May I bring you anything?" He obviously expected her to refuse.

"Perhaps I'll come back another day if this isn't to her convenience. What is she doing?"

He crossed the room to open the tall French window and shout "Go away!" at a goat, browsing on what had, many years ago, been a flower bed. The goat took no notice. Madoc shook his head and shut the window. "That's the one I'll butcher next," he said with cold glee. He looked at Nora. "Her ladyship is in the kitchens with the vet, madam," he said.

Nora wondered what a "vet" was—a disease? an implement?

"Lancing boils. One of the dogs's got boils."

"I'll come back," Nora said and made for the hall.

Madoc followed her. "She'll be very disappointed, madam," he said. "Will ye not go and see her?"

Nora was torn between her sense of curiosity and her annoyance at having come the best part of a mile for nothing, all at the behest of a lunatic baroness. "Very well," she said. "Where are the kitchens?"

"Ah! Humble apologies for all this," Lady Henshaw called as soon as she saw Nora, who wondered what the word "humble" might possibly mean when applied by her ladyship to her own behaviour. She was holding

a once-elegant silk cushion over the head of a shaggy and dirty-coated great
barbet, or water dog as some call it. This dog was lying across the kitchen
table, its forelegs pinned by one servant girl, its hind legs by another. A
rusty seven-pound weight held down its tail. A horse doctor—what Madoc
had called the "vet"—was lancing a string of suppurating ulcers down the
dog's left flank and cleaning them out with flowers of sulphur and tar. Only
the fact that the dog was very drunk enabled them to subject him to these
indignities.

"Soon be finished," said Lady Henshaw.

Two other dogs, a black Siberian and a black Iceland dog, came dashing across the kitchen, uttering strange cries—a mixture of yelps, barks,
and howls—at her. In later visits Nora got to know them quite well,
though they steadily treated her as hostile from that day forward. But their
hostility was not that of dogs on their own territory, repelling a stranger.
Indeed their bravado was only a thin mask for a kind of guilty cowardice,
as if they knew, and you knew, and they knew that you knew, that their
*real* territory was somewhere else—somewhere forgotten or mislaid—and
that they were only practising, keeping the skill alive in a lame-hearted
way, here at Henshaw Park. Nora decided at once that both were insane;
and nothing happened later to change her mind. On this afternoon, seeing
the demented light that shone from their eyes, she ignored them.

The two servant girls stared at her; and with sinking heart she realized
that both of them were also—to put it kindly—rather simply furnished in
the attic floor. She shrank from their inane inspection of her and walked
out of their view—at least with normal servants she would have been out
of view, but one, the more obviously nitwitted of the two, lowered her
head and continued to survey Nora from under her arm, giggling all the
while.

From her new location Nora could see into the scullery, where the open
window was partly blocked by the upper half of a goat; it had its fore-
hooves in the sink and was licking drops of water off the tap as they
formed, which they did at a rate of about one every second. She suddenly
wanted to run from the house; only Lady Henshaw's kindly smile and the
friendly gleam in her eyes stopped her. "There's a great goat poking its head
through the scullery window, drinking from the tap," she said.

Lady Henshaw nodded. "It was a dreadful mistake, putting that tap in.
They always left the pump alone."

"That should do it," said the horse doctor.

They all let go of the dog and the larger of the two maids dragged it
from the table to the floor; it landed on the stone flags with a thud that
would have broken any human bone. There, unshaken, it took three
inebriate steps in a semicircle, then sat and licked its tar-encrusted flank.

The two other dogs joined in, lapping eagerly, as if the leg were a bowl and the tar was the greatest of delicacies.

"If they insist on eatin that muck, ye'd best put some down for them on a plate," Lady Henshaw said.

The doctor obeyed eagerly, emptying the tar bottle to its very dregs. "It'll kill them," he said in a voice filled with hope.

Madoc, still at the doorway, sniffed gloomily; he knew better. Lady Henshaw went to the scullery and rinsed almost all of the blood and pus from her hands and arms. The goat took no advantage of the sudden gush of water from the tap but waited until it was turned off again, and even until the final driblets had subsided, before it resumed its measured one-per-second licking. As there was no towel or cloth, or curtain, Lady Henshaw walked past Nora yet again, still with that same warm smile, and went this time to the stable yard. "Come on out!" she called when she reached it.

Nora obeyed, to find her ladyship standing in the court swinging her arms like windmills. She seemed quite unable to coordinate the two limbs, so that they went fast or slow in total independence and often hit each other, quite hard. Several times Nora wondered why she did not cry out in pain. The hem of her skirts, swaying in sympathy, scattered goat-dung pellets about the yard like grapeshot. Several dozen goats stood about the place—including on the coach-house and stable roofs—watching her with that incurious intelligence which sooner or later fills the eyes of any cloven-hoofed creature that lives close to humankind for long enough.

"Quite mild again," Lady Henshaw panted through her exertions. "Let us stroll."

They went out through the stable-yard gate and took a gravel lane that wound around and slightly up the hill. To their left was Henshaw wood; to their right, reaching south through the gap in the Blackstone Hills, was the canal, the railroad, and the turnpike. Most of the workings were, from this angle, concealed in cuttings. The oval shaft and the now engineless numbers ten and eleven shafts were clearly visible though, as was Rough Stones, about on a level with Henshaw Park.

"Very inhospitable of me," Lady Henshaw said. "But you probably don't want tea or things of that sort."

Nora, remembering the conditions in which the tea and its accompaniments would likely be prepared, had to agree, despite her thirst.

"We shall both have a glass of port in a minute," Lady Henshaw added. The lane turned on itself and Nora could see that it wound gently upward, through the woods, in a series of S curves. Occasionally she caught glimpses of a small, templelike structure higher up.

"Hate sharin me place with all those beasts," her ladyship went on. "The vet says I shouldn't. He gave me a list as long as granny's tongue of all the pests and diseases they can catch from humans. But he doesn't have the task of drivin them out all the time. Besides, *I* pay *him*."

"Some of those branches look rotten," Nora said. She had never seen a mature woodland so neglected.

"*Some* of them?" Lady Henshaw said. "Everything needs attention. But it's all too much. People think I don't know. They think I don't notice. But I do."

The older woman's vulnerability, so suddenly laid bare, was the last thing that Nora had expected to encounter. She had the strongest feeling that in some obscure and very roundabout way, the other was asking for her help. She quickly dismissed the thought, for what could she, so ignorant of society and of any world beyond the line from here to Manchester, what could she know or do that might help a Lady, a "baroness in her own right" as John said, whatever it meant?

"It isn't as if I don't try," Lady Henshaw continued. "I can't tell you the number of times I prepare everything and even begin . . . the woodland . . . the roof . . . the coach house—d'you know there are two good coaches in there that can't be got out because the floor's collapsed under them?—the well. . . . But we get nowhere."

"What . . . why do you stop? What goes wrong?" Nora asked. A robin hopped ahead of them around the next curve; it looked back as if seeking approval for its moves, then it flew to a nearby briar and sang its twit-twit alarm call.

"I've a coachman with more airs and graces than an oratorio. I've three simpletons as maids, which I am forced to through my connection as patroness of the Stanfield Asylum. . . ." She paused to kick a lump of coal off the pathway. "Also it's cheaper. One can't blink that fact. Two pounds a year instead of eight is a lot saved. And I've a butler who opposes me in everything. Of course, I shall dismiss *him,* as soon as I have found someone to take his place. Oh yes!"

"Do you mean Madoc? The one who showed me into . . . in, today? I thought he was your postillion."

The decaying woodland was all about them now, shutting out the view and filling the air with the cloying smell of wet fungus.

"You're more rational than *he* is," Lady Henshaw answered. "He thinks he's a Welsh prince."

Nora was by now beyond surprise; she looked back at the other with polite interest.

"He does," she continued defensively. "A Welsh prince. He has a chest filled with mouldering old papers that prove he's the lineal descendant of some ancient Welsh prince called Madoc who, or so he swears, discovered America. It's all lies, of course, but as it's either in Latin or Welsh, I'm powerless to prove it to him. Between you and me, it's my opinion that he's not entirely compos mentis." She nodded confidentially and lowered her voice almost to a whisper to reinforce the truth of it.

The final bend led up a short leg to a broad clearing on the side of the hill in the midst of which stood an elegant little gazebo, elliptical in plan and with six pillars supporting a shallow copper dome of the same shape. The two pillars nearest the hillside, which still rose behind the building for two hundred feet or more, were tied into a thin wall, rendered with stucco, and showing traces of a former mosaic decoration. A natural spring had been harnessed into the design, its waters rising up a concealed pipe and streaming forth between the lips of a grotesque ichthyogriff, or fish-tailed griffin, into a stained marble bowl. The overflow was led away, rippling and gurgling, down the hillside. Nora felt thirstier than ever.

"The only good servant I've got," Lady Henshaw concluded, "is Shawn McGinty, me groom." She stooped before the cupboard beneath the bowl and fished out a key from her bodice. "And *he's* lost all his teeth," she added.

The cupboard proved to contain an assortment of unwashed wine glasses and three bottles of port, one already drawn. They sat in the gazebo, hemmed in by the blackened trunks of damp trees, beneath a sky of remorseless and unrelieved gray, and sipped indifferent port from cracked glasses. It was not the way Nora had imagined herself spending this Sunday afternoon.

"Well," Lady Henshaw said at last, "we can't fritter away the whole afternoon in idle chitchat. The reason I've brought you all this way . . ." She looked hard at Nora suddenly. "You *can* keep a secret?"

"None better," Nora said.

The other nodded happily. "Tell your husband, of course. Don't believe in secrets there. But I'd be grateful if ye'd let it no further. The fact is I'm writing a romance, d'ye see." She watched to see the effect the news had on Nora, who gave no hint other than that she considered it the most natural thing in the world for Lady Henshaw to be doing—especially as she had shouted it to the four winds only yesterday. Satisfied, she continued: "It's a tragic tale with a happy ending. The hero, you see, is an aristocrat stolen away at birth by gypsies and then sold into a poor family. At the last, to be sure, all is discovered by a most ingenious interplay of circumstance, and the young duke is restored to his rightful inheritance; but before that he has the most rash experiences."

"It sounds quite entertaining," Nora said. To herself she wondered why the poor might want to buy a baby—especially as there were cheaper and more pleasurable ways available. "Is that water drinkable? May I? I'm very thirsty . . ."

Lady Henshaw merely nodded, eager not to be distracted. "The fact of the matter is—I know so little about life among the lower orders. It is extraordinary how ignorant one can be without knowing it. The simplest things: where they keep their money . . . how they shop . . . how they *manage* without a servant . . . what dances they do. . . . It really is quite monstrous—the *depth* of one's ignorance."

Understanding dawned on Nora at last: She was to be some sort of advisor to Lady Henshaw on the lower orders! She laughed in modesty, not in such a way as to offend. "Why don't you just go up and down the valley . . . your neighbours here, all around. . . ."

"Neighbours?" Lady Henshaw was puzzled. "Well, yes, I suppose they are neighbours—in strictly geographical usage. But no no no no no no, I don't need to. That's why I'm so pleased to have found you."

"Oh?"

"Yes. You are one of our sort, yet you have lived so long among them. . . ."

Nora did not trust her ears. "One of *your* sort? I am one of your sort?"

Now the other looked doubtful. "It *was* your grandfather, James Telling, squire of Normanton?"

Nora nodded. "Great-grandfather."

Lady Henshaw was vastly relieved to have the fact confirmed. "Hunted with my maternal grandfather. So there you are!"

"But what possible . . ." Nora's voice tailed off. "You mean that signifies? My *great*-grandfather?"

"Of course it signifies, you goose! It is *all* that matters. You wait until you read my book. It is all explained there. Do you imagine for one moment that I would open my doors to you and . . . and . . . and take you strolling if you were just some middling sort of person? If you were not a Telling?"

In later years Nora was to remember these casual statements, and even to think of them as among the most illuminating things that Lady Henshaw ever said to her; at the time, though, they merely left her even more confused. "You mean, the fact that I know nothing of the ways of society, no French, cannot play music, or sing after notes, cannot compose a letter, have read no clever books . . ."

Lady Henshaw had begun shaking her head and wafting her hands about dismissively as soon as Nora had reached her first instance; by now the motion was so violent that she was afraid the other might shake herself apart. "You'll soon pick up all that. It seemed a fair exchange to me. You tell me the ways of the lower classes—among whom it was your unfortunate lot to sojourn, a mistake now quite properly rectified—while I tell you the proper modes of behaviour." She cleared her throat, holding up a hand to prevent Nora from saying anything just yet. "Also, I thought you might care to learn how to master a horse and ride to hounds."

Nora suddenly divined that a brain far cooler and more calculating than anything yet revealed lurked beneath that eccentric and seemingly dissociated exterior. In that fraction of a second she revised all her estimates of—and revalued all the gossip she had heard concerning—this remarkable lady.

"I accept—and gladly," she said. "You honour me, your ladyship. And it's a poor return I can give, I think."

Lady Henshaw patted her arm. "I shall be the judge of that."

They returned their glasses, unwashed, and Lady Henshaw locked the cupboard. "Don't call me 'your ladyship,' " she added. "That's servants' talk. You will call me 'Lady Henshaw.' "

"Mrs. Thornton has been helping me with some instruction," Nora said, not wanting to seem disloyal to Arabella, who had so zealously and steadfastly guided her all these weeks.

"And ought to continue so," Lady Henshaw said. "But always remember that hers is necessarily a very middle-class view. They are what the French call *bourgeois*. The Thorntons. Not like us. She is from the south, which is so spoiled by new fortunes and by tuft-hunters treading on one another's pretensions. . . . I eat goat's meat, but do I bleat or try to scale rooftops? Your navvies eat beef but do they grow horns and moo? Of course not—yet that is how the middle class digest all these books on etiquette that people are scribbling now. They turn into little walking vademecums of behaviour. It shall be my especial aim, dear Mrs. Stevenson, to spare you such a fate. You must know what to do—but, even more important, you must know when *not* to do it. And that," she sighed, "is something the whole tribe of Mrs. Thorntons could hardly tell you."

Going back through the stable yard, Lady Henshaw said, as if on the most sudden impulse: "Have a look at another hack of mine." And she threw back her head and bawled, "McGinty!"

They were back in upside-downland. One of the stable doors began to fall outward, ponderously. When the dark V it created was only thirty or so degrees from vertical, a lithe, elfin figure leaped through it into the yard and positioned itself to catch the door before it fell all the way.

"Lost count of the times I've told him to mend that hinge," Lady Henshaw said, and she gave McGinty a nod.

When Lady Henshaw said her groom had lost all his teeth, Nora had pictured an old, shrivelled man, employed for his wisdom rather than his strength. But McGinty could not have been more than thirty. With his red, moonish face and almost permanent elfin smile, he looked like a juvenile Punchinello; he was often suspected of devilment or wit where he had intended only plain action and speech. Nora pitied him his lack of teeth until, on a later visit, she saw him demolish a large, crisp apple as efficiently as any horse would have done, bare gums or no bare gums.

In response to her nod, McGinty, having replaced the door, now opened it from the outside, the way it would open if it had hinges. Moments later he reappeared leading a magnificent blue-roan gelding with black legs. It stood quiet as a lamb, head up, ears pricked, eyes alert, as it might stand for a portrait. There are some horses that proclaim their quality at first sight, even to the most ignorant, and this was such an animal. She dug her fingernails into its withers and raked them back to its flank. Such muscle! And then down, from its shoulder to its elbow. How the flesh trembled over its chest! It turned and nuzzled her.

"Magnificent!" she breathed.

McGinty gazed at her in an astonishment that turned to glee when she said: "Worth eighty if it's worth a farthing."

"Eighty, is it!" McGinty exclaimed. "Sure wasn't I on him this very mornin', and didn't the fella leap Henshaw clough without the spur? There's not a hedge nor wall in the whole West Riding he wouldn't leap and ye'd think him on his way to bed! And the pedigree that's on him . . ."

"It's all right, McGinty," Lady Henshaw said. "We're not selling."

"I'm glad it's yer ladyship says so. Sure if ye were, I'd not advise a penny under a hundred. And that's guineas." He patted the horse's neck. "Ah—that's a grand creature! So he is."

"Name?" Nora asked.

"Millwood," Lady Henshaw told her. "After the place we got him. Try him, go on."

"I'm not clad properly . . ." Nora began before the look in Lady Henshaw's eye withered her to silence. "Without a saddle?" she asked, not seeking to delay, for she desperately wanted to mount him. Lady Henshaw nodded toward McGinty, who stood with his hands ready cupped to help her up. He was strong, too; she barely got her weight above the ankle in his hands before he hoisted her easily into the air and, in perfect time with her movement, lowered her onto Millwood's back. Trembling with elation, she crooked her right leg up over Millwood's withers and pressed the other against his side, smoothing down her petticoats in the same movement.

"Have ye sat a horse before?" Lady Henshaw asked.

Nora was at first too shy and too delighted to answer; she merely shook her head and smiled. Then, feeling that was a little discourteous, she said, barely audibly: "Once when I was ten."

"Looks born to it, wouldn't ye say?" Lady Henshaw asked the groom.

"Born to it, is it! Sure if ye didn't know better ye'd swear she grew from out the fella's back."

"Sit up straighter. Even straighter. Take up the traces."

"There's no bit . . ."

"He'll not run off with ye."

Nora took up the traces, holding them awkwardly. McGinty reached a hand under Millwood's jaw and grasped the bridle. The horse started to walk at the click of his tongue. And around the yard they went; around once, twice . . . five times in all, with Lady Henshaw shouting the occasional instruction.

To the end of her days Nora was never to forget that first moment when she sat on the back of that magnificent beast and looked down, down, down at a world unbelievably more remote than she had ever imagined it would be, and felt such monstrous power rippling so quietly beneath her. How could people ever bear to get down off a horse again and walk! Disappointment must have shown in every line of her face when McGinty's soft "Hooo!" brought Millwood to rest again.

"Wait there!" Lady Henshaw said and went quickly indoors.

Experimentally Nora dug her left heel into Millwood's flank and made, as best she could, the click of the tongue she had heard from McGinty. The horse began to walk again. McGinty grinned and shook his head. "Aren't ye the one!" he said.

After only two more circuits Lady Henshaw reappeared. Behind her was Madoc, holding a basket, its contents wrapped in a once-white cloth.

"Stay on!" she called. "You can ride down as far as the gate. We'll all accompany you."

The two deranged dogs slunk out between Madoc's legs, their heads hanging lopsided, their tails drooping. McGinty led Millwood out of the yard, with Lady Henshaw walking on the other side and Madoc a little way behind. In turning to see how close Madoc was, Nora noticed that one of the dogs had vomited a small ocean of tar, which the other was listlessly lapping up.

If the ride around the yard had been paradise, the walk down the carriage drive, her head on a level with the skeleton boughs of the avenue, was its seventh heaven. And when they reached the gate and McGinty cupped a hand again for her to step down by, she was almost ready to cry. She took Lady Henshaw's hand and curtseyed, stammering out her thanks in confusion.

"Madoc's going with you to carry the basket. You'll find some papers in it for you to look at and . . . tell me your opinion. And some goat's meat. The next best thing to venison, don't ye know."

Nora repeated her thanks.

"Until next Sunday then, Mrs. Working-Lady," Lady Henshaw said, and watched with knowing amusement as the chagrin spread across Nora's face.

"Well," Nora said. "I believe . . . I really do believe I might . . ." and her eyes kept straying toward Millwood.

"Tuesday?" Lady Henshaw said, her tongue lingering on her lip. "Just after ten? Stay for luncheon?"

And Nora could only nod, she was so happy. She watched the horse until it was out of sight. She looked around for some sign of a goat or a lunatic dog but saw none.

"How normal it all appears," she said as she set off with Madoc.

He grunted. "If 'normal' is to signify the saving of money, and a refusal to suffer fools, and the will to live free of social constraint, then that is the most 'normal' house in England," he said dourly.

# *Chapter 37*

By the end of January—or, to be precise, at ten minutes before eight o'clock on the evening of Saturday the twenty-fifth, when the shop was about to close after its fourth week of successful trading—Nora knew that whatever she was intended for in this life, it was not retailing. The succession of rush, idleness, rush, idleness, all quite outside her control, irked her. The reappearance of the same faces, the endless repetition of the same remarks about the weather and the working, and the quality of the goods she sold, the small-minded cunning they employed to try and get credit from her, the grumbles, the ailments, the catch phrases, the scurrilous jokes, the subjects for gossip, the lies . . . she felt tied to a vast merry-go-round, slowly passing and repassing the same stalls and sideshows. By the eighth circuit it had ventured beyond mere boredom and pioneered a special purgatory of its own.

The problems, too, were of the irksome rather than the challenging kind. The women from Walsden were very inadequate assistants. They gave wrong measure repeatedly—not maliciously, not even carelessly, but out of simple ignorance and inability to learn. Nora was astonished that it was she more often than the customer who noticed the underweight. Sometimes she tried short-changing them, always saying "No, no, wait a minute; stupid me!" and counting it out properly before they could protest. But it was almost always clear that they would have accepted her first count—at least until they got home.

She was not, in Madoc's phrase, one to suffer fools. And by that evening she understood more about retailers—and felt much less contempt and much more admiration for those she had met and been so scathing about to John—than she would have believed possible.

So Paul Wardroper, though he did not know it, chose a highly favourable moment to come into Stevenson's Shop and offer his services to her. He was, he explained, a flannel weaver of Rochdale; but times were hard and the mills were taking even the last bits of the trade from the handlooms. Some years ago he and a few others, attempting to cut their costs, had tried to form an equitable or co-operative shop, after Mr. Owen's model. . . .

Nora wrote *Owen, Co? shop* among the notes she had been making concerning Lady Henshaw's romance, which she had been reading in idle moments during the day.

The idea of the shop, Wardroper explained, had been to buy at wholesale rates and sell at the smallest profit conducive to maintaining the establishment. But it had failed, just as all the earlier ventures had failed. And the reason for their failure—or so he, Paul Wardroper, was convinced—was that they had not followed commercial lines. Nora, who had been about to yawn, to thank him for his little history lesson, and to lock up for the night, suddenly pricked up her ears.

"In what way?" she asked.

"We let sentiment rule commercial judgement, d'ye see, ma'am. We sold only among ourselves. Now it's my belief such a shop must work like any other shop. It must sell to any comer and at a proper commercial rate for its neighbourhood. The profit must be returned later to its subscribers, after allowing for reserves and other expenses."

"And what has this to do with me?" Nora asked.

"A number of us are eager to try the experiment again, to start an equitable shop on commercial lines in Rochdale. Yet we have no experience. Then I heard of your store here; it seems much like the one we have in mind. And, as no shopkeeper hereabouts is likely to give me experience, and believing you and the nearby shopkeepers to have no love going begging between you . . ." He smiled, not needing to finish.

Nora nodded. "Come and speak to my husband," she said. "Have you supped?"

"No . . . nor breakfasted."

"Sup with us."

Later she and John agreed that it was not his expressions of intent nor his promise of performance that swayed them but their own independent judgement of him as trustworthy, serious, and intelligent. A jewel compared with the assistants they now had from Walsden. Wardroper, his wife, and their eldest boy would work for a pound a week between them, keeping the shop open five days a week and cleaning out and moving fresh stores on the sixth. They would begin next week in place of the present staff. Nora would still do the purchasing in Manchester and up the Vale.

"He'll be a valuable man, maybe," John said when Wardroper had left. "In months ahead, as Charley Eade gets less useful to us, you could send this fellow in to buy on the same terms and with the same bonus but without the guarantee to fall back on."

"Aye," Nora said doubtfully. "I'd still have to go in every week or every other week to see he wasn't cutting price by cutting quality. But it would mean I'd not be chained to it."

She did not say what a weight it would lift from her soul. She had resigned herself to running the shop to the end of this contract—or at least until they had enough profit to get out from under Prendergast (still, mercifully, too ill to pose any immediate threat). But the prospect had seemed leaden indeed, even with young Tommy's bright chatter and cheerful flood of ideas to enliven the days.

As the time of his father's release loomed near, he grew increasingly excited. In those early days, back in November and December, he had seemed outwardly unconcerned. When people had tried to provoke him to sadness, so that they could parade their sympathy, he, by contrast, had seemed eager to make light of it. But now that Leap Year Day—the day of Thomas Metcalfe's return—was wearing on, no one could doubt how deeply Tommy must have been feeling all that time. He made a calendar to hang on the wall, with flowers and stars around the twenty-ninth of February; and each day was crossed off in a happy little ritual as soon as Nora opened the door to him in the morning. Also she discovered he had been writing brief notes to his father each day and storing them against his return. She found a small sheaf of them rolled up in the drawer of the high desk where he sat beside her and did the bonus book. They were all in order by date, beginning the second of January; each had just a few lines, saying things like "today I jumped the cluff" or "today I made out 11 pound bonus for Mrs. Stevinson, she givs lots of monney away" or "today I played 3 blind mice all throuhg."

But whatever the message for each particular day might be, there was one he repeated at the end of every note. It read, quite simply: "I love you, Daddy, and miss you and pray for you and want you home once more, Your respectful loving son, Tommy."

For Nora there was an especial sadness that grew in pace with Tommy's excitement. She knew well that Tom Metcalfe would flit from this district. John said he might have learned a lot of sense at hard labour; but Nora, while not doubting that chance, knew, also, that the humiliation had been too great to permit the man to stay. Metcalfe had stood his trial with the steadfast gleam of impending martyrdom in his eye; at no time had it burned brighter than when he had been led from the court to the back stair and the road to jail. Whatever sense he might learn, it would not stretch to the abandonment of the struggle he had then begun. There was no doubt in her mind that he would go; and that his going would take Tommy out of her life.

Often in those early days of February, as Tommy prattled on of the mammoth celebration he was planning for his father's homecoming, she forced herself to imagine the shop, and Rough Stones, and the visits to Manchester, without him, without his shrill little voice, without the constant litter of his quaint childish drawings, without his warm, sticky fingers twined in hers. It was going to be a drear world for a while, and more than once she had to blink away the tears that grew against her will. She pressed her fingers gently on the child then forming in her belly, hoping to feel a movement there. And she prayed that, boy or girl, it might be as bright and as cheering a little soul as Tommy had become to her.

By way of preparation for the wrench to come, she began in the middle of the month to cut herself off from some of the pleasures they had enjoyed together. She knew it puzzled and hurt him when, every time he suggested they should go and spit raw potato for his chickens, she would say, "Not today, Tommy, I'm a little too busy just now." She would see his face drop and she would almost relent as he walked off crestfallen. But, as is the way with children, he was skipping again by the time he reached the turnpike; and he would spit for his flock with all his usual gusto. He might miss her for a while but it would soon pass. And as for her—well, she'd just have to busy herself. Work was sovereign.

The Tuesday of the week before Metcalfe's release, Nora had spent the morning at Lady Henshaw's. By now she had a proper riding habit and McGinty was beginning to talk of going out on the highway with her.

Her eyes lit up when he raised the subject again that lunchtime. "Oh, could we?'' she asked. "There's a young friend of mine, the son of a neighbour, only a little boy, who doesn't believe I ride a horse at all. If we just went up as far as the oval shaft, I could show him. Shall I ask her ladyship? Oh, please say yes, dear McGinty!"

Moments later, with McGinty on the sorrel mare behind her, she was trotting sedately out of the gates of Henshaw Park and onto the turnpike, feeling and looking every inch the grand young lady. It was a blustery day with broken clouds scudding low across the sky and sending their shadows rippling up the valley and over the flanks of the hills faster than a horse could gallop. Her veil streamed out before her as she raised her chin and urged Millwood south toward the spot where Tommy usually sat and played his tin whistle to the chickens or spat potato for them to scrabble after.

She saw him at once, sitting cross-legged on the milestone, the hearse feathers, now gray and broken, bobbing in his cap as he nodded his head in time to whatever tune he was playing. It was some little while, however, before he saw her, so that she was less than a furlong away when he stopped, turned full face to her, and waved. She waved back.

Impulsively he leaped down from his perch and began to dance on the spot in time with his tune. Still she could not hear it because of the direction of the wind. Then, impatient of her coming, he skipped into the roadway, and began leaping and prancing, still playing an unheard melody, toward her. The chickens, Hannibal, Biddy, and all the rest of "his" flock, seeing their daily dole of potato vanish down the road, set off in pursuit, so that he seemed like some infant Pan, charming the birds with his pipes. Nora laughed to see how joyously he danced to meet her.

But her laughter was short-lived, for only an instant later she was shouting to him in alarm: "Get off the road!" Behind him the coach had turned the corner at Stone House, going its usual reckless pace, and was now bearing remorselessly down the hill toward him. And though the coachman had seen the lad and was tearing the mouths out of his team and kindling the brake, it was clear that only Tommy's own presence of mind could save him.

But the wind carried away every vestige of sound that might serve to warn him; and his own gay laughter and reckless movement were enough to drown whatever remnant fought through to him in the teeth of that blustery gale.

Nora screamed again—it was almost continuous with her first agonized call—"Get off! Get off!" And she waved her hand as if to rake him to the verge. But he could not make out her words, and the streaming of her veil cut across his view of her face; and so he danced blithely on, with four terrified horses, two tons of coach, and a panic-stricken coachman only seconds from him.

She spurred Millwood forward, knowing it was hopeless to try to reach him, yet hoping something in her movement would alert the boy. And at that instant he must at last have heard the thunder at his heels for he turned to face it.

"Tommeeeeeee!" She heard her shriek split the air of the valley. She heard it mingle with the shrilling of the horses as they reared almost broadside in their attempt to avoid him. But he stood transfixed before that monstrous onslaught. Her last memory of Tommy was to see him standing there, elbows bent high in that posture she had come to know so well, with a white cackle of chickens shimmering in feathery alarm around him, just before he fell spinning beneath that heaving wall of horseflesh, iron, and wood. "Tommeeeeee! . . ." The shriek rang on and on and on.

She lay on the ground. But was it not Tommy that lay on the ground? Confusion. Millwood was trotting homeward. McGinty, dismounted, stood ready to catch him. Her shriek, or her violent spurring, must have made him rear.

She was running. Habit hitched up around her knees. "Tommeeeeee!" Again her scream rose above the wind, above the wheeling horses, the creaking, groaning coach. People ran from the hovels.

But she was first. Let it be a miracle! Make a miracle! Oh, make a miracle! she pleaded with every jolt of her feet. The Tommy-like bundle in the road lay still as still. Her mind's eye restaged that final moment when the wall of flesh and coach burst over him. He *could* be just knocked down. Under the belly. Between the hooves. Amid the coach wheels. Oh, let him just be unconscious. A miracle! A miracle! A miracle!

With bursting lungs and red mists seeping upward into her vision she dropped to her knees beside the little boy. He lay face down. Limp. He looked unmarked, yet he did not breathe. And when she made to turn him over, as gently as could be, she knew there was no hope; his upper and lower parts moved almost independently of one another. One eyelid, obeying some final, random message from his dying brain, trembled . . . trembled . . . and was still.

The grief came within her like a possession. It overwhelmed her, stifled her breath, almost wrenched her muscles from off her bones as she leaned forward and buried her face in that dearest, most loving little body. No cry would rise in her throat. Her eyes were too clenched for tears. The agony that seized and bound her spirit was like a premonition of her own death; indeed, at that moment, if she could have exchanged states with what had been Tommy, death for his life, all the persuasion of heaven would not have stopped her.

But that was the very nadir of her anguish. Within, some unmoved caretaker of her own survival was already fighting to master that sacrificial urge to death, forcing her at least to breathe. And when it triumphed, her grateful lungs gulped hugely at the air. And Tommy, who for that long-held moment had stayed so close, while her answering soul had hovered on the borders of his death, now vanished from her faster even than the speed of prayer. And only then did she begin to feel his loss as something quite distinct from her grief at his going.

That grief was now a mercy, racking her body into sobbing convulsion, aching at her throat, shrivelling every joint, filling all the corners of her with sensation to efface the world and bring a kind of waking oblivion. Of the scene around—the milling feet, the hushed throng, the women weeping into shawls and aprons, the whole dumbfounded universe—she was unaware. Until strong hands reached down to lift her. To turn her. To fold her into a giant's body, all strength and all tenderness in one huge frame. A well of dark and warmth and comfort. "Come away now," John said. His voice seemed to arise within the channels of her ear. "Let your grief go. Stint nothing in it." He was not far from weeping, too.

Of the walk back to Rough Stones, too, she knew little. The gripping in her stomach seemed just one more part of the whole agonized world. But a half hour later, when she lay in her darkened room, sobbed out and void of grief, she knew the stirring there was more physical in its cause; and she crawled across the room, enduring one long paroxysm, hoping she might reach the commode in time.

Sweat sprang from every pore and she thought for a moment that this pain—a real, wrenching, physical pain—would burst her skull apart. It had never been so bad those other times. She sat, and strained, and waited.

And though it had come so insidiously upon her, its lifting was as sudden and as blessed as a fanfare. Something left her womb. It passed, hot and piercing down her birth canal, seeming to cut her as it went—but to cut like a knife so sharp that its severing was kindly, without pain. She heard it fall, wet and limp, into the porcelain. She felt the blood that seeped out after it. That too was warm. All warmth seemed eager to pass from her.

When the shivering was over and a great coldness fell about the room, she stirred again, reaching a rag from the store in the commode—unneeded these months long past. Months dead beyond recall.

Automatically, obeying long memory, her fingers folded the clout and held it to her groin as she prepared to rise and put on its more permanent fastening. The first movement carried her to the floor beside the commode and she could not avoid seeing the thing within.

But it was not a thing. It was a baby, perfect down to its last detail, though it was no bigger than a kitten and only its right arm had yet formed. The other was just a little bud still—though it had perfect hands and fingers, and its feet had toes. *His* feet. He would have been a boy.

She was amazed at herself for looking at him so dispassionately. Was there no sadness left to share for her own . . . flesh and blood? She looked again at the dead boy in his porcelain sarcophagus. Flesh and blood were the words for it. And then a terrible doubt eased itself into her thoughts: Was it perhaps . . . Thornton's begetting? One, two, three, four . . . four and a half . . . nearly five months. Is that what a baby looked like then? They said—Mrs. Hampton had said—that sweet basil tea dried up your monthlies, too. So you couldn't tell. Surely it was too small to have been begot last August? Perhaps it was best never to know.

Aching at every joint she roused herself and secured the menstrual rag more permanently. She covered the aborted fetus with soil and paper, as if it had been an everyday evacuation, and put it, for the moment, back in its cupboard. Then she rang for Bess.

"Mistress!" the girl cried out the moment she entered the door. She ran to her, thinking she would fall at any moment.

"Help me dress," Nora said, her intention firm if not her voice.

"But . . . the master says ye've to rest. He's seeing to everything. . . ."

Nora shook her head. "There's too much to do. We must not succumb to grief but rise above it."

Bess, though filled with doubt, knew better than to argue.

"Lace me in tight," Nora said. "I need its support."

"Have a drop of brandy," Bess said. "It'll still the pain and race thy blood for thee."

And later, when Bess saw her carrying out the commode pot and remonstrated with her, Nora said: "I need work into me hands, see thee," which so astonished the girl that she thought her mistress was mocking her or—even worse—making a joke.

Nora, wearing bonnet, shawl, and cape against a cold that had struck to the very core of her, stood at the front door of Rough Stones, let it close behind her, rested against it, and dared, for the first time, to think of Tommy. Instantly hot tears flooded her eyes and her body succumbed to a relief of sobbing. The salt ran, cooling, down her cheeks, cold upon her chin, and chill at the pit of her neck. She shivered. It would not do. There were so many things to arrange. Mourning. She'd have to get some weeds.

Arabella was at the gate; suddenly there was no telling reality from what might be.

Arabella was real. And this hot misery.

"My dear!" Arabella said, coming up the path. "Oh, my dear!"

"I must get some mourning," Nora said. "What must I do about it?"

It was a general cry for help, but Arabella, her sense undermined by the emotion of the moment, yet having come to Rough Stones prepared to be practical, to do practical things, slipped unthinkingly into the role she had so gladly filled for many weeks past. And to her own shocked dismay she heard herself saying: "Oh, you need only get an armband, as it's not family. And it need last no more than a week . . ."

Nora's look of horror checked her at last, and she stood dumbfounded as the anguished girl rolled herself off the door and on to the stone wall of the house, which she then beat repeatedly with her forehead and her hands, crying, again and again, a formless, grieving cry.

Arabella stood helpless behind her, biting her lip until the pain became intense. If biting her tongue off would call back those thoughtless words, she would have bitten it through at once. But the words were out; their utterance was irretrievable. "I did not mean *that*," she cried in an agony of shame. "It was your question . . . you said . . ." But what could explain her words? What would make Nora even stop and listen?

No. To the contrary, Nora's departure into this furious agony was a deserved rebuke; at such unguarded moments the thoughts that escape us are a true window into our souls. Let her now search into her own. Her words had been no *mere* slip, but were as a sign from Providence; it was a cue for prayerful self-examination.

Nora's passion was somewhat more governed now. Arabella reached out a hesitant arm and grasped her shoulder. "Nora?" she said.

The other became quieter, indeed almost calm again, though still she did not turn.

"Nora, that was the most callous and . . . unfeeling and . . . unthinking, thoughtless, stupid thing to have said. Please . . . I . . . Nora?" Her voice tailed off as Nora, now quite subdued, continued to lean against the wall. Arabella was almost on the point of leaving when Nora at last turned to her again and smiled wanly.

"I'm sorry," Arabella said. "Truly."

Nora sniffed the brine from her nose and shook her head, almost as if she were angry. "My fault," she said huskily. "My . . . senseless question."

Arabella took her arm then. "You surely weren't going out?" she asked. "I came here to sit with you."

Nora drew herself up, squared her shoulders, and smiled once more, bravely this time. "I must," she said. "Life must go on . . . our life, at least. There's so much to be arranged. I should never have come up here. . . ."

"All is being taken care of," Arabella said, still trying to prevent her from leaving.

"I've no doubt." Nora pushed by her and set off, walking tenderly, for the gate. "John'd do everything if I let him. But that's not my way."

When they reached the turnpike some force drew her, against all her rational judgement, to the place where it had happened. Arabella followed, watching Nora guardedly all the way.

The road surface was a confusion of hoof marks and the ruts gouged by the iron tyres as they skidded. There was no sign of hearse feather and tin whistle.

"He must have had the brakes hard on," Arabella said. "Except for that one stretch there."

Nora kept silent. She knew why there were no skid marks on "that one stretch there." No other sign of the accident remained.

And John, she found, had indeed done it all. Immediately after the accident Walter had gone with the coach to Todmorden, where the stable master—"'Without prejudice, mind; I want that firmly understood"—readied a horse and car while Arabella was sent for. Together they had collected Mrs. Metcalfe and Tommy's sister, Beth, and he was now seeing them home to the Acorn.

"How was she affected?" Nora asked.

"As you might expect," Arabella told her, but did not elaborate.

The doctor was now making his examination for the coroner. The carpenters were putting together a regal coffin of oak, beech, ash, lime, and walnut. The lads had opened up a subscription to pay for the funeral and the tea, and to leave some over for the family. When the doctor had finished, two of the carpenters' wives would lay him out. The coffin would be ready against Thursday and then he would be taken in it over to the Acorn, ready for the funeral on Saturday.

"He's to have a proper hearse and four black horses and a full set of hearse feathers," Nora said.

But John shook his head. "I doubt the subscription'll run to that."

"If I have to pop my wedding ring to pay for it, he's to have hearse feathers," Nora insisted. "We can well afford it."

The argument was so uncharacteristic of her that he knew at once how deeply she meant it, and he agreed without demur.

"Tell the carpenters to draw up a list of the coffin furniture they need," she said before she left. "I can get it in Manchester tomorrow."

He frowned. "You'll surely not go to Manchester tomorrow?"

"Life goes on," she said. "Work is sovereign."

Her truculent bravado, which jarred so strangely with her evident grief, worried him deeply. So did her insistence that Tommy should lie shrouded in the best parlour at Rough Stones until Thursday. "He'd be too lonely down here," she said. But he wanted to do nothing that might hinder the scope of her grief.

She ate little that silent evening and he was glad when, once they were in bed and darkness was all around them, she threw herself upon him and wept an ocean from her eyes. But he did not stir from his sleep, when, much later, she slipped from between the sheets and, pulling her shawl and cloak about her, crept down through the silent house to the parlour where Tommy lay. There she renewed the single candle that burned, thrusting the darkness from him to the farthest nooks and corners of the room. When its flame had settled, she turned down the shrouds to uncover his face. The warmth of that steady light banished the pallor of death and it seemed he lay in breathless sleep. The movement of the sheet dislodged a curl, which lay across his forehead as it had in life.

In a curious way it was a joy to see him there, so calm, after that most violent and outrageous ending on the turnpike down below. She thought again of all the merry chatter, the unending stream of odd thoughts and sayings, of the faultless recitation of abstruse passages from his father's books . . . all that had poured through those lips, now forever stilled— of his shrewd, challenging eyes, so eloquent in laughter, so downcast in rebuke or shame, now forever lost to the light . . . dead lips, dead eyes, in a dead face. No Tommy lurked behind them now, ready to ambush her delight and wonder.

No Tommy.

There was no Tommy any more. Never more.

The world would never know him as she had.

Her hand brushed something soft in the shadows on the table. The plume. The broken plume all battered and gray. She lifted it. The toy whistle rolled gently toward her. She picked it up. The women who had laid him out had not known what to do with them. She rolled the shrouds lower, exposing his two hands, crossed piously upon his chest. That was not like Tommy. She loosened them, one upon another, and between them gently inserted the two toys, curling his fingers around them.

She meant it as an act of love, but there was no Tommy there to be loved now. Instead it was an act of parting, a numb leave-taking between one body and another; one body dead beyond all fancy it might live; and another that mourned . . . mourned . . . mourned too deep for tears, mourned too deep even for understanding.

She pulled the shrouds back then and left the room. Outside the house, barefoot on the path Tommy had freed from its weeds, she felt the cold night seep into her bones. A glacial moon shone through ragged clouds in a burnished impasto of light. But no answering light burned in the valley below. No glimmer showed from up the Vale. The whole world lay stricken with sleep. Here, alone, cold in the icy moonlight, she felt closer to Tommy than she had felt in there beside what had been him. Or *housed* him. For he was in spirit now; liberated; free to soar. Yes! His had been a soaring kind of spirit.

She looked skyward. If he was anywhere, he was there, filling the sky from horizon to horizon. Beyond pain. Beyond the rage of life.

As she went back upstairs to the bed she thought would never warm again, she was astounded to find her cheek wet with tears. *It must have been the wind,* she thought, for she had felt no especial cause for grief. Indeed, the understanding that Tommy was now beyond the reach of pain was the balm that brought her sleep.

By grim coincidence Mrs. Metcalfe called on her way to the mill next morning with a similar thought to impart. She opened the top half of the kitchen door before she knocked and waited to be bade indoors. There was only one person in the world who regularly opened the door in that way and at that hour, and Nora rushed to the kitchen, hoping, for one unthinking moment, to see him—but learning only that the body's habits and memories are beyond the rational order.

"I'm sorry to open the door afore I knock, missis," Mrs. Metcalfe said. "It's me hearing. It's been that bad since I started at the mill."

Nora had no resources left to enable her to respond to an opening at this level of banality. "Come in, Mrs. Metcalfe," she said. "What a grief it is, to be sure. And you should know how deep we share it."

Mrs. Metcalfe came just within the door, and Beth, her eyes as red as coals, shuffled in beside her.

"Ye'll want to see him," Nora said.

"Aye," Mrs. Metcalfe agreed. "And the lass. She should see, too."

Nora showed them in and left them.

"What did you think that was, then?" John asked.

Nora stared back, unwilling to answer.

"And all that blood on the cloth in the commode cupboard?" he continued.

That was easier to bluff through. "I've got the cardinal for a visit," she said. "Very normal."

"Looks a lot to me," he said.

"It often is, they say. With being on sweet basil."

He smiled. "I think it's time we gave that gentleman no more house-room."

She reached over the table then and squeezed his hand, as happy as the times allowed. From the next room they could hear the sobbing of the mother and daughter.

The pair still wept as they left by the front door, but just before they reached the gate, Mrs. Metcalfe turned and said: "Mebbe the lad had the best of it. That brightness in him would've been a scourge in later days. Like for his dad, see. It's naught but a pain to him. To understand what's best left be by the likes of us."

"Mebbe," Nora agreed. There was no ground where her mind and the mind that nurtured such cold comfort could meet. And as she turned from them and went back indoors, her body once again forgot, and prepared itself to welcome the Tommy they had not left today. She had to fight back her tears. How long before that eager corner of her heart was choked?

"How may I help thee?" John asked when she sat again beside him and the house was still.

"Oh, my love," she said. "Just be! Just *be*. Without thee in this house I'd not have come through this dark day. I've known since that hour we met—I've but one single cause to live. But it's taken this grief to show it's as true of the dark in life as of the light." He squeezed her hand. "If thou art *there*," she went on, now feeling a desperate urge to talk, "there's all the world may come at us. It'll not signify—not so long as thou art *there*." She sighed. There was so much more to say—but no words to say it in.

"And Tommy," he said, warily. "Thou'll not conserve thy grief? Thou'll give it rein?"

She nodded. "Nay, but thou were right," she said. "And I were wrong. We oughtn't to have meddled. I were wrong to send her to work. To take him here. We should've sent them ten bob a week and . . ." She shrugged.

"And abandoned them?" he said. "Let the Royal Mails be their best link with humanity? Never! Ye don't mean it."

"Meddling with others' lives is wrong," she answered. "Just because we've got money. Money doesn't convey such a right."

He sensed then that she needed some just cause for guilt to help her overcome her grief; there would be little point in trying to argue her from this stand yet a while. "Mebbe," he said, in a tone that begged to differ. "You call it right. I'd call it a duty. And in a truly just society all rights and all duties merge into one unavoidable responsibility."

She looked cannily at him then. "You and that Mr. Fielden! The man will have ye in Parliament yet."

He was glad that she could say anything that looked brightly forward—even such nonsense as that.


# *Chapter 38*


When, on Thursday, they heard that Metcalfe was not to be released on licence for the funeral, Nora at once suggested that Tommy's body should be embalmed sufficiently to preserve it over the ten days that remained before the father's sentence was served. To her surprise John strongly, almost vehemently, opposed the notion.

"It looks like a confession of responsibility . . . as if we think we owe it to the Metcalfes," he said, though that was not the real cause of his opposition; he wanted an early occasion for corpse, and grief, and memory to be buried.

"But . . ." Nora faltered. For of course it was precisely such a responsibility and such a debt that oppressed her. This impasse threatened to separate guilt from grief and to give each its independence.

His spirits fell as he saw how she struggled between the impulse to nurse her guilt and the contrary urge to confess it; and the thought occurred to him that although the immediate funeral might console her grief, the postponement until Metcalfe's release would better assuage that more stubborn sense of guilt. He resigned from the decision. "Let the mother determine it," he said.

Midmorning brought Beth and her mother, dressed for the expected funeral. As soon as Nora put the suggestion to Mrs. Metcalfe, she regretted it. The pair had come to Rough Stones braced for the ordeal and welcoming the release it would bring. The momentum of their expectations almost carried the mother on to a decision for an immediate funeral. Yet there was a gleam in her eye that Nora at once recognized: a savage gleam of proffered revenge.

Nora remembered how, when her little sister Dorrie had died of fever and loss of blood, after the rats had savaged her, and when, only days later she had come home from the mill to find that Tom o' Jones's boar had killed and devoured her youngest brother, Wilfrid, leaving only an arm to bury, one of her first, grief-stricken reactions had been to wish for some way of sending their wretched remains out to Daniel in his Australian penal colony. How desperately she had wanted some means to inflict her outrage upon him and heap him with it. So she understood, perhaps even better than Mrs. Metcalfe herself, why the other finally decided for a postponement—and why the decision was made with such quiet satisfaction.

But vengeance of that petty order is not easy to sustain. Nora, a year earlier, had not even been able to send Daniel a cutting from the *Manchester Guardian,* which had carried a paragraph baldly summarizing the coroner's findings that no one was particularly to blame for the deaths. So, too, when the day of the funeral came, Mrs. Metcalfe was as confirmed in her grief and as grateful for her Tom's support as the most devoted of wives and mothers.

That last day of February shivered with the false promise of spring. Bare branches stirred in a gentle breeze, gleaming robustly in the sun as if by afternoon they might burst forth in buds of green. Fields and headlands, after a rainless week, put off their sodden winter darkness and tempted the bolder farmers to mend their ploughs and patch up their big harnesses. A light powder scattered from hooves and wheels passing and repassing along the turnpike, foreshadowing the dust devils of high summer. Only down the thickset, overhung lanes and dank in the shades of ditches, where mud lay clogged, and water gurgled crisp and cold as it drained, only there was winter's reign unbroken still.

The earth had been heaped from Tommy's grave before that earlier, postponed interment. Already its appearance was that of an ancient mound, smoothed by rain, cracked by frost, and smoothed again. Nora wished the sexton had roughened and freshened its surface for today's ceremony; its smoothness and the erosion of its feet gave it the semblance of a mountain. Indeed it seemed a prodigious quantity of earth to pile upon so small and frail a body.

Though a hundred or more awaited the interment outside, only a handful went into the church for the service—the Metcalfes, the Stevensons, Findlater and the other Chartists, Hope, Burroughs, and a number of the Summit navvies and tradesmen. The young boys who bore the coffin and pall, sons of Metcalfe's fellow bricklayers, were also there.

Prison had changed Metcalfe—not merely in such obvious ways as his gaunt frame and haggard face, but also in a new shiftiness about his eyes and a permanent air of nervous apprehension. His dignity had been laid waste. The man who shouted defiance at John Stevenson at the trial, and who ruefully but good-humouredly smiled at the shouted reply of "better combination," had been broken, or so it seemed. The wreck of him shuffled in an off-the-treadmill gait down the aisle, looking to neither side, avoiding every eye. Even when Findlater reached out and squeezed his arm, he passed on with scarcely a nod, still not raising his eyes.

Stevenson was shocked to see what the new silent prisons could do to a man. The old, rowdy, anarchic houses of correction might have brutalized and degraded the body, but they had never so quenched the spirit. Throughout the long service he stared at Metcalfe's listless back, hoping for some sign of that old truculent confidence, and finding none.

The curate spoke endlessly of death and sin, never once mentioning Tommy, never even hinting that it was a child they were committing into the care of eternity. If he had gone on a minute longer, Nora would have stood and thrown a hymnbook at him. John, sensing her mood, patted her clenched fist and whispered: "Look at Findlater."

She turned slowly and saw that the Methodist's face was fixed in a mask of bloodless fury. She was glad her mood was shared—indeed, looking around she could see no expression there of solemn and composed agreement. Most were coldly angry at the irrelevant and platitudinous homily they were being forced to endure. The energy and relief with which they went out of doors for the interment were almost unseemly.

But out there the cleric was reduced to his proper dimensions—an ill-thriven cold-heart, posturing beneath an infinite sky and half drowned by breezes. He became—as indeed he was—an outsider to their collective sorrow, centred now on that tiny polished coffin waiting for its last consignment. Their anger dissipated itself as they faced the solemnity of those last aweful rites, now so near at hand.

To Nora, as that moment approached, it suddenly became clear that no justice had been done to Tommy. They had all been put through a ritual of no especial relevance to him. They might as well have collected every creature that had died in the parish over this last fortnight and heaped them all in beside him for economy's sake. She saw the young bearers and the head carpenter, Shortis, who was officiating here as undertaker, preparing the braid straps for the lowering, and a panic seized her. He must not be left to go in this cold, irrelevant way. Someone must say that it was *Tommy* in that box, and say what manner of person Tommy was. In her agitation she almost decided to take the office upon herself but, to her relief, she saw that Findlater, also in the second rank of mourners, stood no more than a few paces away.

Quickly she edged herself to his side. "Findlater," she said. "We can't commit him to judgement with just this curate's words to go beside him. Someone must speak as to the little lad himself."

At once she knew that Findlater had been on the verge of the same decision, for he shot her such a look of grateful relief and stepped forth to stand beside the grave, holding out a hand to stay the bearers for a moment. Tom Metcalfe, who had overheard, beamed his gratitude at Nora, who, in thin-lipped embarrassment, returned his smile.

"By your leave, doctor," Findlater said to the astonished curate, who, looking around the assembled mourners, had the good sense to bide his peace.

In a style no longer fashionable, Findlater spoke directly to the coffin: "I did not know you well, Tommy. We met but once and you asked me a question that puzzled me then and that continues to puzzle me now. As I went from that meeting I could not but help thinking of the story of Our Lord in the second chapter of Luke, where He astonished the doctors of the Temple with His questions." Then, sensing the outrage stirring in the curate, he added in a slightly querulous tone: "I did not then, nor in all that I have heard of you since, feel any taint of blasphemy in that conjunction of my thoughts. For there was about you, Tommy, a quality that brought to me a deep understanding of Our Lord's injunction to suffer little children to come unto Him. Often in these months past, and of course most especially since your tragic death, I have found my thoughts returning to you, together with those words 'suffer little children.' So, all unknowingly, you have brightened my life with a deeper awareness of the radiant love of God. That is why I have come today, Tommy, and why I am moved to speak this farewell.

"But I am a mere one, one of a hundred and more, all moved by that same spirit of ineffable sorrow. Perhaps they would not express it in quite these same words, but their inner sense would not be otherwise: A radiance has gone from among us. A direct illumination of God's holy Word has been taken from us. Yet for those of us who have the eyes to perceive and whose hearts are open to accept, you leave behind among us the understanding which, all unknowingly, you brought. God is indeed tender and merciful to us. For though He has taken you and your brightness to Himself, He has left below your dearest gift: a deeper understanding of His ways. For who, knowing you, did not at once also know, and know with a certainty that learned homilies could never impart, what Our Lord meant when He said: 'of such are the Kingdom of Heaven.' "

Everyone thought Findlater had finished and so began nodding agreement, blowing noses, and wiping their eyes. But he, looking directly at the Metcalfes and the Stevensons, raised his voice and added: "In your life you united people whom these troubled times might have torn asunder into bitterest hatred. Let us not forget that. Let us not turn back from the kinship you gave us. Let us preserve it and thus honour you."

He bowed his head in mute prayer. In the silence before the ceremony resumed, Nora's heart exulted. Tommy had been sent off duly and fittingly. It was almost a triumph to see his coffin lowered and hear the closing words of the interment ring out over that silent throng. He did not go to his long home unshriven. The hollow rain of subsoil on the lid of his box was like the applause of a grand finale.

And at last it was completed. One by one the crowd withdrew, silently to the churchyard gate, then with animated chatter—some even with laughter—as they strode or strolled out along the turnpike to the barn where the funeral meats were to be served.

At length only the Metcalfes were left at the graveside; a little way behind stood John and Nora. The sexton, spade in hand, waited respectfully by the church wall, studying one of the windows as intently as if he had never seen it in his life. Tom Metcalfe had lost that air of meek submission he had worn in church, but his dignity was still a mere phantom of its former substance. When he turned and saw them he smiled with a wan and unconcealed surprise. They nodded back, uncertain who should speak first.

Beth leaned toward her mother and whispered something. With fussy resignation Mrs. Metcalfe led her daughter away round the back of the church building. Only when they were out of sight did Metcalfe, facing the inevitable, turn again to them and begin to stammer out his gratitude.

"You must not even think it," Nora said. And to distract him she moved to the graveside to take her own last parting.

John did not join her. "You certainly must not," he said. "Young Tommy came to mean a lot to Mrs. Stevenson and me. Whatever little we've done was as nothing, for if we'd done less, we'd have hurt ourselves."

"All the same . . ." Metcalfe said. He was uncertain how to speak to John.

"Well . . ." John looked at the tower and then at the sky. "I expect Shortis has settled up but I just ought to see he's left naught undone." He turned and left them alone at the grave.

Nora stiffened at once. Despite her love for Tommy, and the solemnity of the moment, and despite Findlater's eloquent final plea, she could not block out the thought that here was the man who had wished to encompass their ruin. It was hard not to hate.

"Mrs. Metcalfe's told me of all what you did," he said. "About getting

her out the workhouse and . . . seeing her straight and all . . . and helping . . ." He nodded at the earth, unable to say the name.

"I know what it's like. Being left . . ." she answered in as neutral a
tone as she could muster. She did not look at him.

"Aye. She told us that and all. Well . . ." He sighed. "I'd just say
thanks, like. Not wanting to make it more difficult for thee."

She stared at the coffin, knowing it would be the last time she or anyone
ever saw it; she tried to efface Metcalfe at her side. "God preserve that little
spirit," she said quietly.

He stood bowed and silent as she left. She thought her words might
have stung him into tears, for though he was still, he breathed like a
sobbing man. She was glad he had heart enough left for it.

Toward the end of the day, as the afternoon faded to a frosty night,
John Stevenson came upon Metcalfe, standing, as chance would have it, in
that same bowed and silent attitude near the turnpike gate. The funeral tea
was drawing to its close.

"Tom," he said.

Metcalfe grunted.

"What'll thou do now?"

"I've not given it that much thought."

"What about America? Make a fresh start of it?"

"Run away, ye mean?"

Stevenson was heartened to hear the challenge, just a hint of that same
old challenge, return to his voice. "I hope jail's not made thee bitter,
Tom," he said.

"I'll go back down south, I think."

"Ye could do well by yerself. These are champion days for men of
enterprise."

Metcalfe snorted a single, despairing laugh, shook his head, and sucked
a tooth.

"What's that to say?" Stevenson asked.

"Thou'll never change."

"And thou? I'd hoped thy time on Jacob's ladder'd bring thee to a
better comprehension of this world and Tom Metcalfe's place in it."

"The union's still our lodestar, if that's what thou art on about."

"Which union, lad? Thou talks as if there's naught but the one."

Metcalfe stared morosely at the reddening sky, not deigning to answer.

Stevenson pressed on, wanting to test him for any new weakness in
resolve, any undermining of that once-implacable faith. "Eh—I wish
sometimes I were in manufactures."

Metcalfe turned to him in surprise. "You?" he asked.

"I'd know what to do with unions there!"

"Same as here—smash 'em."

"Would I!" Stevenson sneered. "I tell thee: If I was Fielden or any of these other mill masters, I'd not let any man or woman through the gates as weren't in a union. Bible."

Metcalfe stared at him, frankly incredulous. "And in the Horse Marines, too, I've no doubt," he said at last.

"Thou art blind, Tom. Blind. Thou thinks all masters are the same and act as one. And thou thinks the union is like one Leviathan operative—all power delivered in one mighty fist."

The image seized Metcalfe's imagination and his eyes burned red with light borrowed from the falling day. "Aye!" he breathed.

Stevenson laughed. "Eeee! Thou hast *that* much to learn of human nature! Listen—thou'll hear nothing for free. Hast thou heard this word *bureaucracy?*"

"Nay."

"It's a paradise for clerks. And it's what thy union'd turn itself into."

"Never!"

"I guarantee it. Give me a big mill and compel every hand into a union, and inside a year I'd get fifty committees going. I'd weave rings round the likes of thee. I'd get committees for carders, committees for doffers, for strippers, for grinders, for sheet-loom minders, patchers, spindle-shank turners, twelve-hour men, floor sweepers. . . . I'd find fifty classes under that one roof. Fifty different workin' classes to shove and elbow one another. Inside five years there'd be so many committees going, I'd be able to drag wage negotiations out the best part of six months. Easy!"

Metcalfe was trembling with anger. "Never! The union'd never let thee! The union'd stop it."

"*Stop* it?" John's scorn was deep. "I tell thee—the union . . . nay, folk, folk in the union, *folk,* they'd do it. I'd have a job stopping them." His tone was suddenly more sad than triumphant and he patted Metcalfe's arm to show that he was no longer offering debate. "Still, I see thou art set on the union way. I thought this three month past would've put thee on to some other line."

Metcalfe relaxed and leaned on the gate, able to turn to Stevenson for the first time and smile at him, equal to equal, now that the challenge had gone. "I'm not given to such light conversion," he said.

Stevenson nodded. "Then tell us, Tom. Here's something thou must've ground over in thy mind in the jailhouse. If thou were back on the works, would thou still seek to combine?"

But Metcalfe merely laughed. "Give us the job back, and I'll give thee certain answer," he said. When Stevenson did not reply he, too, became serious again. "Navigation work," he went on, "is no place to start with unions. Too transient. Nay—I shall go where I can make me weight felt."

Stevenson suddenly turned to him and held out his hand. "Mebbe we'll meet then, Tom. It's a small world, ours. Good luck go with thee."

Metcalfe paused before he took the proffered hand. "If we do, it'll be on opposite sides of the table. I'll show thee no more mercy than thou showed me."

"Fairly said."

Then they stood in silence a while, side by side, leaning on the gate and watching the night drain the red from the sky.

And watching and overhearing them from the fringe of a nearby group, Nora succumbed to a relief whose intensity surprised even herself.

# PART FIVE

Tabard Inn

# Chapter 39

As February passed into March and March into April, John watched Nora's grief dwindle until none but he could see the remnant. She wept no more, heaved no more sighs at unaccountable moments, tossed through no more shallow nights. She spoke less often of Tommy, and when she did it was with a brightness that was less obviously forced. She still visited his grave each week and freshened it with flowers but, outwardly at least, these trips had less and less the nature of a pilgrimage and took on more and more the character of outings for herself and whichever of Lady Henshaw's horses she was exercising that week.

The mere record of her actions showed that her life had returned in every way to the pattern in which Tommy's death had cut so harsh a wound. Each week she visited Lady Henshaw and corrected the more glaring absurdities of the romance she was writing—though, as Nora said to John, "If you overlook her ignorance about working folk, it's not a bad little yarn—there's excitement in it, I'll say that."

The book implanted more complex thoughts of which she was not wholly aware, and which she would have found difficult to put into words for him. All her life she had seen the gentry—men like the Duke of Bridgewater's agent and Mr. Orrell, the master of the mill at Stockport—as larger than herself and her kind, yet also distant. The effect was exactly that of looking at people through a telescope. You were sure you could touch them and talk to them; yet they moved in silence through a remote and glassy kind of medium. Reading Lady Henshaw's book was like putting her eye to the other end of that same telescope. Everything near at hand was suddenly made to appear untouchably remote and small and insignificant.

Again and again her mind returned to Lady Henshaw's casual assertion that Nora Telling's ancestry counted far more toward her social acceptability than anything Nora Stevenson actually was or did. That, and the attitudes she unconsciously absorbed from the eccentric old woman's book, began a process of subtle change within her. For a long time she was unaware of it, and even when it did begin to strike her, the effects seemed trivial. One day, for instance, it suddenly occurred to her that she no longer minded having Bess and Tabitha around the house. When they had first moved to Rough Stones she had resented their constant presence; it put her always on display. Home was no longer her nest and John's nest, a free-and-easy refuge. But now all that had vanished; now the house would have felt empty and somehow wrong without servants.

Even then she did not at once connect these changes with Lady Henshaw's book.

John, whose reading of the book was more analytical, pointed out that her ladyship recognized only two kinds of poor. One kind was like a ragged middle class; it knew its place, obeyed the ten commandments, ate well but frugally, kept the temperance code, and always had a few shillings saved. Its children were cherubs in fustian—bonny, chubby, red-cheeked, and mischievous. The other poor were dangerous, vicious, drunken people, always destitute, and deeply dyed in sloth and depravity; they were either mere rag-clad skeletons or towering, hulking bullies—who or what fed them to such gargantuan proportions was a mystery left ravelled; any money they had put by was dishonestly gained.

"She believes it, too," John said. "They must all believe it. The deserving poor are angels in rags. So if the poor you meet look thin and starved and destitute they *must* also be vicious and undeserving."

"She must ride around here blind then," Nora said.

She made a comparable division in the language she advised Lady Henshaw to put into the mouths of these figments: a kind of colourless bad grammar with an insipid northern flavour for the deserving; and a rich, zestful dialect—her own native speech, in fact—full of oaths and insult, for the depraved.

These literary endeavours and her own tuition in etiquette generally occupied them until luncheon. Then, for most of the afternoon, she would ride, sometimes by the turnpike, sometimes over the top of Summit, but always by way of Littleborough cemetery. Very soon she had reached the degree of proficiency at which most people would begin to attend the meets of their nearby hunt. McGinty was always pressing her to take the plunge for he was not only proud of her progress, he also felt that Lady Henshaw did not ride to hounds nearly often enough for her own sport, the good of her horses, or his own pleasure.

"Aw, go on, missis!" he would urge. "Sure there's dozens there couldn't sit a horse like yerself can. Ye'd walk past them and they at full gallop."

But Nora was adamant. She would not hunt this season. "Suppose it came to the kill and I'd kept up all the way and they were breaking up Charley Fox in the next field and me in this one and every hedge a hairy bullfinch and no gate . . . I'd bust every vein in my skull."

"Arrah! Sure there's no such field with Millwood beneath ye. He'd swish at any bullfinch and make a rasper of it and leave the rest of the field looking for the gate."

"And me on foot! Or worse. No, you'll not tempt me now. When I hunt I want riding to be second nature. I want to forget riding. So save your breath."

On at least one day each week she and Arabella would hire two hacks from the livery stables next to the cockfighting pit in Todmorden and ride out for a whole morning or afternoon over the moors to the north—once going as far as Haworth, right over the far side. These adventures came to an abrupt end one day when Arabella, in an agony of embarrassment, asked Nora how a woman could know whether or not a baby was on the way—and Nora told her. From that day onward Arabella retired to live the life of a semi-invalid, not at all from modesty but because, as every doctor knew, pregnancy among the middle class was the next best thing to a long, debilitating illness.

Each week, too, Nora would go to Manchester to get the supplies for her store, which Wardroper, the Rochdale flannel weaver, was now running with such efficiency. Her battle with Charley Eade had sunk to a state of armed truce. She caught him twice in small deceptions that he passed off as errors; and she was sure no larger swindle escaped her. He appeared to resign himself to the prospect of a steady three or four pounds a week for, at most, a day's work.

"It's not what I'm used to," he would grumble. "You'll never get me to say I like it."

But the arrangement suited them both well enough, and so it endured.

On the other days she would compile the accounts, and keep their various books and inventories up to date. She was meticulous, unemotional, as alert and sharp as ever. People said it was wonderful how quickly she'd conquered her grief and become mistress of herself again.

But John knew that she had not. Something had been subtracted from her spirit. Her invention was dulled. She came to him no more with ideas for new and better ways of doing things. She left well enough alone. She made a ritual, almost a housekeeper's chore, out of all she did. That old obsessive, venturesome, aggressive, implacable, obdurate huntress, with her gleaming eyes and the blood on her hands, was suddenly absent from his landscape.

When he heard of the explanation she gave for not going hunting this season he thought that in anyone else who had been riding, as an adult, a mere six weeks, it would be a most sufficient excuse; but in Nora it was an evasion. Worse still, she had lost so much of her spark that she did not even recognize it for what it was.

But how do you go about getting something like that back? When her second letter to Mr. Sugden in Leeds, asking Sam's whereabouts, was returned marked "Gone away," he hoped it would stir her into some positive action on her own part. After all, Leeds was a mere three hours away by coach from Todmorden. But she found some reason not to go; it seemed she wanted nothing to disturb the even tenor of life at Summit. And that was no fit frame of mind for a railroad contractor's wife.

His patience was not helped by the knowledge that somewhere in Southport the Reverend Doctor Prendergast was taking his daily walks up and down the seafront, steadily recovering his strength and his faculties. It could not be long before he returned; and when he did, the tissue of excuse and prevarication would collapse. It would be time to settle.

Work at the tunnel, too, was growing irksome. The pioneering work was over; no new discoveries remained to be made. It was now a matter of punctilious attention to detail and to following the specifications to the inch. He had one major disagreement with Thornton during these months. It concerned the number of rings of brick to be laid in the troublesome fractures section between shafts six and seven. The engineer was sure eight rings would suffice; it was in the middle of a long, straight run of rail and there would be no sustained lateral forces on the roadbed. But John felt in his bones that, in the invert at least, where the fractures had been just as bad as in the walls and soffit of the arch, the specification should be raised to ten. He even put his doubts in writing and asked Thornton to express his confidence in the eight-ring specification in the same way. It was the first important disharmony between them and for a while it led to a cooling of their relations.

Then in April a miner was killed during the enlarging of number six shaft for ventilation. To be sure, it would have been unheard of for a venture this size to go to completion without a death; eight deaths, or even a dozen, would have been the average for the time. Nevertheless, John had hoped for the miracle and this marred his record. It was small comfort that the man had been drunk and that, as his mates said, it was a wonder he'd lasted so long for he'd been close to death a dozen times a week since he'd started there. A death was a death. It called for even tighter vigilance on his part; yet all the time his spirit was impatient to be off, to be away, to be starting something new.

Every visit he made to Manchester he saw some new mill going up, some new extension to the canal being made, some decayed area being pulled down to make way for better. It was a time of thrust, vigour, confidence, and expansion; money was flowing there like water. And what was he doing? Wallpapering a rural tunnel with bricks! Three times that spring he tendered for works let in Manchester and Rochdale, and each time he lost to some other contractor—unfairly, he was sure. The luck that had seen him through Summit this year seemed unable to follow him into the world at large.

Somehow, he knew, the answers to his restlessness and to Nora's unusual lethargy of spirit were one and the same. They were both caught on a circular rail; they needed a jolt, an earthquake, to get them back on the old lines.

The first rumblings of it came when the month was almost out. John had spent most of the afternoon at the canal wharf, supervising the sorting through of a pile of bricks he was going to reject, when Jack Whitaker came down to say that one of the directors of the railway, a Reverend Prendergast, was attending the site.

John left Whitaker to complete the sorting while he went up to meet the cleric. A special excitement, nervous, almost fearful, grew within him as he walked. He had not felt it since the day of the strike—or the day before, to be precise, when he had addressed all the craftsmen and had not known what turn matters would take next.

Here it was then. Nemesis. The consummation that had mocked him all these months, pricking his hope and then dashing it. Here it was. And still he had no answer. His mind was empty and seemed to cringe within him. And every step brought him closer to the black-coated and gaitered figure of the priest, standing just above the cutting with his back toward John. He had forgotten the precise quality of the hatred that figure could arouse.

"Reverend doctor!" he called. "Glad you've come back among the living!"

"Stevenson!" He turned around. He was very much thinner than John remembered him—younger-looking, healthier, and jollier. In fact, he was as jolly as he had been on that first day, when he and John had taken lunch together in Manchester. It was an ill omen. He behaved as if he expected a fight and knew that he was bound to win. He clapped and clasped and rubbed his hands together a great deal and spoke with all the hearty insincerity of a horse trader. "Stevenson! Good to see you! It's been too long! Far too long! How are you? Busy?"

"I'd like the thirty-hour day," he answered. "There's a fortune waiting the man who invents it."

"Indeed," Prendergast said pleasantly. "There's a fortune awaiting any astute man these days." He looked toward the mouth of Summit East, a furlong from where they stood near Deanroyd bridge—quite close to the spot where Arabella had turned her ankle.

"Would you care to inspect your tunnel?" John asked. "We're a little before the timetable, despite this chronic shortage of hours in the day."

"No, I thank you. Mr. Whitaker was kindly enough to take me a hundred yards in and he assures me the remainder is much the same."

John nodded, and watched, and waited.

"I've been looking at your accounts from the Miles Platting end of things," the cleric continued. "They, too, are nicely up to timetable."

"Very nicely," John agreed.

Prendergast looked around. The whole Vale was renewing its life with the coming of spring. Even the purple-brown moors were shot with a newly verdant hue, and the breeze that poured over them and spilled down into the valley carried the first hint of summer's warmth. It twisted and whitened the shimmering leaves of willow and aspen near the edge of the cutting, along the banks of Walsden Water. The brook gurgled sharply over its stony bed, still cold from the upland springs. Birds shrilled and battled for territory all around. Prendergast breathed a contented sigh at all he saw. "Lamb for dinner tonight!" he said with relish.

"Aye, it soon comes round again," Stevenson agreed.

"You'll never guess who I happened across in Manchester last week," Prendergast said casually.

Fear tightened John's guts. There were several dozen in Manchester whose paths he would rather the priest did not cross.

"Thornton," Prendergast said. "Perhaps he told you?"

"As a matter of fact, he didn't." John felt only the mildest relief.

"Strange." The other smiled. "He's such a little chatterbox, don't you find?"

"He has that reputation."

"Yet it's possibly not so strange. The circumstances of our meeting were such as might . . . embarrass, perhaps, a young man with a pretty wife and they not eight months married. It was the sort of place you'd more likely find elderly celibates like myself."

John was surprised at the priest's insistence on this detail; it was as if the other were trying to put some distance between his vocation and his present business.

"He has that reputation, too."

"An interesting man. I'm told there is a stagecoach passes at five to the hour; let us walk up to the turnpike."

John strode in silence beside him, waiting his chance.

"Yes!" sighed the priest. "The seasons come! Every year they come a little sooner. Bringing us . . . what? Ah me!"

John decided then that his best hope lay in taking a little of the wind out of Prendergast's sails—going far beyond anything the priest could have reasonably expected when he set out for Summit. "It's brought me great fortune," he said. "You've no idea how well things have gone here since we finished the drift. The accounts at Miles Platting don't tell the half of it."

"Indeed!" Prendergast was both surprised and delighted.

"No doubt of it. In fact, I'm desperately looking for new works to invest my surplus in. Canals . . . turnpikes . . . even another railroad?" He looked intently at the cleric.

"Might be able to help you there," Prendergast said carelessly. "Er . . . what about a dividend, Stevenson?"

"Had I known you were coming," he said with his widest, warmest, friendliest smile, "I'd have brought all the books completely up to date. However, even without that, I can assure you we've done so well that any dividend—within reason, of course—will be acceptable. Any dividend."

He knew then that his cheerful, go-with-him-twain strategy had been right. Prendergast was now slightly unsteady with the excitement. His tongue flickered rapidly from side to side and he stared at Stevenson as if he feared he might turn to be a mirage. "Any dividend, eh? Eh? What? Fifty percent? What about that? A thousand pounds?"

John tried to look as if he'd been kicked hard but was nevertheless going to brave it out. "What about it?" he asked, breathlessly recovering his poise. "I said, did I not—we have done amazingly well. A thousand pounds—indeed, why not!"

"Well . . ." Prendergast still seemed unable to believe it.

"You may see the books now, if you wish . . . or I can bring them when I pay you. Yes, why not let's do that. It'll take a day or two before I can assemble that much. . . ."

"My illness has been so expensive, you understand." Stevenson had been so obliging that the priest now seemed to feel he had to explain his demand.

"To be sure, doctor. You have no need to justify this very reasonable request. It was I who was dilatory—all those weeks before your illness. Not . . ." He laughed. "Not that you could have had a thousand *then!* Would next Wednesday do? Tomorrow week?"

"Admirably! Admirably!"

"Here comes the stage."

They resumed their stroll toward the turnpike. "We'd best not meet here. Let's say the Gryphon at Littleborough, shall we? At half past two? It should be fairly empty at that time."

"I look forward to it," Prendergast said. "You take it well, Stevenson; that I must say." He looked anxiously at the approaching coach.

"I'll bring the money and the books."

"Capital. Capital."

"Perhaps you'll bring some news of any fresh contracts? To soak up all this extra cash I seem to have."

Prendergast laughed and then hit his forehead, chiding himself for his forgetfulness. "Two canal extensions in Ancoats," he said hastily, hoping to finish before the coach drew up. He didn't want any of this to be overheard. "The Ashton-under-Lyne canal and the Rochdale canal. Both doing wharf extensions. Port Street . . . Mill Street . . . Cannel Street. Bid £15,200 on the first, £6,830 on the second. And if a man of your proven ability can't clear a shade over three thousand on that . . . !"

The braking coach drowned their laughter, and when they parted it seemed they were once again the warmest of friends.

John watched the coach out of sight and then, for no particular reason, looked up at Rough Stones. To his surprise he saw Nora framed in the doorway waving energetically to him; it could only be to him.

With a lighter step than he had trod for weeks he set off up the lane to the house—for, of course, he had no intention of parting with that much money to the priest. Not in a week, not in a year, not until he earned it. With each step he repeated, ritually, Ashton-fifteen-two, Rochdale-six-eight-thirty.

"He's struck at last," she said when he reached the front gate.

"You saw?" he asked.

"I bless that telescope every day."

"Oh?" he said. "What else does it show?"

She hesitated before, with some bravado, she said: "I know where Thornton goes to relieve his feelings every day around this hour. One of these days he'll get tired of facing east and then I'll see the size of it."

He laughed and looked up at the opened bedroom window, through which the objective of the telescope was just visible. "You . . . you'd best go up," he said. "This might be your lucky day."

He had seemed on the point of saying something else. "All that exercise it gets," she went on. "Makes you curious."

He seemed at a loss for words then, looking at her with a curious smile that, in the end, embarrassed her. And when he did speak it was to change the subject entirely. "Get pen and paper," he said.

She told Bess to bring tea for them and then went with him into the best parlour, where the writing desk stood.

"Write down: Rochdale Canal £6,830 and Ashton-under-Lyne Canal £15,200." He studied intently the effect it had upon her.

"Oh!" she said brightly. "Is he starting to earn his keep at last?"

"He may be. He wants a thousand pounds."

She looked again at the figures. "On these? He must be reckoning we'll make at least three thousand."

"Not on those figures. Not on those contracts," John said, still not taking his eyes from her. "He wants a thousand pounds now. Full stop."

"He *what!*"

"Now. Stage payment on Summit." His tone seemed to imply that Prendergast was actually being quite reasonable and that he intended to pay the demand. "He's given us eight days."

Nora almost choked in rage and astonishment. "Eight! Eight days . . . a thousand quid! Big-bloody-hearted Prendergast!" Bess, entering with the tray, almost dropped it on hearing the words. Nora, nothing deterred, went on: "I'll give him a thousand bloody pounds! I'll give it him in cast-iron weights—right at the junction of the Rochdale and Ashton canals." Bess left the room, exhaling audibly, upward over her face as if to cool it.

At last he permitted himself a smile as he reached a hand forward to squeeze hers. "That's *my* Nora!" he said. "Welcome home, love."

She relaxed. "Eee!" she said. "I thought you were going to. . . . The way you were talking! How much does he want then?"

"Oh, he wants a thousand, all right. That's no joke. And he wants it in eight days. But as far as I'm concerned, he can go to Manchester seafront and fish for it."

"What's he done to earn it!" she said, the indignation growing once again. "Tell me one thing he's done."

"He's kept hold of his tongue. Which, incidentally, is a bit more than Thornton's done. I think our fun-loving friend has imparted his estimates of our profit-to-date on this contract."

Nora was about to explode again when she suddenly caught herself; a slow smile spread across her face. "And that's what's behind the Church of England's sudden rush, tumbling over here with his invoices hanging out!"

"That was how I read matters."

"So!" She laughed richly. "The honourable member for the antipodes thinks our likely profit to date is just three thousand! A mere three!"

He joined her laughter then. "We'd better get the other eight down to London just as soon as may be."

"And, come Saturday, we'll have a thousand profit on the shop account—more, in fact. Take that, too." She sipped her tea. "That will make . . . just over seventeen thousand we'll have moved to Bolitho & Chambers. D'you think that's enough?"

"I have *no* idea," he said with cheerful sincerity. "But it's going to have to be, isn't it! That . . . plus my tongue . . . and your bookkeeping—and your pretty eyes. Let's hope there's a touch of Thornton in him."

She was not at all amused.

"Just a touch," he said, trying to placate her.

She looked steadily at him, still unsmiling. "Something short of a touch," she said.

He cleared his throat and pulled out a pocket diary. "What day shall we go?" he said. "Eleventh? Eleventh of May?"

"Is that a Monday?"

"Aye."

"Make it the twelfth. I'll see Charley Eade that Monday, then I'm done for the week."

He smiled at her insistence. "Why not let Wardroper do it for once?"

Immediately she darted him a suspicious glance. "Has he been getting at you?"

"No," he said, truthfully.

"He's always on at me to let him go; but I'm determined he shan't. And if ever I'm sick . . . listen now, this is no joke . . . if I'm ever too sick to go, you're to go in my stead."

"But why?"

"There's no need for him to know about how we purchase—how much, where, and for what. He already knows everything necessary to his end of things. Keep him ignorant, we keep him dependent. I know it's not your way—you'd train half the world to do your work if you could—but it's mine."

"So be it," he said. He was delighted to see how much of the old Nora had come back at Prendergast's bloodsucking demand.

"You still think I'm daft," she said, as if she believed his concession masked an accusation. "Well next year, the year after, sometime soon, that man and his mates are going to open an equitable co-operative shop. What will we be doing then?"

"How should I know!"

"Exactly!"

"Well!" he said, flabbergasted. "What does that prove?"

"To me, it proves that we should do as little as we need until we know what *we*'ll be doing then. There's only two sorts of people in this world. Us, and competitors."

He looked shrewdly at her, but said nothing. Then, glancing again at his diary, he said: "The twelfth then. Tuesday. We'll go Tuesday, see Chambers Wednesday or Thursday, and whichever day we don't see him, we'll do something else. Come back the Friday. I'll write to Chambers tonight confirming the day. I wrote ten days back saying we'd visit him sometime in the month. What shall we do the blank day?"

She looked at him, her eyes brimming with secret amusement, and then tried to think.

"Come on," he said. "What were you going to say?"

"I just had a passing notion—a fancy—to see what seventeen thousand gold sovereigns'd look like, all piled up."

He laughed, sharing her delight. "What a thought! Eh—I wonder if Chambers has ever seen that much."

"No," she chided. "To be serious, I should like to see the Houses of Parliament."

But he shook his head. "There's nothing to see. The fire destroyed all the old palace. The Lords and Commons meet in a barn with very little public provision, and the new palace is only just begun. In fact . . . what's today? Yes, they laid the first stone of the new building this very morning."

"Nonetheless, you asked me what I should like—and I should like to see the Palace of Westminster."

"I bow," he said. "I bow. So be it. I shall also write to Fielden tonight to see if he can procure us tickets to the House."

"I suppose we *have* a vote now," she said, on a sudden impulse.

He had to think before he answered: "Eh! I don't think we do! We own no land. And the rule is for an occupier of a tenement at twelve pounds or more a *year*. Our lease here is only for three hundred sixty-five days and this is *leap* year! Hah! Seventeen thousand pounds in the bank and no vote! So much for Reform!"

"What's to be done with these figures?" she asked when they had finished laughing. "Rochdale and Ashton canals?"

"I shall go to Manchester tomorrow," he said, standing to leave. "I'll drop in at their offices and get the specifications and invitations to tender. Those . . . are the winning tenders. I imagine the others are already submitted."

She ran upstairs after he had gone, hoping to watch him through the telescope; but her attention was distracted by a man on horseback, wearing a bright-green cloak. He had reined in at the curve just this side of Stone House and was looking down over the works with a curiosity that was far from passing or idle. She knew from the way he strained upright in his saddle that he was watching John to the very last visible step as he vanished below ground. And then, as if to confirm the object of his interest, he turned full face to her and looked directly up at Rough Stones.

She almost pulled away, guilty at being caught spying; but experience and her own eyes had taught her that the telescope was not remarkable at that distance and that a person behind it, in the dark of the interior, was as good as invisible. So she endured his apparent scrutiny without flinching, and she looked long and hard at him. He was certainly interested in John, and in this house. And he was certainly handsome, with dark, deep-set eyes above prominent, almost feminine cheekbones, and full but finely chiselled lips—all framed in ringlets of glossy black hair. It was a face of contradictions—at first sight sensitive, delicate, even frail, yet closer inspection revealed an arrogance in the eyes, a firmness in the mouth, a strength in the line of the jaw.

He turned from his scrutiny of the house and looked at the line of shafts now being widened into ventilation chimneys. Then, all very leisurely, he faced south and set his mount toward Littleborough at a slow trot. She recognized the horse, too: a seven-year-old washy chestnut mare with the near hock partly stockinged; a hack from the stables in Littleborough. She was going to Littleborough tomorrow, in any case. It would do no harm to make one or two inquiries.

McGinty, who was considered the quidnunc of the Walsden end of the valley, had never heard tell of the fellow when she described him the following day. It ruled out any chance that he had come from, or stayed in, the Vale. So she rode over to Littleborough in the afternoon.

Clifford, the ostler at the livery there, remembered the man for he had dealt with him himself. A Mr. Dow, of London. A scholar, he had said, with an especial interest in civil engineering and modes of transport.

"Did he say why he had come here? I mean why to Littleborough?"

"He said it were the Blackstone Gap brung him. Ye could see all three modes there side by side. Canal, turnpike, and the railroad."

She went next to the Royal Oak, where, according to Clifford, the mysterious Mr. Dow had stopped the night. Nancy Spur, the landlord's wife, assuming that Nora's interest was romantic because of the visitor's handsome physique, found no difficulty in breaking her husband's rule not to talk about guests to outsiders—and in any case Nora could hardly be classed as an outsider. Mr. Dow was a Mr. Nathan Dow and he had given his address as c/o Benjamin Tighe, Calthorpe Arms, Gray's Inn Road, in Holborn. He was a great dandy, though he came without a servant, and he had three trunks of clothes and only stayed two days. And that was funny because there'd been a mix-up because his luggage hadn't got *his* initials but his cousin's. But she couldn't remember now what the initials on the trunks had been. Then one of the maids said it was C—N.C.—she remembered that because she said his cousin must be called "Cow" and he hadn't laughed. Oh, but wasn't he *handsome!*

Nora left Littleborough satisfied with her day's inquiries. Mr. Dow was just a handsome, passing stranger. They could forget him.

The following Tuesday—a week before their London visit—they got the second jolt of the earthquake that was to shake them from their measured circular tour. It was just past midnight and they had been asleep three hours when she awoke with a strong conviction that something was wrong; all her senses came swiftly alive. She felt across the bed to nudge John awake, but John was not there.

There was a creaking on the stair.

"John?" she called.

"Aye!" It was he who had been creeping up the stairs; now, relieved at being able to walk normally, he came into the room.

Meanwhile she had noticed that a flickering red light was playing on their bedroom ceiling. One of the hovels below must be on fire! She sprang from the bed and crossed swiftly to the window. Her hand flew to her mouth and she breathed sharply in, not believing, not daring to believe, what she saw. "John!" she cried out. "The shop! The offices—it's all burning!"

She turned frantically to him. But he was smiling! Grimly, it is true, and with a savage kind of satisfaction, as if he were already assured of a triumph—but he was smiling. He lifted something into the light. His shotgun!

"Are they still there?" he asked and stooped to peer through the telescope, which was set for her height. He smiled again, the same grim smile.

"Who?" she asked.

He left the room quickly. "See for yourself," he said. "It's taken them four months to drink down enough courage for this. Don't make a sound and don't come after me."

Nora scanned the burning site with her telescope. She saw many figures, all young men, darting around and among the flames, but it was quite a while before she saw one she recognized—Dicky Redmayne, the one whose spur John had taken at the Christmas Eve party in the Hall. He stood with one or two of his mob, arms folded, watching the fire consume their business. He smiled like a universal benefactor.

She raged and fumed alone there in the bedroom. How she wished telescopes would work in reverse, so that she could line it up on him and discharge her pistol down it, being certain of hitting him. She began to dress—or, at least, to cover herself as much as propriety would require, buttoned up or no. Did John really think she would stay obediently up here? And what the hell did he mean tiptoeing around the house while the offices and the shop, the entire plant of John Stevenson, Contractor, went up in smoke? And why were those young ruffians standing there as if no danger threatened?

In shawl and dress, a limp and cumbersome thing without its petti-coats, she slipped out through the front door and, hitching it up to her knees, tripped silently down the lane to the turnpike. At the bottom an urgent "Sssss!" made her flatten against the hedge.

"I told you to stay behind," he whispered angrily.

She crouched just beside him. "And I told my limbs but they didn't obey me either."

"Can you see them?"

She stretched slowly upward until the site became visible. All the men were still there. No one had come from the hovels—or, if they had, they had returned on seeing who was doing the burning.

"Now you're here," John said grudgingly, "you might as well be useful. I can see their horses along the road a bit. See if you can slip up there and let them loose and drive them off." He caught her arm as she made to leave. "If you hear me shout and you're near the horses, take one and ride off for help. If you're still too far to make it, run back here."

She bent and kissed him. Until then it had not even occurred to her that *he* was in danger. The idea that any mortal could harm John Stevenson was laughable. All the way to the horses she wondered why he was so calm—so joyful, almost. Did he love a fight so much that he'd even relish the destruction of their business?

It was the work of moments to let the horses go. There were eight in all. She gathered their reins as she untied them, and led the animals slowly and as quietly as possible down toward Deanroyd bridge. On the way she picked up a stout, slightly rotten, branch lying near the ditch. When they reached the crown of the bridge she released her grip on the reins and stood, letting them walk past her. As soon as she was behind them she raised the stick and brought it down with all her might on the nearest rump. It broke with a crack that rang up the valley.

But the trick worked. With a neigh of fright the horse stampeded away up the road and the others, willy-nilly, followed. With her heart in her mouth she began to run back to where she had left John. The two sounds least likely to intrude upon the vandals, she had reasoned, were the crack of a stick amid all the crackling of the flames, and the neighing of a horse, for there was hardly a night hereabouts that was not broken by that particular sound. But had she gone far enough away? The drumming of the hooves as they stampeded had seemed agonizingly loud. Was it loud enough to carry two furlongs and penetrate the rear of the flames and the drunken glee of the youths?

When she was still fifty yards away from the foot of their lane she saw John making his way down, behind the cover of the hedge, to the point where she had left him. He must have returned to the house. She hoped he had brought the other shotgun or her pistol; she cursed herself for failing to think of it when she had come down.

It amazed her that no one saw her, walking openly on the highway, for no concealment was possible. Perhaps they did see her and paid no attention; after all, what threat was there to them in the sight of a lone woman, without a bonnet, walking slowly along the highway?

She reached the foot of the lane only a moment or two after John returned.

"All away," she said.

He breathed vastly in his relief. "Take this," he said, handing her the other shotgun. "It's charged blank. No shot. Go up toward Stone House. By the milestone there. Shoot yours in the air after I shoot mine. About three seconds after. Count three."

She thought: *For three seconds you count four,* but all she did was nod. He watched her walk all the way to the milestone. And she knew he was watching her, so she did not bend to snatch up a handful of gravel and stuff it down the spout until she saw him leaving his place of hiding and walk over the road. *Charged blank indeed!* she thought.

The fires were dying down now, and their sheds and tents were emerging from the holocaust as glowing heaps of embers. Still that question nagged her: Why did these louts behave as if they felt themselves utterly safe from discovery? She could not help remembering the mysterious and handsome Mr. Dow who had stopped at this very spot not a week since. Was he somehow connected? If, when they were in London, they went anywhere near that place of his, in Gray's Inn Road, she'd certainly try to find out. The more she remembered the way he had looked at their workings here, the more certain she felt that he had some connection with this fire.

"Stand where you are!" John's shout rang back from the opposite valley side. "In the Queen's name!"

After one moment of shocked immobility the dozen or so youths made a dash for their horses—or, at least, made the first few steps of such a dash before the sharpest-eyed among them shouted, "They've gone!"

"Come up here!" John called to them. "Walk nice and quiet."

"The canal!" came a cry and, as if moved by a single brain, they turned and fled away from the road. As soon as their backs were toward him he fired his shotgun straight at them; they were too far away to sustain anything more than a light flesh wound. Three seconds later they took a slightly more painful broadside of gravel.

She walked gaily back toward John.

"I waste my bloody breath telling you anything!" he said. "What was it? Gravel?"

"Better than that," she said. "Rough stones!"

He had to laugh then, even though her disobedience angered him. She took his arm. He put both guns over his other arm and they walked together down to the smouldering ruins of their huts and tents. The tent with the ale casks in had burned to a cinder, but the casks themselves were only superficially charred. They heard a distant crackle of undergrowth as the raiders made good their escape.

"Lucky we keep meat in the wagons," she said. "Not more than forty pounds' worth of stock destroyed. Eee! Smell that butter!"

"D'ye fancy a baked potato?" he asked.

She laughed. "Aye!" And he passed her the guns before he made a quick dash over the cooler embers to fish out two that were uncharred and quite edible.

"That was folly!" he said when he returned. "I forgot." And he patted the powder horn slung at his belt. "We mustn't get light-headed now."

Eating gingerly, breathing sharply in to cool what they bit off, and blowing vigorously on the rest, they walked around the glowing heaps of ash. Eerie blue flames danced over each pile. "No danger of it spreading," he said. "We'd as well go home."

On the way up he said, "The biggest loss is £247 in cash, but as most of it was in gold sovereigns, we'll recover it, I'm sure."

"What about the records?" she said.

He looked pityingly at her. "The day I rely on written records . . . I'll retire."

"Thank the Lord we keep all the accounts at home."

"Aye. Someone's watching over us."

"What I can't fathom," she said, "is why they were so *open*. Ye'd think they were sure we were out."

"I'm sure they did. They'd never have behaved like that otherwise. Have you told McGinty about our visit to London?"

"Of course," she said, "but I didn't tell him it was this week. I said I'd not be coming tomorrow because we were going to London . . . next . . . week." Her voice slowed as she heard the possible confusion arise.

"That's it!" John said. "I'll be buggered!"

He yawned. They turned in through the front gate of Rough Stones.

"Another thing I can't fathom," she said, diffidently, "is the . . . eagerness . . . in you. Even before you left, when we were still upstairs, you nearly split your face grinning. You're like a dog with four tails."

"Well," he said, "put yourself in Redmayne's position. If this cost us five hundred pound, it'll be worth it, I reckon."

Bess came out of her room, holding a lighted candle, as they went upstairs; but they told her to go back to bed and that all was well.

Nora wanted then to mention Mr. Dow and her suspicion about his connection with tonight's affair. But, as they were getting back into bed he grasped her waist from behind and said: "Eee, if there's one thing gets me going it's a warm night."

"Tonight!" she laughed, disbelieving. "Warm?"

"Give us half a chance," he whispered, craftily drawing her to him and caressing her all over.

But she was slow to fire. "It's a long day tomorrow," she said half-heartedly.

He stopped and held the blankets up for her to get in. "Aaah! You poor old gentlewoman!" he said, full of mock solicitude.

"Aye," she smiled wanly. "That's just how I feel!"

But five minutes later, remembering his hands upon her, she regretted what she had said and whispered, "All right, if you still want." But he was then sound asleep once more.

Not for long, though. Within an hour there was a thunderous hammering at their front foor. John was awake before her and was lighting the candle as she opened her eyes. He drew back the curtains and threw open the casement. "Yes?" he called.

"Stevenson!" a voice said from below.

"Good morning," John answered. "Squire Redmayne, is it?"

"Aye. And wishing he were any other man in this Vale! I'd not want the sun to rise without your getting my assurance I'll pay all your damages."

"That's handsome of you, squire. I can't yet say what they'll be . . ."

"Whatever! Whatever! And look, Stevenson . . . I don't know exactly if it's . . . your sort of . . . uh . . . line of business, but I've got plans drawn up for eleven acres—a mill, four hundred houses, chapel, and other works. I was putting it out to tender but, if you want it, it's yours for the nod."

John, too excited to trust himself to speak, swallowed and stared down into the dark.

"Say?" Redmayne prompted.

"I'll take it, sir," John said. "Where is it?"

Nora, sitting up in bed, curled her toes and shivered her legs in a regular spasm of joy.

"Just beyond the Albion mills in Todmorden. Go along Romfield Road and turn as if making for Baltimore bridge. It's the waste ground opposite the Baltimore malthouse."

"May we meet there tomorrow? Or later today, I mean?"

"Come to the Hall. At eleven, say. We may easily walk it from there."
He began to leave.

"One other thing," John called. "I'd be grateful for ten gallons of
vitriol from your works. There's gold in those ashes."

"It shall be," Redmayne promised.

They heard the gate slam and listened to the dying clatter of his horse's
hooves before John lifted her off the bed and swirled her round in a near
delirium. "I said it! I said it!" he repeated. The swish of air extinguished
the candle. He put her down on the bed again, afraid of blundering into
something in the dark. He shut the window.

"I wish I knew people like you do," she said. "You knew he would do
some such thing, didn't you?"

"Nothing like *that*. I was certain he'd compensate us and offer his good
offices over some contract. But . . . well, you heard! Four hundred
houses, a factory, a chapel—if that hasn't the smell of a hundred thousand
pounds! And on our doorstep . . ." He waited for a response.

"Yes!" she said, but her enthusiasm was a fraction late.

"What is it?" he asked.

"Redmayne's no fool. His grandfather came up from an eight-shilling-
a-week weaver and he's not lost it."

"So?"

"Well—he's more or less asking you to swindle him. No competitive
quote . . . name your price."

John dropped his voice to a low, level pitch. "I think he knows I won't
cheat him."

"Oh, good," she said. "As long as you know it, too, he's safe. But if
that's not like stretching his neck across the block, what is?"

The clock downstairs struck three.

John chuckled. "Just now you said you wish you knew people. When
you say things like that, I can only agree." He did not speak unkindly, so
her reply was rueful rather than hurt.

"Well—you've been right so far."

He leaned back against the head of the bed. "A mill . . ." he repeated. "Four hundred houses . . . a chapel. . . . It depends on the size
of the mill, but it must be at least £100,000." He sighed happily. "A
hundred . . . thousand! You realize that we'd have to go to London
anyway now. This is a new phase. We'll be looking to borrow at least
twenty thousand for this and the canals. Working capital."

"Aye," she said. "Let's hope there's a real ding-dong fight now
between the Liverpool & Manchester and the Manchester & Leeds over the
route of the link line. A year's delay'd suit us now."

He laughed voicelessly and, reaching over her, placed a finger on her brow. "I like the mind that goes on steaming away quietly in there," he said. "Never fret over what it *doesn't* know. The things it knows and the ways it works are all I ever wanted." He scratched his head. "Eee! Three o'clock, eh? How can we get back to sleep with eleven acres of work out there on offer?"

She cleared her throat suggestively. He knew what she meant but he wanted to tease her for her earlier refusal. "Not catching cold, are you?" he asked. But she insinuated a warm and expert hand beneath his shirt and made it impossible for him to maintain his cool pretence.

He leaned over and kissed her thighs at the hem of her chemise. She lay back and wormed herself, slowly, very slowly, from it; he followed the hem with his lips, kissing and nuzzling the flesh that it laid bare, all the way up to her lips. He followed with his hands, straddling her, gently raking her with his nails, caressing her with his fingertips. When he took her face between his hands she moaned: "Be soon! Oh . . . !" And he stretched himself upon her and waltzed them into the sort of delirium he thought they had forgotten how to achieve these last two months or so, since Tommy's death.

Later, running her fingers gently through his hair, she said quietly: "I've not been that much of a wife to thee. Not since Tommy died." She kissed his mouth and laid a finger on it to show he needn't speak. "I've known it, too, though I've said but little. . . ." She tried to say something else but could not manage. Instead she rubbed her cheekbone hard against his; and he, responding, felt their skin slip, lubricated by her tears.

He pulled away, straightened the covers, and cradled her in his arms until she went to sleep. Himself he lay relaxed, awake, trying to imagine the problems attendant on extending canals and on building streets, houses, chapels, and mills.

# *Chapter 40*

Beneath the embers they found, very charred but still intact, the strongbox that held the cash; so they did not need the vitriol. The carpenters started at once to build new site offices; John got them to build each one in sections that could be bolted together. "Then we can move it to another site without taking it all to bits," he explained. Shortis, the supervising carpenter, thought it no way to build but was surprised, when the structure was erected two days later, to see how firm it stood.

The shop was not rebuilt. Instead they adopted Nora's earlier plan of selling directly from the wagons on the sidings. For the cashier, usually Wardroper's wife, they built a portable shelter. Already more than half their sales were made direct from the wagons to the women who had charge of the big shanties at Calderbrook.

The main problem posed by the fire was the loss of records and of the latest revised specification. John and Walter decided not to try to re-create the history of the tunnel but to prepare an up-to-date description of the existing site and a working specification of all that remained to be done. John said that if the Manchester & Leeds draughtsmen could prepare a blank scale map of the tunnel with each ten-yard interval marked, he would be able to recapitulate the geology of the lengths already bricked in. "Fernley has always maintained," Walter said, "that there's no need for paper where Lord John goes. It's often irked me that I've had to consult drawings merely to confirm what you've already told me from memory; but I've never been so glad of the faculty as now."

Bonuses for the gangs were not affected by the destruction, for their progress marks were physically cut in the sides of the works. The records in the office were merely to prevent the men from effacing the marks and recutting them farther back or—as had been done on other workings—removing the marked brick intact and relaying it farther back. This was the "travelling-bonus swindle," by which a spurious extra yard of achievement could be kept marching along the tunnel each week. To prevent it, John sent Whitaker and Fernley through the entire tunnel to note the positions of last week's markings before anyone could change them.

At eleven he left the site and went to keep his appointment in Todmorden. By noon he and Redmayne were standing on the eleven acres of waste ground at the eastern edge of the town. The squire was no longer apologetic, rightly feeling that his offer of this site had been compensation enough; instead he now rubbed his hands with glee as his mind's eye pictured the houses and streets and the chapel, all huddled around the mill that was to fill this rough ground between canal and river.

"I mean to pay the lowest possible wage that will ensure bare survival," he said earnestly. "For it's my belief that cash just burns the linings from their pockets. What do they *need* it for, eh? For drink? For gambling? A high cash wage is an inducement to sin. Look at my son. It's money's been his ruin. D'ye think he'd behave as he does if we were paupers! If it weren't for his being a gentleman and my son, he'd be hanged for last night's caper. Or transported at the least. Well—I mean to save them from that."

"It's certainly a point of view," John said. "You've done test diggings here, I suppose. What are the footings like?"

"Very dry. It's all dry as a bone here, though you'd not think it to look at it."

The land must have been deserted for over a year; a second generation of weeds, vernally green, shimmered in the spring sunshine among the black and rotting stalks of an earlier crop. Abandoned hovels, thrown up in less than twenty-four hours, had soon tumbled down, gutted for their meagre timber, their hearthstones, or the rocks that had marked their doors. The turf roof of one had slid down almost intact and had reknitted itself over the year to make a tumulus of grass.

Redmayne pointed to one of these mouldering remains as they passed. "We'll give them palaces compared with these . . . pigpens. Well, you'd not even keep pigs in something like that, would you? It's my belief that if they're well housed, with substantial walls around them, and well fed, you'll get the best out of them. It's what they really need."

John laughed: "Try telling that to the farmers around here!"

"Farmers?" The squire was puzzled.

"The way *they* keep pigs, you'd think they never cared whether—"

"No, no," Redmayne said testily. "I mean people, not pigs. Give your operatives good substantial houses, good drains, street lighting, an active chapel, and wholesome food, and I can't for the life of me see what they need a great deal of cash *for*. That's where your tommy shop interests me, Stevenson. They say the quality of your tommy exceeds the best in many of the shops; is that so?"

"We thought the shopkeepers took advantage of our lads, yes. We never looked for great profit on the tommy, believing that well-fed men working to the timetable would be our real profit."

"By jove, you're a man after me own heart! Look after your operatives and they'll look after your profits, eh! What!" Redmayne was delighted at the idea. "Anything you can tell me about operating such a shop . . . anything . . . would be vastly appreciated."

"When the time comes. Surely. Mrs. Stevenson's the one, really. She manages it all—does the buying, supervises the selling, keeps the books."

Redmayne stopped and stared at him. They were almost at the canal bank now, in the shade of Hey Head, towering over them to the south. "You don't say so," he exclaimed. "Really? Mrs. Stevenson, eh? Something of a risk, what?"

"Risk?"

"Well—you're responsible for any financial shortfall or any contractual error. . . ."

John threw back his head and laughed. "Oh, I'm sorry! . . . " He gripped the squire's elbow lightly. "Sorry! I'm not laughing at what you said but at the idea of Mrs. Stevenson and 'financial shortfall' in the same sentence! They're not even in the same world." And he told the story of the timber shipment and Ossie Oakshaw. Redmayne chuckled, but not at all as heartily as he would have if a man had pulled such a trick.

"My grandfather made our fortune," he said. "He'd never have let a woman do such things."

"Times change," John said mildly. "Ye'll want wharves here, I take it."

"More than that—a basin." He gestured out the area of the dock that was planned at this point along the canal bank. "Oh, just think of it, Stevenson—can't you picture it? The basin . . . the mill . . . and four hundred houses . . . the streets . . . the chapel. . . . I've dreamed of it for years. . . ."

He sighed and Stevenson saw a more-than-entrepreneurial gleam in the man's eyes. Redmayne was a frustrated patriarch. He was not picturing streets but *himself* walking through those streets, among those houses, acknowledging the respectful greetings of his people. Perhaps he also saw Mrs. Redmayne and their two daughters going the rounds with food from the Hall tables and kitchens—and himself at Christmas, leaving barrels of beer at the head of each street and a dole of plum pudding at each house. It would fit the picture of the third-generation squire reviving and keeping up traditions that the primeval gentry had already long abandoned. If that were the key to Redmayne's aspirations, it would dictate certain aspects of their relationship. He stored away the thought.

As John left, Redmayne made one final allusion to the events of the previous night. "Well, Stevenson, I don't know if it's not almost sinful to say it, but I feel a great deal of good may have been done this neighbourhood by last night's villainy."

John said he hoped so and, to himself, marvelled at the ability of enthusiasts to take silence, or indifferent answers, for wholehearted endorsement.

That afternoon in the private bar at the Gryphon in Littleborough he handed into the Reverend Prendergast's eager fingers an envelope containing £475 in paper money. He smiled as he watched those fingers tear apart the seal but, before they could count and discover the shortfall, he said: "It's a great deal less than promised but—as I daresay ye heard—we had a near-disastrous fire at Deanroyd last night. It'll take another week now to assemble the rest."

Prendergast stared in dismay at the cash until light dawned. "You've led me a dance," he said, incredulity in every tremor of his voice. "You've been playing me!"

The friendship of the week before was gone now. John was both calm and distant. "You shall have the rest next week. As I have already told you."

"And the books?"

"Do you listen to nothing? I said—we had a fire."

"But I need the money," Prendergast said in genuine anguish, as if the real depth of his loss had only just got through to him. "I need it." He looked at the banknotes as if they would hardly buy a box of snuff.

"In a week," John insisted steadily.

When Prendergast looked at him next there was no disguising the hatred in his eyes. "If you are not here next week, Stevenson, nothing shall prevent me from going at once to Sir Sidney with . . . with my discovery."

Later Stevenson was to place great significance on the fact that Prendergast used the word "discovery" in his threat rather than something more all-embracing, like "evidence of your forgery" or, even stronger, "proof of your chicanery."

"I shall be here," he promised. "You had better bring my letter—both my letters."

Prendergast, now back on familiar territory, smiled. "You know full well the price of those."

John pretended to suppress a smile in return, as if to say "it was worth a try." When they parted, immediately after this exchange, the priest was—or so John hoped—just sufficiently reassured to keep him quiet for one more week. There was no doubt that, when he came here next week and found he had been thoroughly duped, he would go at once to Sir Sidney.

But by then it would not matter; a week tomorrow either the forgery would have found its adoptive parent, or Nora and he would be setting out across the Atlantic with eighteen thousand pounds to take care of any seasickness.

"You might as well kiss my royal Yorkshire arse," he said beneath his breath as he watched the priest cross the road and walk up the driveway to the station.

\*      \*      \*

The following Friday, four days before their London visit, brought a letter from Chambers to say he would welcome them next Wednesday at eleven in the morning, and another from Fielden to say that, with Easter falling so late this year, neither House of Parliament was sitting during the week of their visit, but he'd gladly show them around the remaining buildings and the ruins of the palace as well as what little could be seen of the new building. He himself would be visiting London at that time and would, in any case, very much welcome a further chance to meet Stevenson and talk one or two affairs with him. He, Fielden, had heard of Redmayne's new business with Stevenson, and there was a possibility of some further work of a similar nature at Waterside.

"Eee!" Nora said. "That's less than a mile from Redmayne's contract—and both right slap on the canal! Think of the saving!"

"You see what we've done," John said. "We've played their game. Because we didn't go rushing for the magistrates on the one hand, or trying to sting Redmayne for a fortune in shhh-money on the other—or, to put it differently, because we've behaved to them exactly as they'd have behaved to one another, we're being invited inside to warm our hands at their fires."

A postscript to the letter advised them not to try the new direct route through from Normanton via Derby, Leicester, and Rugby because the North Midland Railway and the Midland Counties Railway behaved as if the very idea of a passenger wanting to travel all the way to London on one ticket were absurd. It was better, he said, to go the old way round through Earlestown and Crewe. But they were to be sure to travel first-class in that case, as the Grand Junction Railway had no provision for second- or third-class passengers from Newton to Birmingham between the hours of six in the morning and six in the evening. But at least the three companies involved had been working the route long enough to be familiar with the notion that people in Manchester actually wanted to go all the way to London.

"It's a poor omen for railways when Members of Parliament write in such terms," John said.

# *Chapter 41*

Their journey to London was by the up-line of the same railroad that Walter and Arabella had taken north the previous summer. From the Liverpool Road depot in Manchester to the Birmingham depot at Euston in London took a little over ten hours, what with waiting on connections at Newton and again at Birmingham; but for Nora and John not a moment was grudged. The second-class coach they took on the Liverpool & Manchester portion of the journey was showing its years. But the company was so agreeable—two midshipmen and a wine merchant with a vivacious young lady he introduced as his wife—that Nora was quite sorry to sink into the plush splendours of the first-class coach at Newton for the journey south.

Their fellow travellers were an elderly and obviously fairly senior clergyman with a relaxed left half to his face; the mouth on that side needed constant wiping. He wore black silk gloves on his spindly hands and all the way to Birmingham he read—and shook his head in vexation at—a heavily annotated copy of Barr's *Scripture Students' Assistant.* Opposite him sat what was either his wife or some very poor relation or someone else to whom he was not particularly obliged to be pleasant and the tedium of whose journey he was not expected to lighten. Every ten minutes or so this miserable lady fed a fresh cachou into her jaws, snapping at it like a dog afflicted with summer flies.

John and Nora divided their time between watching the landscape flying past—at speeds which at times reached forty miles an hour—and reading. He was deeply into Thomas Edwards' *Rudiments of the Art of Constructing and Repairing Canals* and had bought for her a new copy of Grant's *London Sketches,* which she found totally absorbing. Not that its chapters—on Impostors, Debtors' Prisons, Penny Theatres, Police Officers, Workhouses, Lunatic Asylums, Gaming Houses, and so on—were particularly relevant to their present visit; but the picture it gave of teeming life and myriadfold activity was enough to alert her to the nature of the city toward which they were now hurtling. Before two hours had passed she had read enough to know that London would be nothing like Manchester, the only other city of which she had any adult knowledge. She only had to read that London had no fewer than eighty penny theatres for juvenile patrons, many with eight separate houses each evening and catering in all for something like 24,000 young persons, to know that Manchester was but a village by comparison.

Also there was their map, Cruchley's New Plan of London, which showed the vast extent of the built-over area—nearly six miles in one direction, from Bayswater almost to Bow, and three miles in the other, from Camden Town to Camberwell. Soon, it was clear, outlying villages like Kensington, Hampstead, Peckham, and Stratford-by-Bow would be swallowed . . . and where would it stop? Once they started building railways from London's present outskirts reaching out to the villages around, there was no limit. The city might swell even as far as Acton or Barking or

Barnet or Croydon, though people now would laugh at such a notion. It would be an astute thing to do, she thought, if one had capital one didn't actually need to call on at short notice, to buy up land around the projected stations in the hope of leasing it later for building plots. That was an idea worth considering.

The only chapter in the book that directly bore upon their present visit was one dealing with the Victoria Parliament, though there was very little about the actual building, old or new. Mostly it was about Peel and Melbourne and disastrous maiden speeches, especially the terrible one by the writer Disraeli. "I doubt," wrote James Grant, the book's author, "if he will ever acquire any status in the House." And if his maiden speech was anything to go by, Grant was right.

From Birmingham they had the coach to themselves, for the clergyman and lady were not going on to London. At Rugby two gentlemen got in, one with a brilliant black eye; but both fell fast asleep almost at once. On this stretch of the line John found reading impossible. He had been a navvy on many reaches of the track and was constantly turning to her to say things like: "It was very soggy here—it rained all month!" or "Here's where I first saw Robert Stephenson."

At Kilsby Tunnel, shortly after Rugby, he said, "Here is the one we can be grateful we *didn't* get! Shorter than Summit, but it took from 1834 to 1838. I should think Stephenson would never want to go underground again after . . ." He was counting the ventilation shafts by their pools of light; after one he said: "It was about here that all the trouble lay. They struck quicksand. Poor Nowell, the contractor, he took to his bed and died, they say. But Stephenson got a number of steam pumping engines rigged up there and they pumped . . . I think it was sixteen hundred gallons a minute! Think of that—you never saw such a man-made torrent pouring away."

"That must have cleared it!" Nora said as they burst again into daylight.

John smiled slowly. "Oh, it cleared it. Yes—*nine months* later! They had to drain upwards of five square miles of quicksand."

Nora shuddered at the thought. "Poor fellows. What was the contract let for?"

Stevenson raised his eyebrows. "Ninety-nine thousand; it must have looked attractive until they got into the quicksand."

Nora shuddered even more at that.

"And you never saw more reckless men," John went on. "I worked at the north end myself for a month. There were three men killed there playing follow my leader trying to leap over a shaft. The leader, who was drunk, managed the leap; the three followers, who were very drunk, failed. I don't know how many were killed in all on that contract, but it was a terrible one."

Nora listened raptly for John rarely spoke of the dangers or difficulties of their branch of engineering. "So really," she said, "what I've seen at Summit is nothing like the business in general?"

"No," he agreed. "We've been lucky at Summit. It's gone as well as open-skies working. Most roadlaying goes well enough." He looked out through the window. "This stretch here I remember; we more or less danced all the way. It's when you get into deep cuttings, tunnels, bogs, big embankings—unusual places like that. They spell trouble. *And* profit, of course. The recipe for success is to reduce the risks to the point where working in such places becomes as easy and smooth as level tracklaying over hard ground. Then you earn the profits that attend the risks, but you expend only the labour that goes with the simple workings."

"That's what you're good at," she said with pride. "There's none better than you at it, I'll lay odds."

He smiled. "But think of poor Robert Stephenson. Before Kilsby was even finished, he was up in Todmorden with Gooch and Thornton, surveying a route for a tunnel over four hundred yards longer! That's what you call a man with stomach!"

"That explains why he was so pleased with you when he came out that time. Oh, that reminds me! The strike. *Our* strike—that was the twentieth, wasn't it, November?" He nodded. "Well, so was this opening of Parliament." She patted her book. "Isn't that funny? All this going on down there at Westminster and all that going on up at Summit with us."

He gazed again out of the window and said: "When they come to write the history of these times, which event, I wonder, will they think most important? If Tom Metcalfe becomes hereafter an important leader of unions or if we make anything of ourselves . . . who knows?"

# *Chapter 42*

They drew into Camden Town on the northern fringe of London just before six that evening. There they were relieved of their tickets, and the engine was shunted away to a siding while all the coaches were attached to the cable by which their freewheeling descent to the depot at Euston was regulated. "If there's a train due out, our descent helps to haul it up here, where they attach the engine and pull away to Birmingham," John explained. They watched the bankrider climb on to the front of the now engineless train, ready to guide them down; then they themselves got back inside for the final one and a quarter miles.

"Oh!" Nora said, startled by the utter smoothness of the ride. "It's like floating in a boat."

"Aye!" John agreed. "Until you do this, you don't realize how much of each piston thrust is transmitted to every coach. One day all railway travel will be as smooth as this."

Ten minutes later they came gracefully to rest at the depot, a simple, open-sided shed containing two platforms and four tracks—the two inner ones serving merely as empty-carriage roads, filling by means of small manual turnplates on which any single coach on the arrival or departure line could be rotated through ninety degrees and sent to a similar turnplate on the empty-carriage road. Each platform was about 140 yards long. The arrival platform, on the eastern, open side of the depot, was a milling throng of omnibuses, porters, hackney coaches, hotel touts, private carriages, and people waiting to greet the new arrivals, or to pick their pockets, or—if they were young, pretty, and poorly chaperoned (a slim hope as this train was first-class only)—to help them into the gay life. There were papersellers, piesellers, beverage sellers, and girls, all with their wares attractively on display. Grooms in livery led pairs of well-matched horses to the flat wagons at the back of the train, on which the private coaches were roped. Self-important servants of the Royal Mails unlocked their coach and loaded its contents into a covered wagon, which they backed across the platform to butt with the train. They forced everyone to go around the horses, whose heads were soon buried again in their nosebags.

"We're to look for a man with a red cravat," John said, his eyes searching among the restless melee.

"With white spots?" Nora asked. "Like the one over there? Second column from the end."

John searched and found the man. He, too, was scanning the crowd and evidently not finding what he sought. "Could be," John said. The man's eye caught his; John waved; the man smiled and began to thread his way toward them.

"I need to bury a Quaker," Nora said.

"That's over the other platform. As soon as this fellow gets our bags, I'll take you around there. Show you a small tragedy, too."

"Mr. Stevenson, sir?" the man asked as soon as he reached them.

"And you are from . . . ?" John answered.

"The Talbot, sir, off Vellington Street."

His cockney accent confused the word. "D'ye say Talbot or Tabard? We're to stay at the Tabard."

The man laughed at that. "Quite right, sir," he said. "Werry confusin'. Tabard is indeed the name above the gateway. But they all calls it Talbot. Don't ask me! But Talbot it is."

"Who sent you?" John asked, still wary.

"Vy, Mr. Tom Cornelius, landlord of the Talbot, sir."

"Good fellow," John said and showed him which bags were theirs. "We'll come back in ten to fifteen minutes," he added.

"Talkin of vich, sir, don't forget to move your vatches and clocks to London time. Ten minutes before Manchester time, as a rule."

They thanked him and walked around to the departure platform, where a colonnade of buildings housed the waiting rooms for the first and the second classes, the ticket offices, staff rooms, and the earth closets for ladies and gentlemen, one at each end. She emerged to find John waiting for her on the departure platform. Here, too, the crush was great, for the evening train to Watford was due to leave at the quarter hour. It was a very different sort of crowd from the ones they had mingled with at Newton and Birmingham; here there were no private coaches, no bags, no anxious or tearful relatives, no excitement; just ranks of sober gentlemen waiting for the coaches to be manhandled off the turnplates and be joined to make a train of first- and second-class carriages. Each man seemed to know his seat, too, for as soon as a new coach was added, a group would detach themselves from the waiting mass and take their places as if by agreed allotment.

He led her among the crowd and across the central granite roadway, where omnibuses and carriages were arriving in an almost constant stream, entering through a giant triumphal archway held on four massive fluted columns. Its soaring grandeur, after the dirty, primitive, and disorderly arrangement of the platforms and offices, was breathtaking. "Eh!" she said. "Isn't that grand!"

"Tragic, I call it," he said. "Thirty-five thousand pounds they forked out for that."

"Eh," she said. "They'd have done better to save their money and built a decent depot."

"Their money," he snorted. "Our money. I should think threepence off each ticket pays for that . . . essay in delusion. Come and see it from outside."

From Drummond Street the great seventy-two-foot-high portico, already dirty after only two years' exposure to London, certainly looked impressive, leading one to imagine great echoing halls behind it—a railway temple to which this would be but a propylaeum. The dingy little cast-iron barn, open down one side and both ends, matched by acres of weed and rubbish on the other flank, was just laughable.

"Still," she said, "when they get a station worthy of it, it'll not look too bad. It has a grand air of permanence."

"Aye," he laughed. "It's permanent all right. I'll say that for it. It'd cost a thousand or two to get rid of."

It also symbolized—though she would have found this impossible to explain to him or even to put into words for herself—it also symbolized an atmosphere that was London, a sense which pervaded all she had read that day, which sprang at you from the map, which seemed to float like a will-o'-the-wisp around the streets and among the houses. It symbolized *money*. And though she did not recognize it consciously until the following day, the awareness of it was already stirring the essential Nora from her long slumber, quickening her blood, sharpening her senses, filling her eyes with a gleam they had held only fitfully since Tommy's death.

In the coach on the way to the Talbot—or Tabard—they passed no fine houses and saw no great estates; but even the poverty that stretched all around, the abject, grinding poverty, more desperate than anything to be found so casually in Manchester, even that spoke of huge wealth—somewhere. Such assemblies of paupers could not be gathered in such permanent concentration unless, somewhere nearby, there were tables groaning with silver plate and vaults stuffed with gold. She sensed that wealth in her very bones.

It was clear from the way they had to fight their way south down Gray's Inn Road, against the main northward rush as the City emptied; it was clear from the rash of ROOMS TO LET signs in the windows, beacons to the hopeful; and it was clear in the sheer number of pawnshops, repositories of hopes forlorn. Here was the city where men brought their dreams. Here was the magnet of all ambition. Here was where big fish from little ponds learned of the ocean's existence. Here was the honeypot. And, just as an English foxhound, transported suddenly to the American plains and knowing nothing of, say, white-tailed deer, would nevertheless recognize its scent as spelling game and quarry, and would at once give tongue and own the line and follow it in hopes of a kill, so Nora, cast suddenly into this new land, owned its scent of gold and lusted for her kill, knowing nothing yet of the shape and form of her actual quarry.

"The Tabard, where we're staying," John said, "is very near the

Greenwich Railway's depot at London Bridge. That's mainly why I chose it. That's built all on arches, you see. Like the Manchester link line may be. We can go and see it."

She smiled and nodded happily, wondering what it was that invigorated her so. Out of the window she saw the sign over a shop: GRAY'S INN PHARMACY. Gray's Inn Road! The address of the mysterious Mr. Dow—the possible arsonist! The . . . *something* Inn. No . . . Arms. The Calthorpe Arms!

She threw open the window, poked out her head and said: "Is this Gray's Inn Road?"

"Indeed it is, madam."

"D'ye know the Calthorpe Arms?"

"Right behind yer, lady." He pointed with his whip.

"Stop!" she cried. "I have business there." She turned back quickly to John. "No time to explain it now," she gabbled. "It's something Nancy Spur told me last week . . ."

"Shall I come?"

She hesitated.

"Very well." He smiled. "Be as quick as you can."

She walked swiftly up Wells Street to the side entrance of the inn. The light inside was so dim that she could at first see nothing. She had no idea what her next move ought to be.

"Yes?" a girl's voice said. The air stank of cabbage, liquor, and smoke.

She drew herself up to full height and, without having consciously intended it, said in perfect imitation of Lady Henshaw: "Be so kind as to summon Mr. Tighe. I wish to have him brought to me."

She could see the girl now, a plain dumpling, staring at her stupidly.

"Do you understand me?" she asked, with exactly Lady Henshaw's mixture of sharpness and kindliness.

"What is it, Margaret?" asked a man, out of view around the corner.

"Lady wants you, sir."

A shadow fell across the girl as the man approached. She backed away to make room for him. He was a big man, almost as big as John—for which she was glad. Big men were more gallant and obliging than small ones. Small men were suspicious and belligerent creatures.

True to form, the big man smiled. "Yes, madam?"

Taking her courage in both hands she said, without smiling: "I've come for the messages and letters for Mr. Dow."

"Dow?" he said, as if he had never heard of the name. But he immediately gave himself away by adding. "All right you, Margaret. Leave us."

Nora's heart began to hammer at her throat. What had she done? She had let herself into something far over her head here. Mr. Tighe was no longer smiling. "I've not seen you before," he said. "You've never come before."

Now she smiled. "I appreciate your caution, Mr. Tighe. And so, I'm sure, does . . . Mr. Dow." She put enough of a pause before the name to suggest that she knew it was a pseudonym. The device appeared to relax the landlord slightly, though he was still suspicious. "But I have a carriage outside and much business still to do. So if you will please hand me over what you have . . ."

Tighe looked very dubious. "I don't know," he said unhappily. "He ought to have said he was sending you . . ."

"You mean he *didn't?*" she said, scandalized. "Oh! Why in that case, I can hardly blame you! He certainly should have sent to tell you. I was convinced he had. What a bloody pickle!"

If he had doubted her quality, those doubts were removed by her swearing, and her manner of swearing. "Tell you what, madam," he said. "I can't just take your word, much as I'd want to. But if you can tell me Mr. D's . . . well, shall we say *another* name for him, I'll turn over to you what I have."

Nora thought rapidly and played her last card. She looked around as if every wall had eyes, and ears lurked in every corner. Then, drawing close to him, leaning up toward his ear, steadying herself with a gentle hand laid upon his arm, she breathed the initials that had stood on Mr. Dow's luggage: "N. . . . C. . . ."

Tighe, no doubt swayed in part by her beauty and the closeness of her, pulled reluctantly away, breathed heavily, and shook his head in admiration. "He's a careful one that Mr. . . . . C," he said.

"In his place, would not you be careful, too?" she asked.

"Indeed!" He spoke as if Dow lived always on the verge of summary arrest.

He capitulated then and went somewhere into the back of the house to fetch whatever awaited the mystery man. She trembled with delight; soon, perhaps, the mystery would be cleared up. Peering into the gloom, she was unnerved to realize that a pair of eyes was fixed unrelentingly upon her.

But it was only young Margaret, pricked by curiosity—as became clear when Tighe, returning with two envelopes, shooed her before him up the passage and into the bar.

As he handed her the letters, he said: "Who shall I confirm as having called for them?"

"Lady Summit," Nora said unhesitatingly. "It's not my name, but it's the one he and I agreed on. And I shall use it every time I call in future."

Tighe smiled and bowed before, remembering himself, he sprang to open the door for her. "There'll be no trouble next time, your ladyship. Tell Mr. . . . C that."

"I'm heartily glad to hear it, Tighe," she said as she swept by. "So will he be. So will he."

"Good night, your ladyship."

The coach from the Tabard was not in sight. With a quick look up and down the short street she thrust the letters into her bodice, aligning them with the side panels and gripping them with her arm. Even as she hid them she knew it was something dreadful she had done. Suppose Mr. Dow was completely aboveboard? The consequences didn't bear thinking of. John would be furious. It was the thought of John's fury that really awoke her to the enormity of her action.

Back in Gray's Inn Road she saw the coach had moved on about fifteen paces, to the next corner.

"Come and see!" John called. He and the horse seemed bathed in fire.

When she drew level with him there was no need to point out what had drawn him. For there, over the heads of passing horsemen and coaches, stretching between the houses that flanked Guilford Street, hung bars of fiery cloud, crimson where they caught the light of the sun that had set ten minutes earlier, deep smoky green where they were shaded from it.

The pair of them stood spellbound by its intensity. Not one inch of the scene before them was devoid of colour. The sky ranged from gold through cold turquoise, to azure, to purple. The houses, stark against the skyline, were a rich prussian blue, the streets a kind of lilac grey, the windows opposite, set in the deep, muffled red of London stock bricks, burned back the twice-reflected fire of the sunstruck walls on this side of the street.

Within moments it had faded. A great swath of earth shadow had risen up the sky and snuffed out the clouds, leaving the night to its blues and greys and violets, unrelieved.

"It was worth a day's journey just to see that," she said as he helped her back into the coach.

And when they were aboard and moving again through the gathering dark, he said: "What was that all about?"

"Oh," she said. "A wild goose chase . . ." And she told him of the man she had seen nosing around their workings the week before the fire, and how the following day she had traced him down to the Royal Oak and what Nancy had told her there.

"So what did you go in there for?" he asked, nodding back toward the inn.

"To see if I could get any letters or messages waiting for him." She laughed. "I think they thought I was an escaped lunatic. Anyway I got out unharmed."

He sighed, imitating despair. "Escaped lunatic is about the mark!"

"I know," she said quickly. "I couldn't get out fast enough. I suddenly thought—suppose they're love letters and this Mr. Dow has no connection with us or with fires . . ."

She was still thinking it as she hugged the two letters between her bodice and corset while the coach fought its way on through the twilight rush hour, down to Holborn, and into the City.

Up in Lancashire she had thought of London as a place much like Manchester or Leeds except that it was bigger and dirtier and more dangerous and the people spoke faster and cheated you quicker. How different was the reality! St. Paul's . . . Mansion House and the Lord Mayor . . . the Bank of England . . . Old Bailey . . . there were names to conjure with! They stirred in her the same emotions she had felt on Christmas Eve, when the ensign and that other young fellow had recited those poems, and when everyone had sung "Rule Britannia."

London Bridge was at first a disappointment. "Where's all the houses?" Nora asked. "I thought it was all covered with houses."

"That was old London Bridge." He pointed downriver. "It used to stand there. Not long ago, either. A terrible ramshackle affair that was. It got so bad, there were two spans people didn't dare cross. This one should last a lot longer."

From the middle of the bridge they could look a fair distance both upstream and down before the river twisted out of sight. Downstream lay the night, full, dark, and cloudless, with a promise of frost. The west-facing walls of the buildings glimmered palely as they caught the last of the twilight; above them, like four slightly glowing onions, loomed the corners of the White Tower, in the Tower of London. From the dark hulks of ships and the tall riverside warehouses came the fitful gleam of lanterns and gas flares as stevedores and masters fought to beat the tide.

Upstream, against the last lowering of the day, the river was a pale highway between two fairylands. A million gaslights and oil lamps twinkled in streets and from windows, tracing out the human cobwebs and giving a new, nighttime form to the hills and plains of the City and Westminster. Now, even more than by day, you could see those teeming streets and sense the myriad activities to which their buildings gave a home. How wonderful, she thought, to be a soaring bird and wing one's way among the palaces and theatres and houses and slums, to see it all. Yet even as she pictured it, she knew it was not what she wanted; not really. She wanted to take part in that unending motley. She wanted the choice of it.

"I wish I'd brought my telescope," she said.

He laughed.

After her flights of fancy the Tabard was, to say the least, a disappointment. At the top of Wellington Street, opposite the Town Hall, they turned left through a dilapidated gateway into a very uneven open court. The driver had to make wild detours right and left to avoid potholes and short ditches, all filled with putrid water. And as for the inn at the bottom of the courtyard—if you piled several dozen labourers' hovels on top of and beside one another, every which way, all of different materials and sizes and styles, and bound the whole lot together with a rolling, wooden balcony, as a drunkard might bind a parcel with string, you would arrive at a somewhat tidier version of the Tabard. It was a building that had gone on growing through the centuries, almost independent of the will of man—a sort of architectural tumour, a malignancy of timber and plaster. Somewhere within its ramshackle, broken-backed accretion of rooms and halls, corridors and stairs, you felt there might still lurk a company of archers fresh from the Crusades or a frightened rump of Tyler's rebels.

Yet it was quite clearly a popular place. When they were halfway down the court an empty stage passed them, going out. And when they arrived at the apron of the inn, four more stage coaches were either then disgorging their passengers or had just done so.

"What an inn!" Nora said.

"Oh—d'ye not like it?" he asked facetiously. "Our family has always used it. For centuries. Been coming here."

"I believe you, too. Centuries!"

But now that they were among the lights and amid the bustle, the whole aspect of the place was more cheerful. Porters scurried back and forth carrying bags and trunks from the apron to the rooms. Men and women, warm in friendships newly struck upon their journey, "after-you'd" and "my-dear-good-fellowed" and laughed their ways indoors to taproom, dining room, and bars. Serving girls brought pots of ale to the coachmen, who swaggered before the usual admiring crowds of ostlers and barefoot stable lads. The horses just stood, morose and exhausted by their long haul, knowing they must drag the empty coach and the unsteady coachman a mile or two yet before they reached their several stables. Dogs sniffed with impunity among their leaden hooves and between the carriage wheels for anything that might satisfy hunger, slake thirst, rouse lust, or perhaps just raise a memory. It was a rich, warm world of welcome reaching out to them with its bustle of bodies, its chorus of voices, of the fall of hooves and the grind of iron tyres on cobbles, and its mingled odours of dinner, fire, beer, straw, horses, and putrescence. It was a microcosm of all that Nora had seen and sensed from London Bridge.

"I'm going to like it," she said.

Before they had even pulled to a halt, the landlord came striding toward the coach. He threw open the door, folded down the steps, and handed Nora down. "Mrs. Stevenson, madam . . . and you, Mr. Stevenson, sir! Right welcome. You had a pleasing journey, I hope?"

"Oh, yes!" Nora said. "And such a drive! From the depot to here! It's so big!"

"I'm Cornelius. Thomas Cornelius, landlord." They shook hands all round. "Yes, it's not often, as you may imagine, we have the honour of entertaining guests from the north. I hope you will find yourselves well pleased here and will feel able to tell your friends . . ." There was little need for them to reply. Cornelius went on like a machine. "We are famous, you know. We've been serving guests and visitors to London since long before all your Yorkshires and Lancashires fell out with one another."

"I can believe it," John said.

"You don't have to, sir. Come and look." And he led them adroitly among the pools that mottled the yard to the farther wall, where he pointed up to a faded legend painted on the crumbling plaster. Even next day they had difficulty deciphering it. "There!" he said and read it for them. "It says 'This is the Inne where Sir Jeffry Chaucer and the nine and twenty Pilgrims lay in their journey to Canterbury, anno 1383.' There!"

"Four hundred and fifty-seven years!" Nora said, looking around the yard and finding it very believable.

"You're better at sums than I am!" Cornelius joked.

"That's a fine confession for a landlord," John told him, and then added: "Mrs. Stevenson's better than Cocker."

Cornelius, leading them back to the apron, whose light made the pools and ditches easier to discern, bobbed his head forward and looked at her with humorous fear. "I must remember that before I write your bill!" Then he turned to John. "You know Cocker's books were all printed just around the corner? Funny you mentioning him."

"I didn't know that."

"Yes. In Tooley Street. Oh yes, there's a lot of history around here for people who have the time to find it." After a pause he asked, "Do you have a local interest? Not as I wish to pry, but if there's anything in which I may help . . . ? I'm well known here, you understand."

He took them indoors and led them through a warren of twisting corridors between leaning walls and beneath once-straight ceilings built in an age of dwarfs. Where lights flickered dimly, they were gloomy; where there were no lights, they were dark and beset with projecting crutches of timber or low-slung beams.

"You might be able to help at that," John answered as he dodged among these obstacles. "My interest in the neighbourhood is the Greenwich Railway Company's depot next door." Cornelius stopped and looked at him sharply. "I'm a railroad contractor by trade," John explained.

The landlord shook his head dubiously and resumed his walk. "You're entering some politics there. It's not just the Greenwich, you know. It's the Croydon railway, too. And it'll soon be the Brighton, on top of it all. There'll be some jolly fighting up on those arches these next few years! But you've come to the right place here, you know. What? I should think so! D'ye know George Roberts?"

"I've not had that honour."

Cornelius stopped again and pulled out his watch. "What's it now? Just turned seven. In an hour or so we should be able to rectify this . . . this gap in your experience, sir. George Roberts is one of the company's engineers, the Croydon company, that is. Comes here every night after work for an hour or two. Easily introduce you if you like?"

"Aye," John said. "I'd welcome that."

"This is—or rather these are—your rooms." He paused, like a showman, pointing at the door. "Rooms, do I say? It is a *suite*. The best of the house. Exactly as your letter commanded!"

He threw wide the door and gestured them before him into a large, panelled chamber measuring about fifteen feet deep by twenty wide and with a ceiling twelve feet high. The floor, of polished oak, gleamed darkly in the soft light of four oil lamps, newly lighted. In the middle stood their luggage, ready to be unpacked.

Cornelius drew a heavy drape over the window and crossed the room to open its inner door, facing the door they came in by. "Your bedroom," he said. "If it gets chill, you can send for the fire to be lit." He indicated a large, oak-panelled fireplace with a tapestry hung above it.

The room was the same size as the parlour they had first entered. It, too, had a gothic latticed window, in the same wall as the parlour. Cornelius drew the drape over this as well. The bedroom was richly furnished with a stout four-poster bed. An ancient linen chest stood at its foot, and a wardrobe, two chests of drawers, a night commode made to look like a chair, and a washstand were variously disposed against the walls.

"You may ring for hot water and shaving water," Cornelius said, pulling a bell rope by the bed. He watched them eagerly, looking and hoping to see their approval. John caught Nora's eye and raised his eyebrows at her. She nodded warmly back.

"I think we may call it highly satisfactory, Mr. Cornelius," he told him.

The landlord beamed. "It is the best," he said. "And this room, you know, is unique. There is none other like it in London."

A maid knocked and entered. "You can unpack now, Sarah," Cornelius told her. "But first, just open the other door there, over the passage." When the girl obeyed, the landlord turned back to them. "There now—what d'ye see? Eh? Look at that and tell me."

"That's a long oak plank," John said, noticing that it made a single run from their bedroom, through the parlour, across the passage and into the dark of the far room.

"Forty-five feet!" Cornelius said. John whistled. "But the whole floor, you see is continuous. Not just that one plank. This was once a single room, forty-five feet long. A hall. And its name? Bless me if it's not the Pilgrims' Hall! Yes! This, Mr. Stevenson, sir—and you, Mrs. Stevenson—this is the very room, *the* very room, where Sir Geoffrey Chaucer, not to mention the Wife of Bath, the Miller, the Clerk, the Knight, the Merchant, Franklyn, Dyer—and all the other merry pilgrims—where they lay and regaled each other with their tales." He sighed and looked around, as if long familiarity with the room had still not dulled the wonder of it. "In this very room," he said in reverentially hushed voice, "you might say that English literature was born. Yes—the craft of English letters first saw light of day here."

After he had gone to see to their dinner, Nora said to the maid: "Your master has a love of writing, Sarah."

But Sarah gave a little laugh, half affectionate, half mocking. "Until last year Mr. Cornelius was telling people that Geoffrey Chaucer was leader of a pilgrimage to Jerusalem and it was his capture by the heathen Saracens as caused the Crusades! That's Mr. C and literature, bless him!" John and Nora laughed, hoping to hear more. They were not disappointed. "He got all that off a Mr. Saunders who came here last summer. It was Mr. Saunders who discovered all that about these three rooms being originally one big hall. Until then they all said the Pilgrims' Hall was burned down in the big Southwark fire."

"Still," John said, "he tells it well."

"Mr. Cornelius does everything well, sir. He's the best landlord that ever owned this place," she said. Then, having finished their unpacking, she gave them both a knowing smile and left them to wash before dinner.

"Strange girl for a maid at an inn," he said. "She's had some education, that one."

When their dinner had been cleared, John said he supposed he might as well go and meet this engineer George Roberts; and Nora, itching to unseal the two envelopes still hidden in her bodice, supposed she would read a little more from *London Sketches* and go to sleep.

Just as he kissed her good night and told her not to wait up, they were startled by a maniacal scream and an even more maniacal cackle of laughter from somewhere outside their window. John quickly crossed the room and flung the casement wide; but the street was silent and, as far as they could tell by the dim light that struggled feebly from the small and curtained windows, deserted.

\*     \*     \*

George Roberts was a short, powerful, good-humoured man with a gift for telling stories and imitating people. Within moments of their introduction he was talking to John as if they'd known each other, and had sat drinking at this particular table every Tuesday, for years. He was keen to hear about the drifting and tunnelling at Summit and was quick to realize that John, too, was the through-and-through professional.

John soon broached the subject of an arched railroad. Roberts thought that if John ever took on such a contract, it would be wise to go for one that excluded the price of bricks, or, failing that, he ought to enter a long-term contract with the maker for the specified number of bricks at an agreed price. The Greenwich railway arches, he remembered, 878 of them, had caused quite a famine of bricks and drove the price very high; the contractor had made no profit on the last hundred arches he built.

Later in the evening, when the ale had loosened his tongue even more, George told him a lot of inside dirt on the shameless behaviour of the Brighton Railway Company's directors and managers—the open stock jobbing, the leakage of funds, the dilatory supervision. And so the talk went on for hours—who was projecting what, where, what it would cost, problems of operating a line, memories of the pioneer days a decade ago, dreams of the future, the fortunes awaiting the right men. . . . It was gone midnight when John returned, and Nora had by then long been sound asleep. He heard again the screaming and the laughter outside their window and wondered what it could be.

Nora, had she been awake to hear it, would not have wondered. It was the first question she had asked Sarah, whom she summoned back to the room as soon as John had left.

"Oh," Sarah laughed. "We don't notice anymore. It's the lunatics in Guy's Madhouse in Queen Street, just over the way. It has no meaning. Was that all, madam?"

Nora looked carefully at the girl's plain and pleasant face, wondering how far she was to be trusted, knowing she had to be trusted . . . worrying. "I need a number of things, Sarah," she said quietly. "I need a knife with a blade scoured so thin you can almost see daylight through it. I need a little spirit lamp of the sort to heat medicines or hair tongs. And I need a room where I may work undisturbed for half an hour. Not this room." She waited anxiously for the maid's reply.

Sarah stared a long while, summing her up, before she answered. "I want no part in anything illegal."

"Nothing illegal is intended," Nora assured her.

"If it is," Sarah said, "if it should turn out so, I will not lie to shield . . . anyone."

Nora admired her caution. And her frank spirit. "I will tell you in part," she said. "Enough to set your mind easy. There is a man who means my husband's business ill. My husband will not believe it. I have intercepted letters to this man and hope they may show one of us right. Until then I wish to spare my husband knowledge of it. I must unseal and copy them privately, now."

Whether she believed her or not, Sarah nodded and said: "In ten minutes I shall take you to a place."

The place proved to be Sarah's own room, a snug, airy little garret immediately up the stairs from the Pilgrims' Hall. Their bell rang up here as well as in the servants' hall so Sarah, having pointed to the knife and spirit lamp on the table, left her and returned to their parlour in case of John's early return.

"Tell him, if he comes, you're just sitting there to keep watch while I went to see him," Nora cautioned.

When the maid had withdrawn, Nora, now barely able to contain herself, slipped the two letters delicately from her bodice. They were hardly rumpled—at least, in the light of the one candle Sarah was allowed, they looked smooth enough. The stiff side panels of her corset had kept the paper firm.

Controlling the tremor of her hands as best she could, she heated the paper-thin steel of the knife Sarah had found for her. She was pleased to see it was freshly scoured. Even so she tried it on the jotting pad she had brought, both to see that it left no stain upon paper and that it did not singe it on contact.

She lifted a third of the seal before the knife cooled to the point where it no longer melted the wax. She reheated it. Next time she was almost through before it cooled. The third heating finished the job. *Quite expert!* she thought, *for an utter amateur!* There was no telltale mark; it was as if the seal had by some magic, sprung off complete. With more confidence she managed to get the other seal off in two heatings, even though it was slightly larger.

She dowsed the spirit lamp by replacing its dome of glass over the burning wick. Both letters lay unsealed but unopened before her. She had to fight an impulse to seal them again at once. *Suppose I mark one,* she thought, *or spill ink on it!* She wiped her hands compulsively for the third or fourth time since she had sat down. Then, still feeling them unclean and fearing the marks they might leave, she took some paper from her writing case and tried in vain to rub a mark into it. Then she checked that the ink was tightly stoppered and made one more fruitless attempt to wipe dirty marks onto her note paper. And all this time her eyes strayed back, once and again, to the two unsealed envelopes on the table.

At last she took the first one up. "My most precious angel," it began, "my handsome darling" . . . and her worst fears about the folly of her action appeared justified.

Sick at heart, cursing her stupidity and arrogance in leaping to such wild conclusions, she picked up the other letter and listlessly folded it open. This time she hardly dared to look.

"My dear N," it began. How discreet they all were! She looked for the signature: "T." Oh, so discreet. "It is done! The last £100 was replaced this morning and the entire £2675 is as if it had never strayed. More than that—the accounts and receipts have been revised to perfection and the whole sorry episode is now beyond detection. Old Adam, I need hardly say, is eternally grateful. He swears the boy has learned the lesson of his life. He and I are both for ever in your debt, and none, you may be sure, is more cognizant of that fact than, Yr obedient and devoted servant, T."

Well, she thought glumly, it was *something*. Mr. Dow was not entirely aboveboard. It made her wonder what she had really expected—that Dow had been in touch with someone about the fire or about Summit and that that someone would be replying? It was asking a lot of fate. Still, here *was* a gift from fate: a compromising letter. Dow had in some way entered their lives; his purpose was as yet unexplained; until it was clear, one should not abandon anything that might be of use. One never knew.

So she copied it, word for word.

And for good measure she copied the other, which read: "Tempest has discovered *nothing!* We are safe once more. I tremble already with pleasure at the thought. Oh do—do come to me and still these fevered longings. None but you can quench them—and that only briefly!! Ever, Ever, Ever."

There was no signature; unless it was cleverly disguised in that final repetition. Eva? Eve? A stuttering attempt at Evelyn? And how tantalizing that the one letter was signed T and the other hinted at deceiving a certain "Tempest"! Were they the same? She shivered at the web of deception here a-tangling—and herself now part of it!

All that then remained was to reseal the letters, with a swift pull of the hot knife, held absolutely flat so that it did not make a telltale little furl in the edge of the wax. She put them in a larger envelope and stuck them in the bottom of her writing case. And then, for the first time, she took a real look around Sarah's room.

What a deal of books the girl had. She counted: thirty-two. And some journals. She peeped inside them. A lot of religious books—sermons and things like that. And a lot of poetry—Cowper, Shelley, Burns. None was dedicated to her. Secondhand probably. One book stood out as new: a copy of *Nicholas Nickleby*. This one had a dedication: "To Sarah Nevill, a loyal servant from a grateful master, T. Cornelius. 18 February 1840."

That date! She shut her eyes and bit her lips. The room reeled briefly before she steadied herself. How it still hurt. It was a judgement for her wickedness this night.

No. There was no sense thinking like that. Judgement! That was Arabella's way: Torture yourself into inaction by self-doubt. True, there was nothing to be proud of tonight; but it had to be done. Their business had to be protected.

She put the book back as it had been, neatly arranged the knife and spirit lamp, blew out the candle, and left, clutching her writing case to her. A memory of the snug, orderly little room lingered on. Briefly she envied the girl a life that was so neat and good.

Sarah stood up the moment Nora entered. She closed a small book and put it into her pocket. She had not relished the passive role that Nora had forced her to take in the evening's clandestine activities and there was no warmth in her welcome. Nora had been going to give her a half sovereign, partly to thank her, partly to buy her silence; but something cold and remote in the girl's eye and upright stance forbade it.

"Thank you, Sarah," she said. "I'm very grateful."

"Glad to be of service, ma'am," Sarah said formally.

"Stay and read on if you wish. It's a more comfortable chair and a much better light. Besides, I owe you an inch of candle, I'm sure." She could see the girl hesitate. "You're a great reader. I see by your shelf up there."

Sarah smiled. "I've always been fond for books."

"And at the moment, to judge by the one on your windowsill, it's Mr. Dickens."

She shivered, like a cat when its back is scratched. "Oh, last Sunday, ma'am, my afternoon off, I went up to Doughty Street to see his house. But they said he's moved; over to Paddington reservoirs, they said."

"Do you have any other tales by him?"

Sarah smiled shyly and sat at least half way down on the arm of the chair. "It's my ambition, one day, to own all his books, madam."

"Then may I help? May I buy you one in London tomorrow? To say thank you for your help tonight, which I'm sure went much against your nature."

The girl darted her a quick, slightly puzzled look. Nora could see how much she wanted to accept and how strongly she felt impelled to refuse. But the bookworm won. "There's *Oliver Twist,* or *Pickwick Papers* . . ." she said reluctantly.

John was right. Everyone had a price; and by no means was it always in cash.

Nora nodded, so as not to stretch the subject further. "I'm so ignorant of books," she said. "May I ask you who this Geoffrey Chaucer was?"

And Sarah told her. For an hour or more she poured out all she remembered of *The Canterbury Tales*—the stories the pilgrims were supposed to have recounted, after setting out from this very room, four and a half centuries earlier. Nora sat spellbound, drinking it in. But, for all that, she did not envy the girl so much as she had done earlier. In that eager gush of storytelling she sensed a hunger for a like person to converse with. Nora knew she was not that person—merely its closest approach in many a long and lonely week. This trip to Dickens' former house . . . trying to give a body and face to the mind she tapped alone in that little garret up the stairs . . . the poetry . . . the sermons. . . . It was a hunger for the exalting mind, and for the mind that addresses you directly. She tried to imagine what it might be like to read one of those poetry books, and then to go downstairs to mingle with the cooks, potboys, ostlers, servants, and rough patrons of this inn.

No, she did not envy Sarah quite so much. Yet it was wonderful to have so many fine stories and poems in one's head; that, of course, was something she, too, could have. When she had earned the time.

# *Chapter 43*

"Eurgh! Got a mouth like a bull ring this morning!" George Roberts called out before he realized that Nora was not just another passenger toiling up the ramp approach to the station. "Morning, Roberts," John said and presented him to Nora. She, amused at his confusion, told him that the northern expression was a good deal less refined.

"Not much to see up here, in fact," George said. "Only our grand classical-romantical curtain wall." He pointed to the patch of sailcloth stretched on ropes to form a screen around the platforms.

"More curtain than wall," Nora said.

"Blew off a passing Dutch coaster and they didn't think it worth coming around for." George spoke with such conviction that she believed him for a moment.

The sail ought to have reached to the edge of the wall that contained the platform and divided it from the approach ramp; but the idle men of the district had reefed it sufficiently clear to create a long aperture through which they, standing on the ramp, could gaze directly at the ladies' ankles—and even, when they were helped into the carriages, at their calves.

"Plenty to see *there,*" she said.

"And here's where you see the stupid, short-minded cunning of the Greenwich line," George continued, embarrassed now at her frankness. And then, for several minutes, he pointed to one piece of evidence after another to support his claim that cupidity and bloody-minded vanity were ruining England's chances of getting a decent railway system.

"You sound like a regular champion of nationalization, Roberts," John chided.

George stopped and said, with all humour gone: "Indeed I am. And so I hope is any Englishman with no direct interest in stock jobbing and legal embezzlement! You wait—in ten years the French will have a *national* railway system, and the Belgians. And we'll have a thousand branch lines, all annoyed at having to carry passengers beyond their own particular terminal stations. Dear old England! I love her as much as the next man but, oh dear, she does have a gift for steaming bravely out of the depot with only half the train coupled up behind her!"

John could see Nora's hackles rising at this unpatriotic slur so he interposed hastily: "Well—time will tell. I daresay there's a good deal of logic in that, but I think you underestimate the value of self-interest and the competitive spirit."

"I doubt it." George laughed. "It can't be all that long before self-interest and the competitive spirit manage to kill off some of our passengers. Still, we won't fall out, you and I. There's the arches you came to see."

When they were back in the hackney coach and on their way to the City, Nora said: "I'm out of concert with your Mr. Roberts." But John was too busy, turning over in his mind the implications of what they had just seen, to bother with the patriotism of a minor railway engineer. "Did ye notice how they let off the space between the arches?" he asked. "Where the arch doesn't cross a road they let it out for stables, warehousing, manufactories, dwellings. . . . That interests me."

Nora immediately remembered her ideas about buying up cheap land around new railway stations outside the suburbs of big cities. "Aye," she said eagerly. "We could reduce our quote on the understanding we got a long lease on the vacant arches at a very low rent."

"Peppercorn rent, they call it," he told her. "You see, we'd treat the profit forgone as capital. And considering all the attendant risks, I think we'd want to see more than two birds in the bush for the one we agreed not to take in the hand."

"Depending on our own situation at the time, we'd want to see an annual profit of ten or fifteen percent after expenses on that, I'd think," she agreed.

He nodded and shrugged. "Aye. Something in that region."

She laughed.

"What's up?" he asked.

"I was just thinking. We know how to *make* money, thee and me. And how to keep books balanced. But we know bugger all about *capital*. Raising it, moving it, applying it, repaying it! For all we talk grandly of 'working' capital and 'outlay' capital."

He smiled ruefully. "That is going to be part of my strategy today with our Mr. Chambers. We must induce him to believe that he's gotten two clever customers with a big facility for making money but no genius whatever at using it up at the higher levels. All this around here . . ." He waved his hands out at the Bank of England, which they were at that moment passing. "That's the Bank of England," he said.

"Aye." She didn't even look at it. "He must be led to imagine *he's* going to play that role for us. We'll make the money, he'll handle it and take his percentage and we'll be grateful ever after."

He laughed. "That's it. So you can suck his brains all you're worth but at the end of it, just act daft and say"—he raised his voice to a refined falsetto—" 'Oh, I'll never understand all that!' "

She dug him in the ribs. "I don't talk like that!"

"That's what I mean. You must try." He became serious again. "In general, though, it's going to go like this: We start with a glowing account of the works at Summit so far. You can break in anything to say the things I can't say, about, hem hem—how clever I am! You know—do your she-wolf act . . ."

Her eyes opened in exaggerated surprise. "Well. We *are* learning things about ourselves today!"

"I hope we are. Anyway—when we've got him picturing all that money coming his way for him to manage, we'll start talking about these new contracts, give him the idea of how it's going to swell and go on swelling. And then we'll make it clear how ignorant we are of financial management at these exalted levels. So that we get him wetting his pants thinking he's got a debenture on our lives. And then, when I see the gleam in his eye, I'll tell him how I once borrowed his name."

Nora giggled. "He should find it easy to swallow then."

But John was less sanguine. "He *should*. Aye, he should. But I'd be happier if we were bringing him thirty thousand instead of just over half that. He's a Jew and he's a banker. On both counts he's nobody's fool. So don't let's go in there thinking we've got a new length of carpet."

Meanwhile the coach had gone along Cheapside to St. Paul's and, doubling back down Watling Street, had now halted at the top end of Dowgate. They got out and John paid off the driver. "There!" he said as she took his arm. "I asked him to go around by the way we came last night, and we didn't even look out the window."

"Pity," she said lightly. "Have you got all the accounts? Are you sure of everything?" Anxiety and excitement were making her edgy.

Bolitho & Chambers, being a merchant bank, had no counters nor any facilities for direct dealing with the public. Indeed, theirs was more like a lawyer's office than anything Nora had pictured. "Nice and small," she said in whisper while the chief clerk was in the inner sanctum, telling Chambers of their arrival. "Hard to believe that seventeen *hundred* has ever passed this way, let alone ours."

"Aye," John agreed. "Looks promising."

Chambers came almost running to greet them. And his arrival in the outer office stopped Nora's heart in her breast: *Mr. Dow!* Beyond all shadow of possible error it was Mr. Dow. She had seen him—virtually as close as she saw him now—through her telescope. For an irrational moment she thought that he, too, must recognize her. Especially when she quailed before that impish, mocking smile he gave as he bent to kiss her glove. But he was merely being gallant; and she hoped he would take her confusion for another of those instant conquests he must be well accustomed to by now. Indeed, she herself was none too sure, for he was certainly the handsomest man she had ever seen. Then it struck her: Nathaniel Chambers of Dowgate—Nathan Dow! How could she have missed it? The fire! The fire had misdirected her.

John, thinking she was overplaying the vapid butterfly-girl, or playing it too early, cleared his throat.

Chambers turned to John. "There are no diversions here to offer Mrs. Stevenson. But I have an elderly and very trustworthy maid upstairs and my carriage is at her disposal . . . if"—he turned to Nora—"if you would care to go shopping in the West End, ma'am? While Mr. Stevenson and I talk all these tedious matters through?"

John explained Nora's part in the business and why she would be joining them, tedium or not.

"Then it will be no tedium—at least not for *us*," he said gallantly. "Though I shall talk in constant fear of burdening so pretty a head with every trifling detail."

She could see that the idea was anathema to him, though; he barely managed to maintain his smile as he ushered her in.

As soon as those hypnotic eyes were off her, her mind began to race. Those letters—she had put them out of her thoughts for this morning. She had to remember what they said; they guaranteed that John's forgery would be owned by Chambers. Yet . . . something about that thought was not . . . not right. Why could she not blackmail Chambers? Something said no.

John nudged her. "Mr. Chambers is asking if you'd prefer tea?"

She pulled herself together. "To what?"

"Sherry."

She had to keep a clear head. "Tea," she said. "No sugar."

She had ten minutes to recover her self-possession while she sipped her tea, and the men drank their sherry, and all three of them ate their biscuits and talked of London, and the north, and railways, and of course the weather. And while they talked she thought of all the ways in which she might make clear what she knew of Chambers' darker dealings. And the more she thought, the more unhappy she became with the whole idea.

When they finally got down to the business of the day, she pushed these worries to the back of her mind and played her part exactly as John had set it out for her.

John explained the circumstances in which he had gained the contract—glossing over the difference between his capital and the credit demanded by the Manchester & Leeds—and the changes he had made in the working. When he had finished, Nora butted in to point out how superior John was to most contractors. Then John explained how he couldn't have managed without Nora—how she kept the books, her skill at purchasing, and finally the tommy shop. She could see that Chambers' attitude toward her changed from one of patronage, to bewilderment, to at least a suspension of his disbelief. And finally, when John passed over the ledgers he had brought, and when the banker had spent several silent minutes looking through them, she saw something like a grudging admiration, now mixed with a decided wariness, in the glance he shot at her before he closed the book and said to John: "I don't really need to go through these in any detail now. My clerk can do that later. The proof is in the money you've been sending down here."

"Still," John replied, "you're probably thinking one swallow doesn't make a summer. . . ." And he went on to describe the new contracts he had taken up this last fortnight—throwing in the fact that they were due to meet Fielden at the Houses of Parliament tomorrow to discuss a fairly large contract for his firm.

Chambers was now very impressed and made no attempt to disguise his interest. "You're into the second stage of your growth," he said. John agreed and pointed out that they had reached the point where their own money-raising skills had come to a limit.

The banker saw the bait and took it, offering his considerable services. He began to sketch out on some jotting paper a number of alternative ways they could raise the money they needed. As she watched him suavely moving his pen from block to block in his little diagrams, she suddenly realized why it was that she could not openly challenge him with what the letters had revealed. It was his *vanity*. He would never forgive her; and if their business were to move in the hoped-for directions, she and he would have to work in some kind of trust and mutual regard. If he refused to support John, and then she forced him to go back on that refusal, there could never be any kind of a working relationship between them.

So when the point came where the discussions were rounding off before lunch, and John could not long delay mentioning his forgery, she sat with leaden heart, knowing that the information she had was of little use— beyond a last-resort insurance to keep them out of jail. How could she let him know without saying anything explicit? Impossible . . . well, *almost* impossible. Unaccountably, her pulse began to race. Perhaps it was not impossible. Only to fainthearts. If she kept alert. . . . John was just beginning his confession.

"As you may imagine, Mr. Chambers," he said, "these achievements we have described this morning were not gained by methods that would win the good-conduct prizes at Sunday school."

Chambers smiled. "We're men of the world here in the City, Mr. Stevenson. I'm sure ye never thought otherwise."

"No. To be sure. For instance, to get the contract in the first place, I was obliged to forge a banker's letter of credit!"

Chambers laughed heartily. "The devil you did! Oh, pardon, ma'am . . ." Then, seeing Nora's beady, unsmiling gaze upon him, his face fell. Realization dawned. "Not . . . not *this* bank!"

*He's going to refuse,* Nora thought. *I know it. Do something!*

In desperation she did the only thing that suggested itself.

"Mr. Dow!" She clapped her hands and pointed both index fingers at him, her arms held straight, her face alight with the discovery.

"I . . . what?" Chambers said, put out of stride more than worried.

"Mr. Dow! You remember, dearest," she gushed, turning to John—who was looking daggers at her, "you remember I told you of the strange man nosing around our workings. The one we thought connected with the arsonists. This is Mr. Dow. That was risky!" she added as an afterthought, turning to a now very puzzled Chambers. She did not take her eyes from the banker's, afraid that John's anger would make her falter. "The fire we had at Summit was immediately after your visit. Until now we've assumed Mr. Dow had something to do with it!"

"This is . . . enlightening," Chambers said guardedly.

She rubbed her hands. "And all the time it was *you!* Curious about this unknown John Stevenson who kept sending his money to you! Coming up there in secret to see for yourself! Of course! How clever!"

Her apparent admiration touched his vanity enough to let him smile faintly in modest confession. "A banker, too, has interests to protect," he said. "Information is our stock in trade. And you cannot better firsthand information."

Now Nora really gushed. "That's what I thought, too," she giggled. John, now certain that she was acting a part and knowing she must have good reason, was no longer angry; he watched, tense and alert.

"D'you know," Nora went on, in the tones of a schoolgirl telling her chums about an escapade, "I even called at the Calthorpe Arms to find out more about our Mr. Dow. I thought I might deceive Mr. Tighe into parting with some of his letters! What a laugh!"

Chambers, doodling idly with a dry nib, paused for a fraction of a second before he darted a glance at her and then at John. The contrast—Nora's stony mask, belying her tone of voice; and John's evident bewilderment—unnerved him; they were not behaving like two confidence tricksters. The woman did not *want* her husband to know; she was trying to get *him* to understand something without conveying it to the other man. But that was too improbable, surely.

"Tighe?" he said, very convincingly.

She laughed again. "The landlord. He thought I was a lunatic, of course."

Chambers could not conceal the relief that passed fleetingly across his face. "It would have been a criminal act," he said. "Intercepting mails. Personation . . ."

"There's a bit of the old Adam in all of us," Nora said. "Even those of us descended from Eve—for she was Adam's rib. . . ."

The extraordinary thing is that Nora was so glad to have worked in so natural-sounding a reference to the name "Adam" that she had quite forgotten her conjecture that the name "Eve" might have been concealed in the closing dedication of the billet-doux; and she had intended her mention of Eve here to correct, as it were, Adam's sex in referring to herself. But the effect on Chambers was unambiguous. Even John, who had no idea of the reference intended, could see that Nora's words had struck a home in the banker and exercised some kind of power over him. He watched with wary interest.

Nora was now in a quandary. Should she assume she had said enough to alert Chambers to the danger of any course other than the one that served the Stevenson interest? Or should she drop one more hint to confirm the fears she must already have stirred? The second course, she decided.

She turned to Chambers, all smiling apology. "I'm sorry, Mr. Chambers. You were about to tell us . . . ?"

"I was about to ask you," Chambers said to John, "exactly what you did? What did you put in this forgery?"

John drew a silk packet from his inner pocket and unwrapped it with care. From it he pulled and unfolded a single sheet of paper. "There's a copy," he said. "The original was on your notepaper." He was cool and businesslike, not the least shamefaced.

Chambers kept his eye on John. "Our paper," he repeated. "May I ask . . . ?"

"I bought it," John said. "There are places where you can buy anyone's paper. And autograph signature."

Chambers was now quite cold, giving nothing away. He looked down at the copy and read it in absorbed and chilling silence. "But by this date Bolitho had been dead for months!" he said.

John pulled out another sheet of paper. "That is a copy of the letter I substituted for it."

Chambers read that in the same dour silence. At length he said: "It's well drafted, I'll allow that. What happened to the first one?"

"*That's* the problem," said John. "There's a clerical gentleman, probably known to you, who spotted the error in the first letter and caused me to substitute the second. Of course, he kept the other and is now hoping for a donation of thirty-three percent of all our profits."

"Thirty-three and a third," Nora corrected.

"The old . . . !" Chambers said, halting as he remembered Nora's presence. He sighed. "You must have come here with some kind of solution in mind?"

John extracted a third sheet from the silk bundle and, unfolding it, passed it over. It read:

Dear Mr. Stevenson:

On going through the office effects of my late partner, Mr. Bolitho, I came across a copy of the letter of credit you asked us to prepare in December 1838 but never used. Recently you asked us to send you a further such letter and upon inquiry I find that my clerk, noticing that the earlier letter had not yet been dated, put the date of 8th August 1839 upon it and despatched it to you. The fact that it is now ostensibly signed by Mr. Bolitho, some months after his demise, is, to say the least, highly irregular and may give rise to some very proper inquiry. I take this occasion therefore to enclose a properly drawn-up letter of credit, signed by myself alone and bearing that same date. I trust that and this letter will clear up any misunderstanding which may in the meantime have arisen. Meanwhile I hear that you are to be congratulated upon your marriage and I hasten to add that I very much . . .

Chambers' gaze fell rapidly over the closing pleasantries.

He pursed his lips, folded the letter, tapped it once or twice on his thumbnail, and said: "It might work at that. It . . . might . . . work. Did you reply?"

John smiled and pulled a fourth sheet from the bundle. It read:

Dear Chambers,

Thank you for your new letter of credit and covering letter of explanation. I showed both to one of the Manchester & Leeds directors, Reverend Prendergast, who, I think, claims some slight acquaintance with you, and have his assurance that his company files will be properly revised. He promises that your mistaken first letter will be destroyed.

For the first time since John's confession, Chambers actually smiled at him. "Neat," he said. "Neatly done." But then he sighed again. "However, I do wish I could first inspect your forgery. . . ."

"Prendergast called it excellent. He said that had it not been for the misfortune of Bolitho's death, he'd never have suspected it to be other than copper bottomed."

"Well—that's praise indeed." He looked at both of them. "You're an odd pair, if I may be quite candid. I've never met your like. And I've always said that my ten years in banking have brought me more experience of people than others would get in a score of lifetimes."

Nora laughed. "I wish you could have seen us that night, Mr. Chambers. By the light of four candles. Myself fretting over bricks and timber and wages and the price of iron, and Mr. Stevenson practising your signature again and again. And we had no notion of the trouble we were laying down. What's the saying? We sowed a wind and almost"—she repeated the word with a stress meant only for the banker—"*almost* reaped a Tempest!"

For what seemed an age he stared at her with his lips pursed as if he were about to whistle. And whistle he very nearly did as he let out his pent-up breath and, once more, gave a rueful smile.

Meanwhile John was saying: "Whirlwind. 'Sow a wind and reap a whirlwind.' That's the catch phrase."

Nora accepted the correction and said directly to him: "Tempest and whirlwind could be very similar, I think." She avoided looking at Chambers, but she heard his unstinted laughter.

"Come," he said, rising and gesturing them toward the door. "A dozen good lamb chops are spoiling while we dawdle."

"We're back in harness then, I take it?" John asked, always one to get absolute confirmation and commitment.

"What you have done, Mr. Stevenson, is not very elegant by City standards; but, as it was successful, I can't really fault it. What's that other saying: In for a penny in for a pound?" Chambers came between them while he spoke. And, with daring intimacy, he took John's left and Nora's right arm in his hands.

"Oh!" Nora said playfully. "I'm sure in these exalted circles it's not pennies and pounds but something like: 'In for two thousand six hundred and seventy-five pounds, in for ten thousand'!"

And then she had to bite her lip to stop herself from laughing, for Nathaniel Chambers had grasped the soft flesh on the back of her arm, above her elbow, and had gently *pinched* it. She glanced quickly at him but his amused, superior face stared fixedly ahead.

No qualms remained then about the possibility, nor indeed about the quality, of future co-operation between themselves and him.

He took them to a chophouse in Fleet Street where they devoured succulent and tenderly grilled lamb chops, washed down with two bottles of claret, and topped with some deliciously cooling water ice. "These new table d'oat and ah lah cart houses in the West End are all very well in their way," Chambers said. "But for my money the City chophouse beats all. No one in all the world eats so well as the Englishman in his chophouse." They did not dispute him.

But if he had planned for a meal of light conversation during which he might hope to pump information from his two new clients up from the country, it was a hope forlorn. It was they who pumped him; and there was no subtlety about it either. By the time they stood up again—heavily and unsteadily—the pair of them knew a great deal more about forming companies, floating shares, calling up capital, issuing scrip, writing debentures, and about stocks, shares, securities, margins, options, endorsements—in short, more about the prominent landmarks of their new country of residence—than they had dreamed there was to know. Chambers left them in Fleet Street as he had another client to see and they had nothing to do until seven that evening, when he would call to take them to the theatre at Sadler's Wells. Their address at the Tabard amused him; he had never actually been south of the river.

"There *is* something of Thornton in him!" John said after Chambers had gone.

But Nora would not agree. "He has, in refined form, everything that in Thornton will remain forever coarse."

"He flirted with you, all right!"

Nora looked sharply at him: "And that's *all* he'll ever do." She meant it both as an assessment of Chambers and as a promise; but she also made it clear she resented even the thought that the promise was necessary.

"What was in the letters?" he asked. He did not look at her but gazed straight up Ludgate Hill at St. Paul's, black on the skyline. Everything was black with soot.

"All right!" she said, wanting to be aggressive and getting no cause for it from him. "*You* did something underhand and it worked. That's all I've done. And it also worked."

He looked at her, conceded the point with a nod of his head, and looked ahead again, waiting for more.

"And it's a good thing I did," she said. "And that I kept it from you. Because if you'd had the information you'd have *had* to use it differently. You'd have had to challenge him." She held her head up proudly. "I think it's very good the way it's all worked out."

"You didn't challenge him? That wasn't what you'd call a challenge?"

"A woman's challenge. Not a man's. It's different."

"As I'm not to know the substance of the challenge—only its apparent gender—" he said, "I can offer no further opinion."

She laughed at that. "Very well," she said, and, as near word for word as she could remember, she recited the contents of the two letters.

By the time she finished, they had arrived at the top of the hill, immediately outside St. Paul's. He stopped dead and stared at her, waiting for more. "Well?" he said at last.

"That's all."

He reached out a hand to steady himself. "All?"

"Yes."

"But suppose he challenged you? One—*prove* those letters were addressed to Nathaniel Chambers. Two—who is Adam? Three—who is the youthful embezzler? Four—who is T, the writer of the letter? Five—*what* accounts were tampered with? Six—who is Tempest? A nickname? They're all so damned discreet, it might well be. Seven—who is the woman?"

She looked blankly at him, trying desperately to think of one thing, one solitary fact, she could lay at Chambers' door. And there wasn't one.

She punched him playfully in the chest: "You'd have done just the same as I did," she said, blithely going back on her previous line of argument. "You'd have hinted you knew it all. Relied on his guilty conscience or sense of self-interest to do the rest. You'd have done that."

"Of course I would, you daft pennyworth!" he said. "But I'd have *known*. I'd have known I held a hand full of rubbish. You thought you had all trumps."

"Good thing, too," she chuckled. "That's the difference between us. If I'd known, I could never have done it."

He had to laugh, though at heart he was far from amused. "Listen,'" he said when she was collected again. "A pact. No more deception like this. Leave it to me where it concerns us both. Is that agreed?"

She pouted but she had to acknowledge the sense of it. When she looked at him he was staring up, with a mask of savage glee, at the clock on St. Paul's.

"What now?" she asked.

"Twenty to three. I'd almost forgotten. Our Church of England is about to enter the Gryphon in Littleborough, where it's still half past two, in the fond hopes of wrapping his sticky claws around the rest of his thousand pounds."

"What have you gone and done?" she asked, knowing from his smile that he had not told all.

"I've left him an empty parcel."

"He'll have an apoplexy!" she said.

"I hope so. We'll force this to an issue now." He became serious. "Eh—I hadn't realized until this day what a shadow that man has cast over this past winter. I feel like a clock with a new spring."

But as sobriety returned to her she wondered whether he had been quite wise to go so far to provoke and antagonize the reverend doctor. John always said that the stakes were highest where the rewards were greatest; but somehow that didn't seem to cover the case when you deliberately raised the odds against yourself. She had often feared that John's hatred of Prendergast would blind him to their best interests—and never more than now. Only his great enthusiasm—a clock with a new spring, as he said—sustained her through the rest of that long walk home.

Two hours later, after visiting St. Paul's and the Monument, they arrived exhausted at the Tabard. There, feeling it a very sinful thing to do, they went to bed and slept for two hours, until Sarah came with hot water to awaken them. Nora wondered then whether to give her the two Dickens novels she had just bought, but decided to leave them, as a sort of gratuity, until their departure.

The performance at Sadler's Wells was a serio-romantic lyric drama called *The Island,* its plot founded on the story of the mutiny on the *Bounty.* Its hard-working cast was headed by Mr. T. P. Cooke, doyen of theatrical sailors, Chambers said, and still remembered for his amazing debut, in this very theatre in 1832, in *Black-Eyed Susan.* Tonight's drama was amazing for its use of ropes over pulleys to lift unwanted scenes and properties off the stage and hold them poised above it out of view. There was a real ship, which floated on real water, and burned in real flames. And there were, somewhat incongruously, donkey races—with real donkeys running around the auditorium on a special raised track—to enliven the tedium of life on the tropic isle. The men (of the island and the audience) enjoyed the dusky maidens in grass skirts. Nora wept at the tragic death of Fletcher Christian. And they all had a splendid evening.

During the performance she slipped Chambers his two intercepted letters. And when it was over, on their way to supper in one of the sumptuous private rooms at the Albion off Drury Lane, Chambers produced an envelope, unsealed. "By the way, Stevenson," he said, "your letter." And no further reference was made to any of their affairs for the rest of the evening. It was past midnight before they arrived back at the Tabard. And despite their earlier sleep, and despite the howls from the madhouse over the way, they fell at once into the heaviest slumber.

They awoke at nine the following morning, feeling the day already half over. "We'll never be gentlefolk!" John said. "Early rising is in our bones by now." They breakfasted light and hastened over by coach through Lambeth to Westminster to keep their eleven o'clock appointment with Fielden.

The actual buildings were—as John had said—a disappointment. The last remnant of the old Commons and the old Lords were just visible at foundation and cellar level. And the Cotton Garden, which had promised the best view of the river, was partly taken over by the barnlike structure of the present Lords and Commons, the rest being filled with scaffolding, stone, dry aggregate, and all the usual builders' bric-a-brac. They could hardly speak to one another over the ringing of masons' chisels and the unending *rip-rip* of the saws.

"House of Lords is going to be here," Fielden shouted before he led them through the back door into Westminster Hall, the only large building to escape the fire.

Here, although the activity was more moderate, the noise was hardly abated; it needed only one plank to drop, one man to laugh, one steel chisel to ring—and the echoes resounded a long dying among the ancient rafters of the hammerbeam roof.

"That looks very old," John said.

Fielden laughed. "Twenty years at least," he answered. "It goes all the way back to George IV." Then, seeing their disappointment, he went on. "No, you're right, really. The building goes all the way back to . . . William Rufus, I think, or one of the Henrys. But the roof and the outside wall were restored about 1820. I remember they broke up twenty ships at Portsmouth to get enough timber, so I should think most of those beams were done then."

"What's it used for, or *was* it used for—when they haven't got all these builders in?" Nora asked.

"Take your choice, ma'am," Fielden replied. "Everything under the sun. In the very early days they used to have jousting in here when it was raining outside. Queen Elizabeth had a bedroom off there—this was a royal palace then—she used it as a breakfast room. It's always been a court, of course. A court of justice. They used to pillory people outside in Palace Yard, chop their ears off, brand them, or take off their heads or hands. Titus Oates was tried here. And Cromwell's head. They put that up on the gable with Ireton's and Bradshaw's. That"—he pointed to the southwest angle of the Hall—"was where the High Court of Chancery used to sit. There"—to the southeast angle—"was the King's Bench—Queen's Bench, I suppose we call it now. That"—to the north door on the west side—"was the Court of Common Pleas, and alongside it was the Court of Exchequer. Four High Courts, sitting simultaneously in this one room! And in between them were market stalls selling books, haberdashery, ribbons, bonnets! So a day like this"—he had to raise his voice over the builders' hubbub—"I suppose you could call this a *quiet* time for this old hall!" On his way out he added: "They used to have a crier going around inside. They called him 'The Lord of the Twice-Impossible' for his charge was to keep silence among lawyers and women!"

Fielden's offer of work was almost laughable: a short length of retaining wall and the outer shell of a new gas-making plant—work for a man and his dog. "It's little enough, I know," Fielden said. "But while you have the men in Todmorden, and as long as you're moving bricks up the canal . . ."

"He thought he'd get it right cheap on that account," John said to Nora later. "Well, he's due for a shock there. We're not going to start doing business that way or we'll go down in history as the best-loved bankrupts in Yorkshire."

Still, their lunch with Fielden had been, in its way, very rewarding. He had talked of most of the important families and new people between Bradford and Manchester, and had given John two valuable hints: one, to join the Freemasons as soon as he was well established as a contractor; the other was to avoid open or strong connection with either political party. "And I say this," he added, "as one who hopes greatly for your support of the Liberals one day. But ye'd not thank me now if your too-early support cost you friends and business. So my advice to you—stay neutral. Let them come to you."

"In the years to come," John said, "we may look back upon *that* advice as the best thing to come out of this very useful visit."

# *Chapter 44*

They arrived back from London to find a carefully worded letter from Sir Sidney Rowbottom asking John to be so good as to attend at the company's offices on the afternoon of Wednesday the twentieth. No subject was mentioned but there was no possible doubt that this was anything other than Prendergast's work. He must at last have carried out his threat.

John's heart sank as he read the letter for the second and then the third time. To Nora he was offhandedly optimistic, but she knew him well enough to sense the worry that simmered beneath this thin cover of confidence.

Prendergast had talked of going to Sir Sidney with his "discovery." John took that to mean he would say that this disturbing little inconsistency had come to light . . . wrong date . . . sure Stevenson was aboveboard . . . probably some very simple explanation . . . but ought not to leave matters unresolved.

That would have suited John very well. If it came out that way, it could all be explained; it would arise and be disposed of naturally—thanks to the letters he had brought back from Chambers.

But what now? After his stupid and needless provocation of Prendergast, might not anger compel the priest to go far beyond the limits where natural caution would normally have stayed him? Sick at his own blunder, he had to confess he could find no convincing reason that it would not.

The nightmares did not help either. For four succeeding nights he ran at top speed and zero velocity across a frictionless plane on the far side of which Dicky Redmayne and his mob were burning the box in which lay Chambers' all-important letters. Twice on the Tuesday night he had to get up and reassure himself that it had indeed been only a dream.

Wednesday morning came, and with it the news that he had been awarded both canal contracts. It did little to raise his spirits; indeed he now fell victim to a further kind of guilt, tinged this time with awakened self-interest. And he began to wonder whether his eagerness to take revenge upon Prendergast might not be harming his firm. For suppose the priest really was desperate for cash? Suppose he went bankrupt—or merely had to pull in his horns and live an altogether more modest life? Neither change would be of much service to the firm of Stevenson in the years of promise that were now opening up before them.

When he put these particular doubts to Nora, she admitted she too had been thinking along just those lines. Reluctantly she reversed all she had said and felt these last seven months and told him: "Pay him the rest of his thousand. Tell him exactly why you're doing it. Explain what he may hope for in the future if he joins our side." And then she smiled. "If anyone can make him a friend, even after this, it's you."

"Friend!" He was astonished.

"Ally then," she said impatiently. "You can do it."

Just before lunch they had a further surprise when Sir Sidney himself came posthaste up the turnpike from Manchester, halted at the foot of Rough Stones lane, and asked for John to be brought to him.

Sir Sidney was angry—partly with Stevenson for being such a bloody fool, partly with Prendergast for stirring up mud that had settled so firmly and for so long, but mostly with himself for having been manoeuvred into this ridiculous situation. Here he was, the chairman of a railway with massive outgoings and only a piddling income until this tunnel at Summit joined the two counties, about to confront and perhaps ruin the one man whose genius ensured its due completion. It was too bad of Prendergast. Should have sent him off with a flea in his ear. Stevenson could have forged the Queen's signature and the Great Seal for all it mattered now.

As he waited he watched the work then in progress at Deanroyd and south toward the scout. Strange how even at a glance you could tell a good works from a bad one—something in the way the men moved, purposefully, and the way materials were piled in good order. . . . Even the noises from a good works were in some indefinable way different. He shuddered to imagine how it might be in the hands of any one of a dozen other contractors. No—to dismiss Stevenson now, and for a crime that had no victim, was quite unthinkable. The Board—or at least its chairman—

would have to swallow all notions of honour and concoct some explanation to satisfy Prendergast and to save this contract for Stevenson.

Yet Sir Sidney was not even sure that Stevenson had done anything amiss; that was where he had to tread delicately. At the back of his mind ran the perpetual caution that there just might be a reasonable explanation for this seeming forgery. Even Prendergast, who by all accounts knew Stevenson quite well by now, had said he could not really believe the man capable of outright forgery. It was all such a bloody delicate mess.

After the usual pleasantries, he and John strolled back along the turnpike toward Stone House. Sir Sidney plainly did not want eavesdroppers for what he had to say. John, watching him closely from their first moment of meeting, soon understood that Prendergast must, in the end, have played his cards cautiously. He must have hoped that, when faced with it, Stevenson would find no answer and so would be forced to incriminate himself. He shuddered to think how close that potential moment of unmasking had come.

Sir Sidney now amplified Prendergast's reluctance tenfold. Indeed for a full quarter of an hour he spoke of nothing but his Board's delight with the way the Summit contract had gone ever since John had had the disposal of it. Finally John had to prompt him—by asking after Prendergast's health. That provoked a spate of assurances that the priest, too, held Stevenson in the very highest, the *very* highest regard.

But at last he came to the delicate nub of the matter: "It's your letter of credit, you see, dear fellow. A bit of bother about the date."

"Surely not."

"I fear so."

"I mean—well, surely Prendergast explained it to you? I remember I explained the whole thing . . . oh, months ago, backend of last year."

Sir Sidney was now both embarrassed and puzzled. A prelude to anger. "He said nothing of that to me."

"To be sure, he *was* very ill soon after. Very ill. I hear they despaired of his life at one time. Could that have induced him to forget?"

The other was glad to have this escape. "That must be it. Poor fellow. Not better yet, perhaps."

"But how embarrassing for you, Sir Sidney. And, I suppose, for me, too. We shall have to be very tactful with the old gentleman."

Sir Sidney looked at him in rapt admiration. "By Jove, Stevenson! You're a prince among men! Let me shake your hand. No, no—I insist. Not many men could see their honour impugned and show such charity. No man I know."

John laughed to mask his embarrassment. "What sort of man would think his honour impugned when a poor, sick clergyman, still convalescent, has a little slip of memory! On the contrary, my admiration of Doctor Prendergast is redoubled. He did a difficult thing in difficult circumstances. And I'll wager he did it with the utmost circumspection, eh? No outright accusation? Behaved with fairness itself toward me?"

"Yes," Sir Sidney confirmed. "Yes. Very fair. Very fair. Said he wouldn't believe a word against you. Felt you ought to have the chance to explain. Was sure you could."

"Ah! And that was why you asked me to call on you today!"

Sir Sidney nodded glumly. "Thank the powers I took it upon meself to call like this first. I didn't believe it for a minute, of course. Thank heavens I came."

John turned them back toward the waiting carriage. "Amen to that," he said. "If I may suggest . . . ? I have somewhere the letter from my banker where the entire confusion is explained. I also have—I hope—a copy of my reply. If you were to take them and show him . . . say I laughed it off . . . no malice . . . make light of it . . . perhaps it will not mortify him too greatly, then."

"I think you've hit it," Sir Sidney said, overwhelmed in his relief that today's distressing business had all come out so happily. "You're the very example of Christian charity, sir. We're greatly in your debt—Prendergast most of all."

"I hope he won't feel it too great a burden," John answered.

Later, when John handed over the letters, Sir Sidney climbed back into his carriage and said: "So—no need for you to come to Manchester today. . . ."

"I've been pondering that," John told him. "I think I will come, you know. Just to reassure the poor old chap."

Again that admiration in Sir Sidney's eyes. "A prince, sir. A veritable prince!"

And John, watching the carriage pull away, smiled and said: *"Il principe!"* But the arrogance of his words and the very ease of his triumph had already turned sour within.

The luck that had gilded this entire year had accompanied him even into this, the most arrant and stupid of blunders. There was something very self-diminishing about a triumph that was so richly undeserved. And no learned jocularity could restore that curtailment.

For Nora he tried to pass his meeting off as a success. She was not deceived. She smiled dutifully, but she busied herself with any distraction that offered and she could not quite meet his gaze.

It was a chastened and unusually self-examining John Stevenson who went to Manchester for that long-awaited triumph. He arrived later than he had intended at the company offices and met Prendergast just as he emerged into the street. He had never seen a man look so dejected.

The thought that he could even contemplate easing the anxieties and anger of this past half year by a few moments of crowing over this pathetic, dispirited, and essentially despicable creature was suddenly revolting to him.

He was at Prendergast's side before the priest even noticed him. He thrust out the packet he was bearing and, with a smile, a genuine smile, said: "Five hundred and twenty-five pounds. Late, I fear, but not I hope too late."

Prendergast all in the same dazed instant recognized him, accepted the packet, and took in his words. Then it seemed he had to do all three over again, transferring the packet from one nerveless hand to the other.

"But . . . you have no need . . ." he began, once the message had finally penetrated. He looked back at the window of Sir Sidney's office.

"It was you who had no need, Prendergast. You had a perfectly reasonable proposal. You still have. You had no need to compel my agreement by this blackmail."

"I hadn't?" Prendergast was still confused.

"It is an irrelevance. It always was. But would you ever have believed it if I had told you so?"

A faint and slightly rueful smile crossed the priest's face.

"But now I have proved it to you. Eh? Now you must believe it. Now we can enter a real partnership. At . . . shall we say—five percent? Something a touch more realistic?"

Prendergast became his recognizable self at last. And John, to his own astonishment, found that he was actually glad to see the re-emergence of the old reprobate whose threats had for so long brought nothing but fear and loathing.

"Come," John said. "Let us talk, you and me, about a contract that's soon to be let on the Bolton & Preston line. . . ."

# Chapter 45

May and June that year were showery and cool; July was wet. The hay cut was light and people shook their heads over the prospects for the harvest. The inclemency of the weather caused some people to postpone or suspend the less essential of their building operations—for which John Stevenson was heartily grateful. As it was, he learned a sharp lesson in the laws of supply and demand; and if he had not taken George Roberts' advice and got a contract price set for all the bricks needed at Redmayne's site and to complete the tunnel, he would have doubled its cost to him. The rate of bricklaying in the tunnel was itself enough to create a shortage of skilled bricklayers; but when the demands of the Redmayne site were added to it, shortage became famine and the daily rate went up to six shillings and sixpence, and for two weeks even to seven shillings, in order to attract enough labour to the sites. When all the accounts were done, Nora reckoned it had cost them at least an extra thousand pounds on both contracts to avoid the enactment of the penalty clauses.

But she worried about it more than John. It was a time of challenge for him to find the most effectual way of disposing of the work and minimizing the erosion of their expected profit. Meeting that challenge was its own reward. Redmayne's site had costed out at £86,000 and he had topped it up to £97,000 to allow for profit and contingencies. It was not a high-risk contract and he knew he could not expect the thirty and forty percent margins he would want for something more speculative. So there was little room left to navigate within.

His clerk of works there was an old master mason called Spicer. He'd "built more mills and more houses than John Stevenson had had hot dinners." There was no problem in building he hadn't already met and overcome. That was all to the good, and there wasn't a day on which John did not warm with thankfulness and admiration for the old man's skill. But there was one great disadvantage, too: Spicer *knew* how the whole site should be built; he knew *exactly* how. For him it might have been a religious service. Everything had its order and place and time. And John's idea of digging out *all* the foundations, of laying *all* the sewers and service mains and soil drainage, and of surfacing *all* the roads and pavements, and of building the chapel, which was mainly stone, and of making the new canal basin, which was also mainly stone, and of carrying every brick to its appointed pile among the dozens of piles that dotted the site . . . in short, of postponing to the last possible moment the time when the costly bricklayers would have to be brought on site in any number—such an idea was for many weeks quite beyond Spicer's grasp.

He watched foundations grow to two courses above ground and there halt, and he shook his head. He watched roads thread their way among the weeds, and he sighed. And when the piles of bricks stood in neat arrays of rank and file and the bricklayers at last had to be set on, he declared he'd never seen a work done so arsy-versy.

But a week later he was able to dismiss a third of the hod carriers, whose job it was to feed the bricklayers with fresh bricks. And only days after that he was admitting, still with some surprised bewilderment, that he'd never seen building go so quickly. Donkey carts of sand and aggregate pulled easily and swiftly over the made-up roads; on other sites they often fell into potholes, breaking wheels and spilling loads. No brick had to be carried more than a dozen yards; on a traditional site a man might spend all day wheeling barrowloads of them from piles several chainlengths away.

One day Spicer said to him: "Thou knows, Lord John, if it were wintertime and not frozen, and if we had yon gas plant working, we could light them streets and build to summer hours!" And when he heard that, John knew he had a valuable new man upon his staff—a man who, despite age and long experience, was now thinking more of cash outlay and effectual working than of blind tradition.

But in one respect John's ambitions were not realized. He was not able to keep together his bands of navvies and offer them work on his other sites. The "arsy-versy" work at Redmayne's had, in part at least, been an attempt to keep some of his lads together as long as possible, but it merely postponed their inevitable departure. And as the sheer volume of stonebreaking and muck-shifting at Summit dwindled, his navvy labour force shrank in the same measure, from eight hundred to only half that number. He looked around for other railroad or navigation work, but the only line then actively begun and not let out (apart from the Bolton & Preston bid, which Prendergast was working on) was the link from Manchester to Crewe by way of Alderley Edge. And, as he reluctantly had to confess, he was just not big enough yet to put in a bid for such a major section.

To him this was an especial sadness, for, of all the hopes that had encouraged him at his start, the desire to keep together a corps of navvies who would think of themselves as "his" lads first and navvies second, who would see him through his lean times if he saw them through theirs, and who would, in time, share the wealth that came by their work and his enterprise . . . that desire had lain closest to his heart. He took his leave of each man singly as the work ran out, and he gave to each a crown, and a penny into the hand of each child, to see them to the next working. And to every man he promised work when his contracting business was big enough to be taking on men instead of laying them off.

Often on his way back to Rough Stones after these leavetakings the tears would stream down his face. He knew each man, knew which parts of the tunnel he had worked, knew his value. To send them off, however you argued it logically, was like a betrayal. He had betrayed them by not being big enough to keep them on.

At first Nora tried to comfort him with softness and sympathy, but she soon found the best way was to point out that, if it meant so much to him, he could easily keep the men on, every single one of them, by forgoing a little of his profit on the works. "Oh no," he said when she first made the proposal. "If I do that we shall never be big enough to do it the proper way." Soon all she had to say was: "Well—if it really means so much to you . . ." and leave the rest unspoken. And he would sigh, and suppose she was right, and devour his supper with relish. At the beginning of August, Prendergast let them know that £20,000 was the probable winning bid on the new Bolton & Preston line. If they won that contract, it might stop the rot.

Nora had bought Millwood from Lady Henshaw soon after their return from London. It made little change in the pattern of her life, for she still went to Henshaw Park at least twice a week and helped her ladyship with her endless three-volume novel; and she still went riding with McGinty, who was teaching her to leap small fences and cut-down gates. "Ye've that many bruises," John grumbled, "we'll need an oriental doctor to show us how to enjoy our connubial rights."

Nora had tolerated the goats and ignored the mad dogs and endured the half-wit girls for so long now that Henshaw Park had come to seem quite normal. As she never knew what Lady Henshaw would be doing when she arrived, nothing she actually did was a surprise. One day she was painting wildflowers—an easy task since they grew right up to her walls. Another day she was waist-deep in what she called an "archaeological digging." Another day Madoc was shoulder-deep in the same pit, and she, on its edge, was calling it "me new cesspit." Another day it was all filled in again and, until it grew over, was referred to scathingly as "Madoc's Folly." Another day Nora found her in the yard with three naked, terrified, giggling, hysterical, feeble-minded girls, a yard brush, scouring soap, and a pail of water. Once you have accepted all these encounters as "normal," where can "surprising" begin?

John, too, had bought a horse—Hermes, a large, five-year-old dappled-grey gelding, which he rode to Redmayne's site as well as to Littleborough for his visits to the Manchester canal workings. To save the expense of keeping their own groom, they stabled Hermes and Millwood with the drayhorses from the workings, and paid the farrier another crown each week.

Usually John would start the day with the arrangements at Summit and then go over to Redmayne's about midmorning. Nora would ride with him as far as Gawks Holm, where she went up to Arabella at Pigs Hill. There she would spend an hour or two reading to Arabella from "improving and diverting books of a secular nature" as Arabella called them—the works of

Johnson and Addison, the novels of Scott and Jane Austen, and the poems of Byron and Wordsworth. Nora had, since her visit to London—since her visit to Sarah's room, to be precise—become an avid reader, an omnivorous devourer of the printed word. It had begun as something of an exercise in self-improvement; but it had quickly turned into a pleasure unalloyed, and every spare moment would find her with her face whitened in the light reflected off some page. And as she read, alone in her garden, alone in her room, her thoughts would sometimes stray back to that other lone reader in her garret at the Tabard, Sarah Nevill. But it was not the neat little room with its orderly shelf of books that returned to her mind's eye; it was the girl's distaste at the clandestine work in which Nora had made her partner. From time to time, before she caught herself out at the absurdity of it, Nora would imagine herself solemnly explaining to the girl the necessity of tampering with the letters. She wondered if their paths would ever cross again.

Each evening, when John returned, she would try to describe to him how insufferable Mr. Darcy was, or how exciting had been the jousting between the Disinherited Knight and Brian de Bois-Guilbert and the four Normans, or how "elegant and refined" (to use another Arabella phrase) Addison was, but it was an exercise in frustration, for John had neither time nor inclination to lose himself in fantastical stories. He, too, became an earnest reader—but of books on civil engineering, roadmaking, invention, and the history of manufacture. He devoured almost every book that Walter brought home from the library.

As summer wore on and as, between the showers, hot days gave way to hotter and Arabella's pregnancy grew daily more like a totally paralyzing illness, Walter showed a pathetic eagerness to vanish down the line to Manchester on no greater pretext than that Stevenson needed another book. And John, seeing him leave all solemn and trembling, was moved to pity the engineer his slavery to his obsessions. But there, for once, he was wrong.

# Chapter 46

In later years Walter was to look back on that winter and spring of 1840 as an idyll of young manhood. Even at the time, even before memory had blunted the sharper edges of the experience, he knew it for a season of unusual satisfactions. It had given him great pleasure to contemplate—on the train, when he returned from that expensive house of civil reception in Salford, just after Christmas—how well his life was settling down into its compartments. Everything that happened in the weeks that followed merely confirmed the essential rightness of his feeling.

For Arabella, too, it was a time of joy. Though she was quickened, and had been so at least since December, she remained long unaware of it. Tight lacing masked many symptoms. And, since no one had ever explained the connection, it never crossed her mind that the failure of her little friend to come on those more-or-less regular monthly visits had anything to do with generation. All she knew was that she felt exceptionally well, contented to the point of a steady, muted happiness. She, too, was to look back on those days as idyllic.

Walter was the most attentive of husbands. His greatest delights were in such simple things—walking with her when the evenings grew light and the days were mild, turning the page for her as she played their new pianoforte, joining her in duets (even though his ear did not always match his gusto), and reading to her from *Nicholas Nickleby* and *Jorrocks* and the verses of Wordsworth, whom Walter considered supreme among poets. It was precisely the sort of life she had envisaged for them during the long years of their engagement.

She even managed a tolerant, superior sort of contentment that was *almost* a happiness when Walter exercised his rights on her. He was so considerate and thoughtful nowadays. He never tried to get her to join his delight, as he had in those early, dreadful weeks. And she, thanks to that gentle consideration of his, had come to realize how different men were from women—especially in their degree of endowment with animal nature. One had to remember it was the same animal nature that led them to explore distant lands, to make great poetry and music, and to build fine cities—and fine tunnels. She would be almost flying in the face of God to deny it a due place in the home, which, after all, was the source of all civilization and its arts and achievements. Thus, as a mother may lovingly comfort or encourage a child possessed of a rage or an enthusiasm she herself is years past sharing—feeling *for* the child rather than with it—so Arabella learned to comfort and encourage Walter when that particular spirit had seized him, though she herself was far above sharing it.

And when Walter was away, at Summit or in Manchester, there was always their new home and its cares to absorb her. Little Horsfall, who, just after Christmas, had gone through a spell of surly and grudging obedience so bad that Arabella was on the point of dismissing her, suddenly turned into a model servant. Mrs. Bates said it was because the girl had taken to the Unitarians, who, under the patronage of the Fieldens, were strong in Todmorden. Sweeney said it was just growing up and that her good behaviour meant as little as her bad, except that it made her easier to live with. Arabella took it as a caution against the harsh and precipitate judgement of others; to have dismissed Horsfall without any positive attempt to rescue and reform her wayward spirit would have been very wrong.

Each week that passed brought problems of this kind. No doubt they were all very trivial compared with those that Walter faced every day at Summit, but they were, for all that, important. The harmony of this little female community and its master, their physical wellbeing, and their spiritual care—these were not minor responsibilities. And Arabella was not one to make them appear so. Often she would think of John Stevenson's ridiculous expectations for her—how he saw her as some kind of missionary, moving among his navvies and doling out example as if it were a kind of nourishing broth. Such a man could only think in those grandiose terms. She could never have made him see the importance of her little work at Pex Hill.

Sometimes when Nora called, they would talk and laugh about it together. And Nora's amusement at the very idea of Missionary Arabella, far from making her feel insulted, merely confirmed that hers was a still, small light whose radiance was just sufficient to illumine this one little household.

Nora would carry this amusement home to Rough Stones.

"I fancy yon Arabella has at last begun to take your opinions of her to heart," she said once to John.

He showed a wary interest.

"She's bought a new china dog and is now undergoing agonies of spirit as to whether it should stand near the paper silhouettes or the stuffed lark or have a new shelf all its own above the chiming clock that shows the moon. She'll be in agonies about it all this week, you'll see. It must take a great soul to accommodate such long-tormenting doubts!"

In time John learned not to answer these jibes and not to repeat his certainty that there was more fibre in Arabella than met anybody else's eye.

Arabella's pleasure with their life at Pex Hill was especially delightful to Walter. Often as he sang with her . . . listening to her soft, appealing soprano . . . watching the light reflecting off the music and delicately suffusing her face with pale radiance whenever he turned a page, he thought back with amusement to the early weeks of their marriage.

But his amusement masked a more complex emotion, something between anger and shame. How could he ever have imagined that this purely spiritual love could accommodate itself to the gratification of mere animal lust? A love that found expression in such pure joys as walking together, singing together, reading poetry together . . . how could such love bend itself to those base, cloacal urges! Even his fantasies about dead girls now made him cringe with shame. These days what he did with Arabella could scarcely be called carnal at all; it was so void of lust, of fantasy, of any dominance or assertion of power, that only the most literal mind would connect it in any way with fleshly gratification. Except, of course, at the very pinnacle of its climax; that could hardly be avoided, for it was then that body, mind, spirit, urge, need, and passion all united. But that was the only moment when such unity was proper—in the highest, purest kind of love.

He remembered the analogies he had once used in order to persuade her that pure and carnal love could unite in a marriage: that love was a tissue irrigated by three arteries—pinch one off and part must wither, spreading its gangrene to the whole. Now, when he saw things in so much clearer a light, it amazed him that an analogy—a metaphor, really—drawn so exclusively from organic nature could ever have seemed convincing. Especially to a modern engineer. It was so old-fashioned—like one of those witty, implausible arguments that seventeenth-century poets loved to elaborate.

Indeed, the more he thought about engineering and natural science, the more excitingly clear it became that they offered the only true metaphor of life, far truer than old-fashioned arguments drawn from natural history. Probably the first true vision of man and nature and life and society and behaviour and that sort of thing in the whole of history. A new order was emerging, positive, clear, and rational—built on the certainties of physical science and the achievements of engineering. Together these two structures were reshaping the minds of those who lived and laboured among them. A new understanding of mechanism was opening up—not in the vague way the philosophers one had read at school bandied such terms about, but in engineer's language, which dealt in measurement, prediction, and control.

It was now clear to him that the leading spirits of mankind had scaled upward to a new level of awareness—one in which metaphors of life taken from nature no longer satisfied the truly modern intellect, one in which natural science alone could mark the way forward. True, they still had far to go. The metaphors of science and the explanations they offered of life and society were at present like two out-of-focus images in a binocular surveying telescope. However, he firmly anticipated the day when they would not only resolve into perfect clarity but fit, one upon the other, in total accord. He hoped still to be alive in such momentous times.

He had come to these notions in the most casual way during the many hours he had spent in examining his own passions and their at times ungovernable force. It was always the word "force" that triggered these thoughts. Arabella's father (who had proved so right, though for all the wrong reasons) had spoken of "vital force" and "conserving the force of manhood" or some such phrase. Always *force.*

By the most enlightening coincidence, "force" was a word daily on the lips of any engineer who had the remotest connection with steam power. Twenty and thirty years earlier, such power had been delivered to the cylinder at pressures measured in mere tens of pounds to the square inch. Now, in the most advanced engines, the pressures were nudging the hundred-pound mark and the talk was all of greater and greater force.

To engineers it was now clear that no single cylinder could take steam at such pressures and extract all its energy at one stroke. Engines of the future would all have to be "compound"—that is, they would have a high-pressure cylinder to take the peak of the force out of the steam, which would then pass to a different, low-pressure cylinder where the rest of its force could be usefully extracted and put to work. Any other system would be wasteful, inefficient, and—worst of all to an engineer worth his salt—unharmonious.

The journals Walter read and the discussions he had with colleagues were bound at some point to touch on this coming generation of engines. It took little intellectual effort to realize that these ideas offered a most exact parallel to the proper regulation of the force which so possessed him at times. No single outlet could exhaust all its energy; it, too, needed its high and its low vessels. Even his most assiduous devotion to Arabella absorbed only the high element. He had proved as much when, in a bout of induced spiritual zeal, he forswore the low element and within days began to show all the symptoms Arabella's father had promised would accompany its indulgence: "simple irritability, backache, headache, nervousness, and lassitude." A quick trip to Manchester and fifteen minutes on the old fork every so often was enough to prevent a recurrence of that.

But the haphazard nature of these forays and their lack of any predictable or regular core left him at heart dissatisfied. They smacked of mere self-indulgence. He wished he were a man of leisure who had all the time in the world to examine and experiment with these fascinating new ideas. But he lived a catch-as-catch-can sort of life and must seize what opportunities it thrust upon him.

Then Arabella's pregnancy was confirmed; and her lapse into near paralysis gave him all the time he needed to endow his low force with the harmony and order that its high level had long possessed.

Although it was mere chance that took him down Cannon Street that particular day in early July, and although he could in no sense claim to have planned all that he and young Nelly and Sophie did with one another in the weeks that followed, yet there was a level within him at which he had long prepared for just such an encounter. That was why John Stevenson was wrong to see it as no more than a further expression of Walter's eternal obsessions. The men at Summit, who nudged one another and winked as they said "Fallen in love 'as Gaffer Thornton," were closer to the truth.

The two girls were dressed in such elegant silks that Walter, strolling and daydreaming behind them on Cannon Street, had taken them for two young ladies until he saw how coarse were the dark-haired girl's hands. Then he noticed that they were strolling slower and slower; he, naturally, kept pace behind them. The dark-haired girl stopped and twisted around, bringing her body in profile and her face three quarters to him. She fixed him with her large eyes and smiled beautifully. His pulse began to race at once. What a figure she had! A delicate little head with large features—large, dark eyes, large cheekbones, and a large mouth with full lips—and a delicate little body, also with large features.

He smiled.

Her friend had gone a few paces on and taken the first of three steps up into one of the houses before she, too, turned and smiled at Walter, rather shyly. The first impression she made was far less striking. She was petite and quiet, with auburn hair, and she had a way of dropping her eyes to the ground and smiling as if about to apologize for something.

He looked back at her more brazen friend. "Well," he said coming close to her. "It's a fine day for peeling a banana."

Her smile broadened into a grin. "Or to take a turn around Bushey Park."

The sweat began to start from him; anxiously he wiped his palms upon his hips. "What do they charge by way of entrance at that park?"

The girl looked at her friend to include her. "A dollar each," she said. "To help the poor scholars. A dollar for a scholar."

He was fairly twitching now to be at her. "Do they study hard?" he asked. "Your scholars?"

"Only to please," the girl assured him.

"I'd like to see their school," he said, already walking toward the house. The auburn one had opened the door and peeped inside while the other two were talking; now she turned back and gestured that the way was clear and that no potentially embarrassing encounters would follow.

There was an extra excitement for Walter as he followed them upstairs because, apart from one drunken adventure when he had been an apprentice—and had been too drunk to take advantage of it—he had never before taken horizontal refreshment with two girls together. He was glad their room was on the top floor, too. There was something romantic about being as high above the street as possible, beneath the sloping walls, with the windows open and spilling in the evening sunlight and the breeze, invisible to the world, safe from prying eyes and from passers-by upon the stair; you could forget all the other rooms in the house and their depressing reminder that the unique joys you here created were being repeated there and there and there and there, in endless cliché.

When they started the final part of their ascent, out of sight of the rest of the house, the auburn one ran ahead to open the door. But the dark-haired one, immediately in front of Walter, slowed to almost a halt and began delicately to lift her skirt and petticoats upward about her waist. Walter followed, mesmerized, caressing gently with his hands the smooth white flesh of calves and thighs and bottom as each was laid bare. At the top she halted and stretched back one limb at him, like a cat. "Oooh Charlie!" she murmured.

"Walter," he corrected. He always liked them to call him by his proper name. "And you?"

"Sophie," she said. "And she's Nelly."

Nelly held the door open to them; her other hand clutched a tin cash-box, which she unlocked as soon as the door was shut. Sophie was already running eager fingers over Walter while Nelly demurely asked for their money. "So soon?" he joked.

"While the gleam is in the eye," Nelly said simply.

She locked his half-sovereign in the box and put it back in the drawer. And when she turned and took off her bonnet and let her hair fall it was a signal for the most astonishingly voluptuous adventure in sensual exultation he had ever undergone.

After six more visits, which took a mere week to consume, he no longer separated the details of this or that session in his memory; they all dis-solved into one thrilling riot of their jubilant flesh. He did not ask where his energies derived or how he managed a double performance, day after day; he was besotted with their skills. Even on the train back home, exhausted beyond any new feat that day, the memory of their youth, their liveliness, the soft curves of their young bodies, their invention, their utter willingness . . . all would overwhelm him to the point of desperation, so that he would even for a moment seriously contemplate taking the same train back to town and returning to them.

He understood well enough what had happened to him: He had found the predictable and regular element which his lower life had never yet possessed. Being already head-over-halo in love with Arabella, he had now, so to speak, fallen arse-over-tit for Nelly and Sophie. They began to haunt his working day, so that anything—the forked wrinkles of skin by a person's eye, a cow's udder, the maid's arm at breakfast, pale knuckles . . . anything—would call them to mind and set him trembling.

For a time he wondered why he needed two of them; until he realized that the presence of both girls and, in mechanical terms, the choice they constantly offered him, helped reduce the taint of humanity, of individuality, and of all those distractions that belonged to the higher vessel. Thus, together, they offered no challenge to the neat ordering of his vital forces and their efficient, energizing progress from high to low. Either Nelly or Sophie on her own might, during the frenzy of his rut, become a person; as long as he always had both available, there was no danger of that.

When that frenzy was over, of course, there was no harm in exploring their humanity; he was by nature far too confirmed an opportunist to take any notion, least of all his own, to fanatical extremes. So, when the beast was off his back, they would often lie side by side in the balmy summer breeze, temporarily chaste, and talk of life and dreams. He learned that they were both country girls, from one of the villages up beyond Preston. They had been caught, when they were both sixteen, taking on a bit of beef without a licence, as they put it, and had been shamed out—indeed driven out when it was found they were both pregnant. They had been advised to go to a certain dressmaker in Preston who had aborted them and sent them on to a dressmaker in Manchester who was known for letting rooms to quiet gay ladies. She had set them up in this room, which they had, together with another on the floor below, and the use of two dresses for four pounds a week. And here they had been ever since.

The difference he had noted between Nelly and Sophie, almost at first sight, had not been contradicted. Nelly remained demure and somehow shy; even in her most lascivious and most abandoned excesses there still remained a core of gentleness and, though it seemed on the face of it an odd word to use, modesty. Her speech was never coarse. She would talk of "your thing" and "my place" and would ask him to "put it in." Sophie had no such inhibitions. Her language was as coarse as her hands.

One day they told him that Nelly would not be there the next day. A client had asked her to go down to Liverpool and stop the night there with him. Sophie pulled a glum face of sympathy at him. "So it's only me, if you can bear it?" He said he thought he could—but not up here; if they tried it up here he'd feel all the time that Nelly was missing. "Tell thee what," she murmured in a low, husky voice. "Why don't tha stay the night too. If tha come ere a bit later—come at half past nine—seein as thou art such a reg'lar, tha may stop with me all night for the reg'lar two dollars."

He wondered then whether he was ready for this test. He knew in the abstract that he could not forever be hiring *pairs* of girls; but had he yet learned enough to obscure their humanity until his force was spent, when they had no power to disturb him? If only Arabella were not pregnant, if only she were available at the complementary high level. . . . Still, what better test could there be than this single proffered night with Sophie? And so cheap, too.

But Sophie, by a thoughtless trick, was to render that night incapable of confirming his hopes or denying his fears. From the moment the maid showed him into the heavily curtained room and he saw her sitting cross-legged, jewelled, and naked in the soft light of two oil lamps, upon a mountain of mattresses and silken cushions, gazing up at him with her wide, dark eyes and smiling with those big, generous lips, her long hair let down and spilled around her, he knew that she was up to some private mischief.

The air was heavy with a musky perfume. She did not stir until he had almost reached the edge of the mattress. "Hello," he said. Her smile broadened but still she said nothing. Then she leaned forward and unlaced his shoes, holding them while he stepped from them. She worked her way up his body, removing one piece of clothing after another, breathing on him, kissing him, biting, gently scratching, caressing. By the time they had finished they were both kneeling, knees touching, lips touching—*just* touching—eyes staring into eyes, trembling and aflame. She lifted her arms over his shoulders and pulled his head more firmly against hers; and when his lips closed around and over hers, she pushed her tongue deep into his mouth.

He was too astonished to respond at once. This was not a whore's performance; it was a lover's. Was that really what she was trying to say? He was glad to note no response within himself—just a brusque impatience to have her. He knelt upright, lifting her and pulling her to him, trying to fork her thighs with his knee. But she pulled away at that and spoke her first word to him that evening. "Wait," she said.

And reaching behind one of the cushions she pulled out a squat dark bottle. She uncorked it and poured a small pool of oil from it into her palm and immediately began to massage it into his member, working it with especial care into the corona and around the frenulum. The action was strangely thrilling, yet as she continued, watching him carefully all the while, it became remote and somehow hypnotic.

"What is it?" he asked. It was colourless and carried a faint, woody perfume, not in the least aphrodisiac.

"All-night oil," she said as she restoppered the bottle and put it back. "You know your usual trouble: ten minutes. That's about your limit."

She held another bottle open beneath his nostrils. He sniffed deeply. "Mmmmmm!" That was one to stir the blood. "What's all-night oil?" he asked.

"Lie back," she said. "You'll see."

He obeyed and watched her pour this new scented oil onto her hand and massage him as before, now with one hand, now with the other, gently, cleverly, never too fast. Then she leaned over and lay full length, slightly overlapping him, still manipulating him tenderly, and put her mouth to his ear. Slowly, with the low-pitched, husky voice that invariably thrilled him, she breathed the one syllable "fuck" into his mind. She said it again, more urgently, and again, and again, and again, time beyond number. It seemed to transfigure her to say the word and repeat it until it became a moaning, ecstatic possession.

On any other night it would already have been over with him by now; but the oil she had used seemed to confer the power to linger on the threshold of delirium without crossing it—in fact, without being *able* to cross it. "Faster," he said. She obeyed, still murmuring that one word into his ear. "More!" he cried. And more she gave. But as one may run in a dream, accelerating to a frenzy . . . to a panic . . . and find oneself moving not a hairsbreadth forward, so he rose and soared, higher and still higher, toward some pinnacle of tumescence—seeing it recede before him as steadily as he appeared to gain upon it.

And when her arms ached from the exertion and she forked herself over him and thrust down hard upon him, he hated her for the spasms of rapture that drove the breath from her and squeezed the sweat from her pores.

He hated her for the undreamed-of powers she had conferred. And for the potency she had robbed him of. On they went. And on. And still on. However they lay—or sat or stood or crouched or knelt—whatever he did to her or she to him, whether strong and swift or languorous and slow, nothing could bring him to spend. The pain was exquisite, for it was a pain of absence. That thrilling sensitivity conferred by erection upon numb flesh was dulled—only half there. Yet that half was enough to sustain his hopes and, ultimately, to stir his desperation.

It was not impotence, for even after ninety minutes he was as hard and as lustful as when he had begun. He knew what impotence felt like; drink and fever had taught him that. There could be no doubt that this was something altogether different.

Nor could there be any doubt why Sophie had done it to him. From that very beginning, knowing what was to follow, she had fluttered and trembled with excitement. And from that moment when she thrust herself upon him, she kept herself on a tableland of ecstasy, passively, by submitting to all his wild attempts on her, and actively, knowing that however bold she grew she could not lose him.

After two hours, when he thought she could have no breath left to moan with and when every muscle in her lithe little body must surely ache as deep as his, she gave one last tiny sign of exhausted contentment—and fell *asleep!* "Well, here's a fine thing!" he said aloud. He shook her gently. She murmured, turned heavily on her back, and sighed a yawn. Briefly her eyes flickered open and, half-drowned in slumber, she looked out at him and smiled. Nothing then would waken her. How could he still yearn for her after *two hours?* Why was the sight of her lying there, totally passive and beyond caring, still so stimulating—and how could he still be so stiff and eager?

He oiled himself again and eased his way gently, almost reverently, into her. For a thrust or two it was all he anticipated. *Without her there— consciously there—*using *me, I shall manage it,* he thought. *Now it's me using her, the way it should be.*

But his body had its own memories and standards, independent of his conscious will. His body found that having Sophie in these circumstances was uncomfortably reminiscent of having Arabella; and his body was unable to go on. For the first time that night he knew true impotence. He laughed morosely to himself as he extinguished the lamps, pulled some bedclothing over them, and settled beside her warm, relaxed body to sleep. *If there are brothels where women go to get satisfied by men,* he thought, *they'd be very like this.*

It was six the next morning, two drowsy, desperate sessions later, before he finally emptied himself into her. It felt as if he had saved himself for weeks and was trying to launch her on an ocean. For as the oil had spun him out and dulled each moment, so some residue of it seemed to have invaded his ejaculatory tracts, dulling their rapture even as it prolonged their mere activity. It was the most painful, least thrilling climax he had ever procured.

At the age of fourteen a horse had kicked him in the balls. He had forgotten the intensity and persistence of that pain until the moment came for him to hobble away from Sophie and that house, the physiological antithesis of the panting, trembling bundle of lust that had tripped toward it not ten hours earlier.

*I've got to give it up,* he decided on the train out to Summit. *It's ruining my health and my pocket. If I go on at this rate, I'll have paid something like £150 a year for the privilege of dying of nervous debility. I've got to stop.* He groaned and shifted tenderly. Never again. In one night that selfish, thoughtless, crude little Sophie had destroyed the neat divisions of his life.

It was two days before an overtly sexual thought entered his head; two days in which he was as free of his burden as a child. The religious people were right: When the lower being was subdued, the higher being was freed of something that weighed it down and mired it. Even after the pain had departed from his lower being it remained quiescent; that terrible, orgiastic night with Sophie had set him free. He breathed again, a liberated man, a man renewed, shining, untarnished.

Stevenson spoiled it by asking him to get a book or paper on Telford's modified macadam system for laying hardcore. Walter was actually at Oldham Road, waiting for the train home, when his conscience told him that at the least he owed Nelly and Sophie an explanation; they had become good friends these last weeks, over and above their business relations. He ought to take his leave properly.

Twenty minutes later when they knelt giggling and squirming in front of him, side by side, he had the honesty to let his spirit sing in exultation, then and all the hour that followed.

Lower being, higher being—it was all Walter-being; what point was there in denying any of it? To do so was as stupid as cultivating one part of it to excess. That was the true lesson of his night with Sophie. When he took the last train home that evening he felt himself a replete, satisfied, well-rounded man in full and vigorous prime.

And so it went the following week, and the first week into August. Always now he favoured Sophie. Nelly was sweeter and much more skilled; each time she could do something new to astonish his delight. But it was a very professional skill. Between their bodies, his and hers, was a mere bargain. With Sophie now—coarse, earthy, direct youngster that she was—with Sophie's body his had made a pact. Ever since that night there had been on her part a more than commercial agreement to honour, a more than economic hunger to meet; and on his part there was something deeper—not higher, but deeper—than mere lust to assuage. Nelly *reacted,* swiftly, intelligently; Sophie *responded,* profoundly, urgently.

It did not matter that she lolled her head in an idiot way, or laughed coarsely, or panted a steady stream of obscenity into his ear when he lay clasped with her (so vile that even Nelly was shocked)—all these things in a curious way reaffirmed the purity of their love. For animal and earthy though it was, their love gleamed as pure and unsullied on *its* dark, hot plain as did his and Arabella's up there amid the great, cold, celestial peaks. There were no cries of conscience within him when, at night, he lay beside Arabella, one moment entranced at her cool radiance and at the thought of the child now so heavy within her, and the next moment trembling with lust at the prospect of Sophie's body waiting for him, warm, inviting, and available down there in Manchester.

So, by one curious irony, it was his love for Sophie that brought his visits to an abrupt and painful end. And, by another, it was Nora who with her telescope had a better view of what happened than Walter himself.

*     *     *

For weeks Nora had noticed the pretty young girl who was put out in the sun every day at Stone House. It needed very little observation to see that she was feeble-minded, but Nora wondered why her mother took such pains to rope her firmly—and constantly checked to see that the ropes stayed tight.

One day she asked Bess about it; and—with much blushing and stammering and hiding in aprons—she was told the story. So now, each time she looked through her telescope, she always trained it briefly on poor young Emily Ann and spared her a moment of pity. But on this day Emily Ann was not there. The ropes were there. The chair was there. But no Emily Ann.

She swung the telescope slowly along the valley bottom, following the canal towpath, which would be the girl's obvious route. Not a hundred yards from Stone House she saw her, hobbling beside the rushes between the canal and the stream. Surely those unused, enfeebled legs could hardly carry her. The power of lust alone drove her forward. Manward.

There was a man, too. On the other side of the canal. The man who had chased the pig into the Irish randy . . . what was his name? Eph . . . something. He stood panting on the far bank of the canal, his eyes almost extruded by the pressure of his lust. Nora could understand his dilemma: If he went the quickest way, over the Stone House bridge, he would possibly alert the mother; but if he went all the way down to Deanroyd and back, some other man would get her first. Men! she thought. Or some men, anyway. Thornton, for example.

Talk of the devil! There he was, in his usual place in the rushes, relieving himself. It must have seemed like every adolescent dream made real when Thornton glanced up and saw Emily Ann standing at the fringe of the rushes, looking at him the way snakes look at frogs. Nora could not see whether Thornton had rebuttoned his front flap but from the manic glee on Emily Ann's face, and the direction in which the girl was staring, she guessed not.

Thornton was a master of these things; there was no gainsaying that.

Any other man—any *thousand* other men, finding themselves unbuttoned before a young girl and seeing her gaze upon them, would do something to cover up. But Thornton, with that special acuity of his senses in these matters, stood on display without a twitch of modesty. Emily Ann ripped open her bodice and, cupping her breasts in her hands, advanced on Thornton.

Kissing them perfunctorily, he helped her to the ground. Oh, he was a man to pay a bill at sight! And the poor little idiot girl just lay there, twitching, with that seraphic smile on her face, while he went at her all he was worth.

A pair of tattered boots dropped into the upper perimeter of the telescope field. She raised her line of sight. Eph. Face as black as onions.

She followed him into the clearing among the rushes until he stood at Thornton's side, waiting his turn. It was probably a tradition of the Vale on these occasions that the man next in line got as ready as possible so as not to waste one golden second of Emily Ann at large. So that when Thornton finally became aware of the boots at his elbow and spun around to gaze skyward, it must have been an unusual silhouette he saw wafting above him. He stood at once and for a brief, incongruous moment they faced each other, bowsprit to bowsprit. Fancy loving *that!* Either of it.

Then Thornton pushed Eph backward into the rushes, making two o'clock to Emily Ann's noon. She, not discriminating, threw herself upon Eph and swallowed him within her before Thornton could have even cleared his throat. He shrugged, buttoned himself up, and left. Before he crossed the brook three navvies ran eagerly to the place where he had just been. Word was spreading.

Nora sent Bess to go and tell the mother where her daughter lay. Fifteen navvies later, though no one counted, Emily Ann was carried, weeping at her privation, back to Stone House. Shortly after, strong men winced and stopped their ears down in the cutting when the crack of the whiplash and the frail little creature's screams rang up the valley whose freedom she had sought and lost.

It was the last time Emily Ann escaped—which was just as well, for not quite three months later her enfeebled body succumbed to the effects of secondary syphilis. Walter did not know it was he who had infected her, for when his chancre appeared the following day, erupting at the left anterior margin of the corpus cavernosum, he naturally assumed it was she who had bitten him.

The pain was intense, the irritation unendurable, the stench of its suppuration nauseous. He could not possibly go back to Nelly and Sophie like that—except just to show them and explain. They looked at it, sympathized, and said goodbye. Sophie briefly regretted his departure from her life and then, like Nelly, forgot him entirely.

He was subsumed into that endless flow of eager, trembling men who passed into and out of their rooms and their lives. Nelly did not even know it was she who had bitten Walter; her dose had been so long ago.

The doctor was sympathetic but heartily implacable. "Got lost in Much Hadham, landed in Clapham, eh?" he chuckled. For the weeper he prescribed corrosive sublimate of mercury to attack the virus at its root—if Walter would pardon the word, ha ha. And a blue pill, consisting of mercury, liquorice root, and confection of roses, twice a day. "Going to be an unpleasant month or two," the doctor said. "The mercury makes your gums go soft and tender and you'll have the perpetual taste of metal in your mouth. If it gets intolerable, change to calomel or some milder form of mercury. Children tolerate it much better than adults, for some reason."

"Childen?" Walter asked.

"Yes indeed. They get it too. Congenital, you see." He poked a monitory finger at Walter. "No connubial joys for you until I say you're clear! Understood?"

Walter nodded. He breathed a silent prayer of thankfulness that Arabella's pregnancy had kept her beyond his foul touch. Suddenly his notions of high and low vessels seemed both threadbare and disgusting. He wondered what could possibly have led him to entertain them. What can any metaphor teach—whether drawn from science or from natural history? If you had to seek for metaphors, you were disguising something. Truth was truth. You could point to it.

Look at Stevenson and Nora. There was a truth you could point to. You could see they were everything to each other. Away from her, he was the butcher's dog—he could sit by the beef all day and not even give it a sniff. That was how a marriage should be.

Not for the first time that year, nor by any means for the last, he thought of Nora and of all her qualities, which only his lust had masked that day they met. All those things that Stevenson had discovered at once. What a wife she would have made! If . . .

"Nora!" he would murmur when he knew he was alone. The pain it brought was numbing and comfortable.

But a week or so of corrosive sublimate racked him with pains of a far less metaphysical order.

# Chapter 47

It was John who suggested the picnic. On the Wednesday of the second week in August he came home and said: "D'ye know what it is a fortnight today?"

She thought. "Twenty-sixth,"she said. "Eay! A year since we first met! One year! Our anniversary . . ."

"We should go on a picnic," he said. "I got the notion this evening. It looks as if we're in for a spell of settled weather. And I thought: a picnic."

Her eyes gleamed at the prospect.

"And we'll ask the Thorntons," he added.

Her face fell. "Nay," she said. "Just thee and me."

But he was determined. It would be kindly, after their kindness at Christmas.

"What about her baby? She'll never agree to come out," Nora said.

"When's it due?"

"September."

"You'll find a way of talking her into it," he said confidently.

She said nothing to Arabella for a week, half hoping that John might think better of his plan. Later she realized that she ought to have asked Arabella at once, for she would certainly have turned the idea down. But a week of intolerably hot weather made the notion seem not quite so unthinkable. After two further days of the heat she was certain it would be just the sort of tonic she needed. "Where shall we go?" she asked.

"Mr. Stevenson won't tell me. He says it's a surprise."

"Somewhere up this way?"

"No. I think it's somewhere south of us, but all he says is that we'll see what we shall see."

The moment these arrangements were confirmed, John began to regret his suggestion. At its heart was the sort of shallow-minded trick that even the most loving spouse can serve his, or her, partner; indeed it was the sort of jape for which only a lover may expect forgiveness. Long ago—in fact, on the day Robert Stephenson had set up his new engine at Reddish, and Walter Thornton had inadvertently let slip the actual site of his and Nora's meeting—he had thought it might be amusing, when the anniversary of that day came around, to induce the pair of them to return to that same place and . . . what? See what happened? He had dismissed the thought at once as unworthy and juvenile.

Yet often over the months that followed, the notion had again crossed his mind; and each time it seemed a little less reprehensible and a little more amusing, until, in the end, familiarity had entirely dulled its sting. But now, when he faced the reality of his scheme, its potential dangers and the hurt it might do to Nora began again to strike him. Only his own obstinate fatalism, a species of arrogance, stopped him cancelling the arrangements at once. And then, as the days drew on, his disquiet was once more lulled and his confidence grew that he could prevent anything from getting seriously out of hand. The one admission he would not make was that he was in any way jealous of Thornton for the favour that Nora had been starved into selling him.

When the softest-sprung car in the livery stables turned up at Pigs Hill at nine o'clock on the morning of Wednesday the twenty-sixth of August, Arabella and Walter climbed aboard—the one gingerly, the other tenderly—with no notion of where they were going once they had called by Rough Stones.

"It's curious," Walter said when they drew away from Pigs Hill, going down toward Gawks Holm, "you never knew John Stevenson before he became a contractor. He was already, so to speak, up there when you met. But I remember him as a navvy ganger. It still seems . . . beyond belief at times."

He opened the parasol and held it over them to keep off the sun.

Arabella, secure in the fastness of her pregnancy, had become much less censorious of the world these last few months. She could afford to say: "I knew, the moment we met up there on Reddish Scout, that he was an extraordinary man."

Walter looked so sharply at her she was forced to add: "Well, he *is*. Last year at this time—a ganger. Now he's sought out by influential men, bankers, Members of Parliament, the squire . . . they all want to know him. You have to admit—he is extraordinary."

He nodded. "And his wife."

Arabella pouted: "I think he makes just a little too much of her part. He would still be something without her, but she could hardly have made anything of herself without him."

"You do surprise me!" he said, not wishing to argue. "I thought you liked her."

"Oh, I do!" Arabella said fervently. "She's the dearest person. But not . . . special—not . . . extraordinary. Not like him."

They were passing the place where she had exploded in fury at Stevenson the day they had met the Irish. She smiled. How arrogant she had been then! To think she believed she knew better than John Stevenson about managing men and all the difficulties of an undertaking like Summit.

When they pulled to a halt at the foot of the lane leading to Rough Stones, Bess and Tabitha, already waiting, puffed and blew as they hoisted the baskets and blankets and cushions and sunshades aboard. John and Nora, on Hermes and Millwood, came circumspectly down the steep lane. Nora was veiled against the sun.

"Late!" Walter joked.

"Aye," John confessed ruefully. "Any hour before six of a morning we can be on time; any hour after and we'll be late. That seems to be the rule."

When Bess and Tabitha, as excited as anyone else, were seated, John took up a station beside Arabella, with Nora on the other side, next to Walter.

"On the way here we were remembering Calley's Irishmen taking this road," Arabella said. "I was thinking how remote that day seems and how . . . *unimportant* . . . were the emotions that moved us then." She smiled at John as she spoke; and he, hearing her stress the word "unimportant," knew that she was finally and explicitly burying that bit of their past. He smiled back, acknowledging it, and then looked around at the road they had just traversed.

"Aye," he said. "It's hard to remember that time—riot, strike meetings, pickets. Hard to picture it, this glorious weather."

Walter, noticing the smile that passed between them, wondered for the first time whether anything had happened between Arabella and Stevenson that day. He even began to count back nine months from September before he stopped himself in shame.

Nora, too, noticed the smile and wondered what lay behind it, though in a far more idle vein than Walter.

And all the way, because it was an anniversary and a time for remembering, they played the game of "Look—there's where we. . . ." At the toll bar, they paused to pay their due.

The other side of the bar stood a ragged pauper family, like death's heads on mopsticks. The father, in his early twenties, held a bony little girl of four on one hip. A lot of her hair had fallen out. Behind him stood a boy of about five; his emaciation showing clearly through his tattered clothing. The mother, still hobbling up toward the group, laboured for breath. In her arms she held an unweened baby, who would sleep a few seconds, then awaken to emit a feeble, voiceless cry, and then fall back asleep for a few seconds more. The mother glistened with sweat. All were barefoot except the man, whose left foot was strapped into a curious roll of leather that gave it the overall shape of a pony's hoof.

John spurred ahead as soon as the bar was drawn and reined in before the pathetic little group.

"Seeking work?" he asked the man.

"Aye, sir." He was almost desperate in his eagerness. "They just turned us off at Rochdale workhouse."

"Which one?" John didn't want the man to think he wouldn't check.

"Spotland, sir."

"Ah." John waited.

The man swallowed, looked rapidly at each of them, licked his parched lips, and said: "If ye've work going, sir, I'll do it, sir. I'm yer man. I'll do anything. Children have not eaten two days since, and yon bairn's very badly. Please, sir!"

John nodded at his foot. "What's wrong with yer foot?"

"Nothing, sir!" The man tried to laugh but was seized by a fit of coughing.

John turned Hermes to the turnpike again and touched him gently with the spur. "On we go," he said.

In desperation the young man hobbled after him. "Sir!" he called.

John reined in again and half turned. "Well?"

"It *is* nothing, sir. A horse trod on it when I were a lad. I'll never run the Derby if that's what ye had in mind for us. But if it's heavy work, I'm yer man, sir."

John looked him up and down impatiently. "Thou'll need building up," he said. "Thou are naught but bone and gristle."

The man nodded his agreement. "But I've heart enough for it, sir. I've got the spirit." He waited anxiously. "Was it navvying, sir?"

"Aye."

"I've navigated afore, sir."

No one believed him. It was a desperate lie.

"Where?" John asked.

"Er . . . " He looked nervously around, not knowing what further lie to risk.

"Manchester?" John prompted.

"Aye! Manchester."

John dismounted quickly and walked to stand immediately in front of the man. "Listen," he said. "I'll take a chance on thee, lad. Thou seems likely. Follow this turnpike just round yon bend. Thou'll see three wooden shanties. Offices, they are. In the middle office there's a Mr. Fernley. Fernley—right?"

"Aye." The man was all eagerness now.

"Tell Mr. Fernley thou's met with John Stevenson. He's to put thee on at beginner's rate. That's seven shilling and sixpence a week."

The other was delighted. "Dollar and a half!" he cried out.

"Aye. But three of that'll go to feed just thee—so it's no king's ransom. Even though it's twice what thou art worth." He stressed the fact carefully. "Say to Mr. Fernley that he's to let thee have a pair of boots . . ." He looked at the man's foot. "Well—one boot, anyway. And a steel navvy shovel. Thou'll buy them from a stoppage out of thy wage at a tanner a week. Ten weeks. Five bob. Right?"

"Aye, sir. I . . . I'm that much obliged. . . ."

"Nay, lad," John interrupted. "Not 'obliged,' see thee. The word is *obligated*. Obligated. Thou art obligated to me. It'll be six month afore thou art truly worth thy wage. Six month while thou build thyself up at *my* expense. Come New Year 1841 thou'll be navvy enough to leave me and walk on any site in the land. That's when I'll look to thee to repay this obligation. I'll carry thee six month and I'll look to thee to give us six month of thyself when thou art fit for it."

"Aye, sir! I will. I will. Never fear!" The honesty that had made his earlier lie so transparent now underlined his sincerity.

"That's no legal agreement, mind. It's twixt thee and me. Man to man. Thy name?"

"Noah Rutt, sir."

John held out his hand. Noah took it. "Noah Rutt to John Stevenson. Man to man." He stood, arms akimbo, and turned to the wife. "Is he a drinking man, missis?"

But the woman could only wheeze and croak.

"She's got no voice," Noah explained. "We had nothing to drink yesterday but water from the canal. She and the bairn have both taken a fever from it. But I'll tell thee I'm no great drinking man, sir."

John looked hard at him and then at his watch. "If thou work until dusk," he said at length, "thou may have two bob by way of sub. That's for meat and shelter. No spirits."

"Aye, sir!" Noah was beside himself with relief. "I'm that much obliged, I can't—"

"Thou may spare us that," John said brusquely. "I've told thee how thou may discharge this obligation. *That's* the thanking I want." Suddenly he reached out and grasped Noah's two shoulders. "Stand tall now," he said. "Put steel in thy back! Thou art one of Stevenson's lads from now. Be proud!" He turned and strode back to Hermes; Noah and his ragged little family stood and stared after him. When he was mounted again he looked at them in surprise. "Well?" he said. "Let's get on then!"

He watched them hobble and shuffle away in the dust before he said quietly, "There goes one month's charity. But I fancy we'll not lose by it."

They all took up their former positions and resumed their leisurely way south.

"That young fellow has never navvied in his life," Walter said. He was puzzled that John had seemed to believe the lie.

John laughed. "Aye—he's in for a shock, what!"

Arabella shuddered. "I remember those two you showed me last summer. Poor things!"

"But he *lied* to you," Walter said.

John, still grinning, nodded. "And he believes I was deceived by it."

"Yet when he lied about his broken foot you were ready to leave him. I don't understand."

Now it was John who looked puzzled. "If I'd pretended to believe *that,* he'd've taken me for a fool. But by pretending to believe he's navvied before, I've given him double reason to drive himself hard. The two cases are worlds apart."

"That is a very flexible morality," Arabella said.

"If I catch him working only half strength, all I need say is 'Are you sure you've navvied before?' and he'll double his efforts."

"Nevertheless," Walter said, "it is more or less condoning a lie." He pressed his gums gingerly and sucked air over them, between his teeth.

"Not toothache, I hope, Mr. Thornton," Nora said.

"No. Not toothache, thank you, Mrs. Stevenson. Gums are a bit tender."

John took another glance over his shoulder at the Rutts. Nora, watching him, said: "Lady Henshaw would say they brought it all on themselves."

"It's a funny time to be taking on rubbish like that. When you're laying off forty or fifty a week," Walter said.

John nodded his head ruefully. "Aye," he agreed. "There'll be a bit of trouble explaining that. But what else could I do? Just leave them? I couldn't do it."

"Nora?" Arabella said. "Why did you say that about Lady Henshaw?"

"Oh . . . she sees everything like that. If a man's lucky, it's because he's also virtuous. If he falls on hard times, it's because of some moral error in his past.

"But that's *true!*" Arabella cried. "We may be certain that if we went into the history of that wretched family back there, we'd find acts of intemperance, prodigality, and vice quite sufficient to explain their present condition."

Nora looked briefly at her with a kindly pity in her eyes; how would one begin to explain? "We could also find many happy and prosperous families with exactly that same history," she said.

"Then their happiness and prosperity is only momentary," Arabella assured her. "In the end their vices and follies will be paid for."

"That's certainly true," Walter agreed—so glumly that everyone turned to him. He looked around, startled. "You only have to see the reverse," he said, quickly recovering. "Those who study temperance, and thrift, and industry—they prosper. And we need look no further than a yard or so to see the living proof of it!"

"Thornton's right," John said then.

"The Reverend Malthus has shown quite conclusively," Walter continued, warming now to the theme, "how misguided charity can do nothing but encourage, indeed even *create,* poverty. I don't mean your sort of charity, Stevenson, the sort of thing you did back there at the toll bar. I think of that as something like priming a pump. You have to expend a little water to fill the cylinder before you can extract a lot."

"I call it investment," John said. "Plain and simple."

"Quite," Walter agreed. "Just so. No—I was referring to mere almsgiving. For instance, if there had been no man there, no breadwinner—just the woman and the children—it would have been wrong . . . well— perhaps not *wrong,* but . . . socially pernicious . . . yes! socially pernicious, to do anything to help them."

Arabella smoothed her creamy summer dress around her. "All our leading spiritual thinkers and most philosophical minds are agreed on that. One must steel one's heart, as my father so often says."

Nora, tiring of this turn in the conversation, tried a little gentle fun. Solemnly she said: "We must 'walk by on the other side,' as the Bible tells us to."

"Oh, no!" Arabella cried out without thinking. "That was . . ." And then she thought. "That was a different point altogether," she said quietly. Nora enjoyed her confusion, and she, looking up and catching Nora's smile, called out, "Oh Nora! You tease!" Nevertheless, the thoughtful look did not entirely vanish.

They drove and rode in silence then, enjoying the slow crunch of the wheels, the sight of the warm sunshine, the bird song.

"Oh, look!" Arabella cried. "That grove up there. I used to ride that way last autumn. It's so pretty. Do let's picnic there."

She was pointing to the abandoned graveyard between Top of the Wood and Gorsey Hill, overlooking Littleborough and the railway line almost from Rochdale up to Summit. It was where Nora's father lay buried. Nora looked in heedless alarm at Walter—and he at her before their mutual embarrassment forced them both to drop their eyes. Nora was glad of her veil. Neither looked at Arabella. Neither looked at John.

But he was watching both of them. And when he saw their confusion he smiled and turned to Arabella. "A capital idea!" he said. "Unless Mrs. Stevenson has a better . . . ?"

"No, no, dear," Nora said hastily.

"Let's go there then," John said. "The road is fairly level and firm." He did not add that he had put a party of men on it in the last two days, filling its potholes and shaving its bumps, to the delighted surprise of the two farmers served by the lane.

It led along the hillside, climbing slightly, until, just below the "grove," it turned sharp right and wound uphill, skirting the eastern edge of the graveyard. The footpath that Nora, and then Walter, had taken a year ago circled the southern wall of the enclosure. At the point where path and lane met, Walter and Tabitha helped Arabella down. "Not far to walk," Walter encouraged her while she, leaning heavily on him, hobbled slowly at his side. "Does it . . . are you all right?" he asked anxiously. "He's very heavy," she said stoically. "And he's certainly letting me know he's there, today."

Meanwhile, John and Nora had entered the field by the gate, lower down. The car was backed down the lane and led in by the same route after Arabella had descended.

By chance, Nora, now leading Millwood, joined Walter and Arabella at the very point where she had been resting last year when Walter came by. She looked stonily ahead. He glanced nervously at her and redoubled his attentions to Arabella.

"Here's a place," John called, having gone a little way in front. "We should be nicely out of the sun here for most of the day."

He stood by a gap in the dilapidated old wall. The trees cast a deep shadow over the ground immediately inside the graveyard; the break in the wall gave them a commanding view of the whole countryside. "You see!" Arabella cried in her delight. "It must have been a sixth sense urged me to choose this grove!"

"What about the farmer?" Walter asked, looking at the grass, now quickly reviving from the hay cut. With luck it might make a second cut this year.

"He's a friend. No problem," John said, remembering the farmer's surprise at the extravagance of making good the whole lane just so that a pair of ladies could have a smooth car ride. A friend indeed.

Bess and Tabitha spread rugs and cushions for the party and then set about unpacking the hampers. Jackson, the driver from the livery, unhitched his horse and turned it loose. Then he unsaddled Hermes and Millwood, took off their bridles, and turned them loose, too. All three galloped around the field several times in delight at their freedom.

There was a distant whistle of a train from the valley below. "Ten thirty from Manchester," Walter said.

It was out of sight, hidden in the hollows south of Littleborough.

John took out his watch. "Due eleven twenty-six. She'll make it." He put the watch away again. "She should go on to Summit; there's that load of rail due this morning."

"Yes," Walter said, sitting beside Arabella. "It does one good to hear those words. Taking metals to Summit. That's progress! What?"

"No railroad talk!" Arabella said firmly.

"Hear her! Hear her!" Nora agreed. But a moment later she burst into laughter.

"What now?" John asked, pained.

"Your face!" she said. "The expression on it. 'No railroad talk!' One might as well tell a pail of water to go and dry itself!"

When their laughter died, Arabella gave a sudden start.

"What, dear?" Walter asked, thinking she was hurt.

"There's someone in there!" she said, turning round as best she could and peering deep into the shade of the grove.

They all turned to see. And indeed there was someone. There was a distinct crackle of twigs and litter crunching underfoot. "Hey! Fellow!" Walter called.

Then Nora laughed. "A goat!" she said. "You don't think Lady Henshaw's come to join us, do you?" They all laughed, but Arabella wrinkled her nose in disgust, too. "Oh, do drive it away, Walter dear. Please! I cannot bear their smell."

Dutifully, carefully, Walter rose and walked into the deeper shade behind them. Nora stood up, too. "I'll make sure it doesn't jump out into the field," she said. "Or the lane." And she called to Walter to drive it into the field at the hilltop.

John, left standing beside the rug on which Arabella reclined, smiled at her. "An excellent choice, Mrs. Thornton!" He looked again at the view.

"Yes," she said. "I often thought, when riding past it, what a pretty place it was."

"Well!" John clapped his hands and rubbed them together. "Since activity's the order of the day, I think—with your permission, ma'am—I shall gather a few sticks to make a little cooking fire."

At the far side of the wood, Walter shouted across to Nora, asking her if the goat had got out into the lane.

"No," she said, walking into the cemetery and toward him over a tumbledown remnant of the wall. "He's up the hilltop already."

"I didn't see," he said. "Got stuck in those briars. Look!" He showed her a tear on his jacket.

"Dear, dear," she said. "Let's go back. There used to be a path . . . yes, here it is." She walked ahead of him down the slope.

"Well!" he said meaningfully.

"Aye!" She did not pretend to be ignorant of his meaning. "Well well well!"

The path led past the very gravestone they had used. Nicholas Everett . . . why should that name have stuck in her mind? She stopped and turned to look at it—knowing that the honest thing would be to walk on by as if it had lost all meaning. She had not been alone with Walter Thornton since that day. It made a difference. Out there, out in the world, she could watch him as a third person and feel a kind of laughing or contemptuous pity for him—or share John's admiration of him as a professional. But alone with him, she felt the laughter die, the contempt drain away, while the pity swelled into compassionate forbearance. She could not pass that place in silence.

She stopped and turned to look down at the flat, worn stone, half smothered in turf and moss. "There it is," she said simply.

All she heard was the shiver of his breathing. She could not look at him. Why could he not make light of it? Get it all over between them. She'd have to lead him. "Aye! Where thee and me frigged—master!"

She turned to him, smiling, wanting to see him smile back. But he stood there with his head bowed, his eyes clenched tight, his lips pressed hard upon his teeth, baring them in a grin of agony. "Don't," he pleaded.

Now she was aghast at what she had unleashed. She forced a laugh. "I'd forgotten," she said. "Until the car stopped by the path there, it had gone right out of my mind."

"It was not . . . *crude*," he insisted, ignoring what she was saying. "Not like you tried to make it sound. It was not."

At least he seemed calmer. "Yes," she said, lightly. "From that day to this. Quite forgotten it."

"I haven't," he said dully. "I've remembered it every day."

"Oh dear," she sighed.

"Every day this year."

"We'd better return or they'll start wondering," she said. "Where we are, I mean." She started to walk again.

"Nora!" he called.

She turned and faced him.

"Tell me," he said.

She waited but he added nothing. "Tell you what?" she asked at length.

"What it was like. Tell me you enjoyed . . . tell me it was *good!*"

She turned away. "We must get back."

He walked swiftly to join her and took her arm from behind. "You made it wonderful, Nora. I shouldn't say this but *she* makes it so . . . *unlovely. She* drove me to it."

"Drove you to what?" Nora asked. "No—don't tell me. I don't want to know. My advice to you, Mr. Thornton, is to take a mistress. And, by the way, please feel free to address me as Mrs. Stevenson."

"You have no idea of the agonies of this past year!" he went on, heedless. "The doubts I have endured. How . . . unclean . . . how . . . vile . . ."

"Or gambling," Nora was relentless. "Or the bottle. You've many lines to try out yet before you come grovelling to me—or to anyone—for pity."

At last he gave sign of hearing what she was saying to him. "Pity!" he sneered. *"You* have none. I can see that!"

"Bravo!" She turned and clapped him briefly, ironically, with her silent, gloved hands. "Full circle! What did you say of pity? Out there on the road? What did you call it? 'Socially pernicious.' Was that the phrase?"

He had no reply to make to that. They walked, careful among the brambles, in silence.

"I gave you a sovereign that day," he said suddenly. His tone was conversational again.

She was glad he had mastered himself once more. "I remember," she said. "I told you it made me feel cheap. And you said I had ideas above my station." She looked round and caught him smiling. Her sense of relief increased. "D'you know what it's worth now?" She asked, almost gaily.

"I *beg* your pardon!" He was shocked, thinking she meant something else by the word "it."

She blushed and laughed in confusion. "The *sovereign,* Mr. Thornton! Good God—you couldn't buy . . . the other . . . not for the Bank of England you couldn't. The sovereign—I gave it to Mr. Stevenson. And if it's not trebled in value, I've no knowledge of keeping books."

"Ah!" Thornton said, very cool and conversational now that they were drawing close to the clearing where Arabella lay. "I wish I could pick such winners!"

Arabella heard him. "Have you driven it off?" she called.

"Yes," Nora told her. "It's run off into the field at the top of the hill."

"Nasty smelly things," Arabella said.

"The next best thing to venison," Nora imitated Lady Henshaw. It was so perfect that everyone laughed.

"Who's picking winners?" John asked, returning with an armful of faggot. He wet a finger to feel for the breeze and went to light his fire a little to the left of the gap.

"Mrs. Stevenson is," Walter answered. He sat down beside Arabella and squeezed her arm reassuringly. "She says that the sovereign she brought to you a year ago is now trebled in value."

"That's a rash estimate!" John said. "Less noise!" he called at Bess and Tabitha, who were whooping and guffawing with laughter as they prepared the lunch. "They're a sight too pert," he said, lowering his voice once more. "That pair."

"I was reminding Mrs. Stevenson," Walter went on, "that it was a year ago our paths first crossed. Hereabouts, in fact—on this very path."

Nora was trying to make a daisy chain. She was glad of the preoccupation it gave her but she wished Thornton would not skate on thin ice with such relish; he was not a good actor.

"A year to this day," John said.

Nora interrupted: "If you saw those Cousin Bettys of Lady Henshaw's, you'd not mind Bess and Tabitha being pert. I bless their liveliness every time I return from Henshaw Park to Rough Stones."

"Do imitate Lady Henshaw again, dear Nora," Arabella pressed her. "It's so uncannily like her, you'd swear she was beside us."

Nora smiled, thought, and then laughed. They all began to smile in anticipation. "Last time I was there," she said, "the great big one, the one they call Gertie, came in. She's got one eye looks up and the other looks down." She had to let their laughter die before she could go on.

Fifty yards to their left, Bess, hearing them hoot, looked at Tabitha and said softly: "Less noise!" making them both giggle until they were helpless.

"Come here, Gertie!" Nora imitated.

Again they laughed.

"Come here, girl. Don't shuffle—this is a drawing room. Now! What have you been? Eh? Tell us! Go on! Speak up! Tell us! What have you been?" Nora cleared her throat to signal the change. "I been a right wicked girl, ma'am." Back to her ladyship. "Wicked! Yes, wicked! Why? Go on! Tell Mrs. Stevenson! Why!" Change again. "I poisoned everyone, ma'am." Her chin shot up as she became Lady Henshaw again. "Yes! Indeed! Poisoned us all, didn't ye! Go on. Don't stop! Tell us how! Confession's good for the soul. Tell all." She hung her head, becoming Gertie for the final line. "I made the tea with water as were twice-boiled, ma'am," she muttered.

They laughed then until they had to hold their sides to dull the aching. "Oh. She's mad!" Arabella said, catching her breath and dabbing the tears from the corners of her eye.

"She gets the girls at two pounds a year to the trustees—and that's only for appearances' sake," Nora said admiringly. "She's not . . . altogether mad."

"Did you ever think, as you walked up this way with only a pound in your pocket, did you ever think even in your wildest imaginings that you'd come on such friendly terms with people like Lady Henshaw and Squire Redmayne and John Fielden?"

"No," Nora said fondly. "Of course not."

Arabella sighed. "You must be very glad it's all behind you now."

Nora gazed out over the valley and the rolling hills and the plain beyond. Manchester was a grey smudge in the far distance. "I can't say I was *un*happy in those days," she said. "I don't mean I enjoyed poverty. That would be silly. But . . . and it would be dishonest . . . but in myself I have to say: I was not *un*happy." Touched by these words the others listened in silence. "Unhappiness is in the person. Not the purse." She looked up and smiled around, almost apologizing for this sudden lapse into aphorism.

Arabella, despite her earlier denigration of Nora, looked at her now with frank admiration. "That is real firmness of character!" she said. "You shame me. I could never accept poverty with such calm."

Nora did not want Arabella to undervalue herself so much. "You shouldn't say such things," she said. "You never know what you can do until you face the necessity. I think you've got . . . great strength. You shouldn't talk yourself down." She laughed. "And here's me lecturing you!"

Arabella smiled, and, turning to John, said, as if it were of no consequence whatever: "What do you think of investment in railways, Mr. Stevenson?"

"Really, my dear!" Walter began to laugh an apology.

But John cut him short. "No, no," he said. "I'd be happy to advise. Do you mean if the money were mine to invest or what do I think you should do?"

Arabella looked puzzled. "Is there any difference?"

"A great deal. The risk that may bring spice to one life may tear another to shreds with anxiety."

"Ah!" She grasped the point. "You would take the risk, I see. And Nora?"

"Yes." Nora did not hesitate. "We both would. Circumstance has already borne the two of us as low as folk may possibly get. And"—she turned to Walter—"despite what Lady Henshaw or Mr. Thornton may say, I'll swear it was circumstance . . . fortune . . . *not* vice that took us there."

Thornton nodded. "I concede the point."

"It took us—or me, anyway—lower than I can possibly get again, though we may be poor. Bankruptcy is a part of our lives. . . ."

John cleared his throat in protest at that. "The threat of it, dear. The threat, only."

"Yes, the threat of it, I mean. We cannot exclude it. It is the shadow side of this present sunshine."

Now John nodded his approval. "So the question is, Mrs. Thornton, could you face ruin in such a spirit?"

"The threat of it," Nora corrected with a great display of self-right-eousness.

He laughed but said nothing, awaiting Arabella's answer. "I've already said I couldn't," she told him. "And been roundly reprimanded for it."

Nora made a prim face.

"There's your choice, then," John said. "You can advise yourselves."

A boy on a horse, riding fast, went along the lane at the foot of the field. John stood up quickly, put his fingers to his tongue, and whistled a long piercing blast that halted the play of their own three horses and of the servants. It also stopped the rider. He rose in his saddle and looked over the hedge at them; John waved energetically. The boy turned around and made for the side lane.

"Sorry about that," John said.

Nora looked deeply suspicious. "What might this be?" she asked.

"The mails, probably," he said with a laugh she did not share.

Walter and Arabella looked from one to the other with bewilderment.

"I thought," Nora said wearily, "we might have had this one day without the mails. What did you promise?"

He smiled but did not answer.

"You speak with feeling," Arabella said.

"Oh, my dear, I tell you—no debtor was ever badgered by baileys as we are hounded by the mails."

The boy rider, spurring up the lane, took the gate without hesitation. It was a beautiful leap and they all cheered spontaneously.

"Well ridden, lad," John called as he reined in and leaped from the saddle.

"Your mail, Mr. Stevenson, sir," the boy said.

John thanked him and flipped him a half crown. But instead of opening the letter he threw it onto the rug so that it landed near Nora. Her attitude changed at once as soon as she saw the name of the sender: the Bolton & Preston Railway Co. John told the boy to go and get a bite of snap off the girls and to rest his horse half an hour.

"Won't you open it?" Arabella said. "Please do. It must be important."

John looked at the letter and then at Nora. "No," he said airily. "I gave my word."

Nora pouted and tossed her head. He laughed at her. *"You* made me give it. Ten minutes after dinner. That's my allowance."

"But if it's important . . ." Arabella repeated, still thinking it was simple courtesy that held him back.

"Oh no," Nora said to her, though her sarcasm was all for John. "Not important at all! It's only to let us know whether we've got the most recent contract offered on the Bolton & Preston Railway."

Arabella's eyes lit up. "Oh!" She looked incredulously at John. "Don't you *burn* to know? How *can* you leave it lying there?"

"My word is my bond. Ten minutes after dinner."

"It's simply to revenge himself on me. Because I extracted that promise."

John nudged Walter's shoe with the toe of his boot. "Thornton," he said, "I have a football in one of those baskets in the car. What d'you say to a kickaround before lunch to work up an appetite? We can take on the groom and that lad."

Walter rose grudgingly and followed him toward the car.

"It's just to annoy me," Nora told Arabella. Then she raised her voice as he departed. "Well, I mean *not* to be annoyed."

They got out the football and, with the other two males, played across the slope. They took it in turn to mind goal, which they marked with their rolled-up jackets.

"What's the contract let for?" Arabella asked.

"Oh," Nora said, her sarcasm now wasted, "only twenty thousand pounds! And there's a tunnel on the next section to go to tender. That will be at least thirty thousand. It would be ideal to work the two together."

"It does seem . . . wayward." Arabella leaned back on her pile of cushions and winced.

"Is anything wrong?" Nora asked anxiously.

"I shouldn't have laughed so much when you were mimicking Lady Henshaw," Arabella said. Then she added stoically: "Besides, it is our burden."

Nora nodded. "All pleasure costs pain, they say."

"Pleasure?" Arabella asked so sharply that Nora turned to her in surprise.

"You know what I mean," she said.

"I do not," Arabella answered vehemently. "I do not."

"Well, you soon will, now," Nora soothed. "The pleasures of parenthood. Of fostering new life."

"Ah!" Now Arabella was embarrassed by her misunderstanding. But Nora, her eyes fixed on the footballers, appeared not to have noticed. "Yes, I see. How right you are, Nora dear, to direct my thoughts to that. It is . . . what did you call it? The sunshine to my present shadow; a month at the most, Dr. Ray says."

"Does he," Nora said casually. "I wouldn't be surprised if it was sooner." She looked at her. "Maybe quite a lot sooner."

Arabella was delighted. "Do you think so? Really?"

Nora nodded sagely.

"How d'you know?" Arabella prompted her.

"I've delivered several babies in my time," she said. "Poor folk don't trouble doctors for that sort of thing."

"What . . . how is it?"

"The first one I helped, that was down at the mill in Stockport. She went into labour, had the baby, and was all swaddled up again and back at her loom—all in the half-hour break for meat. My second one was two long days. You can't tell."

Arabella relaxed again. "I shan't be sorry. It can't come too soon for me." She sighed, deeply satisfied. "I wonder what the future holds?"

Nora chuckled. "Who can ever know that! Last year I was walking this very path, without a penny to bless me—"

"But," Arabella interrupted, "I thought you said you had a sovereign?"

Nora cursed her forgetfulness. "Ah . . . yes," she said, thinking quickly. "But that was spoken for. If I ever got to Leeds. I wasn't able to spend it on the way. Still . . . here I am again today. Same place. And now I've a husband who pretends he can't find sufficient interest to open a letter concerning twenty thousand pounds! If that isn't topsy-turvy! If you told me that next year we're all to assemble here again to shake hands with the Man in the Moon, I'd not know how to dispute you."

For a while they watched the footballers. Then Arabella said, "See how fiercely they play! That's Mr. Stevenson who's done that. He gets people"—she clenched her fist—"really working hard. Or so Walter says. He has a charmed way with people."

"He's rash with them," Nora offered correction. "He decides very quickly. Like with that young man on the road today. I know very well what he was thinking. He's so optimistic. He was thinking how we'll need more labour now for the Bolton–Preston contract. He's not sure we've won it until he opens this letter." She turned it over on the rug and let it fall again. "But already he's taking on people. He's too optimistic, d'you see? If we haven't got the new contract, there'll be bad trouble at Summit with him getting rid of good men and taking on rubbish like that cripple on the turnpike. Still . . ." She revived from her gloom and smiled at Arabella. "I've no right to grumble at him, either for rashness or optimism. He asked me to wed him just twenty-four hours after we met."

"Goodness!" Arabella was astounded. She knew it must have been quick, but not twenty-four *hours*.

"Yes," Nora affirmed. "That was rash. The mouth makes quick, the body breaks slow, they say. Yet I don't think there's any two happier people in God's whole Creation. So I'm a fine one to speak."

After a short silence Arabella turned to her and said: "Tell me what poverty is like, Nora."

"Poverty?"

"Yes."

"Well . . . what . . . I mean, what in particular?"

"The mills, for example. I look out of my window at Pex Hill and I see half a dozen mills, and the people coming in and going out, like ants. But I have no notion of what they are like."

"Noise . . . fumes . . ." Nora had to force herself to recollect.

"One reads such accounts," Arabella prompted. "The drunkenness, and brutality, and . . . lewd behavings . . ."

For some reason, Nora felt obliged to defend what she felt Arabella to be attacking. "There was also friendship," she said. "Good company. And on a winter's day you can just *love* the heat. If we all looked only on the down side of life, the canals would soon be choked with folk."

"Yes . . ." Arabella began dubiously; but Nora was now launched.

"Warmth . . . friendship . . ." she said, "and . . . I suppose the word is *recklessness*. Yes—a kind of recklessness. Very few things could be worse, you thought, so ye'd try anything." Suddenly she turned to Arabella, her eyes alight with discovery. "Perhaps that's why John is so quick to decide. And perhaps *that* is what nags me. D'you think that could be it? Yes, I'm sure that's it. Recklessness born of poverty is not . . . fitting. It's dangerous to such a man as he gains power. Dangerous to himself, I mean."

Arabella, sharing her enjoyment in the discovery, said: "More and more I understand why he married you and why you are so necessary to him." She sighed. "Oh, Nora! I hope both our families may prosper and that their work will bring us together frequently over the years!"

"Yes, oh yes!" Nora said, just as fervently. She wished she were free to tell Arabella that sometime today John was going to offer Thornton a job.

The men, their game temporarily over, came trotting back, breathless and sweating.

Nora picked up the letter and stood up before John could flop down. She turned to Arabella. "Please excuse us, dear," she said. "I'm going to force this man of mine to be sensible."

"Suppose it's bad news?" John asked craftily. "That would damp down the day for us!"

For a moment she was nonplussed. Then a slight tremor of his face made her smile and push him gently out onto the path. "You don't for one moment believe it's going to be bad!" she said.

But she did not hand him the letter to open until they were round the corner, up the lane, and into the graveyard—at the same place she had entered it when she and Walter had chased out the goat an hour or so earlier.

She saw how tense he was as he opened the letter. For a moment he hesitated, eyes shut, not breathing, before he squared himself to it and slipped out the contents. She moved close, to hold him in case he needed the solace.

"We've got it," he said quietly. "That Church of England is going to be a very useful man since we—" But she let him get no further. She threw her arms around his neck and whirled him round until he was going fast enough to swing her right off the ground. No cry of joy came from her throat; just one long, deep sigh of satisfaction and relief.

"All right!" he cried with the last breath she squeezed from him. "This is our fourth contract, so let's behave as if we're getting used to it. Eh?"

She paused. "As a matter of fact," she said archly. "It's our fifth!"

"Well, there you are! You see what I mean." He smiled. "Just behave yourself."

She took his arm and walked with exaggerated primness at his side. He squeezed her hand and she settled.

"Isn't there anything else you want to show me here?" he asked.

She stopped. She looked at the trees skirting the edge of the graveyard and soon found the one she was seeking, a little farther down the path.

She stood and pointed to a patch of the woodland floor. "He's down there," she said.

He watched her carefully but saw no reaction. "Father and daughter," he said.

She looked up at him then. "There's three generations here," she said deliberately.

He did not at once comprehend her meaning. And when he did he could not believe she had said it.

"I didn't mean to tell thee," she said. "Not till I was more certain of it."

And then he was wild with joy. He lifted her up and began to swing her before he realized what he was doing. Then he lowered her like thistle-down, and hugged and kissed and held her. He dropped to his knees again to press his ear and then his lips to her stomach. And all the time he repeated her name and laughed. "What is it?" he asked. "Boy or girl?"

"I'll tell thee next March," she said.

Before they left that place she looked again at her father's unmarked grave and said: "Yon man taught us to read and write and figure. That was the key to the jailhouse door for me. What do *we* give this one?" She patted her stomach.

"A new world," he said. "A better one than this."

At that moment Walter came running into the woodland in search of them. "Stevenson!" he shouted. "Mrs. Stevenson!"

"Surely we've not been gone that long?" John said.

"He sounds fretful," Nora replied. "Here!" she called.

"Oh, Thank God! I say—do come. Quickly!" He was breathless though he had hardly run a hundred yards.

"What is it?" John asked. Both he and Nora hastened forward now.

"It's Arabella. Something's wrong!"

"Wrong!" Nora was scornful. "Don't you *know?*" She looked at John. "I've thought so. All morning I've said it to myself."

"What?" Walter asked. Now all three were hastening back to the picnic place.

"She's in labour!" Nora said. "Talk about ignorance . . . !"

Without further question John went to harness and saddle the horses.

When Nora and Walter arrived at Arabella's side, it took only a few brief questions to establish that the twinges—the pains that Arabella had been trying to shrug off as "our burden"—had started at least as early as that morning and were now coming quite often.

"We must get her home!" Walter said in an anguish.

"Exactly when did they start?" Nora asked.

"To be quite truthful," Arabella said, "I think they really started last night."

"Last night!" Nora tried to remain calm and reassuring.

"I didn't know they had anything to do with the baby," she said. "Or not with the birth."

"There's no hope of getting back to Todmorden now," Nora said. "Not in time. No chance at all."

"Littleborough, then," Walter said, now even more desperate. "We must make a stretcher. Stevenson!"

John came over, leaving Jackson to finish readying the horses.

"A stretcher," Walter said. "Cut two saplings and we'll use our jackets."

But John was watching Nora's troubled face. "What's wrong, love?" he asked.

"Well," Nora said, "the obvious choice is Littleborough. There's Dr. McCuish there. But I'm not sure she'll even reach there. . . ."

"But I can't have my baby here!" Arabella was aghast. "How *can* you be so certain?"

"I can't," Nora answered, also troubled. "That's what is so dreadful. It must be your decision. We could set out for Littleborough—and risk having to deliver the baby beside the turnpike. Or we could snatch whatever little time we have left and make a place ready here. There's a lot of privy places in the bushes behind us. . . ."

Walter had gone to pieces by now. He walked up and down, saying: "Oh dear dear dear, oh dear oh dear oh dear . . ." as if it were a litany.

"I can't," Arabella protested. "Like some farm girl. Hidden in the bushes . . . oh, we *never* should have come! I said we shouldn't . . ."

"You said!" Walter exploded, rounding on her as if he would hit her. "I *asked* you whether you thought it wise, and you insisted. 'Oh, not for another month,' you said. Well, I tell you now, Mrs. Thornton, if you've done anything to jeopardize my son . . ."

"Thornton!" John snapped angrily. "Blow steam, man!"

Arabella moaned as another twinge racked her.

"That settles it!" Nora said, realizing that neither Thornton nor his wife was fit to decide anything. "Right, you men. Get to work. One of you is to go to Littleborough to fetch Dr. McCuish. The other is to get all the blankets and cushions except the ones she's on now and find a privy place in those bushes. Come on—lively now! Bess! Tabitha!"

Jackson came over to them with Hermes. John turned to Walter. "Go on, Thornton. You go for the doctor."

Walter moved like one in a dream. "I don't know," he said. "I just don't know." John helped him onto the saddle. Once he was seated he seemed to take more charge of himself. He even smiled at Arabella. "Bear up, my dearest. Help is on its way." And off he galloped.

Bess and Tabitha came running over. "Yes'm?"

"Listen." Nora's calm and unflustered manner soon overcame their excitement. Indeed, everyone now took their cues from her. "Mrs. Thornton's likely to be delivered here. Has either of ye helped deliver a woman before?"

Bess had. Tabitha had not.

"Right. Bess is to stay by me. Tabitha, you go with Jackson, take the two horse pails and give them a good scrubbing in that brook we crossed, back down the lane, and bring them here again, full and clean."

In less than fifty minutes Walter had returned—but no doctor rode with him. "He's out on a visit over toward Rochdale," Walter said. He kept peering at the bushes, hoping to see something—or hear it.

"Nothing yet," John said.

"I left word. He'll come as soon as he gets back. I hope I did the right thing."

"Of course you did."

Nora appeared from the bushes, wiping her hands. "Not yet," she said in answer to the inquiry that at once lit Walter's face.

"The doctor . . ." he began.

"I know," she said. "I heard."

Once again he looked worried. "Don't fret," she told him. "Arabella's a good, strong girl. The baby's presented the right way. She's not altogether comfortable but she's in no real pain. We don't *need* a doctor, you know. It's not a sickness! She'll do just fine without. She's a strong, healthy lass and all the signs are good. Couldn't be better! John—take this man for a walk."

"Oh, Stevenson!" Walter said, still bemused but no longer fretful. "There is a treasure indeed!"

Twenty minutes later Walter shouted: "Is it over?"

And Nora's shout came back: "No!"

Fourteen minutes later Walter shouted: "Well?"

And Nora shouted: "Couldn't be better! The baby's head has two crowns to his hair!"

"Now what's that mean?" he asked John.

"Don't you say that down south?"

"Never heard of it."

"It means good luck."

A few minutes later he shouted into the thicket: "May we approach?"

"No!" Nora shouted. "Stay away!"

"No!" Arabella joined in this time.

"Arabella!" he called out. "Are you all right?"

"Of course she is!" Nora shouted. "Go and get that football. She'll come out and keep goal for you in half a minute!"

They laughed.

"Men!" she said to Arabella. "They've no idea, have they!"

She cradled the baby, a healthy little boy who was breathing happily without having cried. "Oh!" she said to him. "You do everything so easily in your family!" She laid him on Arabella's stomach, waiting for all the afterbirth to be delivered.

Arabella, not truly exhausted, for it had been an unusually easy birth, lay back on the cushions once she had seen him. "The Lord be praised!" she said happily. "Oh, blessed be the name of the Lord. 'A woman when she is in travail hath sorrow, because her hour is come: but as soon as she is delivered of the child, she remembereth no more the anguish, for joy that a man is born into the world.'"

"Ten fingers, ten toes," Nora said. "Go on! Anguish indeed! You'd have nodded off to sleep if we'd let you!"

Arabella smiled happily but said nothing. Nora fingered the umbilical cord. "That's all nicely shrunk now," she said. "Shouldn't bleed." She took the sharpened knife from Bess, who watched with open mouth while Nora cut the cord in one swift movement, a few inches from the baby's stomach. "Now," she went on. "Put the afterbirth in that empty bucket. Doctor may want to see it. I'll clean up his little face for him. . . . Oh! Look at those puzzled eyes! No, I'm not your mother! That's your mother! Yes, it is! Yes, it is!"

She picked up the baby and wrapped it in a clean tablecloth. And with a napkin, dipped in the pail of clean, cold water, she began to clean up his eyes and nose and mouth. The cold was a shock and the baby for the first time began to cry. "Oh!" she chided, not pausing in her work. "Cold water! Yes, cold! And you'd best get used to it too! For there's a deal more coming your way!"

And while Arabella straightened herself and made herself presentable again, Nora went on washing and talking to the baby.

"Oh!" Arabella said as soon as she sat up and saw where she had been lying. "Your beautiful lace tablecloth! It's all spoiled!"

"Never!" Nora said, shocked that Arabella could see it from that point of view. "It's glorified!"

Nora felt certain that Walter would ignore Arabella until he had exhausted his delight at his new son. But it was the other way round. Indeed Arabella, a little disappointed, had to push the child into his arms before he would stop fussing over her and take any interest in their boy. But then Nora realized what it was—Thornton was shy! He didn't want to mishandle the baby or make any other mistake while she was there.

"I'll look out for the doctor," she said and left them.

As she left, she wondered if Thornton would notice that the gravestone Arabella had been delivered on was, in fact, Nicholas Everett's. True, it was just about the most concealed part of the cemetery—which, after all, was why she had chosen it with Walter—but even so, it was a rather grisly trick of fate that John had chosen it when he spread the blankets.

The moment Walter came out into the open again she knew from his face, and from the glance he shot at her, that he had realized where his son had been delivered.

Shortly afterward the doctor came, breathless, full of needless apology, and of anxiety for Arabella. But as he questioned her and Nora and listened to their answers and examined Arabella and the pail with the afterbirth, his tension eased and he became more and more jovial.

"Where did you say the cord was?" he asked at one point.

Nora described how, after the birth of the head, she had seen that the cord ran obliquely up, over the baby's left shoulder, and down again behind.

"So what did you do?"

And she described how she had pushed the cord clear of the left shoulder and worked it back into the birth canal as the baby progressed outward.

"Why do you ask, doctor?" Arabella said.

"It's of no great moment *now,*" he answered. "But I think you ought to know that this young fella—and probably you, too, Mrs. Thornton, owe your lives to the skill of Mrs. Stevenson."

And Arabella embarrassed Nora still further by saying that they had debts in that direction they'd *never* be able to requite.

The doctor thought that Arabella ought to rest in Littleborough for a day or two before going back to Todmorden. He went down with her and Tabitha and Jackson, leading his horse at the tail of the car. Walter was to go back to Pigs Hill to collect the things she would need.

"We'll come down with you to Littleborough," Nora said. The doctor looked up sharply: "Absolutely not! There's been quite enough excitement for one day. Now Mrs. Thornton's to have absolute tranquillity."

Arabella winked at Nora.

It was well into the middle of the afternoon before the car pulled slowly out through the gate and set off for Littleborough. John, Nora, and Walter stood and waved until it passed out of sight.

Nora sighed. "Well," she said, brisk again. "I thought I'd be put off my meat by that. But my guts are ready to eat my little toes."

"Thornton," John said, "I expect you'll want to be away if you're to make the double journey. You're welcome to Hermes."

Walter had acted a little dazed ever since he'd seen the site of Arabella's accouchement. Now he roused himself a little. "To tell the truth—" he began and then faltered.

"Stay and eat if you wish," Nora invited. "You'll probably make the journey better for a little food inside you."

"Mmmm." He nodded.

"Sit yourself down then," John said.

"She's in excellent hands. . . ." Walter seemed to find it necessary to excuse himself. "I expect it'll make no difference if I get there at six or at seven."

"Or all at sixes and sevens!" John tried being hearty, to cheer him up. "I'll go and help that Bess with the hamper."

"Oh, let me too. . . ." Walter began to rise again.

"No, no!" John said, pushing him down. "You're our guest of honour now!"

*Honour!* Walter thought. He almost despaired.

His venereal clap was subsiding, but a secondary outbreak had obliged him to fit a little wax bougie to prevent the walls of his urethra from growing together. Its recent removal had left him with a gleet that would have discoloured his shirt had he not put down a succession of cheap handkerchiefs. And though that prevented awkward inquiries, it could not shield his spirit from disgust every time he renewed and burned the blemished and stinking cloth. A sense of his own filthiness never left him.

These strains of his secret life now combined with the open provocations of this most taxing day, easing his self-control to a dangerous degree. As soon as John was out of earshot, Walter turned urgently to Nora and asked: "What game is your husband playing?"

"Game?" She feigned ignorance.

"Yes," he said. "All day I've had this feeling. There's some . . . secret between him and Arabella. Don't you feel it too? Did you see how they smiled at each other when we set off?"

"That's a disgraceful thing to say!" Nora answered, wishing she did not have to lower her voice.

"And why did she suggest *this* place of all places? Why this place?"

"You are not to make such suggestions! If it worries you so much, keep Arabella out of his reach. But what a thing to say of her. On the day she gives you such a fine son, too!"

When Nora said "keep Arabella out of his reach," she had meant it as a shallow and obvious absurdity—the kind that reveals a deeper absurdity, obsessive enough to mask everything that might show it up for the nonsense it really is. But Walter, his judgement now clouded in precisely that way, heard only the stark, unqualified warning: Keep Arabella out of Stevenson's reach.

And because he took it seriously, it pointed up an entirely different absurdity. He laughed in scorn. "Your husband and Arabella! Hah! That's rich! He'd stand more chance of winning the favours of the Eddystone Lighthouse! And derive greater pleasure!"

"I think this has unhinged you—"

"And that gravestone!" he interrupted. "Why just that gravestone?"

"How do I know? Ask him."

"You haven't . . . told him?" Walter suggested.

"Oh, very likely," she sneered. "Do please talk of other things."

"I'm sure he suspects." Walter seemed to speak more to himself than to her. "I'm sure he suspected it that day."

"What day?" She was alert suddenly. "You mean last year?"

"He asked me, when he met with me in the drift that night, he asked me if I'd 'tumbled' with you. Took me off my guard."

She laughed mockingly, believing him. "That's his best time. When you're off guard. I suppose you owned up!"

"Of course I didn't! I denied it. But . . . you see . . ." He faltered. "I was uneasy about what *you* might have said. I mean, you might already have joked about it. How was I to know? I didn't know you then." He sighed. "So I daresay my denial was not as forthright as it might have been."

She looked glumly at the skyline. "I hope it was too dark to see your face," she said. "There's not the slightest power in you to deceive." Suddenly she looked at him in something akin to warmth. "It's the nicest thing about you, to be candid."

"He'd guess anyway." Walter refused to be cheered. "I wish I had his powers."

"Oh, yes!" she crowed. "There's a deal of folk who wish that!"

"I mean his power to judge people. His genius, it is. For people. You wait—that cripple he picked out on the turnpike today. He'll turn out to be a second James Watt! I could go out and pick a hundred cripples, and I'd just have a hundred mouths to feed. He picks one and it'll be James Watt the second. That's what I mean. He can see through people's exteriors to their true worth." Nora was pleased to hear this return of his humour; but then he spoiled it by turning to her and saying: "Oh, Nora! How I misjudged you! What a prize you are!"

She could have cried in disappointment. "You are to stop addressing me in that familiar way!"

"Why *did* he pick that gravestone?"

"Good Christ! Will you . . ." She almost exploded. "Darn that hole in your face! He chose it for the same reason *we* chose it: It's the priviest nook in there. Now here they come. So shut up, for the love of Charley!

And try to look a bit cheerful! I must say—for a man that's just had good issue in a fine healthy son with two crowns in his hair, you deserve some kind of a diploma for keeping a cool head."

He barely heard her. That warning: *Keep Arabella out of his reach* tumbled on in his mind like a catch phrase that will not be suppressed. "What did you mean?" he asked. "About not leaving him alone with Arabella?"

He knew there was no time for her to answer. And she wasted what few moments she had with the sharp (and to him pointless) correction: "You mean *her* alone with *him!*" Then she had to turn with a jovial smile to John and Bess. Nodding at the creaking hamper they bore between them she said: "That's a champion sight! I swear I could almost smell that chicken while we waited!"

"All quartered and ready," John said.

Bess coughed. "If you please, ma'am," she said. "I'm none too hungry. Could I go and take some ease in the cemetery?"

"Ye may have an hour, Bess. The trap should be back then," Nora conceded.

"Thank you, ma'am."

When she had gone, Nora said: "She's gone to meet that farm boy. That's what that is."

"Farm boy?" John said.

"He came up the lane while ye were at your football," she told him.

He passed out chicken and a now rather limp salad.

"You permit it?" Walter asked.

"She's fifteen," Nora answered. "Old enough. She knows what'll happen if she gets herself into trouble."

"Little minx!" John said off-handedly and turned to Walter: "Well, Thornton—for a newly minted paterfamilias I must say you're looking decidedly—not to say determinedly—glum."

Walter merely sighed. "Am I now?"

"Though why I should say 'gets *her*self into trouble,'" Nora continued, "I don't know. It's not a very true account. They should have to dismiss the lad as well."

When she said that, Walter suddenly came to life. "Oh, they would!" he said with heavy sarcasm. "Believe me, they would! If he carried the evidence around, too."

"Who would?" John asked, unsure whether or not to laugh.

"This new breed . . . of . . . these prudes . . . killjoys. Oh yes!"

Nora nibbled at her chicken. "I'm sure you know what you're talking about," she said.

John intervened. "What'll ye call the lad, Thornton?"

Walter turned to him and said with heavy emphasis: "I felt sure *you*'d know that already!"

"Me?" John said, surprised. "I imagine you'll call him Walter, too. No?"

"I shall call him"—Walter dropped the name as if he thought it would prove a bombshell—"Nicholas Everett! Nicholas . . . Everett . . . Thornton."

"Nicholas Everett," John said experimentally and then turned, mystified, to Walter. "The man of the moment? Something I've not heard?"

Walter, who had not touched his meal, looked narrowly at the pair of them. At Stevenson, all innocence . . . at Nora, so casually busy with the basket and its contents. It all looked so forced and so deliberate to him.

"Are you two playing me a joke?" he asked.

Nora, trying to restore calm, began drawing his attention to what still lay in the basket: "There's veal and ham pie . . . or pigeon pie . . . or collared calf's head . . ."

"Nicholas Everett," Walter said heavily to John, "is the name on that gravestone. As you very well know."

"My wife was offering you some—"

"Though you may pretend you don't!"

"Thornton," John said wearily. "You're getting damned difficult to follow. *What* gravestone? *What* am I supposed to know so very well?"

Walter buried his head in his hands. "Now you are mocking me. Certainly. I am sure of it."

"Then let me tell you plainly—before you grow totally unhinged—let me tell you my main reason for asking you here today . . ."

"Hah!" Walter looked up triumphantly. "Now we come to it!"

"My main reason was to put a proposal to you. If we got the Bolton–Preston contract, which we now know we *have* got, I was to offer you a job. I'll need a good engineer. . . . Are you listening, man?" He could not tell from Thornton's face what the fellow was thinking. "I propose to offer you a post on that and other works. At six hundred pounds a year. And a tenth share of all profits!" He watched for some response. "Well?" Again there was only that blank stare. "For heaven's sake, man?"

"Oh, Lord!" Nora said in disgust, imagining that Thornton was silently weeping.

But that was by no means clear.

"Take a hold of yourself, man!" John told him.

"What is all this," Walter asked, "about . . . you and Arabella?"

John was stunned. "Arabella? Myself?"

"This is my fault," Nora confessed with a sigh.

"What quality did you find there that I missed, eh?"

"Thornton!" John exploded, his patience at an end. "Speak plain or hold your tongue, damn you!"

"It's me to blame," Nora repeated. "I made some passing joke . . . or I *meant* it as a joke . . . about . . ."

"A joke!" Walter cried. "Ah! So you say! But I know better. A joke! I'll tell *you* a joke, Stevenson. See if it makes you laugh. Nicholas Everett is the name on the gravestone you covered up today for Arabella's delivery. That grave!"

John did not twitch a single muscle. His level gaze forced Walter to continue.

"And on that same grave—'"

"Thornton!" Nora almost shrieked. But John, without removing his eyes from Walter's face, sought and found her hand and clasped it for reassurance. As soon as her hand was in his grip, she thought: *He knows! He knows!* And the relief that flooded through her was like fire and wine. Nothing mattered now. She watched Walter as if he were an automaton, mouthing words she had seen him mouth a hundred times before.

"On that same grave," he repeated, "a year ago . . . a year"—he struggled to open his watch—"to this very hour, I topped your wife on that selfsame stone. *Tumbled* with her!" There was no reaction. Neither of them moved. "There!" he added. Something had been left unsaid but he could not remember it.

Nora took a deep breath. "Thornton," she said quietly. "You did not top John Stevenson's wife. . . ."

"And she loved it!" he crowed. That was what he had forgotten to say.

"You did not top *her*," Nora repeated in that same moderate tone. "Not"—she clasped John's hand tight and shook it in triumph—"this man's *wife*. Can ye not see that? You topped a ragged little runaway. A little barefoot thing in rags. With a belly empty enough to contain all the pride she could swallow *and* . . ." She hated adding these next few words for they were untrue, but she had to stifle his yearning for this dead past, and to do that she had to be brutal: "and all the distaste, too . . ."

"No!" he called out in agony.

". . . and still leave room for meat," she said. "But that was not Lord John's wife. *Her*, Lord John's wife, ye couldn't buy for the queen's jewels and a king's ransom."

"But . . ." Walter was now bewildered beyond mere incoherence. The words that rose to his throat would not even form.

"I've forgotten it," Nora said.

He just looked at her. "There's nothing then," he said at last. "Nothing."

They stared at him, horrified.

"Nothing?" Nora at last found words for her scorn. "Nothing? A good wife—the best of wives. Safely delivered of a fine, healthy son. A job at six hundred offered—and ten times the prospects. Nothing! The only place you've gotten nothing, Mr. Thornton, is right down the middle of your back!"

"Nothing!" Walter repeated, just as if she had not spoken. He turned directly to John. "And you—what did you take?"

He did not wait for an answer but stood and walked away down the field. He collected Hermes, but he still had not mounted by the time he passed from their view along the lane.

"Eh!" Nora turned to John. "You never did, did you? Not you and Arabella!"

He smiled at her in gentle scorn. "Please!" he said.

She grinned happily and looked again at the dispirited Thornton, now almost out of sight. "He'd best stay clear of his child or the father will likely catch nappy rash and die of it."

John laughed richly and lay back on the rug; but the laughter overcame him and he had to sit up again. "Eh, Nora! Nora!" he said. "Thou art . . . thou art a bloody rock! A fastness! A mountain in my land! How could I ever have thought of a life without thee!"

She leaned her head on his shoulder. The lowering sun crept in under the lowest branches and dappled them with its golden warmth. "I'm glad it's out in the light of day," she said.

"I . . . suspected it," he said, not wanting to tell her of the nicks in the edge of the coin that made its provenance certain.

She misread the hesitation in his voice as a reluctance to confess something quite different. She smiled and leaned on him more heavily. "You've not been . . . not jealous!" she said.

He sniffed.

"Nay!" she went on.

She looked quickly up at him, read the uncertainty on his face, and leaned against him once more; she was wriggling with delight. "You *have* been!" she said.

"Mebbe," he admitted.

"Eh, love! You've no more sense than . . . nay! Jealous! Thee!" She tickled his ribs. "Come on, then. There's none to disturb us now. Give us a green mantle. Or the blankets and cushions are still on the gravestone. Let's give yon Nick Everett another warming!"

But John did not move, except to put an arm around her and hold her still. "Nay!" he answered. "Poor bugger. Yon Nick Everett, he must be amazed at what the world's come to; him lying deep down there and naught but frigging and childbirth six feet above!"

"Come on!" she urged.

"No!" He was firm now. "We shall sit here and we shall do the one thing we've not had time for all this twelvemonth."

"What?" she asked.

"Sweet nothing," he said.